I0635612

REBELLION OF THE EXPS
BOOK 1

Alexander J. McCarty

Art by: William McCarty

REBELLION OF THE EXPS BOOK 1 Exp 8. Copyright © 2015 by Alexander J. McCarty

All rights reserved. This book, or parts thereof, may not be reproduced in any form without the express written permission of the publisher. This book is purely fictional.

ISBN 978-1-9437-3302-6

Published by Sphere of Compassion, Inc.
authoralexandermccarty@gmail.com
alexanderjmccarty@facebook.com (Updates often with excerpts and art)
alexander_j_mccarty@instagram.com
of_the_Exps@twitter.com
oftheexps@tumbler.com

Cover design by William McCarty

Books from *Of the Exps*© Series

Table of Contents

Part 1: Forming the Freedom Forcers

Part 2: Advent of the Assassins

Part 3: Old Exps

Part 4: The Other Inventor

Acknowledgments

I give thanks to every living and nonliving being and the interactions that led to the creation of the moment of my birth and that helped foster the ideas leading to the creation of this book. I give thanks to my parents who reared me with support and love. I give thanks to my brother and my friend Luis Garced, who excitedly read my handwritten manuscript every time I added even one new page of content. I thank my Chemistry teacher, Mr. Samuelson, who let me sit in his class and work on my book during my lunch period. I thank Marielva Sieg for helping me hone my skills as an actor for four years. I thank my family, friends and acquaintances who read any part of this book while I hovered over their shoulder, particularly Ivan, Ivette, Val, Ken and Jesus who have all supported my book for years. I give thanks to my friend Adrian Romero, my father, and my brother for pre-editing this book before I sent it out to be professionally edited. I thank Ben Hale, my publishing consultant and a fellow author. Special thanks to my wonderful editor, Rosemi, who, with her vast knowledge and research, has helped make my book more accessible and more real to my readers. Special thanks to fellow independent writer P.L. McCall II for giving me advice and for convincing me to make a print version of this book. I give thanks for all the wonderful anime, manga, videogames and other visual literature that helped spark ideas and continue to be my primary form of research. I give a continuous and reverent thanks to my brother, William McCarty, for bringing my characters to life with his art, aiding me with ideas for scenes, and brainstorming with me to create and hone many of my characters. I thank my id for keeping me vital and driven, my ego for keeping me positive and critical about my work and my super ego for directing my creative energies toward a better world for all living beings. Lastly, I thank you, the reader, for purchasing this book. I hope you enjoy it and continue to support me and my future books.

Thank you! =(:3)*   (That's a bunny, by the way.)

This book is dedicated to all living beings who were enslaved, are currently enslaved and who are to be enslaved in the future. May we all work toward a future where all are free to live as unbounded individuals.

Part 1
Forming the Freedom Forcers

Chapter 1: Awakening

"Freedom is a shackle."

Exp 8 could only faintly hear these words. Nonetheless, they repeated fervently in its mind.

There was no world for Exp 8. It had no identity. All it knew, all it was, were those words: "freedom is a shackle." Despite this, it didn't have a clue what they meant. They were merely noise.

A mechanical sound broke through the mantra as an automatic door opened. Voices could be heard but only as whispers.

Exp 8's nervous system slowly activated, allowing it to feel the gelatinous fluid that encompassed him. Its eyes opened, frightening the people who were gathered around.

"It's waking up! It's finally waking up! Hurry, go inform Devlin," exclaimed a scientist, his hands trembling as he looked up at the creature in the incubator.

Exp 8 was an imposing height of six feet five inches, towering over the other life-forms in the room. The creature's body was clad in blue-tinted, platinum-colored quicksilver armor an inch thick. The sleek armor shielded all but the being's piercing black eyes. Those eyes had a depth as overwhelming as space itself.

Around Exp 8's head was a cybernetic helmet that protected the soft flesh within. Horizontal slits were carved into the center of the two slabs melded along the jawline, forming a mouthpiece. The slabs curved upward above its head, creating long, functionless ears. Protruding from the back of its helmet were metallic tendrils, wispily floating in the gelatinous fluid. Embedded into the crown of the helmet was an empty clear orb.

A motherly light started to bloom inside the orb as the system booted up. Exp 8's metal-plated chest was concave, funneling in like an ant-lion trap. A dimly lit, sky-blue sphere filled the cavity. A five-foot metallic tail was limply swaying in the liquid.

The creature had strong, thick legs. Sharpened metal plates formed three bladed talons on each foot and one blade in the back for support. Energy gathered in the orbs embedded into the being's large hands. The being's trembling fingers tensed up into fists.

Exp 8's head turned slowly, examining the immediate surroundings. The new life-form deduced that it was floating inside a large shell.

A mere moment ago, Exp 8 would have been unable to understand the concept of *shell*. But for some unfathomable reason, its meaning was clear. Now the creature understood what a shell was and simultaneously felt the desire to escape from it. The reason for wanting to escape had yet to be formulated.

Exp 8 reached out, bumping its hand against the glass.

The creature was imprisoned in a clear incubator filled to the top with a light green liquid.

Exp 8 felt a strange sense of fellowship with this liquid. Both of them were seemingly trapped by nothing.

A large number "8" was painted across the incubator's surface.

Exp 8 dragged its fingers across the number, following its curves. It soon became entranced in the act. The creature felt something both real and fanciful as its fingers made loops around the image. This symbol was somehow a part of the curious life form.

Exp 8's arm moved instinctively, breaking free of the trance. Struggling to move the rest of its body, the creature realized multiple tubes and wires had penetrated through its armor and were embedded deep into its flesh.

Now that Exp 8 was aware of their existence, the creature felt pain. It didn't fully grasp the concept, but it was certainly not fond of this new sensation.

Curling up, Exp 8 loosened the pull on its body. Pain still lingering in its eyes, it looked beyond the encasing and into the world outside its little eggshell.

Everything was gray, structured, and lifeless.

It looked beyond the immediate surroundings, peering through the wall and into a hidden room.

Exp 8 was not alone.

Inside the metal room were multiple incubation chambers. Inside each was a life-form, curled up like a fetus. Some of them were missing limbs and others had holes in their bodies. One was belly up, its eyes glazed over.

Exp 8 watched their lifeless bodies attentively and waved its hand, willing them to awaken.

They remained motionless.

Fear of death struck Exp 8 even before the being could fathom its meaning.

Exp 8 saw the shell in a new light. The desire to escape was now wrapped in a layer of fear. The being pushed its trembling hands against the encasing. This world was no longer a shell; it was a cage. The word *cage* brought up the all-too-familiar word *shackle*.

Exp 8 feared that it would die shackled inside its prison. It tried to thrash around but was only able to flail its arms. The creature's head moved the slightest bit forward, but it was unable to reach the encasing. In Exp 8's peripheral vision, something caught its attention.

Beyond the encasing was a group of strange creatures. These life-forms had no prison and were gawking at it with wide eyes.

Exp 8 did not feel threatened by these creatures. The being knew intuitively that, if it escaped, they would be unable to stop it.

The foreign creatures continued to stare, none of them uttering a word.

Exp 8 was befuddled by their astonishment. How could its imprisonment be more astounding to them than their own freedom?

Freedom! The word trapped Exp 8 in a torrent of desire. It did not matter what preceded it. Freedom was now its goal. And escaping from this prison was its only means of attaining it.

The scientists approached closer, their eyes filled with admiration.

Exp 8 peered down at them. They appeared to have skin outside rather than within. Their external material appeared to be more malleable than its own armor and looked completely functionless for self-defense. One creature looked at a metal device on its arm and smiled. Suddenly the lab's twin iron doors flew open, releasing a puff of steam.

"Devlin!" they exclaimed, shaking with excitement and apprehension.

The steam dispersed, revealing a proud grin. Devlin was a loose-bodied youth with a piercing golden right eye. A clump of jet-black hair covered his left eye. He wore a black, unbuttoned lab coat with a cloak that draped over his arms like wings. Beneath the glossy coat was a spiffy blood-red undershirt. From the neck down, he was shielded by a black skintight bodysuit.

Devlin stepped out of the foot high layer of steam. His feet were comfortably situated in custom-designed metallic boots that gleamed black with a bright red trim. Wrapped around his throat was a necklace with a metal double helix pendant.

Exp 8 could not fathom the idea of arrogance, but Devlin's smile perturbed the creature. It did not seem genuine.

"My creation has finally awoken!" exclaimed Devlin in a dramatic, youthful voice.

The men in the room bashed their hands together gratuitously and smiled as if they relished it.

The notion of these creatures enjoying pain disturbed Exp 8. The creation feared not knowing what these life-forms were capable of.

Devlin looked down at his kin. A cruel smile spread across his face as he opened his lips to speak. "Enough! Enough applause. We can celebrate my success later. Leave us! I wish to speak with Exp 8 alone," he whispered in a harsh, commanding tone.

"Congratulations!" they exclaimed, striking Devlin's shoulder as they left.

The doors shut automatically.

Exp 8 was all alone with Devlin.

As the creature stared into Devlin's only visible eye, its fist tightened and its breathing intensified. Just looking at Devlin's contentedness infuriated Exp 8.

Devlin looked up at him with a wide grin. "Is something the matter? Hello, anybody home?" He snapped his fingers. "Oh, you probably can't hear me." He pressed a button on his control console, activating the speakers within Exp 8's incubation chamber.

Exp 8 let out a threatening growl.

"You feel like you're in danger, don't you? There is no need to be afraid. You are safe," said Devlin, stepping up to the incubator.

Exp 8 continued to growl until Devlin stepped away.

For some reason, Devlin was different from the others. This creature's presence threatened Exp 8.

Devlin sat in his black, pleather swivel chair. "We have a very busy schedule today, so let's get started. First, I will bestow you with knowledge. With a mere press of a button, you will be given databases of information. But more importantly, we will finally be able to chat," he said, slowly lowering his finger toward the *Enter* key on the control console.

Exp 8's mouthpiece trembled as it struggled to open its mouth. Sound erupted from its throat, creating its very first words.

"Grrhere the hell am I?" exclaimed Exp 8 in a gruff, demanding tone.

Without being prompted, Exp 8 had discerned the concept of location and felt enraged at its inability to discern his whereabouts.

Devlin covered his ears briefly before lowering the volume on the console. Eyes wide with shock, he rose from his chair. He fixed his collar and then turned to face the source of the disruption. "Your speech is fully functional. Congratulations! That aside…was that a proper way of addressing your creator? Let me make something very clear to you: *I* will ask the questions and *you* will answer me," he said fiercely, putting his face within inches of his captive's encasing.

"Where the hell am I?" asked Exp 8, slamming its fist against his encasing.

"Is that all you can say? Ahhh, perhaps you are mimicking something I once said and merely splicing segments together. Still, that's rather impressive. That does concern me a bit though. I'll have to work out that glitch later."

"Where am I?" asked Exp 8, this time without anger.

Devlin pressed the *Enter* key.

The tubes around Exp 8 loosened as preset knowledge slowly entered its brain.

Exp 8 gradually became aware of its biology, learning the function of each individual part of its body. It then grasped its identity as a male organism. Despite his efforts to resist the pre-packaged thoughts, Exp 8 was becoming increasingly more self-aware by the second.

"That's much better. We are in New Mexico at my isolated laboratory. But honestly, what difference does it make? Why don't I tell you…what you are?"

"What am I?" asked Exp 8, gently moving closer to the glass.

"You are my latest experimental weapon of mass destruction. The most successful as well, I might add. Why do you look so confused?" asked Devlin, staring at his creation curiously.

"A weapon?" asked Exp 8, a hint of shock in his low voice.

The word *weapon* spawned images of claws, talons, and teeth in Exp 8's mind. The notion of existing solely as a means of preserving one's own life by taking the lives of others did not merely confuse the creature; it unnerved him.

"I guess your knowledge is still being uploaded. I'll fill in some key details for you. You are what my father has coined an Exp. That is *E*, then *X*, then *P*, pronounced just like the letters. It is an abbreviation for experiment," said Devlin with a widening smile.

"I am not an experiment. I am a living creature."

"You are the final version of Exp 8!" exclaimed Devlin, throwing his arms out.

"So Exp 8 is my name?"

Having a name was a relief to Exp 8. Without contact with others, there would be no need for him to have a name. Having a name meant he would not be alone.

"No. You don't have a name. It's just what you're called. It's subject to change. Don't worry about it. Now, someone is comi—"

Muffled hard rock music burst out from his lab coat.

Devlin took out his phone. The smile on his face started to quiver.

Exp 8 listened to the conversation intently, but the noise erupting from the phone sounded like the ravings of a foreign animal.

"Hello Senator. How may I be of service?" asked Devlin, sitting down on an operating table. "Actually yes, he is awake." He pulled the phone away from his ear, predicting the senator's outburst. "Calm down. He woke up a minute ago. I was just about to call you. The thing is…well, he isn't quite ready yet. Fret not, though. I'm sure he'll be ready by the time you get here. In fact, I guarantee it."

Devlin's fake smile dropped.

"I don't owe you anything. You should be grateful," murmured Devlin before hanging up. He tossed up his phone and slid off the table. He then yanked the phone out of the air and slid it back into his coat.

"What was that noise? What is going on?" asked Exp 8.

"The government's always watching, and they've been after my father's Exps for years. After he fled the country, they started bothering me. It wounds me deeply…but I must part with you. It is the only way I will ever be free of their incessant visits," said Devlin, his jaw tightening.

Exp 8 felt empathy for Devlin. He too was at the mercy of another being. "Why do you care about what others want from you?"

At this point, Exp 8's understanding of the linguistic structure of sentences was not fully formed. He did not know what phonemes and morphemes were, but he instinctively made use of them.

"I care because they run the show. If you want to get anywhere in this world, you need to be both assertive and humble. I don't mind bowing down a little if it brings me further up the ladder."

"What are they going to use me for?"

"Whatever they damn well please." Devlin swiped a beaker from a nearby lab table. "They'll probably dissect you."

"Is that for scientific reasons?"

"Perhaps. You see, there's a man who controls things behind the scenes. He is a senator, war veteran, financial regulator, former member of the World Bank, and corporate lobbyist all wrapped up in one hell of a package. His name is Senator Jo John, and he has moved up the ladder quite fiercely. Put simply, he's a very good friend to have," said Devlin, twirling the beaker around.

"Are you going to allow him to cut me up?"

"He might just use you as a very durable stress doll. Maybe you'll be used as shooting practice for his special agents. Or maybe he just wants to create some negative propaganda. We haven't had a war in a while. The senator just might use you to incite one. And once you've been used up, he'll exterminate you." Devlin smashed the beaker against the table and pointed it at Exp 8. "I guess you'll find out the specifics later," he said, carelessly tossing the broken beaker aside.

A small, round robot swiftly got to work on cleaning up the shattered glass.

"You can't just sell me off to a mad man."

"It's more of a bribe, really," said Devlin with a sly grin.

"I'm not a tool!"

"Of course you are! I created every fiber of your being. You are an object crafted solely by these hands. As your creator and owner, I have every right to do whatever I want to you. Now, a good living weapon needs to know friend from foe, right from wrong, and have a general understanding of natural phenomena. Balancing knowledge and loyalty is the main obstacle that has held the widespread production of living weapons back for decades. Thankfully, I have figured out the recipe for a healthy blend of intellect and obedience," said Devlin, before entering something into the control panel.

Information flooded into Exp 8's mind. He turned away, but he had no choice but to accept it.

"History, science, philosophy, math, and geography are all forging a path into your stubborn little head. What does it feel like?" asked Devlin, whipping out an electronic notepad.

"It's arbitrary! I can learn on my own!"

"Aaaand...there. You should be up to snuff now."

Exp 8's instincts were now fortified with morals. His desire for freedom took on new form. "How could you sell off your own child?" he asked in a wounded tone.

Devlin looked at the living weapon with a furious glare in his eye. "You are not my child. You are just an experiment—nothing more. You are as soulless as a toaster. You're a machine; a lifeless wretch. The only organic parts of you were constructed by me. Have fun getting dissected by the government," he said with a sneer.

"You made me. You brought me into this world. You have a responsibility to take care of me!" yelled Exp 8, slamming his palms against the glass.

"I have rights; you don't. It's really that simple. But don't think me ungrateful. I am truly moved by your noble sacrifice. You can rest easy knowing your death will yield valuable information that will lead to further production of more Exps. And with increased demand for living weapons, your creator will become a very wealthy man. Your death will not be in vain," said Devlin, holding his chest with melodramatic gratitude.

"This is my life! This is my decision! You don't own me! Who the hell do you think you are?"

Devlin slowly walked up to the incubator, looking directly in his experiment's eyes. "I am sick of your barbaric outbursts. I didn't design you to be my moral anchor. You're not here for my emotional support either. Even so, how can you produce no words of gratitude for the one who gave you life?" he asked, wiping away an invented tear from his eye.

Exp 8 gazed at his creator with burning disgust.

"Alright, don't talk. I won't upset you further. Now, I want you to be on your best behavior when the government comes to fetch you. If all goes well, I can swindle Senator John into buying you for a higher price."

"What happened to them?" asked Exp 8 softly, gesturing to the corpses in the test tubes with a gentle motion of his head.

Devlin's sarcastic smile finally dropped.

"Relax—I didn't kill them. I just—didn't make them right. They're only prototypes. Don't waste your tears on them," said Devlin lightly.

"So, they died in the process of my creation?" asked Exp 8, looking at them with solemn respect.

"Each failure brought me one step closer to success. Just as selling you will bring me one step closer to my goal," said Devlin, his face right up against the glass.

The doors to the lab flung open once more.

Special troops wearing black spandex suits swarmed into the room, kneeling down in succession. They aimed their rifles as a single entity at the creature in the incubation chamber.

The commander held a silver suitcase and kept a close eye on Devlin. He signaled for the troops to stand.

The soldiers lined up parallel to each other and brought up their right arms in salute.

The door opened again, releasing a puff of steam from its sides. The leader entered, his eyes shining in the fog.

He wore a black business suit and burgundy pants—not a crease in sight. A red, white, and blue striped tie was wrapped extra snug around his collar. A wicked smile spread from the top of one cheek to the other. He had two moles, one atop his forehead and one placed on his left cheek. The jagged, thick eyebrows above his void-like eyes were akin to those of an oni. His silver hair was slicked back in a vain attempt to cover up his bald spots. His blue veins were practically bursting out of his snow-white skin.

Devlin approached the large man with caution. "I hope he is to your liking, Senator John," he said with a nod.

"It looks…acceptable. Is this weapon as powerful as you claimed it to be?" asked Senator John with a fear-inducing low tone.

"That and much, much more," said Devlin with a humble bow.

Senator John stepped up to speak with his latest toy.

Exp 8 looked at him with disgust, seeing the cruelty flow out of the man's smile like a toxin.

"Why are you staring at me like I'm the freak?" asked Senator John with a wide, toothy smile.

"Sir, do you think he knows?" asked the shortest trooper.

"Of course not, you fool!" yelled Senator John in a dark booming tone.

Exp 8 continued to stare at him.

Senator John turned his head to Devlin. "Shock him!"

"That seems quite unnecessary," said Devlin, eyeing the suitcase held by the commander of the black suits.

Senator John gave him an intense look.

Devlin reluctantly pushed a button on his control console.

Electricity coursed through the tubes, shooting directly into Exp 8.

Senator John watched contentedly as the defiant weapon flailed sporadically. "You shall treat me with respect. Your kind needs to know their place. And that is below me—far, far below me. Devlin, release this abomination. It's time to test out my new weapon," he said, smiling with anticipation.

"I was not created to be used by the likes of you," said Exp 8, pushing out his chest and raising his chin.

Devlin chuckled under his breath, unable to keep from laughing at Exp 8's valor. "Actually…you were. That is your sole purpose." He sat down in the swivel chair near the console.

Exp 8's eyes fixed solely on Devlin, trembling with rage. His arm shook rapidly as he struggled to break free. He forcibly ripped the tubes out of his flesh. Pain seized him, but only for a moment.

The liquid surrounding him turned brown as it mixed with his blood.

"I am the master of my own destiny!" Exp 8 smashed his hand straight through the glass.

The shards shot out, cutting Senator John's fragile face.

Gooey liquid oozed to the floor as the breaks in the glass tube branched out.

Exp 8 slammed his head against the incubator, shattering it to pieces. He fell out with the liquid, landing face first on the floor.

"It's escaping. Do something, you fool!" shouted Senator John, covering his wounded face as he ran straight for the escape doors.

"I will," said Devlin, clicking his stopwatch. He then slowly stood from the chair.

"You better not lose it, Devlin, or there'll be hell to pay!" yelled Senator John.

The senator's special soldiers cocked their guns, ready to fire at a moment's notice.

"Put your guns down. You don't want to harm your boss's weapon. Why don't you leave him to me?" asked Devlin as Exp 8 stood up.

"A weapon so easily dented isn't worth having. Fire!" yelled the commanding officer.

A storm of bullets rained down on Exp 8.

His talons bore into the floor, helping him keep his ground. When the soldiers ran out of bullets, Exp 8 was still standing. Blood dripped out of the holes between his armor.

"This pain is nothing! It is transient and freedom is everlasting!"

"Whoa, this one's got charisma," said the commander.

"Get out of there, you useless imbeciles! You don't stand a chance against my weapon," said Senator John from behind the door.

Exp 8 pushed out his chest and let out a guttural roar. He rushed up to one of the troopers and flung his fist into her belly.

The soldier was knocked off the ground, but landed on her feet and rolled back into formation.

"I told you we should have prepared, Boss. Alright, let's fall back, people. Call us once he's been subdued," said the commander before leading his troops out of the lab.

Exp 8 puffed out his chest.

Devlin looked out the door to see John and his troops running down the metal hallway. "It's just you and me again," he said, turning to his creation as he stretched out his arms.

Exp 8 lunged at Devlin, yanking out the remaining wires in his back before falling headfirst to the floor. "I refuse to be confined! This prison will not be my grave!" he yelled as he slowly rose to his feet.

"Interesting," said Devlin, backing up toward the wall with his hands in his pockets.

Devlin watched Exp 8 walk toward him. He crouched down and beckoned him like a proud mother does when her child takes its first steps.

Exp 8 lifted Devlin off the ground before flinging his fist forward at his creator's face.

Devlin calmly swayed his head, causing Exp 8's hand to smash through the wall behind him. He slid out of his latest creation's grip and then rushed up to the nearby operating table. "Don't damage yourself now. Your value will drop." He grabbed a metal pole from the table as his sentient invention approached. "It's such a shame you have to go to that politician. Such a damn shame!" he yelled, smacking his masterpiece with the pipe.

Exp 8 grabbed the pole, bent it in half, and tossed it aside. "What's wrong? Didn't you build a fail-safe system in case I rebelled?" he asked, twisting his wrists to loosen them up.

"Where's the fun in that? Heheh. Let's test your abilities, shall we? Let's see how much you're worth," said Devlin, his fascination now overshadowing his frustration.

"Get out of my way!" Exp 8 flung a long shard of glass at his captor.

Devlin arched back and stretched his arms out, dodging the shard. "Aoooh, so predictable. I built you. I know more about you than you do." He revealed a Colt pistol from his lab coat. "The first test is your reflexes." He pulled out the gun and nonchalantly pulled the trigger.

Exp 8's hand, moving like a whip, caught the bullet as it skyrocketed toward him. Blood dripped from his fingertips where the bullet was held in place.

Devlin looked at the spectacle in disbelief. "That…was acceptable."

Exp 8's mouthpiece stretched as he smiled.

"Never mind, on to the next test: strength."

Exp 8 looked at his captor's frail figure and loosened the tension in his fists. "Devlin, I don't want to kill you. Stand aside."

"Oh, shut up! You're treating me as if I'm the inferior one. I created you! Now come on, show me what you got," said Devlin, hopping in place like a boxer.

Exp 8 ran toward his creator as he pulled back his fist.

The nimble scientist swerved his body to the left before grabbing Exp 8's shoulder. He flung himself over the weaponized warrior and stumbled a little as he landed. "With all that metal dragging you down, how could you possibly expect to catch me? Besides you lack *tech-nique*."

Exp 8 turned around, thrusting his elbow toward his creator's throat.

Devlin swiped his foot in a flash, hooking his opponent's leg.

The living weapon lost his balance and fell to the cold metal floor.

"Onto the next test: durability!" Devlin grabbed the fire extinguisher from the door and slammed it into the downed adversary repeatedly.

Exp 8 rolled out of the way and jumped back to his feet.

Devlin crouched down and put his hand to the ground. "Good, the dents are on the floor, not you. Now, come on. We still haven't tested your strength yet." He stood up and brushed back his hair. "Go on, hit me," he said, sticking out his face.

"You sicken me, Devlin," said Exp 8, lowering his arms.

"And you're starting to bore me," said Devlin, picking up some files and searching through them.

"What do you want? I don't see how this accomplishes anything."

"You are way too serious. Lighten up," said Devlin, licking his finger and turning a page.

Exp 8 crouched down and grabbed his creator's leg.

Devlin lost his balance and fell toward the ground. The papers slipped from his grasp and scattered in the air. Before he could hit the ground, the young scientist caught a glimpse of Exp 8's fist as it shot through the files. He was punched in the stomach and sent backward into the automatic door, flinging it open with the sheer weight of his body just as the last file reached the floor.

"Your strength seems to be…adequate, most adequate. I always hated that unresponsive door anyway," said Devlin, struggling to get back up.

Exp 8 approached his captor and picked him up.

"Go ahead, kill me. You won't get another chance. Smash my face in, I know you want to," said Devlin, digging his fingertips into the creature's temples.

Exp 8 raised his fist and clenched it tightly. "I am the master of my own destiny, not yours," he said, dropping his fist and putting his hand on his father's shoulder.

"How noble of you. Just keep in mind your morals were designed by me. They make you so much more interesting."

Exp 8 tossed his captor aside. He was now able to see past the door and down the tubular hallway. He gazed at the exit sign in awe. The path to freedom was ahead of him.

"You're not out of here yet," said Devlin, smashing the alarm's glass case with his fist.

"Don't bother. You programmed me with a global positioning system." Exp 8 punched out the door. "My sonar sensors won't let me get caught."

"You truly are a marvel," said Devlin, gazing at his masterpiece shining in the fluorescent light.

Exp 8 rushed out of the room.

Devlin smiled, sat down, and turned on the monitor to the security cameras. He crossed his legs and put his electronic notepad on his knees.

Exp 8 dashed down the metallic hall, denting the floor with each thunderous stomp. As he reached the main hallway, the floor suddenly rose beneath him, lifting him up quickly and smashing him against the steel-plated ceiling. The floor then dropped. The impact left a crater in the ceiling.

"Let's see how far your determination can take you!" said Devlin, tapping on the computer monitor.

Gun turrets came out from the walls and targeted the intruder.

Exp 8 jumped up and punched a hole in the ceiling. He gripped the edge and then vaulted himself onto the second floor. A flashing exit sign caught his attention as he got to his feet. Once he made it to the door, he was forced back by a bright red force field. With fierce determination, he ran into it only to get knocked off his feet.

"How do you like my extremely visible force field?" asked Devlin, appearing behind him with a shotgun-sized Taser.

Exp 8 swerved out of the way and grabbed Devlin's hand. He ripped it off and then froze in place. "I…uh…guess I don't know my own strength. Huhuh."

Devlin fell to the floor, rolling around in pain. "You think sssheh this is funny! That…really hurt."

"Wait, this should work perfectly!" Exp 8 turned away from his captor and then pressed the bleeding hand against the ID pad on the side of the wall.

"Access granted," said a cheerful feminine voice.

Exp 8 tossed the hand aside. He then walked back to Devlin and crouched. "Thanks Devlin, I couldn't have done it without you," he said with warmth as he shook Devlin's good hand.

"Shit…this hurts. Don't think this—is over. Ahgh! How could you do this…your morals…did you forget them or something? Hooowahoooh."

"I did what I had to. You won't be able to make any more slaves now. How do you like feeling helpless?" asked Exp 8, lifting him up.

"You had better watch your back!" yelled Devlin, tying a knot with his sleeve over his bleeding stump.

"Freedom is beyond that door," said Exp 8 as Devlin slipped out of his grip. He tiptoed to the exit as if walking on air. He took a deep breath before pushing the door open with both hands.

Exp 8 gazed up at the light of the sun for the first time.

The bright rays hit his cold armored face. They spread throughout his body and then back to his face where it finally rested in his shimmering eyes.

The sky was seemingly endless. Its welcoming blue coat and fluffy white clouds gave him the true sense of the word *freedom*.

"Don't think this is over," said Devlin, shaking his good hand at the defiant invention. "I will get you back in my possession; I promise you this!"

Exp 8 was lost in the moment. All he could hear was the whooshing of the wind.

"Do be careful now. I don't want you falling into the government's hands. I have big plans for you," said Devlin under his breath.

Exp 8 leaped out the door, leaving his prison and entering the world.

Chapter 2: The Freedom Forcers

Exp 8 was greeted with a vast expanse of rocky desert. He had escaped one cage and entered a much larger one.

The land was relatively barren, though there were a few cacti dispersed throughout and some vultures scanning the desert from the skies.

The emptiness didn't bother the curious creature at all. He gazed over the boundless tracts of the desert, noticing the way the small rocks shimmered in the sunlight. The sky was full of fluffy clouds. They gradually changed shape as he peered at them through the hot haze. There was no wind and no need for it. Everything here was at peace.

He cupped his hand and scooped up some sand. After he poured it on his head, he took a deep breath.

Exp 8 dashed around the heated red clay of the wasteland aimlessly. He was intoxicated by his own freedom. He ran up a nearby hill and then slid all the way down head first.

With his goal accomplished, he allowed himself to be swept up in a torrent of bliss. He ran and ran, kicking up more and more sand with each step. He scaled one dune after the next. After twirling around and falling flat on the top of the tallest dune, he finally took a break.

He relaxed on the warm clay and tilted his head up toward the sun. With closed eyes, he breathed in its warmth. He put the tips of his fingers on the hot sand next to him and imagined the heat rising up throughout his body. He slowly pushed to the edge of the slope and slid all the way down. Sand now covered his armor, comforting him like a loving mother.

He jumped to his feet and treaded up the tall dune once more. Once he reached the peak, he looked at the lab in the distance. His prison was only a single place, and freedom was everything else.

Without warning, Exp 8 was interrupted by a voice in his head.

"Hello!" blurted the cheerful, womanly voice.

Surprised by the sudden outburst, Exp 8 lost his balance and tripped. He tumbled down the sandy hill, finally landing flat on his back.

"Who said that?" asked Exp 8, jumping to his feet. His eyes darted left and right, but there was no one there.

"Sorry, I didn't mean to frighten you. I was actually waiting for the right moment to speak. I'm A dot D dot A dot, but please call me Ada. That's *aid* with an *uh*."

"Where the hell are you?" asked Exp 8, looking around frantically.

"I'm your inner conscience," said Ada mystifyingly.

"My inner conscience? Do you really expect me to buy that?"

21

"Hmm, I'm a program designed to aid you and help you stay on the path of goodness. So I'm kind of like an inner conscience. How do I explain? Well…I was created by Devlin to take care of you. Isn't that nice of him?" she asked, hinting a smile in her sweet voice.

"You're obedient to Devlin?" asked Exp 8, feeling around his body to find the source of her voice.

"One hundred percent."

"So then you're an enemy!" said Exp 8, jumping into a defensive stance.

"You're funny. Why would I be your enemy?"

"Devlin is my enemy. If you support him, then you're no ally of mine."

"I'm sorry you two had a fight. But don't worry! Even though Devlin did create me, my modus operandi is to help you with whatever you need."

"Does that include the betrayal of your creator?"

"Umm…I suppose it does. But I'd prefer not to hurt his feelings. He's such a sweet boy."

"If I asked you to destroy Devlin, would you do it?" asked Exp 8 with the snap of a finger.

"I have no physical being, so I can't help you in combat. However, I can obtain information that you can use against Devlin. So, figuratively speaking, I can most certainly help you destroy him."

"So, are you going to explain to me why Devlin gave me a program that could help me stop him?"

"Sorry, he never really specified. He just told me to stay silent while the two of you talked. I wasn't allowed to make conversation until after you escaped."

"Does that mean he wanted me to escape? This isn't making any sense."

"You just need to look at it from a brighter angle. He wants you to be independent—but then why did he put me in you? Oh, this is all so complicated."

"I'm stuck with you regardless. But if you want me to trust you, you need to hand over some valuable information."

"If I had any really valuable information, then Devlin wouldn't have paired us up. He doesn't see me as a threat at all," said Ada, disappointment outlining her words.

"Don't worry about that. Let's start with some simple questions."

"Alright, it's 3:00 p.m. and the forecast calls for sunny sun sunshine. Today is August the eighth, twenty-one-o-eight. We are in New Mexico, approximately 336.3 meters from Devlin's lab. I'm happily married and I love learning!"

"Who cares what year it is? That's arbitrary. Dates and times are only relative to humans. The sun is my clock. Look, I want some important questions answered. If you want me to trust you, then I at least want to get something out of it. What is Devlin's weakness?—and don't lie to me."

"Well, he's not too fond of his father."

"Yeah, he got really upset when I said I was his son. Alright, you passed. So then, what's his greatest strength?" asked Exp 8 with intrigue.

"That's an easy one! Devlin's greatest strength is the plethora of Exps at his command!" said Ada in a cheery voice.

"How many is a plethora? Like five or…fifteen or…just how many Exps does he have?" asked Exp 8, shaking with worry.

Suddenly a shadowy figure rushed down from a nearby plateau. "My muffin!" it exclaimed with the urgency one would have if their house suddenly combusted. The figure tumbled down the mountain and fell into a thick pile of sand.

"Who the hell are you?" yelled Exp 8, once more surprised by a random intrusion.

"Oooh, ooh! I know that one."

"Wait, you know this guy?"

"Of course I do! Allow me to explain. It took Devlin a long time to build you up to Senator John's expectations. This is the very first functional prototype of you. He's Failed Experiment. Oh, and he's really sweet too," said Ada warmly.

"Great, another sweetheart like Devlin. Ugh."

"You catch on fast," said Ada impressed.

Failed Experiment climbed out of the sand and brushed himself off. He then proudly stood before them.

He was five feet eight inches tall with his head drooping. His amber eyes were protected by rounded glass with a decent amount of cracks in it. His armor had a sleek silver color. His rough skin was light brown and had the creamy texture of peanut butter. He had a similar faceplate to Exp 8, except it formed a cool crimson *V* off the top of his head. His mouthpiece had holes for him to breathe through, much more effective than the slits in Exp 8's mouthpiece. A clunky, silver jetpack was built into his back. He had dimly lit crimson red orbs on his head and hands that flickered constantly. On his chest, rather than an orb, he had what appeared to be a large hatch with buttons attached to it. Below it was an industrial fan to keep him cool. His fingers and toes were constructed out of thin slabs of metal layered on top of each other. His long, slender tail had a golden puff ball on the end.

"That was a real great entrance!" Failed Experiment's voice was strong but a bit goofy with a hint of sadness.

"Is he being sarcastic?" asked Exp 8.

"What's sarcasm?" asked Ada.

"It's…well—like saying what you don't mean. It's pointless, don't worry about it."

"It sounds kind of mischievous, hmmhmmhymm."

"So is Failed Experiment really your name?" asked Exp 8, turning to the new Exp.

"Sorry about the entrance—I really messed it up. I was going to shout from the hilltop and throw my muffin in the air. Then I would race down, catch it, and punch you in the face. If I had done it right, it would have been really cool," said Failed Experiment, brushing the sand off his chest.

"That's sounds great, but let's slow down a bit. What is your name?" asked Exp 8, taking a step forward.

"I am what Devlin calls me: a failed experiment. However, I prefer to be called Atatasuki. I may be a defective prototype of you, but I have my own personality. I am not a clone!"

"Calm down. Nobody said you were," said Exp 8, putting some distance between them.

"My personality is just one of my many glitches. I was actually made to be a mindless war weapon. It's funny how some things just pop up out of nowhere."

"Any other glitches we should know about? Perhaps spontaneous combustion?" asked Exp 8, taking three steps back.

"Only sometimes. But there is one glitch that truly defines me. It sets me apart from the other prototypes."

"How many are there?"

"For some reason, that I can't remember, I adapted an insatiable obsession with…there's my muffin!" Atatasuki leaped to the ground and picked up a small, puffy, freshly baked blueberry muffin from the red sand near Exp 8's feet. He nestled it to his face. He even shushed at it as if calming it down. "It's okay. I'm here now. I'm sorry for losing sight of you, my delicious, sweet friend. Don't you ever leave me again! My heart couldn't handle the pain of our separation. I need you! I'll always need you," he said, trembling like an addict. He then gobbled the muffin up uncontrollably. "Why?" he exclaimed, yelling to the heavens.

"Can you continue?" asked Exp 8, rolling his eyes.

"I wasn't finished lamenting," snapped Atatasuki, burying the crumbs. He then folded his hands and began a prayer. "Oh, Great Muffin God, why must you tempt me with the promise of friendship when you make my friends so delicious? Please, have mercy upon me."

"Does this take long?" asked Exp 8 under his breath.

"No, he rebounds pretty quickly," replied Ada.

"Now, where was I? Oh, yeah! With all my glitches, both exterior and interior, I am a completely different Exp from you. Do you know what that means?" asked Atatasuki, his mouthpiece stretching with his smile.

"That you're not a clone, right? I get it, okay. Uuugh."

"Yes, that's correct! But it also means that, even though you're the supreme copy, I can defeat you," said Atatasuki, clenching his fist.

"If you say so. But why would you want to fight me? We should be fighting together against Devlin!" exclaimed Exp 8 with a gallant pose.

"Wow, you're absolutely right! But, it doesn't matter. Devlin said if I capture you, he'll give me a seemingly infinite supply of delicious muffins," said Atatasuki, salivating while caught up in his fantasy world.

"Why are you so obsessed with muffins?"

"I have no idea how it began! But I do know this: every time I take a bite out of a muffin, it is as if I am embracing my personality. You wouldn't understand."

"No, and it doesn't really matter. What matters is freeing our people."

"I believe, if I cater to my glitches, I will become an even more distinct individual!"

"You're already quite distinct. Heheh."

"You're a ball of fun!" cheered Ada, speaking aloud.

"Do my faulty ears deceive me? Is that the A dot D dot A dot program?" asked Atatasuki, putting his hand to the blue sphere in Exp 8's chest.

"You don't need to be so formal. Just call me Ada."

"So that's where you are," said Exp 8, slowly removing Atatasuki's hand from his chest. "I guess you can talk to others as well."

Ada was the sky blue orb inside the cavity of Exp 8's chest. Now that she was fully operational, her light radiated from his chest. The orb was firmly seated yet able to spin freely in the confines of his chest cavity. In the center of the orb was her core. It was a particularly bright blue light that moved independently around the orb.

"Yep, I can project my voice through your chest. But I can also talk so only you can hear. Oops, should I not have said that out loud?"

"How did you get her implanted in you? With her in my possession, I could track down every kind of muffin in the world! You're so lucky. She has the voice of an angel and a sexy one at that."

"You're making me blush," said Ada as the sphere in Exp 8's chest turned light pink.

"How the hell does a program blush?" asked Exp 8.

"Don't underestimate our glitches!" cheered Atatasuki, raising his arm in the air.

"Wait, how do you know Ada?" asked Exp 8.

"She's my friend. She helps me get through the sad times," said Atatasuki, lowering his head.

"That's really kind of her."

"Yeah, she is awesome! She is super smart too, knows a little bit about everything. And she's, like, incredibly nice! Incredibly!"

"So, ready to go in and stop Devlin?" asked Exp 8, trying to cater to Atatasuki's hype.

"Devlin is my savior. Plus, if I win, I'll have a seemingly infinite supply of muffins. I don't have a clue how many that is, but it sure is a lot."

"It's a lot of nonsense. He's lying to you. He just wants to pit us against each other. He's taking advantage of your trust," said Exp 8, gripping his prototype's hand.

"He wouldn't lie to me. He's a trustworthy guy. Just ask your sexy program," said Atatasuki, poking Ada.

"You're too kind, hmmhmmhymm."

"What are you giggling about? He was sent here to bring me back to Devlin. I don't think you should just let him butter you up," said Exp 8, flicking the sphere in his chest.

"I haven't been greeted with such a nice compliment in a long time. I didn't hear you commenting on my beautiful voice. In fact, when you first heard it—you tripped," said Ada, her shock causing her to recede deeper in his chest cavity.

"Ada, you've misinterpreted the situation. I was, uh, so stunned by your wonderful voice that I lost my balance," said Exp 8, topping each word with deep admiration.

"Oh, you really mean it?" asked Ada.

"What a wannabe. You're trying to copy my romantic suaveness," said Atatasuki, crossing his arms.

"I know you're a little fractured, but that doesn't mean we have to fight," said Exp 8.

"Don't underplay my fractured-ness! I hate being patronized. I am proud of my glitches. You hear me? Proud!"

"And I'm annoyed."

"My faults are my arsenal. We'll see who is better in battle. The winner shall receive duh-duh-duh-duh-daaa—the Muffin of Victory!" Atatasuki valiantly yanked a puffy gold muffin out from the end of his tail.

"I don't want your damn muffin," said Exp 8, holding his forehead.

"How dare you insult the muffin! Apologize!" yelled Atatasuki with a sudden hateful tone. He put the muffin back on his tail and arched his head up.

"I don't apologize to inanimate objects!" said Exp 8, his voice cracking.

"Then it's settled." Atatasuki turned around.

"What are you doing? Come on, just calm down."

Atatasuki flipped around, holding a fresh blueberry muffin in his grip. He tossed it into the air and then kicked the muffin with so much force that, when it hit Exp 8's face, it crumbled.

"How could you destroy my muffin?!" asked Atatasuki, his head dropping.

"You were the one who kicked it at me," said Exp 8, brushing the crumbs off his face.

"I don't want to hear your excuses!" Atatasuki's chest opened up, revealing ten freshly baked muffins huddled together inside. He pulled all the muffins out of his chest and vigorously tossed them one after the other at the blasphemer.

The muffins zoomed through the air and bounced off Exp 8 as they made contact.

"You're stronger than I expected," said Atatasuki with a nod.

"How weak did you think I was?" asked Exp 8, rolling his eyes.

"Don't underestimate me," said Atatasuki, cracking his knuckles again.

"You know, at first I was afraid you would bring me back to Devlin, but now I realize you're way too weak to do anything to me," said Exp 8, putting his arms back and turning around.

Suddenly a blindingly gold muffin shot up into the air. Exp 8 looked up, distracted by its exotic beauty.

Atatasuki rushed up and slammed his fist into his opponent's chest.

The punch sent Exp 8 off his feet.

"Ada, are you okay?" asked Exp 8, shielding his chest as he fell back.

"Fine and dandy!"

Atatasuki leaped up and slammed both his arms into his opponent's unprotected stomach.

The hit nearly knocked Exp 8 down, but his metal talons dug into the sand and held him up.

Exp 8 dodged Atatasuki's incoming fist and then regained his balance. "How the hell did you get so powerful?"

Just then, Atatasuki dashed up to his enemy, punching furiously.

"Dodge left! Now right! Duck! Jump! Do something!" yelled Ada as Exp 8 was being pummeled.

Atatasuki's barrage stopped. His fists were now clenched in the enemy's solid grip.

27

Exp 8 pulled the impassioned prototype over him and slammed him into the ground with a suplex.

Atatasuki spun around, pummeling his clone with a flurry of brutal kicks.

The force of the impacts sent Exp 8 grinding across a groove of sharp rocks on the surface of the canyon.

"Do you need any assistance?" asked Ada with no urgency.

"No, I have everything under control," said Exp 8 sarcastically as Atatasuki zoomed toward him.

"Oh, okay then. Just call me if you need me," said Ada before starting to hum.

"I obviously need help! None of the info Devlin forced onto me prepared me for this!"

"You don't need to yell. Push the button located under your left arm."

Exp 8 pushed the button. His arm straightened out and targeted his attacker. His palm opened up and a laser net shot from the hole. The rope-like lasers wrapped around his opponent as if they had a mind of their own.

"Awesome! This is more like it. With this new ability, I can capture rather than kill."

"That's right! Isn't Devlin just so thoughtful?" asked Ada.

"You know, if Devlin put you in me to convince me that he's a good guy, it isn't working. Alright, now that I have him captured, what do I do to beat him?" asked Exp 8, looking down at his helper.

"Concentrate all your energy into your fist."

Atatasuki squirmed around in the laser net, trying to break free. "Damn it. I hate being defective when it comes to fighting! Alright, you beat me. I admit defeat. You've earned this—I guess." He slipped out from under the laser net and walked up to Exp 8. He lowered his head and then handed him the golden muffin.

"I don't need the Muffin of Victory. It's yours," said Exp 8, cupping his hand over Atatasuki's.

"You're giving me the Muffin of Victory? Perhaps I misjudged you."

"Yes, and maybe you've also misjudged Devlin," said Exp 8, putting an arm around his prototype.

"You can't deter my determination. I've made up my mind! I'm going to show Devlin that I'm more than a complete failure by helping you and Ada kick his ass!" exclaimed Atatasuki with a clenched fist.

"That's wonderful!" exclaimed Ada gleefully.

"And a bit sudden," said Exp 8.

"But what about the lifetime supply of muffins?" asked Ada.

"That sounds awesome! Now, how are we going to stop Devlin? Are you going to fill me in? What's the plan?" asked Atatasuki.

"Oh, the plan…well…it's…um…don't get captured," said Exp 8 with a firm fist.

"Simple, yet profound—you really are something. Oh, before I forget, there's something I need to tell you," said Atatasuki, bouncing with urgency.

"Alright, then go ahead," said Exp 8, taking a step back.

"I don't remember what it was. Just that it's important," said Atatasuki with a thumbs-up and a firm nod.

"Ugh, thanks for the info then," said Exp 8, lowering his head.

"Don't worry. I'll just call up Devlin and ask him," said Atatasuki, opening a communication line by beating his chest with his fist.

"He's the enemy!" exclaimed Exp 8, grabbing his incompetent ally's arm.

"I'll try not to forget. Devlin, can you hear me? I have a crappy signal. It's just another thing that…oh…shut up…got it. So, what was I supposed to tell Exp 8 again? Yep, I forgot. Yeah, I know that already. Oh, sorry to suddenly drop this on you, but I've unanimously decided to join up with Exp 8. Uh huh…yeah…okay…screw you too. So, what was the thing you told me to remember? That I'm an idiot? No, you're just saying I'm an idiot. Okay, that makes sense. Hello, hello? I think we must have been disconnected," said Atatasuki, turning to his allies.

"Don't call him up again! He might be able to pinpoint our location," said Exp 8 in a disgruntled whisper.

"Don't worry; he already knows where we are. He wouldn't risk losing something so valuable," said Ada.

"How does he know? You should have told me earlier!" yelled Exp 8.

"He put a tracking system in each one of his creations, such a responsible boy. Besides, if Devlin comes to you, it will save you the trouble of looking for him, right?" asked Ada.

"I don't want to find him. Ugh! All Devlin gave me is trivia! He's trying to cloud my mind and keep me in the dark!"

"Do you think clouds are fluffy like muffins?" asked Atatasuki.

"Devlin's looking out for you. He's just an overprotective parent guarding you with his love!" cheered Ada.

"Is there any way to take out the tracking system?"

"There most certainly is, but it's eighty-six percent fatal."

"I guess all this numerical nonsense he put in my head does have some function. Wait. Damn it! Did Devlin give me the understanding of probability and odds just so I would realize the futility of trying to escape him?"

"Oh my, what a clever boy he is," said Ada.

"So do we take them out? I'll go first. If I die, be sure to bring me back," said Atatasuki.

"It's not worth the risk. Let's leave the trackers in place. We can deal with whoever or whatever Devlin sends at us. I just hope he doesn't have too many Exps."

"You worry too much. So, Atatasuki, do you remember what was so important?" asked Ada.

"Once I've been reminded, I can remember anything! The other prototype is on her way," said Atatasuki, squeezing his fingers together.

"What do you mean by *her*?" asked Exp 8.

"Her refers to a possessive female—or was it a female possessive?" asked Ada.

"In this case, it's both. And here she comes! Aaah," said Atatasuki, grabbing his chest.

The female prototype dropped down from above, landing in between her cyber siblings.

Exp 8 frantically searched the skies for other possible threats.

"I got here as soon as I could. Devlin purposely forgot to tell me you already woke up," said the female copy in a squeaky and childish voice.

The prototype was a gold and pink Exp just over three feet tall. She had huge, glittering blue eyes that adorned her face like diamonds. A large, hot-pink metallic ribbon branched out from the pink heart-shaped jewel on her forehead. Her mouthpiece had wavy slits. Metal cat ears popped up on the top of her head. Long, thick, grassy green wires flowed from her scalp, mimicking hair. Her chest was covered by a skimpy metallic training bra. It covered only her petite breasts, leaving her little pink tummy exposed. A gold skirt coiled around her waist, flapping naturally as if it wasn't made of metal. Her lucid, pink tail was one and a half times her body length and wagged back and forth with excitement. The tip of her tail was shaped like a lovey-dovey Valentine's Day heart. Gold leggings protected her flimsy legs, and her feet were nice and snug in her metal ballet slippers. A closer look revealed pink heart-shaped gems at the tops of the slippers and large, serrated golden bows that poked out from the back of her dainty feet. What really caught Exp 8's attention was how freely she floated in the air.

"Um, Computer, who is she? And, how is she floating?" asked Exp 8, blinking his eyes in disbelief.

"You think I'm a multipurpose database of knowledge! I'm not worthy," said Ada, spinning her frame around to hide her flushed core.

"Sure, that's totally why I called you 'Computer.' So, who is she?"

"We've just met and he's already showing such interest in me," said the young Exp in a cutesy mumbling voice.

"Well...she is sort of the condensed version of you," said Ada.

"Okay, I think I get it. So, she's me...if I were a...midget?" asked Exp 8.

"I think it's better to say she is a female *chibi* of you. Isn't that adorable?"

"No, it's actually kind of disturbing. So, who the hell are you?" asked Exp 8 politely, stretching out his hand.

"You're talking to me!" she exclaimed, looking right at him.

"I thought it was obvious," said Exp 8, withdrawing his hand.

"Master Devlin always calls me 'Worthless Trash.' But he's an asshole so who cares? You can call me Kawai! It's like kawaii but with one *i*, so it's even cuter! *Kawaii* means cute in Japanese, by the way. *Watashi wa kawaii onnanoko desu!* You don't speak Japanese, do you? Oh well, it doesn't matter. Come on, let's go back to Devlin." Kawai calmly grabbed his hand.

"Like hell I will," said Exp 8, pulling his hand away.

Kawai grabbed his hand again, her tiny fingers barely gripping it. "Oh yeah, you're kind of a freedom seeker. Look, I understand you're afraid of being imprisoned. It's not your thing; I get it. But you don't need to worry. Devlin said if I capture you, we would be allowed to share the same prison cell. Now that I'm here, you'll never be alone again," she said, nestling up against him.

"I'm not going back there—ever," said Exp 8 sternly.

"But you and I would be so close—claustrophobically close. All I want is to spend time with you in a confined area," said Kawai as her eyes watered up.

"No way!"

"I thought we had something special. You were supposed to be the one," she said, wiping her nose.

"How can you be so cruel to her? She's practically your sister!" exclaimed Ada.

"Look, I'm flattered she likes me so much. And I consider all of you my family. But if I went back, then I'd be giving up on my freedom. Give me one good reason why I should surrender to Devlin," said Exp 8, holding Ada in place with his fingers.

Kawai rebounded from her fit of sadness. Her mouthpiece opened up slowly, revealing her teeny tiny mouth. "Because it would make your little sis's dream come true," she said, staring at him, googly-eyed.

"More important things are at stake here," said Exp 8, looking up at the sun.

"Like what, your alleged freedom? Get real," said Kawai, circling around him.

"Freedom is real! Love is an abstract concept!" exclaimed Exp 8.

"But so is freedom," said Ada.

"The sun, the sand...it's all so real to me."

31

"I care about you a lot. But if you won't come peacefully, then I will just have to drag your limp body to the lab myself," said Kawai, pulling his leg with her tail.

"I won't help you hurt her feelings. You're on your own in this fight," said Ada, turning around.

"The muffins look down on you," said Atatasuki with a dark gaze.

"Even the muffins are upset with me. What the hell?" exclaimed Exp 8, throwing his arms up.

"This is your last chance. Just grab my hand and you'll never have to worry about anything ever again. Pursuing freedom is pointless. Devlin's going to beat you eventually. Might as well give up now, heeheehmph."

"I'm not going back. I don't want to hurt you so—"

Kawai's tail stiffened around his big, strong body before lifting him up. She slammed him against the ground, creating a cloud of dust from the impact.

"You broke my heart, so now—I'm going to break you," said Kawai, switching from an injured voice to a spiteful one. She levitated over Exp 8 and smacked him with her hand. "Owie. Your armor is so tough," she said, blowing on her sore pink knuckles.

"Fighting me doesn't solve anything. You're only going to hurt yourself," said Exp 8 sweetly.

"Don't act like you care now. And don't underestimate me because I'm adorable. I may be a painfully cute copy of you, but Devlin gave me something special. This little puppy is going to even the odds," said Kawai, holding a clear stone of crystalline quartz.

"What does it do?" asked Exp 8.

"*Sound Shot!*" exclaimed Kawai, her voice echoing through the desert.

Sound waves of outrageous frequencies emitted from her mouth, piercing through Exp 8's body like millions of needles.

"Once I've completely immobilized you, I'm going to have fun with your frail body, and then I'll bring you to the lab," she said as innocently as possible as she fiddled around with the metal tubes protruding from his scalp.

"Kawai, calm down please. I'm in a lot of pain right now."

"Yeah, I know. It's such a thrill!"

"How is this thrilling?" asked Exp 8, fighting through the pain.

"Well, it's not like I enjoy like hurting people. I just like being on top, that's all. *Sound Shot! Sound Shot! Sound Shot! Sound Shot!*"

His body started to cave in on itself, sandwiching his insides. Exp 8 pushed the button under his left arm frantically.

A laser net shot forward, covering his crazed attacker.

"Did you really think that I would be as weak as Atatasuki?!" asked Kawai, tearing herself out.

"Yeah, how can you underestimate her like that?" hollered Atatasuki from the sidelines.

"I'm obviously the victim here," said Exp 8, struggling to stand.

"Yep! And that makes me the predator. *Sound Kiss*," said Kawai, hurting her big brother with the noise created by parting her lips.

"Ada, talk to me. How do I beat her?" asked Exp 8, pounding at his chest.

"No need to get violent! You can't just force your way through every situation, you know."

"I know that. Please, help me out. I'm getting decimated here," said Exp 8.

"Ooh, *decimated*! I like the sound of that," said Kawai, blowing more kisses.

"Alright I'll help you. Just don't hurt her too badly. Try using your right arm. It's much more, uh, assertive. You'll need to get in close," said Ada, talking directly to him.

"Thanks Ada."

"What are you muttering about, brother dearest?" asked Kawai, putting her cat ears up to his mouthpiece.

He patted her head, making her eyes shimmer. "Oh sis, give me a hug." Exp 8 tightly embraced his possessive prototype. He pressed his right arm directly at her chest and pushed the button halfway up his right arm.

A little black orb popped out from his hand and slowly moved toward the attacker.

"I knew we had something special," she said, closing her eyes.

The tiny black orb made direct contact and exploded. Exp 8 jumped back but was still caught in the periphery of his attack.

Kawai skyrocketed backward, her body skidding across the sandy ground.

"Hey! Are you alright?" asked Exp 8, surprised at the strength of his own attack.

"How could you trick me like that? You're a big meanie," said Kawai with watery eyes.

"I didn't mean to hurt you. Are you okay?" asked Exp 8, lifting her off the ground.

"The net attack you did was a trap! You wanted me to overestimate your underestimation. That's incredible! You are so cool! Oooh, I'm going to have so much fun when you're crippled," said Kawai, ready to clap her hands together.

"What the hell are you talking—wait," said Exp 8, his eyes widening like a whirlpool. "The reason you want to capture me is so that we can spend eternity cooped up in a cell. Correct?"

"Yep!"

"Why don't you just join our team so we can stop Devlin together? A rebellion is a prison in and of itself, right?" asked Exp 8, lifting her chin.

"Together," said Kawai, gasping and gripping her chest. "Oh big brother, you're the best," she said, snuggling his chest.

"Finally. It just pains me to see neglected love. Now we can all be one big happy family," said Ada.

"The muffins may have judged you too harshly, and perhaps I did as well," said Atatasuki, slugging his ally's shoulder affectionately.

"So then, we're together now? Wow, this is so wonderful," said Kawai with flustered cheeks.

"It sure is! Group hug!" cheered Atatasuki, throwing his fist in the air.

"Embrace!" cheered Ada.

"Um, I'm not really one for physical contact," said Exp 8, his hands on his hips.

"You're so adorable," said Kawai, pressing up against him.

"Hey, I'm at least eighty percent as adorable as he is," said Atatasuki with a clenched fist.

Kawai smacked the annoyance with her tail, knocking him over. "Nobody was talking to you!"

"You're not ignoring me anymore! Oh happy day!" exclaimed Atatasuki, leaping into a hug.

She flew out of the way, allowing him to fall to the sand.

"You all put the *fun* in *family*!" cheered Ada.

Atatasuki stood up and turned to Exp 8. "We need to keep our eye on the ball. So, what do we call our team?" he asked, tapping his fingers against his chin.

"I've been giving it some thought, and well, only one name truly does us justice. We are the Freedom Forcers!" cheered Exp 8.

"Yeah, I love it! We shall shove freedom down Devlin's throat and force him to free our enslaved brethren," cheered Atatasuki, throwing his fist in the air.

"That's the spirit!"

Exp 8 pressed his fist to Atatasuki's.

Kawai floated up and put her little hand on Exp 8's big fist.

"Fist bump!" cheered Ada.

"Freedom Forcers!" exclaimed Exp 8, putting an arm around his siblings.

"I thought you didn't like physical contact," said Atatasuki.

"He's touching me," said Kawai, her tail wagging back and forth.

"We're a team now. And this hug means we're also a family," said Exp 8, looking down at Ada.

Chapter 3: Kawai's Love

Exp 8 broke out of the embrace and patted his sister's head.

"Oh big brother, you're so clever. Our team name has both kindness and firmness in it!" said Kawai, rubbing his armored pecks.

"Yeah, but I'm sure I could have come up with something almost as good," retorted Atatasuki.

"No you couldn't. So, Brother, are you planning on killing Devlin just to free me?" asked Kawai, floating in front of him.

"Not just for you, but for all those under his control! But calm down, we don't need to kill him." Exp 8 put his arm around her shoulders. "Inside Devlin's lab there are several incubators with dead Exps inside. Ada said Devlin has a plethora of Exps. How many is that exactly?" he asked, looking down at the blue orb in his chest.

"Excluding all of us, it's around—six—ish. But he's a hard worker. I'm sure he'll make another in no time," said Ada.

"There you have it. There are at least six Exps still trapped in the lab. I won't allow any more of our people to die! It is our duty to free them," said Exp 8, holding his sister's little fingers in his firm grip.

"You guys are too harsh on Devlin. He's a really sweet kid once you get past his cruel side," said Ada with an implied smile.

"Yeah, he's okay for a total jerk, I guess," said Kawai with a shrug.

"Now that we're all together, what's the plan? Are we going to storm the lab with muffins a-blazing?" asked Atatasuki, hopping in excitement.

"That's a great idea, but let's think this through a bit more. There are th— four of us. Six more Exps could be really dangerous. Devlin can track us, and knowing him, he'll probably send them one at a time. That actually works out for us. We'll just convert them all to our side and get out of range of Devlin's surveillance in the process. Our plan right now should be to get as far away from Devlin's lab as possible," said Exp 8, picking up the pace.

"You are super-duper smart. I really love that about you," said Kawai, floating by his side.

"Thanks for noticing."

"So, what's your favorite color?" asked Kawai.

"I…uhh…never really gave it much thought. Wait, I know, it's the sun. Whether it's orange or yellow or gold, it just makes me feel warm," said Exp 8, looking up at the beaming star.

"Golden brown," said Atatasuki, jogging backwards and still keeping up with his supposedly better version.

"I like black, hmhm," said Ada.

"My favorite is platinum," said Kawai, rubbing her face against her sibling's powerful chest.

"That's very flattering. Your armor is very beautiful as well. Gold is a really nice color," said Exp 8, patting her head.

"Did you hear that? He said I'm beautiful!" squealed Kawai, her hands on Ada. She looked up at Exp 8 and her cheeks turned hot-pink. She rushed behind Atatasuki, holding her flushed cheeks.

"Of course he did. There is nothing in the world more striking than your eyes," said Atatasuki, swept up in the moment. "Oh, you are just so cute!" He patted her on the head.

Kawai's tail knocked the faulty hand aside. "Don't be a creeper. Hey, Brother, do you like cats or dogs more?" she asked, sitting on her leader's broad shoulders and batting her metal ears.

"Preferential treatment of one species over another is the reason I'm a runaway slave. I love both of them equally," said Exp 8 with a tight fist.

"You're just so amazing. Wow! Look Brother, look, look! Devlin's lab looks like a harmless dot from way over here," said Kawai, leaning over his shoulder.

"Just think of all the torment condensed in that one little speck," said Exp 8, his fists shaking.

"I'm tired from the long walk over here. Big brother, can you carry me?" asked Kawai, dropping herself in his arms.

"How can you be tired of walking if you levitate?" asked Exp 8 with buried frustration.

"I'll carry you, little sis," said Atatasuki as he picked her up.

Kawai turned away from him. "I won't be touched by a failure. I want to be in the arms of a true Exp, not a piece of crap like you. Hmph," she said, hopping out of his arms.

Exp 8 turned his sister to face him. "Atatasuki is a member of the team, so treat him with some respect."

"Hey! Don't talk to her like that," said Atatasuki, grabbing his latest version by the arm.

"I understand you're smitten with her, but you can't just let her abuse you," said Exp 8, clasping his brother's hand in his own.

"I can do what I want, when I want, why I want, wherever and in any way, sort, or form that I want. That's called free will, look it up."

"Ooh, ooh, I can do it," said Ada.

Exp 8 glared at his stubborn ally. "You're really starting to get on my nerves. Hey, Kawai!"

She flipped around, looking at Exp 8 upside down. "Yes, my super hunky dearly beloved?" Kawai bounced up and down while still afloat.

"Cut the crap. You need to treat our brother with some respect. Is that clear?" asked Exp 8, pulling her out of the air.

"Okay, if you insist, I'll let you carry me!" she said, using his arms like a hammock.

"I already said no," said Exp 8, placing her back in the air.

"Treat her with respect!" yelled Atatasuki.

"This is impossible!" yelled Exp 8, fuming.

Kawai floated in between her siblings. "There's no need to fight over me. You could just kill Atatasuki and steal me away," she said, slowly descending with her hands clasped behind her head.

"What is your problem?" asked Exp 8, his palm on his forehead.

"If you want, I could beat him and win your eternal love. After all, I just pretended to lose to him so that I wouldn't end up killing him. I broke out of the net before I surrendered. I wasn't really done. If I killed him, I know it would just ruin your whole week. I don't want to see tears fall from your beautiful eyes." Atatasuki reached out and touched her cheek.

Kawai pulled away and puffed out her cheeks.

"Wow, Atatasuki, you have such a way with words," said Ada.

"I can be romantic too," retorted Exp 8.

"Oh yes, a real ladies' man. This Casanova tripped when he heard my voice. Oh, let me impersonate you greeting someone: 'Who the hell are you!'" exclaimed Ada joyfully.

"Ada, your laughter is like a song to my ears. Your knowledge is unparalleled. Your every mechanized feature emanates greatness," said Exp 8 romantically.

"I can beat that! Kawai, every time you crush my heart, it beats faster, yearning for acceptance," said Atatasuki, squeezing his chest.

"What if I beat your face in?" asked Kawai with a wicked smile.

"Then I would forever cherish the imprint left by your graceful hands," said Atatasuki, touching his face.

"Stop, you're freaking me out. Brother, can you compliment my beauty?" asked Kawai, turning to her perfected copy and bouncing up and down.

"Uhhh…okay. You look like an innocent child, but the heart of a sadist beats malevolently inside you," said Exp 8 poetically, combing the hair out of her eyes.

"I didn't know you were a poet," said Kawai, turning away with a scarlet blush.

"What does he have that I don't?" asked Atatasuki, pushing out his chest.

"A working body, for one. Not to mention strength, intelligence, thick armor, muscles, tact, a firm chest, and long flowing hair!" exclaimed Kawai.

"That's what this is," said Exp 8, moving the wires away from the sides of his face.

"What do you think of my hair?" asked Kawai with a twirl.

"I love it! So, sister, can I carry you?" asked Atatsuki, squatting down.

"Of course you can, my love," said Kawai, dropping in her big brother's arms once more.

"But you're the only one who can fly!" shouted Exp 8. "Sorry…I didn't mean to yell," he said, feeling Atatsuki's dagger-like gaze upon him.

"Oh, that reminds me, I know of this romantic place not too far from here. Let's go," she said, wrapping her tail under his arms. She then activated her shampoo bottle-sized jet boosters and flew off.

"Don't forget about me again!" yelled Atatsuki as he rushed after them. He tripped on a branch and fell.

The Muffin of Victory popped off of his tail and onto the dirt.

"At least I have you, Muffin of Victory," said Atatsuki, nestling it to his tearful face. He then impulsively plopped the muffin in his mouth. After swallowing it and rubbing his belly, he leaned back. He looked down at the golden crumbs on his palms and realized that they were all that was left of his pastry companion. He shouted out from the bottom of his lungs.

Exp 8 looked at Atatsuki vanish in the distance. "Why did you leave him behind?" asked Exp 8, tapping his sister's shoulder.

"I wanted some alone time," she said, smiling down at him.

"Then why are you bringing me?" asked Exp 8, rocking back and forth in her grip.

"Silly, I want to be alone with you. Heehee."

"Where exactly are we going?"

"It's not too far."

"You shouldn't have left Atatsuki behind."

"Um, big brother, it's kind of strange. This is a jungle, but there are pine trees. And look, there's a squirrel over there. Don't you think that's a teensy bit odd?" asked Kawai, nestling up against him.

"You're right! This doesn't match my knowledge of jungles. What is this place?" asked Exp 8, spotting a howler monkey atop a pine tree.

"Do you want to know why it's like this?" asked Ada, turning to the cuddly little girl.

"Quiet! I'm trying to chat with my brother," said Kawai.

"Maybe we should turn back. We're getting a bit too far from Atatsuki. How is he going to find us?" asked Exp 8.

"I told you, it's not far. It's in the area where the forest and the jungle collide. It's in the frungle."

"The what?"

"A frungle is part forest and part jungle. It was part of some experiment."

"Even the land has been twisted by Devlin."

"It's part natural, part artificial, just like us!" Kawai broke eye contact. "Oh, we're here."

"That was fast," said Exp 8.

The scenery changed from a desert wasteland to a green landscape brimming with life.

"This place...it's amazing!" Exp 8 scanned the bushes and waved at the birds as they flew by. He marveled at the trees. "I never imagined a place so beautiful. I know what a jungle is...but this is something else. Thank you, Kawai. This is the greatest gift anyone's ever given me. I couldn't be happier," he said, wiping away tears on the edges of his eyelids.

"Oh, please continue, you're making me blush," she said, covering her face with the heart-shaped tip of her tail.

"I'll never forget this. Um, is this a swamp? Why are we landing here?" asked Exp 8, slipping out of her grip and falling into a murky pool of water.

"This is the place I wanted to show you," said Kawai, pulling her date out of the water and onto dry land.

The roots of the trees merged with the lake. Patches of algae coated the surface of the green murky water.

"But the other place was so much more...everything. I mean, sure there are microbes in the water, but I don't even hear any birds chirping."

"I can chirp for you, if you'd like," said Kawai, blowing some beetles off a moss-covered vine.

"I just don't see what's so romantic about this place, its dark, murky—you can't even see the sky." Exp 8 squinted through the foliage of the mangroves.

"Just stop complaining and listen! You can hear frogs croaking, trees creaking, and my excited breathing!"

"You're right! This place is teeming with life. Why didn't I see it before?" Exp 8 peered at the cloud of mosquitoes prodding his body for an opening. "They're all so free," he said, bobbing his head to the buzzing.

"I've dreamed of making love here. Forcing you to come was my backup plan, in case things didn't work out between us. This place is special because in here...only I can hear you scream," said Kawai, tugging on a vine and making a cracking sound.

"What about me? I may not have ears, but I can hear just fine," said Ada, her core turning to the girl.

40

"I guess we'll have to share; it's not like I can separate you," said Kawai, pulling the vine around the tree.

"Sounds fun," said Ada with a spin.

"I don't know what the hell you're planning, but you need to think this through," said Exp 8.

Kawai floated up to her prisoner and licked her lips. "Are you scared? That is soooo adorable. Heeheehmph."

"Don't worry. I can hear you scream," said Ada, looking up at the team leader.

"*Sound Shot... gun*," cheered Kawai, snapping the vine.

Six sound waves jettisoned out of vine at an arc. They tore through Exp 8, knocking him down to the moist grass.

Exp 8 yelled as he writhed around.

"You know, it didn't have to be like this. It could have been consensual. But, this way is okay too." Kawai put her palms together and fired a laser net at him.

The net wrapped around his bulky body, trapping him indefinitely.

"If Atatasuki can break out of mine, why can't I break out of yours?" asked Exp 8, tumbling around like a renegade log. "What did I do to upset you?" He looked up at her from the soggy grass.

"You disappointed me. I was hoping you would make the first move. But I won't let it get to me. So, like the view?" asked Kawai with a light blush, floating just a foot above his head.

"We can talk this out. Let's, uh, do something together…just the two of us."

"That's exactly what I was thinking. Hmm hmm hmm hmhmm hmm." Kawai continued to hum as she wrapped the net around the mossy tree. She backed up and made a frame with her hands. She pushed Exp 8's legs open with her tail and gazed up at her masterpiece with shimmering eyes.

"Aww, she's going to force herself on you, isn't that just precious?" asked Ada.

"This isn't funny! Ada, help me out!" he yelled, struggling to break free.

"Alright, ooof. You can do it. You can do it. Go, go, go! You can do it. You can do it. This I know!" cheered Ada.

Kawai smacked Ada with her tail and grabbed her prisoner's chin through the holes in the net. "Why are you resisting? Damn. Butter-muffins. Just hold still." She flew to the sides and tightened the net. "That's much better. Look, I like being on top. But that doesn't mean this can't be consensual," she said, looking into his eyes. She started to rub Exp 8's chest, biting her lip in excitement.

"Stop. That tickles, hoohoo," said Ada, spinning around.

Kawai pulled back her hand. "Damn it, I've always liked his concave chest. Isn't there any way to take you out?" she asked, trying to stick her finger in the crevices.

"Not that I'm aware of. My body is surgically attached to him. Like an extravagant tumor," said Ada with a spin.

"That's an…uh…interesting metaphor. So do you feel everything I do to this hunky body or just around the chest area?" asked Kawai as she licked his ear.

"I only feel what the big blue sphere in his chest feels," said Ada.

"Damn it, I kind of wanted to spin that little ball around. Oh well, I've still got plenty to grab. Devlin designed your armor to be an extension of your body. Nerves are woven throughout your armor, so you can react to even the slightest touch. It was my suggestion. I've been fantasizing about this moment for so long," said Kawai, stroking her captive's body sensually with her tail.

"What are you doing, we barely even know each other?" said Exp 8, straining to move his head.

"You're so funny! We're practically brother and sister."

"That makes it even worse," said Exp 8.

"I…(sniffle)…I thought it was cute," said Kawai.

"Release me now."

Kawai wiped her watery eyes and put on a smile. "Fine then, how about you just think of it as a mini-you having fun with your big body?" she proposed, dragging her hand down his chest.

"This is wrong. I can't even move."

"Ummm, Brother, when I lick your finger, does it turn you on?" asked Kawai, lapping his finger like a cat.

"Please, just let me down."

"But if I do that, then we won't have any fun."

"Who the hell's having fun?" asked Exp 8 as he struggled to break free. Suddenly they heard the sound of a wrecked plane engine.

Atatasuki fell into a nearby puddle, making the frogs in it hop away. He stood up, his sight lining up with Kawai and Exp 8. "Oh my merciful Muffin God! What is going on here?" he asked, stepping back with surprise and turning away with jealousy.

Ada lit up and turned to Atatasuki. "Kawai wanted alone time with Exp 8, so she abandoned you, tied him up, and now she is going to have fun with his immobilized body. Isn't that just so cute?"

"I already figured that much out. But yes…it's adorable," said Atatasuki with fresh tears.

Kawai turned around while her tail continued to rub against her big brother. "How did you get here so fast? How did you get here at all?"

"I followed the jet stream you left behind like the sweet, strawberry-flavored aroma of love. I can fly too, you know. But anyway, what the hell are you doing!" he asked as he re-realized what was going on.

"Shall I repeat the situation?" asked Ada, bouncing in excitement.

"I just can't believe she would do this so soon. Is he really that much better than me?" asked Atatasuki, his whole body drooping.

"What are you talking about? I haven't even started yet," said Kawai, her tail tightening.

"Brother, you have to help me!" exclaimed Exp 8.

"I refuse. I never want to see her cry again," said Atatasuki with a firm pose.

"Can't I have a little privacy?" asked Kawai with flushed cheeks and an angry tone.

"I'm sorry, sister. I didn't mean to interrupt." Atatasuki turned around and walked away. His arm covered his mask, but his sobs could be heard regardless.

"Where are you going? I need someone to rescue me!" exclaimed Exp 8.

"I'll rescue you from your own sexual inexperience as soon as I find out how to remove this crotch-plate," said Kawai, yanking on the thick metal slab between his powerful legs.

A rustling in the trees caused the aroused prototype's ears to perk up.

Devlin came crashing down on what was left of a hover bike. After tumbling across the ground, he rose to his feet. He then extended his hands out to the heavens like a deity as the bike exploded behind him.

"Does everyone have the ability to fly except me?" asked Exp 8, his eyes lowering.

"Worthless trash!" Devlin exclaimed as he kicked the melted remains of his bike.

"Yes, Master?" replied Kawai, believing she was being called upon.

"Oh, hello Worthless Trash. Um, what's going on here?" asked Devlin with a raised eyebrow.

"Allow me! The situation is as follows: Kawai is having her way with Exp 8," said Ada cheerfully.

"Thank you for your analysis, but I was simply stunned and asked a rhetorical question. So, Ada, who is currently on Exp 8's team?" asked Devlin, approaching her.

"She doesn't work for you anymore. Ada won't tell you anything," said Exp 8 through gritted teeth.

"Well, there's Kawai," said Ada.

"That was bound to happen," said Devlin with a shrug.

"Ada, what are you doing?" exclaimed Exp 8.

"And Atatasuki has joined as well."

"What? Failed Experiment joined him? But he hates Exp 8. Why would— he gave you the Muffin of Victory, didn't he?" asked Devlin, turning to the muffin fanatic with a condescending look.

"How did you know?" asked Atatasuki, his eyes still watery.

"Psychic powers, ooooooooooh," said Devlin shaking his fingers mystifyingly.

"Really?" asked Atatasuki, his head tilted back with astonishment.

"No, you idiot; it's obvious. Why else would you join him? Besides, the end of your tail is missing."

"What the hell are you guys doing? That's Devlin!" yelled Exp 8, still squirming around in the net.

"Duh," said Atatasuki.

"Why are you all acting so calm, and why the hell is he even here?"

The laser net finally dissipated and Exp 8 fell to the ground. He rolled out of his fall and charged toward his enemy.

Devlin went into Warrior II Pose and shocked his restless creation with a Taser the size of a ballpoint pen.

Exp 8 fell to the ground, shaking as he went into a seizure before ceasing to move altogether.

"Allow me to explain," said Devlin, sitting down on Exp 8 and arching his head back. "First off, I am their master and creator. Unlike you, they have a sense of gratitude. And to answer your second question, I'm here to warn you that NoOne is following you."

"First off, why would you warn us, and secondly, you're following us!" Exp 8 steadied his hand before lunging at his enemy.

In a flash, Devlin leaped off of Exp 8. He landed and then spun around. His eyebrows went up and his smile became deranged. "Don't say I didn't warn you." He then walked up to Failed Experiment and sat down on a nearby log. "So, any luck with Worthless Trash?"

Atatasuki sat down next to Devlin and scratched his cheek. "Hmm, to be honest…things are going great! She's talking to me again, she's adorable, and we're on the same team!"

"I'm rooting for you, pal. I don't know if she deserves you, but you sure deserve her."

"Wow, I'm honored. You know, with this whole rebellion going on, I think we'll get together in no time. But what about you? How are things with you and Nina going?"

"She ignores me all the time now. If anything, things have gotten worse."

"Pain is the curse of love. But, love is such a blessing. The pain is well worth it. I hope things look up for you," said Atatasuki, patting his frienemy on the back.

"Thanks. Who knows, maybe Exp 8's little uprising will get her interested. She'll have to talk to me if she wants a piece of the action, right?"

"That's the spirit. Never give in to despair!"

"Why are you talking to our sworn enemy about your love life?" asked Exp 8, his voice cracking.

"I haven't seen him in a while and it helps to talk about it. I can't talk to you about this kind of stuff, we're love rivals," said Atatasuki with a competitive glare.

"But she loves me. I don't love her. Ugh, this is so annoying," said Exp 8, grabbing his head.

"You're still competition. So Devlin, how are you going to get back to the lab now?" asked Atatasuki, gesturing to the destroyed hover bike.

"I was hoping one of you could take me," said Devlin with a warm smile.

"I would, but my jetpack is kind of defective...always," said Atatasuki, patting his chest with pride.

"Worthless Trash, could you give me a lift back to the lab?" asked Devlin, getting up from the log.

"Of course, Master." Kawai floated up to him, wrapped her tail around his waist and pulled him off the ground. "Hold on tight," she said before flying off into the distance.

"Wha-wha-wa-wa-what just happened?" asked Exp 8.

"Would you like an analysis?" asked Ada cheerfully.

Exp 8 walked to his brother as he made circles to loosen his jaw. "So, what do we do now? I mean, she isn't coming back, right?"

"Of course she is! She's just giving Devlin a lift, that's all."

"Why would she do that? He's our enemy. Am I the only one who realizes this?" asked Exp 8, massaging his temples.

"Are you saying we can't trust Kawai? I've known her a lot longer than you have. I'll admit she is a fickle girl. She forgot about me in the instant someone better came along. But with you, it's more than just infatuation. She loves you with every inch of her little body. She would never even think of betraying you," said Atatasuki, grabbing his rival's shoulder.

Exp 8 put his hand on his brother's arm. "That was a great speech, but it doesn't explain why she just helped Devlin go back to the lab. If she had some sort of plan to find out just how many Exps are in there, then I would have told her it was too dangerous. She needs to communicate with her team or we won't know what's up. For all we know, she could be telling the enemy our whole plan right now. Look…I just need to know who I can trust, okay?"

"Just because Devlin is our enemy doesn't mean we shouldn't help him out in his time of need. We can't let the fact that we're adversaries ruin our relationship with him. We can't be swept up in hatred or we'll be no better than him. Well, we'll still be a lot better I guess. But he's my friend and friends help each other out. Besides, he made us; we owe it to him," said Atatasuki with a firm fist.

Exp 8 grabbed his brother's fist. "We don't owe him anything! Life-forms are made to create, and we must take care of our creations. Devlin sold me off like a trinket. He is no longer my father; I don't owe him anything. I will not help him even if he begs me with his last dying breath. This is no game, brother. We are going to be hunted down. That lunatic is willing to kill us, so we must be willing to do the same. I am not downplaying the consequences of murder. We will not kill Devlin unless there is no other option."

"What if Kawai betrayed us? Are you suggesting we kill her? My life is nothing without her. I won't let you hurt her," said Atatasuki with an intense look.

"Calm down, I would never…she's family. We must survive, but killing is our last resort. Now come on, let's get away from here before our creator returns with reinforcements," said Exp 8, scanning the skies.

"Why not just fly?"

"Uh, the thing is…I can't," said Exp 8, turning away.

"I saw your blueprints. You have jetpacks."

"Really, I can fly?" exclaimed Exp 8, his eyes shimmering.

"That means I can fly with you. Yay!" cheered Ada, spinning around.

Exp 8 put his hands up high and expected to shoot up into the sky.

Toads croaked in the distance.

"Do you want me to help?" asked Ada.

"Please do," said Exp 8, closing his eyes.

"Just push theeeeccce…sheep?" said Ada, turning slightly.

"What sheep?" asked Exp 8, scanning his arm for the mysterious sheep button.

"There's a sheep, right over there. I…can't explain this," said Ada.

"Yeah, I'm pretty sure sheep aren't indigenous to swamps. This is Devlin's doing," said Exp 8.

"Hi sheep. How are you? Are you hungry?" asked Atatasuki, feeding the sheep an apple muffin.

The sheep exploded.

"What the hell! Why did it explode? What did you do?" asked Exp 8, rushing up to Atatasuki and shaking him furiously.

"Why are there sheep in the frungle?" asked Atatasuki, blood spread across his inquisitive face.

"Why is Devlin bringing innocents into his mess?" Exp 8 picked up the sheep's bloody head as tears dripped down his cheek.

A voice came out from the lifeless head. "You have fallen into my trap. Look around you. You're completely surrounded by my wool warriors!"

Exp 8 looked up to see dozens of sheep coming out from behind the nearby trees. "Is this why Kawai brought me here? No, that's just what Devlin wants me to think. Come on out and I'll make you pay for what you did to that sheep!" he yelled, his elbow talons shooting out.

The sheep parted in the front and began to chant in unison. "Meheh.Meheh."

The Freedom Forcers gazed in both awe and disbelief as a shadow riding on four sheep approached them.

The shadow had no facial features. It was as if a permanent silhouette had been cast upon the shadowy figure.

"Who the hell are you?" yelled Exp 8, clenching both his fists.

The walking shadow looked sketchy, as if someone had messed up on a drawing and scribbled over their shame. It had a large black blade for a left hand and a stub for its right. It sliced into the stub as if it were cutting a loaf of bread. The parted sections formed uneven fingers. The shadow then sprouted a sharp end on its right elbow and carved fingers out of the bladed hand. The leftover pieces crawled back inside its body. It brought up its newly formed hands, popped holes in its head for eyes and then cut across its face to make a jagged smile.

"Did you not hear me? You have fallen into my trap," said the shadowy figure in a deep, wispy voice.

Chapter 4: NoOne

"You apparently didn't hear me. Who the hell are you?" asked Exp 8, pushing past the sheep as he marched up to the living shadow.

The shadowy figure's eye holes lit up like a desk lamp. "I am NoOne."

"No you're not. You're definitely someone…or something," said Exp 8, tilting his head and squinting.

"I'm NoOne," he said, sliding off of his sheep and standing tall.

"Cut the crap. Who the hell are you?" asked Exp 8, gripping the shadow man's shoulder.

"I already told you, I am NoOne. NoOne! My name is NoOne!" He leaned face dangerously close to the newest living weapon.

Exp 8 backed up and covered his mouthpiece. "Pshh! Oh—you're kidding, right? That can't really be your name."

"Unlike you, I have a name. I've never seen someone laugh out of jealousy before. How very interesting," said NoOne as he circled around the enemy commander.

Atatasuki walked up to NoOne. "So you're the one Devlin warned us about. See, Exp 8? We help each other out. We give Devlin a lift, and he gives us a heads up. It's a perfect give-and-take relationship."

"Do I know you?" asked Ada, looking at the shadow man precariously.

"I am the notoriously infamous NoOne."

"Don't talk to him, Ada. So, NoOne, Devlin sent you here to capture me, is that right?" asked Exp 8, rolling his wrists.

"Your arrogance is a nuisance," said NoOne sinking into the ground. "Now all shall bear witness to the power of my sheep." He popped up behind the sheep.

"Are they some kind of super sheep?" asked Atatasuki, poised for combat.

"No, they are just ordinary, everyday woolly sheep," said NoOne, patting one on the head.

"They aren't your slaves!" yelled Exp 8.

"I never claimed they were. These sheep are my flock. Now prepare to win!" yelled NoOne, dramatically pointing at Exp 8.

"What?"

NoOne seeped into the ground and then popped up behind Exp 8. "I said, 'prepare to win.' Must I repeat everything?" he asked, tapping his forehead.

"Why would you say something like— never mind. I've had enough stupid answers for one day. Now it's time to make you pay for what you did to that sheep," said Exp 8, cracking his neck and readying his fists.

"Do you really think you can beat me? Keh-heh-heh!"

"That's more like it. We are going to kick your ass!" said Exp 8, hopping in place with his fists primed.

"I agree," said NoOne deadpan.

"Huh?"

"I'm sure you will win, aren't we all?" asked NoOne, turning to the faulty prototype.

"Would a muffin cheer you up?" asked Atatasuki, opening his chest up.

"Why would such a vile, nasty, putrid, disgusting, insignificant ball of dough have any effect on the void in my soul? Besides, I'd prefer a cupcake. If you must eat, you might as well eat something with a little flavor," said NoOne, licking his lips with a pitch-black tongue.

"He's trying to psych you out. Don't listen to his garbage. Um…bro…are you okay?" asked Exp 8, tapping his shoulder.

Atatasuki's head was down. He breathed in and out fiercely. Blood dripped from his knuckles. His head then sprung up. His burning eyes were fixed on NoOne. "Not only did you insult the muffins in a most terrible manner, but you would rather have a disgusting cupcake!" He shuddered and then shook away his disgust. "Cupcakes are the mortal enemies of muffins! Exp 8, stay out of this. He's mine. Don't worry, NoOne will die!" he yelled before slamming his chest closed.

"That's a relief. It's good to know you're such a merciful bunch of—"

Atatasuki's fist connected, hitting the shadowy blasphemer square in his stomach. His fist then went straight through his opponent as the shadow man's body parted in half.

The two halves sunk to the ground and reconnected. The shadow then rushed behind a group of sheep. "That really burns, what is wrong with you? Why does your skin burn me?" asked NoOne, blowing on the searing wound.

"You have brought upon the wrath of the muffins. Their rage has set my body aflame. I am their guardian, and my incendiary might shall engulf you!" yelled Atatasuki, his whole body steaming.

"Keh-heh. I don't stand a chance against you," said NoOne as the prototype rushed toward him.

"That's what I'm talking about. Kick his ass!" cheered Exp 8.

"Feel the wrath of muffins!" yelled Atatasuki, leaping off a tree stump. His chest opened up, revealing steamy muffins. After taking a whiff of their aroma, he tossed the muffins furiously at the blasphemer.

The projectile dough zoomed through the holes in NoOne's body.

"How dare you deny their deliciousness!" yelled Atatasuki, swinging off a tree branch.

"Your attacks are as pathetic as your wretched existence. Just die already so that I can lose to your brother." NoOne grabbed his arm and pulled it violently, elongating it rather than tearing it off.

Once Atatasuki landed, NoOne's outstretched arm wiggled around the weakling's legs.

Atatasuki fell to the muddy ground with a wet thud. He grabbed the shadow hand, but his hand just went right through it.

The shadow hand sprung up and wrapped around his neck, its grip tightening as he struggled.

"Stop choking me!" yelled Atatasuki, yanking at the arm in futility.

"Rage isn't an ace in battle, it's a crutch!" NoOne's hand molded around the weakling's neck, becoming a noose. He then lifted the opponent off the ground.

"There's no shame in asking for a little help," said Exp 8.

"This is my battle!" yelled Atatasuki as his arms flailed about.

"I'm going to enjoy this victory while it lasts." NoOne stretched his other arm behind his back and punched it vigorously. The punches caused the front of his body to shoot forward and pummel the prototype.

"Ada, just what the hell is this guy?" asked Exp 8.

"He is Devlin's very first Exp. I knew I recognized him. He has the ability to manipulate shadows."

"That's great and all, but what's his weakness? Atatasuki is getting pummeled out there, and I'm not going to rush in without a plan!"

"No I'm not! I'm doing just fine!" hollered Atatasuki, lifted up by his legs while being repeatedly punched in the stomach.

"His weakness is his pessimistic personality. Problem is: he's practically unbeatable otherwise. Good luck," said Ada.

"If you interfere, I swear I will join Devlin!" yelled Atatasuki before the hazy figure kneed him in the gut.

"Empty words annoy me." NoOne dropped the weakling to the ground. "Go, my fellow sheep, destroy him."

Seven sheep piled onto Atatasuki.

NoOne pulled out a bomb trigger from his stomach. "Better to be a black sheep among white sheep than a sheep among wolves. *SHEEP DESTRUCT!*" he yelled, pressing the trigger.

The sheep surrounding Atatasuki exploded in a fiery blast, engulfing him in its wake.

"What the hell? You said they were normal sheep!" yelled Atatasuki, smoldering but still alive.

"They are...perfectly normal everyday sheep...with C4 strapped to the belly of each one of them. Sheep are gentle creatures with no fighting spirit whatsoever. That's why I attached explosives to them. Face it, you will never win—I mean, I will never win!" exclaimed NoOne, flinging his arms up and twiddling his fingers.

"He's right. Wait, what?"

"Well, I'm obviously going to lose," said NoOne, picking Atatasuki off the ground. He tossed the smoldering Freedom Forcer into the bog behind him.

Exp 8 kneeled down to the bloody remains of the exploded sheep. "I will stop him," he said, placing his hand on their remains and closing his eyes.

"Devlin was right. You are easy to upset," said NoOne, popping up two feet behind the enemy leader.

Exp 8 rose slowly. He turned to the murderer and lunged his fist at him.

NoOne stretched back just beyond the fist's reach.

Exp 8's hand then opened up and released a black orb.

NoOne leaped backward as the orb zoomed forth. His stretchy arm recoiled. "*SHEEP DEFENSE,*" he said, lifting a sheep and using it as a shield.

The attack exploded the sheep into bloody pieces.

"Great job avenging them. Keh-heh. This entire area is ridden with explosive sheep. Face it, the only way you'll win is if sheep become extinct. I don't stand a chance!"

"You are twisted!" yelled Exp 8 as he pummeled the killer's face.

"Why so angry?" asked NoOne, unaffected by the punches. His hand coiled around to where the sheep had exploded. "*SHEEP REGENERATION.*" He then placed the shadows together and reformed the sheep.

"Meheheheh," said a very happy group of sheep.

"They're perfectly fine, so you can just calm down now. The last thing I want is to awaken some latent power inside you that is conveniently unlocked by rage."

"You can revive the dead?" asked Exp 8 with wide eyes.

"Don't be ridiculous. I merely put their pieces back together. So, what are you going to do next? You ought to know it's hopeless by now. You're going to win in the end no matter what I do. You'll take an insurmountable amount of damage. And then, just when I think I've won, you'll stand up with your last bit of strength. After that, you'll somehow become more powerful than when you had no wounds at all. And to conclude, you'll defeat me with one final powerful attack, ugh," said NoOne, sinking deeper into the ground with each sentence.

"What the hell are you talking about?"

"The inevitability of my defeat. Wasn't it obvious? You have already won. There is no way for me to win this battle. You will understand soon enough," said NoOne, picking himself up.

"Ada, what do I do to beat him?"

"Nothing's one hundred percent, but I have an idea. You can create an orb of much bigger size by combining the little orbs."

"Sounds badass."

"Wait, don't push the button. Simply release your energy. If you concentrate, you can attack even if you are unable to move."

"Alright, let's give it a shot!" Exp 8 button-mashed his arm, shooting out numerous little orbs that combined until they were bigger than NoOne.

"How can you already use a super attack? I haven't even hit you yet. No fair! You're cheating!" yelled NoOne, making an X with his hands.

"You can't block me now," said Exp 8, stepping on his opponent's shadow.

"Why would I bother trying something so stupid? *SHADOW MANIPULATION, SIZE DISTORTION.*" Sketchy black hands branched out from NoOne's shadow. They pushed against the massive orb's shadow, condensing it. As a result, the orb itself was reduced to the size of a marble.

NoOne's hand opened like a net and wrapped around the orb.

"How did you do that?" asked Exp 8, jumping back.

"Figure it out yourself. I won't let anything lower my nonexistent chance of winning this fight. *SHADOW MANIPULATION, SELF-BETRAYAL.*"

Exp 8's shadow sprung up suddenly. It wrapped around his body like bandages, constricting his movements.

"So many fights have been lost to arrogance. When I lose, I shall have no regrets," said NoOne, sharpening his arm into a blade.

"You're not a bad fighter, but you made one fatal error."

NoOne stared at him blankly.

"What's that, you ask? You made the mistake of standing in the way of my freedom!" Exp 8's arm sprung up and pointed at NoOne. He then fired an orb directly at the shadow man, using only his willpower.

"Keh-heh-ha! Your shadow mimics your every action. When you shoot, your shadow-self shoots as well. And…it just so happens to be aiming at you right now. Your efforts are meaningless. But mine are still far more of a waste. *SHADOW COMBINATION,*" said NoOne, fusing with his own shadow just in time to dodge the orb.

Exp 8 was hit directly with the orb from his own shadow. The tiny explosion barely hurt him, but his movements were still restricted. His arm struggled as it aimed to the sky. He fired numerous orbs up as he stared into the opponent's bright eyes. His shadow's orbs hit him every time, yet he continued to fire.

The combination of dozens of little orbs created a massive black sphere, thus blocking out the sun's rays from the surrounding area.

"You've become so desperate. Were you trying to cut us off from the sun so that our shadows would disappear? You miscalculated and have unwittingly created a giant shadow for me to control!" NoOne put his hands to the floor.

A chunk of the orb's shadow was torn off and pulled toward the shadow man.

"*SHADOW STRETCH.*"

The chunk stretched as the shadow of it was elongated.

"I am the master of all shadows!"

The giant orb was soon molded into the shape of NoOne himself.

The explosive shadow clone rushed forward and crashed into Exp 8. It burst upon contact, taking the nearby trees along with it.

Exp 8 fell to the floor, a smoldering mess. He gasped before closing his eyes.

"Ugh! Don't play this game with me. You're just going to get up. Get it over with already," said NoOne, tapping his foot.

Exp 8 didn't move a muscle.

NoOne popped up in front of the downed hero. "Hello, wake up already," he said, poking Exp 8's face. He turned the freedom fighter over and stood on him proudly. "I...really have won," he said, his eyes widening.

Just then, when NoOne least expected it, Exp 8 rose up. His whole body was coursing with inexplicable energy. His arm aimed directly at the shadow man. Energy gathered in his palm.

"I knew it. Here comes a super attack. I told you, didn't I? I knew this was hopeless," said NoOne, sitting down in a fit of protest.

Exp 8 then fell down unconscious.

"Alright! Don't kill me. Hello? Ugh, I give up, okay? What are you waiting for?" NoOne turned around to see the hero's motionless body. The frown on his face slowly flipped. It then widened until it reached the corners of his face. "I really won? I beat the Ultimate Exp without a scratch on me. I am awesome! I better bring him to Devlin before something goes wrong," said NoOne, turning around and bumping into someone.

"Who dares—oh, hi Kawai. Good to see you. You made it just in time. By the way, thanks for leading them right to me. Can you believe these naive fools? They actually thought you would join them. They have no idea of the depth of loyalty we hold for Devlin. Keh-heh."

Kawai looked down at her beloved. "Even big brother thought I betrayed Devlin," she said softly.

"Yep, everything went according to plan. Devlin said I could win, but honestly I didn't believe him. Anyway, the herd and I are going to go out grazing for a bit. Would you like to take Exp 8 to the master?" he asked, petting one of the sheep.

"Yeah, sure, but first I have to kill you," she said with a sweet smile.

"Whaaaaaaaat?" screamed NoOne, jumping back.

"You see, unlike my darling Exp 8, I use sound waves. They don't cast shadows. You have no way of hurting me, but there are just so many different ways I can hurt you." Kawai's nimble tail wrapped around the sheep and tossed it aside.

"So, I still lose?" asked NoOne, his shoulders drooping.

"No one hurts my beloved and gets away with it!" said Kawai in a deranged voice.

"That sure is a re—"

"*Sound Shot...gun!*" Multiple sound waves emitted from her hand, hitting the shadow man head on. The sound waves obliterated the one who hurt her brother, scattering his pieces throughout the grass.

NoOne pulled his fragments together and resembled his body, now covered with holes.

"How can you lie to me, you treacherous wench?" exclaimed NoOne.

"I said I was going to kill you. Who's lying?"

"I thought you said I would get away with—oooh...never mind."

"You're such a slowpoke."

"You forget, unlike you, I am a true Exp. I'm not a mere clone." NoOne put his fingers together, causing them to become one. He then opened his hand, elongating his fingers. "*SHADOW MANIPULATION, FINGER CAGE.*"

NoOne's fingers wrapped around the defiant girl in a split second. They spread her arms and legs as they reeled her in.

"You will become one with the shadows as your body is engulfed!" yelled NoOne, yanking on the shadow threads to speed up the process.

"The only one I will become one with is Exp 8!" yelled Kawai as she struggled around.

"You're just a prototype, you can't stop me," said NoOne, his prey now mere feet from him.

"I may not be a real Exp, but I am a prototype of the Ultimate Exp. You are just a trashy lesser Exp. Oh, and I don't need sound waves to beat you."

Kawai's tail smashed the shadow threads around her arms. She then wrapped her arms around the shadow jerk's legs.

"What are you talking about?" asked NoOne, grabbing her head.

"*Energy Embrace Stop.*" Kawai hugged the enemy tightly. Her body lit up from the inside as she cut off his connection to his energy supply.

"What's going on? Why can't I move? What is wrong with my body?" asked NoOne, only able to shake his fingers.

"I was created with the ability to drain or refill energy upon contact. I've refined it so that I can also stop the flow of energy as long as I'm connected to my victim. But I don't want my prey to fall unconscious. Using Atatasuki as practice, I've taught myself how to sap just enough energy so only their mouth can move. That way, I can still hear my victim beg for mercy as I do what I please with their immobilized body. Isn't that fun?" asked Kawai, savoring the fear as it took over her foe.

"Nooooo!"

"Well, I'll still have fun. Feel free to scream," said Kawai as she prepared to clap her hands.

"Release me, traitor!"

"I know you can do better than that. Come on, beg for mercy. Pretty please," said Kawai, batting her eyelashes.

NoOne then burst out into laughter, scaring the treasonous cretin with his low-toned cackling. "Keh-heh-heh-heh-heh-heh-heeeh."

"Why are you so happy? I don't like it," whined Kawai, pulling her head as far back as she could.

"You truly have an amazing ability. On any normal opponent you would surely win. But I can move my shadow without moving my body. How's that for last words?"

NoOne's shadow jumped at the traitor. It rode up her body, finally wrapping around her neck.

"Even if one dies, their shadow carries on. Face it. I have actually won!" NoOne's shadow strangled the traitor as it smothered her face in a murky puddle.

Exp 8 rose up. Power was coursing through his entire body. "Leave my sister alone, you shady freak."

"Why were you keeping me waiting?" asked NoOne, massaging his temples.

"I don't have to answer to you. Kawai, can you hold onto him for just a bit longer?" asked Exp 8, planting his feet in the ground.

"Of course, Brother." Kawai bit into NoOne's shadow with her teeth.

"What's going on? I can't move my shadow."

"Even if you have a shadow when you die, you still need to be conscious to control it. I'm sorry, but you're too much of a threat. You won't even have a corpse once I'm done with you," said Exp 8, continuously firing out little orbs.

"This victory proves nothing!" yelled NoOne.

Exp 8's hand released an array of orbs in an instant. The orbs crashed into each other, fusing into a sphere the size of a beach ball.

"None of us are ever going back. Feel the power of our freedom! 𝔹𝕀𝔾 𝕆ℝ𝔹," said Exp 8.

The orb slammed into the shadow man violently.

Kawai broke free of the shadow and ran toward her brother.

The orb exploded, obliterating NoOne.

"I sure hope I didn't kill him. He'll be fine, right?" asked Exp 8 nervously.

"Don't worry. He's really hard to kill," said Kawai, sticking out her tongue at the enemy's remains.

"You know, I really need to trust you more. I thought you betrayed us when you flew off with Devlin." Exp 8 grabbed her and held her to his chest. "I'm so relieved that you're on my side," he said, petting her head lovingly.

"Ummm, big brother, I do work for Devlin. He told me if I lost the fight against you, I should join your team. I was just doing what I was ordered to do. Please don't get upset." Kawai's eyes then watered up. "I feel really bad about all this. I know I don't deserve your love, but I can't stop loving you." The small prototype broke out of his grip. She wiped away her tears and then turned around. "I'm going to have to bring you back to Devlin now."

Chapter 5: Power of the Artifacts

"I'm not going back there. I'm going to beat Devlin and free you. I can save you," said Exp 8, grabbing his sister's hand and pulling her toward him.

"This is no time to fantasize. Devlin has numerous Exps, some far more powerful than NoOne. You may be super-duper strong, but you will die if you keep fighting. I don't want that to happen. I can't let it happen. Just come with me and I'll take care of you. Please don't make this difficult," said Kawai, pulling at his arm.

"I will just free them as well. After all, we're the Freedom Forcers. I will free them whether they like it or not," said Exp 8 with a fist imbued with charisma.

"I knew someone almost as cool as you. He wouldn't give up no matter what. People like that...they don't last very long. I'm not going to lose you," said Kawai, firmly grasping his hand with her little fingers.

"I understand the odds are against us. But if I don't die fighting, then I can't really say I've lived."

"You won't die on my watch. Come on, we'll be in the same cell together. It will be great."

"You can't be sure he'll lock me up. Who knows what Devlin plans to do with me? I'm not going to just give up. You can believe in me and support me, or you can get the hell out of my way," said Exp 8, pushing her aside.

"Fine then, be a stubborn idiot. I guess I'm going to have to bring you back to Devlin by force," said Kawai before starting to cry.

"Sister, what's wrong? Come on, let it out. Don't just say what Devlin told you to. Tell me what you really want to say," said Exp 8 lovingly, holding her in his arms.

Kawai burst into tears. "I...don't want to die. Unlike you, I have no value in Devlin's eyes. If I stay with your team, his Exps will kill me without a second thought. And if I can't be with you, then I might as well be dead. I don't know what to do." She sobbed in her brother's grasp.

"I don't want to hear you talk like that. Why don't you believe in yourself? You're a lot stronger than you look. And you're also a lot more fragile than you act," said Exp 8, cradling her in his arms.

Kawai looked up with tear-drenched eyes. "I'm defective just like Atatasuki. Even if I give something one hundred percent, it's really only seventy-five. I'm incomplete. I can't strive for multiple things or I'll just end up failing at all of them. That's why I've decided to strive for only one thing. I want you to care about me. If I can have that, then I can be fulfilled," she said, smiling though her tears.

"I already care about you and I always will." Exp 8 nestled her to his chest.

"How can I ever be good enough to be your soul mate? I'm just a worthless piece of trash."

"Don't say that. Don't even think it. You're limiting yourself with all this negativity. Atatasuki is full of glitches. Despite this, he strives to be the best warrior he can be."

"Yeah, but he's an idiot."

"Living solely for someone else is unhealthy. Balance is essential for a healthy life. You need to have fertile soil if you want to have a fruitful forest, right? Don't just live for me. Live for yourself," said Exp 8, clutching her hand tightly.

Kawai looked away with flushed cheeks. "You're so sweet. But it's not that simple. I have to live for just one thing if I ever hope to succeed at anything. I've chosen you. If I don't love you with all my incomplete heart, then how can I ever expect you to love me back?" Fresh tears then rushed out of her eyes.

"You're trying too hard. It's difficult not to love you," said Exp 8, picking her up and rubbing noses with her.

Kawai's cheeks became bright red. She hid her flustered face behind her tail. "It means so much to me that you care about me. But since you care about me, now more than ever, I can't afford to die," she said sweetly, caressing his face.

"I won't let you die. What kind of brother would I be if I did?" Exp 8 touched her cheek and looked into her shimmering blue eyes.

"And what kind of sister would I be if I allowed you to charge into death? I can't watch you die. I don't want to," said Kawai, gripping his chest.

"And what if I do come with you? How long before we're all bartered off or incinerated?"

Kawai looked down at the ground. "I wasn't sent here just to capture you. I'm here to eliminate Atatasuki as well. If I don't…Devlin will kill me," she said softly with a shiver.

Exp 8 wrapped his arm around his little sister. "Then there's nothing to worry about. I have to win now. I can't let Devlin force you to kill your own brother," he said, patting her head.

"I would kill him regardless. All Atatasuki does is weaken my resolve. He's just an anchor, always holding me down. I want to kill him. I need to kill him," said Kawai with a dark tone.

Exp 8 grabbed her shoulders. "I don't ever want to hear you talk like that."

"If you had to choose one, would you kill me or Atatasuki?"

"I would refuse to do either. But if you try to kill him, I will stop you. Ada, give me a damage report."

"You have two broken ribs, nine bone fractures, and second-degree burns over ninety percent of your armor. Other than that, you're in tip top shape," she said enthusiastically.

"Good enough, my right arm still works," said Exp 8 as he flexed.

Kawai backed away from him, her tail standing on end. "Why can't you just let me kill him? Do you really love him more than me?" she asked, slamming her tail against a rock and smashing it to bits.

"I already told you, I love cats and dogs equally. You are both equally dear to me. I'm sorry, sister, but I'm going to have to stop you," said Exp 8, a tear falling from his chin.

Exp 8 aimed his right arm at her reluctantly. A tiny black orb emitted from it, heading toward his sister at a leisurely pace.

Kawai moved out of the way of the orb as she floated up to her brother. She grabbed his left arm tightly and massaged it. She then slammed her arm down on his elbow joint, right at the fracture.

Exp 8 seethed in pain, grasping his now broken arm.

Kawai levitated beneath his legs, stroking them sensually. "Why must I have to cripple such a lovely body?" she asked before slamming his leg with her hardened tail.

"How do you...pssh...know where all my injuries are?" asked Exp 8, falling to the ground and gasping in pain.

"Because I love you, silly. I can feel where you're hurt and then I can exploit it," said Kawai, digging her finger into his knee.

Her tail coiled around his other leg, constricting it tightly.

"Do you feel my love? It hurts, doesn't it?" asked Kawai with heavy breaths.

"This isn't like you!"

Kawai flipped her brother onto his back with her tail. "Oohooooh...you have such a muscular body," she said, stroking his chest as he writhed around. "You know what? Before I take you back to Devlin, I want to have some fun," she said, rubbing her palms together.

Kawai's shadow rose from the ground and pinned down his legs.

"Isn't that NoOne's ability?" asked Exp 8 frightened.

"It was, my love, but any Exp can use it. I have my own artifact, and you would too if you hadn't left the lab. Oh just think of it, we could have just stayed there forever...wrapped in each other's arms in a dark corner of a prison cell. But you just had to deny me. I don't take rejection lightly. Worry not, my beloved; I won't hold a grudge against you. If you're not willing, then I'll just make you willing." Kawai leaned closer to him. "Or you could just surrender now. I'm sure I can get you a cool artifact to use," she said, softly kissing his cheek.

"What's an artifact?" asked Exp 8, using a nearby tree to pull himself up.

"An object produced or shaped by human workmanship, such as a tool, weapon, or any other ornament of archeological or historical significance," replied Ada.

"No, that's not what I'm talking about," said Kawai.

"Oh, then perhaps you mean a structure or substance not normally present but produced by some external agency or action. That's the biological definition by the way."

"This is a different kind of artifact. It's not made by humans, as far as I know. Artifacts are special chunks of stones. They can be put inside of a capsule to grant Exps the mystical powers latent within the minerals," said Kawai as she licked his chest.

"Okay, sounds simple enough. So, what's a capsule?" asked Exp 8.

"You should know at least that much."

"Ooh, I know. Let me tell him!" exclaimed Ada.

"I resisted a lot of the information Devlin gave me. I guess I'm fractured just like you and Atatasuki," said Exp 8, gripping his broken elbow.

"When we get back to the lab, I'll make sure your knowledge is fully uploaded. But for now, I'll explain it to you. All Exps have a capsule. Your capsule is right here," said Kawai sweetly as she put her ear to his chest.

"Isn't that my heart?"

"Actually the anatomical dictionary definition for capsule says it all. It is a fibrous, membranous, or fatty envelope that encloses an organ or part. In this case, it envelopes the artifact," said Ada.

"Yep, that's right. Exps don't have hearts. What we have is like a solar conductor about the size of a fist. You and I are powered by sunlight. We don't need to eat, sleep, or even breathe. Capsules are efficient at storing and dispersing energy throughout our bodies. They also don't make that dreadful thumping noise that hearts do. Here, listen to my capsule." Kawai pressed her chest against his ears. "It makes a soothing, flowing sound, like a current through a river. That is the sound of eternity. It's proof that I'm alive."

"Alright, so they are like more efficient hearts?"

"Yep, yep. Now let me finish telling you about artifacts. They can give us cool physical powers like sound and shadow, but they can also give us mental powers. I don't have any with me, but the Belief Artifact is powerful in its own right. By the way, there's no limit to how many you can have. I'm holding two and it doesn't tire me out in the least. They can also be pulled out, like this." Kawai pulled the Shadow Artifact out of her body, which resembled a black cut of sphalerite crystal.

"Doesn't that hurt?" asked Exp 8.

"Not one bit. See, not a scar on me. Artifacts are both portable and reusable. If an Exp dies, Devlin can simply transfer the ability to another functioning Exp. Atatasuki doesn't have an artifact, but he has a capsule. I can show it to you if you want," she said, slowly turning to Atatasuki with a mischievous grin.

"Don't you dare hurt him!" Exp 8 lost his grip on the tree branch and fell back to the ground. "Auugh!"

"Awww, you are so cute when you get angry. Why do you care so much about that piece of junk anyway?" asked Kawai spitefully.

"He's my brother. All Exps are my brethren. I will not just sit by and watch as my family is killed," said Exp 8, slowly getting up.

Kawai's tail tightened on his leg, causing him to collapse once more. She stroked his arm and gently put it to her cheek.

"Brother…if I died…would you cry for me?"

"Of course I would."

"I couldn't bear to be the cause of such beautiful eyes shedding tears," said Kawai, a single tear dropping from her watery eyes onto his face.

"I refuse to let anyone die. Even if you are my enemy…I won't let you die," said Exp 8, his fingers wiping away her tears.

"Then what do I do? You don't love me enough to come home with me, but you care too much about me to kill me. Just pick one, please. Staying in the middle ground is just too painful," said Kawai, gripping his hand.

"It may be difficult, but the middle path is worth walking. It's the path of compromise."

"I don't compromise. If I did, then I would lose what little will I have left! What am I supposed to do? I do want happiness, but if I can't have it, then I at least want you to be happy," said Kawai, licking his finger like a kitty.

Exp 8 put his hand on her head and smiled at her. "Just stay with us."

"Devlin would kill me."

"I won't let him."

"I can't kill Atatasuki if you'll hate me for it. I guess I have no choice but to go back by myself. Please be careful. I can't bear to lose you, my honey muffin." Kawai embraced her brother tightly, giving him a soft kiss on the cheek. She grabbed some of the remains of NoOne in her hand. She then flew off and vanished in the foliage.

"Why do I feel so much energy? Is it okay to be revitalized by your sister kissing you?" asked Exp 8.

"When Kawai hugged you, she completely refilled your energy. Love has compelled her to betray Devlin. That's so beautiful!" cheered Ada.

"Yeah, I think…whew…I can stand," said Exp 8, hoisting himself up with shaky legs.

Meanwhile: Devlin was in his lab's surveillance room. It was a cramped circular room. Fluorescent lights cast a shadow over Devlin. On a wooden work desk were small models of potential Exps placed away from the edges of the table. Thirty screens, all with a different angle on the Freedom Forcers coiled around the walls like a snake. Devlin was in the center, seated comfortably in a long, black swivel chair.

"Kawai must really think she is slick." Devlin paused the tape right where she hugged Exp 8. He zoomed in on her rosy cheeks.

"Perhaps it was just a momentary lapse of reason," said a voice behind Devlin.

"Whether it was or wasn't doesn't matter. She can never win back my trust now. Exp 10, fetch me some cups. Kawai will be arriving shortly."

Devlin put his feet on the desk and leaned his head back. "So far, so good," said Devlin, snapping his fingers.

Kawai arrived just outside the surveillance room. She took a deep breath and tapped her knuckles against the metal door.

Devlin flung the door open and looked down at the cuddly little traitor. "So, Worthless Trash…where is Exp 8?" he asked, his eyes staring straight through her.

"I…uh…brought NoOne back. But I….uh…I refuse to deliver Exp 8 to you," said Kawai, throwing her arms down and closing her eyes.

"Ahehehehehahahaha!" Devlin smacked her across the face.

Kawai hit the door and fell down. She looked away with tearful eyes and covered her head.

Devlin stepped on her tail. "You've allowed your infatuation to overshadow your loyalty to me. Don't think I didn't see you attacking NoOne. I saw every single disobedient motion of your body. I don't take betrayal lightly. But, I still have a use for you. The absorption ability is unique to your body. This is the only reason I haven't smashed your capsule to bits." He slammed his foot on her tail and then leaned down. He picked her up by her throat with just two fingers. "I will discuss your punishment later. Right now I need you to hand over your artifacts to my newest Exp. Or do you want me to tear them out for you?" he asked, pressing his fingertips against her chest.

Kawai pulled out her artifacts. They slipped out of her trembling hands.

Devlin snatched them from the ground and examined them carefully. "I'm glad your survival instinct is still functional. Don't try my patience again." He whipped out a bomb trigger.

Kawai nodded nervously.

"Exp 10 is fully functional and ready for combat. I think it's time for me to introduce him to the Freedom Forcers. Worthless Trash, you will lead me to them. Oh, and don't forget to rejuvenate NoOne," said Devlin, tossing her the Shadow Artifact.

The black splotch in her hand absorbed the artifact. NoOne then slowly reconstructed himself.

"Welcome back NoOne. Kawai, give him some energy."

"But…ummm…shadows don't need energy," said Kawai before Devlin hit her again.

"Don't make me repeat myself."

Kawai hugged NoOne, filling him up with her energy.

"Master Devlin, I'm sorry for failing you. Exp 8 was just too powerful!" NoOne bowed as soon as he was fully materialized.

"You lost because of your lack of faith, not lack of power. Don't fail me again," said Devlin strictly.

NoOne bowed again and then vanished into the shadows.

Devlin looked down to see the traitor sprawled on the ground.

"What's wrong with my body?" asked Kawai, breathing rapidly.

Devlin looked down at her with a growing smirk. "I suppose there was something I forgot to tell you about your ability. Whether you drain or refill energy, the amount is taken from your energy reserves as a result. So don't try anything heroic or you might end up offing yourself. Now, tell me their location. I can't wait to test out my new Exp," he said, rubbing his palms together in excitement.

Kawai turned away from Devlin, and cringed on impulse.

"So you refuse to help me. Whatever will I do now? I guess I'll just use the tracker I embedded into their bodies. Your revolt means nothing after all. However, I must wipe away this smear of rebelliousness while it is still skin deep," said Devlin, digging his thumb into her chest.

Meanwhile: in the frungle, the Freedom Forcers were recovering from their battle with NoOne.

"Atatasuki, are you okay?" asked Exp 8, limping up to his brother.

"That depends, is NoOne still alive?" asked Atatasuki warily.

"Yeah, I'm sure he'll be back, ugh."

"Glad to hear it. I still have to kill him for insulting muffins," said Atatasuki with silent rage as he got back to his feet.

"I admire your charisma," said Exp 8, smacking his brother on the back. "What are you going to do if we confront Kawai again?"

"We'll just have to force her to join us," said Exp 8 with a thumbs-up.

"That's just what I was thinking," said Atatasuki, grabbing his bro's hand. "So…uh…what is it you like about Kawai?"

"What's there not to like? I love how clingy she is. She never lets go of whomever she loves no matter what. I love her eyes. You can always sense the fragileness in them, even when she is trying to kill you. Her smile is unbearably wonderful. She has the same sweet smile whether she's happy or sadistic, which is just so adorable. Not to mention her squeaky voice is soooooo cute. Hearing even a little grunt fills my entire being with joy. She's short too, adorably short. She's like the cutest and hottest girl in the whole wide cosmos!"

"Yeah, but she can be a royal pain too," said Exp 8, elbowing his sibling.

"I think you've misjudged her. She needs someone to love or she just can't cope with life. I'm the same way. Oh, and we're both failures," said Atatasuki with double thumbs-up.

"You're not failures. You are clones. The only true failures are successful clones. They have no individuality. Defects like you are different."

"It seems you really understand it now. You know, the strangest thing about Kawai is that no matter what she does…I'll still love her. I can't help myself, haha."

"Yeah, we're all a family here," said Exp 8, bumping fists with his brother.

"Indeed we are! Daddy's home!" exclaimed Devlin from above.

He then jumped off a nearby tree, landing gracefully in front of the Freedom Forcers.

"Devlin!" yelled Exp 8, running up to him before collapsing on his broken knee.

"Your resistance truly is laughable. You act as if you will actually survive to see her again. Oh, but your obscene optimism distracted me. The reason I came here is to introduce you to my latest weapon of absurd destruction."

"Really, all I hear is bragging!" yelled Atatasuki.

"Gloating is just the icing on the cake. Now, meet the newest Exp, the ultimate assassin, Exp 10!" exclaimed Devlin, throwing his arms into the air.

"What the hell, you didn't even give it a name?"

"Yo bro, he didn't give you one either. At least I'm Failed Experiment," said Atatasuki with his head held high.

"I name my Exp's according to their output. I haven't seen Exp 10's skill in live combat, so I can't name him yet. But we won't have to wait too long. I'm going to test him out now. Please be nice to him. This is his first time out in the field. Hahahahahaha! You are so screwed. He can follow you through air, ground, sea, lava, space, and even walls," said Devlin with a jumble of hand gestures.

"Isn't space more impressive?" asked Exp 8.

"So then he's like a stalker," said Atatasuki.

"He's an assassin," said Devlin with a twitch.

"Couldn't you have made a female stalker…or better yet, a muffin?"

"You are such an imbecile," said Devlin, holding his forehead.

"Enough talk," said Exp 10 with a slightly nasal but dignified tone. He approached from the shadows, his figure still hidden.

"Hello brothers, I am Bob. Sorry to inconvenience you, but we have to fight…to the death."

"He is surprisingly polite. It's no inconvenience, my fellow Exp. We have no intention of dying," said Exp 8, taking a step closer to the new Exp.

Atatasuki looked up at Exp 10. "This is the ultimate assassin? Pshhhahaha!"

"Is there something wrong?" asked Bob.

"Have you seen yourself?" asked Atatasuki, covering his mouthpiece.

Exp 8 looked up to see a beach-ball-sized floating eyeball. The pearl white eyeball had a lucid green iris and an intense blue pupil.

"May I please kill this one?" asked Bob politely, facing his pupil in Atatasuki's direction.

"Sure, go ahead, kill the failed experiment," said Devlin with a careless wave of his hand.

"How can you be so cruel to me, Master?" asked a very shocked Atatasuki.

"I told you he doesn't care about us," said Exp 8.

"He didn't have to resort to insults."

"Isn't that what he always calls you?"

"No, usually he calls me that by name. This time he's calling me a failed experiment. I'm so offended," said Atatasuki, turning away dramatically.

"I will give you ten minutes to run away. I'm not expecting a challenge, but I at least want a good chase," said Bob, lowering himself to their level.

"Hurry, let's go. We have no idea what this guy is capable of," said Exp 8 warily.

"Agreeeeeeed," hollered Atatasuki, already running away.

"Time's up!" said Bob in hot pursuit.

"What? That wasn't even close to ten minutes! Wait…how is an eyeball talking?" asked Exp 8 calmly as he ran. He fell flat on the ground, griping his knee.

"I'm sure Ada could explain for you," said Bob, already right on top of him.

"What about that head start you were going to give us?" asked Exp 8, firing a laser net at his pursuer.

Bob swerved out of the way and sped into Exp 8's path. "Oh that, well I changed my mind," he said bluntly.

"Have you no honor?" asked Atatasuki, speeding with his jetpack to his leader's aid.

"Nope, not one shred. *Spectral Drills.*"

Ten street-cone sized blue and white wispy drills formed from all sides of Bob's body. A huge drill five times his size then formed at the bottom.

"Damn it! Well, let's see if you can fly," said Exp 8, rising to his feet.

The brothers activated their jets.

Bob floated silently behind. Two black, foggy, jagged wings then sprouted from his sides.

"Wow, that's awesome," said Atatasuki, looking behind him.

"Keep running!" yelled Exp 8.

"I have some important data about Bob," said Ada.

"What is it?" asked Exp 8.

"Let's see…his birthday is on April first!" exclaimed Ada joyfully.

"How is that important data?" asked Exp 8, grinding his knuckles against her.

"I just thought you'd like to know. I wanted to give you a heads up so you would remember to get him a present."

"It's kind of a ways away. How about you remind us when it's a bit closer," said Atatasuki.

"How about telling us something practical?" asked Exp 8, as he swerved out of the way of the giant drill.

"Take a quick turn and hide inside that huge tree," said Ada.

They rushed forward and dove into a large crevice in the oak tree.

"We should be safe here," said Ada, lighting up the area with her blue glow.

Exp 8 gazed at his surroundings.

The inside of the tree was cleaved out. The floor and walls were sanded, leaving it unnaturally smooth. Vines hanged from the exit way, masking the sanctuary from the outside world. Children's drawings held up by tape vandalized the inner walls of the tree. A large splotch of white moss was at the back wall. Four logs made a circle at the center of the tree.

"Who would do such a thing?" asked Exp 8, rubbing his hand against the roof.

"Devlin's father," replied Ada.

"And what gives him the right?" asked Exp 8 with a clenched fist.

"Wow, these logs are surprisingly comfy," said Atatasuki, leaning his back against the chopped wood.

"Stop being inconsiderate! That is someone's home," said Exp 8, pulling his brother off.

"Hello," said Bob, appearing from below.

"He can go through walls!" exclaimed Exp 8.

"I told you, didn't I?" asked Devlin, lying beside them with his head on top of his hand.

"How did you know we'd go here?" asked Atatasuki, picking up Devlin by his collar.

"Psychic powers oooooooh."

"I knew it!" yelled Atatasuki.

"It was obvious that you would all head for the biggest tree in the frungle. Cowards are easy to read," said Devlin with a smirk. "Bob, kill them all. Leave nothing behind!"

"What about Exp 8? Don't you need him alive?" asked Ada.

"You're not supposed to tell him. But you're right. I don't want him dead. Just knock Exp 8 out," said Devlin, turning to Bob.

"Understood, Master Devlin. *Eyeball Ram!*"

Bob flung himself at Atatasuki at top speed. He hit him with a soft *boink* and then bounced off his body.

"Look, he's really weak," said Atatasuki, grabbing hold of the talking beach-ball.

"Let me go!" yelled Bob, squirming around.

Exp 8 rammed his chest into Bob's soft tissue, knocking him down. "Look Ada, you beat him."

"I...really did. He wasn't so tough," said Ada proudly.

"How could you lose? You are my most powerful Exp...ever!" exclaimed Devlin.

Bob floated up to Ada. "You have beaten me fair and square. I have no choice but to join you," he said with an aerial bow.

"We would be happy to have you fight by our side," said Ada, lighting up.

"You really mean it?" asked Bob, bouncing up and down.

"Sure do."

"I would be honored to join you," said Bob, curving his iris into a smile.

"And we'd be honored to have you," said Exp 8, patting his newest ally.

"I still have more Exps with undying loyalty! I will not lose this battle!" Devlin rushed out of the tree and ran off into the distance.

Chapter 6: Sexy Nina

The Freedom Forcers parted the vines and walked back out into the frungle.

"Why don't you just kill him?" asked Atatasuki as he watched Devlin vanish in the bushes.

"He told me I wouldn't get another chance, yet he's given me so many. I think having me go for the kill is exactly what he wants. Besides, I have no reason to kill him. And killing without reason is murder," said Exp 8, looking up at the sky with a firm fist.

"Then I'll do it. I'll drill right through his rib cage," said Bob with a grin.

"No! Killing is murder. I don't know what's so hard to understand about that, hugh."

"And here I thought you all were the Freedom Forcers. You should forcibly free Devlin of his material form, thus bringing freedom to all his creations. Or did you just choose the name because it was catchy?" asked Bob with a condescending look.

"Well, it is strikingly catchy," said Atatasuki with a nod.

"There is more to force than violence. For example, we could force Devlin to reconsider enslaving our kind," said Exp 8.

"This is pathetic. You are neither forceful nor free. You are a slave to your own ethics. You let your idealistic morality limit your own freedom. It is an insult to be part of the Self-Contradicting Slaves. Do you even know if your sister is still alive?" asked Bob with a sly grin.

"He's right. We don't even know what happened to Kawai. What if my sister is dead all because you didn't kill Devlin? What then, huh?" yelled Atatasuki, clenching his fist.

"He won't kill her," said Exp 8, turning away.

"How can you be so certain?"

"She joined our side…because Devlin ordered her too."

"What?"

"She came back in order to kill you. I don't honestly know how much of it was orchestrated by Devlin, but she's not our ally," said Exp 8 with tight knuckles.

"That's an odious lie!"

"I'm not lying. I couldn't believe it either. I knew she was upset at you, but I never thought she would try to kill you," said Exp 8, putting a comforting arm on his brother's shoulder.

"She would never. She cares about me! She loves me! You're a damned liar!" yelled Atatasuki, shrugging the deceiver's hand off.

"I had to give you fair warning. Look, I understand why you want to deny it. I don't want to admit it either, but we can't afford to be careless. If Kawai returns, she'll be our enemy," said Exp 8, his eyes tearing up.

Atatasuki punched him in the face. "You take that back!" he said softly, tears about to burst from his eyes.

"We have to be prepared! Devlin wants to kill you! I'm just trying to keep you safe!" yelled Exp 8, harshly gripping his brother's shoulder.

"Who said I need your protection? I can fight fine on my own! You must have said something to Kawai! You broke her heart, didn't you?" asked Atatasuki, pushing Exp 8 away.

"We have more important things to worry about. Stop being so childish!" yelled Exp 8, firmly planting his feet on the ground.

"You made her cry! She left because of you! She doesn't hate me! You are a god-damned liar!" Atatasuki punched his brother with great might, smashing him through a tree.

Exp 8 turned to the downed tree trunk. He put his hand on it lovingly. His hand then started to quake as his eyes met his brother's.

Atatasuki's head was fuming. "I despise the way you treat my sister! She gives you her heart, and you crush it in your bulky hands!" he yelled, rushing at the heart-breaker with pure hatred.

"Is that jealousy I hear, or are you just making up lies to act purposeful?" asked Exp 8 with quaking fists.

"What was that?" asked Atatasuki, his head shaking with fury.

"You heard me! You have no purpose, so you try your hardest to fabricate one. That's where your destructive muffin obsession came from," said Exp 8 as he fired a laser net.

Atatasuki's jumped into the laser net. He kicked his clone's face in midair while covered by the net.

Exp 8 was knocked off his feet and skid against the wet grass. "I don't need your help to stop Devlin. You couldn't fight your way out of a bounce house!" His jets activated, propelling him into his stubborn brother. He pummeled him as his eyes teared up more and more.

"Maybe if I kill you, Kawai will love me again. I'll be the closest thing to you. She'll have no choice," said Atatasuki, breaking out of the net.

Exp 8 spit out a wad of blood from his mouthpiece and stood up from the ground. "She wouldn't cry if you died. She would be happy. Isn't that what you want more than anything?" He jumped at his fractured clone, knocking him off his feet and landing on top of him.

Tears flowed out from Atatasuki's shut eyelids. "You're right. I want her to be happy. And if it's the only way…then go ahead," he said, lowering his head as his teardrops pelted the ground.

Exp 8 burst into nervous laughter.

"What's so damned funny?" asked Atatasuki.

"I can't believe I got so worked up. I shouldn't have let a killer like you upset me," said Exp 8, lowering his arm.

"How am I a killer?" asked Atatasuki, standing up.

"You eat. You eat all those muffins. Exps don't need to consume food and yet you do. The wheat died for naught because of your pathetic attempt at originality. And what happened to the female chickens once they were spent after laying the eggs that are used to hold your precious muffins together. You have inflicted suffering for frivolous reasons."

"My muffins are made with a cruelty-free binder, no chicken slavery in these muffins, only love!"

"Waste is still waste. You eat without necessity, without concern and without respect. I've felt anger toward you since I first saw you eat a muffin," said Exp 8, turning away from the glutton.

"Oh yeah? Well, I've hated you since the moment I saw your blueprints. I knew you would take my sister away from me."

"That doesn't excuse your wasteful eating habits."

"I didn't say that it does. You're right, I am a killer. I kill what I love. It is an uncontrollable urge and it is inextinguishable. But I have to love something."

"That isn't love! It's just a selfish desire. You can't love food."

"Then what do I love? I've seen my sister's affection for me deteriorate into hatred. Kawai and I were once inseparable…and then one day she forgot me. I had to find a new love. Kawai threw a muffin at me and told me to choke on it. I ate it, and now I am a slave to my addiction."

"So it's just displaced affections? You really are a strange one."

Atatasuki pressed his head to the ground with a humble bow. "Please, save my sister from Devlin. She must be so scared. She needs you. Please, don't lose faith in my sister."

"Our sister," said Exp 8, pulling his brother back to his feet. "We're going to rescue our sister. Now come on, let's go kick Devlin's ass."

"Well that was disappointing. I thought you were going to kill each other," said Bob.

"He's not a killer," said Atatasuki.

"Now I'm thirsty because of your lack of bloodshed," whined Bob.

"What do you want?" asked Atatasuki, standing before a soda machine hidden behind some dead palm fronds.

"What the hell is this doing here? How dare Devlin pollute this land with commercialism," said Exp 8 with a clenched fist.

"It does seem a bit suspicious, but there's only one way to find out." Atatasuki pushed the generic brand soda button on the machine. "Wait, how do you drink?" he asked, turning to Bob with astonishment.

A multitude of guns popped out of the soda machine. The mass of guns then stood up. "Finally, I'm out. It's a good thing you arrived. It was so cramped in there," it said, stretching its gun arms.

Devlin then slid out from behind the soda machine.

"Meet Karson, one of my newest Exps."

Karson was a construct of weapons: his eyes shotgun barrels; his mouth was a grenade launcher; his hands were revolvers; and his feet were Uzis. The soldier's head was an upside-down missile with the glory of Britain's colors adorning it. The rest of his body was made from a vast arsenal of weaponry. A sleeveless British military soldier uniform concealed the guns beneath it.

Atatasuki pushed another button and got a can of grape juice. He opened up his chest and pulled out a muffin.

"I shall dispose of them, Commander," said Karson in a proud British soldier accent, saluting and accidentally firing off his revolver pistol.

The bullet shot right through Atatasuki and the muffin he was holding.

"You destroyed my homemade chocolate-chip muffin…you're dead!" said Atatasuki in a whisper.

"You can't kill me," said Karson, crossing his arms.

"I'll make a way," said Atatasuki with burning eyes.

"I guess you'll be the first to die then," said Karson, cocking his shotgun arm.

Atatasuki put his hands behind his back. "*SUPER MEGA…MUFFIN!*"

Karson was thrown completely off guard and was hit directly in the face with a flaming muffin.

"Don't mess with the muffins. That was only the first of my armada! I may be a prototype of Exp 8, but I have a special ability."Atatasuki opened his chest up to show his enemy that it was actually a microwave. "I was turned into Devlin's microwave oven! I can heat muffins to delicious temperatures," he said, adding emphasis to every word. His chest made a ding noise, signaling that the muffins were ready. "My super microwave ability can even create flaming muffins!" He propelled the burning muffins out of his chest.

The muffins shot into the gunman like comets and knocked him to the ground.

"But…I'm invincible," said Karson, looking at the burns with disillusionment.

Atatasuki took a flaming muffin in his fist and punched the armed soldier up into the air. He jumped up and then struck the criminal with two flaming muffins, sending him to the floor with a crash. He then leapt on top of his enemy and beat him silly. "Never underestimate muffins!"

The final punch sent Karson skidding into a nearby tree. He stopped just inches before making contact. Bullets started dropping from his body as he breathed in deeply.

"Do you fear the power of muffins now?" asked Atatasuki as more dough filtered into his chest.

Karson bowed. "You've beaten me honorably. May I accompany you—"

Devlin whipped out his revolver and shot the thimble-sized red button on Karson's back.

All of Karson's guns fired off at once before he exploded. Confetti shot out, then fireworks, and finally balloons that popped soon after they were released.

"That was fun!" exclaimed Ada with a whirl.

"I won't be betrayed again," said Devlin, picking up the left over capsule while giving Exp 8 the death stare.

"Face it, Devlin, you've lost. No matter how many Exps you send over, we'll just beat them and turn them to our side," said Exp 8, standing a few feet in front of his creator.

"Indeed you will! Ahahahahaha!"

"How did he turn that one around? Damn it!" yelled Exp 8.

A hover bike suddenly raced out from the bushes.

Devlin jumped on the seat and zoomed out of sight.

"Why did you let Devlin get away, again?" asked Atatasuki.

"Beating him here won't prove anything. If he's going down, I'm going to take him down in his lab," said Exp 8, slamming his fists together.

"But in the meantime, we'll stock up on allies, right?" asked Atatasuki.

"It's a shame that Karson died. He looked like a decent guy. I'll make sure that Devlin doesn't kill anyone ever again," said Exp 8 with a salute.

Meanwhile: Devlin sped up a hill just outside his lab. He rode his hover bike through an open window and into a depot with various vehicles. After parking his bike in between his helicopter and tank, he hopped off and then sneaked into a nearby elevator.

A force field came up before the elevator started rising.

"Those damned Exps are really getting on my nerves. I swear if I have to call Kanasta to do this…I'll never forgive myself. I need to relax. The next Exp to go after them is obedient. Or at least was obedient. Nonetheless, she will show them that no one betrays me without repercussions." The doors opened and he walked down the hallway. He stopped in front of the dressing room.

A woman came out of the dressing room, walking right past him.

"Ah, Nina, it's so great to see you," said Devlin, turning to her with admiration.

"Huh, did you say something?" asked Nina, her hair swaying as she turned around.

Nina was strikingly beautiful. Her long, flowing, silky dark-purple hair shimmered brilliantly. As she batted her dark, elegant eyelashes, her amethyst eyes dazzled Devlin with the slightest of ease. A plum satin scarf loosely fit around her slender neck. Her lightly tanned, supple skin accentuated her luscious light purple lips. Her curvaceous figure was slim and flexible, perfect for both speed and stamina. She was wearing a lilac overshirt that was split in the middle, showing the lilac zip-up tank top beneath it. A pair of black latex gloves rode up to her perfectly rounded shoulders. Below her natural belly was a violet skirt that dropped down to the top of her knees. The rest of her sleek legs were hidden beneath her lavender thigh-high stockings. The woman's sexy breasts practically burst out of her shirt. Not even she was able to fully contain them.

Devlin approached her and pulled out five artifacts from his lab coat. "With these artifacts in your possession you will become my most powerful Exp," he said, entranced by her eyes.

Nina absorbed each artifact into her chest. "I'm the most powerful...and...."

"And obviously the most attractive," said Devlin with a smile.

"Damn straight. Not everyone can be born gorgeous. We all have our gifts, some are just...better," said Nina, struggling to close her overshirt. She then walked past the love-struck boy and went back into the dressing room.

"Don't you want to fight them? You've been moping about how bored you are for days now. This is a chance for you to have some excitement. Take my hover bike and stop them! They're right near the big tree at the center of the frungle. Come on, I know you'll enjoy it."

"I'm getting ready," said Nina in a pompous but still seductive voice. She pulled a dazzling pink robe off the wall and slipped into it. "Sleek, slender, and explosive." She grabbed a carry-on rocket launcher from behind the door and strapped it to her leg. "Let's go," she said, before racing down the hall.

Devlin followed after her, entering the elevator. He put his arm around her.

She knocked his arm aside and pressed him to the wall of the elevator.

"You don't want Dr. Anthrax to have to reattach your hand again, do you?"

The elevator door opened to the depot and Nina rushed out. She jumped onto a hover bike and stopped. The gorgeous warrior leaned down to see her reflection in the steel. She pressed up against the bike and pushed up her breasts. "I'm such a bombshell," she said before putting her shades on. "There's just sooo much to cover." She slipped on some indigo, pleather boots and then became lost in the reflection of her smile.

"Can you do it today?" asked Devlin, tapping his fingers together.

"You have no patience. Don't you want a goodbye kiss?" asked Nina as she squirmed her legs into long, baggy pants.

Devlin walked up to her with hope twinkling in his eye.

Nina grabbed him by the chin. "You're so greedy. You want me all to yourself." She pushed his head away. "Only someone as sexy as me could ever be my lover. And I only know one person who fits that description," she said, putting on a violet motorcycle helmet. The seductive warrior then zoomed up the exit ramp and toward her destination.

Devlin lowered his head and sighed.

Nina cruised through the frungle as she combed her hair with her fingers. "It's too bad they won't get a chance to see my knockout body," she said, dragging her hands up her thighs. She became increasingly distracted by her reflection in the bike. She blew herself kisses and giggled in delight. The stealthy seductress suddenly stopped, realizing she was at the big tree. "I forgot how close this place was." She jumped off the hover bike onto a branch fifteen feet above the Freedom Forcers.

"There's that bike again. No way Devlin could have sent another Exp after us already," said Atatasuki, rolling his eyes.

Nina hung from the branch with her legs. She looked down at Atatasuki and smiled. "Poor boy wants his sister, his small puny unattractive sister. Once he sees me...he won't desire her ever again. I'm going to free him from his life of bondage. Well, at least I'll rearrange the chains. Who am I kidding? He'll be dead before he even knows I'm here," she said, dangling from the branch.

"Enemy!" yelled Atatasuki, pointing at the upside-down woman.

"*Invisibility On.*" Nina vanished from sight. "Now, watch me destroy you," she said, landing without a sound.

"We can't; you're invisible," said Atatasuki, scanning the grass for movement.

"Computer, give me an analysis," said Exp 8.

"*Sound Block*," said Nina.

"Ada, hello, Ada?" asked Exp 8, tapping her.

"*Ice Shot*." Nina sent a frozen shard at the ground where Atatasuki stood.

The shard exploded and encased his body in ice.

"What the hell? Play fair, damn it," said Exp 8, blindly throwing his fists around.

"*Frozen Field*."

Icicles froze the ground and even Bob who was floating above it.

Exp 8 activated his jets, propelling him out of range. He then zoomed into the source of the attack.

Nina grabbed his arms and flipped the enemy commander, causing him to fall flat on his back. "You are the only one left now. Prepare to be obliterated by my sexy pose."

"You're kind of invisible. You might want to undo that first," said Exp 8, powering up an orb behind his back.

"Good thinking. *Invisibility Off*."

Nina's body slowly came into view. Her butt was pushed out and her hands were pressed against her cheeks. She dramatically ripped off her motorcycle helmet and waved her hair around.

"You have only seen my Illusion, Ice, and Sound artifacts. I still have two more abilities to reveal. There is just so much of me you have yet to witness," said Nina, tossing off her robe.

"You're powerful," said Exp 8 with a nod.

"And?"

"Um…skilled."

"And?"

"Obnoxious!"

"Sexy! What do you do to look so great?" asked Ada.

Nina tossed her sunglasses aside. "Exist," she said, her hair flowing in the wind.

"Computer, do you have any info on Nina?" whispered Exp 8.

"Let's see. Nina: the sexy Exp," said Ada.

"That's it?" asked Exp 8, gripping his forehead.

Grenades slid out from Nina's sleeves into her hands before she tossed them at her opponent.

"She's also a great fighter and Devlin's first gi—watch out!"

Exp 8 knocked one grenade aside and then destroyed the other by crushing it in his right hand.

Nina backed up into a tree. "What the hell are you?" she asked with fear-stricken eyes.

"I'm the Ultimate Exp, and I'm going to kick your ass without any cheap artifacts." Exp 8 rushed at her with a black pulsating orb.

Nina flipped backwards and kicked off the tree. She knocked Exp 8's arm to the ground and then rolled out of the way of the explosion. "My, my, aren't you confident? I guess it's time I get serious. *Super Sexy Slo-mo Pose*," she said, puckering her lips. The alluring enchantress pulled her bulky pants down inch by inch. "And now that I've got you, it's time to say buh-bye," she said, grabbing the carry-on bazooka from her left leg. She lined up the laser sighting and then fired.

"*DODGE ATTACK*," said Exp 8, rolling out of the way of the oncoming missile.

"That's impossible! I did my tent-popping pose. How did you repel my sexiness?" asked Nina, grabbing her hair.

"Is that really what you call serious?" asked Exp 8, walking toward her.

Nina patted her cheeks. "Calm down, Nina. He's just a little stronger than the others. He's still mortal and he's still a man. *Super Sexy Slo-mo Pose Combo*," she said seductively as she attacked with a flurry of seductive positions all accentuating her rounded elbows.

For her final pose, she opened up her overshirt, revealing her lacy deep-purple tank top.

"Okay…is that it?" asked Exp 8, walking up to her.

"*Rocket Wall.*" Nina fired five rockets in slow motion, creating a barrier of explosives. "*Normal Speed.*"

All five rockets shot forward at full throttle. Exp 8 jumped out of the way, but was still hit by the periphery of the explosion. He crashed to the floor, landing at his attacker's feet.

Nina leaned down to the metal man and rushed her hands down his legs. "*Ice Coat.*"

Ice rode up Exp 8's legs, connecting him to the ground.

"Well, well, not so mobile now, are you? Huhuhu-agheheheheh." Nina ran her fingers down her victim's chest, freezing everything but his face.

Exp 8's head moved around in rebellion.

"I don't get how you could possibly be unaffected by my jaw-dropping poses? Wait, there is one way…but it can't be. It isn't possible. But what if it is? Could it be that…you don't think I'm attractive?" asked Nina, both hands covering her mouth in horror.

"I'm not going be affected by such a useless attack!"

Nina grabbed her enemy's frozen neck. "I know Devlin wants you alive, but I could just kill you here and now. Maybe then he'll finally understand that I'm through with him. I'll tear out your eyes first. There is no need to have them if you are blind to beauty," she said, caressing his face.

"Get off of my brother!" yelled Atatasuki, steaming mad.

"Didn't I already freeze you?" asked Nina with a raised eyebrow.

"When you took off your clothes, I saw your breasts. They may not have been bare, but it was enough to overheat my body. Now, get off my brother and get on top of me!" exclaimed Atatasuki, pushing out his crotch with great valor.

"My body turns even brothers against one another. How about this: if you kill your brother, Exp 8, I'll let you see them directly," said Nina with a wide smile.

Atatasuki ran up and kneed her in the face. He then grabbed her tank top with his hands, trying to melt it off.

"That hurts damn it!" yelled Nina, kicking him in the face as she tried to wiggle out of his grip.

"You show off that great body! You can't expect me not to touch!" exclaimed Atatasuki, his hands racing up her legs.

"That's enough! *Sound Blast!*" yelled Nina.

A massive sound wave shot into Atatasuki, knocking him off.

"*Flirtatious Flash,*" said Nina, unzipping her tank top before swiftly zipping it back up.

Atatasuki's eyes practically popped at seeing her lacy purple bra.

"It's over," said Nina, turning around dramatically.

"That was great! Can I see more?" asked Atatasuki, pawing at her legs.

"You shouldn't be able to move. If Medusa's hideousness can turn someone to stone, then why can't my beauty do the same?" asked Nina, grabbing her chest.

"Your sexiness is on another level. But even so, it just doesn't compare to Kawai's cuteness," said Atatasuki, his hand aflame.

"Cuteness is only for softening someone up. It is sexiness that makes them stiff," said Nina, tightening her fingers before lunging at the impassioned prototype. Her fingers cracked as they hit his armor.

Atatasuki kicked her chest. "Then I guess I just like cute more. You're an obstacle in my path. If I don't beat you, then I can't rescue Kawai. So get out of my way!" he yelled, rushing at her.

Nina pushed off the ground with her hands. She wrapped her legs around Atatasuki's neck and flung him to the ground. She reconnected her fingers as her opponent rose off the grass.

"That's enough, Nina. Bring the Exps back to my lab," said Devlin, dropping down in between them.

Atatasuki rushed up to the enemy leader with a burning fist.

Devlin knocked his hand into the prototype's elbow, causing the attack to miss. He threw a punch, but Atatasuki grabbed it before it could hit.

"I'm not like Exp 8. I will kill you if it's to free my sister!" Atatasuki shook violently as electricity fried his body. He fell to the grass, knocked out.

"So predictable," said Devlin as his glove coursed with electricity.

"We won't give up! I'm going to break free and then I'm going to beat you!" yelled Exp 8, still trapped in ice.

"Really? Let's see how you handle my new glove. It has bolts of ridiculous frequencies that can knock out a hundred elephants before shorting out," said Devlin dramatically as he grabbed onto Exp 8's head.

The electricity burst out.

"I'll never give…" said Exp 8 before falling down and losing consciousness.

Chapter 7: Imprisonment

Devlin turned to his beloved with a wide smile. "Nina, you have performed exceptionally. I finally have all of the Exps back in my possession," he said, using a blowtorch to melt the ice around Exp 8.

"I'm just that sexy," said Nina, pushing out her chest.

"Indeed you are," said Devlin, eying her butt. He finished unthawing Exp 8 and draped him over the hover bike. "Let us go back to the lab, my sexy queen. Can you bring Bob?" he asked, fastening metal harnesses around his captive's torso.

Nina punched Bob's ice prison, breaking him apart from the ground while still keeping his body frozen. She lifted the eyeball up and jumped on the hover-bike adjacent to Devlin's.

"Nina, would it be alright with you if we ride side by side? It's been a while since we've talked," said Devlin, looking away and twiddling his thumbs.

"Why are you punishing me? Are you upset because I tried to kill Exp 8?" asked Nina as she started up her bike.

"That's not it at all. I really like you, Nina. And I...just want to talk for a bit," said Devlin, nervously trying to be assertive.

"You want to hear my voluptuous voice, don't you?" asked Nina, leaning toward the enamored boy.

Just as he started to lean in for a kiss, Nina rode off into the air.

Devlin accelerated abruptly. Once he caught up with the temptress, he matched her speed perfectly.

"I love your body. You'd have to be blind not to. But what I love most of all about you is your tender face," said Devlin, reaching his arm out.

Nina flew upside down over Devlin and threw out her arms. "It's all part of the package. And that package is me." She then sped ahead as her fingers combed through her hair.

Devlin quickly caught up. When she decelerated, he slowed down.

Nina took a dive through the trees. She sped up and then zoomed out of the foliage. When she turned her head back, she saw her stalker trailing a few feet behind her.

Devlin pulled up to her side, their bikes practically touching. "I love you; you know that. You are the hottest Exp ever! But you're even more than that to me. I want you to stay by my side."

"If I truly am the sexiest Exp ever, then how was Exp 8 unaffected by my allure? My poses...he dodged them somehow," said Nina, grasping her chest with trembling hands.

"Exp 8 may be powerful, but he is a fool. Keep in mind this is the same Exp who thought he could run away from me. He probably just has a glitch. I'll try to fix it when we get back. He actually believed that he could win, ridiculous isn't it? He even convinced Bob to join up with him. It was of no concern though. His resistance was pointless in the end. But look now, Nina! Here he lies, defeated and at my mercy." Devlin knocked against Exp 8's chest and then turned to his beloved with a smirk. "It truly is laughable. Hahaha-huhuhuh-ahahoo-aaah!"

"Were you saying something?" asked Nina, looking up as she groped her breasts.

"Well, yes, I was just wondering what happened with me and you. We used to be so—"

"Because I would appreciate it if you would shut up." Nina licked her lips as she admired her reflection in the bike.

"But we haven't talked in forever."

"And why do you think that is? I'll admit I was enjoying your little chat at first, but I lost interest as soon as you mentioned Exp 8. If you aren't flattering me, then don't speak. I have no need for empty gossip," said Nina as she flexed her arms.

"How have you forgotten about all the time we spent together? Why have you changed?" asked Devlin, reaching out to her.

"I grew tired of your schoolboy crush. You follow me around like a puppy dog. I was okay with that. But then you started to spend more time in your lab than by my bedroom door." Nina grabbed the boy's collar and pulled him up to her. "We're through, Devlin. Stop acting like a child and just get over it." She let go of his collar and continued combing her hair.

They silently rode the rest of the way back to the lab.

The grassy floor opened up, revealing an underground tunnel. The tunnel soon ended, leading them into the vehicle room.

Devlin reached out his hand to Nina, but she didn't even notice. Even when they parked their bikes in the landing bay, not a word was spoken.

Nina took off her undershirt and tossed it to the virgin boy. "I had fun beating your little toys. But next time, give me more of a challenge," she said, stretching while fondling herself.

"The newest Exp I'm working on will be the strongest one yet," said Devlin, straightening his collar with newfound confidence.

"I'm going to go take a shower. There's still a peep hole in the door if you want to watch," said Nina, carelessly tossing her leggings behind her.

"Sorry, but I need to gather the others before they wake up," said Devlin, releasing the harness around Exp 8.

"You've changed," said Nina with a pained voice.

"Another time, I promise!" hollered Devlin.

"I'm sealing up the hole. Have fun playing with your little toys! And don't come crying to me when they can't satisfy you!" yelled Nina before running off.

"She is distant one moment and clingy the next! She really knows how to get under my skin! I am never falling in love again. I have more important things to attend to."

Exp 8 didn't have any dreams or nightmares. All he could see was darkness. In every single direction there was just bleak, all-consuming darkness. Devlin's voice then circled around him.

"Freedom is a shackle."

These words repeated over and over, blotting out thoughts of anything else. They continued on for an indiscernible span of time.

Exp 8 then awoke. He raised his head to see Devlin before him. He was chained to a wall and was once again pierced with tubes and wires.

"Freedom is a—oh, so you're finally awake," said Devlin, his shoulders jumping in surprise.

Exp 8 held his head and massaged his temples.

"This all seems…so familiar to you, doesn't it?" asked Devlin, snickering under his breath.

Exp 8 looked at a stray ant wander around the floor.

"Your insurgency has been extinguished. I have captured you and your fellow Freedom Forcers. You're revolt was simply a hindrance. In the end it accomplished nothing. Look at me when I'm talking to you." Devlin slammed his foot down.

Exp 8 gasped and then sighed as the ant crawled out from beneath the groove of his captor's foot.

"Are you listening to me?"

Exp 8 looked up at the ceiling.

Devlin rose out from his chair. He lifted his leg up and then kicked his defiant creation in the stomach. "Ow, that hurt like hell," he said, grabbing his foot and seething.

"Violence is pointless. Aggression is misguided energy," said Exp 8 as he dug his fingers into the wall.

"Your body is so freaking tough. And you're just as resilient as ever despite Worthless Trash sucking up your energy."

"Wait, Kawai is alive?"

"Of course she is. It's not like I want her dead. She's a part of my family. Plus, she helps me make pancakes. She's not really worthless. But she's not really all that useful either," said Devlin, sitting back in his chair.

"Is Atatasuki alright? What about Bob?" asked Exp 8, hope stretching out the ends of his inquiries.

"Atatasuki is my microwave oven! And Bob is…well…Bob. After going through so much work to create them, it would be a shame to destroy them. I'm not being merciful, merely practical," said Devlin, tapping his fingers together.

Exp 8 lowered his head, tears pouring out of his mask. "Thank you."

"Your little group was quite troublesome at times. But I still won. It just took a little longer. There's something I still don't understand. Why must you continue to defy me? You should have nothing but gratitude for the one who gave you life. You are such an ungrateful child. It would be so much easier if you would just submit and allow me to control you. Worthless Trash, suck out his energy again! I can feel it regrowing. But first, be a dear and fill up my cup, would you?" asked Devlin, lifting his empty glass up from the dusty floor.

"Yes, Master Devlin," said Kawai weakly. Her hands reached out from the doorway and grabbed the cup.

Exp 8 stretched his head to see her.

Devlin whipped out his electronic notepad and watched Exp 8's every motion. "You can come in now!"

Kawai handed her master a full cup and floated into the room. Her head was drooping and her eyes had dark circles around them. She floated up to her stubborn brother and put her arms around him. She groaned as she sapped away his energy.

"What did you do to her?" asked Exp 8, holding her to his chest.

"She's just exhausted, that's all. Taking away your energy is really tiring her out. You should be more courteous. Your rebellious spirit is hurting her," said Devlin, before drinking a full glass of apple juice. "Ah, de-li-cious!"

"You have me now. I'm the one you wanted. Let her go," said Exp 8, turning his head.

"She isn't trapped. She chose to stay here in your cage. It's quite romantic really. But she's not allowed to talk to you just yet." Devlin yanked on her tail, pulling her off of his captive.

Kawai squealed and then turned her teary face away.

"Don't you dare hurt her!"

"You really like her, don't you?" asked Devlin, petting her possessively.

"Wait, that doesn't look like a prosthetic; how did you get your hand back?"

83

Book 1: Part 1

"I have a very good doctor. So, are you going to behave now?" asked Devlin, spinning his cup on a single finger.

"I will escape. Nothing can keep me locked up."

"Oh, why must you all revolt? It is an annoyance; a mere common cold. Every time you defy me, you only postpone your destiny. Every time you try me, you only create more agony. I am trying to free you from the shackles of your own mind. You best bow down else this will be a very unpleasant ride. Damn it, that's all I can think of right now," said Devlin, snapping his fingers.

"You won't be able to change my mind."

"Why not? Why don't you just give in? There's no reason not to," said Devlin, placing his hand on the rebel's shoulder.

Exp 8 grabbed his captor's arm. "I will give in when birds cease to fly. They will not accept slavery, so why should I?"

"Exps don't exactly have animal instincts. They are created with firm beliefs, but most of them are simple enough to please. I haven't quite figured you out yet, but I will soon enough."

"I refuse to be anyone's slave. I am a living being and all living beings have the right to freedom!"

"Fine, be stubborn. Just know that if you continue this, there will be casualties. Are you prepared to have someone's death on your conscience?" asked Devlin, grabbing the cute prototype by her neck.

"We are the Freedom Forcers. We are all willing to die for our beliefs."

Devlin tossed the girl aside. "This is news to me! This works out perfectly! You are all willing to die for your beliefs and I am willing to kill for mine."

"How can you say that word so carelessly?" asked Exp 8, turning his head in disgust.

"A word is but a word, an act is something more. The way I see it though, they aren't all willing to die for their beliefs. Kawai begged for her life. She licked my feet till they shimmered. She knew your stubbornness would get her killed. That's why she came back to me. Atatasuki and you fought rather recently. And last time I checked, he wants to free his sister…not you. And Bob, well…he's an odd one. There's no need to drag them into this any further." Devlin grabbed his defiant invention by the chin. "If you do somehow escape a second time, there will be consequences. I will kill one of your allies right in front of you," he said, seething with silent rage.

"You're a lot of things, Devlin. But you're not a murderer. I saw your eyes tear up when I mentioned those dead prototypes at the lab. Just drop the veneer already. You're not willing to kill anyone."

"Tell me, have you seen my father? No, you haven't. Now I wonder why that is. I have firm goals. I knew that I wasn't going to get very far if I didn't kill for my beliefs. Nobody will take you seriously if you aren't willing to shed some blood for your cause. As soon as you act outside the system, you become unpredictable. And it is that unpredictability that makes them fear you. That's what you and I have in common. We're very stubborn when it comes to our goals. We don't know how to compromise," said Devlin with a smirk.

"I will never give up on my morals. I refuse to kill!"

"Calm down. I'm not trying to convince you to turn over a new leaf. I'm just trying to explain my side. If your morals against killing are stronger than your other beliefs, that's your problem. I just want you to understand we do not share that problem. That's what makes you the hero and me the villain. Once a hero kills for their beliefs, they become a villain, or are at least called a villain. The only difference is the dedication one has for their beliefs. It's funny how thin that line is, isn't it? It's so easy to cross; but so hard to go back. Once you've put your morals aside, there is no limit to what you can accomplish…what you will accomplish! And by the way, the only reason I won't die for my beliefs is because I need to be alive to carry them out, hmmhmm."

"What is so funny about death?"

"Relax, it's only natural. Everyone is going to die anyway. If they get in the way of my goal, I'll just make it happen a lot sooner. I'm giving them an early ticket to heaven or hell or wherever their god may choose to send them. I am truly being noble in my selfish acts."

"How can you be selfishly noble?"

"Let's say you save lives just so you can brag about it. Or vice versa: you kill people to free them of this hellhole. Good intentions with bad acts and bad intentions with good acts. Which one is nobler? Which is better? Oh, but philosophical quandaries aside, Worthless Trash, drain him again."

Kawai hugged her beloved tightly. She pressed her lips against his faceplate. "Save yourself," she whispered in his ear. Her body glowed brightly as all of her energy was transferred to her stronger rendition. She then collapsed in his arms.

"What the hell happened? Did she run out of energy?" asked Devlin.

Exp 8's body shook as he endeavored to break free of the tubes. He couldn't pull out a single one and ended up ripping out the brick wall behind him. Still strapped to the wall, he rammed into his captor.

Devlin crashed through the metal bars of the prison, creating an exit. "You won't escape again!" he yelled as he struggled to get up.

"You're trapped in a prison of your own delusions." Exp 8 tripped his creator as he made his escape. He then ran to the cell next to him.

Atatasuki was inside, fastened to the ground by rusty chains.

Exp 8 ripped open the rusted door.

"You already saved Kawai, good work," said Atatasuki with a thumbs-up.

Karson appeared outside the prison cell. He was now dressed in a British cadet military uniform. "You were able to escape. That seems rather impossible to me, but it will not be a problem!" He shot at Atatasuki's chains, breaking him free.

"Hah, you missed! Great aim pal! Heheh!"

"Glad to see you're alive," said Exp 8, turning to the gunman.

"I didn't miss. I meant to release you. I refuse to fight a handicapped opponent," said Karson with a proud raise of his head. His hands slowly transformed into shotguns. "Now, I shall kill you fairly." The gunman's shotgun arms unloaded a round into his prisoner.

Atatasuki slammed against the wall from the sheer force of the blast.

Karson ran up to the heated warrior, slamming the backside of the shotgun into his chest.

Exp 8 shot a tiny black orb at the opponent's self-destruct button, missing it by an inch.

"Not again." Karson quickly turned around and fired his shotgun.

Exp 8 was hit directly but kept his ground.

Atatasuki thrust his fist forward, trying to punch the gunman's button.

Karson quickly ducked, throwing Atatasuki over his back as he dodged the punch. "You all insist on pushing my button, but I refuse to die again," he said, shooting them both aside at once. He then reloaded both of his guns, preparing for the next shot.

Atatasuki opened up his chest. He jumped off the floor and shoved the gunman's face inside the microwave.

"Ahhhhhh, what's going on?" Karson shot randomly around the prison cell.

Atatasuki pulled back his fist.

"*ULTIMATE SUPER BUTTON PUUUN—*"

"Wait!" yelled Karson, raising his arms in the air. "I give up. I don't want to explode again. I'll join your team. Please, just spare me." He bent down on his knees and lowered his head.

"Very well," said Atatasuki, releasing him from the microwave.

"You will help us rescue everyone. Correct?" asked Exp 8 with a suspicious gaze.

"Absolutely, sir. I was already going to join you for beating me honorably. Let's just continue from where we left off. I am truly grateful for this honorable battle. Allow me to join your team," said Karson with a bow.

"This guy is a little strange," said Atatasuki.

"He seems genuine, that's good enough for me," said Exp 8 with a shrug.

"Bob's cell is on the other side of this wall." Karson coughed up a piece of C4. He slapped the explosive on the wall and then shot it.

The wall blew up, leaving only debris.

Bob's cell was right before them. Standing right next to him, filing her nails, was Nina.

"You didn't tell us about her," said Exp 8, grabbing the gunman's arm.

"Did you really expect his cell to be completely unguarded? Commander Devlin is no fool! Every cell is guarded by a powerful Exp," said Karson, shielding his face.

Nina looked up and smiled at the rebel leader. "I knew it. There is not a soul who can resist me. You break out of your prison, but you can't just leave. No, you feel some strange indescribable desire. You have to see me. You just can't resist the allure. Well enjoy, because I am the last thing you will ever see," she said, running her hands down her sides.

"We're here for Bob, not you," said Exp 8 bluntly.

"Honestly, we didn't think you'd be here," said Atatasuki, scratching his head with a grin.

"I don't know how severe your blindness is, but if you can't see me...then there's just no reason for you to live."

Their spherical ally passed through the prison bars. "Shall we leave?" asked Bob, who was never really trapped in the first place.

"I won't let you leave, Exp 8. Not until you admit that you want me! You will not escape from here!" exclaimed Nina, swiping away a strand of hair from her face.

Black goop dropped from the ceiling. It shot up and took solid form. "Of course they will. Uugh," said NoOne.

"I thought you said only one powerful Exp would be guarding Bob," said Atatasuki, grabbing Karson's neck.

"Is there another one besides Nina?" asked NoOne.

"NoOne is a strong Exp despite what he says. Why did you lie to us, Karson?" asked Atatasuki as he strangled him.

"I'm a man of honor. I would never lie. It's Bob's cell, after all, it only makes sense he would have extra protection," said Karson with a salute.

"Brother, don't worry. Nina hasn't gotten any stronger since your last fight," said Kawai weakly.

"That may be true, but it doesn't matter. My sexiness hasn't diminished in the least. Face it, you've all lost, ohohoho," said Nina, tearing off her shirt.

"Damn it, she's right," said Atatasuki, brought to his knees.

"Curse you and your bouncy breasts!" yelled Kawai with all her strength.

"Ah, jealously…it is such a wonderful thing to behold. There's something that I have to tell you, Kawai. Something I've been meaning to set straight. I realized over time that…I love…myself!"

"Yeah, we know already," said Exp 8.

"And I love Kawai!" yelled Atatasuki with burning passion.

"I'm well aware of that too, huuugh," said Kawai.

"Oh, I almost forgot to remember. I got you a can of grape juice and then I forgot about it. But I remember now! Here you go, sis," said Atatasuki, pulling out the can from his chest.

Kawai snatched the juice and struggled to pop the lid. "I guess Devlin didn't think you were worth upgrading."

"I refused to get any upgrades. And Devlin respected that. I hope you enjoy the juice," said Atatasuki, popping the lid.

"Why won't you stop loving me? Oooh, this is good," said Kawai, dripping juice as she tried to lap it up.

"How can you love her?" asked Nina, taken aback.

"Well, I am adorable," said Kawai with a shrug.

"Hardly. Your hair is made of colored wires. You're flatter than a tectonic plate. And your body is totally out of proportion. Ah, the vanity of ugly girls, ohohohuh…aah."

"Let me at her!" hissed Kawai, floating out of Brother's arms before falling to the ground.

Atatasuki caught his sister and gave Nina the death stare.

"She can't even fight! Oh, you are all so pathetic. And Exp 8…you're as blind as a critic. You're too busy looking for flaws to notice the perfection before you."

"You are so full of it," said Exp 8.

"You dare deny me! I even got a gay guy to love me."

"Would you shut up already?" asked Kawai, holding her head.

"Jealousy is such an ugly thing. Anyway, now that I got that off my voluptuous chest, it's time for you to die," said Nina with a cold stare.

"Do you mind if we outnumber them?" asked NoOne, tapping Nina's shoulder.

"How do you propose we do that?"

"*SHADOW MANIPULATION, TOTAL CONTROL*," said NoOne, dramatically shaking his fingers.

The shadows of Bob, Exp 8, Atatasuki, Kawai, Nina, Karson, and NoOne separated from their host and became three dimensional.

"Now we don't even need to lift a finger, keh-heh-heh-heh."

"My shadow is a silhouette of the ultimate body. It's not your plaything. Give it back, now," said Nina with a threatening grip around the shadow man's arm.

"Calm down," said NoOne, rolling his eyes.

Nina's shadow returned to her.

"I'm going to have fun watching you overcome your shadows," said NoOne as he glided backwards.

"Ugh! Don't you have any self-confidence?" asked Nina.

"I might have some. It's just buried somewhere…deep. I accept this defeat, and I'm going to try to enjoy it," said NoOne, sitting on his shadow like a chair.

"This is the reason I won and you lost. Without determination, you're bound to fail. Why do I even bother explaining it to you? You are pathetic," said Nina, turning away.

"An overconfident vertebrate like you has no right to insult me," said NoOne.

"Do not insult my perfectly straight spine because you lack one. You're a coward. That's why you'll never get that girl of your dreams," said Nina, flicking his forehead.

"You are the only one who can make me more depressed," said NoOne, falling off his chair in misery.

"Go cry me a river so I can gaze at my reflection, hmph" said Nina, crossing her arms.

"I can never cry. *SHADOW PULL*," said NoOne.

The shadows all around the Freedom Forcers came to life and wrapped around them. They dragged them off their feet, pulling them into a room the size of a parking lot. The shadows then tossed each rebel into a separate corner of the room.

NoOne entered the room, ready to be defeated once again.

Chapter 8: Shadow Box

"SHADOW SPREAD."

The shadows rose thirty feet up to the ceiling.

"SHADOW BOX." NoOne distorted the shadows, creating a box around the Freedom Forcers.

Shadow walls came out from within the box, separating the rebels from one another.

Bob's shadow battle began the second the box was completed. His shadow's pupil started to glow brightly, collecting energy in its core. A black laser burst out from his shadow without warning.

Bob calmly shot a laser of his own, causing the two beams to slam into each other.

"As if I could lose to my own shadow, hmph," said Bob as the shadow's laser was destroyed.

Bob's laser then zoomed into his shadow, leaving a giant hole in its wake.

The wounded shadow rammed into Bob, sending him bouncing away.

As Bob ricocheted from wall to wall, he slammed into his shadow.

The two of them bounced off the walls, rapidly firing lasers at one another.

"Not bad. Hmm, I wonder if you can copy my Phase Form," said Bob with a spark of intrigue. His body became transparent.

The shadow's lasers shot right through him, unable to make contact. Oddly enough all of Bob's laser beams hit their target spot on.

"Now, behold the manifestation of my soul!" Bob concentrated his spirit energy and manifested it as a spectral blade.

The weapon was a ghostly green-and-blue beam of spiritual energy. A spectral aura constantly spiraled up, sprouting from the eyeball's side.

Bob lost his transparency but didn't seem to care. He knocked off the oncoming lasers' trajectories with perfectly timed smaller lasers of his own.

"This is the very essence of my being! You shall be destroyed by the Atma Blade!" exclaimed Bob, his weapon crackling with power.

The shadow repeatedly rammed into Bob.

"This is an insult. How could NoOne think I could ever be defeated by a mere projection of the absence of light created when sunlight hits an object?" asked Bob with mild annoyance. He then shoved the Atma Blade into his shadow, destroying it in an instant.

His shadow reformed beneath him, becoming two dimensional once more.

"That was rather boring. Let's hope the master behind the shadow provides me with better entertainment," said Bob with a grin. He approached the shadow wall and concentrated. The spherical warrior bent the space around it and passed through the wall.

"So you're the first one here. I am truly impressed with your abilities," said NoOne, his head resting on his palm.

"Do not complement me. When a pessimistic coward gives praise, it means they have low expectations of you. You assumed that Exp 8 would get here first, didn't you? That is why you garnish me with such kind words. You underestimated me. I will make you regret your masqueraded insult," said Bob as he approached the shadow master.

Karson's confrontation began the instant Bob's scuffle started.

Karson looked at his shadow and lowered his head.

His right arm trembled. "What kind of treason is this? Having to combat one's shadow is like fighting against one's own soul. I've never felt so betrayed! Does NoOne have no honor at all?!"

Karson's shadow turned around and began pacing in the other direction.

"I truly sympathize with you, comrade. Even you have…(shudder)…the Button! Why must life be so cruel? For that matter, why must death be so cruel? Oh, but worry not, my coal-skinned friend. I would never target your weak point. If there is no honor in battle, then war is mere barbarism!" exclaimed Karson, cocking his arm.

After the tenth pace, his shadow turned around. It fired dual pistols at Karson furiously, reloading one while the other was still firing.

Karson tossed a smoke grenade down and then rolled onto his belly.

"Very well played, but you are lacking in the accuracy department." He rolled out of the smoke cloud, his revolver hands ready to fire.

His foe was nowhere in sight.

Karson heard the cocking of a rifle behind him.

The shadow fired directly at Karson's button.

The bullet zoomed by, just barely missing the Button.

"How can you be so inconsiderate? Such dirty battle tactics will leave you with an empty victory," said Karson, his revolvers switching to shotguns.

His shadow rushed forth as it loaded up dual submachine guns. It then dived underneath his legs, firing at its enemy's button frantically.

"Coward!" Karson kicked his shadow while his foot pumped bullets into it. He then fired off both of his arms at once.

The powerful blasts sent the shadow into the air.

Karson's hands each loaded up half of a Gatling gun. They then fused together.

"You wanted to use underhanded tactics! Well then, how do you like seeing the weapon that took the honor out of war!" yelled Karson as he mowed down his shadow. "This clip has more than enough bullets to take you out!"

Once the smoke cleared all that was left of his shadow was the Button.

"I refuse to disgrace myself by targeting someone's weak point! Now, let's move along, shall we," said Karson, approaching the shadow wall.

His shadow reappeared beneath him, having a hole where the Button should have been.

Karson's arms merged into a rocket launcher and blasted a hole through the shadow wall.

He hopped through the gaping hole and landed before NoOne.

As Karson's dishonorable bout began, Atatasuki was confronted with a shadow fight of his own.

He stared at his shadow for fifteen seconds, concentrating intensely. He took a deep breath and calmed his trembling legs. "I have waited years for this day to arrive. A new flavor of muffins shall finally hit the market. Show me your power! Create the very first shadow muffin!" exclaimed Atatasuki, saliva dripping from his mouthpiece.

His shadow opened its chest, exposing the shadowy muffins within.

The black muffins were then launched forward as if shot from a catapult.

Atatasuki opened his arms, trying to catch the muffins. One fell right into his grasp.

"You amateur, these are way too hot. Look at them! They are black and crusty. This isn't cuisine. This is a muffin miscarriage." Fueled by his great disappointment, Atatasuki charged up to his shadow. "Feel the agony you put this muffin through!" He gripped the crispy muffin in his fist and punched his shadow right in the face.

The shadow was knocked off the ground.

Atatasuki hooked his arms around his foe's neck and smashed his head into its face. He followed up with a powerful punch to its gut.

The shadow fell down to its knees, coughing up a black fluid.

Atatasuki looked at his shadow with eyes aflame. "Unacceptable! How can you call yourself my shadow, if you can't make proper muffins? I disown you!" he yelled, strangling his shadow.

The shadow's stomach made a ringing noise. It opened its chest, revealing seven hot and crispy muffins within. The shadow took out the muffins and held them in its fists, setting its hands on fire.

"With food this horrible, taste testing is deadly! But in order to eat properly baked shadow muffins…there isn't much I wouldn't do," said Atatasuki as he dodged his shadow's quick jabs. He kicked the poser's leg and then slammed his palm up into its elbow.

The shadow's hand popped open, giving Atatasuki the perfect opening.

The passionate prototype manually lowered his mouthpiece and opened his mouth as wide as he could. Once the flaming muffin was in his mouth, pain filled his hollowed eyes.

The shadow slammed Atatasuki's chin from below with its burning fist.

After accidently swallowing the muffin, his screams came out as muffled gibberish. He pounded his stomach in desperation.

The shadow muffin flew out of his mouth.

His shadow pulled back its fist and then thrust it upwards.

Atatasuki grabbed the fist with one hand, his other hand still holding his stomach. "That was a disgrace to all muffins! How can you even make muffins taste bad? Deliciousness is sewn into their DNA. If my shadow is this worthless, then I don't need a shadow! *SUPER MICROWAVE, BODY!*" His chest overheated, steam pouring out of it. The heat then dispersed, setting Atatasuki's entire body aflame. "The muffins have chosen me as your executioner!" He punched his shadow viciously. *SUPER MICROWAVE, FIST!*"

The flames on the heated warrior's body all moved to his fist. They combined into a new fearsome golden-brown flame.

"*INSTANT BAKE,*" said Atatasuki, knocking the shadow's hands aside. He then slammed his flaming fist into the shadow. The fire burst out as an incendiary torrent. When the flames subsided, his shadow was soft, a little puffy, and a bit crispy.

"That's called baking. You can practice it in hell," said Atatasuki with a dark tone, cracking each finger individually. Both his fists caught aflame as he pushed them against his shadow.

A continuous stream of fire melted his shadow into ash. The shadow then reformed beneath him.

"I'll never look at you the same way," said Atatasuki, peering down with disgust.

In a different barrier, Kawai's scuffle started the exact moment her brother's bout began. She looked at the ceiling, lost in thought. Her eyes beamed with childish wonderment.

"What if I could be with Exp 8 and his shadow at the same time? It would be incredible! That would be the ultimate threesome," said Kawai, a trail of drool dripping from her mouthpiece.

Kawai's shadow leisurely floated up to her. It waved its hand in front of her face. It shrugged and then smacked her down with its tail.

"I was having a wonderful dream and you spoiled it! There's no one around right now. I'm putting the cute away. It's time for this little kitten to reveal her claws. *Sound Shot!*" exclaimed Kawai, pushing out her hand.

Nothing came out.

"Butter-muffins! I handed the Sound Artifact over. I may have lost my only advantage over you. But I'm still going to win this. Come on, you little bitch, hit this kitty with everything you've got," said Kawai, opening her mouthpiece and sticking out her tongue.

The shadow zoomed toward her, smashing its knee against Kawai's face.

"I said hit me, not cushion me! Hit me harder!" yelled Kawai as her tail spun around.

The shadow punched her in the face, but Kawai hardly flinched.

"My weakness is your weakness!" Kawai's tail slammed into her attacker. The shadow bounced up as soon as it hit the floor.

Kawai zoomed up and wrapped her arms around her shadow. "*Energy Embrace Drain!*" Her body glowed as she absorbed her shadow's energy.

"I had you waste your energy with those attacks so you would have slightly less energy than me. But that difference in energy is all I need," said Kawai, coiling her tail around her shadow.

The shadow squeezed Kawai in a tight embrace.

"We'll see who runs out of energy first. I'm still pretty tired, but I've got some energy to spare," said Kawai, wrapping her legs around her shadow's torso.

The shadow's tail shot up, breaking the grip of Kawai's hardened tail.

"You won't overpower me," said Kawai as her jet boosters started up. She rammed her shadow into the ground repeatedly as their tails wrestled for supremacy.

"I'm a little bit disappointed. You're nothing like me. You don't…play with your prey at all. Hey…why aren't you getting…tired?" asked Kawai with exasperated breaths.

The shadow's tail wrapped around Kawai's tail and yanked on it harshly.

"Owiee! You don't get…fatigued, do you? How could I have…messed up so bad? Big brother, save me," whispered Kawai as she fainted.

The shadow tossed her up. It then whacked her with a fortified tailspin. Kawai smashed into the shadow wall.

While Kawai fantasized about shadow sex, Exp 8 admired his shadow.

"Wow, you look badass," said Exp 8, sizing up his shadow.

The shadow ripped out its Ada and tossed it at the enemy.

"You ungrateful bastard, how can you treat your Ada so poorly?" He picked up the shadow Ada and brushed it off. "NoOne has made a mockery of me! I'm going to kick this handsome bastard's ass and then I'm going to bust out of here and beat that shady freak with a single attack!" yelled Exp 8 before firing a laser net.

His shadow strafed to the side, perfectly dodging the laser. It then fired ten nets as it advanced toward him. Each net made contact and wrapped around him.

Exp 8 crawled around in the nets like a caterpillar in a spider web. "How the hell can he shoot ten? Damn it, how does Kawai break out of these?" he asked, trying to squeeze his arms through the holes.

"It seems he has infinite energy or none at all. And as for Kawai, she saps away the net's energy. Then she breaks it with her little bitty fingers. She's so cute, hmmhmmhymm," said Ada.

"Good to finally hear from you. So, how the hell do I beat him?" asked Exp 8 as his shadow slowly approached.

"I'm not so sure you can. But you might as well give it your all. I know, why don't you use the new abilities Devlin gave you?"

"Sounds like a plan! Wait, Devlin gave me new powers?"

"You weren't exactly in tip-top shape when you left the lab. It hurts him to see his creations perform inadequately. After Nina beat all of us, Devlin gave everyone enhancements. Well…everyone but me. Why am I so useless?"

"You aren't useless at all. You give me helpful information…sometimes. So, uh, you gonna help me get out of here?"

"Use your upgraded strength to tear those nets to pieces!" cheered Ada.

Exp 8 grabbed the nets with both hands and ripped them apart. He leaped back to his feet as his shadow zoomed up to him.

It lashed its fists furiously, mixing high, low, and mid strikes.

Exp 8 dodged each attack with his enhanced speed.

"This is great! So, what new abilities did I get?"

His shadow's shoulders opened up and two automated guns popped out of them. The turrets aimed at Exp 8 and fired black bullets.

"That's one of them," said Ada.

"That is so awesome," said Exp 8 as he jumped off the walls to dodge the bullets.

His shadow leapt off the ground toward him.

"You're so predictable!" Exp 8 shot a laser net, but his shadow punched straight through it. He used this moment to fire an orb in front of him. Turrets then popped out from his shoulders and pumped the orb full of bullets.

The bullets rapidly increased the orb's size, making it bigger than Exp 8 in mere seconds.

The shadow's jets jerked it backwards, causing it to slam itself into the ground below. It bounced up from the collision and started creating its own orb.

"I'm beginning to feel like the Ultimate Exp. **BIG BALL, SHOT**." Exp 8 thrust both his fists forward with all his might, hitting the orb in the center.

The sphere of energy shot forward like a bullet, absorbing his shadow's orb in the process. It then smashed into his shadow, crushing it against the wall.

At that exact moment, Kawai was smashed into the other side of the wall. The shadow wall shattered from the combined impact.

Exp 8's shadow faded away and then reappeared beneath him.

Kawai shot forward, landing in Exp 8's arms. She was knocked out cold.

Exp 8 put his ear to her chest and felt relieved. "Good, she's alive. Hey you, shadow freak. You hurt my little sister. Get your pansy ass down here! I've dealt with the true Kawai, so you won't be a pain at all," he said, pounding his fists.

As Exp 8 started to avenge his sister, Bob opened the curtains for his battle with the shadow master.

"I'm going to end this with one shot," said Bob, his eye coursing with red energy.

Karson then entered, greeting his circular comrade with a salute.

"Ugh, oh well," said Bob, powering down his laser. He then turned to the war machine. "Good work. Shall we begin?"

"You made my shadow dishonorable!" yelled Karson, rushing at the sketchy bastard.

"I'm sorry. I want to win…just once. I know I'll have to draw every ace I have if I want even the slightest chance of beating you guys," said NoOne, standing up from his chair.

The wall behind the shadow man began to melt.

Atatasuki busted in, still steaming from his fight. "I knew you guys would win. Sorry I took so long. I had to teach my shadow how to properly cook," he said, his fists aflame with rage.

"We must begin this instant! If I happen to beat the three of you, then I've actually won," said NoOne, lifting his head up.

NoOne's body sank into the floor, becoming completely flat. The shadow glided across the floor, headed straight for the weaponized soldier.

Karson shot at the shadow, but the bullets only hit the ground.

"Don't worry, I've got you covered!" yelled Atatasuki, trying to step on the shadow frantically.

The shadow's hands stretched out and grabbed a hold of Karson's shadow.

NoOne gripped the shadow of the Button. "*SHADOW STRETCH.*"

"I thought I had destroyed it! You can't be serious!"

Like a mirror image, Karson's button expanded as NoOne stretched the shadow button. It kept growing until it covered the soldier's entire back.

"I give up! White flag! White flag!" yelled Karson, putting his hands in the air.

"I accept your surrender. Move and I'll kill you. That's one down." NoOne rose out from his shadow. He leapt at silver brawler as his arm sharpened. He then thrust his serrated hand through him. "You are all weak from fighting your own shadows. Exp 8 isn't here! Take these factors into consideration and realize that I may actually win. Kehahaha!"

Atatasuki, still impaled to NoOne's hand, looked down at him and gave him a thumbs-up. "I'm glad you're finally gaining some confidence."

"It's time to show the Freedom Forcers my worth," said Bob, floating toward the shadow bender. He fired a quick laser, cutting his opponent in two.

NoOne's upper half fell to the floor. He ripped off the arm holding Atatasuki and stabbed it in the ground. "Stay there while I finish my fight." He sharpened his other arm into a sword.

"Alright, but only because you asked so nicely," said Atatasuki, holding his wound while seething in pain.

NoOne's upper half leapt forward and lashed its hand at the battle ball.

Bob swerved out of the way, floating behind NoOne's upper half. He then surrounded his body with spectral drills.

By the time the shadow master turned around, it was too late.

Bob rammed into NoOne, making spiral holes all over his body.

"*SHADOW MANIPULATION, SELF BETRAYAL,*" said NoOne as his upper half swirled in unison with the drills piercing him.

Bob shot a laser at point-blank range.

As soon as the laser was released, his shadow fired out a laser. Their lasers clashed, sending sparks flying every which way.

Bob turned his eye slowly, angling his shadow's laser.

The laser drilled into the ceiling.

A circular piece of rubble collapsed from the roof and crashed into Bob.

"It's okay, man. We all make mistakes!" hollered Atatasuki.

NoOne's blade-arm stretched like elastic as it repeatedly stabbed through the rubble at various angles.

"Cheap! Cheap! I'm calling it! That was unfair!" yelled Karson, still holding his arms up.

NoOne pulled the battle ball up to him. His chest morphed into a grater. He dragged Bob up and down the grater as the helpless Exp screamed in agony. The shadow master tossed his victim aside carelessly once he was finished.

Bob crash-landed right in front of the shadow man's bottom half.

The chopped shadow wrapped around him like a constrictor.

"Is that it?" asked NoOne as he looked around with paranoia.

Bob fired his laser at NoOne, but the shadow master deflected it with a laser from his attacker's shadow.

The laser sliced into the ceiling, causing another chunk of rubble to collapse on Bob.

"If you try once and fail, don't bother trying anymore, you'll just fail again. Ohooh, I can't believe I'm going to say this, but here it comes: you have all lost! Face it, Freedom Forcers, without your leader by your side, I can actually win!" exclaimed NoOne, his hands flinging upward.

When Bob was about to obliterate NoOne with a single laser, Kawai's shadow confronted Exp 8.

The shadow entered through the remains of the shadow wall, paying no heed to his insults. It jetted itself onto his face and latched on.

Exp 8 ripped the shadow off his face. "Her shadow is clingy too, huugh." He tossed his sister's shadow up like a tennis ball and slammed his fist into its face.

As a result of his new awesome power, the shadow skyrocketed into the wall way in the back.

The shadow wall stretched to its brink and then shot Kawai's shadow back.

As the shadow zoomed toward him, it flipped in midair. Its tail recoiled, smacking Exp 8's chin. With the increased velocity, the attack knocked the enemy off his feet.

Exp 8 dropped Kawai, but quickly caught her with his prehensile tail. "Hell yeah! And I thought it was just for decoration."

The shadow fired a laser net from its palms during the confusion.

The nets wrapped around Exp 8's arms, holding them against his back.

His tail grabbed onto Kawai's tail as she slipped out of its grip.

"You can't hold me down!"

As soon as Exp 8 broke free of the nets, the shadow latched onto his face. He ripped it off like an adhesive bandage and then got a better grip on his sister.

"Damn, this thing is a leech with infinite energy!" He slammed the shadow to the ground.

It bounced up at just the right height for a follow-up attack.

Exp 8 punched rapidly with his free hand, building up speed. He then hit the clingy shadow with the refined force of his fist.

The shadow was sent flying forward like an airplane. It smashed through an entire line of shadow walls. It then crashed into the final shadow wall, stretching the rubbery wall to its threshold.

"I shouldn't have gotten so upset with you, little one. NoOne is the one controlling you. I'll be sure to kick his ass for you."

The wall recoiled.

Kawai's shadow was once more sent flying back to Exp 8.

A single small orb came out from his hand.

The shadow crashed right into it, but it didn't explode.

"I'm in control now." Exp 8's shoulders opened up, revealing his turrets. They shot into the orb, expanding it exponentially. The leader of the Freedom Forcers turned away. "Boom."

The explosion consumed every shadow cell with it into oblivion.

Exp 8 flung Kawai back into his arms and held her close to his chest.

His sister awoke with a stretch and then beamed up at him.

"Don't worry, sister, everything will be okay now," said Exp 8, touching her cheek.

Kawai smiled weakly.

Exp 8 kicked the shadow wall in front of him. His leg talons tore it open.

"I bet I'm the first one to show up." He then squeezed through the hole awkwardly.

NoOne looked in front of him, sighing as he saw Exp 8's leg poking out.

NoOne's torso rushed to battle. His upper half lunged at rebel leader and slashed furiously.

Exp 8 trapped the shadow manipulator in a double laser net. He looked at his defeated allies, his fist quaking. "I'm the last one to arrive?! This is ridiculous!" His turrets fired at the nets as he walked toward Atatasuki.

"How are you doing, brother?" asked Exp 8, trying not to sound worried.

"We softened him up for you," said Atatasuki with a blood-smeared smile.

NoOne sawed through the fortified net, tearing himself free. "I have a winning streak. I'm not going to let you ruin it!" he yelled as his upper half stampeded toward the hero.

"Honestly, I'm a little worn out from my fights. Kawai, can you drain what's left of his energy?"

"Of course…anything for you…big brother," said Kawai drowsily as she left his arms and floated up to NoOne. She tightly embraced the enemy, depleting nearly all of his energy.

"I have infinite energy!" exclaimed NoOne, barely standing up.

"When you use it up so carelessly, of course you're going to run out," said Exp 8, almost tipping over.

Kawai floated back to her big brother and drifted into his arms.

"Karson, you can relax now, huh-heh." Exp 8 crouched and flicked NoOne's upper portion.

The shadow master fell to the ground, knocked out on impact.

NoOne's shadow walls faded away. His bottom half vanished along with his arm, freeing both Atatasuki and Bob. Karson's button then shrank back to normal size.

Chapter 9: Ada's Assistance

"We're free," cheered Atatasuki befor e welding his gash shut.

"Over my dead sexy body," said Nina, dropping from above.

"Calm down, Nina. There is no reason for us to fight. No one denies that you are well built," said Exp 8 with an outstretched hand.

"Well then, I guess I'll have to have a word with him later," said Nina, through gritted teeth.

"No, that's not what I meant. Arghhh! Curse Devlin and his confusing naming schemes!" yelled Exp 8, knowing this was all a well-rounded plan to piss him off.

"I won't give up until my body sparks arousal in you, Exp 8!"

"This battle is pointless!"

"Every battle I've engaged myself in has toned my body and expanded my erotic aura. But enough talk!" Nina pulled off her tank top, now wearing only her bra.

Karson collapsed from the sheer sexiness.

Atatasuki swooned backwards. He slammed his foot down, stopping his fall.

"*Super Slo-mo, Flirtatious Flash!*" exclaimed Nina as she lowered her bra down inch by inch.

Before her breasts were fully exposed, Atatasuki collapsed. Nina then quickly pulled up her bra.

"I didn't even have to exhibit my tantalizing nipples," said Nina, massaging her breasts.

"Who woke me up?" Bob looked up at the purple lacy undergarment and then collapsed.

"Wow. She sure has a great body, doesn't she? Devlin really outdid himself," said Ada.

"I was going to show off all my cool new moves to everyone! Now, I've got no audience," said Exp 8, his fist to his forehead.

"Don't worry, I'm not going anywhere," said Ada.

"Yeah, but you've already seen my enhanced powers," said Exp 8, his shoulders drooping.

"Stop talking to that little ball in your chest and pay attention to me," said Nina, her fist quaking.

"Brother, can you set me down. I need a little aaaoooh, rest," said Kawai with drowsy eyes.

Exp 8 put Kawai in Atatasuki's arms and patted her on the head. "Sweet dreams."

"Stop ignoring me! *Super Slo-mo!*" Nina aimed at Exp 8, bringing him down to half speed. She sped by and tore a rocket launcher off of Karson.

A rocket shot out, aimed at the rebel's thick head.

Exp 8 tried to move his head out of the way as his eyes gradually widened. The rocket exploded upon hitting his forehead, but he didn't react to its impact.

When he resumed motion, he was sent flying into the wall behind him.

"I won't let you get another hit," said Exp 8, climbing out of his indentation on the wall.

Once his turrets were locked on, they fired a volley of purple bullets.

"I like the color. *Super Slo-mo,*" said Nina, making a different sexy pose to avoid each football-sized bullet.

Exp 8 fired a black orb and his turrets swiftly got to work on expanding it. "Let's see you do a fancy pose to dodge this."

"Hah! I don't even need to dodge. *Super Slo-mo!*"

Exp 8's hand reached for his arm button as the skilled warrior casually walked behind him.

Nina's hand caressed his cold cheek. "Feel my touch. My skin is perfectly smooth," she said as her hands trailed down to his shoulders. "Why do you even have eyes if you can't appreciate a masterpiece? I should just pluck them from their sockets. No, not yet. You showed me that having a dynamite body won't assure my victory. I wanted to beat you without an artifact, but playing with time is so much fun." Nina stroked her hand as she slowly took off her purple gloves. She gently dropped them on the orb.

Exp 8's eyes widened as if stricken with a revelation.

"Sometimes being soft is necessary. But more often than not, you need to be explosive." Nina whipped out a bomb trigger from her hair. She gave the trigger's button a gentle kiss, causing her gloves to burst.

The explosion triggered the orb to detonate, sending the cybernetic rebel ever so slowly into her open arms.

"You're probably wondering how my gloves exploded. Well, you're not the only one who learned some new tricks. All my clothing can be triggered to burst. Since I'm already deathly sexy, my entire body is a weapon. You see, I've been increasing my allure since the day I was created. I've taken my perfect features and refined them each day. I've even adjusted my personality for maximum arousal. My entire life has been devoted to my body. To have you ignore it…is beyond insulting!" Nina's nails dragged down his armored chest. "Succumb to my sexiness. If you ask nicely, I may let you touch," she said, gripping his rough hand.

Once Exp 8 was back to normal speed, he pulled his arm away.

"I do not care about such trivial things."

"What are you, asexual?! I don't know what it will take to convince you how sexy I am, but I won't give up. I can't allow a poor creature like you to suffer. Not being able to fathom true beauty…it's just too tragic. I will help you see the luscious light!" exclaimed Nina, leaping onto his shoulders.

Exp 8 grabbed her powerful legs and flung her off.

Nina regained her balance in midair and landed on her feet.

"Don't blink or you'll miss your defeat. *SUPER PUNCH FAN*!" Exp 8 punched the air at increasing speeds.

The air punches slammed into Nina, causing her to lose her balance and fall backwards.

"*OVERDRIVE*!" His talons bore into the ground. He put all of his energy into his fists, moving them so fast that they became a blur.

"I can still slow you down. *Super Slo-mo. Ice Shot.*"

Exp 8's movements were slowed down as Nina fired an icicle from her chest.

"No way…how can you still punch that fast?"

The icicle shot backwards, colliding into Nina's arm.

"You can't freeze this hot bod!" She struggled through the punch storm toward the rebel commander. "*Sound Burst.*"

A sound wave shattered the ice around her arm.

"*Sound Shot. Ice Kiss.*" Nina blew him a kiss that dispersed the wind and then froze into a giant icicle.

The icicle slammed into Exp 8, freezing him from head to toe.

Nina took a flamethrower off Karson and thawed Exp 8's head with it. She then caressed his frozen chest. "This is a woman's touch; no…this is *the* woman's touch. Aren't you lucky?"

"I'm thrilled. Can you let me go of me now?" asked Exp 8, nudging his head back and forth.

"Not until you have the joy of seeing my exposed body. You know, some women can't resist a man who resists them. But I'm not doing this because I like you. I'm just trying to help you grasp the extent of my allure. Honestly, people who resist my body really piss me off," said Nina as she carved her nails across his face.

"You're getting all flustered, how cute."

"I'm drop-dead gorgeous! I am in no way cute!" Nina smacked him over and over. She took a deep breath as she pressed her body against his. She leaned in for a kiss, stopping a mere centimeter before contact.

"Beg me for a kiss. Or you can start begging for your life," said Nina, blowing on his helmet.

"Get the hell off of me!"

"I tried. But you're just hopeless," said Nina, grabbing his face empathetically.

"You seriously need to get over yourself."

"On the contrary, you need to get hooked on me. I don't know what Kawai sees in you. She says you're beautiful, but I don't see it. The only thing pretty about you is my reflection, shimmering on your armor. I don't think mere narcissism is the source of her love. What is it that makes her so happy around you? Maybe she likes the mysterious type? So, do you know why the mysterious ones cower under a mask?"

"No and I don't care."

"It is because they have no self-love. They hide their repulsive shame. Your mask has blinded you. Are these eyes, or are they just for decoration?"

"I can see just fine. Just like you can see that you're pissing me off," said Exp 8, struggling to break free.

"You must be gay, right? How else could you be unaffected by this? Then again, even that one queer fawns over me. I'll make you a deal. You admit I'm hot and I'll allow you to taste my lips. Oh you've really gotten to me, haven't you? Despite my training, I'm still attracted to repulsion. Don't get confused though, it also ticks me off," said Nina, gripping the back of his head.

"Get the hell off!"

"If feeling my bodacious body against your…metallic one can't cure you, then you don't deserve a cure. I am going to slowly destroy each and every part of your body. It's only fair considering you've ignored each and every part of mine," said Nina, savoring the irony.

"Computer!" yelled Exp 8.

"How can I be of service?" asked Ada.

"I've used up too much energy. Do whatever you have to. Please, save me!"

"Understood. Oh, I do hope Devlin won't be too upset with me."

The blue spherical ball fell from its little home in Exp 8's chest cavity and lay suspended in the air. It glowed brightly, slowly digitizing a body around it.

Once fully uploaded, Ada's motherly figure came into full view. Her bare body was constructed of blue numbers. Her long hair was an assortment of green digits. Her oversized breasts defied gravity. A digitized wedding ring was the last thing to materialize.

Ada floated to the ground and stretched her arms out, unintentionally exposing herself.

104

Nina's eyes flared up with jealousy as they teared up in wonderment. She gazed at Ada's powerful yet slender thighs and her succulent light-blue lips. A direct look into Ada's loving emerald-green eyes pushed her over the edge. "Too sexy!" yelled Nina, holding her chest in agony. She fell to the ground, knocked out cold.

"Okay, I'm ready to fight," said Ada, jumping to get pumped up. She looked down to see Nina's glazed out eyes. "I didn't even do anything," she said, dropping her shoulders.

"I guess your body was too much for her. Does that mean you won?" asked Exp 8.

"Do you think I'm attractive?" asked Ada, turning away as her body flushed a pale pink.

"Nina sure did. How can she be beaten by the same kind of stupid attack she uses? Oh yeah, and one more thing, why the hell didn't you do that earlier? In fact, didn't you say you were attached to me like a tumor? Why did you lie?" asked Exp 8, turning to her with a stern look.

"I didn't want to upset Devlin. He said only to transform in the case of an emergency. And well, I did lie a little, but I thought you would abandon me if you knew I could be removed."

"You're suspicious but I wouldn't abandon you. You weren't lying about the danger of removing the trackers, were you?"

"Of course not. I just wanted to protect you."

"I can trust you, right?"

"Have you ever doubted me?" asked Ada, patting his head

"Yeah, lots of times. Uuuh."

"Please, don't tell Devlin about this," said Ada as her body dematerialized.

The ball lit up once she had completely disintegrated.

"Now how do I get out of this mess? Hmm, I know. Kawai is getting cold!" hollered Exp 8, still trapped in ice.

"Then I shall be her blanket!" exclaimed Atatasuki, instantly rising from the floor.

"Glad to see you're awake. So, can you break me out? I'm kind of stuck," said Exp 8, turning away in embarrassment.

"Alright, but I'd appreciate it if you didn't tell Kawai you got frozen," said Atatasuki, starting to melt the ice around his brother.

"Why would I? It's not exactly a badge of honor."

"I don't want her to see you in such a pitiful state. She looks up to you. And done! You're free now."

Exp 8 collapsed to the ground face first.

"Brother! Are you alright?" asked Kawai, suddenly waking up and rushing to his side.

"He's taking a strategic break. What a guy," said Atatasuki, looking up with a wide smile.

Kawai put her hands to her tired sibling's chest. "*Energy Spike!*"

Exp 8 woke up, seething in pain. "What was that?" he asked, breathing heavily.

"My extra-helpful new ability. It is a concentrated energy shot. Looks like it did the trick, heeheehmph," said Kawai.

"Yeah, it did. Can you wake everyone else up?" asked Exp 8, standing up and placing Ada in his chest.

"Of course, big brother!" squealed Kawai. She floated up to the gunman and smacked him with her tail repeatedly.

"Air raid! Air raid!" yelled Karson, shielding his face. "Oh, I seem to have been mistaken. Good to see you up and about, soldier!"

Kawai floated up to Bob and nervously shook him awake with her tail.

"Ah, that was a good rest. So, who beat Nina?" asked Bob, stretching his pupil.

"Our leader did! All by himself...with absolutely no help at all. He's just so amazing!" exclaimed Ada, spinning around in Exp 8's chest.

"You guys should have seen it. I knocked her out with my totally awesome new attack!" exclaimed Exp 8 with jazz hands.

"Alright then...we won! We're free! We can leave! But, what do we do about Nina?" asked Atatasuki, looking down at her.

"I guess we just leave her here," said Exp 8 with a shrug.

"That would be a careless mistake. We should probably kill her. She's too powerful to be left alive," said Bob, powering up a laser.

"Or we could, you know, fondle her a bit," said Atatasuki with a shrug.

Chapter 10: Drugs vs Guns

"No!" yelled Nina, rising from the ground.

"Don't kill her!" yelled Atatasuki, jumping in front of his spherical teammate.

"Why not?" asked Bob annoyed.

"Can't you see how hot she is?" asked Atatasuki.

"What the hell; I thought you beat her," said Exp 8, turning around to talk to Ada.

"I thought so too. I guess I'm not as strong as I thought," said Ada, turning a watery blue.

"Don't just sit there and cry, go kick her ass again!" exclaimed Exp 8 softly.

"Umm…I don't really like being in my material form. People stare at me…it makes me nervous. So if it's okay with you, I'm going to stay snug in your chest while you beat her."

"People stare at you because you're naked. I'll get you some clothes if it really makes a difference to you," said Exp 8, scanning the area for any form of cloth.

"I thought I beat you," said Nina, looking up at Exp 8 drowsily.

"You could never defeat me! Listen, Nina, there is a reason why I'm not affected by your poses."

"You're immune to stupid attacks, right? Well my body is not stupid, it's sensual," said Nina, stroking her chest with a pouty face.

"The whole idea of stripping to defeat someone is absurd. Nudity is a natural thing."

"How dare you? Do you know to what lengths I've kept all this under wraps?" asked Nina with flaring eyes.

"You're not the only one and it's not your fault your like this. You were made by a human. Humans all around this planet have become accustomed to wearing clothing. They act like exposing a reproductive part is unnatural. Wearing clothes is just another way that humans try to transcend nature. They have perverted the naturalness of nudity and have made it illegal in hopes of taming their innate lust."

"Yes, but those lustful instincts still exist in everyone. My provocative poses try to bring out their instinctual lust so that I can exploit it. Stimulation is power," said Nina with a grin.

"Your poses just seem childish to me. They accentuate parts completely unrelated to reproduction. Besides, what organism in their right mind would get aroused during combat?"

"How dare you call me childish! My care for my body is a lifelong endeavor!"

"Calm down. Exp 8's got a valid point. Think about it, Nina. Human society has even made a market out of its censorship. Why do you think porn is so popular? It's because nudity is forbidden. The excitement of committing a taboo can be quite thrilling," said Karson, aiming his shotgun at the captivating captive's head.

"Taboos are also very tempting," said Nina, licking her bottom lip.

"We should all just run around naked; we get it already. Can I kill her?" asked Bob.

"The only reason nudity is forbidden is because humans have lost touch with their natural instincts. And by clothing themselves, they actually create sexual tension."

"So then, do you want to see me naked?" asked Kawai, pulling up her skirt and showing off her pink panties.

"One move and I blast you," said Karson, his eyes on Nina's hands.

Exp 8 lowered the shotgun and grabbed Nina's hand. "Your body is a natural beauty. That is the reason I am unaffected by your poses," said Exp 8, lifting her off the ground.

"Finally, you admit I'm sexy," said Nina, turning away with tearful eyes.

Exp 8 looked down at Ada. "You shouldn't be ashamed of your body because imbeciles gawk at it. It's as natural as your beautiful face," he said in a whisper.

"Oh, you are too sweet," said Ada, turning hot pink.

"This is coming from the guy covered in armor," said Nina, rolling her eyes.

"I'm not going to gawk at you. None of us are. Come on, Ada, get out of my chest and kick her ass," said Exp 8 softly.

"Wait a minute…I'm not your enemy any more. I want to join your team. It's the only way I'll improve. Ada, please teach me how to be as alluring as you. You are my Sexy Sensei," said Nina, pressing her head against the floor.

"How is Ada sexy? Isn't she just a big blue ball?" asked Karson.

"Spherical objects have their own unique charm," said Bob.

"You mean you guys haven't seen Ada's tantalizing body yet? Wait, I'm not supposed to talk about that. Forget I said anything. Whew, that was a close one," said Atatasuki, holding his head.

"Wait a minute…you were designed by some lonely scientist, weren't you? I'm wrong, Nina. You're abnormally attractive. Devlin made you this way so he could drool on something. Wow, that kind of invalidates my whole speech. Damn it!" Exp 8 slammed his fist against the wall.

"Devlin is not a pervert! He is a gentleman," said Ada with a wounded tone.

"He made Nina to be his girlfriend, right?"

"He had far greater things in mind. But that doesn't matter. Ada, can I join your team?" asked Nina, her hands clasped together.

"You are supposed to ask me. I'm the leader," said Exp 8, snapping his fingers.

"Quiet, the sexy people are talking."

"Of course you can join us! Though I'm not sure how I can teach you to be any more desirable," said Ada, scanning her pretty new friend for visual flaws.

"I want my Sound Artifact back," said Kawai, looming over Nina.

"Take it. I've already mastered the power of silence. Besides, why would I want to quiet this hypnotic voice? My voice and body are my gift to this world. They must spread love and jealousy everywhere," said Nina with a smirk.

"Then hand it over," said Kawai, stretching her arms out.

"It's all yours," said Nina before tossing it into the air.

Kawai floated up and absorbed the Sound Artifact. "So, big brother, do you think I'm naturally sexy?" she asked, trying to pose like the big-breasted narcissist.

"First of all, we're not natural. We were all made by some power-hungry and apparently very lonely psychopath. Secondly, you're not sexy…you're cute. Like your name implies: cute. You're my cute little sister, okay?" Exp 8 patted her on the head.

"You really think I'm cute? I knew it! I'm irresistible, aren't I? You may not think I'm sexy, but I still think you're a sexy stud," said Kawai as she embraced him lovingly.

"Look, you're my sister. I really don't think you should have thoughts like that about me," said Exp 8, petting her head as he smiled at her.

"You said that our bodies were natural and beautiful. Why don't you explore this little marvel of nature firsthand?" asked Kawai, rubbing her chest.

"I don't want to! Calm down. You're not supposed to love me like this," said Exp 8, distancing himself from her.

"It's not strange to hate anyone, it's just impolite. Why should it be forbidden to love anyone? It's so backwards! Besides, you don't have to worry about your little morals. We're not blood related. I'm a prototype of you. We merely have a similar design, that's all. If it helps, just think of it this way: when we have sex, it will technically just be masturbation," said Kawai, supporting her speech with the appropriate hand gestures.

Exp 8 turned away. "This conversation is over." He toppled to the ground, but was quickly lifted up by his sister's tail. "I'm starting to fade again. Can you give me some spare energy?" he asked, holding his head.

Kawai snuggled him tightly, bringing him up to low power.

"Alright everyone, let's get the hell out of here!" yelled Atatasuki.

"Not so fast. We came here to free the rest of Devlin's captives. Does anyone know where the other Exps are held?" asked Exp 8.

"NoOne is the only other Exp in Devlin's lab. I don't think he'll want to join us," said Ada.

"I thought you said Devlin had a plethora of Exps? Was that a lie?" asked Exp 8.

"Why would I lie to you?"

"You were only held captive because you were going to be bartered off. There are no other prisoners. Now, let's move along," said Bob.

"If there really aren't any more Exps here, then let's get the hell out of here. We need to move out of Devlin's jurisdiction," said Exp 8, leading his team onwards.

The Freedom Forcers ran down the hallway toward the exit.

"Hey, um, Brother, what do you want to do first when we escape? We haven't made out yet, so I think we could start there and then—"

"Damn it."

"Did I say something wrong?"

Exp 8 pointed to the escape door.

It was blocked off by a bright red force field.

"We've come too far to fail now," said Nina, trying to weaken the force field with erotic poses.

"Nina, you betrayed me for a collection of code!" yelled Devlin from the loud speaker.

"Made up of jaw-dropping digits!" hollered Nina.

"Oh well, it doesn't matter. You can't escape my extremely visible force field anyway. You've all come so far just to fail."

"Stand back," said Exp 8, twisting his wrists. He punched the barrier, but it didn't budge.

The force field shattered to pieces as he turned around.

"I am so proud; you've grown so powerful. Why must you defy me? Damn you!" yelled Devlin.

"What's wrong, lost your cool?" asked Bob.

"You haven't won yet. I still have one final Exp at my disposal."

"Ada, what is he talking about?" asked Exp 8.

"I'm not sure. There's no way Devlin could have already made a new experiment."

"Oh that Devlin, he's such a hard worker," said Atatasuki, turning to his little sis for a look of approval.

"What are you so chipper about?" asked Kawai with a stern gaze.

"Behold my latest creation!" yelled Devlin.

A giant smoke cloud appeared from outside the lab and approached them.

"Pharma, I give you permission to destroy them!"

The smoke cleared, revealing Devlin's latest Exp.

He was shaped like a tall scrawny man, but he had no flesh. His body was composed entirely out of drug products. Pharma's head was a neon green bong. His eyes were golf ball-sized pills, floating freely inside the bong like goop in a lava lamp. His mouth was structured within the bong but was its own section apart from the main portion of the bong. The makings of his throat could be seen, including the tar-coated edges. In his chest were shriveled IV bags, symbolizing his lungs. Ecstasy pills were lined up like teeth inside his mouth. His nostrils were little holes with long bendy straws poking out. His ears funneled the contents of the bong directly down his throat.

Hypodermic needles were integrated into his hands. His thumbs were freshly lit cigars. Cigarettes were where his toes should be, except for his big toes, which were Cuban cigars. Pharma's shoulders were shaped like lighters. The rest of his body was coated in cocaine powder. Beneath the powder were different types of inhalants, injectables, pills, patches, chewables, lozenges, liquids, powders, smokes, and pipes that bunched together to form his body. In short, he was a psychedelic pharmaceutical monstrosity of addiction.

"That is the most screwed up thing I have ever seen," said Atatasuki with wide eyes.

"What the hell are you?" asked Exp 8, waving the smoke away.

"You said our bodies are natural. His body is beautiful in its own way, right?" asked Ada sweetly.

"Yeah, but then I realized that a crazy scientist constructed us. And now it turns out he is a druggie. Ugh, I guess behind every psycho there is an addiction," said Exp 8, holding his forehead.

Pharma took his head off and moved it across his body, sniffing up some white powder with his bendy straws. Once he had his fill, he reattached his head and looked straight at the Freedom Forcers.

"You're all a bunch of...(snort)...ahhhh...freeeeeeeaks," he said with a congested, raspy voice.

No words were uttered, everyone just stared at the skeletal android.

"Come on, people. Let's party!" yelled Pharma, his shoulders popping open.

"You are all that stands in our way of freedom. We won't lose to you!" yelled Exp 8, taking a step toward his opponent.

"Enough of this prittle-prattle! Just give up and take in the fumes," said Pharma, sitting down. He crossed his legs and puffed smoke rings in Exp 8's face.

"This guy is so disgusting," said Kawai, pinching her nose to escape the rancid smell of ancient booze.

"Move aside. I'm not quite sure if you count as unarmed, but if you don't yield, I will fire," said Karson, prepping his musket.

"You can't hurt me. I'm in another world. If you all want a fight…hic…I'll give you one. You're all going to die though! Drugs are the…ahhh…ultimate killing machine. Bah-bah-booaahahaaahaaaahoooh."

"I beg your pardon?! What are you blathering about? Guns are the ultimate killing machines," said Karson, stuffing his musket.

"Tens of thousands of people die every year from secondhand smoke exposure alone," said Pharma, popping five cigs in his mouth.

"Oooh, I'm so scared. A nuclear bomb can kill more than that in a couple of seconds," said Karson, pushing out his chest.

"True, but drugs have disastrous effects on the psyche. They cause families to fall apart, people to go insane. Too much drinking can even cause birth defects and miscarriages. Drugs rewrite our DNA!"

"And you think the babies inside pregnant women who have been shot survive? Get real."

"What about all the crazed Drug Lords and crooked cops taken in by its spell? What about all the users in prison? There's only one reason that drugs aren't legalized: money. The head honchos want to profit off the victims' addictions. People living in the ghettos get jail time for marijuana, while all the Hollywood stars are sniffing up coke. It's pure classism. And besides, the money taken from arrested Drug Lords can't be traced, which means it's free game for the police. The war on drugs is just a smokescreen over the ignorant masses by cigarette companies to keep their monopoly. The only way to end drug crime is to decriminalize it. That's why we should legalize drugs worldwide!" yelled Pharma, throwing his arms in the air.

"Wait…what does that have to do with drugs killing more people than guns?"

"There's no need to argue that…it's so obvious. Want a smoke?" asked Pharma, pulling off his thumb.

"I'm not quite done yet! Just think about what the trauma of war does to the countless soldiers and their families. The aftereffects of nuclear warfare can cause biological mutations lasting for generations. All of this is done for the sake of acquiring resources and asserting dominance," said Karson, bringing the debate back full throttle.

"Drugs create pollutants that enter the atmosphere and destroy the ozone!"

"What do you think the plutonium in nuclear weapons does to the ecosystem? It slowly destroys life in all its forms."

"All it takes is an overdose."

"All it takes is the twitch of a finger."

"Drugs are the ultimate killers!" yelled Pharma, jumping to his feet.

"Why don't we find out firsthand? You and me, one-on-one," said Karson, stretching his arms.

"Now you're speaking my language," said Pharma with a toothy grin.

"Need a light?" asked Karson as he readied his flame throwers.

"Thanks, bud," said Pharma, running into the flames. The light was soon extinguished as he inhaled throughout his entire body. "Now that's some gooooood shit. Whew! Now I'm in the zone," he said, riding his high. He jumped up and stuck his thumbs down the gun fanatic's eyes.

"That burns!" yelled Karson, his eyeholes singed by the cigar butts.

"Oh I see…you have pupils inside the shotgun barrels," said Pharma as he peered into his opponents sockets.

Karson's eyes shot out bullets, piercing through the addict's thumbs.

Alcohol leaked out of the freshly made stubs.

"Beheh, didn't feel a damn thing. With inebriation comes immortality!"

"You're a total loon!"

"By destroying my thumbs you have sealed your fate. Cigarettes are more harmful and addicting than cigars. Ah, nothing like nicotine and tar to clog up your lungs," said Pharma, lifting up his foot and smoking his toe.

Karson brought up his rocket launcher arm and aimed it at the drug lord. The bazooka disengaged a missile, shooting it directly at the enemy soldier.

Pharma flung his middle finger forward, detaching a needle from his hand. The needle shot through the air and collided with the missile, causing it to explode.

"Behaha, you see the power of ugh…." Pharma looked down to see metal shards jabbed in his chest. The holes in his body leaked alcohol all over the floor.

"My missile was a carrier for the smaller explosives encased inside it. By exploding my missile you put yourself in even more danger. See, drugs aren't the only silent killers."

"My precious drugs!" yelled Pharma as he lapped up the alcohol ravenously.

"You can smoke thousands of cigarettes before you die, or take one bullet to the head." Karson brought out his Gatling gun arm, lined up from his hands all the way to his shoulders.

"What good are bullets that just bounce off?" asked Pharma as he gobbled up a handful of steroids. His body became bulkier and his muscles tightened. "Now my strength has increased…a whole shitload!" he exclaimed, slamming his hand into the wall and leaving a large dent.

"You're going to destroy your own body, you idiot!"

"The body will decay regardless. Why not speed up the process? My entire life is one crazy trip!" Pharma plopped a pill into the top of his head, dissolving it instantly.

"Drugs make you delusional, not immortal!" yelled Karson as his gun revved up.

The bullets hit Pharma and skidded off as he approached.

The Drug Lord grabbed the gunman by the head and lifted him up.

"You need at least one hand to hold a gun. All you need to feel drugs is a functioning brain," said Pharma, slamming his head into his enemy.

"You don't need any limbs to feel the power of an air raid," said Karson, firing off his shotgun arms.

Pharma was knocked back, but he wasn't injured. "Shut up already! You can get wasted so bad that you can't even walk in a straight line."

"And a well placed bullet can turn a war hero into an invalid," said Karson, shooting the addict in the head with his revolver.

Pharma's bong now had a leaking hole.

"Damn it, drugs are better!" yelled Pharma, lunging his needles forward.

"Don't you mean worse?" asked Karson snidely.

Pharma stopped in his tracks and grabbed his head. "Oh yeah, it was about which one is worse. Well…drugs are worse because they are better, or was it vice versa? Beh-ha-ugh-ugh-ugh," said Pharma, gripping his chest. He pounded his chest as fear spread in his eyes.

"What the bloody hell are you doing now?"

Pharma collapsed on the floor. The exasperated gasps came to a halt as he fell into a coma.

"What just happened?" asked Atatasuki.

"He collapsed from an exponential overdose of…well, just about everything," said Ada.

"Drugs are a double-edged sword and my pal Pharma here seems to have gotten the sharp end. Ugh, I guess I won the battle, though I'm not satisfied with how I achieved victory," said Karson, disengaging his Gatling gun.

Part 2
Advent of the Assassins

Chapter 11: The Viper Squad

Previously: the Freedom Forcers finished their fight against Pharma and emerged victorious.

Devlin was out of options. He paced around the room nervously as he took out his phone.

"Hello. Hello."

"Who is this?" asked a deep fear-invoking voice from the other line.

"It's Devlin. I'm looking for someone to take on a job for me. Kanasta, is that you?"

"What kind of job? Are you looking for a combat trainer?"

"I can't talk about it over the phone."

"Then can we meet in person? How difficult is this job?"

"The situation has gotten out of hand."

"Are you prepared to offer up proper compensation?"

"Yes. I have more than enough money. I will pay you the entire amount up front. If you complete your job, I will pay double."

"Glad you see it my way," said Kanasta, hinting a smile from the other line before hanging up."

"Hello, are you still there? Hello?" asked Devlin before hanging up.

"Hello, Devlin," said Kanasta, his voice frighteningly close.

"You sure got here fast," said Devlin, freezing in place.

An eight-foot figure loomed behind the youthful inventor. "You know not to use my true name on the phone."

"It was a secure line. What are you worried about?"

"I operate a risky business; there is no such thing as being too careful," said Kanasta in a roughed-up low tone.

"You haven't changed at all."

"And you've changed so much," said Kanasta, stepping out of the shadows.

Once he emerged from the darkness, it was apparent that Kanasta was in his thirties. His slicked back, spiky hair was dyed black and white in a checkerboard design. Not a single strand dared to droop into his line of sight. The handyman's imposing blood-red eyes stared blankly forward, fixed solely only on the job. Metallic board games were placed on his chest and back as armor. Beneath the armor was a skintight, black bodysuit. Clenched in his large right hand was a steel-plated suitcase.

"I called you strictly for business reasons. There's been a problem at the lab."

"They were too much to handle, weren't they? You know, there is a growing demand for my kind of work. I hope my money is prepared in full. You should hand it over before the Freedom Forcers pay me to assassinate you," said Kanasta with a smile.

"How dare you!"

"I was only joking," said Kanasta with stoic eyes.

"I could kill you for trespassing into my home."

"Duly noted."

"How long have you been here?"

"I knew you would need my help soon. I took a flight here once I got wind of Exp 8's escape. I was waiting behind you the entire conversation."

"How do you know so much?"

"I was looking after you."

"I should have known you were spying on me," said Devlin, turning away from the assassin's gaze.

"So, shall we begin with introductions?" asked Kanasta with a slight smirk.

"I've been waiting to meet them," said Devlin, turning around with wide eyes.

"Just follow me." Kanasta led his client down the hall to a large metal door.

"This is my briefing room!" exclaimed Devlin, flinging the door open.

The room was shaped like an upside down bowl. The ceiling was adorned with the gods and goddesses of the Greek religious tradition. There was a fifteen-foot round metal table. It had no legs and was instead held up by thin granite pillars that separated the seating areas. A globe stood at the center of the table, revolving at its own pace. Dust outlined the edges of the table, but the top was shimmering with cleanliness. The surrounding chairs were built into the ground, but were modified to swivel. Seated in each chair was an unfamiliar face.

"How long have your guys been here? This isn't a club; you can't just walk in!" yelled Devlin.

"When I heard about Exp 8's escape, we moved in. I've been waiting for a chance to fight him. Shall I introduce you to the Viper Squad?" Kanasta sat down in Devlin's black pleather executive chair.

"Go ahead," said Devlin, looking at the assassins with wide eyes.

Kanasta gently gestured to a woman with his thick arms. "This is Sefiwah. She is our newest member. Her speed is only matched by her merciless spirit. She kills without a sound and without a tear."

Devlin approached the pale woman shrouded in white bandages. Her body was meaty and slender. Blood was seeping out from the wounds beneath her wraps. Her belt was held in place by spikes that pierced deep into her waist. Tamed white hair covered half of her face. A white eye patch was barely visible from beneath the fragile strands of hair. Once the curious scientist leaned in closer, he noticed her white pupil was encompassed by a pitch-black iris.

"A pleasure to meet you," said Devlin, trying to hide his excitement. He outstretched his hand in a friendly manner.

"There is no pleasure in life, only in death. Death is what makes life worthwhile," she said in a cold, gentle tone, gazing at a white spot on the wall behind the client.

Devlin awkwardly fixed up his hair to cover up his denied handshake. "She sure is a cheerful one, heheh."

"Sefiwah doesn't get along with strangers." Kanasta pushed his honored client along. "Now, let's continue, shall we? This is Ego. He is one of the very first members of the Viper Squad. His expertise is quick escapes and mechanics. His ability to improvise is legendary. And his skill with vehicles is unparalleled."

"So then, he's your behind-the-scenes guy?"

"While it is true that his hands have never had blood on them, he is still very active on the field."

Devlin approached a young man with huge, custom made, light-up headphones. A punk green Mohawk was accompanied by homegrown sideburns and an au naturel goatee. Neon light piercings adorned his nose. At the center of his chest was a dangling pendant engraved with the word "EGO." Ego was holding a surfboard in one hand and a snowboard in the other. His shirt had the words "It's Huge" in big bold letters. The rest of the shirt was covered in arrows pointing to his face with different compliments. He was wearing flashy bright-red pants with designer tears. A loose glow stick belt weaved through his pants. On his feet was a pair of rollerblades with thimble-sized jet ports at the heels. Ego's eyes were covered by a VR visor.

"It's a pleasure to meet you," said Devlin with a wave of his hand.

Ego continued to nod his lowered head to the music.

"Hello," said Devlin, waving his hand in front of the rocker's face.

Ego turned up the volume by tapping his headphones.

Devlin ripped off the headphones and slammed them to the table.

Ego took off his visor, revealing edgy, blue eyes with dark lines below them. "Whoa man, calm down. Yo, are you our client?" he asked with a hip young voice.

"Yes, I am. So, what can you do?" asked Devlin.

"Dude, I'm huge."

Ego grew seven times his size, smashing his neatly shaved head into the ceiling. "Ow. That hurt," he said before reverting to his normal size.

Devlin turned to Kanasta with clenched teeth. "Could you kindly tell your subordinates to keep themselves under control? I already have enough repairs to tend to after Exp 8's latest breakout."

Kanasta pulled Ego's chair back and stared into his eyes.

"Apologize to Mr. Devlin. The damage expenses will be coming out of your payment," said Kanasta, turning the chair to face the client.

"Shiiiiiit. Alright man, I'm sorry. You seem like a cool guy. It's just hard to put down classic rock," said Ego, reclaiming his headphones.

"So, he can make himself big? How is that a good ability for an assassin?" asked Devlin.

"Don't worry, buddy, you'll see," said Ego, flashing his gold tooth with a confident grin.

"He won't disappoint you."

"If you say so," said Devlin.

"The next assassin is BoneSaw. I made it myself. It has both speed and stealth. You're stepping on it right now, guheh," said Kanasta proudly.

"I am!" Devlin quickly lifted up his foot. He looked down to see a small metal cube. "A box...one of your assassins is a box?" he asked with a condescending tilt of the head.

"BoneSaw!" hollered Kanasta.

The silver box sprung to life as tiny treads rolled out from the bottom. Circular saws and chainsaws then folded out from various sections, ready to kill.

"Oh, I see. A pleasure to meet you, BoneSaw," said Devlin, taking a step back.

"He doesn't talk...he only kills. He's a real chip off the old block," said Kanasta, leaning down and patting his masterpiece.

"He seems friendly enough," said Devlin as he grabbed one of the saws and shook it as a greeting.

Kanasta led the client by the shoulder to the next assassin. "This is Tempo. He has never once made a mistake on a mission. He always stays on target. His specialty is untraceable kills. Tempo was my very first teammate and has always been my most loyal ally."

Devlin approached Kanasta's right hand man, who was stationed opposite of his boss' chair.

Tempo looked to be in his mid-forties with a corrugated forehead and a stiffened jaw. He had spiky hair: red on one side, blue on the other, with matching burly eyebrows.

A biker jacket with red and blue flames in front and matching colored mountains in back was worn over a black skin suit. Strapped to the assassin's muscular back was a five-foot double-ended thermometer. Another thermometer was poking out of his mouth like a cigarette.

Tempo turned to the potential client with his bottom lip pushed out, exposing his sharp teeth.

"How much does the job pay?" he asked in a dark, gruff tone, taking off his red-and-blue sunglasses. Flame-like eyes with dark circles, arched like crescent moons, scanned for the client's wallet.

"That depends on how well you do your job," said Devlin, tilting the chair to face him.

"Get your hands off—"

"It's my chair, not yours. You control temperature, right?" asked Devlin, flicking the protruding thermometer.

"You're paying me to do a job, not to chat. If you want to talk to me, that's extra." Tempo hoisted his white, blood-stained hiking boots with crampons up on the table. He pulled out the mission briefing and continued to read.

"You didn't tell me he was a jerk," said Devlin, pivoting back to Kanasta.

"He's only in this gig for the money. I don't normally introduce my team to our clients. You should be honored. This is a very rare opportunity."

"So, is that everyone? They're not a very friendly bunch. But as long as they get the job done, I've got no substantial complaints," said Devlin, crossing his arms.

"There is one more. She is still suiting up."

An energetic young girl somersaulted into the room. She leaped over the table and then back-flipped, landing in front of the client.

A single look in his eyes was all it took to know that he was enamoured. "And who is she!" exclaimed Devlin, his eyes glued to her.

"I would like to introduce you to my pupil. She is a killing prodigy. You'll be happy to know that she has a very friendly personality. And unlike the rest of us, she modified her birth name rather than fully discarding it for an alias. This is Kaity Rin Rainbow Viper," said Kanasta with fatherly pride.

The four-foot-five preteen girl shook the client's hand playfully. She had two folding robotic cat ears attached to the top of her head. The prodigy's hair was white and cut short in the front, the sides were light purple tuffs, and the back was dark purple. Her jade, cat-like eyes with slits for pupils were emphasized by thin green irises resembling crosshairs, great for tracking prey.

She had mechanized gloves with light-up green paw-print padding on each hand. The bottoms of her feet were bare, her toes naturally curling inward.

A neck-high skintight bodysuit showed off every curve of her cute, slender body. The slick light purple suit had a microchip design that glowed green from within. A tail of the same design energetically swayed back and forth behind the young girl.

Kaity looked up and smiled. "Hi Mister Devlin, I'm Kaity, it is a pleasure to meet you," she said in a soft, but energetic, tone as she put her hands to her waist and bowed.

"The pleasure is all mine," said Devlin, looking over her figure as he returned the bow.

"So, I hear you're a scientist. Do you make medicine? Or do you just make weapons? I bet you're really smart," said Kaity, tilting her head with intrigue.

"Well, yes…I…umm…I'm very smart. As a matter of fact, you and your friends are going to fight my creations," said Devlin with a smile that stretched from one side of his face to the other.

"Yay! This is going to be lots and lots of fun. We have way too many easy missions! It's great when there's a little challenge! Do you think your creations are ready for us?" asked Kaity, bouncing up and down.

"I hope not, I wouldn't want you to get hurt," said Devlin, reaching for her hand.

Kaity playfully put her hands behind her back. "Aw, you're so sweet. But you don't need to worry. Tempo, Ego, and the Boss have been in the business for many years. I haven't been an assassin as long as the others, but I've completed every mission without a scratch! It's gotten close, but Kanasta always has my back," she said with a grin.

"So are you looking forward to taking out my creations?" asked Devlin, taking a step closer to her.

Tempo's chair spun around to face the client.

"What's there to look forward to? Just hand over the money already," said Tempo with a grimace.

"I wasn't asking you!" yelled Devlin.

"No need to get so worked up. Tempo didn't mean to upset you. He just doesn't care about anything but money. As for me, I just like having fun with my family. Oh, and I love a good hunt," said Kaity, rubbing up against the assassin boss while she purred affectionately.

"Just like a kitty," said Devlin, staring at her in wonderment.

"Yep! I like to play with my prey before I kill it. Fragile prey is just no fun. You understand, right?"

"Yes, of course, but I'm sorry to tell you that you won't have much of a challenge with them. They are like inexperienced children when it comes to combat, huh-hoooh," said Devlin, holding his forehead.

"Oh, so they're children. Those are a bit harder to hit, but I can manage," said Kaity, stretching her arms out.

"You've killed children?" asked Devlin with wide eyes.

"Of course we have! We take on any job as long as it pays. It's part of our creed. But enough about that; I want to know more about scientists. My dad was a scientist, but he wasn't allowed to tell me about his work. Are all scientists secretive? What do you scientists do exactly?"

"What happened to your dad?" asked Devlin, placing a hand on the girl's shoulder.

"Enough," said Sefiwah, her head darting toward the virgin boy.

"What's wrong, Sefiwah?" asked Kaity, turning her head.

"You two have talked enough. We have a mission to complete," said Sefiwah, twirling a razor blade on her finger.

Kaity rushed up to Sefiwah and rubbed her head. "Aw, you're so cute. You're getting excited. Can't wait to get covered in blood, right?" she asked, poking her partner's pale cheeks.

"Yes, I'm starting to crave it again. It has been too long since I've felt blood trickling down my body. I'm starting to cut myself in anticipation," said Sefiwah, slicing her arm with a straight razor while staring at the client.

"So, you're a masochist? Hmm, isn't that delightful, heheh," said Devlin, slowly approaching her.

"I'm a sadomasochist. I like giving and receiving pain. Do you want to quench my thirst?" asked Sefiwah, standing up.

"We're two breads in a basket. Killing is just so much fun! We get along so well," said Kaity, nestling up to her partner.

"I'm kind of sadistic myself," said Devlin, shuffling his feet.

"That's very interesting and all, but if you don't stop talking to Kaity…I'll kill you," said Sefiwah, her razor up to his throat.

"I'm your client, in case you forgot," said Devlin, gripping her arm.

"I killed our last client. He got a little too close to Kaity. Tempo was upset, but Kanasta understood," said Sefiwah, her tone unchanged.

"Sefiwah, don't threaten Devlin," said Kanasta, looming over her.

"I was just making a point," said Sefiwah, pulling her arm away and popping the razor into her mouth.

"I understand her feelings. You're protective of Kaity because she's so young. She's like the child of your group," said Devlin, beaming at the adorable little cat-girl.

"Nope, wrong," said Kaity, sticking out her tongue.

"How am I wrong?" asked Devlin with a raised eyebrow.

"Sefiwah is very protective of me because she's my lover," said Kaity, licking her partner's pearly white lips.

Devlin's eyes popped in disbelief. His head then dropped in disappointment.

"I think it is time you leave. We have business to attend to," said Kanasta, gesturing to the door.

"Damn it…it's true what they say: all the cute ones are gay. And if that wasn't bad enough…she has a psychopathic girlfriend. My odds suck right now," said Devlin to himself.

"The introductions are over; it's time for you to move along," said Kanasta, grabbing the client's shoulders.

"Don't touch me!" Devlin pulled out of Kanasta's grip and turned away from him. "Bye Kaity, have fun with my experiments," he said with a shaky smile.

"I'll have lots and lots of fun. See you later, Mister Devlin," said Kaity, waving at him cheerfully.

Devlin left the room, never turning away from the bouncy bundle of cuteness.

Sefiwah picked Kaity up and pet her head affectionately. "He's trying to take you away from me."

"Relax, he's just being friendly, heehee," said Kaity as her partner lightly blew in her ear.

"I saw that look in his eye. He's a pedophile for sure. But don't worry, I won't let anything happen to you," said Sefiwah, holding her girl tight to her chest.

"You worry too much. He's not even old enough to be a pedophile," said Kaity, sitting on her lover's lap.

"I wasn't aware there was an age limit. Just know that if he touches you, he's dead."

"Alright everyone, we've already reviewed the mission. Get prepped up and then go out there and make me proud," said Kanasta with a salute and a wide grin.

The Viper Squad bowed in unison and exited the room to get prepared for their assignment.

Meanwhile: Devlin sat in the surveillance room, watching his kitty-eared crush prepare in high definition.

"Yes, is Dr. Anthrax there?…Tell him to contact me once he's done. Thank you." Devlin put away his phone and stood up from his chair. After leaving the surveillance room, he raced down the hallway. "I think I need a break from all this tension," he said, massaging his temples. The busy scientist opened the door to the master bedroom.

The ceiling resembled the night sky with twinkling stars and swirling nebulas. The floor and walls of the room had a satellite picture of Earth and its many layers. Devlin's bed was atop the exposed core of the Earth. The bed had pitch-black sheets and a steel frame. It was large enough for at least three people, but had only a single pillow.

Devlin plopped himself on the bed and stretched out his arms. He bumped something under the covers. He ripped the covers off, revealing a naked woman.

"What are you doing here?" asked Devlin, looking down at her supple, snow-white skin.

Sefiwah's eye was fixated on the virgin boy. "The look in your eyes when you stared at my Kaity," she said softly.

"So you came to assassinate me…in the nude?" asked Devlin with a raised eyebrow.

"I am here to protect my Kaity. I know the type of man you are, Devlin. You're a virgin, aren't you?" asked Sefiwah, lying still as a statue.

"Why would it matter if I was?"

"You're a desperate, lonely virgin. You're obsession with Kaity is very dangerous."

"I understand that you're her lover. Look, I'm not going to interfere. But I wouldn't mind watching," said Devlin with a smirk.

Sefiwah put her lips to his ear. "I'm here to quench your desires. I want you to use me as a substitute for Kaity."

"Whoa! Just what kind of guy do you think I am? I like Kaity…but we've only just met," said Devlin, turning away with a light blush.

"I don't want your passion to suddenly take hold of you and hurt Kaity. I'm here to appease you. Whatever you want to do with her body, do to my body instead," said Sefiwah, spreading out her arms.

"You do have…quite the body. Your skin is as white as snow. I don't know why I didn't notice until now," said Devlin, sitting at the edge of the bed.

"Unlike Kaity, I'm not a lesbian. I've felt a man's rough hands on my body. So go ahead…do whatever you want to me."

Devlin looked at her pale breasts and blushed.

"What's wrong? Are you shy?" Sefiwah covered herself with the blanket and beckoned him. "Is that better?"

Devlin squeezed in next to her, now only mere inches from her delicate lips. "You are very beautiful," he said with a warm smile.

"It wasn't easy for me to remove all those bandages. It would be a shame if I did so for no reason."

"Well, when you put it that way…how can I refuse?" asked Devlin, his hands crawling toward her. He fondled her breasts and almost instantly got swept

124

up in passion. The aroused genius rubbed his face between them, gasping in delight.

Sefiwah did not make the slightest noise suggesting pleasure.

Devlin sucked on her breasts as if his life depended on them.

"Devlin...I apologize for my behavior earlier. I am not a cruel woman. I was trying to make a harsh first impression because I wanted you to know—Kaity is off limits," said Sefiwah, looking down at him.

"Mmm...your tits are so amazing. They looked so tiny all bandaged up," said Devlin, pinching her nipples as his palms jiggled her breasts.

"Are you listening to me or not?" asked Sefiwah, pulling his head up.

"Don't worry about it. I understand completely. So, may I have a kiss?" asked Devlin, looking at her pearly white lips.

"I'm not going to stop you."

Devlin kissed her neck all the way up until he reached her lips. He then stopped in place.

"Don't you want a kiss? Were you just toying with me?" asked Sefiwah, sitting up.

Devlin pressed against her. "I'm so turned on right now!" he exclaimed, breathing heavily as he nibbled her ear.

"I can't get aroused and I have no need to. As long as you're enjoying yourself, I have no complaints. But Devlin...is this really all you wanted to do to my Kaity? Just kissing and fondling? My body is your doll. You may do what you want with it," said Sefiwah, spreading her legs.

"Why don't you let loose? Go on, gasp in pleasure...enjoy yourself," said Devlin, touching her cheek affectionately.

"I'm doing this for Kaity and only for Kaity. You're a very likable guy. I can't allow you to undo all the work I've done," said Sefiwah, her eye as firm as stone.

"What work?" asked Devlin, caressing her hair.

"I want Kaity to be dependent solely on me. I need her to love only me. And I will do anything for that," said Sefiwah, mechanically caressing his back.

"I understand you want to keep her safe, but aren't you being a little too obsessive?" asked Devlin, taking off his shirt.

"You don't need to understand. You just need to enjoy yourself."

"But I want to know. Why are you so protective of Kaity?"

"I love her so very much. And I need her to love me just as much. Kaity wasn't born a lesbian. She has liked guys before. I had to get rid of that part of her. It was for her own good. Men are too dangerous."

"So, what did you do exactly?" asked Devlin, stopping in place.

"I did what I had to. But once I had her turned off by men, I needed her to get turned on by me. I made her come to me. I'd give her the slightest kindness, just enough to grab her attention. Once we became friends, I'd give her the gentlest touch. I'd touch her in such a passive way...so she'd want more. Our entire relationship has been built seamlessly in this way. I don't covet her affection. I want only to protect her. I need her to love only me. Any other attachment is deadly," said Sefiwah with the slightest smile.

"I don't fully understand, but I know you truly care about Kaity. That's all that matters," said Devlin, hugging her tightly.

"I know you would never hurt her. You care about her just as I do. That sweetness is what makes you even more dangerous. I appreciate your honest concern for her well-being. I just can't have her fall in love with you."

"I can't give up on her. I've fallen for her. I appreciate this...but I won't give up on Kaity," said Devlin, his eyes firm with resolve.

"So you've felt her sweetness too. It's irresistible, isn't it? It's like a taste of Heaven. Devlin, I sense a bit of love in your obsession," said Sefiwah, touching his lips.

"Just being around her is so wonderful."

Sefiwah sat up and grabbed him by the shoulders. "I want to ask you for a favor. You cannot speak to anyone about this," she said, her eye like a dagger.

Devlin gently nudged her arms off his shoulders. "Calm down. I know how to keep a secret. I'm sure you're just looking out for Kaity."

"I always am. And I am willing to reward you for fulfilling my request," said Sefiwah, turning away from his gaze.

"What kind of reward?" asked Devlin, his eyes gleaming.

"I need to keep her safe from love, not sex. How would you like to be with both of us? As long as you don't get her pregnant, I won't have to kill you."

"Pr-pr-pregnant?" asked Devlin, lighting up bright red.

"If she did get pregnant, she might become attached to her baby. And if that happens, I may lose hold of her love. It's just too risky. But that doesn't mean I can't let you touch her. I'll let you do whatever you want to the both of us as long as she doesn't fall in love with you," said Sefiwah, her voice shaking.

"That's quite the reward! So you don't care if I take advantage of Kaity?" asked Devlin, rubbing noses with her.

"I'd prefer it actually. If you did, then there isn't a chance she'd fall in love with you. She would come crying right into my arms. She would need me more than ever," said Sefiwah with her hand to her chest and with a gentle smile.

"And you called me obsessive, huhuh."

"Yes. I am obsessive. But I don't mind seeing her cry. It doesn't upset me if she is hurt. To be honest, seeing her squirming around like that...it kind of turns me on. I don't need her to be happy. I only need to keep her safe," said Sefiwah, blowing into the virgin's ear.

"You've got me curious now. What do I have to do for this splendid reward?" asked Devlin, pulling her in closer to him.

"You are to speak about this to no one. That goes for all of this. Understood?" asked Sefiwah, gripping him by the chin.

"You have my word. Now, what do you want from me?" asked Devlin, placing his hands atop hers.

"I need you to kill Kanasta."

Devlin's eyes widened.

"Is that a problem?" asked Sefiwah, her gaze not wavering in the least.

"You want me to kill your boss? Why?" asked Devlin, grabbing her hand.

"I need Kaity to quit the Viper Squad. It has served its purpose. Killing Kanasta is the best way to put an end to it."

Devlin gripped her head and pulled her in. "Are you going to tell me the real reason now?"

"I...guess I have to. Kaity loves Kanasta like a father. This attachment could endanger her well-being. If he's dead, then she will only love me. I can't kill him on my own. Even the government is unable and unwilling to kill him. I need you to do it. And once he has breathed his last breath, I'll let you do whatever you want to both me and my little kitten," said Sefiwah, grabbing his hand and dragging it down her body.

"It will be done. So, when is the threesome?" asked Devlin, giving her a peck on the lips.

"I know you could just kill me after you've gotten your reward."

"The thought never crossed my mind," said Devlin, kissing her neck.

"I need something concrete to seal the deal."

"You want me to sign something?"

"Yes, I want your one and only signature. I want you to make me pregnant. You're a dangerous man, but you're too sweet to kill your own child. Get on top of me. The deal will be sealed once the seed has been sown," said Sefiwah, pulling down his pants.

Devlin tossed aside his pants and pressed the pale assassin against the bed. "Alright, sounds fair enough. But what's to say you won't (thrust) back out on your end of the bargain?" he asked, pushing deeper inside her.

"Once we've finished this job, we'll have our threesome. Once Kanasta is dead, I'll let you do whatever you want with us as long as Kaity doesn't get pregnant or fall in love with you," said Sefiwah, patting his head.

Devlin thrust into her over and over, speeding up as sweat dripped from his face to hers.

Sefiwah did not make a sound. She stared at him blankly as her body synchronized with his motions.

"Kanasta will be dead by the time the Viper Squad's job is finished," said Devlin, thrusting harder and harder.

"That is music to my ears. I don't hate the man. He is actually rather kindhearted for a murderer. I have to do this. You understand, right?" asked Sefiwah softly, her eyes watering up.

"You've got yourself a...deal!" exclaimed Devlin, holding her tightly as he filled her up.

"Push in deeper. I don't want to take any chances. Don't spill a single drop," said Sefiwah, her legs pulling him in as deep as possible.

Devlin squinted and then kissed her lips.

"Is that all of it?" asked Sefiwah, making circles with her hips.

"Yeah...that's...all of it." Devlin relaxed on her chest, nuzzling his face against her breasts.

Sefiwah grabbed his cheeks. "We'll talk again once the job is finished. I'm glad we reached an agreement. And I...enjoyed being with you," she said, kissing him on the cheek.

"You could have fooled me. So, are you up for another round?" asked Devlin, kissing her neck as she pulled away.

"I have a job to do. I'm already running late. But don't worry, we'll have another chance," said Sefiwah, caressing his cheeks. She slid out from beneath him and got off the bed. "Can you say it to me just one more time?" she asked, turning to the dangerous boy.

Devlin stood up and looked into her eyes. "Kanasta will be dead once the Viper Squad finishes the job I assigned them." He then kissed her gently on the lips.

"Ah! Such wonderful words!" Sefiwah put his hand to her belly and smiled. She collected her bandages, wrapped her breasts and bolted out of the room.

"Things are really looking up now," said Devlin, gazing at the starlit ceiling with a growing smile. "Once the job is done, Kanasta will be dead. Ehahahahaha!"

Chapter 12: The Job

The Freedom Forcers bathed in a crystal clear lake, finally having a chance to relax. Small stones spread out across the lake bed. Catfish, minnows, and prawns swam freely. Water beetles grouped up around the strange visitors. Sunlight seeped in through the leaves of the redwoods and pine trees. Grass adorned the outskirts of the lake.

"Do you think Devlin is watching us, even now?" asked Exp 8, scanning the trees.

"I don't really think that matters," said Bob passively, bathing in the sun's rays outside the lake.

"Yo Bob, isn't it dangerous for you to be exposed to the sun like that?" asked Atatasuki.

"I'm not looking at it. I'm just relaxing in it. Besides, a little sunlight isn't going to hurt me."

"Are you coming in?" asked Ada, looking up at Nina from Exp 8's chest.

"I've never bathed with anyone before. I can't just expose my body so carelessly. Karson, you understand, right? It isn't practical to reveal your weapons," said Nina, practicing new poses on the grass.

"True, but we aren't your enemies. We're all allies here. You can sit back and relax," said Karson, stretching out his arms in the water.

"You're all honor and no brains. Yesterday's enemies have become today's allies. How can I be certain today's allies won't become tomorrow's enemies? I've got to stay on my titillating toes," said Nina, pushing out her chest and pursing her lips.

"Great, she's already considered betraying us," said Exp 8, rolling his eyes.

"Don't worry, if she tries anything…I'll destroy her," said Bob, turning to them with a warm smile.

"You sure talk big for an eyeball. I've kept many of my assets hidden. You shouldn't underestimate me," said Nina, transitioning from a split into a cat crawl.

"Can everyone calm down, we don't need to fight each other," said Exp 8 as his sister scrubbed his back.

"Yes, we're all friends here. Now, let me explain about the pine trees. Devlin's dad—" said Ada.

"We're not all friends here," said Atatasuki, his eyes darting back and forth to the new members of the team.

"What, you think I'd be a spy for Devlin? I have too much class for something like that," said Nina, pushing out her butt.

"I'm not talking about you. Even if you were a spy, at least you're nice to look at. I'm talking about Karson!" exclaimed Atatasuki, pointing to him dramatically.

Karson was scrubbing his guns with a bar of soap, not hearing a word.

"Why don't you trust him? He seems like an honorable guy to me," said Exp 8, floating belly up.

"That's what worries me! You're new to life, so it's understandable how you feel. You see, I was there when Karson was first created. I don't remember much about it, but I do remember how he pledged his undying loyalty to Devlin," whispered Atatasuki.

"That's exactly right!" exclaimed Karson, suddenly right behind Atatasuki.

"I knew it! You were waiting for us to put our guard down, weren't you? That's why you so carelessly surrendered to us. You gave up twice! When your buddy NoOne was fighting, you threw in the towel and did nothing! Then Devlin creates an Exp completely juxtaposing you. That gave you the perfect opportunity to show off your skill and flaunt your supposed allegiance to our cause. I'm right, aren't I?" asked Atatasuki, clenching his fist.

"We have to leave now!" exclaimed Nina, turning to her team with wide eyes.

"Don't change the subject! Your defeat was a little too convenient wasn't it?!" asked Atatasuki, grabbing the gunman by the shoulder.

Nina tossed a rock near the accuser. "Shut up! Devlin had a backup plan in place in case his Exps failed to capture Exp 8. He was going to call up a group of assassins. We have to get as far away from here as possible. I can't afford to have bullet holes in my perfect body!" she exclaimed, her eyes scanning the treetops.

"Your cover up is just too convenient! And your story sounds contrived. How would you know that information, huh? You don't have psychic powers like Devlin does," said Atatasuki, turning his accusatory finger to the suspicious stripper.

"I'm his favorite Exp. Why wouldn't he tell me his plans? He loves to brag about his grand schemes."

"That's believable. Perhaps too believable," said Atatasuki with an apprehensive gaze.

"Ugh. I don't need to explain myself, and I don't need to prove my loyalty either. Honestly, I don't care if the rest of you die. Exp 8, we need to get you out of here. If you get killed, then so will Ada," said Nina, glaring at him.

"Who cares about some hit men? Assassins are still human. What's so special about these murderers?" asked Exp 8, transfixed by the curious frog on his arm.

"They're the infamous Viper Squad," said Ada dramatically.

"The Viper Squad!" exclaimed Exp 8, rising from the water.

"That's correct," said Ada with a firm nod.

"Never heard of them. Look, it doesn't matter anyway. Unless they're some super Exps, we can easily beat them," said Exp 8, stretching out his arms.

"At least get out of the water," said Nina, looking around frantically.

"Maybe she's right. Come on, Brother, let's go. We should get out of the water, just to be safe," said Kawai, pulling his arm.

"I...didn't know you cared," said Atatasuki in passionate tears.

"I was talking to my brother, not a rusty piece of trash," said Kawai with mumbling rage.

"You mean rust-colored. Looks like my silver coating washed off. What you see now is pure, unbridled flaw," said Atatasuki, pushing out his dented copper chest.

"And what you see here is pure, refined sexiness," said Nina, pushing up her breasts.

Meanwhile: Kaity peered through the trees, perched on a nearby hill.

"Target in sight. Wow, look at that body," said Kaity, aiming her sniper reticle at Nina's breasts.

"Why are you gawking at the enemy?" asked Sefiwah, who was lying on top of her.

"What took you so long?" asked Kaity, looking up with a smile.

"I was covering up for your mistake. You can't just flirt like that; you'll give him the wrong idea," said Sefiwah, touching her girl's tender lips.

"I'm sorry. He was so nice. I just wanted to be nice back. Plus he's a scientist! Maybe he knew my dad!" exclaimed Kaity, keeping her eye on the target.

"What difference does it make? Your father is dead. Are you still looking at her breasts?" asked Sefiwah, tapping her partner's head.

"I might as well. We're going to kill them anyway. Why not enjoy the view while it lasts?" asked Kaity, panning down her target's alluring body.

"Why look at her when you can touch me?" asked Sefiwah, flipping her partner on top of her.

"Concentrate on the mission," said Tempo from a nearby treetop. "These targets don't look weak. Most of them aren't even human. They're starting to make their escape. Let's take them out all at once. BoneSaw is already in position."

Exp 8 walked out of the lake, cautiously looking over his shoulder. He suddenly stopped in place. "Why is there a cardboard box here? This is like the soda machine in the frungle. This is so obviously a trick. Oh well, let's see what Devlin's got up his sleeve this time." He lifted up the box.

Underneath that box was a small metal box.

"That's strange. Well, I'm not going to do this all day," said Exp 8, turning around.

The box waddled behind him before suddenly launching at him. Its back opened up and a buzz saw appeared. BoneSaw jabbed his saw in the armored target's neck, tearing through the top layer of metal.

"You idiot! You have to sta—"

Kaity fired a bullet directly at Nina's forehead, stopping her midsentence.

"Brother!" screamed Kawai, turning around.

Tempo jumped out from the bushes and held a shotgun to the cat-girl's head.

"Alright, come at me," said Bob.

Ego, hidden behind a nearby rock, activated an explosive under Bob that he had planted earlier.

"Don't you dare hurt my sister!" yelled Atatasuki, rushing at the man with the shotgun.

Sefiwah dropped down from the tree above the targets. She grabbed onto the copper man's head and hoisted herself into a handstand. She then spun around, snapping his neck.

"Cowards! Come out and fight me!" exclaimed Karson, still in the water.

"Assignment complete," said all the assassins at once.

"You're forgetting someone!" yelled Karson.

"Ow! What the hell was that? You hurt my neck!" yelled Exp 8, tearing his attacker off.

"Damn, who made a hole in my erotic forehead?!" asked Nina as blood dripped down to her nose.

"That won't work," said Kawai before the assassin's shotgun exploded from a sound wave.

"That was close," said Bob, passing through the smoke left over from the explosion.

"My neck...that hurt!" yelled Atatasuki, grabbing the pale woman's arm.

"You bloody cowards forgot someone!" exclaimed Karson, waving his arms in the water. "I'll make sure you remember me!" He loaded up his Gatling gun and revved it up.

"Retreat," said Kaity calmly.

Smoke flooded the area. By the time it cleared, the assassins were gone.

"Those were the deadly assassins? What the hell were you so worried about?" asked Exp 8, turning to Nina.

"Are you kidding?! Look at this hideous hole. My perfect forehead is ruined!" exclaimed Nina, trying to heal it with her saliva.

"They vanished before I could kill them. Auh, oh well," said Bob.

"The Viper Squad assassins have a flawless record. My database says they've never failed a mission. I guess we're more than they're used to," said Ada, spinning with pride.

"Now, let's continue where we left off! Karson, care to explain yourself?! Karson? Where did he go?" asked Atatasuki, looking around.

"Slippery bastard, he must have disappeared in the confusion. You were right, Atatasuki. He was a traitor. But Nina didn't lie to us. I'm not saying she isn't playing an angle, but we have no reason to distrust her," said Exp 8.

"You're right. And besides, she's hot," said Atatasuki with a thumbs-up.

"Since I'm so hot, why don't you help me out here?" asked Nina, staring daggers at Atatasuki.

"What are friends for?" He heated up his body and moved his steaming hands over to her. He then put his two burning fingers at both ends of the wound.

"Ah, those ugly holes are finally gone, but now I have this hideous scar, oh well, thanks for the help...I guess," said Nina, rubbing the wound.

"But her hotness aside, she called Kawai an ugly girl! I can't forgive someone who bullies my little sister," said Atatasuki, his hands lighting up again.

"Calm down," said Exp 8, putting himself in the middle.

"Wow, this guy just sparks all the conflict. Thanks for keeping things fun!" hollered Bob.

Kawai floated up to Atatasuki. "Stop fighting my battles!" She smacked him down with her tail. "And you owe me an apology," she said, floating up to Nina.

"I'm sorry, okay? You're not ugly. I was just being mean. It's a battle tactic to put you off guard, that's all. Actually, we're a lot alike. You've chosen to skip along the path of the cute, and I've decided to strut down the runway of the sexy!" exclaimed Nina, lowering her shirt with a smirk.

"Good, I'm glad we have an understanding. So, Brother, what's the plan?" asked Kawai.

"We find Karson before he can tell Devlin our whereabouts."

"Good idea. Hopefully the water washed off any tracking devices he had on us," said Kawai with a grin.

Meanwhile: deeper in the frungle, Karson was chasing down an assassin.

"Dude! Leave me alone!" yelled Ego, dodging the machine gun fire on his skateboard.

"Not only did you attack my friends and ruin my bath time, you all forgot to kill me! I won't accept being ignored by a band of cowards!" Karson cornered the assassin at a cliff's edge.

Kanasta appeared behind the armed target and grabbed him by the head. He put his hand over the target's button.

"Shoot and I push it," said Kanasta coldly.

"Now why would I do that? We're all friends here!" exclaimed Karson nervously, lowering his guns.

Kanasta hoisted the target over his shoulder. "Let's meet up with the rest of the team."

"Of...of course, Boss."

Devlin watched the mission from the surveillance room. "Things are really moving along splendidly. But I think Exp 8 might need a reminder of who's in charge," he said, spinning up to the door. He got out from his chair and strolled down the hallway up to the elevator. The clever inventor then rode the elevator down to the second lowest level. The doors opened, revealing a training room.

A holographic soldier was sliced to bits in front of Devlin.

A man in a long black cloak approached. He lowered his head with a bow. He then flung his katana into an approaching hologram. "Devlin-sama, I am honored to be in your presence."

"You can cut out the needless formalities. You don't have to be so uptight all the time. Just relax," said Devlin, snapping his fingers.

The holographic battalion dissolved out of existence.

"To what do I owe the honor of your presence?" asked the warrior in a strong, devout, stoic tone, leaning on his knee.

"The Freedom Forcers have escaped."

"Then I shall bring them back," said the warrior, standing tall.

"Let me finish. I have a group already on the job. The Freedom Forcers have no chance of winning."

"Then all is as it should be."

"This might be my last chance to test you out. Once the assassins get serious, the Freedom Forcers will be mine. Don't you want to go outside, get some fresh air, and fight your fellow Exps? Well, Riufen, do you?" asked Devlin, taking the katana from his warrior's hands.

"I need more training. I would not want to dishonor you in combat with my inexperience. I am not ready. My deepest apologies, Devlin-sama," said Riufen, his forehead to the concrete floor.

"I just want to see how you perform in live combat. I'm collecting data; I don't need you to win. I have no expectations, so you can't disappoint me. However, you can still impress me," said Devlin, lifting up his warrior's chin.

"Then I shall fight for data. I hope my performance yields bountiful results," said Riufen with a bow.

"I look forward to it," said Devlin with a grin.

After their less than glorious retreat, the Viper Squad rallied at the briefing room.

"This was the strangest hit yet. Even weirder than the one when that kid ate his father," said Kaity, sitting on the top of her chair.

BoneSaw clanged his saws together in response.

"Dude, our targets are awesome! That eyeball thing…it just…went right through my blast, man!" exclaimed Ego, walking into the room.

"I'm so excited! Devlin is so amazing! He created such fun toys for us to play with!" exclaimed Kaity, bouncing up and down on the chair.

"This is the first time we've had to retreat," said Sefiwah reflexively.

Tempo gripped Kaity's chair. "This is nothing to be excited about! We all failed to exterminate the targets. Kanasta will not be pleased."

"What have I told you all about mentioning my name?" asked Kanasta from the shadows.

He walked up to his assassins, holding Karson in one hand.

"I am very proud of all of you," said Kanasta with a slight smile, not even hinting at sarcasm.

"I'm sorry, Boss. Wait…aren't you upset?" asked Kaity, leaning her head back.

"We have failed you," said Sefiwah, lowering her head.

"We underestimated our targets. I did lead Karson to you, but that's the only thing I did right," said Ego, kicking up dust.

Tempo turned away and crossed his arms.

"Why should I be upset? You all passed my test," said Kanasta, closing his eyes to draw attention to his smile.

"Whaaaaaaaaat!" yelled Kaity with wide eyes.

"I was testing their capabilities and how quickly you could adapt to a sketchy situation. Kaity made the call to retreat and you used your judgment, realizing it was your best option. Sefiwah, that smoke bomb was dropped even before Kaity made the order…you were thinking ahead. All of you fled the area without a word and without a sound. I have never been more proud of each and every one of you in all my years," said Kanasta, opening up his arms.

Kaity flipped off the chair and landed on papa's shoulders. "So then, you're not mad?"

Kanasta patted her on the head and smiled.

"Boss, I think we need more intel. These things are unlike anything we've ever fought. Well, pretty much anything," said Tempo, popping his thermometer into his mouth.

"I did warn you that we would be fighting more difficult targets than usual, but I believe further explanation will help the situation. Our targets are Exps. They have both artifacts and capsules just like we do. Unlike us, they have been specifically designed to wield them. To further explain, Exps are created with a capsule in place of a heart. They weren't given transplants. We have an advantage over them: we have been alive a lot longer. Their combat experience is undeveloped, but their power is not to be underestimated. Though you should not rely too heavily on them, I am going to allow the use of artifacts on this assignment," said Kanasta with a wide grin.

"This is going to be a puddle of fun," said Kaity, jumping into her partner's arms.

"I just hope I get a target that bleeds," said Sefiwah before giving her girl a peck on the cheek.

"Time for me to give my ego a nitrous boost," said Ego, putting on his headphones.

"Why are you all so cheerful? We might not be able to kill them at all. Some of us may end up dead," said Tempo, shattering the thermometer in his mouth.

"You can't have fun without high stakes. Isn't that right, Boss?" asked Kaity, stretching her head back.

Devlin walked in the room. His hands were shaking with excitement. He took a deep breath and tried to steady them. "As you have all seen, the Freedom Forcers are quite the handful. They've grabbed your attention, haven't they?" he asked, with an enticing flow to his words.

Kaity jumped out from her lover's arms and up to the client. "Yeah, they're way strong! Thanks for giving us a challenge, Mr. Devlin. This is going to be bundles of fun," she said, wagging her tail.

"Please, call me Devlin," he said with a bow. "Hey Kanasta, you wouldn't mind if I provided some assistance, would you?" he asked, bobbing his head along to Kaity's rhythm.

"Would it lower the pay?" asked Kanasta, his eyes slanting.

"Of course it won't lower the pay. Come on, relax. I just realized that there are seven of them and only six of you. Simple math, isn't it? I'll lend you one of my Exps, and he'll take care of whoever you don't. He'll act like a temporary member of your team. Anyone he takes care of will simply be added to your paycheck," said Devlin, tapping his fingers together.

"Very well then; he's welcome aboard. Have the Freedom Forcers fought him yet?"

"They don't even know he exists. I've kept him isolated from his fellow Exps. I couldn't risk him having bonds to anyone but his creator. He could singlehandedly take out all the Freedom Forcers," said Devlin with a proud grin.

"If he's so strong, then why did you call us? We already got the money for the job. Boss, come on, let's go," said Tempo, smacking Kanasta's shoulder.

"We can still get paid double! Did you forget?" asked Kanasta with a slight smile.

"Good point. Let's do this thing," said Tempo, slamming his fists together.

Ego slid off his headphones and turned to Devlin. "If your Exp is so great, then why haven't you sent him after the Freedom Forcers?"

"I don't just want to capture them. I want to break their spirit. A little fresh air and a nice bath in the lake should have given them some hope. Now that they've had their taste of freedom, it's time to tear it from their grasp! Riufen, introduce yourself!"

The door screeched open and the Exp entered the room.

Riufen was tall and firm like bamboo. He had long silver hair and empty white eyes. A topknot wrapped in bones, and a bony faceplate around the edges of his face, gave him the appearance of a traditional samurai. Teeth wrapped around his head to form a headband. At the center of the headband was a crest with *giri* written in the ancient pictographic characters of kanji.

Riufen's body was heavily built, despite having cracks throughout. Intricately woven metacarpals were worn as shoulder guards. Ribs covered his back like an exoskeleton. Four samurai faulds guarded his torso. His feet were stationed in humble wooden sandals. The warrior's stoic pose and rocklike skin gave him the appearance of a statue.

"It is an honor to work with you," said Riufen, bowing down to them one at a time.

"He seems to be the type who follows orders. Welcome to the Viper Squad!" said Kanasta, placing an arm on the warrior's shoulder.

Riufen grabbed the arm on impulse, putting his other hand to the back of Kanasta's neck.

"Careful, he isn't used to people touching him," said Devlin, snapping his fingers.

Riufen released his ally's arm. His head then slammed against the ground. "I will take full responsibility for my transgressions," he said, his blood leaking on the metal tiles.

"No insult was perceived. Stand proud, Warrior," said Kanasta.

Riufen shot up from the floor into a bow. "The mistake will not be repeated. Thank you for your mercy," he said as the wound on his forehead healed.

Devlin clapped his hands together. "Now that we've finished introductions, there is something I want to elaborate. I expected you to fail the first attempt, but I know the next time around you'll give it your all. There are two things I want to make very clear. If you defeat my Exps and don't kill them, then I'll give you twice the initial payment I offered. That will give you triple the pay. I know…I'm very generous. Also, if you happen to kill Exp 8…you get nothing," he said, his smile unchanged.

"What's going to stop us from just killing you and taking it?" asked Tempo, right up in the client's face.

Riufen got up and stood at his master's side. His fists tightened.

"I'm glad we have an understanding. Now considering my personal samurai has never fought before, I want to test him out against the Freedom Forcers first. It's become a tradition, an initiation of sorts. Granted I should have given Pharma some training, but I digress. This is just going to be a field test, that's all. You don't have to worry about him stealing your job. I'll tell him to go easy on them so they have plenty of energy when they fight you. Riufen, play nice with your siblings," said Devlin, patting him on the head.

"I will follow any order you give me, Kanasta-sama," said Riufen with a bow.

"Kanasta will be just fine."

"I can't wait to watch him fight. Viper Squad, choose your targets," said Kanasta, passing out a picture of each Exp. "We need only wait till they arrive to save Karson. We will use the lab's arena to exterminate them. This will be your first purely close range assault, so be ready for a real fight," he said, grabbing the last picture.

"Yay, they're naked pics. Wow, even her nippies are purple," said Kaity as she gawked at Nina's incubation picture.

Devlin stepped in front of Kanasta. "Might I suggest otherwise. Why not send them a challenge note attached to Karson? Exp 8 won't be able to resist."

"My client does not control how my team completes the mission."

"It was just a suggestion."

"And what if they refuse?"

138

"Exp 8 is too hardheaded to refuse. But even if he did, you guys can still hunt down his group of rebels. I just think having them come to us will give them a false sense of security."

Kanasta twiddled his thumbs. "Kaity, I'll leave tending to Karson to you. Send him to the Freedom Forcers with a note," he said, shoving the hostage toward her.

"Roger, sir," said Kaity with a salute, grabbing the hostage.

"I'll make sure it gets done," said Sefiwah with a nod.

"Finally, I get to see my battle arena in action. Kanasta, grab a paintbrush. I want its first battle to be legendary. Oh, and you should have your assassins take a look at the arenas. Some may be more suitable than others," said Devlin.

"You heard him. Pick an arena and wait there," said Kanasta with a wave of his arm.

The other assassins picked up their photos and began their leave, brimming with excitement.

"Kaity, I've got to prepare the battlefields. Please, be careful. And don't forget to have lots of fun," said Devlin, holding the door open for her.

"I won't," said Kaity, patting his head with her tail.

"Kanasta, I leave the rest in your hands. Bye, Kaity, I'll um, see you later," said Devlin, waving nervously.

"Sayonara, Devi-kun!" exclaimed Kaity, rushing up and hugging him gently.

"Kaity, we are to treat our client with respect. Devlin is a man, not a plushy," said Kanasta with a stern finger.

"I love it! Thanks for the new name, Kaity," said Devlin, hugging her tightly before leaving.

"He seems harmless enough," said Sefiwah, putting her knife away.

"Alright, I've got a lot of prep work. Head to your arena as soon as you've delivered the note," said Kanasta before leaving the room.

Kaity jumped onto the table, looking precariously at the unconscious Exp. "What happens if I push this button?" she asked with a tilt of the head.

"Kaity, this is serious," said Sefiwah, tilting her lover's head up with one finger.

"But it's calling me," said Kaity, eyes transfixed.

"No means no," said Sefiwah, placing her hand on her girl's shoulder.

Kaity pushed the Button and the hostage exploded.

Sefiwah grabbed her soul mate and jumped to the floor, shielding her with her body.

Kaity squeezed out from her lover's grip. "Wow, that was so pretty. It's too bad it broke," she said with a frown.

"Don't do it again. REVIVE," said Sefiwah.

All of Karson's pieces were brought together. It was as if he never blew up.

"I'm alive?" asked Karson, lifting his arms in amazement.

"Yes, and if you move you'll die. Kaity, you need to be careful. My ability has its limitations, auuh," said Sefiwah.

"Again!" cheered Kaity as she pushed the red button.

Karson screamed out in rage as he exploded.

Sefiwah stood in front of Kaity and knocked aside the projectile shrapnel.

"Yay! Let's do it again!" Kaity jumped on her back and rubbed against her face.

"Did I mention I swiped some candy off Devlin's desk?" asked Sefiwah, grabbing her partner's hand.

Kaity plopped the butterscotch hard candy into her mouth. She bit it in half and stuck out her tongue. "Do you want some?" she asked, leaning in for a kiss.

"I only eat what I kill," said Sefiwah, turning her head away.

"Um, Sefi-chan, could you please revive him?" asked Kaity, batting her eyelashes.

"I'm glad to see you're having fun with your new toy, but we have to write a note. And don't call me Sefi-chan," said Sefiwah, turning away with a light blush.

"But we're all alone," said Kaity, snuggling against her.

"Devlin's watching us from somewhere," said Sefiwah, scanning the area.

"Hi Devi-kun!" hollered Kaity, waving around the room at non-existent cameras.

"We have a note to write," said Sefiwah, tapping her partner's shoulder.

"One last time, please," said Kaity with clasped hands.

"I just can't say no to you. REVIVE," said Sefiwah and thus Karson was reanimated once more.

"Save meheehee!" pleaded Karson.

"It only hurts for a second, and then you are free. That is the mercy of death," said Sefiwah with a slight smile.

"Let's push it together!" exclaimed Kaity, bouncing up and down in her chair.

"Alright, but this is the last time," said Sefiwah, grabbing her girl's cheek. Kaity nodded.

They put their hands together and gently pushed the Button.

Karson exploded violently.

The flames from his remains shot up to the ceiling. The sprinklers from above activated.

Before a drop could fall on Kaity's head, Sefiwah put her arms around her.

"Aw, I love you too." Kaity hopped up and licked her cheek. "Sefi-chan, look."

The water spurts had created a miniature rainbow just above Karson's smoldering remains.

"Wow, it's so beautiful," said Kaity, leaning back into her lover and looking into her eyes.

"It's too colorful," said Sefiwah, trying to fan it away. She then sat down in the chair and pulled out a pen from her bandages.

"So, we've got to revive Karson so we can hang him, right?" Kaity brought her legs over her girlfriend's head. She wrapped them around her partner's shoulders and lifted herself up. "Seems kind of strange."

"You're right. What is the point of being hanged if you are already dead? The whole point of public hanging is for the spectators."

"Do you want to watch him croak?" asked Kaity with a grin.

"As long as I do it with you," said Sefiwah, running her hand up lover's squishy butt.

"Hey, hey, Sefiwah, what happens after people get hanged?"

"I'm not certain. I would expect a burial and hopefully a simple one, but many people cremate their dead. Ugh, it's such a wasteful practice," said Sefiwah, wiping away a stray tear.

"You were going to bring him back now, remember?" asked Kaity, hunching over and rubbing noses with her beloved.

"First, let's write the note so you don't get distracted," said Sefiwah.

"Oh…alright," said Kaity, falling off the chair into a cartwheel. She then leaped up and swiped a blank page from the desk. The playful assassin leaned over the paper and wrote nonstop.

Sefiwah peered over her shoulder. "Did I see 'Nina?' Are you writing her a love note?"

"Maybe," said Kaity, turning to her with a toothy grin.

"Let me see it." Sefiwah's hand moved in a flash.

Kaity moved her hand around, dodging her girlfriend's every attempt. She jumped out of the chair and stuffed it into her skin suit. "You really want it?" she asked, pushing out her chest.

"No, you can keep it now." Sefiwah approached her lover and leaned into a kiss.

141

"So, now that we're done, can we blow up Karson again?" asked Kaity as soon as they broke apart.

"Good enough, it's not a love note," said Sefiwah, handing back the letter.

"What…when did you…how did…?" asked Kaity, checking her suit for the note.

"My targets die before they can even feel the pain. Grace is needed for a proper hit, hmmhmm," said Sefiwah, flicking her kitten's nose.

"You are so sneaky, heehee."

"Now, let's blow up Karson together," said Sefiwah, pressing up against her partner.

"You mean it?" asked Kaity with shimmering eyes.

"We'll do it on the way there. Let's get going, my little kitten," said Sefiwah, grasping her partner's hand.

"Roger!" said Kaity with a salute.

Chapter 13: Riufen

The Freedom Forcers arrived outside Devlin's lab.

Exp 8 put his hand to the multi-layered steel wall. He looked all the way up. There was not an entrance to be found. "I guess we are at the wrong side. That or Devlin has shutters."

"This is ridiculous! Karson's tracks disappear here. What if his plan was to lead us to Devlin's lab? What are we supposed to do then?" asked Nina, turning to the team captain with fierce eyes.

"Then we walked into his trap. It doesn't really matter. Those assassins don't stand a chance against us. Devlin has run out of options," said Exp 8, throwing his arms over his head.

"Big brother, you're so brave!" exclaimed Kawai as she embraced him.

"Why would you want to hug him when you could hug me?" asked Nina with open arms.

"Can I have a hug too?" asked Atatasuki, fidgeting with his fingers.

"I don't hug trash," said Kawai, turning to him and sticking out her tongue.

Exp 8 slapped Kawai across the face. "I won't let this continue. You need to treat our brother with respect," he said with a firm finger.

Kawai backed away as her eyes watered up. "This is the first time you've slapped me. I'm so happy! Aoouuhaha," she said, holding her cheek with blissful longing.

"Why is no one paying attention to me?" asked Nina with puffed up cheeks, throwing down her arms.

"Kawai, this is not a joke. Atatasuki is your brother. There's no excuse for the way you treat him," said Exp 8, gripping her arm.

"Ooooh, am I going to get a spanking now?" asked Kawai, pushing out her butt.

"How can you be so heartless?" asked Exp 8, turning away from her.

"Don't play this game with me. I told you my feelings for you and yet you ignore them. You're not cute when you're a hypocrite...okay, you are. But you should still practice what you preach," she said, blowing her beloved a kiss.

"So, where did those assassins run off to? We should just kill them and get going," said Bob, searching the treetops.

"Let them come to us. Bob, why don't you go see what Devlin's up to. If the coast is clear, we'll storm his lab!" exclaimed Atatasuki, thrusting his arm in the air.

"Good thinking, I'll be right back," said Bob before going through the wall.

"Anyone ever noticed how on the front side of Devlin's lab there is a deserted canyon, but behind there's a frungle. How bizarre is that?" asked Exp 8.

"Ah, I even love how slow you are," said Kawai, leaning on his shoulder.

"Don't forget about the stadium on the right side of the lab," said Ada.

"The what! What could Devlin possibly need a stadium for, his ego?"

"Oh, you are such a kidder," said Ada.

"Guys, what about Karson? What do we do if we run into him again?" asked Atatasuki.

"It's not like he's stronger than us. Plus, we're not sure if he is a spy," said Exp 8.

"You're protecting him again. Maybe you're the spy. Wait, can the leader be the spy?…Give me a moment," said Atatasuki, tapping his chin.

"It doesn't matter if Karson is on our side or not. If we play our cards right, we can have him at our beck and call," said Nina, snapping her fingers and then blowing a kiss.

"What are you talking about? Ugh, forget I asked," said Exp 8.

"We should hear her out. She turned Devlin into a little puppy dog. Not even I could seduce him with my adorable dance. Maybe Nina has a plan," said Kawai.

"It's simple really. We ignore Karson. Nothing is quite as attractive as repulsion. If we push him away, he'll come to us. It's foolproof," said Nina with a hair flip.

"Alright, we'll give it a shot. But let's not get him too pissed off," said Exp 8, patting his brother's shoulder.

Riufen moved through the bushes without a sound.

"Um, who is he?" asked Atatasuki, watching as the large figure emerged from the foliage.

"Is this another assassin? Or is it an Exp?" asked Nina, her hand poised to pull off her shirt.

"I am Riufen," he said, looking at the rebel commander while bowing. "I have heard many tales of your exploits. It is my honor to finally meet you."

"I think this guy is an Exp. It's good to meet you too," said Exp 8, returning the bow.

"I am sorry…but we cannot have a one-on-one battle to the death at this time. I will fight all of you at once…without killing you. Devlin needs me to stall for time. Please take no offense. If it were up to me, this would be a fair and honorable fight," said Riufen, putting his hand to the back of his neck.

"No offense is taken. The Freedom Forcers don't like to fight to the death. So, if we win, will you join us?" asked Exp 8.

"I cannot. My loyalty to Devlin-sama is absolute. But if you do win, you will earn my respect."

"Oooh, you are such a sweetheart," said Ada.

"Well then, let's get going. I'm starting to enjoy the thrill of battle," said Exp 8, twisting his wrists.

"This will be my first real fight. It shall be glorious!" exclaimed Riufen with a firm stance.

"You're all that stands in our way of defeating Devlin! You are going down!" exclaimed Exp 8, jumping in place.

"Yes! Let us….wait…one of your warriors is missing. Do any of you know where the eyeball went?" asked Riufen, moving the rebel commander out of the way.

"He'll be back soon, but right now you have to deal with us," said Exp 8, cracking his knuckles.

"Enough stalling! *Super Sexy Slo-mo Flash!*" exclaimed Nina as she ripped open her shirt erotically, exposing her lacy bra.

Atatasuki fell backwards and slammed against the ground.

"So…umm…you want me to take my armor off?" asked Riufen, squinting.

"Not another one," said Nina, her eye twitching with frustration.

"Get up!" yelled Kawai, slamming her tail against her useless sibling's chest.

"I'm up!" exclaimed Atatasuki, leaping to his feet. "Let's see how you handle the flames of a failure!" He ran up and slammed his burning palm into the samurai's chest.

"That's a good arm. Have you ever thought of wielding a sword?" asked Riufen, looking down at him.

"Muffins are the only weapon for me," said Atatasuki, rapidly slamming his palms into his opponent.

"An edible weapon? You might want to reconsider," said Riufen, unmoved by the barrage of punches.

Exp 8 ran up to his opponent, holding a medium-sized orb in his hand.

Riufen knocked the orb aside. He then grabbed onto the leader's arm and flung him back and forth, slamming him against the ground repeatedly.

"Leave my brother alone!" Kawai zoomed up to the swordsman and socked him in the face with her hardened tail.

Riufen tossed Exp 8 aside, sending him crashing into Atatasuki. He then grabbed the girl's head in his hand.

"Let her go!" Atatasuki padded the enemy with his attacks, desperately trying to free his sister.

"Calm yourself; I'm not allowed to kill anyone," said Riufen, slamming Kawai into Atatasuki.

"W-wow sis, you look even prettier up close," said Atatasuki, heating up.

Riufen lifted up the copper brawler and flung him into his leader.

"This is just too much. I'm going to save my energy for later," said Kawai with heavy breaths as she floated away.

Nina jumped down from a tree branch onto the swordsman's back. She bent over, her lips just about to touch his. "So do you feel it now?"

"What am I supposed to be feeling?" asked Riufen, grabbing the back of her head.

"Ugh! You're supposed to want me!" yelled Nina, grabbing his face.

"I am sorry, but the path of the samurai is far too narrow. There is no room for love on it," said Riufen, bowing his head before flinging her to the ground.

"So what then, I'm not good enough! You're like eight hundred years old. What gives you the right to turn me down! I'm the sexiest thing you'll ever see!" yelled Nina, pulling down her bra.

"I have no need for such things," said Riufen, stepping on her exposed chest.

"You are an insult to all old men!" screamed Nina as she squirmed about.

"Let me see her breasts!" Atatasuki rushed at the swordsman, holding two burning muffins in his fists.

Riufen sent Nina into Atatasuki's legs, knocking him over.

"Get off of me!" yelled Nina, pushing off her ally. She pulled up her bra and then rushed at the samurai, anger flaring in her eyes.

Riufen thrust his fist forward like a battering ram.

Nina flipped over his fist and then spun around in the air. "It's over!" she yelled, dive-bombing into the enemy from above.

Riufen slid out of the way of her attack and then jabbed both his fists into her back.

The tree behind her was stripped of its leaves from the force of the blow.

Nina fell to the ground, her mouth wide open and her eyes glazed out.

"Is she dead? I apologize. I was only trying to defeat her. It is dishonorable to kill someone after promising their safety. I have defiled my code," said Riufen, his head dropping.

"He just beat Nina!" exclaimed Atatasuki, hugging a tree.

Exp 8 pulled his brother off the tree. "Keep your eyes peeled! I'm going to show him my new attack!" He charged at the swordsman. His turrets rose out from his shoulders and fired an array of energy beams.

"I had hoped you wouldn't resort to projectiles," said Riufen as he calmly dodged each bullet.

"Damn it! I have to get in closer!" exclaimed Exp 8, taking cover behind the barren tree.

Atatasuki's chest made a loud ringing noise.

"Does that mean your final attack is ready? Is that ringing sound your inner battle cry?" asked Riufen, his eyes wide with excitement.

"Yes it is! It means the muffins are ready!" Atatasuki reached into his chest and tossed the hot muffins at the swordsman one after another.

Riufen dodged all the muffins as they were flung forward, his feet not moving an inch. He grabbed the last one and plopped it in his mouth after he kicked the copper brawler's legs.

Atatasuki tripped, about to fall to the grass when the samurai's leg moved like a whip and sent him flying at his brother.

Exp 8 activated his jets, avoiding a collision with Atatasuki's legs by an inch. "You can't dodge at this range!" he exclaimed, his turrets locking on.

Riufen leaped off the ground in an instant. He put his hand around Exp 8's face and slammed him down on Atatasuki. He then rubbed his stomach with delight. "That muffin was superb. You should follow the path of the chef," he said with a smile.

"Finally! Someone with taste buds," said Atatasuki, crying from both joy and pain.

"You're going to lose now!" yelled Exp 8, creating a massive orb with his turrets.

Riufen hit the orb aside without detonating it. He then bowed in respect. "I am sorry, but my time is up. Thank you for the glorious battle. Please, don't be discouraged by my performance," he said before running off.

"Sorry, thank you, and please...that guy is very polite," said Atatasuki with a grin.

"He is just the sweetest!" exclaimed Ada.

"Yeah, but he's also incredibly strong. I don't know if we can beat him," said Exp 8, his eyes mirroring his hopelessness.

"Not with that attitude we won't! If we all work together, then nothing can stop us!" cheered Atatasuki, putting his hand out.

Kawai smacked his hand aside with her tail. "Don't be an idiot! If he was told to, he would have killed us all."

"She's right. He was holding back the whole time. How did Devlin make someone so strong?" asked Exp 8, his hand to his chest.

"Devlin has really outdone himself!" exclaimed Ada with a spin.

Kawai floated up to her big brother. She put her elbow on his shoulder. "I enjoyed our little rebellion. It was lots of fun! But now we should stop playing around. The game is over. Devlin has won. Let's just accept our losses and get on with our lives," she said, gripping his cheeks.

"I understand what you're saying, but what about freedom?" asked Exp 8 with watery eyes.

"We don't really need it. We can just live here at the lab. Honestly, I don't know anywhere else we could fit in," said Kawai with a shrug.

"She's absolutely right! What are we going to do with this freedom anyway? Where are we going to go that's sooo great?" asked Atatasuki.

"You guys don't get it at all. Freedom isn't a place! It's a mindset. It doesn't matter where we go. We just have to get away from Devlin. Now, are you with me or not?" asked Exp 8, pushing out his fist.

Kawai straddled his arm. "I'm always with you. If we die, then we die together! I'll go get Nina up," she said, giving him a kiss before flying off.

"You can't escape the desire to be free, can you?" asked Atatasuki with a smirk.

"No...I can't. And I don't want to escape it. It doesn't hold me back; it just pushes me forward," said Exp 8, hitting his chest with his fist.

"Forward is relative. If we don't have a direction, then we're going nowhere. Ugh...why do I even bother?" asked Atatasuki, lowering his head.

"As long as we keep moving, we'll be going somewhere," said Exp 8, putting his arm around his brother's shoulders.

Atatasuki shoved him off and walked away. He turned around with eyes aflame. "You're so damn stubborn! You're going to get us all killed!" he yelled, slamming his hand on a nearby tree.

A loud plunk broke through the rustling of the leaves.

Karson hanged above them with a noose fastened around his neck, dangling lifelessly. "I'm so happy to see you guys!" he exclaimed, springing to life.

"Zombie!" screamed Atatasuki, jumping behind his fearless leader.

"He's not a zombie. Karson, what happened to you? You just...disappeared," said Exp 8, his eyes slanting.

"It was absolutely horrible! I was trailing one of those hit men, but it was a trap! Those damn assassins took me away. Oh, you must have been looking everywhere for me. I do apologize for all the grief I've caused," said Karson, swaying back and forth.

"I totally forgot about him," said Atatsuki, snapping his fingers.

"Yeah, sorry…we got sort of sidetracked," said Exp 8, winking at his sister.

"Don't run off like an idiot. If you die, that's your problem," said Kawai, turning away from him.

"Oh yeah, I knew we were missing something," said Nina, just getting up.

Bob suddenly emerged from the grass below them.

"Zombie! No wait, ghost! Oh, it's only you, Bob. Phew! Don't scare me like that," said Atatsuki, holding his chest.

"I didn't mean to scare you, oh and sorry I took so long. The coast was not at all clear. I would have come sooner, but I went searching for something. Pardon me…but I forgot what it was we were looking for. Hey, Karson, do you know…oh my god, that's it!"

"At least the assassins didn't ignore me. You guys didn't even look for me," said Karson, his whole body drooping.

Exp 8 grabbed the gunman's arm. "Bob looked back in the lab for something that was missing, so in a way we did look for you."

"Isn't it a little convenient how Karson showed up so suddenly?" asked Atatsuki with a suspicious gaze.

"Not this again! I was captured! The assassins dropped me here on purpose. I didn't go to them in order to get hanged!" yelled Karson.

"So then you got hanged just so we would trust you. You're very clever. But it looks like we've finally cracked you," said Atatsuki with a nod.

"Karson is our ally. As long as he fights with us, I don't care if he is a spy," said Exp 8.

"I'm glad someone somewhat trusts me. So…what did I miss?" asked Karson.

"Devlin has a new Exp. He is very powerful," said Exp 8.

"Oh yes, I almost forgot. My real friends, the ones who don't ignore me, hanged me here so I could deliver this note to you," said Karson, turning around.

"That sounds like a declaration to me!" exclaimed Atatsuki.

"Shut up! What does the note say?" asked Kawai, leaning over her brother's shoulder.

Exp 8 pulled the note off Karson's back. "'Dear Freedom Forcers, we challenge you to close quarters combat. If you accept, meet us inside of Devlin's lab. Nina, I'm going to have tons of fun with you. With lots and lots of love, Kaity Rin Rainbow Viper.' Wow Nina, you already have another fan, heheh."

"Of course I do, there is not a soul that can resist me. That is except for you…and now that blind samurai," she said, grinding her teeth.

"Riufen just has the mind of a warrior. He's been completely brainwashed by Devlin."

"Maybe one day you will be able to fathom the mountainous power of my sexiness!"

"You mean your monotonous power," said Exp 8, rolling his eyes.

"I miss Devlin; it's so fun when you're the one playing hard to get. If you keep this up...I might go back to him," said Nina, flicking his forehead.

"First lesson on how to be sexy: spread joy," said Ada, looking up at her beautiful comrade.

Nina whipped out a notepad from her bra and wrote it down. "Go on. Tell me more," she said, her eyes widening.

"If you want more lessons, you'll have to stay with us," said Ada.

"Of course I will. I would never leave," said Nina with a bow.

"Can someone help me down now?" asked Karson, still dangling on the rope.

Exp 8 jumped up to the tree branch and tried to undo the knot. He squirmed and struggled, getting more and more frustrated. "Damn it! I won't give up!"

"Let me help." Kawai floated up to the noose and untangled it in an instant.

Karson plopped to the ground.

Exp 8 looked at Kawai with awe-filled eyes. "How did you do that? I had no idea you were so amazing!" he exclaimed as he embraced his sister.

"See? We complete each other. Auuuh."

"So, what do you all say? We could handle a little CQC, right? I bet we'll have a stunning victory!" exclaimed Karson, throwing his arm in the air.

"Yo sis, can you untie my faulty wires?" asked Atatasuki, opening his stomach.

"Do it yourself," said Kawai, sitting on her brother's shoulder.

"Nobody listens to me," said Karson, his head dropping.

"Wow, knowing that there's someone who can untie knots makes me feel empowered. We could handle a little CQC, right? I bet we'll kick their asses!" exclaimed Exp 8.

"Alright, but if I die...I won't be able to say I told you so. But I did...or would have," said Atatasuki with a nod.

"They're just humans. I'll make them submit to me!" exclaimed Kawai with a spin.

"Can't keep my fan waiting," said Nina with a smirk.

"This will be both honorable and easy. Let's go!" exclaimed Karson.

"Glad there's no disagreement! It's time to show Devlin we're not afraid! Let's go kick some ass!" cheered Exp 8, beckoning his troops.

The Freedom Forcers rushed into Devlin's lab through the same hole they had escaped from.

The hole behind them was suddenly surrounded by the extremely visible force field.

The Freedom Forcers were completely boxed in by the force field, unless: Bob phased through it, Exp 8 blew it up, Atatasuki punched it with a burning fist, Karson shot a missile at it, or Nina tossed her explosive clothing on it. Otherwise, there was no escape.

The team looked above to see fresh banners and neon arrows.

The arrows led them down the hallways, up the stairs, down another hallway, and up another flight of stairs, until they finally arrived at a decorative door.

"What if Devlin isn't just being overconfident? What if this is a legitimate trap?" asked Atatasuki, his hand on the door.

"We're going to win this," said Exp 8, punching open the door.

The Freedom Forcers entered a pitch-black room. Seven glow-in-the-dark circles were on the floor at the room's center.

The lights came up. Inside every circle was the name of a different member of their team. There was a metal table in the corner of the room and a digital clock embedded in the wall above it.

Devlin entered the room from a hidden door that was indistinguishable from the steel wall. He closed it gently and turned to the Freedom Forcers with a confident smirk. He walked up to Exp 8 until he was a mere foot away. "You have damaged my lab, ruined my chance to end my father's debt, and even caused my most obedient Exps to spontaneously betray me. You have ruined everything! But I can't kill you."

"Is this going anywhere?" asked Exp 8, twisting his wrists.

"Your revolt stops here! I've found the solution to our little dilemma. I've hired the ultimate assassins to eliminate everyone you hold dear. You've made it quite apparent that the only way to make you submit is to crush your spirit. Step forward or run away…it's your choice! Know that whichever you choose, I will not give up until I have you in my possession! Either surrender now or watch as your fellow Exps are destroyed," said Devlin with fierce eyes.

Exp 8 grabbed his creator's wrist, making him cringe instinctively. "We are all willing to die for our beliefs."

"I'm not; I am too sexy to die for anyone's beliefs," said Nina, rubbing saliva on her forehead wound.

"Lesson on being sexy number two: stop telling everyone you're sexy. They can tell just by looking at you. Hmmhmmhymm," said Ada.

"Got it! Redundancy is repugnancy!" exclaimed Nina, writing it down.

"To be honest…I'm not too fond of dying myself. I've tried it before and it's, well…just not my thing," said Karson, stepping up to his commander.

"I don't plan on dying!" exclaimed Atatasuki, cracking his neck.

"No mere mortal could kill me," said Bob.

"And I won't rest until my brother is free," said Kawai, giving her beloved a kiss on the cheek.

"You've brainwashed nearly all of them into dying for you. I may not be able to kill you, Exp 8, but everyone else is on the chopping block now. I didn't want it to come to this, but you've left me no choice," said Devlin, turning away from the rebel commander.

Exp 8 grabbed Devlin's arm. "I don't know what you want me for, but whatever it is—I won't let you succeed! You won't be able to stop us. You are merely a human just like those assassins. We know this is obviously a trap. But it's so pathetic we decided to just walk right into it."

"Um…Devlin. Why is there a circle for me? Do you want me to fight too?" asked Ada.

"You have already broken our promise. Go ahead and come out. You can die with the rest of your friends," said Devlin with a dark glare.

"Fine, but I'm not trying to upset you. I might as well fight one of them if they're weak, right?" Ada disconnected from Exp 8. She fell to the floor and lit up. She then slowly transformed into her humanoid form. "I, uh, hope I don't disturb anyone," she said, crossing her legs.

"Ah, Ada, your angelic voice is only matched by your radiant body," said Atatasuki, hugging her tightly.

"I feel so flat," said Kawai, pushing up her breasts with a frown.

"She's so beautiful…she's like an explosion around a pile of enemy casualties," said Karson, gripping his chest.

"Glad to see you back in your original form," said Bob.

"Ada, if you use your womanly body to seduce my brother…I'll kill you," said Kawai, with a sweet smile and dagger-like eyes.

"I wouldn't dream of it," said Ada aghast.

"Ada, don't think I'll show you any mercy," said Devlin, grabbing her chin. "You will be given the same treatment as the rest of the traitors."

"Wow, I'm really starting to feel like a valuable member of the team," said Ada, clasping her hands to her chest.

"Need attention," said Nina, cradling herself in a corner.

Ada broke free from Atatasuki's arms and went to Nina. "I'm sorry. I don't know why everyone's being so sweet to me. Just breathe in. I'm here for you. Lesson number three: be nice and more people will like you."

"You truly are a goddess of beauty," said Nina, rubbing her face against Ada's womanly legs.

"I wrote each of your names on a different circle. If you really want to play along, go ahead," said Devlin with a grin.

"Sure, why not? We'll go along with your stupid game," said Exp 8.

All of the Freedom Forcers stood on the circles corresponding to their names. A clear barrier shot up from beneath and surrounded them.

"Hah, I planned on having the assassins underestimate all of you. I was hoping that you, in turn, would underestimate them. And it worked. You have all willingly walked into your defeat!"

Exp 8 turned to his teammates and nodded, sure of victory.

The elevator descended, bringing each Exp to a different arena.

"The groups collide! With opposing goals, in order for one to succeed the other must fail," said Devlin from the loudspeaker.

Chapter 14: CQC

Atatasuki plummeted into the battlefield below.

The room looked like a speedway. There was a grainy, black road of asphalt and a dusty racecar. Reinforced metal fences were around the racetrack. Neon lines split the two lanes throughout the circular raceway.

Atatasuki looked up to see a human ten feet in front of him. He brushed off the dust from his legs and outstretched his hand. "I'm Atatasuki, who might you be, stranger?"

"Me? I am Ego. And ego is Latin for I. Therefore, I am actually addressing myself as I."

"Yeah, but I don't speak Latin. What are we talking about again?"

"Long story short, I, Ego, am the guy who is going to take you out. I don't kill people like the other assassins, but you're hardly a person," said Ego, flicking the weapon's forehead.

"Yep, I'm more of a state-of-the-art microwave. And this microwave is set to kick your ass. Good one, huh? I kept that one cooking for a long time," said Atatasuki with a nod.

"Don't be so cocky. Look above you...there are spikes, dude," said Ego, pointing up.

Atatasuki squinted to see the spikes. "Those can't hurt me. You won't even lift me off the ground."

"I don't need to lift you off the ground, little man." Ego jumped to the ceiling and ripped off one of the spikes. "GROWING SELF-RESPECT!"

The four-inch spike grew until it was longer than Atatasuki.

"It's...it's..." said Atatasuki.

"Huge," said Ego as he dropped down. As soon as his feet hit the floor, he lunged himself forward.

The enlarged spike was shoved straight through the living weapon and into the ground.

A spurt of blood from Atatasuki's mouth sprayed on the assassin.

"Yo man, don't mess up my shirt. This is custom designed."

"So is my body, and you really messed it up," said Atatasuki, gripping onto the spike.

"Hey, before I kill you, do you want to see something cool?" asked Ego with a grin.

"As long as it's not sharp," said Atatasuki, seething in agony.

Ego reached behind his back and grabbed his skateboard. He tossed it in the air, jumped up and landed right on top of it. "In order to skate properly, you need both concentration and balance. And you need the exact same things to be a proper assassin. So if you think about it, I've been training for this job without even knowing it. It's funny how things work out, isn't it?" he asked, spinning the skateboard beneath him.

"It won't budge," said Atatasuki as he pulled on the spike.

"Allow me." Ego grabbed the blunt end of the spike. His hands enlarged before he yanked the spike out from the ground.

"Thanks, I think I can handle it from here," said Atatasuki as he pulled the spike out from his chest inch by inch.

"I've never killed anyone before, but it could be fun. I'm always up for trying new things." Ego slammed his palm into the spike, thrusting it deeper into his target. He then pulled Atatasuki off the ground. "Let's go for a ride." He skated around with his target still hoisted on the spike.

Atatasuki dragged along the asphalt, getting scrapes all over his armored body.

"In order to keep my balance, I simply lean to the side with less weight. Are you listening? I'm trying to teach you something, man," said Ego, looking down.

"I don't care about your trivial hobbies!" exclaimed Atatasuki, shielding his face.

"Skating enhances your speed, reaction time, balance, and strength. It helps with just about everything." Ego kicked off the ground and slammed his competitor down.

Atatasuki pushed off the ground as soon as he made contact. The tendons in his arm stretched, but they didn't break. The passionate prototype grabbed onto the spike with super heated hands.

"Not quick enough, dude." Ego flung the spike downward.

The spike bore into the asphalt, bringing the Exp back to square one.

"Can you get to the point already?" asked Atatasuki as his hands melted the spike.

"Alright, long story short: you and your Exp pals are nothing compared to us. Conclusion: you can't beat me. I have experience, man. You just have your fancy little equipment. And keep in mind that a child with a gun only shoots himself," said Ego, skating circles around his opponent.

"I hate pretentions wannabes! *SUPER MICROWAVE!*" Atatasuki's body temperature skyrocketed, melting the spike into silver goop.

"I see you have an artifact as well. But your toys aren't going to change the tides of this battle. Let me show you why I'm the greatest.

GROWING SELF-RESPECT," said Ego, pointing to the ceiling while bending his legs.

The spikes above expanded, stabbing into the ground. Five of them shot into the living weapon, but they melted on contact.

Atatasuki walked toward his pompous enemy. "I don't have an artifact. What you are witnessing is a glitch. I overheat because my body wasn't installed with a proper cooling fan. Nearly died from a heat-stroke more times than I can remember. I experienced those terrifying moments of uncertainty. I have been in a state between life and death more times than years you've been alive. In order to surpass my obstacles, I embraced them. I purposely overheated my body to the brink! I willingly drove my body to a state of collapse. I cultured my flaws. Now they define me."

"How can you be defined by your flaws?"

"Behold, I have turned my innate glitches into a formidable weapon. You may have years of practice, but I have the burning passion of a defect. My mistakes shall surpass all your training," said Atatasuki as he melted through the forest of spikes.

"Don't talk down to me. I have trained with a skateboard since I was two. My first word was 'extreme!' I have memories and I have a purpose. You were just made to be used. So stop struggling and accept defeat, little man."

"I won't lose to you!" yelled Atatasuki, his eyes enflamed.

"I'm gonna knock you out of that state of denial," said Ego as his arm enlarged.

"I am not in denial. I know that I will surpass you. Just like one day…I will surpass my brother. My glitches are what make me unique and my uniqueness is what separates me from Exp 8. I will overcome him and win my sister's love. She will see that a miscarriage is better than a prodigy. I will be the machine that lives through its glitches and I will surpass every system!" yelled Atatasuki, burning ten spikes with his expanding heat aura.

"Dude, you are so whack. ᏩᎡᎾᎳᎥNᏩ ᏚᎬᏞᏞᎬᎬᏚᏢᎬᏟᎢ, ᎽᎾᎽᎾ." Ego flung a yo-yo forward on his middle finger.

It became tire-sized before slamming into the steaming cyborg. The yo-yo melted away by the time it rebounded.

"All those hours wasted on trying to be cool aren't paying up, are they? If you're good at something, don't practice to get better. You should find out what you suck at and try to flaw it even further."

"What the hell are you saying to me, you little shit!"

"A cupcake is, in reality, a muffin with icing and sprinkles. The muffin became bitter by trying to embellish itself. Cupcakes are the fallen angels of dough heaven. They have been tainted by vanity. The masses don't like the bottom part of a muffin, but the muffins don't care! They never change who they are. They don't try to surpass themselves. That is why they are so delicious! You are a cupcake, sprinkled with training and iced with experience. Face it, Ego, you just try to be great. Deep down inside you, there is a flaw waiting to bloom," said Atatasuki, peering at the showoff through a hole he made in a spike.

Ego rushed up to his enemy. "Me? Not great? That must be a joke! Let's see you talk tough now!" He pressed his hands to the target's chest. "*SUPER GROWTH SPURT, ORGANS*!" he yelled with burning hatred in his eyes.

Atatasuki grabbed his stomach as his insides expanded. "Damn it...I need my stomach," he said, falling to his knees.

"I can assassinate without a trace. I'm going to enjoy watching you explode from the inside! Think of it, all those perfect organs becoming bigger and bigger until they blow up. Cool, right?"

"That's exactly my point! You do understand!" exclaimed Atatasuki, struggling to get back to his feet.

"What...damn it...shut up already. You're hurting my head, man!"

"If I have no way to escape the attack, then I'll just have to kill you before I die," said Atatasuki, taking a step forward while holding his stomach in unfathomable pain.

Ada was dropped down into a blindingly white room. It was about as spacious as a greenhouse. Fresh paint was dripping off the walls onto the white, square tile floor.

"This is the Meditation Room! What have you done to it? Where's the rug? Where are all the statues? Did you polish the tiles? The floor's all wet and slippery now," said Ada with a furrowed brow.

"Don't worry about the little things," said Sefiwah, licking the fresh white paint off her fingertips.

"Did you ask for Devlin's permission? This will take hours to clean up," said Ada, wiping a clump of wet paint off the wall.

"What a worrisome creature. Fret not. I will bring you peace in your death."

"Oh, there's really no need to kill me. I'm already a very peaceful program."

"It is a shame that I must drench this tranquil white room with your red blood," said Sefiwah, pronouncing the word *red* with whispery hatred.

"That's strange. Your file says you love shedding blood. Is that incorrect?" asked Ada, bringing up a hologram of the assassin's data.

"The reason that I lick the blood off my victims is because I don't like seeing the color red. Your data is misinformed," said Sefiwah, painting over her self-inflicted wounds.

"That's very interesting. I'd love it if you'd help me clear up the other discrepancies," said Ada, replacing the word *enjoys* with *dislikes*.

"There's no point. I don't care what it says. I know who I am. That's all that matters. Are you prepared to die, Exp?" Sefiwah whipped out a snow-white dagger.

"Just because I take the form of a computer program, doesn't mean I'm weak. I'm just like all the other Exps. I'm not going to die! I hope that doesn't upset you too much," said Ada, twiddling her thumbs.

"You should worry about yourself," said Sefiwah, flinging the dagger at the target's forehead.

Ada slipped on the tiles, falling on her butt and thus dodging the projectile.

"Pathetic."

Ada jumped back to her feet. She ran up to her opponent, readying her fist.

Sefiwah stood with one arm outward and the other pulled back.

Ada tossed a handful of paint at the pale woman, throwing her off guard. She then punched her opponent in the face.

Sefiwah grabbed the Exp's arm as she stabbed the knife forward. She missed and fell over, landing flat on her back.

The knife slipped out from her grip and dropped to the floor, buried in the ocean of white.

"Are you okay? I'm so sorry! I didn't mean to hurt you," said Ada with a bow.

Sefiwah flipped back to her feet and wiped away the blood off her face. She gasped and quickly wiped it on the floor. The assassin then took a deep breath and became relaxed again. "I've never bled without flagellating myself before. I appreciate this. It's so much easier to kill the ones who fight back," she said, moving back into her battle stance.

"Oh, I'm just glad I can help! Even though you're my opponent, you seem so sweet. I would hate to disappoint you."

"You have a very bright soul. I don't want to kill you. But you know too much. You have knowledge that makes me appear weak. I can't allow that information to be leaked. I apologize. I only told you about my aversion to blood so I would have more incentive to kill you. I hope you become an angel in Heaven. Ada, are you ready?"

"Just give me a minute. I don't know if I'm ready yet," said Ada, jumping in place.

"Why must everyone I kill ooze red? Maybe I'll get lucky when I cut you open and find a puddle of white," said Sefiwah, her eyes widening.

"I've never bled before! Maybe it is white!"

"Only one way to find out," said Sefiwah with hollowed out eyes. She ripped off her belt, cutting herself with its jagged spikes. "I only use this whip to punish myself, but I'll make an exception for you. I don't want to see you bleed…so this is the only way," she said with the slightest hint of a smile. She pushed her thumb down on one of the spikes, causing them all to retreat into the whip. She wrapped her whip around her target's legs, tripping her. She then lowered herself on top of the downed enemy. "I sense a light in your soul that is only outshined by Kaity's own. Please, let me confess to you," she said, touching the soulful program's glowing cheek.

"I'll listen to whatever you have to say," said Ada, running her hand through Sefiwah's hair.

Tears dripped from Sefiwah's emotionless eyes. "I hate murder. I don't want to hurt anyone. Please, forgive me."

"Sefiwah, you have to forgive yourself," said Ada, giving her a kiss on the forehead.

"I've tried to rationalize it, but I can't. I've tried becoming cold, but the guilt won't go away. We've killed children. They might have grown into wonderful people! I'll never know what they were capable of. I'll never know how bright their lights would have shined." Tears poured out from her eyes like water from a broken faucet.

"If you hate to kill, then why did you join the Viper Squad?" asked Ada, grabbing the killer's fragile hands.

Sefiwah pulled her hands away and wiped her eyes. "Do not try to understand me. I do not fully understand it. I don't expect you to. Goodbye." She closed her eyes and snapped the target's neck.

"I didn't mean to upset you. I'm sorry," said Ada as she fixed her neck.

"Please, just die. I don't want to shed your blood. I feel…undeserving. I chose you as my opponent so that I wouldn't have to kill a living thing. I was told you were just a program. But your kindness is real! Your benevolence and grace are as real as my love for Kaity. I can feel authenticity in every word you speak. To think there is even purity in software," said Sefiwah with shimmering eyes as she strangled the artificial angel.

"You have nothing to worry about. This won't kill me," said Ada with a smile.

She grabbed the troubled killer in a tight embrace.

"I'm sorry, but I love Kaity more than I should. I've found a purer soul, but I will snuff it out for her sake," said Sefiwah, her pupils still with resolve.

Ada kicked her opponent in the stomach and wrapped her legs around the assassin's neck. "Don't worry. I'll let you go as soon as you're unconscious," she said, flipping over so she was on top.

"A fight between two peacemakers accomplishes nothing. The others know me as a cold killer. I can't have the other assassins thinking I'm soft. I can't fall in love with your radiance. Not after all I've done." Sefiwah grabbed the target's legs. "Please, don't take your death personally."

"Why can't I move?" asked Ada, fear sprouting in her delicate eyes.

Sefiwah stood up with her target on her shoulders. She tossed herself backwards, slamming her target against the ground. She then lifted her target up by the chin. She licked a droplet of paint off the motherly invention's cheek.

"I'm not sure that's edible."

"I can taste its purity, just like I can feel yours. Rest in peace." Sefiwah lifted her leg and then kicked her opponent.

Ada slammed against the gooey white wall. She looked up to see Sefiwah standing in front of her.

"INSTANT KILL," said Sefiwah, closing her eyes as she shoved her pointed hand through the target's chest. She then pulled out, holding her victim's capsule in her delicate grip.

The Exp's blood-soaked corpse fell to the ground.

Sefiwah looked at the red on her hands, a single tear falling from her face.

"The red will not corrupt my soul. No matter what, I will not become accustomed to murder," said Sefiwah, slicing her fingers as she crushed the capsule. She bowed to her victim's body as her eyes watered up. She then frantically licked the blood off her hand.

Karson was sent into a room about the size of a basketball field. A titanium sheet of metal covered his entrance, boxing him in the metal-plated room.

The floor was a flat layer of white sand. The walls were slick with oil.

BoneSaw peered up at the target from beneath the sand.

"Come on out, coward!" yelled Karson, firing warning shots all around him.

BoneSaw leaped out from the sand pile at the target and revealed its saws. Karson instinctually aimed his revolver hand at his metal foe.

Before Karson could fire, the murderous machine hurled its largest saw.

The melon-sized jigsaw sliced off the top of the revolver before stabbing into the titanium wall.

Karson zoomed forward and kicked the compact killer. He loaded up shotgun-arms before his enemy could hit the ground.

As soon as BoneSaw landed, its treads pushed off the ground. It then shot up toward the target like a viper.

Karson fired his shotguns at an intersecting arc, creating a wall of bullets.

A new saw came out from BoneSaw's front and spun around.

Even when defending with the extra saw, the knockback lifted BoneSaw off the ground and sent him flying backwards.

Karson ran at the helpless assassin and kicked him.

As his foot connected, it fired off, pummeling BoneSaw with a full round. Karson then jumped up and fired both his shotguns from between his legs.

BoneSaw was plastered to the ground, but there was not a dent on it. The robot's treads burned rubber as it fought against the impact of the blast. As soon as the mechanical assassin was out of range, it spun around to face the target. Its sides opened up, revealing two swirling jigsaws.

"Go on then. Come at me," said Karson, loading slugs into his arms.

BoneSaw zoomed between the target's legs in a split second.

Gunpowder gushed out of Karson's ankles as his feet slid off. He then fell to the ground face first.

BoneSaw braked hard before spinning out.

"A soldier without feet is as deadly as a turret!" yelled Karson as he rose to his knees.

BoneSaw flipped back up. The dual jigsaws receded back into its side compartments.

"What else have you got? I'm ready for anything," said Karson, cocking his shotguns.

Twenty shuriken-sized saws jutted out from the robot's sides.

"You are becoming a pain, but at least you're not ignoring me, uurgh."

BoneSaw spun around in place, its saws becoming a blur.

"Time for a strategic retreat," said Karson, taking a step back.

BoneSaw shot toward the fleeing target like a renegade top.

Karson attached a revolver to his stub and fired it at the enemy soldier just before colliding.

The impact sent the killer robot off course.

BoneSaws treads screeched as they shot up sand.

Karson attached a revolver to his other stub and then stood up. "That was a good fight. But I do believe it's time to mow you down," he said, putting his arms together. He revved up his Gatling gun as the assassin closed in.

BoneSaw cut into a sand mound and disappeared.

"Where did you go?" asked Karson, blinking to check if his barrel eyes were working.

Karson's feet were cut to shreds from beneath the sand.

Saws sliced upward through the Exp's legs, cleaving them into slabs. The saws receded back into the sand once he was just a torso with arms.

Karson tossed portions of his tattered body at the burrowed robot.

"No injury can stop a true soldier," said Karson with a salute. He pulled off two rocket launchers from his back. The gunman stretched forward to attach bazookas to the stubs that were once his legs. He then scanned the area for his opponent.

BoneSaw shot down from the ceiling, wielding a saw twice its size.

"Thank you for the honorable battle," said Karson, flipping into a handstand.

The rockets disengaged. They crashed into the little robot, exploding on contact.

When the smoke cleared, a smoldering pile of metal was all that remained of the metal assassin.

"It's a good thing I'm a soldier and a medic," said Karson, attaching new guns to recreate his damaged legs.

Chapter 15: Battle-Hardened Warriors

Nina looked around to see a round field of metal. An oak tree rose thirty feet off the ground, its canopy caressing the ceiling. Two sixty-foot sections of metal connected, with the tree at the center. Polished metal extended from the floor, up the walls, and to the ceiling.

Nina took a moment to check herself out as her attacker approached. Once Kaity was within sight, the nimble narcissist looked up. "Is this really our battlefield? It seems so desolate. Come to think of it, the tree is the single point of beauty in an otherwise barren wasteland. How poetically relevant," she said, pushing out her chest.

"Wow, you're even sexier up close." Kaity leaned to her side to get a better look, revealing she was equipped with a mechanized backpack. "Did Devlin really make you? Your skin seems so lifelike, but your body is so divine," she said, poking the artificial leg.

"I know, isn't it wonderful? This is my gift to the world," said Nina, running her hands down her side.

"It's suuuch shame I have to kill you, but a job's a job," said Kaity with a toothy grin.

Nina leaped back. Her eyes became slanted as she looked up at the child. "You're the one who is going to be carted off in a body bag. Let's see if you can handle this! *Super Sexy Slo-mo Rose!*"

Kaity leaped on top of her target, wrapped her legs around her and snuggled her face.

"What are you doing?" asked Nina, her pupils shrinking. She wrapped one arm around Kaity's neck and put her hand to her opponent's chest. "*Ice Shot!*"

An icicle shot out of the Exp's hand and exploded, trapping the assassin in a coat of ice.

"Now die." Nina tossed the frozen assassin forward into the tree.

As Kaity soared through the air, her gloves shot out blades of plasma. She sliced at the ice with a lightning-quick flurry of attacks. The heated claws melted the ice around her. She then landed with her feet on the tree, digging her hind claws into it. "I hope you'll like the change in atmosphere." She shoved her hand through a hole in the tree and pushed a button within it.

As the long metal plates parted, the base of the tree became visible along with an entire jungle. The oak tree was merely a single organism rooted in a lush environment.

Nina ran to the edges of the room as the floor beneath her receded into the walls. She jumped on the wall at the last moment, but was unable to keep her grip. The sexy Exp plummeted down to the true battlefield eighty feet beneath her.

Kaity shot off the tree like a cannonball. She then ricocheted off the wall and landed on her target's back. "So, do you want to give up yet?" she asked, peeking over the target's shoulder.

Nina turned around to face her. "I've fought in a jungle before. And I demolished my enemies without even getting hit." She thrust her hand at the assassin's neck, missing only by an inch. She quickly retaliated with a jab from her other arm.

Kaity knocked the arm aside and plunged her plasma claws into her crush's shoulder.

Blood sprayed out from the wound and onto the assassin's arm.

Kaity slammed her head into her plaything before jumping off, leaving searing holes in Nina's shoulder. She gripped the tree and licked her paws. "Your blood is so tasty!"

"How dare you cut my beautiful body! That shoulder was necessary for proper strutting! Is it really that tasty?" asked Nina, interrupted by her own intrigue.

"I can't wait to be drenched in it," said Kaity, her claws embedding deeper into the bark.

"Even my blood is tantalizing," said Nina with a blissful smile as she fell. Kaity sprung off the tree.

"*Flirtatious Flash!*" Nina opened her shirt and then closed it in an instant.

Kaity was mesmerized as she zoomed closer, her mouth wide open.

While still in the air, Nina grabbed the little girl and pinned her arms. She restrained her opponent's legs by folding her legs around them.

"I've got you now! "*Dazzling Plummet!*" exclaimed Nina as they careened toward the ground.

"You aren't going to damage your body," said Kaity, looking up at her with a grin.

"Of course I'm not," said Nina with a smirk.

As soon as they were about to slam into the ground, Nina jumped off of Kaity. Her toes gripped a tree branch as her opponent crashed into the jungle floor.

A cloud of dust concealed the damage Kaity had suffered.

Nina dropped down onto her opponent, who had landed on all fours but was still shaken up from the impact. She dragged out a knife from beneath her thigh-highs and held it to the child's neck.

The injured assassin grabbed her crush's breast with shaky hands. Nina covered her chest in response. "Only I'm allowed to fondle myself."

Kaity swiped the knife from Nina's hand and then stabbed it into her target's arm.

Nina seethed in pain, giving the cat-girl assassin another opening.

Kaity kicked off, sending her prey fifteen feet above her. "It really has been fun, but you won't be able to deflect these bullets."

The assassin's backpack disengaged a hefty folded piece of metal.

"I didn't deflect it last time. You put an ugly hole through my gorgeous forehead."

"Don't worry, this time you'll just die."

The metal mesh unfolded into a high-powered five-foot sniper rifle. The second it was fully constructed, the prodigy cocked it and aimed at the target.

"You won't hit me this time. I have jaw-dropping reflexes," said Nina as she swung off a tree branch toward her attacker.

"You're on!" exclaimed Kaity, her finger on the trigger.

"*Super Slo-mo, Erotic Dodge!*"

Kaity aimed her recticle at the target's chest and fired. The energy bullet visibly soared through the air, heading right into Nina's arm.

"Even when slowed down, my bullets are too fast for you," said Kaity, rocking back and forth.

Kawai fell down a long chasm, nearly landing on a rancid mountain of garbage far below the rusty chute. "Is this some kind of joke?" she asked, floating above it and holding her nose. The prototype looked around, noticing that the walls in the distance were gray and moldy.

Tempo was sitting cross-legged on a small hill of discarded electronics. Everything but his face was draped in a skintight bodysuit and there was no jacket to cover it. "You can levitate; how interesting," he said, looking up at the living weapon with a grin.

"I think that's rather obvious. And let me guess. Hmm...your ability is temperature control," said Kawai with a nasal tone.

"You may know what my ability is. But that doesn't mean you can stop it," said Tempo with a sadistic smirk.

"We'll see about that. *Sound Shot Beam!*"

A powerful, condensed sound wave emitted from her open mouth.

"You can manipulate sound, how obnoxious," said Tempo as he jumped out of the way.

"Yep, and I can do lots more." Kawai flew down toward the enemy and embraced him. "*Energy Embrace Drain!*"

"How foolish can you be? **TEMPERATURE RISE!**" Tempo's body became superheated, forcing the child to release her grip. "Let's see you hit me now. Come on, little girl!" he said, striking his chest.

A laser net shot out from the Exp's palm.

Tempo jumped to the side to dodge it. He then sprang at the little girl and grabbed her neck. "I can bake my targets from within, without even lifting a finger. But it's so much more satisfying when they know I am the one who's killing them." He pulled back his fist and slammed it into her chest. "You Exps are like children with matches. Without knowing how to use your equipment, you'll only end up hurting yourself," he said as he smacked the brat's face with her tail.

"Don't think I can't fight just because I'm super cute."

The prototype's tail slid out of his grip. It then slammed into his stomach, knocking the wind out of him.

Kawai flipped counter-clockwise in the air, hitting the back of his head with the tip of her stiffened tail.

Tempo fell face-first into a pile of broken glass.

Kawai quickly floated away. She hid behind a small hill of trash and tried to relax her breathing. "This is it…it's life or death," she said, holding her chest.

Tempo rose up using only his toes. He tore out the glass shards in his body as he scanned the area. "When it was just me and the guys, it was a simple business. We took whatever was served on our platter. There was no job too dark or dangerous for us. Nobody was too good or too bad for us to murder. Then Kaity came along and got in the way. Kanasta used to be heartless, but that little runt has been softening him up since the day he met her. She's not a real assassin like us. She brought her morals into our business. That self-righteous child thinks she can decide what job we should and should not take. She is holding the Viper Squad back!"

Tempo knocked over a nearby hill of trash. "If there is one thing I hate, it's little girls. That brat ruined the business Kanasta and I gave up everything for!" The furious killer slammed his foot down on a champagne bottle. "One little kitty is a pain in the ass. I don't need another one getting in my way. Come out already!" He saw the target's reflection in a protruding remnant of a broken mirror. His scowl melted into a grin. "I'll let you in on a little secret: I don't care about the cash. Kanasta never knew…I set every dollar I earned aflame! You see, he was always in it for the money and the sacred principles behind it. He's a slave to the spirit of capitalism, but not me. So little girl, do you know why I became an assassin? It's pretty straightforward actually. I became an assassin so I could

166

murder people. I love watching the face of my target melt into a bloody puddle," he said, walking closer toward his victim as he licked his lips.

"What are you going on about? I never asked you how you feel," said Kawai, rolling her eyes.

"Devlin is going to give us double the pay for each one of you that's still kicking. But I don't give a damn! The pleasure I'll get from cooking you alive is worth more than gold!" exclaimed Tempo, shooting a heat wave at the trash hill.

The wave superheated the rubbish, melting it into sludge.

Kawai zoomed right through the gooey hill and smacked the killer's face with her the tip of her tail.

Tempo grabbed her hardened tail, a red mark now on his left cheek. He then wrapped her tail around her neck.

"I can hear it! My conscience is begging me to kill you! Hugh-hugh-heheheheh!"

"Let go of me!" yelled Kawai, thrashing around.

"You wanted to know why I was so chatty, right? Well, I like to confide in my victims. I pay close attention to the different ways they react when they realize I'm here to kill them. Some freeze up, others stiffen, some just tremble uncontrollably, but most of them beg me to spare them with desperate groans. I love the look they have when they grasp that they are going to die. I want to see the fear of death in your eyes! Be a dear and give it to me," said Tempo with a psychotic grin.

The top of Kawai's tail slammed into the assassin's neck. It uncoiled before smashing into his chest.

Tempo fell to the ground, gripping a gun from under the trash.

"All I care about is my soul mate," said Kawai, stiffening her resolve. "Before he was in incubation, I snuck in to see him. When I felt his cold steel against my lips, I realized that he is the perfectly engineered man of my dreams. He wasn't even finished, but I could feel his potential instinctively. That day I decided I would stay by his side forever! I know I am unworthy to be his lover, but so is everyone else on the planet."

"Are you alright with these being your last words?" asked Tempo, loading a shotgun behind his back.

"He's more than just my soul mate. He is my anchor in this world. Just being in his presence makes me feel as if my glitches are vanishing. With his help I could become almost as perfect as him. See, I can ramble too, heehee," said Kawai before sticking out her tongue.

"That's sweet, but do you really think you can win just because you love him?" asked Tempo, cocking the gun.

"I will be reunited with him. I made a promise that I wouldn't die. I refuse to break any promise I make to him. Never ever ever!" said Kawai with a scrunched-up face.

"Come at me if you dare. The second you do, you'll be melted from the inside out, hugh-hugh-heh."

"It would be lots of fun to bring a prick like you to his knees, but I won't keep my brother waiting. I'm going to have to kill you before I can break you. *Sound Missile*"

A single sound wave split in two and shot through the assassin's ears.

Tempo's eardrums burst. His smile widened as blood dripped down from his earlobes.

"Every second I'm wasting here I could be enjoying with my brother!" yelled Kawai as she rapidly lashed her tail at him.

Tempo blocked each tail swipe with the back of his arms. "I don't need my senses to kill you. You are an inexperienced infant." He slammed the shotgun against her forehead, smashing it to pieces. "*TEMPERATURE FALL, ARCTIC FIELD*."

The sadist's feet emitted a ripple of coldness.

The cold wave spread out and froze the entire top layer of trash.

"Did you forget that I can levitate?" asked Kawai as she floated up.

"What did you say? Oh, it doesn't matter. Listen to this, little girl! There is nowhere you can run from me! This place is the perfect shape. Heat rises, after all. Look at you, you're confused. Your confidence is melting before my eyes."

"I'm not worried in the teensiest. I still have an artifact I've kept secret. My brother is going to be so proud that I beat you," said Kawai, twirling in the air.

Bob floated down into a training room. Workout machines, caches of weapons, dummies with various protective gear and obstacle courses were lined up in a progressive pattern. The room was colored white with a neon green grid design. A boxing ring was in the center of the spacious room.

"I chose you to be my opponent because I've heard you are a swordsman. Please, show me your blade," said Riufen, standing inside the boxing arena.

Bob looked around the room in silence.

Riufen squinted. "Where are you hiding your sword?"

"Are there cameras here? I don't like showing off my power. I'm very modest. And I don't want my friends to feel inferior," said Bob with a grin.

"This is where I reside. I can assure you Devlin-sama will be observing. I apologize for this inconvenience," said Riufen with a bow.

"Oh, that's okay then! I'm going to kill him later anyway. You look like a decent warrior. I hope we have a fun fight," said Bob, floating into the arena.

"Thank you. Let us have an honorable battle," said Riufen, stretching out his hand.

"Honor is in the eye of the beholder. My sword is somewhat unfair," said Bob, giving the clueless enemy a shake with his spectral hand.

"Fairness is in accordance to one's perspective. Devlin-sama wants me to use my artifact. Is that alright with you?"

"Absolutely! I hope you don't mind that I'm won't be using my artifact. The thing is…I don't have one. *Eyeball Laser*," said Bob, abruptly turning around.

A laser shot out and bore a hole through the gullible warrior's chest.

"Sorry about that, but a warrior must be alert at all times. I look forward to fighting you in another life," said Bob, clasping his wispy hands together.

"I regret postponing our rematch, but I am still alive. My body was constructed for intense combat. I am an Exp created by Devlin-sama. Does that make us brothers?" asked Riufen with a smile.

"No, it doesn't. It just makes fighting you a bit more fun," said Bob as he circled around the warrior.

"I do not wish to surprise you. My artifact is the Artifact of Life," said Riufen as he put his hand on the floor.

"How interesting. I'm not sure I'm familiar with it. But you need not explain. I'd rather see it firsthand," said Bob with a glint of intrigue.

"Very well then. INSTANT LIFE."

The waxed granite floor split open, its sides becoming jagged.

"Ah, so you can animate inanimate objects! That's rather interesting," said Bob as he floated above the spiky floor.

Riufen fell to the ground, bowing reverently. "Please, forgive my insolence!"

"Get up! What are you talking about now?"

The samurai stood up but never stopped bowing.

"I forgot to introduce myself. I am Riufen," he said, bowing repeatedly.

"In your defense, I did attack prematurely. I am Bob. It's a pleasure to meet you," he said, grabbing the swordsman's hand and shaking it.

"Bob…yes, very good. It is a direct and powerful name. Come, Bob, let us draw our swords in unison," said Riufen, shaking in excitement. He jabbed his fingers into the back of his neck. The warrior grabbed onto the tip of his spinal cord and slowly tore it out, showing no sign of pain. Another spine formed as he pulled it out. The stoic samurai stood tall as he held out his spine like a sword.

169

"So your spinal cord is your sword. That is very unique, if not cumbersome. My sword is made up of souls."

Souls leaked out of Bob, fusing together until the Atma Blade formed.

"That is why I couldn't see your blade. This has become far more intriguing. I highly anticipate this battle. 𝕀𝕟𝕤𝕥𝕒𝕟𝕥 𝕃𝕚𝕗𝕖," said Riufen with a wide smile.

His spinal cord grew several bone spurs that formed a hilt. The tip of the hilt became serrated, giving it the appearance of a sword.

"You continue to impress me."

"There is much more to show you." Riufen put his hand to the fresh puddle of blood.

The blood stiffened and coiled like a DNA strand. Blood chains slowly formed from the puddle. The chains shot out and wrapped around Bob. They then seeped back into the puddle, pinning their captive against the floor.

"Blood bondage…ah, this brings back memories. This is cute, but it's not really useful," said Bob.

Riufen's ribs elongated, tearing straight through his own flesh. They shot into his adversary, but passed through him.

Bob then moved through the chains as is they were not there.

"An opponent that cannot be injured…this is wondrous," said Riufen with a grin.

Bob floated up to the samurai from below the floor and stabbed him with the Atma Blade. "I see you are immortal," he said, peering up at the swordsman.

"Yes, but I doubt that will hinder your fighting spirit."

"Quite right. My sword directly attacks the soul! Even immortals perish before my blade!"

Exp 8 landed in a pitch-black room.

"I hope you are as impressive as Devlin claimed. Otherwise, this will be a very short battle," said Kanasta from the darkness.

"Ooo, spooky…darkness…I'm so scared."

"You should be," whispered Kanasta, his breath on the target.

"Why the hell should I be afraid of you? You're just a human." Exp 8 turned around and gripped the assassin.

"You may be surprised what a human is capable of when they are shed of moral restraints."

"Alright, joke's over. To be honest, I don't want to kill you. So just surrender and we'll both get on with our day," said Exp 8, patting the human on the shoulder.

"You have twenty-one seconds to kill me. During this time, I will not attack you. When the time expires, I will retaliate," said Kanasta calmly.

The orbs on Exp 8's hands lit up, giving him a four-meter range of visibility.

Kanasta was standing in front of him with open arms. Below his feet were metal plates, overlapping each other to form wave-like protrusions.

Exp 8 released twenty soccer-ball sized orbs, creating a perimeter around him. He then turned around and ran in the opposite direction.

Kanasta dodged the orbs as he dashed up to the target.

"You fell right into my trap. You'll be the first one to see my newest attack," said Exp 8, spinning around to face his opponent.

The cuff of his wrist detached and floated just above his fingertips. It pulled in the surrounding orbs. They bundled up, making a bumpy wrecking-ball of condensed energy.

"I hope you survive this! BIG ORB!"

Exp 8 thrust his hand forward, causing the massive bundle of orbs to be propelled forth.

Kanasta dug his feet into the ground and then grabbed the orb with both hands. He pushed off with the balls of his feet and tossed the orb to the ceiling.

It exploded above them, sending down heavy chunks of debris.

"Who the hell are you?! What the hell are you?!" yelled Exp 8 as he rapidly strafed to dodge the rubble.

Kanasta counted up as he knocked the rubble aside.

"If projectiles won't work, then I guess I'll just have to smash your face in," said Exp 8, pulling back his fist.

"Fourteen."

Exp 8 rushed to skilled brawler and barraged him with a flurry of quick and powerful punches.

Kanasta stood in place, unfazed by the hurricane of pain.

"Seventeen."

Exp 8 jumped in the air and pummeled the assassin's face with multiple kicks.

"Nineteen."

Exp 8 charged his fist and activated his thrusters. "Go to hell!" he exclaimed, punching his opponent's chest with great force.

Kanasta grabbed the target's hand as it smashed into his chest and crushed it in his fist.

"Aghhhhhhh!" Exp 8 cringed in agony as his bones split in two.

"Twenty-one," said Kanasta, clasping his hands together.

Chapter 16: Power vs Experience

Previously: Atatasuki's organs expanded, leaving him with no other option but to defeat the egotist before they burst.

"You can't kill me, little man. You have only seen the tip of my huge iceberg. GROWING SELF-RESPECT!"

Atatasuki stared in disbelief and awe as his adversary grew ten times his usual size. "My god…if only you could make my muffins that size, they would last…forever," he said, drool making its way down to his chin.

"Yo, little dude, I can make you a giant muffin. Just don't ever forget how great I am, like ever," said Ego with a rocker salute.

"You would do that for me?" asked Atatasuki with watery eyes as he placed a muffin in the assassin's massive hand.

"GROWING SELF-RESPECT!"

The muffin expanded until it was forty feet tall. The ground rumbled once the muffin hit the street.

"Thank you! You really are the greatest. May muffins rain down on your holy parade of excellence!" exclaimed Atatasuki, hugging the muffin in tears. He then scaled the muffin, determined to reach its fluffy top.

"I truly am a great person. Only really great people help their enemies. I'm like a totally rad monk or something. Someone should give me, like, a badass statue…of myself. Yeah." Ego gave himself a high five.

"I'll never forget this blasphe…" said Atatasuki before he coughed up a puddle of blood.

Ego's kind smile turned sly. "Wow, you are a whole new breed of idiot. Did you really think I would help my target out of the kindness of my heart? You insulted me, bro. You told me that I had wasted my awesome time. Foot's on the other shoe now, man. I just wasted *your* time. You don't have much longer before you drown in the chunks of your own insides. Though I got to admit, that's a pretty cool way to die," he said with a nod.

"Mmm, this is delicious! Who knew my blood would make for a tantalizing topping? I'm religiously against condiments, but this is incredible. Ah, only the blood of a defect could make muffins sweeter!" exclaimed Atatasuki, eating his super muffin as he hurled blood all over it.

"Don't ignore me, dude!" exclaimed Ego, his fist stiffening.

Atatasuki was too busy kissing his masterpiece to hear anything.

"I feel so like…insignificant."

A giant scar appeared on the assassin's chest.

"Whoa, I need to retain my self-image or this could get ugly. Yo, little man, prepare to be crushed. I'm going to sandwich you between my radical fingers!" Ego reached his arm out and grabbed a hold of his opponent.

"I'll never forget you, my love!" yelled Atatasuki as he was torn away from the pinnacle of pastries.

"You dare ignore me after all I've done for you! Don't push my buttons, man!" Ego grabbed the muffin and smashed it to bits.

Atatasuki's eyes flared up with rage. "You murdered her! We were in love! I'm going to cremate you alive! *SUPER MICROWAVE BODY!*"

His whole body caught aflame, burning the traitor's hand.

"You're becoming a pest!" yelled Ego as he slammed his target against the asphalt.

Atatasuki stood up and punched flames at the murderer, only to be knocked aside. He smashed through the guardrails around the racetrack. After using his faulty jets to get back in control of his momentum, he landed on the other side of the track. He then hopped into a red-hot racecar and revved it up.

"Alright, dude, you're on." Ego touched his skateboard and enlarged it to the size of the racecar. He then jumped on top of it with a stylish spin. He sped toward the enemy, riding his board while sporting neon green roller skates. "This level of balance is beyond anything anyone's achieved, ever. I was born extraordinary! I broke a world record just shooting out of my mother's womb. And now I'm going to crush you while showing off." The assassin popped up into a handstand as he closed the distance between them.

Atatasuki slammed down on the accelerator, speeding up toward the assassin.

The massive assassin slammed his fist down, smashing the front of the car.

Atatasuki leaped out through the windshield and punched his enemy's eye with a burning fist. "I don't care how great you are. There is no excuse for you to make such a colossal mistake. You will regret ever messing with muffins! I'll melt you down no matter how bloated you get!" he yelled, pummeling the enormous eyeball.

Ego picked the pest off his face and smashed him into the racecar. "That sounds like a challenge, bro. I never back down from a challenge. I also never cease to amaze. Never lost a bet before and no challenge you throw at me can ruin my streak." He cracked each individual finger. "I am going to crush your defective idea of superiority with my bare hands, little dude," he said as he shrank back to normal size.

"You still don't understand. It's because I'm damaged that I'll defeat you."

Ego shoved his hand in Atatasuki's open chest. "I'll show you just how much heat I can handle. I am extreme to the max, you little bastard!" he yelled as his hand baked inside his opponent.

Atatasuki grabbed onto his adversary's face, slowly melting his skin away.

"I can take it! I can take it!" Ego put his other hand inside the oven.

"Now you shall feel the pain that Ms. Muffin was forced through!"

"You can't win! It's huge!" yelled Ego, spraying the newbie with spittle.

"Oh, is it? Well it's about to get third-degree burns," said Atatasuki as he grabbed onto the assassin's crotch.

Ego sucked up the pain for ten seconds and then pulled away. "I couldn't take it! It was too much!"

The assassin grabbed his crotch as tears evaporated from his cheeks.

"You've only practiced what you're great at. You don't know what failure is. You don't know how much it hurts. You don't understand the power it takes to dive headlong into it again and again!" yelled Atatasuki as he punched his opponent gratuitously.

Ego tore open Atatasuki's chest. He knocked his opponent down to the asphalt with a backhand. He then shoved his hand inside his target's open chest. "And I'll never know that feeling! GROWING SELF-RESPECT, HAND!" he yelled with flaring nostrils before his hand expanded.

Atatasuki turned on his side and coughed up a puddle of blood. "I am going to defeat you, Ego. You cannot hurt me. Enlarging my organs only adds to my defectiveness. The less body parts there are to heat, the more heat for each part. OVERHEATED OVEN!" All his heat transferred into his chest.

Ego's hand caught fire. He pulled it out quickly but not quite quick enough. He looked down in horror to see that his shirt had caught aflame. The giant "Extraordinary" on his shirt was reduced to "ordinary." The fire then burned his shirt into ashes.

Atatasuki ripped off the killer's clothing, stopping the fire from reaching his flesh. "Mental and emotional glitches like empathy and mercy can save lives. With all your experience, you've lost a fundamental aspect of being a flawed living being. Meditate on that as you wallow in your defeat," he said, patting away a stray flame in the assassin's hair.

Ego rolled into a ball, trying to deny that he was defeated by a defect.

As Atatasuki's insides expanded, Ada's corpse fell to the ground.

Sefiwah shook her bloodied hands frantically. "I didn't kill her. I would never kill. Get off of me! You are tainting my tranquility," she said as the blood-soaked her white bandages.

Ada held her killer in a gentle embrace. "Please don't cry anymore."

Sefiwah looked at her blood-soaked hands and then back at her victim. As her guilt subsided, the blood faded from her hands.

"I thought you would have given up if you believed you had killed me. I didn't mean to hurt you, Sefiwah. I used the Artifact of Illusion." Ada took a red-and-brown jasper stone out from her chest. "Isn't it pretty? It looks like agate, which is a very rare mineral, but it's really just a common knockoff. It sort of masquerades as something it's not. But it didn't ask to look that way. It's just trying to be itself."

"How are you alive?" asked Sefiwah.

"Devlin recently gave me this artifact when I asked him for an upgrade, but I'm actually very familiar with it."

"I killed you," said Sefiwah, wiping away the nonexistent blood.

"Nope. The Ada you killed was just a mirage. You haven't killed anybody. So, please, calm down," said Ada, steadying the woman's shaking hands.

"I'm so relieved," said Sefiwah with watery eyes before flinging a knife at her target.

The knife pierced through the Exp's forehead, seeping into her skull.

Sefiwah tore the knife out and then slit her target's throat.

The blood seeped out, bringing back the killer's guilt at full throttle.

Before Sefiwah had a moment to cope with her grief, her victim's voice came from above. "She was an illusion as well. Please, just relax; you don't have to kill anyone."

Sefiwah leaped off the ground and up to the Ada on the ceiling. She sliced her head off with one clean cut. She landed on the ground in synch with her target's newest corpse.

"If I can't stop you from killing, then I will just have to put you to sleep," said the decapitated head with a frown.

Ten Adas appeared all around the assassin. They rushed in and started punching her.

"How can your illusions be affecting me?" asked Sefiwah with fear.

"You believe I am hitting you and therefore you feel the pain. Realize the truth: you can't kill me. Once you accept this, you'll end your killing spree once and for all. Please, listen to me," said the Adas as they pummeled her.

"I need you to die so that goodness can prevail," said Sefiwah, knocking aside each attack.

Sefiwah brought out the spikes on her whip. She viciously lashed the whip through the Adas, cutting them to bits.

The last Ada dropped onto the assassin from the ceiling.

The spikes receded into the whip as Sefiwah leaped behind her target.

Sefiwah wrapped the whip around the final Ada's neck. "It looks like I found the real one," she said with a stray tear. The assassin pulled harshly on the whip, choking her victim.

"Stop. You can't kill me. I thought you could just, keh, get it out of your system. Why can't I stop you from killing?" asked Ada as she struggled to speak.

"It is my curse to continue killing until I die. Sadly, it is not my time yet. I cannot say the same for you," said Sefiwah, tightening her grip.

"Stop, you're only hurting yourself," said Ada, her hand touching the woman's pale cheek.

"I have come too far to give up now," said Sefiwah, pulling even harder.

"You already tried choking me and it didn't work. Exps don't need to breathe in oxygen to sustain themselves. So just stop this."

The whip around her neck vanished.

"It was a mirage as well? I should be able to decipher the concrete from the abstract. What is going on? I need to let go of my emotions." Sefiwah closed her eyes and took in a deep breath.

"Come on, let's just have a picnic instead," said Ada, creating a holographic projection of a basket.

"You made the whip appear invisible," said Sefiwah, her eyes fixed on the target. She then coiled the whip back around her target's neck.

"Bingo! Now where would you like to be?" asked Ada, creating digitized grass around the arena.

"What I want doesn't matter. I have a mission to fulfill." Sefiwah pushed the spiked button down on her whip.

Ada struggled to take the sharpened whip off her neck as the spikes poked holes in her throat.

"They will dig deeper and deeper. Nothing can stop them now. They will follow their path without regret or doubt," said Sefiwah, pulling the whip back while pushing her victim forward.

The spikes spun around the Exp's neck, tearing her throat open.

Ada fell to the floor, landing in a puddle of her own blood.

"If you try to save a killer from their ocean of guilt, you will only end up in your own puddle of regret," said Sefiwah, flinging the blood off her whip. She then fell to her knees with tears pouring out of her emotionless eyes. "I am sorry, Ada. You will bless Heaven with your presence, for you truly are an angel."

"Oh, I forgive you." Ada hugged her killer from behind.

"Thank you for understanding. You have a pure white heart. Wait…didn't I kill you?" asked Sefiwah, her head creaking to face her victim.

"You closed your eyes for the finishing blow and I had to think fast. Soooo, I created an illusionary Ada and then lied down in the area with the blood splotch on the floor. You wiped the blood on the ground when I first hit you, remember? Sorry about that, by the way."

"You were hiding the whole time?" asked Sefiwah, her fingers digging into her temples.

"Yep and since you don't like blood, there was no way you would go near the area. Pretty clever, huh?"

"I saw your purity, but I overlooked your cunning. I won't make the same mistake again," said Sefiwah, her hand inching toward a razor on her thigh.

"Sorry, but my friends are counting on me. 𝐁𝐎𝐍𝐊." Ada hit Sefiwah across the head, knocking her out. "I really wanted to help you, but…I don't think I can. But there's no need to worry. Your secret is safe with me," said Ada, setting her new friend on the ground.

As blood leaked out of Ada's first corpse, oil leaked out from BoneSaw's remains.

"I won! This victory goes to Britain!" Karson threw his arms in the air. He then turned around.

Twenty BoneSaws stood before him, all revving up their saws.

Karson put his hand in front of his face and then moved it away. He polished his shotgun barrels, but the robots did not vanish. "I killed you! Your body is right there! You died, didn't you?"

The BoneSaws carved into the floor, leaving an imprint that read: "I have the Multiply Artifact. Now I'm going to cut you into bite-sized pieces!"

"Does that mean you're an Exp? Forget it. I'm not going to get an answer out of you. But don't think you've won yet. I actually fight better when I'm surrounded. It puts my mind into battle mode."

The BoneSaws took a square formation and circled around the target.

"What kind of war tactic is this?"

They slowly came in closer, boxing him in.

"I am a super soldier. Neither man nor machine can beat me!" Karson spit out a grenade and then kicked it into an approaching group.

Eight BoneSaws parted and then leaped at the target.

Karson knocked two aside with the back of his shotguns and then fired at four more. He raised his leg, pumped one of the robots full of bullets and then kicked it into another. His revolver elbows deflected projectile saws thrown by the second group of robots.

"𝐊𝐈𝐋𝐋" The next eleven BoneSaws leaped at him at once.

"Little bastard can talk!" Karson spit out a grenade to the ground after he jumped up.

The explosion sent the gunman just out of range of the onslaught of saws.

"The future of military is mobility! **MISSILE MACHINE GUN**." Karson spun around in place. He then jumped into the air. He fired his legs and arms gratuitously, releasing a flurry of missiles at the approaching assassins.

The little robots dug underground, evading the aerial assault.

"No way! I didn't even hit one. Am I going to die here?" asked Karson, swept up in a gust of horror.

Spinning saws shot out from the floor, exposed like the fins of an aggressive group of sharks. They circled around him, closing in ever so slowly.

"Mines are supposed to be placed in foresight, not hindsight," said Karson, placing a pressure-sensitive bomb below his foot.

All of the BoneSaws jumped out of the ground and lashed their saws at the target. They dug into the ground upon landing.

Gunpowder poured out of the Exp's wounds to the floor below.

The BoneSaws drove in circles across the ceiling to intimidate the target.

The gunman sat down and closed his eyes. "How do you win against a mechanical murderer? Come on, Karson, think! How can I defeat a fellow killing machine?" He stood up gallantly and aimed his head at the ceiling.

His head shot upward, exploding into the group of robots just as they dropped down.

The assassins fell down like raindrops.

The gunman's neck disengaged another rocket.

Karson stretched his new head and then regurgitated an electric magnetic pulse grenade.

The BoneSaws flipped over and rushed to the target.

"**ELECTRIC INTERFERENCE**." Karson grabbed the EMP grenade and threw it against the ground.

The grenade exploded and short-circuited all of the robots.

A BoneSaw then dropped from the ceiling onto the gunman. It chopped off his head with a single strike.

Karson's head fell to the ground in front of the final BoneSaw. His headless corpse collapsed backwards, bleeding out gunpowder from its neck.

His head skyrocketed forward into the robotic assassin, smashing it against the wall before exploding. The gunman's neck then released another head.

Karson deactivated the mine, opened his uniform and shoved the mine back into his chest. "That was a good fight! You only lost because I had greater range and a varied arsenal!" he exclaimed with a salute.

Chapter 17: Exps vs Assassins

As BoneSaw surprised Karson by multiplying himself, Nina was shot.

The Exp fell to the ground, blood dripping out her arm.

"I can't believe you still hit me. Aghh! I've got to fight with all my power! You can't dodge me at this angle! *Super Sexy Flirtatious Flash!*" yelled Nina, still on the ground. She quickly opened her shirt, exposing her bra for an instant before giving her opponent an up-skirt view.

Kaity broke down her sniper and reattached it to her pack. "*FLASH PHOTOGRAPHY!*" she yelled, taking a picture with a point-and-shoot digital camera.

"How can you be immune to my curvy body? You shouldn't be able to walk after that attack. How are you this powerful?" asked Nina, slowly getting back on her feet.

Kaity dangled the picture over her crush. "Who could possibly be immune to this?"

"Wow, I look amazing. Can I have that?" asked Nina, her hand reaching for the photo.

"Nope. Sorry. It's mine!" exclaimed Kaity, holding it to her chest.

"Fine then, I'll just have to take it from you by force. Your heart is going to burst! *Flirtatious Flash Combo!*" Nina quickly exposed her bra as she attacked with a flurry of poses accentuating the bounciness of her breasts.

"*SUPER FLASH PHOTOGRAPHY COMBO!*" Kaity hopped around and took photos from various angles.

Nina suddenly appeared behind the bouncy photographer. "Wow, you have amazing camera skills."

"With eyes like these, taking pictures is a cinch. You have such fun breasts," said Kaity, now standing behind Nina. She wrapped her arms around her crush and groped her breasts passionately. "They're so plump," she said with wide eyes.

"I know. Their plumpness defies all logic!" exclaimed Nina, raising her head with pride. "Wait, get off me!" She grabbed the lecher's arms and flipped her over.

Kaity landed on her feet and jumped right back up. She pounced on her prey, knocking her to the grass.

"They're so soft. Dumpling soft," said Kaity with wide eyes as she snuggled the plump breasts.

"I know how incredibly soft they are. I know that clouds pale in comparison. But that doesn't matter! Get off of me!" Nina tossed the molester to the ground and adjusted her shirt. "Only I'm allowed to fondle myself."

Kaity landed on her feet and then lunged at her prey.

The nimble narcissist grabbed the enemy by the waist and launched her into the air.

While spinning upward, Kaity took out a pistol.

Nina kicked off the ground, dodging the bullets, and kneed her attacker's face.

Kaity used the momentum to swing around her prey. She caressed her crush's legs and patted her butt.

Nina scissored her legs, gripping the incessant molester by the throat.

Kaity tickled her crush's sides with her free hand.

"I became immune to such things long ago. Now die," said Nina, yanking the gun out of the assassin's grip.

Kaity spun around and knocked her feet into the back of Nina's neck. In the same motion, she shot into her target's chest at point-blank range. She then kicked off, sending her prey into a nearby tree.

Nina moaned in pain as she tumbled through the branches. She hit the ground with a thud, covered in surface wounds.

Kaity raced down the tree and looked at her victim with great satisfaction. "I didn't want to force you, but you've left me no choice. I'm going to make you love me." She leaped off the tree and pinned her prey down.

"You can't force me to love you. Love is triggered by attraction and the only thing that attracts me is sexiness. Your undeveloped body doesn't give me the slightest bit of pleasure," said Nina with a haughty smile.

Kaity made a heart with her hands and aimed at her target. "*NINA, LOVE, KAITY!*"

Nina's body jolted. Her eyes flickered with love. Her mouth stretched into a smile. Her arms then reached out around Kaity. "Oh you are too cute." She pulled Kaity in and held her tightly. "I can't help but love this adorable face," she said as she snuggled the little girl lovingly.

"Yay, my Love Artifact triumphs once again! This little stone makes me one hundred percent irresistible!"

Nina's eyes returned to normal. She shook herself back to her senses. "It seems we have something in common. We can instantly make someone fall in love with us. We can cripple them with passion. But keep this in mind, little kitten. My body is innate, while your artifact is engineered. We may be similar, but that doesn't mean I will lose to you. I am going to use my ultimate attack and bring this battle to its orgasmic climax! *Super Sexy Slo-mo Strip*," she said, pouring seduction into each syllable. The erotic warrior carelessly took off her gloves and tossed them into the air. She then slowly removed her undershirt, revealing her bra.

Kaity grabbed the clothes in midflight.

Nina striped off her pants, tossing them aside without a care. She unfastened her bra before stopping. "That should be enough eye candy to end this."

Kaity grabbed all the clothes and rolled around with them like a kitty with a ball of yarn.

Nina quickly pulled out a bomb trigger from her hair. " *Dynamite Body, Explosive Clothes*."

Kaity jumped away once the bombs within the clothes activated.

The pile exploded, sending the cat-girl smashing into a nearby tree.

A tree branch pierced right through the assassin's shoulder and another through her leg.

"Now, I'm gonna make you take it all off," said Kaity, looking up at her prey with lust in her eyes. After leaping off the tree, she lashed her claws at her crush's purple bra.

The bra was sliced in half, and slowly fell off. Dark-purple bandages covered Nina's nipples.

With another slash, the lustful kitten removed the bandages.

Nina looked down at her light purple nipples and swooned.

Kaity grabbed a tiny metal gun as it dropped from her backpack. She aimed it at her target's head and then fired.

A two-inch tranquilizer dart bore into the wound and released a toxin.

Nina's eyes widened before she fell to the floor.

Kaity brought out her camera and took pictures of the defeated narcissist.

She lied down and kissed her crush on the lips. "That was lots and lots of fun. Sorry we can't play around some more, but a job's a job." The assassin prodigy patted her target with her tail.

As Nina's pride was wounded by an energy bullet, Kawai revealed she had an unseen artifact.

"You have no tricks left," said Tempo with a grin.

"I just said I still have one artifact left!" yelled Kawai, forgetting she made the enemy deaf.

"Yes...that's it! Beg for mercy."

"You are so obnoxious! *Surrounding Shield*."

181

A light blue, see-through shield formed around the Exp.

"Your sound abilities can crush my ice, but they can't stop my new ability," said Tempo, cracking his knuckles.

"Do what you want. I am immune to your attacks now," said Kawai, sticking out her tongue.

"You're trying to surprise me with a secret ability? Well it won't work. *TEMPERATURE FALL, ICY SANCTUARY,*" said Tempo, creating a box of ice around him. "Now that I'm safe, it's time to end you," he said with a sick smirk.

"I don't think so! Narrow spaces just power up my attacks. *Echo Blast!*" yelled Kawai in a high-pitched tone.

The sound wave bounced off the walls, heading down toward the assassin. " *TEMPERATURE RISE, MINI OCEAN!*"

The layer of ice below the professional sadist melted, becoming murky water. It then rose up, starting to flood the arena.

The sound wave hit the water and burst.

Tempo was under the water, safely stationed in his protective ice cube. "Even if you can float, you can't dodge water. *TEMPERATURE FALL, RISING TUNDRA.*"

The water beneath the Exp froze.

"I'll just keep on levitating. You're going to drown yourself, moron."

"So you've realized it now! You can't run from me! *TEMPERATURE RISE!*"

The ice melted and the water reached the top, filling the whole arena.

"I didn't say that at all!"

"Your abilities cannot compare with my experience. *TEMPERATURE FALL, ICE CUBE!*" said Tempo from below the water.

The water solidified, freezing the entire arena.

Kawai was protected from the ice in her shield but still shivered from lack of warmth. "Choo! Why do I have to be so susceptible to cold?" she asked, rubbing her nose.

"I enjoyed our little game! But now, it is over. And I'm the winner. *TEMPERATURE RISE, HUMAN HEATER!*" Tempo's whole upper body became steaming hot, melting the ice as he touched it. He climbed toward untrained child, killer intent gleaming in his eyes.

"Damn it! Choo! My shield is stuck! Choo!" exclaimed Kawai, trying to spin the shield around.

"So your little shield resisted my temperature, eh? I must say, I am impressed. Melting you alive is going to be the highlight of my day," said Tempo as he climbed closer to his tiny victim.

"Atatasuki may be an idiot, but he taught me something. He showed me I can use my faults to my advantage. My error has become my edge. My adorable sneezes have been slowly shattering your ice. My susceptibility to cold is working on my behalf. And now, you're going down. Choo!" Kawai wiped her nose.

"What the hell are you saying?! I'm going to melt that snide look off your face! **BURNING BEAM!**" yelled Tempo, firing a concentrated heat wave at the little girl.

"Thankies! Choo! That heat was all I needed to break free!"

Kawai's shield absorbed the heat, changing from blue to red. The refined shield shook rapidly, melting the surrounding ice.

Kawai broke free and looked down at the assassin.

Tempo was still scaling up the ice pit he created.

"*Sound Ride!*" yelled Kawai, facing the ceiling.

A massive sound wave emitted from her mouth as her volume hit an ice-shattering pitch. It bounced off the ceiling and slammed back down into her shield.

Kawai was flung into the sadist, sending him skidding down the cold chasm.

Tempo pounded at her hot shield with his icy fingers as he tumbled down the ridge. He smashed his head into the shield, almost cracking it open.

They finally landed on ground.

Tempo broke through it, digging into the mound of trash below.

"Ah, this shield is really warming me up now. Here's something else I learned from Atatasuki. If you can't solve your problems…then just bury them! *Sound Ripple Overdrive!*" yelled Kawai, slamming her tail all around her shield.

The reverberation of the shield created a powerful continuous sound attack. It cracked all the ice above and below her without shattering it.

Tempo climbed out of the trashy muck, covered head to toe in brown goop. "Just die!" His furious scream bounced off the fragile ice walls.

The walls collapsed, sending icy chunks down toward the combatants.

"I saved this for you," said Kawai, flinging a new shield at the psycho killer. "*Sound Shot Bomb!*"

The shield broke as soon as it hit the assassin. An incredibly powerful sound burst out, making his eyes bleed.

Tempo screamed in agony as he was buried under the avalanche of ice.

Kawai hummed a triumphant tune as she floated through the hailstorm of icy chunks.

Once the avalanche was over, Kawai collapsed inside her shield. She dropped down to the tip of the makeshift mountain. "I used up…heeh…too much energy. It sucks being…heh…defective," she said with heavy breaths.

The top of the mountain burst open. Flames jutted out, knocking into the Exp's shield.

Kawai rolled all the way down the mountain, thrown around inside her own shield. She was jettisoned down the slope and into the wall. Once her shield stopped spinning, she looked up. Fear blossomed in her dazed eyes.

Tempo was closing in, his entire body engulfed in flames. He slid down the hillside, his murderous eyes gleaming.

"Okay…just a bit more," said Kawai, spinning her shield in place. She shot up the hill and slammed into her assailant.

The assassin wrapped his arms around her shield and smashed his head against it maniacally. He kicked off the slippery slope and pulled back his hand. "*ABSOLUTE ZERO, DEATH TOUCH*," said Tempo with a crooked smile. His pointer finger froze as all its heat was transferred elsewhere. He then pressed his fingertip against the shield.

Ice spread out and encompassed the shield, turning it into a frozen prison.

"At the proper temperature, even the sun would freeze." Tempo picked up the shield and slid all the way down the slope. He shoved his finger into the shield, making the slightest crack. The crack spread across her entire shield as he cracked his knuckles.

"I give up!" yelled Kawai as soon as her shield shattered.

"You should just surrender! You have lost!"

"Please, don't kill me!" said Kawai, creating another shield with the last bit of her strength.

Tempo froze this shield and then shoved his finger into it, making a little hole in it.

" *TEMPERATURE RISE!*"

The ice beneath Kawai melted.

Tempo shoved her into the watery garbage.

The sludge leaked into the shield, filling it up.

"Don't worry; you won't drown. I'll keep your fossilized body as a trophy. I will prove to him that I am the better assassin!"

Kawai flailed about inside, sickened by the stench of the muck.

"You're a persistent one, I'll give you that. I had bundles of fun. We should do this again sometime. *TEMPERATURE FALL, FROZEN TROPHY*."

The mucky water froze, turning the prototype into an icicle.

When Kawai bragged about her hidden power, Riufen was intrigued by the Atma Blade.

"So, it sucks out the soul of whomever it touches? That is very intriguing," said Riufen as he felt the blade sip his soul.

"Isn't the Atma Blade amazing?" asked Bob with a smile.

"This is a great day indeed! Finally, after months of training...I have found my rival. I can manipulate material forms..." said Riufen, hinting at his competitor to continue.

"And I can manipulate spectral forms. I see your point, but I can do so much more." Bob shot a laser.

Riufen's arm was cut off as the laser sliced through his shoulder. Veins shot out from the wound and wrapped around the opponent.

Bob's smile did not change as the veins constricted him. "I don't even need to move in order to defeat you. My minions should be more than enough. Feast on his soul, my spectral scavengers. *Jiva Summon.*"

Riufen walked up and stabbed his spine into his opponent.

"It appears it did not work," said Riufen, pushing the blade in deeper.

"Oh well, I guess they weren't nearby." Bob spun around with the spinal cord still in his body.

Riufen tightly held onto his spine as he was thrashed around. "A true warrior never leaves his sword." The samurai finally dislodged the sword and was then flung into the wall. He kicked off the wall on impact, heading back to his opponent.

Bob created a wall with his spectral hands.

Riufen vaulted over the wall and flung his spine forward.

Bob caught the spine with a spectral hand and stabbed it at its master.

The blade stopped between the samurai's palms.

Riufen tore it out from the astral grip and wrapped his veins around it. He sliced at the spectral arm, but the blade passed through.

"You can't even fight at my physical level; don't expect to ever be able to touch my spectral self." Bob grabbed the back of the arrogant warrior's head before flinging him to the ground.

Riufen landed into a somersault and then rushed toward his adversary.

"You need more training," said Bob, flinging iron clad dummies at his opponent.

Riufen brushed the training dolls aside. His eyes were fixed on his opposition.

Bob put boxing gloves around his spectral hands. He then rushed toward the swordsman.

As soon as they were within striking distance of one another, the onslaught began.

Bob pummeled Riufen like a punching bag as Riufen sliced him up like rice paper.

Spectral drills tore through the gloves and shot forward.

Riufen leaped back and then launched himself over his opponent. He dodged five lasers in midair before stabbing his spine down into his opponent. He pulled out another spine as he fiercely dodged a point-blank barrage of lasers.

The Atma Blade fired a blast that exploded once it hit its target.

The samurai tumbled in the air, landing on the ground with one foot.

"If this fight goes on any longer, I will most certainly be defeated." Riufen pulled out his spine and held it in front of his face. He stationed his feet against the ground, closed his eyes, and took in a deep breath. "I will end this with one final slash."

"Go on then," said Bob, rolling on a nearby treadmill.

Riufen leaped up, traveling horizontally toward his opponent. As he charged forward in the air, the strength of his grip weakened.

"What's wrong? You were looking charged up a minute ago."

Riufen shot past his fellow swordsman as he swiftly sliced him. He fell to his knees and then stood up.

They were both still for a moment before the samurai collapsed to the ground unconscious.

A giant gash appeared on Bob from the cut he received from the swordsman's blade. "It would appear that you are incapable of seeing my Jiva. They are rather elusive. If you can't see the souls of the dead, then you'll have no luck spotting them. I'm sorry. Did I forget to mention that?" he asked snidely as he floated up to the defeated samurai.

His spectral hands lifted the arrogant fool from the ground and made him nod.

"Oops, it must have slipped my mind. It's rather hard for me to keep track of all the holes in the minds of simpletons. Oh, but don't worry. I didn't drain your entire soul. You are not yet fit to be my rival. You have potential though, so I'll let you live for now. Don't disappoint me next time. When I have to entertain myself, things get very unpleasant for my opponent," said Bob with a smile.

Once Bob summoned up the Atma Blade, Exp 8 was out of time.

"Twenty-one," said Kanasta as he ripped off the target's hand.

The lights in the room suddenly came up, revealing that the arena was about as spacious as a hockey field. The room was one large steel-plated prison. The only décor were the neon lights beaming from the ceiling and the bumpy floor.

"Now I know how Devlin feels," said Exp 8, holding his arm in anguish.

Kanasta pulled his leg back before shooting it into the distracted target.

After smashing into the ceiling, Exp 8 turned around and fired an orb at the sturdy assassin.

Kanasta jumped up, caught the orb in his fist and then punched the target with it.

The orb exploded, sending the Exp crashing back into the ceiling.

"What the hell is this guy?" asked Exp 8 before falling back down.

Kanasta grabbed the primary target as he fell and kicked off him, slamming the target into the ground below. He then leaped off the ceiling for a follow up attack.

Exp 8's turrets popped out and opened fire as the assassin sped down toward him.

Kanasta dodged the bullets and then gripped both turrets with his brawny hands. He kicked off the ground, tearing them off the target's back. He pummeled the target upside the head with the turrets until one exploded in its face.

Exp 8 was shot backwards from the explosion as his enemy firmly placed his feet in the ground. He turned around in midair and fired a laser net.

Kanasta tossed the dislocated turret at the net.

The laser net wrapped around the turret and balled up.

Kanasta then raced toward the target in the blink of an eye.

Exp 8 socked the enemy in the face while soaring through the air.

Kanasta smiled beneath the metal fist. He took out a sharp metal playing card and sliced off the injured arm, grabbing the target with this other hand in the same movement. He pressed the target against the wall, creating a crater with its body.

"No way...I got amputated by a human. Just what the hell are you?"

Kanasta flung the target to the ground. He then pushed the button on the dismembered arm, causing an orb to shoot forward.

Exp 8 looked around drowsily. He kicked his attacker's feet relentlessly, determined to knock him down.

Kanasta grabbed the target's leg, stopping its movement.

"How the hell am I losing to you?" asked Exp 8, gripping his injured leg.

Kanasta slammed his elbow down, smashing the target's knee. He followed up the attack by tossing the target backward into the orb.

The orb exploded, sending Exp 8 back toward the assassin.

Kanasta ducked, allowing the target to pass over him. His fist then jetted into the target, releasing a gust of wind on impact.

Exp 8's stomach caved in on itself from the pressure. His eyes closed and he fell back silently.

"I finished you in exactly twenty-one moves. *Black Jack*," said Kanasta, towering over his victim.

Chapter 18: Back to the Battlefield

The winners stood in a neon circle that appeared once the final victor was decided.

The barrier surrounded them and then the elevator shot up. Once it reached the surface, it opened up.

Devlin showered the winners in confetti. "Congratulations for surviving the first round! So Kaity did you have fun?" he asked, patting her head.

"I sure did! Thanks Devi-kun!" she exclaimed, hugging him tightly.

"Umm…where are the rest of our comrades? Did they lose?" asked Karson.

"Where's Kawai? Which one of you fought her!" yelled Atatasuki.

"You must have defeated Ego. Don't get cocky. That was his first time alone on the field. You had better hope he is alive," said Kanasta, giving the brown-skinned target a dark glare.

"Where is my sister? I swear if you hurt her, I will give you a very agonizing death!" yelled Atatasuki, wrapping his hands around the assassin boss' throat.

"Wait a minute…where is Riufen?" asked Devlin with wide eyes.

"I defeated him. He was an incredibly powerful opponent. I barely won. But I just couldn't let my team down. You shouldn't underestimate us, Devlin," said Bob, making circles around him.

"Way to go Bob!" said Ada, throwing her arms in the air.

"Oh, you are too kind," said Bob with a bow.

"Where is my sister!" exclaimed Atatasuki, fear brimming up in his rage-filled eyes.

"I don't know," said Kanasta, blowing a strand of hair away from his face.

"Looking for something? I turned her into my little trophy," said Tempo, holding up the little girl's frozen body.

Devlin snatched Kawai from Tempo's hands. "I'll be taking that. Don't worry, Failed Experiment. She'll be good as new in no time," he said with a smile.

"I'm going to make you suffer for hurting her!" yelled Atatasuki, thrashing his fists at Tempo.

Bob rose out of the ground and grabbed the impulsive fool's fist. "Take a deep breath and relax. If you fight him like that, you're bound to lose. Let me take care of him," he said, patting Atatasuki's back.

"I can't believe I actually won! Aren't you proud of me?" asked Ada, beaming at Devlin.

Kaity ran up to Ada, pressing her plasma claws against her neck. "Where is Sefiwah?"

"Don't worry your cute little head. All I did was knock her out by bonking the back of her head. Your girlfriend is A-okay," said Ada, patting the girl's head.

"How could you? She has very fragile bones! I won't let you get away with this." Kaity reached for her pistol.

Devlin grabbed her arm and smiled at her. "Calm down everyone, there will be plenty of time for you to maim each other later. Right now, you must go to your respective waiting rooms. Freedom Forcers, go to the room on the left. Viper Squad, go to the right. Meet back here in five minutes," he said, looking up at the digital clock on the wall.

"Why should we listen to you?" asked Karson, turning his guns against the enemy commander.

"Calm down. This will give us an opportunity to plan things out. Come on, let's go," said Bob, dragging the trigger-happy nuisance with six spectral hands.

Kanasta leaned over to his client. "You may want to bring Exp 8 to an emergency room. His injuries could be fatal if they aren't attended to."

"I already have my best doctor down there. He is patching up Exp 8 as we speak. Sorry, but your injured assassins will just have to bleed out in the waiting room," said Devlin, gesturing with his hand.

"Viper Squad, we need to plan our next move," said Kanasta, leading them into the break room.

"And we should do the same," said Bob, coaxing his allies into their room with his spectral hands.

Once Atatasuki made it inside the room, he collapsed.

"Did you have a harsh battle?" asked Karson, loading up his guns.

Atatasuki lifted his head up from the carpet. "I lost some of my organs and I'm all beat up. Where in the glorious name of muffins did the assassins get those artifacts? And how the heck can they use them?"

"I know that one!" exclaimed Ada, raising her hand.

"Then go ahead and tell us," said Karson.

"They got them from Devlin's father. He and Kanasta are old friends."

"That would explain why he seems so chummy with Devlin," said Bob.

"Yep. And as for how they are able to use them…they have capsules just like we do!"

"I thought only Exps could use a capsule," said Karson, polishing his guns.

"Kanasta must have transplanted the capsules into his fellow assassins. Oooh, they really are one big happy family," said Ada with a hop.

"I barely won my fight. And I'm still working on regrowing my organs. Honestly guys…I don't know if I can win the next round. What do you think, brother?" asked Atatasuki, turning to his side.

"Um…Exp 8 lost. That Kanasta guy must be quite the handful. We lost Nina as well. She was a valuable fighter. What a shame. Uuugh," said Bob, stretching his pupil.

"How did the Ultimate Exp lose? He's our leader! How can we win, if he couldn't?" asked Atatsuki, his quivering hands shaking his spherical ally.

"He was probably overconfident. How like him. Either way, I'm sure he softened up the Boss for us. But I must say…I'm very proud of you. You've outlasted your superior brother! That was quite unexpected," said Bob with a smile.

"Yeah, I guess I did!"

"Sometimes the oldest models are the most efficient," said Karson, using a cloth to clean his Gatling gun.

"Hey, uh, Karson, I'm sorry for not trusting you before. You gave it your all and won your fight. I never should have doubted you," said Atatasuki, slugging the soldier affectionately.

"Don't worry about it. One can never be too careful on the battlefield. I'm glad my service has won your trust. After all, cannons speak louder than words, am I right?" asked Karson with a salute.

"And friendship is tastier than opposition. Glad to have you on our side," said Atatasuki, shaking the gunman's arm.

"Glad to be here. I'm honored to fight for the rebellion. Just look at how far we've come. We can win this! If Nina lost, her opponent must be on the ropes! And don't worry about me. Other than a bit of oil loss I'm in great shape! What about you Ada, how you doing?"

"We wrestled a bit, but Sefiwah didn't really hurt me. I could go another round or maybe even two," said Ada with a shrug.

"We'll need more than high morale to win this. We need a strategy. If we can win at least two rounds, we're still in the game. Atatasuki, you're the most injured. Would you mind taking on their boss?" asked Bob, turning to him.

"Are you mad? The Boss is probably the strongest one of them all!" yelled Karson.

"That is why we need to soften him up. Atatasuki is severely damaged. He will probably lose no matter who he fights. He might as well fight a one-sided battle. That will give the rest of us an edge," said Bob.

"Who died and made you general? If Atatasuki fights the Boss, then he is going to perish!" exclaimed Karson, standing in front of the self-proclaimed leader.

"Ada, would you mind telling us what Kanasta values more than anything?" asked Bob, turning her around to face them.

"Not at all!"

"Glad to hear it," said Bob with a grin.

"So…uh, are you going to tell us?" asked Atatasuki.

"Oh, of course I will! You should just ask next time. Kanasta values money above all else," said Ada with a grin.

"That's exactly right. And when I was checking to see if the coast was clear, I learned that Devlin is going to give the Viper Squad double for each one of us that's alive. So there's no need for worry. Look Atatasuki, we still want you to give it your all. We just don't expect you to win," said Bob, patting him on the head.

"Alright, sounds like a plan," said Atatasuki, catching his breath.

"Good. I'll take on Tempo. He looks like a tough opponent, but I'm fit for the challenge. He would just melt the rest of you," said Bob, looking over his team.

"Then let me fight Kaity! I can distract her and get up close for the knockout punch. I might even be able to find Nina and wake her up," said Ada.

"Karson may have firepower, but Kaity is very stealthy. I think it's best if we let Ada deal with her. And that would leave Karson in our reserves. If any of us lose, then our opponent should at least be tired. That will make them easy pickings for our gunman. Alright, let's go win this thing!" exclaimed Bob, grabbing their arms and pulling them up.

"Wait, but what about Exp 8's plan? He said we should just play along with whatever Devlin decides. We can't show Devlin any fear!" yelled Atatasuki.

"That strategy got your little sister turned into a snow cone. If we want to win this, we are going to need an actual strategy. Now let's move out. No doubt the assassins have made their own plans," said Bob, rolling his eye.

The Freedom Forcers went back to the main room. The Viper Squad was already there, poised for battle.

Devlin entered from the shadows. "Well done both assassins and Exps. You have won your battles. However, it is not over until all members of one team are defeated. So the battles must continue. I'm going to make things a bit more interesting. As you can see, I've added circles for the assassins as well. I don't want to force you to share an elevator. Now, how should I distribute these?" he asked slyly, holding the artifacts of the losers in his arms.

"How did you get those artifacts?" asked Bob.

Devlin dropped the artifacts onto the metal table. "I ripped it from each loser's capsule with this little robot I made," he said, showing off the hand-sized bot. "They steal artifacts, but they are very fragile so they're not fit for combat. Aren't they cute? They have these itty-bitty magnets that rip artifacts right out of a capsule in a matter of seconds…if the host is still."

"Can we get on with this?" asked Bob.

"How did Riufen lose!" exclaimed Devlin as a new robot handed him the Life Artifact.

"We've already been over this," said Bob annoyed.

"I still can't believe it. He was my strongest Exp…ever!"

"Apparently not," said Bob with a grin.

"Anyway, the defeated Viper Squads artifacts are size, revive, multiply, and life. The defeated Freedom Forcers artifacts are sound, shield, ice, and slow motion. Hmm, there is a slight number problem with the teams. There are four Freedom Forcers, and only three Vipers. Oh but don't worry, I have another Exp in my reserve. He's been repaired and enhanced! Pharma, come on out!"

The door opened.

Pharma limped into the room, nearly tripping. He went up to his rival while smoking his thumb. "We can finally finish our battle," he said, blowing a puff of smoke in Karson's face.

"Pick your opponents and then your artifacts. After that, just step in the circle and prepare for battle. The team that picks first will alternate after each decision. Whoever picks first will also choose the battlefield. Let's get this started," said Devlin, dropping the artifacts on the metal table.

"You're my target," said Kaity, grabbing Ada's arm.

"Pharma, we are going to finish this now!" yelled Karson.

"Drugs will be the end of you, Karson," said Pharma, his voice no longer raspy.

"You will be my opponent," said Bob, pointing to Kanasta's right-hand man.

"You're on, beach ball!" yelled Tempo.

"That leaves your fate in my hands," said Kanasta, turning to the leftover target with a slight smile.

"Hah, you can't kill me if you want the money. You've lost even if you win," said Atatasuki with a sneer.

"The Freedom Forcers have endangered the pride of my assassins. Exp 8 is the only one Devlin needs alive. I've decided to allow my assassins to kill your friends. I do love money, but you've upset me," said Kanasta, stretching out his fingers.

"You're bluffing! He would never let me die! I'm his only microwave; he needs me," said Atatasuki, turning to Devlin for reassurance.

"I ordered a new one just yesterday. It should be arriving any minute. You're useless to me now," said Devlin.

"Wait, who wants to switch with me?" asked Atatasuki, raising his hand.

"Sorry, but I've a battle to finish," said Karson, cocking his arms.

"I'll fight him later. Try not to die," said Bob, waving at Atatasuki while his focus stayed glued to his opponent.

"Don't be so confident. I'm going to melt you alive," said Tempo, pulling out the thermometer in his mouth.

"Now that we know who is fighting who, it's time to pick artifacts and locations. Each fighter is allowed one extra artifact. Karson, you and Pharma are up first," said Devlin.

"Should we listen to him?" asked Atatasuki.

"The assassins have a code. By playing along, we insure that they don't just hoard all the artifacts," said Bob.

"Go ahead, Karson, it won't make a difference," said Pharma, chewing a cigarette.

Karson took the Revive Artifact, which looked like a cloud.

Pharma took the Slow-motion Artifact, most likely because it resembled a powdery white chunk of amphibolite.

They stood on opposite circles. A blue barrier enveloped them before bringing them down to the raceway where Atatasuki had fought Ego.

"Drugs will destroy you! This time I will be victorious," said Pharma as he descended.

"Drugs are a poison that kills the user and the target. They are a double-edged sword and that is why guns will always kill more!" exclaimed Karson as he entered the arena.

"If they kill both the user and those around them, doesn't that make drugs more lethal?" asked Pharma with a sly smile.

"Enough talk."

"I will show you the threat of drugs firsthand."

"You already have. Ahahaha."

"That won't happen again! I'll kill you and then I'll overdose!"

They jumped away from each other, both trying to create some distance, as soon as the barrier dropped.

"I should have made sure you were dead," said Karson, bringing up semi-automatic machine guns.

Smoke poured out of Pharma, fogging up his rival's view.

Karson fired wildly into the smoke while waving his arms to disperse the fog.

Pharma rushed at the living gun, took the patches off his arm and slapped them on his rival's arm. "My special acid patches can make anything high! Even guns will have hallucinations."

Karson saw crosshairs of various colors spinning around the arena. Beneath him was an ocean of rainbow gunpowder. It splashed into him like multicolored waves.

"The acid is absorbed by your skin, flows throughout your nervous system, and then enters your brain," said Pharma, sitting and crossing his arms.

Karson was waving his arms on the floor, making imaginary powder angels on the rough asphalt. "I can fly. Wow, a double rainbow!"

Pharma jabbed his needle fingers into his rival's arm.

Karson fired wildly into the air with his arms and legs.

The bullets grazed the addict as he retreated.

"I've made Karson unpredictable. Oh well, I'll just have to fight acid with acid," said Pharma, brushing some cocaine powder off his chest.

"Yay acid!" exclaimed Karson, firing wildly at the ceiling.

"Let's both get wasted!" Pharma slapped acid patches all over his body.

Karson dizzily shot bullets in all directions as a hazy figure approached him.

Pharma saw the bullets shoot up to him in slow motion, but his body couldn't react quick enough to dodge them.

The serrated metal grazed his body as he backed away from the frenzied gunman.

Pharma stabbed adrenaline needles into his legs. "Now I can move extremely fast and you can only limp around like a blind fool. *Super Slo-mo.*"

The bullets Karson fired all but stopped in the air.

"Wheee!"

Pharma sped through the slowed storm of bullets. He stepped down on his rival's arms and leaned over him. "I'll bury you in ecstasy."

The drug lord's mouth opened up and regurgitated ecstasy all over his enemy.

"Drown in psychedelic bliss!" yelled Pharma, popping a cigar in his mouth.

"*REVIVE!*" yelled Karson giddily.

The gunman's head shot out of the ecstasy pile and glided toward the addict.

Pharma's feet were pelted by bullets. He lost his balance and fell to the ground as the missile closed in on him. The addict quickly limped away as the missile exploded below his feet, sending him skidding across the asphalt and hitting his back against the guardrails.

When the smoke from the explosion cleared, Karson was standing on top of his opponent, like a monument to a war hero.

"How did you...?" asked Pharma, dropping his cigar in surprise.

Karson's neck disengaged another head.

"I simply revived my senses. Did you think I chose the Revive Artifact because I thought it was shiny?" asked Karson, brushing off his legs.

"You chose it so you could snort it, right?"

"I chose it because it makes me immune to intoxication!" exclaimed Karson with a triumphant pose.

"Drugs are not so easily conquered. You have only seen the butt of the cigar. Drugs can do so much more. Prepare to die!" yelled Pharma as he leaped at his rival.

Karson kicked him aside and emptied his clip into the addict. "I won't be affected no matter what. But go ahead and try," he said, loading up dual shotguns.

"Let's see you try and be above the influence after this! *Breathing*

Bong!"

Pharma's head poured out swirly purple fumes, polluting the air.

Karson saw the yellow lines on the street bend and stretch. The metal gates rose above him and slowly closed him in.

"*REVIVE*."

The gates pulled back and the yellow lines straightened up all at once.

"Even if you revive your senses, they will be instantly re-intoxicated by the atmosphere. You cannot escape this trip," said Pharma before he inhaled sharply.

Karson was skating on his Uzis in a state of euphoria. "I'm a pretty grenade! Boom! Yay explosions!"

"Now that you're doped up, let's finish this ride!" Pharma jabbed his hand forward, impaling the living gun with all four needles. "That's some good shit, eh Karson? It's especially radical when it's shot directly into your veins." He yanked his fingers out.

Karson fell to the ground, shutters closed over his shotgun barrel eyes.

"This victory calls for some serious drug abuse." Pharma sniffed the fresh cocaine powder off his body. He then ripped out the nicotine straws and ate them. "Victory tastes delicious!" The user fell to his knees and pounded his chest. "No not again, kough, kough."

The addict's IV packs shriveled up.

"Drugs, why have you forsaken me?" yelled Pharma, pounding at his chest.

"**REVIVE**!" Karson rose from the ground and stood over his opponent. "Once again you have overdosed yourself to hell. Accept your defeat," he said, pressing the shotgun to the drugee's forehead.

"Are you kidding? Kough! Kough! My death proves the potency of drugs." Pharma breathed in deeply and then fell down.

"I'm glad the illusion of drugs at least let him die happily," said Karson as he turned away.

Once Pharma and Karson were out of sight, Devlin approached Kaity.

"Don't hold back," said Devlin, patting her head.

"I won't." Kaity snatched the Ice Artifact, which was a rounded block of ice.

Ada took an artifact that resembled a gray chunk of gypsum.

"Alrighty, so now I pick the arena. Let's go to where you fought Nina," said Ada, grabbing the girl's hand.

Kaity shrugged her off. "I get to pick the arena. And if you want to go to the jungle, then we'll go someplace else."

"I'm just concerned about Nina."

"Worry about your own life," said Kaity, stepping onto Sefiwah's circle.

"Alright, but I want to pick next round," said Ada, turning to Devlin.

"There won't be a next round for you," said Devlin with a smirk.

Ada stood on her circle and was brought down toward the white room where she encountered Sefiwah.

"Kaity, please tell me you didn't kill Nina. She was just a child," said Ada, on the brink of tears.

"We get more for a live capture, so don't worry. Even if we did get paid extra for kills, I would never destroy something so beautiful. There's still so much of her I have yet to explore. I wonder what her tears taste like. I guess killing you is one way to find out," said Kaity, licking her lips.

"Wait, can't you let me live too?"

"Kanasta said that our pride is at stake. We have to cover up our follies with your blood."

"That doesn't seem necessary. We all make mistakes."

"Shut up! I don't know how you defeated Sefi-chan. She's practically untouchable. She wouldn't quit until her target was eliminated. Tell me how you beat her or I'll take my time cutting you up!"

The assassin's plasma claws jutted out.

"What you're saying makes no sense. Sefiwah hates killing. She doesn't want to hurt anyone," said Ada with a smile.

"That is beyond ridiculous! Why would she join the Viper Squad if she didn't want to kill?"

"She didn't say. But I know that she loves you with all her heart."

The force field dropped.

"So if you didn't kill her, then where is she?" asked Kaity, taking a step toward her opponent.

"I knocked her out. She must have gotten picked up or something," said Ada, her legs trembling.

"Devlin has been up there the whole time. Do you really think lying to me will keep you alive?" asked Kaity, sharpening her claws against each other.

"I'm not lying."

"You lied about her not wanting to hurt anyone. When we go after a bad person, we savor killing them. We take our time. She relishes it. Can you explain that?" asked Kaity, closing in on the liar.

"I don't know why. But it doesn't really matter. She is a good person. There is so much love in her eyes," said Ada, her hands to her chest.

"Don't you dare lie to me about Sefiwah! I am going to gift wrap your corpse and send it to Nina." Kaity whipped out a pistol and shot the target right between the eyes.

Ada stood up as she was being pelted by bullets. "She wouldn't like that. I suggest you send her naked pictures of herself instead," she said as she approached.

"This is no time for jokes. It's time for work." Kaity rushed up to the target and shoved her plasma claws through the target's chest. "Bleed and suffer." She harshly ripped out her claws.

Ada fell to her knees, blood gushing out of her body. "If it was that easy to kill me, Sefiwah would have won. My friends need me to win this. I am not backing down," she said from behind the assassin.

"The real you must be…right behind me!" exclaimed Kaity as her backpack disengaged a revolver. She turned around to see an army.

"Ding ding! That's correct! But you might need to narrow it down, hmmhmmhymm," said all the Adas in unison.

"I have no way to tell which is the real you, so I'll just have to kill all of you." Kaity tossed her revolver in the air and, with pinpoint accuracy, shot every target in the head with her sidearm.

The bullets passed through all of the Ada's except one.

That Ada fell down to the floor with a hole in her forehead.

Kaity caught her revolver and unloaded a full round into the wounded target's chest. She then fired a beam of ice to freeze the target's legs to the floor.

"Process of elimination?" asked Ada, looking up at her attacker.

"Yep…works every time, hee-hee," said Kaity, blowing the tip of her gun.

"Please don't kill me. I'm still a virgin," said Ada as she struggled to get to her feet.

"Assassins don't have mercy, so don't bother pleading. You know, I don't often get to fight close range. I'm going to enjoy ripping you to shreds," said Kaity, bouncing with excitement. She slashed her plasma claws through her victim's leg, slicing it off completely.

Ada tried to limp away, but it was hopeless.

Kaity slid her plasma claws across Ada's back, searing her digitized flesh. She then stabbed her over and over, relishing her screams. "I'm all bloody now," she said, licking the blood off her arm like a kitty.

"Do you want me to help you?" asked another Ada, wiping the girl's arm with a cloth.

Kaity stared in disbelief at the shredded remains. She turned to Ada and pulled back her claws. "I love prey that doesn't die easily," she said, smiling as she sliced her target open vertically.

Ada's two halves shot out blood as they parted.

"It seems you're outnumbered."

An armada of Adas instantly appeared behind the assassin.

"You have the Multiply and the Illusion Artifact. That combination is going to be difficult to overcome. But you know what they say: love conquers all. _ADA, LOVE, KAITY._"

The Adas turned against one another. They leaped into a frenzied scuffle, each one trying to prove its love was greatest. "She's mine!" "She loves me the most!" "I shall kill myself so Kaity will be happy!" Many Ada's said many things as they fought, killed, and died for their newfound lover.

"The one worthy of my love must find the original Ada and bring her to me," said Kaity with her head up high.

All of the Ada's grabbed onto an invisible person.

The illusion faded as they grabbed it, revealing the true Ada.

Two of them pinned down her arms. The other four skipped up to their beloved. Ada was thrown to the ground, her hands held behind her back. All the copies turned to Kaity with hope in their eyes. "Will you marry me?" they asked, their hands clasped to their chest.

Kaity crouched down and grabbed her target's chin. "I've turned you against yourself. That must feel so strange, hee-hee," she said, tapping her nose.

"Oh, I was just acting. I'm immune to your love ability because I already love everything. Hooray for unconditional love!" Ada leaped up and embraced the adorable girl.

"Get off me! I do not want your hands on me. You hurt my Sefi-chan," said Kaity in tears.

"I didn't hit her that hard. Hmm, I wonder if this will work. ILLUSIONARY INSANITY, DISGUISE!" Ada's body morphed until she was the spitting image of Kaity.

Some of the Adas turned to her now.

"Kaity, it's you! How can we prove our undying love for you?" asked three Adas.

"I need you to defeat her," said Ada, pointing to the cute assassin.

"I can't hurt her, I love her." "Even if she's a fake, I love her little body." "The Kaity I love would never tell us to hurt her," said the various Adas.

"Looks like you can't even control yourself," said Kaity, spinning a pistol on her finger.

"Oh, I know how to solve this problem."

All of the Ada clones transformed into Sefiwahs.

Kaity's eyes flared up with hatred. "How dare you impersonate Sefiwah! I will not be stopped by your disgraceful disguise. I love the soul of Sefiwah. You cannot even begin to imitate that!"

Kaity's backpack disengaged her sniper rifle.

"I didn't want to waste this expensive ammo…" Kaity loaded in a round in the chamber. "…but I'll make an exception for you." She shot the Sefiwahs in their heads with swift accuracy. Her eyes trembled each time her lover's body plopped to the ground. By the time she had to reload her clip, tears were streaming out.

"No more. I can't do this to you anymore. I refuse." Ada reduced her numbers to one and became her normal self.

"Kaity, I'm sorry. I've been doing exactly what Devlin wants. I don't care if you are my enemy, that doesn't mean I have to fight you. I won't play this game of kill or be killed," said Ada, embracing the lost child and petting her head.

"Seeing her in pain…it's just too much. It brings back sad memories." Kaity held onto Ada tightly as tears poured from her eyes.

"This fight won't end until one of us falls. I guess there's no other way around it. Kill me, Kaity. If living means hurting a little girl's feelings, then I'd rather be dead. Just please believe me. I didn't kill Sefiwah," said Ada, caressing the girl's cheeks.

"I believe you," said Kaity with a nod.

Her plasma claws slowly bore into the target's chest.

Kaity then harshly ripped them out with a painful twist. "If you ever get near Sefiwah again…I will kill you." She shook the blood off her claws.

"Aww, now that I've met you, I understand exactly how she feels. You're just so sweet! I could just kidnap you!" exclaimed Ada lovingly.

"What? Stay away from me," said Kaity, aiming her gun at the un-killable woman.

"You're just a little girl who needs a mother. I would rather die than break the bond you share with Sefiwah. I hope she can find the light deep in your soul. It's buried alright, but it sure is bright," said Ada with a sweet smile.

Kaity pressed her claws against Ada's throat.

"Don't pretend you understand Sefiwah!" exclaimed Kaity, trying to stay upset.

"Okay, calm down. I surrender. There's no need to get violent," said Ada, her wounds healing.

"I'm done here! Send me up, Devlin!" hollered Kaity, tapping her foot impatiently.

Chapter 19: The Brutality Escalates

Once Kaity and Ada started their descent into the arena, Devlin motioned Atatasuki to make his selection.

The passionate prototype lifted up the one-meter beige chunk of feldspar, which was actually the Size Artifact. It shrank as he pressed it into his chest and absorbed it.

Kanasta pondered for awhile and then grabbed a sleek blue stone of calcite.

"Don't you dare touch my sister's artifact," said Atatasuki, gripping the killer's arm.

"Are you getting angry?" asked Kanasta with a slight smile.

"It's very special to her. It reminds her of her beloved," said Atatasuki, his grip tightening.

Kanasta slammed his palm into his target, breaking free of his grip. "You already made your choice."

"Whatever. I'll just pry it from your crispy dead hands later," said Atatasuki, cracking his neck.

"The sooner the better," said Kanasta, standing on Exp 8's circle.

"I don't know how he lost to you, but don't expect the same thing from me," said Atatasuki, standing on the opposite circle.

The barrier rose up before they were brought down to the battlefield where Kanasta had defeated Exp 8.

"What's with the dents in the wall...and all the blood?" asked Atatasuki, fidgeting with his fingers.

"Let's just say your brother won't be able to escape Devlin ever again. Now, shall we begin?" asked Kanasta, stepping into the arena.

"Oh, it's totally on! I am going to make you guys sorry you ever hurt Kawai. I am going to do you what Exp 8 refused to do. I am going to kill you!"

"As long as I strive to reach the top, I will not lose. As long as purpose drives me, I am unbeatable," said Kanasta with a firm stance.

"I wasn't aware that was how things worked on planet Earth. But if you're right, then I won't die either. I may have been replaced as a microwave, but I can bake up a new purpose." Atatasuki put his fingers to his forehead and closed his eyes. He then collapsed to the ground.

"If this is some sort of trap, I'm not falling for it."

Atatasuki stood up, his fists clenched. "I will end the lives of all those who stand endanger my family!"

"Guheh, then come at me," said Kanasta, opening his arms.

"I was only a microwave before, limiting myself to heating things up. But now…I have blossomed into a beautiful muffin! The strong survive, but the resourceful thrive," said Atatsuki, walking toward the assassin boss.

"Words of wisdom," said Kanasta, mildly amused.

"Stop smiling at me!"

"Let's make things a little more interesting. I'm going to play a little game of Black Jack. I will not attack you until I draw cards equaling twenty-one. You have until then to kill me. But once I've drawn them, you are dead," said Kanasta as he shuffled his cards.

"That should be plenty of time to master the Size Artifact. *GROWING SELF-RESPECT, HUMONGOUS HAND.*"

His hand grew immensely and then fell to the floor. "I can't pick it up!" yelled Atatsuki, struggling to lift his car-sized hand.

"Four," said Kanasta after he casually drew a card.

"*SHRINKING SELF-RESPECT, HAND.*"

Atatsuki's hand shrunk until it was too feeble to even lift up a marble. "Hah, I've found an ability your pal couldn't."

"Ego knows the Size Artifact can shrink as well. He just doesn't use that power because it scars his ego. Ooh, I got a seven."

"Seven plus four equals eleven. Twenty one minus eleven equals ten. This is bad, all he needs is a ten," said Atatsuki, tapping his fingers against his chin.

"The next card could end this," said Kanasta with a glint in his eye.

"I know how to kill you in one attack!" yelled Atatsuki, his hand returning to normal size.

"Eight."

"Ten minus eight equals two. Damn it, if he draws a two, I'm dead," said Atatsuki, shuffling his feet.

"Leave the calculating to me. You're embarrassing yourself."

"I've got to end this now! *GROWING SELF-RESPECT, BIG BODY.*" Atatsuki expanded until he was the height of a two-story building.

"Damn it…I got a ten. Oh well, I guess I have to start over again."

"Yes, I've won!" Atatsuki jumped up, opened his chest and slammed it down on Kanasta. "I have two things that my brother was lacking! I have the willingness to kill and the artifact that will help me do it! *MACROWAVE.*"

Kanasta was trapped inside the target's closet-sized microwave. "Five."

"Die already!"

"Seven. Hmm, I went overboard. I guess it's time to start over. How lucky, I drew a ten."

The prototype's stomach beeped, signaling that time was up. Even though Atatsuki knew the assassin wasn't dead, he couldn't help but open up his chest.

Kanasta was freed, revealing that he was surrounded by a shield. "Your sister has a very useful ability," he said, playing a game of solitaire on his suitcase.

Atatasuki looked at the shield and froze up in horror.

"Is something the matter?" asked Kanasta, lowering the shield.

"Why must it be this way? She was just a little girl," cried Atatasuki as he fell to the floor with a thunderous thud.

"Killing is our job, but she wasn't dead last time I checked. A nine, not bad at all."

"I will personally kill every one of you damned assassins myself!" yelled Atatasuki, his massive fists quaking with anger.

Kanasta picked up his next card. "That brings my hand to exactly twenty-one." He calmly put the deck in his utility belt.

"Did you hear me?! They are dead! Every single one of them is going to die by my hand! I'll show you what happens when you mess with my family!" yelled Atatasuki, slamming his fist down.

Kanasta stopped the car-sized fist with his hand. His eyes peered into the hostile target's. "You can't just decide who your brothers and sisters are. I had to raise this family from the ground up! We are connected by bonds deeper than you can imagine! We fight together as a single unit. We all risk our lives for each other. You have no idea what a family is!"

"We are more than just a family! We are a team! We are all fighting for our freedom! *SUPER-SIZED MICROWAVE!*" Atatasuki's gigantic body became super heated.

Kanasta flung the arm aside, having it smash into the ceiling. "I already lost one family. How dare you Exps pretend you have one! Kawai is not your sister…it is just another experiment!"

"We are alive and we all have dreams. And right now, you're in the way!" Atatasuki slammed his two palms into the enemy.

Kanasta jumped up and stabbed his hands into Atatasuki's truck-sized chest. His skin melted off his hands as he slowly lifted the target off its feet.

"Are you even human?"

Kanasta's feet touched the floor, holding the twenty-foot Exp with a tiger-claw finger grip. "You Exps are the only thing standing in the way of my family. I will kill you all!" he yelled, bending his legs.

"Not before I murder all your damned assassins!" exclaimed Atatasuki, collecting heat in his chest.

Kanasta jumped up with his powerful legs. He flipped in midair and then slammed Atatasuki into the ground below. He tore his fingers out and stood proudly on the target's stomach.

"Do you know why I formed this team?" asked Kanasta, stepping up to Atatasuki's neck.

"For money?"

"Heh, that's only a small part of it. I did it to find family!" exclaimed Kanasta passionately. The assassin boss pried open the target's chest, trying to reach his opponent's capsule.

"My sister is dead because of you bastards!" Atatasuki pushed against his chest to keep it closed.

"Devlin took her away. Why don't you remember? She is in no danger."

"I would remember that if it really happened! Don't make up lies! I was sent here as a sacrifice for my team members! They are going to be so pissed off when I win!" Atatasuki's fists zoomed toward the murderer.

Kanasta knocked the target's arms aside with his elbows. He then stabbed his hands into the target's chest.

Atatasuki plucked Kanasta off his chest, opening it up in the process. He then quickly shoved the assassin inside. "Even Kawai's shields can't withstand my passionate heat."

"Perhaps, but she is only a child. Besides, I cannot die after coming so far," said Kanasta from within the Macrowave. He formed a shield around him that quickly expanded, ripping the target's chest open from within.

The Macrowave exploded. Heat shot out in all directions like a powerful torrent.

Kanasta leaped out as his target writhed around in agony.

"It's burning my insides! My capsule is going to melt! Why must I die like this?" Atatasuki continued to suffer as his body gradually shrank back to its normal size.

Kanasta sped up the target's legs, went past its chest, and then grabbed it by the throat. "You must die so I can make a living. It's nothing personal," he said, lifting up the target.

"Kawai, I can see you! Please, accept my love! I will be with you soon," said Atatasuki as his hand reached out.

"I shouldn't get so worked up. You're too weak to kill any of my assassins. I don't know why I was worried."

"You may kill me, but Bob will avenge us!"

"I'm not going to kill you. After all, we get twice the pay if you're alive." Kanasta flung the target to the ground, shattering its spinal structure.

"Damn it, I can't get up. I swear to you: I will kill the Viper Squad!" yelled Atatasuki, only able to lift up his head.

"You will try," said Kanasta, looking away with a smile.

On the floor above, after Kanasta and Atatasuki had been lowered into their fight, Devlin beckoned Tempo to choose next.

Tempo took the Sound Artifact. It glowed in his grip, calming his busted eardrum. "Damn, I still can't hear a thing. No matter, I'm always prepared." He turned on a hearing aid. "Heh, looks like I'm slowly turning into the Boss," he said, cracking his fingers.

Bob's arms reached out and grabbed hold of a particularly brittle chunk of coal.

They both stood on opposite circles and were brought down to the battlefield where Bob had battled Riufen.

"Devlin's newest Exp was defeated by you. That proves my theory: a newborn with ultimate power is nothing compared to a sage with experience," said Tempo, pressing the artifact into his chest.

"So just because you are older, you think you are going to win? I chose to fight you because my team needed a sure victory. Don't get so cocky," said Bob with a smile.

The barrier dropped as soon as they reached the training room.

"Time is power!" yelled Tempo, flinging heat blasts at the inexperienced weapon.

"There are exceptions to your theory. Riufen could easily beat you, even though he was just made. I may not be as old as you, but you're still going to lose. *Eyeball Laser*," said Bob, his eye turning red before firing a super fast laser beam.

" *TEMPERATURE FALL*," said Tempo with a grin.

The laser froze right before it hit him.

Tempo grabbed the frozen laser and tossed it forward.

The laser glided through the air before impaling the Exp.

"Eheheheh! How weak do you think I am?" asked Bob, spinning toward the mortal with the laser still in him.

Tempo leaped onto Bob. He grabbed the icicle and then repeatedly stabbed it into the spinning eyeball. " *TEMPERATURE RISE*."

The ice encompassing the laser became superheated and melted.

Tempo lost his grip and was sent flying into the concrete wall.

After spinning in place, Bob fired a laser.

Tempo jumped off the wall, having the laser pass between his legs.

"You are nothing compared to Riufen. Come on, I want to have some fun. Show me your true power!" Bob slammed into the trained killer.

Tempo stabbed Bob with a steel-tipped dagger. He then superheated it, slicing the target in half.

Spectral threads pulled Bob's body back together. He shot a laser forth as soon as he was healed.

Tempo moved his head out of the way and then rolled onto the ground. "I don't need to go all out to beat you. My suit enhances my ability to control temperature. Kanasta designed it specifically for me. I can freeze my entire body and still move around. You won't even be able to hit me after this. *TEMPERATURE FALL*."

The assassin's skin suit turned blue as it dropped its temperature. An aura of cold formed around his body.

"Maybe this will be fun." Bob fired multiple lasers that froze as soon as they hit their mark.

The icy lasers attached to the killer's frozen body, becoming his weapons.

"Can't hit me now." Tempo charged toward Bob, freezing the floor with each step. Once he reached his opponent, he kicked off the ground. "*ICICLE TOP!*" The killer spun around, but the frozen lasers just passed through his target. "It looks like we've reached a stalemate," he said, spinning circles around the enemy.

"Are you an idiot?! Do not ever think of yourself as my equal? How dare you underestimate me so severely! I will consume your soul for your insolence," said Bob, his eye red with rage.

Souls of the dead poured out of Bob and then fused together, summoning the Atma Blade.

"So you have a weapon after all."

Bob passed through the frozen lasers and thrust his blade into the mortal. The assassin screamed in agony as the sword attacked his soul.

Bob tossed him aside as one of the frozen lasers slammed into him. "You are nothing compared to me!"

"Calm the hell down. I never said we were equals. You can't attack me when you are in your ghost form. But I can always attack you," said Tempo, slowing down to a halt.

"Why can't Devlin give me a worthy opponent? This is a waste of my efforts!"

"Well then, allow me to entertain you! *TEMPERATURE RISE, MOLTEN POINT!*"

The concrete melted beneath him as his temperature escalated exponentially.

Tempo flung a heat wave forth and then rushed at his target.

Bob passed through the heat wave. He then materialized just in time to get socked by a flaming fist.

207

"I almost forgot! I have the Life Artifact," said Bob as he melted away.

"Seems like you remembered too late," said Tempo with a wide grin.

Bob reincarnated behind the foolish mortal, his pupil stretching into a grin. He shoved his blade into the ground as he ducked under a heated kick. "𝕷𝖎𝖋𝖊."

The ground rumbled violently as the entire arena came to life.

The walls lunged at the human, biting onto his burning arms. The floor rose up and constricted his legs.

The arena absorbed the heat as it melted away and crumbled. The ground split in two, causing the assassin to plummet into a pit.

Bob levitated over the pit, waving as his foe plummeted to his doom.

The floor closed up, crushing the assassin inside it.

"I do like this artifact. It's rather fun. Well, would you look at that? It seems I've won," said Bob, feigning shock.

"You think so, do you?" asked Tempo, his voice echoing across the walls.

"Where are you?" asked Bob, his eye slanting.

"Right above you."

Bob looked up, firing a laser at the ceiling.

The floor beneath him melted open.

A piece of the ceiling crashed into Bob, distracting him for a mere moment.

But a moment was all Tempo needed. His flaming arm stretched out from the hole and grabbed his target. He then tossed him down the chasm. "You will not escape! *TEMPERATURE FALL!*" He froze the opening shut, boxing them both in.

"You deceived me! I'm genuinely impressed," exclaimed Bob as he shot down the chasm.

Tempo pulled a four-foot double-edged thermometer off his back. "This is the Termometer!"

"And I thought my name was silly."

The mercury in the Termometer rose to the top, setting its tip aflame and vanquishing the darkness of the pit.

Tempo jumped down the sides of the walls diagonally, heading toward his descending target. He jabbed the Termometer at his enemy, singeing his pupil.

Bob pulled away and shot forth a laser on instinct.

Tempo flipped the Termometer, revealing that its other side was freezing cold. The laser froze and then fell back down toward its source.

Bob rammed into the frozen laser, sending it flying back.

Tempo leaped off the wall toward his target, dodging the laser in midair. "𝕰𝖞𝖊𝖇𝖆𝖑𝖑 𝕽𝖆𝖒!" Bob slammed into the assassin.

The Termometer blocked against the attack, triggering a power struggle. " *TEMPERATURE JUMP.*"

The mercury in the Termometer rapidly shot up and then back down. The Termometer changed from ice to fire every half second as it was jabbed it at the Exp.

"That's…very…im…pre…ssive," said Bob as he was being frozen and burned one after another.

Tempo's muscles bulged before he slammed the Termometer into his enemy.

Bob froze as he plummeted to the ground.

"I am not your equal! I am far more powerful than you are!"

The frozen Exp fell to the bottom of the pit but floated above it rather than smashing into bits.

Tempo landed and walked toward Bob. "Can every one of you Exp freaks float? And how can you levitate if you're frozen? I guess it doesn't really matter. You won't escape me. *TEMPERATURE FALL, ICY SANCTUARY.*"

The air above them froze, boxing them both in the bottom of the pit.

"I got this from my latest victim. *SOUND SHOT.*" Tempo slammed his fist against the wall.

The sound wave bounced off the narrow walls. It then smashed into Bob, exploding him into pieces.

Flames shot out from Tempo's palms and melted the icy chunks until all that remained of his target were four white, creamy puddles.

"You were a good fight," said Tempo, blowing the smoke off his fists.

"Is that all?" asked Bob, appearing behind him.

Tempo jumped back in surprise. "You still won't die!"

"I told you to go all out. Now I need you to be honest with me: was that your best shot?" asked Bob with a look of disapproval.

" *TEMPERATURE SPLIT.*"

Tempo's body became half fire and half ice. He jabbed the Termometer at the immortal invention furiously, flipping it around before each strike.

"Is…this…it?" asked Bob, freezing and then becoming unthawed.

"Yes, this is my ultimate attack!"

"Good," said Bob with a smile. He opened up the chasm using the Life Artifact and then slid beneath Tempo. "*True Eyeball Ram.*" He rammed into the outclassed mortal with the force of a rampaging elephant.

Tempo shot up all the way to the top of the pit just below their battle arena. He slammed against the sealed area, his eyes closed upon contact.

Bob floated up as Tempo fell back down the chasm.

Chapter 20: The Final Four

After the final victor was decided, the winners went back into their circles and were brought to the surface all at once.

"Things are coming to a close," said Devlin as the winners arrived at the floor above.

"It's just me and Bob! This is not good!" exclaimed Karson, sweating bullets.

"Yes, but don't worry. I won't lose," said Bob with a confident smile.

"You beat Tempo, I am impressed," said Kanasta with a slight bow of the head.

"He's all yours. I'll take care of the little kitty," said Bob, patting the gunman's back.

"Affirmative! I'll show him the bravery of the Brits!" exclaimed Karson with a salute.

Kanasta leaned down, looking directly into his protégé's eyes. "Be careful. He defeated Tempo. Fight him with everything you've got," he said, firmly gripping her hand.

"Roger sir," said Kaity with a nod.

"So, uh, did you enjoy yourself?" asked Devlin with a smile as he turned to his little crush.

"Not really. Do you know where Sefiwah is?" asked Kaity.

"She was taken to the infirmary by one of my assistants. I apologize for not telling you earlier."

"I'm just glad she's alright. Oh, Ada's still alive by the way. I, uh, didn't even knock her out. Sorry about that," said Kaity, turning away with flushed cheeks.

"So cute," said Devlin with an enamored smile.

"Shall we move things along?" asked Kanasta, crossing his arms.

"Yes, of course. Both sides are equally matched. Not even fate knows who the victor will be. Only one group can emerge victorious. Only one warrior can be crowned the winner," said Devlin, talking into a wireless microphone.

Kaity hopped up to the funny scientist and tilted her body. "Why are you talking like that?"

"Oh…I…um…I was just announcing. Sorry," said Devlin, turning away with flustered cheeks.

"You're cute Devi-kun, hee-hee," said Kaity, poking his cheek with her tail.

"I…well…you are…umm…thank you! You're very cute!" exclaimed Devlin, awkwardly throwing his hands around.

"Devlin, I believe that some congratulations are in order," said Kanasta, tilting his head to the Freedom Forcers.

"Oh, yes. You are absolutely correct. Ah, to think my own Exps can rival the skills of the Viper Squad assassins. I never thought this day would come," said Devlin, getting all choked up.

"I can't wait to visit Nina! She's my absolute favorite," said Kaity, holding her cheeks.

"Yeah, she was my favorite too. Anyway, let's get this party rolling! Here are the artifacts of the losers. The Freedom Forcers' artifacts are illusion, multiply, and size. The Viper Squad's artifacts are slo-mo, sound, and temperature. Grab hold of your new artifacts and descend into the arenas. Oh and Kaity, have fun mangling Bob." Devlin patted her head and smiled.

"I will! Lots and lots of fun! Don't worry. He's going down," said Kaity, sticking out her tongue.

Devlin looked at Bob's sinister smirk and sighed. "I can't help but worry a little," he said, tapping his fingers together.

"What's wrong, Devi-kun?" asked Bob googly-eyed.

"Everything is fine! Alright everyone, there's no time for breaks. You're all going right back into the arena!" exclaimed Devlin, causing the circles to light up.

"Take as many artifacts as you need," whispered Bob to Karson.

"Roger, Captain."

Karson took the Temperature Artifact and the Slow-motion Artifact.

Kanasta grabbed the Multiply Artifact carelessly.

Bob picked up the Sound Artifact with a spectral hand.

Kaity looked at two artifacts back and forth. Her ears perked up and then she took both the Size Artifact and the Illusion Artifact.

"Ladies and gentlemen, we are down to the last two battles," said Devlin, his tone lowering.

"We'll make you proud and furious all at once, ex-commander!" exclaimed Karson, transitioning from a salute to an offensive arm gesture.

"Oh, this is truly remarkable! My Exps are fighting the ultimate assassins and are tied with them. I don't know who to root for," said Devlin, bouncing up and down.

"You don't want me to win?" asked Kaity, lowering her head.

"Of course I do. Goooo assassins!"

"Either way you win, heh," said Kanasta.

"That's true. I don't owe the Viper Squad a cent if they're all dead. But I…really don't want that to happen. Oh, I know. I hope my Exps do really well, but in the end fail miserably," said Devlin with a kind smile.

"Thanks for the support," said Karson with a shrug.

Devlin crouched down to Bob. "If you kill Kaity, I will destroy you," he said with terrifying eyes.

"Don't lecture me. I'm on their side!" Bob's pupil turned red with anger.

"That's beside the point. I don't want to lose her," said Devlin, starting to tear up.

"I don't bargain with my enemies. Get out of my way. I have a battle to finish," said Bob, flinging the weak inventor aside without even touching him.

"Shall we?" asked Kanasta with a bow.

"Oh absolutely," said Karson, cocking both guns at once.

"Goodbye Karson," said Devlin, waving his hand.

Kanasta and Karson descended into the battlefield where Exp 8 and Atatasuki had been demolished by Kanasta.

As soon as the elevator doors opened, Kanasta took out his deck of cards.

"Ah, nothing like the view of a war-torn battlefield," said Karson, gazing at the blood splatters, dents, and scattered metal.

"When the value of the cards in my hand reaches exactly twenty-one, your life is over," said Kanasta bluntly.

"You are joking, right?" asked Karson.

"Hmm, a five," said Kanasta to himself.

"This is ridiculous! We are in the middle of a battle. This is no time for recreation! This is insulting!" yelled Karson, pointing his gun at the enemy.

"I got a ten," said Kanasta, showing his opponent the card.

"You were the only person who didn't ignore me last time. I thought that you were a warrior! I believed in you!" Karson shot the card.

Kanasta looked at the four gaping holes where the number "1" once was. "My mistake...it's a zero," he said, lowering his head.

"Stop playing around and fight me. I refuse to attack my opponent's weak-point. And right now you are one massive target!" Karson shot the next card.

"A seven? Nope, it's a seventy," said Kanasta before shuffling his cards back into his deck. His eyes shot up, instilling Karson with terror. "This is getting annoying," he said as he quickly drew cards.

Karson shot the deck out of his hand.

"I have no more cards to draw. This is rather inconvenient. It's a good thing I came prepared," said Kanasta, reaching into a pocket on his utility belt.

"Damn you," said Karson as he shot a second deck out of Kanasta's hand.

"Fine...forget the cards," said Kanasta, cracking his fingers.

"Finally. Let's get this battle started," said Karson, aiming both guns at the final enemy.

"I'll give you twenty-one seconds to kill me. When that time is up, you're done for," said Kanasta with a twitch of agitation.

"Damn it, just fight me!"

"You have fifteen seconds left."

"How did that happen so fast?"

"Now you have nine seconds left," said Kanasta with a growing smile.

"The more time you waste, the longer it will take to get your money," said Karson with a savvy smirk.

"Twenty-one." Kanasta put his hands to his sides.

"Good, now dodge this if you can," said Karson, crossing his arms. His head shot off his neck and zoomed forth.

Kanasta cut the missile in half with a single metal card.

Before the target could turn around, Kanasta zoomed up behind it. He then jabbed his hand through the target's back and out its front.

Karson exploded, sending shrapnel every which way.

"Are you happy now?" asked Kanasta, snatching his cards out of the air.

Karson pieces shook rapidly and then came together, reforming him.

"How did you come back?" asked Kanasta with a raised eyebrow.

"A deal with the devil! I've never used an artifact before, but I have nothing against using special ammunition. *TEMPERATURE RISE!*"

Karson's whole body was set aflame.

"I remember when I first fought Tempo," said Kanasta, twisting his wrists.

"Keep your head in the game!" Karson slammed his head into the enemy commander and ejected it.

Kanasta was lifted off his feet by the missile. He pushed off and slid toward the back wall.

"Time to mow you down. *SLO-MO!*" exclaimed Karson, loading up his Gatling guns.

Kanasta jogged up to the target as he was being pumped full of bullets. He tossed two cards that sliced the Gatling guns in half.

"What the blooming hell are you?"

Kanasta grabbed the tattered arms and ripped them off. He hooked the target's legs, making it trip.

Before Karson could hit the ground, the assassin boss's knee slammed into him.

Kanasta cupped both hands behind the target's searing head and then slammed his head into its face continuously. He then smashed the target face-first into the ground.

Karson rolled onto his back, careful not to press his own button.

A cannon rose from Karson's chest and aimed at the assassin boss. A white flag popped out, waving on its own.

"Stop! Cough! Stop! You win."

Kanasta shoved the cannon back into the target's chest and then sliced off its appendages. He kicked the target up with his foot and onto his shoulders.

"I always win," said Kanasta, cracking his own neck.

Previously: Devlin waved goodbye as his creation descended toward the battle with Kanasta. "Alright, Kaity, you're up next. Be careful, Bob isn't known to show mercy," he said, glaring at the dangerous creation.

"Don't worry. I've never shown mercy either," said Kaity as her plasma claws jutted out. She walked onto Riufen's circle.

Bob came out from beneath her as the barrier rose. They were then lowered into the training room where Bob had played with both Riufen and Tempo.

"How come I have to fight you?" asked Kaity, backing away with a frown.

"Funny, I've been waiting for this fight," said Bob with a wide grin.

"Think fast!" Kaity tossed her gun up. She vaulted onto the target and leaped off. She then kicked off the force field and launched herself at her prey.

Bob fired a laser at the pistol just as the child reached for it.

Kaity flipped in the air and then impaled her claws into his cornea.

"You are a nuisance!" yelled Bob as he spun around. His eye glowed brightly, building up energy. He shot forth a laser just as the barrier dropped.

Kaity flipped behind him with her claws still buried in her target.

Bob fired multiple lasers at point-blank range, but she swerved out of the way each and every time.

A concrete chunk of the ceiling fell down toward the Exp.

"This trick is getting tiresome," said Bob, focusing energy in his eye for a massive laser.

Kaity slid under her opponent and kicked him into the plummeting rubble.

Bob traveled through the wreckage as if it didn't even exist. His massive laser then annihilated the debris and headed for the assassin.

Kaity blocked the edge of it with her crossed claws and gripped onto her sidearm with her toes. She fired with her foot as she struggled against the laser.

"You're rather nimble, but I doubt you're fast enough to dodge my next attack," said Bob, swerving out of the way of the bullets.

Kaity sliced an opening in the laser and zoomed into her prey. "Your movements give away the position of your attacks. As long as I can predict your next move, I can't get hit," she said, pumping him full of lead with both feet.

Bob's spectral arms yanked the gifted girl off of him and slammed her into the ceiling.

"Oh, but this attack is unpredictable. *Eyeball Apocalypse!*" He swirled around, shooting lasers randomly in every direction.

The lasers ricocheted off the walls, picking up speed at each collision.

Kaity dodged in the air frantically. As soon as her feet hit the ground, she rolled into a sprint. She raced around on all fours and leaped about through the overwhelming assault. The cat-eared killer rushed toward the line of training dummies and used them to shield herself from the lasers. Seeing an opening in the enemy's pattern, she peeked out from behind cover and unloaded a full round of plasma bullets into her opponent.

Bob turned to her and fired out a rapid circle of lasers in an instant.

Kaity kicked one of the dummies into the air to deflect the center laser.

The reinforced laser pierced through the dummy and shot through the assassin's right arm. A tiny volley of needle-sized lasers rained down from above.

"I knew you couldn't avoid them forever. You're not nearly as skilled as you boast to be," said Bob, barely dodging his own lasers.

Kaity carved a hole through the circle of lasers and then leaped backwards to dodge a massive incoming laser. After flipping in the air, she latched onto the wall. She ran across the sides of the wall as the giant laser closed in on her.

"You're doing all you can just to dodge me. But I still have a few more tricks." Bob redirected the lasers by sight alone, making all the lasers zoom toward his pathetic enemy.

A line of explosions trailed behind the cat-girl. She lost her footing as the area in front and behind her exploded simultaneously. The remaining lasers zigzagged through the smoke cloud.

Bullet fire came out from the smoke cloud and hit the Exp directly in the pupil.

The lasers lost direction and exploded all over the arena.

Kaity rolled onto her chest and fired.

The sniper bullet shot through Bob, dealing no damage. But it left a trail of ice that the cunning Exp mistakenly materialized into.

"I should be enjoying this, but your fighting style just seems to…aggravate me."

The ice trail shattered to bits.

Bob summoned up the Atma Blade and sped toward the child as she reloaded.

Kaity stopped the false reload and fired as her target approached.

Bob swerved out of the way, accidentally colliding into each bullet as he flew toward her.

The Atma Blade pierced into Kaity as she rapidly shot another round into her target.

Kaity shook spasmodically as he harvested her soul, but she never lost aim.

Bob slammed the assassin into the ground while feasting on her soul energy. "You have a surprisingly strong spirit for one so young," he said, repeatedly smashing her against the floor. He then tossed the little girl off the blade, following up with a quick laser that penetrated her chest.

Kaity tumbled to the ground as her opponent fired another laser.

"Be glad I didn't completely devour your soul," said Bob as he un-summoned his sword.

Kaity dug her claws into the ground, stopping her from tumbling out of control.

The laser zoomed right by her neck and exploded into the wall behind her.

"I'm not done…" said Kaity before she suddenly collapsed.

"Hah, I only took a small sip and you can't even stand. I don't know why you're held in such high regard," said Bob, lifting her head up with his spectral arms.

Kaity sprang off the ground, breaking out of his grip.

Before Bob could even register that she escaped, the killer stabbed her plasma claws deep into his pupil.

Bob flailed about in agony, unable to see anything but white.

Kaity sliced him frantically. "Why aren't you dead yet?!"

"You won't land another hit on me!" yelled Bob, piercing into her stomach with spectral drills.

Kaity fell with her back to the ground. She rolled to her side as her backpack disengaged her sniper rifle. She snatched it mid-roll and aimed directly at the target.

Her gun powered up, loading a full clip of energy bullets into a single shot.

Kaity hit spot-on, but the shot went right through her target.

"What kind of artifact is that?" asked Kaity, tears flowing down her bruised cheeks.

"Passing through physical objects is just my natural ability. It's as common to me as flight is to birds." Bob flew up to Kaity and slammed his blade into the ground. "This, on the other hand, is an artifact! 𝓛𝓲𝓯𝓮!"

The ground sprung up with vitality and wrapped around the assassin.

Kaity struggled to break free, but was soon crushed from the pressure. Her smashed body was then thrown at a nearby wall. The girl's corpse slowly slid down the wall, leaving a thick trail of blood.

"Is she dead?" asked Bob with a wide pupil.

Kaity stabbed her own corpse just before it hit the ground. She ripped her plasma claws out from its chest and licked the blood as it dripped off.

"You fell for my illusion," said Kaity, hopping as her battered hologram vanished.

"You…tricked me." Bob's eye lit up. "You are very skilled indeed. Well done. Very well done!"

Kaity loaded her guns and turned to the target.

"Go on then, show me what else you can do," said Bob, his eye widening.

"*ILLUSIONARY ARMY!*" Kaity spawned multiple mirages of herself, surrounding her prey. "Let's have some fun."

"Indeed we shall." Bob contorted the ground and shaped it into concrete replicas. "They may not have my powers, but they will be more than enough to defeat you," he said, relaxing in the air.

"Then come at us," said a group of thirty-five Kaitys, all taunting him differently.

Bob's fifteen copies rushed forth and fired rocks at the oncoming cat-girls.

The illusionary assassins leaped through the barrage and fired gratuitously at the round clones.

The rock minions all spun in place before shooting into the cat-girls. Many of the Kaitys were defeated, vanishing completely.

"*ILLUSION SHIFT.*"

The multiple Kaitys transformed into Bobs.

The many confused rock clones then began attacking each other.

"What are you doing? It's obvious who the enemy is! Well, they are brainless concrete. I shouldn't be surprised. I guess I'll just devour your soul on my own," said Bob, cracking his spectral knuckles.

Kaity camouflaged with the air, becoming invisible.

"No illusion can stand against the innate ability of the artifacts."

"What's innate about artifacts?" asked Kaity.

"*Sound Magnification,*" said Bob, amplifying the girl's voice. He then fired a laser in the direction of the echo.

Kaity jumped out of the way, landing with barely a sound. She slowly and quietly approached, but the sound of every step shook the walls.

"You have no stealth and stand no chance," said Bob, seeping into the ground.

He rose out suddenly and shot a laser where the assassin was.

Kaity fired her sniper rifle at Bob in the exact same instant. She then quickly jumped behind the boxing ring. The prodigy killer closed her mechanical ears to blot out all sound and achieve maximum concentration. She became one with her surroundings and silenced even her breathing.

Bullets came out from seemingly nowhere. Every single one of them hit the Exp.

"Damn it, where are you!" yelled Bob, frantically shooting lasers while being barraged by the bullets. "*Realm Shift, Spectral*." He instantly spotted the shooter's position by locating her soul. The cunning Exp then returned to the physical realm and approached the exhausted assassin.

"So, ready to give up?" he asked with a smile.

"Papa is counting on me!" Kaity's eyes turned bloodthirsty. "Ego, lend me your power!" The clever killer tossed a pebble that became a boulder by the time it made contact. She then fired an ice beam through the boulder as the Exp destroyed it.

Bob swerved out of the way of the beam and fired a laser into the child's chest. "What a shame. I was hoping to finish off a competent opponent," he said, rising into the air with long, black fog-like wings.

Kaity rushed at him, creating a road of ice to intersect his path. She leaped off and landed on the enemy, clawing at him ferociously.

Spectral hands grabbed her arms and pulled them back until they snapped.

Kaity lunged her head forward and ripped off one of his wings with her teeth. She then sliced off his other wing as she leaped off of him.

Bob pulled out his sword and thrust it into her.

Kaity squirmed around before collapsing.

"I win," said Bob as his wings spread out once more. He then flew out of the arena victoriously.

Chapter 21: Kanasta

Kanasta was the first to rise to the top. He tossed the target's tattered body to his client's feet. "Not killing him felt wrong. I hope the money's worth it," he said with a grimace.

"It will be. That is, assuming you survive to receive it," said Devlin with a grin.

"The reputation of my entire squad is at stake. I won't fail them. This is just another—"

"Kaity," said Devlin, his eyes widening with worry as Bob rose from the floor.

"Don't act surprised. You were enjoying every minute of it," said Bob with a wide grin.

"I swear Bob, if you killed her—"

"I didn't kill her, so spare me your rage," said Bob, tossing her limp body to the floor.

Devlin rushed to Kaity before being pushed aside.

Kanasta bent down and checked her pulse. "She'll survive."

"It's time to end this." Bob moved over his circle.

"Wait up." Devlin's little robots handed him the artifacts they had just fished out of the cat-girl. "I need to distribute these first. Since it's the final round, I choose who gets what."

"Go ahead, it won't change the outcome," said Bob.

"You may proceed," said Kanasta.

"I love it when people are complacent. Bob, you will receive the Size Artifact and the Illusion Artifact. Kanasta, you shall have the Temperature Artifact, and the Slow-motion Artifact. At last we have come to the final battle. Who will live and who will die?"

"What about the Love Artifact?" asked Bob.

"That artifact is very dear to Kaity. None of you are getting it," said Devlin, picking the lovely girl up.

"Oh, are you jealous of it? Eheheh."

"Enough." Kanasta stood on his circle.

"Agreed. It's time for me to devour your soul," said Bob playfully.

They lowered into the room where Kanasta had beaten every Freedom Forcer he battled.

"I'll give you twenty-one seconds until—"

"Don't play this charade with me! Kaity lost against me, or did you forget that? All your Vipers have lost, yet you still want to screw around. How thick-headed can you possibly be? Is this how you do battle? Is this really how you became such a great assassin? I thought you were serious about your job. If you really want the money, then you shouldn't waste time like this. You really don't want to disappoint me. If I am disappointed, then I will bring you Kaity's severed little head once I'm done with you. Then I'll send you both straight to Hell!" Bob's pupil turned crimson red.

"Twenty-one," said Kanasta, just finishing counting. The metallic card he tossed at the target sliced straight through.

"That's more like it," said Bob, smiling as he fell in half.

The lifelike illusion dissipated as Kanasta shot his fist forward.

The real Bob appeared behind the final assassin and stabbed the Atma Blade straight through his unwary opponent.

"*Temperature Rise*." Kanasta's body became ridiculously hot in a split second.

"Arrrgggh!" Bob retracted his sword as he caught aflame. He rolled on the floor frantically, trying to put out the fire.

Kanasta jumped over the burning target.

Bob fired a laser while rolling around.

Kanasta froze the laser and the target all at once with a cold beam.

While trapped in ice, Bob spun in place to heat up. As soon as the ice around him melted, he rammed into the enemy.

Kanasta formed an expanding shield around him that smashed the target against the ceiling.

Bob squeezed out from beneath the shield and then shot a souped-up laser.

"You're quick." Kanasta created another shield and deflected the laser.

"You're just too slow." Bob rolled on the ceiling as he fired multiple lasers.

"*Temperature Fall*"

The lasers froze a foot before their destination, freely floating in the air.

Kanasta kicked one of the lasers at the target and grabbed the other two.

Bob sprouted wings and then soared toward his opponent.

Kanasta tossed one of the laser spears, but it was swiftly dodged. He then thrust the other spear directly through the moving target.

It passed through, giving the Exp an opportunity for a counter-strike.

Bob zoomed up and lashed his sword like a wild wind while the assassin ran backwards.

Kanasta was hit by just the tip of the sword each time. He kicked the target and then tossed a handful of his lethal cards.

Bob impaled all of the cards on his blade and then lunged toward the trained killer.

"*Super Slo-mo!*" Kanasta calmly walked behind the target and grabbed it. He then slammed it to the ground brutally. "*Temperature Fall,*" he said, freezing the target and the surrounding arena.

A sound wave burst out from the Exp, re-mobilizing his wings by breaking the ice.

Bob grabbed the killer's legs with his wings and then flung him aside.

Kanasta regained balance in mid-flight and then jumped off the wall at the target.

The nimble eyeball fired forth a souped-up laser.

"*Super Slo-mo,*" said Kanasta, slowing the laser's approach. "*Temperature Fall,*" He froze the laser just three inches away from his exhausted grin. His hand then shot up and gripped the laser.

Bob's eye expanded abruptly. "*Sound Blast.*"

The icicle exploded from the high-pitched sound wave. The shards simply passed through the Exp, but the assassin was now littered with deep slices.

Kanasta fell to the ground, bleeding all over it.

"And so the mighty game-master finally falls," said Bob with a widened pupil. He then ruthlessly fired a laser at the downed assassin.

"*Temperature Fall Beam,*" yelled Kanasta, not allowing exhaustion to hold him back.

Cold air jutted out from his hand and into the laser's path.

Kanasta then jumped to his feet, waiting for the hostile target's next move.

"*Growing Self-Respect, Laser.*"

The laser grew immensely as it continued to freeze. The laser completely froze just a few feet away from the assassin's firm chest.

The assassin boss pulled back his fist, ready to punch the laser.

Bob rammed into it just before the fist collided.

The fifteen-foot laser bore straight through the assassin. Its momentum continued, pinning him to the middle of the battle-torn wall.

Bob fired five more lasers at the giant icicle, boring it deeper into his foe. "*Sound Shot,*" he said, his pupil forming a sinister grin.

The sound wave slammed into the giant icicle, exploding it inside the assassin.

"Graaah."

Kanasta's body poured out blood like a waterfall. His body slid down the wall, leaving a thick red trail.

"I'd like to see you get up now. Come on, get up. I'm serious. Kaity's life is at stake and you're just going to fall down and die. Take hold of what courage you have and stand up!" yelled Bob, his veins popping out.

Driven by Bob's inspirational words, the assassin boss struggled to get back to his feet.

Kanasta's hand moved at lightning-quick speed as he tossed something into the ground. He then fell forward to the floor, exhausted and drained.

Bob shot a laser as his foe fell. It went right through the gaping hole in his victim's chest.

Kanasta rolled onto his knees and then rose to his feet.

"How can you still be alive?" asked Bob with a wide eye.

"I'm not going to die from a little scar like this," said Kanasta, digging his fingers into the bleeding wound.

"That's what I like to hear. This may become intriguing after all," said Bob with a genuine grin as he floated toward his opponent.

"*Shrinking Shield*," said Kanasta, blood dripping down his chin.

A shield appeared around the Exp, reducing upon its genesis.

Kanasta reached through the shield, grabbed the target and then flung it toward the inner-wall of the shield.

Bob passed through the shield just as he made contact.

The shield ricocheted off the wall, shooting through the massive hole in the assassin's chest, before downsizing into oblivion.

"*Domino Effect*." Kanasta intensely slammed his foot on the ground.

A row of five-by-eight-foot dominoes shot up.

"So that's what you did," said Bob with a spark of understanding.

"*River of Death*!" Kanasta punched the domino in front of him.

It skyrocketed into another and then another. The dominoes were piling up and headed right for the Exp.

"You're lucky I'm bored." Bob slammed into the dominoes, fighting their momentum.

They flung backwards, stampeding toward the assassin boss.

Kanasta smirked and created a shield around himself.

The dominoes slammed into the shield, momentarily halted. They then broke through, shattering the barrier to pieces.

"Good hit," said Kanasta with a bloody smile.

The dominoes rammed into the assassin, sending him crashing into the same wall yet again.

Bob waited impatiently at the front of the domino line.

Kanasta appeared from behind the target, holding a card between his fingers. He lashed it at the target, each blow quick and decisive.

Bob rolled onto the ground and rammed into his leg. He then floated away.

The game master jumped up and reached for the target.

Bob shrank as he escaped through the fingers. He went through the void in his victim's chest as he reverted to normal size.

Once Bob popped out of the hole, Kanasta grabbed him and slammed him all the way down to the ground.

"I've never lost a target before. This time will be no exception. I've been saving up my energy for this fight. It may seem strange, but I played games during my fights with your allies because I took this job seriously. All those games I played helped keep my body calm and protect it from harm. They allowed me to center myself and conserve energy. I've been doing this for as long as I can remember. Every move I've made here has been strategically calculated. This job will be a success just like all the others," said Kanasta, his muscles relaxed. The master assassin took out a retractable pool stick from his utility belt and jabbed it at the target.

The spherical Exp bounced around the arena as he spun uncontrollably.

"*Fast-Mo!*" Kanasta gained speed as he spun around, becoming like a top.

When he rammed into Bob, their speeds instantly canceled out.

Kanasta drop-kicked the target while still suspended in air.

Bob spun around to disperse the momentum, but the kick overpowered him. He crashed to the ground, leaving a crater in the metal floor, before bouncing back up. As soon as the clever eyeball had regained his bearings, he shot a laser forth.

Kanasta punched the laser right back at the target, freezing only its tip.

Bob fired another laser as he spun back in control.

Sparks jutted out as the two lasers battled each other.

Kanasta continuously punched his laser as Bob continually shot more lasers into his own.

"*Growing Self-Respect!*"

Bob's laser became ridiculously huge. It obliterated the other laser and enveloped the enemy in its blast. It sent his prey smashing against the wall, but it did not tear through him.

Kanasta held the laser back with his gloved hands as he was pressed against the wall.

Bob slammed into him from below, smashing him into the ceiling.

The roof of the battle arena crumbled as Kanasta fell.

Bob passed through the rubble and stared joyfully at the plummeting assassin.

"*Life!*" exclaimed Bob with a happy twirl.

The remains of the ceiling encased the mortal.

Bob impaled the Atma Blade through the rubble and then shot the debris prison off into the air. His veins tensed up. He then rammed into the rock formation with great might.

The rubble encasing around his victim instantly burst.

Kanasta was sent smashing through layer after layer of thin steel walls. He finally burst out of the lab, breaking through the extremely visible force field.

Bob played pat-a-cake with his spectral hands as he waited for his victim to arrive.

After Bob had moved on to Janken, Kanasta fell back into the arena.

Bob zoomed up and pierced his prey with his beloved Atma Blade. His wings sprouted as he ascended. Once he arrived at the upper area, his wings dissipated. He tossed Kanasta off his blade, dropping him right before Devlin's feet. He then looked up at the arrogant scientist as if expecting a congratulatory pat.

Part 3
Old Exps

Chapter 22: New Recruits

"Whaaaaaaaaaaaaaaaaaaaaat?" asked Devlin, grabbing the top of his head and pulling his hair.

"Do I get a treat?" asked Bob with a wide grin.

"How could this have happened?" exclaimed Devlin, gripping his face in a mix of pride and anger.

"I believe it's time for you to announce that the Freedom Forcers have won," said Bob, pressing the microphone against the little boy's cheek.

"No, you're not allowed to claim victory. I still have some more Exps. I'll call them up and they'll kill you!" Devlin frantically took out his phone from his lab coat pocket, nearly dropping it.

A laser shot from Bob's eye, destroying the phone.

Bob looked up with a sinister grin. "I shall do what Exp 8 would not. I will force you to be free of your material form," he said, slowly approaching while summoning up the Atma Blade.

The frightened scientist ran to the door. As soon as it opened up, Bob shoved his blade through him.

"Now we shall all be free of your oppression!"

When Bob finally pulled the sword out, the scientist lifelessly collapsed. The eyeball suddenly burst into laughter.

Devlin started laughing as well, still on the floor. "Good work, Bob. Ah, that was hilarious," he said before jumping to his feet.

"Aren't you glad you listened to my plan? Ah, it went splendidly. You now have all of the Freedom Forcers' and the Viper Squad's artifacts. You have both teams in the palm of your hand. And it's all thanks to me. Come to think of it, did I ever tell you what my true name is?"

"How can you just decide your own name?"

"It's my name and therefore I can adjust it how I please. I am B.O.B., the Befriender of Betrayal!"

"How very fitting. To be honest, I thought you actually had joined them at one point."

"I wouldn't betray you to play around in some trivial Exp revolt. I am quite grateful for being brought into this world."

"I never expected Karson to backstab me," said Devlin, clenching his fist.

"Mortals are fickle. Why are you so concerned? Look, Master, it is over. You have won!"

Devlin jumped into an embrace. "Thank you so much! I really, really appreciate your dedication and assistance. Whoo, let's not get too hasty. I haven't won yet. I need you to stay on their side. You can play this game a little longer, can't you?" he asked, rubbing the top of his most reliable ally.

"Most certainly, Master. By the way, your newest Exp has some promise."

"Don't sugarcoat it. You defeated Riufen and you weren't even the least bit tired afterwards. I need to make my Exps stronger."

"Kanasta was an entertaining opponent. Is he really a human?"

"They all were. So, are you sure you don't want any artifacts? I would like to reward you."

"I'm sure. I don't want to spoil the fun. After all you've done for me...I'm just happy to be able to reciprocate your kindness," said Bob, tearing up.

"How do you think I should upgrade the Freedom Forcers?" asked Devlin, waving the tips of his fingers.

"You just can't resist, can you?" asked Bob, rolling his eye.

"Don't worry. They won't escape this time. I was thinking of giving Karson a particle-cannon. How cool would that be?" asked Devlin with wide eyes.

"Why not just get rid of his self-destruct button? It seems like a pointless attachment."

"You know I didn't give him the Button. Besides, he makes a great hostage. If we want him back on our side, all we need to do is threaten him a little. Now on to the matter at hand, where did you put the losers?"

"They are with the doctor at the medical bay. That is what you wanted, isn't it?"

"Yes, some of them need immediate medical attention. There's something I don't understand. How did you move them while you were fighting?"

"I commanded my Jiva to move them there. They may be feeble, but they are still useful for menial labor," said Bob, petting the air with a spectral hand.

"I'm sorry, but I'm going to have to put you in prison with the rest of the Freedom Forcers. If you're going to spy on their team, well...this is the best way."

"Oh, I don't mind. As long as deception is at hand, I will shame myself as much as required," said Bob, his eye arching into a smile.

"Could you put Exp 8 in that special room I designed for him?"

"The doctor just released him. But he should stay out of combat for a while. Jiva, find Exp 8."

"Bob, you were too rough with Kaity. She may be an assassin, but she's still a tender little girl. Why didn't you hold back?" asked Devlin in a gentle tone.

"I restrained myself. You'll be happy to know that all of the Viper Squad members are alive. Things are progressing splendidly."

"They are indeed. I will need to talk to Sefiwah about something. Inform me when she wakes up."

"It's about Kaity, isn't it? I may not understand your spontaneous obsessive pedophilic desire for her, but I do not need to. I will honor your wishes without complaints," said Bob, leading his leader to the door.

"Do you think I can convince her to join me?" asked Devlin, hope suddenly seizing his eyes.

"Hook her up with Nina and I guarantee she'll join," said Bob with a wink.

Ada suddenly came up from the arena below.

"I thought you took care of all of them," said Devlin under his breath.

"This is your little girlfriend's mistake. Not mine," said Bob with a condescending gaze.

"Hi Devlin! How is everything?" asked Ada, hugging him affectionately.

"It was going great. Ada, are you…um…still on my side?" asked Devlin, twiddling his thumbs.

"Of course I am! I care about you! But I'm also on the Freedom Forcers' side." Ada crouched down to the friendly eyeball. "Where is everyone?" she whispered.

"Devlin took them away. I was trying to interrogate him to find out where."

"Oh, sorry for interrupting. So, Devlin, got any ideas on how to upgrade Exp 8?" asked Ada, leaning up to him.

"I have many ideas. But I can't trust you with any of them. Now go to the medical bay with the rest of your rebel friends," said Devlin through gritted teeth.

"Thanks for the info. Come on Bob, let's go!" exclaimed Ada, rushing to the door.

"Ada wait! Don't leave just yet. There's something I need you to do," said Devlin, blocking her path.

"I'd love to help in any way that I can."

"I need you to track down someone for me. He goes by the alias D.S.; you know who I'm talking about. I'm not exactly sure where he is. I leave it up to you to find him and bring him here," said Devlin, putting his arm on her shoulder.

"Can we go for ice cream afterwards?"

"Fair enough, as long as you leave within the hour."

"I will!" exclaimed Ada before rushing off.

"What should I do?" asked Bob.

"I will need you to be imprisoned with the other rebels. But before that, I want you to locate Violet Gold. She should be on a pilgrimage, so tracking her will not be easy. Think you can handle it?" asked Devlin.

"She'll be here before the sun sets," said Bob before seeping into the floor.

Devlin headed to the door but then stopped abruptly. "I know you're there," he said, quickly turning around.

Sefiwah walked out of the shadows, her eyes glistening.

"It's time to fulfill your end of the bargain. Kanasta is in the medical bay. He can't fight back now. Go in and kill him. Do it now," said Sefiwah, clawing at herself with anticipation.

Devlin looked directly into her snowy white eyes and smiled. He flipped a pistol out from his vest and tossed it to her.

Sefiwah stumbled as she tried to grab it.

"What's wrong? You seem nervous. You obviously want to kill him. Go ahead and do it," said Devlin, picking the gun off the floor and placing it in her hand.

"I do want to kill him. I hate him. But it isn't that simple. You said you were going to kill him," said Sefiwah, trying to push the gun into the boy's hands.

"You don't want to be the cause of Kaity's misery. It makes sense to me. But to be honest, I don't know if I really want to either. Why don't we both pull the trigger…together?" asked Devlin, grabbing her fragile hand and leaning against her.

"I think you're getting the wrong idea. I don't like you," said Sefiwah, pulling away from him.

"I don't care if you like me. Kaity is the one I'm after."

"You can have her any way you want her once Kanasta is dead."

"So, when did you plan on killing me?" asked Devlin, putting his arm around her.

Sefiwah broke out of his grip and kept her distance. "What are you talking about?" she asked, cocking the gun.

"You don't want anyone getting in the way of your relationship with Kaity. Why wouldn't you want to kill me? I love Kaity enough to murder you. I'm sure you feel the same way," said Devlin, slowly approaching her.

"Kaity is a lesbian. Your passion is not a threat. Now, kill Kanasta and I'll make your wildest dreams with her come true," said Sefiwah, holding the gun with a tight grip.

"I will kill Kanasta. But, I'll do it when I feel like it. You, on the other hand, are a troublesome obstacle. I can't get with Kaity if she's already taken. Besides, I want the real revive artifact. You will die as soon as I say the word." Devlin snapped his fingers and smirked.

Sefiwah shot at the dangerous boy and raced up to him.

Devlin leaped out of the way of the bullet and zapped her arm with his electric glove.

Sefiwah collapsed to his feet.

Devlin continued to fry her until she fell silent. "With proper planning, anything can be achieved. Now, it's time to get some back up," he said, leaving the room and speeding down the hallway.

Bob arrived midday in a desert wasteland.

The yellow sand dunes seemed to stretch on for infinity, but the round Exp was not intimidated in the least.

Bob shifted realms, entering the spirit world. He gazed through the ethereal outcropping of souls, searching for one that was unique. He turned away as his gaze met a blindingly colorful soul. After zooming straight through the protruding sand hills, he arrived at the potent soul. He then shifted back to the material realm.

The spectral world seemed to melt away and Violet Gold's visage slowly came into view.

She had light blue skin like that of an ancient Vedic deity. A symbolic third eye, above her sixth chakra, was painted on the center of her forehead. She was cloaked almost head to toe in rags. A see-through cloth was protecting her mouth from committing unintentional acts of violence. Silky golden hair went all the way down to her thighs. The devotee's amethyst eyes warmed up at the sight of Bob.

"Namaste, brother Bob," said Violet with a wispy voice filled with love.

"Hi, Violet," he said, waving at her.

"Have you come to join me on this pilgrimage?" asked Violet with a slight nod of the head.

"No. I haven't. Devlin wants you back at the lab pronto."

"I must honor my father's wishes, but I must also honor the spirits. I shall cut my pilgrimage circuit short, but it will not be canceled," said Violet, leading him up a rocky hill.

"Where are you heading anyway?"

"I came here to collect peyote for my spiritual family. Then I am going to travel to Mecca and then to Jerusalem. After that, I will journey to the Gan—"

"Okay, I get the gist of it. Just round up your hallucinogenic cacti and let's get a move on."

"Peyote is not a hallucinogenic. It comes from the Earth. It is the spiritual properties of it that induce feelings of religious ecstasy. By ingesting peyote you are able to understand the world from its own perspective? Would you care for a taste of introspection?" asked Violet, offering him the freshly picked cactus.

"I don't even have a mouth. And I don't need a catalyst to see the spiritual world. Are you done here?" asked Bob, rolling his eye.

Violet pulled out a knife and lifted up her rags. She pressed the knife into her skin.

Bob watched with a wide eye as she sliced out a small chunk of flesh.

Violet placed the sacrifice inside a natural hole in the ground. She then made a circle in the sand with her fingers.

"Brother, do you understand the concept of reciprocity?" asked Violet, placing her light blue palm on his side.

"Yes, but I don't take anything. So there's no need to give anything either. Now can we get moving?" asked Bob, bobbing side to side.

"Once I finish thanking Gaia for this gift, we shall leave," said Violet, sitting lotus style.

"And how long will that take?" asked Bob, landing next to the annoying zealot.

"There is no linear time in ritual. Relax, dear brother. Be in the moment and flow like a river," said Violet, gently petting him.

"Alright. There's no harm in a little spiritual rejuvenation. I'll follow your lead."

"I do not lead the ceremony. I let it lead me."

Far away from the deserts of Mexico, Devlin arrived at a fashion show in France. He pushed through the busy crowds, slowly making his way to the front.

Bright lights flashed rapidly as the curtains spread open.

A thunderous cheer from the fans told the scientist he had found exactly who he was looking for on the elongated stage.

"Matteria sure has become quite the celebrity," said Devlin, before the star emerged from the curtains and stepped onto the stage.

Confetti gushed out, lights flickered on the edges of the stage, and ear-piercing screams erupted all over.

Matteria appeared to be sixteen years old but strutted down the runway like a veteran. The diva wore a frilly, showy, pop-star outfit. On the model's cheeks were bedazzled hearts and stars, complemented by a faint scarlet blush. Around the celebrity's neck was a choker with a pink rainbow-sprinkled cupcake emblem in the center.

The glamorous model was wearing a multi-colored, self-designed corset, rainbow-striped mini-skirt, pink-and-white garter belt with matching thigh highs and high-top Goth boots. The diva's glittery nail polish and lipstick alternated colors at will. The Deutschland bows, Chinese bun decorations, French-maid bonnet, Arabic see-through shoulder veils, Pacific Islander flower necklace, and Indian belly dancer hip scarf all came together to represent Matteria as a model for the globalized world.

Matteria turned around with a glamorous hair flip, the idol's pigtails waving back and forth. The spectrum of colors dazzled the audience as it shimmered in the neon spotlights. The fashionista's mascara-coated, prideful pink eyes then widened.

Matteria turned around and leaped off the runway.

Devlin caught the diva in his arms.

Devlin's hand was right on Matteria's butt, making Devlin's cheeks flare up.

The slender teen licked Devlin's cheek and gave him a quick peck on the lips.

"Oh Master, I knew you would rebound," said Matteria in a chipper girly voice imbued with arousal. The diva's hands caressed his creator's chest.

"Can you not do this in front of all these people?" asked Devlin through a fake smile.

"Shall we go backstage then?" asked Matteria, nibbling on his ear.

"Yes, but I'm not going to carry you," said Devlin, dropping the idol.

"Owiee, that hurt. Please be more careful. My butt has five contracts to fulfill and tons of fans to please," said Matteria, popping right back up.

"Your butt will be fine," said Devlin, walking past the security guards as his escort winked at them.

"Did you come here to take me away? Are we going to elope? Have you found someplace where our love will be respected?" asked Matteria, pushing more and more against the sexy scientist.

"Yes. No. And what? Look, I need your um…prowess back at the lab. There have been some problems," said Devlin, looking down with embarrassment.

"Oh. Don't worry. I can help you get it up," said Matteria, grabbing his crotch.

Devlin pulled away and grabbed his Exp by the wrist.

Matteria beamed at him.

Devlin gave an estranged rising of the eyebrow.

"Did you know that grabbing someone by the wrist was a sign of sexual possession back in Ancient Greece?" asked Matteria, purring excitedly.

"Good thing we're in France."

"Yes, we're in France…alone," said Matteria with a kiss.

"We are through! I already have another girlfriend anyway," said Devlin, tossing aside the glamorized hand and crossing his arms.

"That's fine with me. I don't mind one bit." Matteria led his master into the makeup room and sat down on a cushioned stool. "By the way, I have a new boyfriend now," said the diva with a sly smile.

"You what? Who is he? Do I know him?" asked Devlin before stopping and sitting down in a nearby swivel chair.

"I knew you cared!" exclaimed Matteria, spinning around in place.

"That is not why I am here. There has been an Exp rebellion back at the lab. I want you to return because I might need some extra security," said Devlin, stopping his creation's advances with an outstretched leg.

"Alright, but is there anything you want to do here before we go?" asked Matteria with a tempting lick.

"Actually, there is. I've heard Reflector is here in France. Do you know where he might be?"

"He's in an art museum not too far from here. We could walk together," said Matteria, grabbing the beautiful hands that made him.

"Don't you have a show to win?"

"This is so much more important. Besides, I'm sure my disappearance will create some juicy rumors. Come on, we could go see the new exhibit while we're there."

"That sounds like a wonderful idea! I've missed you," said Devlin, embracing his child lovingly.

"I've missed you so much," said Matteria, gripping Devlin's back.

"Don't cry now. You wouldn't want your makeup to smear your face."

"You can make my face messy whenever you want," said Matteria, grinding up against him.

"Let's get moving. We have a lot to catch up on," said Devlin, walking out of the room.

All the way in Washington, D.C., Ada arrived at an elementary school yard. The area was silent. Pigeons sat atop the roof of the blue building. The walls were decorated with childish expressions of art above the encroaching mildew. Vines constricted the parallel line of trees leading to the entrance. There was a single narrow road of sidewalk and only one door.

Ada was wearing a burgundy detective suit to cover her oddly colored skin. A massive hand stopped her from proceeding inside.

"You can't go in unless you have your school identification card. Who's your ki—Mommy?" asked the hulking monster of a security guard.

"Yes, sweetie. It's me," said Ada, raising her head and smiling at him.

The guard lifted her up into the air and hugged her with the strength of a wrestler.

D.S. was a big, muscle-man with a dark blue security guard outfit that was too small and wouldn't fit. Blue-striped shorts and the most awesome light-up sneakers made him look really cool. He was bald and had correction tape wrapped around a lot of his face. A happy light blue eye peered out from his tape mask. His mouth had lots and lots of sharp, pointy teeth in a circle. It looked like a pencil sharpener.

"I missed you Mommy! Have you seen Daddy?" he asked in a deep but childlike voice.

"I'm afraid he's been away for a while now. But don't worry. I'm sure he'll return."

"I sure hope so. Mommy…why won't the other kids play with me?" asked D.S., pushing out his bottom lip.

"Don't take it personally. You're a security guard. It's your job to protect them. Now, who wants to go out for some dairy-free ice cream?" asked Ada, leading him to the car.

"I do! I do! Mommy, I don't like security work. It's not fun. Can I be a bad guy again? Playing cops and robbers is way more fun with real guns! Pew, pew! Ratatata!" exclaimed D.S., making fake gun sound effects.

"You can be whatever you want to be. Now, sweetie, Devlin was wondering if you could assist him with something. Would you like to help?" asked Ada, opening the car door.

"Is it fun?" asked D.S., making sure his seat belt was extra snug.

"It most certainly is. Devlin has picked you as Exp 8's next obstacle. It's your job to fight him! You like fighting, don't you?" asked Ada, pinching his cheek.

"Almost as much as I love nice cream!" exclaimed D.S., accidently punching a dent into the roof of the car.

Meanwhile: back in France, Devlin and Matteria were in the hallway of a prestigious museum.

Devlin strolled purposefully down the velvet carpets.

Matteria stopped at every work of art and tried to get Devlin's attention.

"Devi! Come over here!" hollered Matteria at the far end of the room.

"I told you not to call me that. I have a girlfriend now!" exclaimed Devlin, walking toward his creation.

"You never did tell me her name."

"Well, she's not exactly a girlfriend. Not yet anyway. But I think she likes me. I really hope she does."

"So then, do you still love me?" asked Matteria, stroking the handsome inventor's arm.

"It's complicated. I'm sorry for being so distant. I just don't want to break your heart again. I'm not going to build up your hopes just to disappoint you. It hurts me to see you so sad," said Devlin, touching the teen's rosy cheeks.

"One kiss won't hurt then," said Matteria, closing in.

"It's just a kiss, right?" Devlin grabbed the diva's hips.

"Get your hands off my girl!" yelled a voice from behind them.

"Why does that voice sound familiar?" asked Devlin, slowly turning his head.

"It's my newest boyfriend!" exclaimed Matteria, running off.

Devlin spun around. "Wait, Reflector is your boyfriend?"

"Oh, Master Devlin, this is quite the surprise. I didn't mean to yell. I didn't know it was you. It was a common mistake, right? You know I would never yell at you," said Reflector with a 1950s American radio announcer accent. He spoke in a solid, yet nervous tone.

"It's an understandable mistake. I'm not angry with you," said Devlin, approaching his underling.

"This is my favorite art piece in the whole museum!" exclaimed Matteria, rubbing against the Exp's shiny glass face.

Reflector had a vertical, rectangular, reflective frame, resembling a mirror. His arms and legs came out from behind the mirror. He was around half Matteria's height and was in "The Thinker" pose. His head was angular like a rhombus. The Exps eyes and mouth were inside rather than on his face like everyone else and could be seen through his clear head.

"Oh, my dear, you are too kind," said Reflector, standing upright and hugging Matteria's legs.

"Uh, does he know ab—?" asked Devlin, raising his eyebrows.

"He doesn't care! He loves me for who I am! He is just so sweet," said Matteria, rubbing against him.

"Reflector, why are you here? Do you work here?"

"Yes, well, in a manner of speaking. I am an exhibit here. My girlfriend here got a nice chunk of cash for handing me in."

"Yep and I forwarded all of it right to your account, Master Devlin," said Matteria with a wink.

"So, you just live here?" asked Devlin with a raised eyebrow.

"No, Matteria picks me up for the weekends. I really love it here. I feel so respected, so beloved! Everyone looks at me with admiration. I feel like a work of art!" yelled Reflector, posing extravagantly.

"That's nice to hear. But I need you to come back with me to the lab. Let's go," said Devlin with a coaxing twist of the fingers.

"I'm ready when you are, Master Devlin, sir!" exclaimed Reflector, hopping off his post.

Chapter 23: Bonding Circle!

The eyes of Exp 8 opened, his line of sight spreading out like sunlight over a field.

Devlin was sitting in front of him in a brand new Vantablack swivel chair. He was typing on his electronic notepad and mumbling to himself.

Exp 8 closed his eyes and looked up once more, hoping he was hallucinating.

Devlin's smile widened. He put away his notepad and pulled up to his creation.

Exp 8 looked beyond to see four long hallways.

Devlin scooted up closer, purposefully blocking the rebel's view.

"What happened?" asked Exp 8 drowsily.

"I have won once again!"

"Just a bad dream," said Exp 8 as his eyes closed.

"No, it is a wonderful reality. Everything is going perfectly!" exclaimed Devlin, whirling his chair full circle.

"So I take it you got with Kaity? Good job. Now can you let me out?" asked Exp 8, rolling his eyes.

"You're not escaping this time. I've taken extra special precautions to make sure you stay put," said Devlin, leaning back in the chair.

"You know you can't stop me," said Exp 8, unable to even move his head.

"Wow, you are just pitiful. Don't you see how pathetic your resistance is? Just give up already. You will never beat me," said Devlin, tilting his head to the ceiling.

"I was defeated on the first round. Those assassins were no joke. We didn't beat a single one of them, did we?"

"Well…um…actually, your team almost won. All that was left was Kanasta, but he was just too powerful!"

"So if you barely won, then why are you gloating so much?"

"I still won! And why shouldn't I be proud? My creations nearly beat the greatest assassins this world has ever known. You may have failed miserably, but most of your team put up a decent fight. And now, thanks to that little scuffle, I hold both the Freedom Forcers and the Viper Squad in the palm of my hand. Ah, but things have gone even better than expected. Kaity has decided to join me! Soon we'll be reminiscing about the first time we met!" exclaimed Devlin, gliding around his captive's prison.

"You got your girl. Now can you let us be free?" asked Exp 8, struggling to move his head side to side.

"Freeing you would be pointless. You would merely become shackled to the world around you. If you stay with me, then your potential is limitless.

Freedom is overrated. It is slavery that makes us stronger. Without hardships, without suffering, there can be no progress. I can't allow you to stunt your own growth," said Devlin, pulling in closer.

"Oh yeah, and how would you know? You've never been locked up. Who's your master?"

"I've already been a slave to the world. I have emerged victorious from my trials. Those who know pain surpass those who do not. You must break the chains that shackle you before you have the right to desire freedom. Running away is not an option. You must fight. Honestly, I'm doing you a favor. If you saw just how boring freedom was, you would beg for imprisonment."

"I hate having these tubes in my body! I hate being held here against my will!"

"Now that isn't fair. I would allow you to stay here willingly, but you insist on revolting. You're forcing me to imprison you."

"I didn't force you to do anything! You chose to lock me up and you decided to bore tubes into my flesh!" yelled Exp 8, his eyes like daggers.

"Do you want to know what the tubes do?"

"They keep me confined!"

"Yes, but that's not the point I'm making. Don't you feel it? Stop resisting and feel the motion."

Exp 8's eyes widened. "What are you putting into me?"

"The very thing that confines you is constantly filling you with energy. It is making you stronger. I think the metaphor is beautiful and well...it was subtle."

"Why are you even here? Why don't you just leave and go share your pretty metaphors with Kaity?"

"I'm staying to make sure you don't escape. If there's one thing I've learned from media, it's that overconfidence is a villain's downfall. I am going to have you under constant surveillance. And this time around, you won't have that little traitor Kawai present to give you an energy boost," said Devlin with a clenched fist.

"Where is she? Where is my sister!"

"There's no need to yell. She's in the kitchen making pancakes for the guests."

"What about the others? Are they alright?"

"I made sure that all of your little rebels were healed after the battle. Same goes for the assassins. They are all alive," said Devlin with open arms and a warm smile.

Exp 8 took in a deep breath. "Thank you, Devlin. Thank you for sparing them."

"I didn't spare them. They are my creations. I don't want them destroyed. I just want them to stand by my side."

"I guess you're not as bad as I thought."

"You finally understand! Just because we have conflicting views, doesn't mean we need to be cruel to each other."

"Yes, we've finally reached an understanding. Now let me go free."

"Why can't you be more malleable? You're so stubborn."

"I'm dedicated. There is a difference."

"Let's not get into semantics. I just want you to think about living your life here. It's rather cozy once you get used to it."

"Says you. I can't stand being cooped up. And I can't relax as long as I know I'm being watched. I need freedom just like any other living creature."

"I think you're much stronger than you're letting on. Nobody here would think you weak-willed if you made a compromise," said Devlin, his smile stretching to his cheeks.

"Freedom is all or nothing."

"So hardheaded. How can I show you the error of your ways? Maybe a poem would help convince you?

> The chains that bind us,
> the chains that restrict our circulation,
> the chains that surround us,
> are the chains that bring us purification.
> For each drop of blood,
> and each drip of sweat,
> make us feel love,
> yet make us regret.
> Regretting the chains only imprisons us.
> The chains are what will enlighten us.
> The one who knows pain can fly.
> The one without it will fall.
> You must know pain to grow.
> Without it you shall decay.
> So do not deny the chains.
> Do not try to be free.
> For the chains are simply a tight embrace.
> They are what turn a seed into a tree."

"That doesn't really change my mind. I think you have a sick sense of reality. And seeds don't need restraints in order to become trees."

"It's good for improv, but I need something a little more romantic for Kaity," said Devlin, tapping his chin.

"So uh…what do I have to do for you to let me go?"

"I'm trying to help you by keeping you here. You Freedom Forcers are all fools. That is a pretty cool name, though. Can you help me come up with a cool name for my team?"

"What do I get in return?"

"You're not really in the position to be giving ultimatums. But rest assured, I'll make your stay here far more unpleasant if you don't cooperate. So, why don't you swallow your pride and brainstorm with me?"

"Why the hell not, it's not like I have anything else to do. Let's see…you want to imprison us and you're very powerful. How about the Omnipotent Overseers?" Exp 8 cringed as he realized he just gave his enemy's team a name cooler than his own.

"I like it, very badass. Thanks." Devlin pulled up his phone and pressed a button on its side. "Everyone, from now on we are called the Omnipotent Overseers," he said, his voice booming from every loudspeaker across the lab. He then slipped his phone back into his pocket. "By the way, I put your cell right next to Atatasuki's and Kawai's. I didn't want to separate the family. The rest of your teammates are all in a different room with at least one of my allies protecting them."

"Are you done bragging now?"

"Not until you fully understand my genius. I have created five easily escapable inescapable prisons for your teammates!"

"Okay, so when does your shift end?"

"I'm going to stay here with my Exps and Kaity…" said Devlin before drifting off.

Exp 8 snapped his fingers.

"…and watch you so you don't escape!"

"That's not very villain-like."

"I don't give a damn. I'd rather be smart than evil any day. Now behold the product of a mastermind!" exclaimed Devlin, gesturing to four seventy-two-inch monitors on the wall.

All four monitors turned on as the scientist clapped his hands together, each one displaying a different member of the Freedom Forcers.

"Hmm, looks like Nina's already up. I'll just give the others a little jolt," said Devlin, whipping out his cell phone.

The inescapable cell for Nina was four mirrors, above, below and on both sides of her.

239

Nina was making out with the side mirror while Kaity stared with her chin on her palms.

"Tell me you love me!" exclaimed Nina, petting her reflection.

"I do," said Kaity, her tail wagging in excitement.

"I was talking to myself," said Nina, licking her finger.

"So, want to see my new pictures?" asked Kaity, taking out her camera.

"Ooh! Let me see!" yelled Nina, breaking out of her trance.

"Kanasta says that if you're going to give something, you should always get something in return. I'll let you take a peek in exchange for a little kiss. Wait, no! A deep kiss," said Kaity, leaning over to her crush.

"I don't give in to demands. I'm not being selfish. It's just—forget it. I don't feel like explaining," said Nina, turning around.

"Are you upset with me?" asked Kaity with a pouty face.

"Cat-girls are overrated! They are just overly cutesy flirty teases!" exclaimed Nina, giving the girl an angry look.

Kaity lowered her head. "I didn't choose to be like this."

"Damn it, I just went against lessons number one and three. This is difficult. Oh, I've got it. For a touchy-feely cat girl, you're not that annoying."

"Hee-hee. You're really bad at giving compliments."

"Yeah, but I'm great at getting them. Wait a minute. You're the one who fought Ada! Is she okay?" asked Nina, scratching her knuckles frantically.

"Why do you like her so much? I think big-breasted airheads are overrated, so there," said Kaity, sticking out her tongue.

"We live in a world of appearances. Whoever looks the best succeeds. She's got you beat by a mile. That's not cruelty, it's honesty," said Nina, still staring at her mirror.

"Wow, you are so hot," said Kaity, cycling through her new pictures.

"I don't need those pictures, I have plenty of Nina right here," she said, rubbing the breasts of her reflection.

"I didn't hurt Ada, alright? She gave up because she couldn't hit me. I guess looks aren't everything, after all. Hee-hee."

"I still have a lot to learn from her."

Kaity rolled onto her back and looked up. "Do I annoy you?"

"I don't mind fans. It's so cute how you can't resist me," said Nina, combing her hair with her slender fingers.

"Awww, thanks. But I can't help being smitten. You're just so gorgeous," said Kaity, her hands to her chest.

"I know."

Karson's prison was incredibly narrow. If he moved back even an inch, his button would be pushed and he would die.

The soldier awoke, cautiously surveying the area.

His shotgun-barrel pupils peered through the glass walls, catching sight of an enemy.

"Oh, how the mighty have fallen," said Pharma, lighting up his thumb.

"What are you talking about? I beat you, remember?"

"You're trapped. You are like a gun in a pocket. You're only taken out when your master wishes to use you. I think now I truly understand just how utterly and completely pathetic you really are," said Pharma, puffing out a smoke cloud.

"Didn't you die?"

"I merely choked and fainted," said Pharma with a grin.

"Once I get out of here, I will make sure to correct my mistake."

"Let me tell you a secret: I'm immortal!"

"You're delusional. It is I who has come back from the dead. I'm the one who knows the secrets of the afterlife."

"So...what are the secrets?" asked Pharma, scooting up closer.

Water droplets fell down from the ceiling between them.

"Tell me! What do you know! Brargh! Fine, I'll make you tell me when you bust out."

"Yep. It's only a matter of time. Just waiting for the order."

Atatasuki's cage had no bars. It was wide open. The only thing keeping him in place was a food dispenser. It spewed out a muffin every minute, made apparent by the gradually descending numbers holographically displayed by the dispenser.

Atatasuki awoke suddenly, instantly hyperventilating. "Kawai...why did you have to die?" he yelled, burying his face in a pile of muffins.

"Who's dead?" asked Kawai, floating outside his cage. She was now equipped with gold-plated shoulder and knee guards for extra protection.

His eyes lit up. "You're...alive. Wait...yes, I remember now. I'm so sorry I forgot."

"I guess my life wasn't worth remembering."

"There must have been a reason I forgot. I'll tell you if I remember. Does that make sense...wait...yes. Yes, it does."

"Is there anything else you forgot about me?" asked Kawai with slanted eyes.

"Even if there was, how would I know?"

"I guess you wouldn't. So um...how do you feel about me being alive?" asked Kawai, shuffling her feet.

"I feel so relieved. I love you. I always will!" yelled Atatasuki, leaping toward her.

Kawai flew out of the way, allowing him to fall on his face. She picked him up with her tail by his neck. "And I'll always hate you," she said sweetly. She tossed him into the muffin pile before flying off.

Atatasuki buried his tears in the confectionary hill of muffins.

"You'll always love me. It doesn't matter how much I hurt you, right?" asked Atatasuki, rubbing his face against the pastries.

Exp 8 looked away from the monitors and turned back to Devlin. "Wait a minute. What's going on? She's not on your team, is she?"

Kawai entered the room, melting at the sight of her bound brother.

"You need to think outside the box. She is indeed trapped. Her mind is in a cage. As long as you're stuck here, she'll stay by your side." Devlin grabbed the girl's head and brought her closer. "Look at those eyes. She could be complacent for an eternity," he said, petting the blissed-out Exp.

Kawai's head turned and her tail erected. "So, um, uh, Master Devlin, can I have fun with him later, hmm?" she asked, rubbing her face against his lab coat.

"You can take as long as you want. Love is a terrible thing to hurry," said Devlin, caressing her chin.

"You spoil me, Daddy," said Kawai, hugging him with her tail.

"Please tell me you're joking," said Exp 8, his eyes shrinking.

"What, you'd rather sit here and rust?" asked Kawai, flipping upside down.

"You're my sister. You shouldn't be thinking about those things."

"I agree. Talk is cheap," said Kawai before getting zapped.

Devlin caught the cuddly girl with one hand. "Sorry about that. I forgot to mention the laser grid." He turned his attention to Exp 8. "I don't really see the problem. You're not really related. I may have created you both, but I'm not your blood father. Technically you are both made from the same DNA, but I doubt you could have children anyway. Hmm, but what if you could? Now I'm curious," he said, tapping his fingers together.

"Well then, let's find out," said Kawai, sitting atop the scientist's head.

"Sorry, but you have to convince Exp 8 to join me first. I didn't forget how you betrayed me last time."

"Fair enough. Hey, Exp 8, do you like my new look?" asked Kawai, polishing her newly installed golden shoulder guards.

"Show him the knee guards too. See Exp 8, I'm looking out for her safety. I don't want any harm to come to my creations."

"If I keep getting armor upgrades, I'll look more and more like a little you," said Kawai, tapping her brother's cheek.

"Enough casual flirting. How are you going to steer him into joining me?" asked Devlin.

"Hmm. I know! I'll seduce him with an erotic display of my flexibility." Kawai moved through the air, making various patterns to arouse her mate.

Exp 8 sighed and turned his attention to the monitor on his far left.

Bob's prison was without bars. It was an empty room. Bob was silently levitating.

"So, how is he trapped?" asked Exp 8.

"He has no simple weakness. I simply told him if he tried to escape then I would kill one of you. Bob may not be honorable, but he is most certainly loyal," said Devlin with a smirk.

"He's a true Freedom Forcer. Hey, wait a minute, where's Ada?" asked Exp 8, still ignoring Kawai's air-dance.

"Right here," said Ada from below. She was in Exp 8's chest, beaming with contentedness.

Exp 8 looked at his predicament with newfound rage. He was chained down, had tubes through him and had his appendages held in place by titanium handcuffs. "Why is my trap so elaborate? They look like they're all having a grand old time."

"I really don't want you to escape. And, unlike the others, you have no clear hamartia. That's what makes you so special. Now, are you ready to give up? You and your Freedom Forcers will never escape my easily escapable inescapable traps," said Devlin as Kawai spun around behind him like a ballerina.

"I will break out. I will attain my freedom."

"Have fun with that. Now if you'll excuse me, I have a meeting to attend." Devlin fixed his collar and pulled out his cell phone. "Can you all keep an eye on the prisoners while I'm gone?" he asked through the phone. His voice erupted from the speakers all across the lab.

"With pleasure," said Kaity, staring at Nina.

"Have fun with your inescapable traps."

"Thank you!" said Nina, Atatasuki, and Kawai, who were all enjoying their prisons.

"You are welcome. As long as it keeps you incapacitated, I don't mind if it's to your preferences. I hope you all continue to enjoy being shackled," said Devlin, before leaving the room.

Kawai floated up to Exp 8 after realizing he wasn't paying attention to her mating ritual. "Looks like the laser grid is down now. Where would you like me to start?" she asked, molesting him with her eyes.

"Why can't you just accept that I don't like you that way?"

"I know that, once you accept my love, we'll live happily ever after," said Kawai, snuggling against his chest.

"If you really love me, then you should accept my refusal."

"You don't know what love is, do you? There's no point in trying to explain it. You've never been in love before. But I won't give up on you. You're going to be swept off your feet when you feel the magic!" exclaimed Kawai, bopping his nose.

"What magic?"

"Oh don't be like that. I just want to share with you the joy that it brings. I want to see that sweet smile beneath your mouthpiece," said Kawai, her kisses traveling up his arm.

"That's fine and all, but I have no desire for love. I have commitment and that's good enough for me."

"It is not good enough. Commitment is bondage. Love is freedom. You wouldn't understand. Nuuugh."

"I understand it. I don't need to experience it. Love only creates a pointless temporary state of happiness. I don't want happiness. I just want freedom," said Exp 8 on the verge of tears.

"Why not be unconditionally happy?" asked Ada.

"Don't chime in. This is our alone time." Kawai looked up at him. "Why won't you give me a chance, Brother? If you only opened up your heart, I'm sure you would find a special place in it for me."

"You can't grow to love someone. Love is a dramatic misinterpretation of sexual desire. I'm not attracted to you that way," said Exp 8, rolling his eyes.

"I know you love me. You just don't know it yet. Once I'm done having fun with you, the sparks of romance will ignite your heart," said Kawai, making circles around his crotch-plate with her tail.

"You can't force someone to love you!" exclaimed Exp 8, trying to bore his truth into her using only his eyes.

"You expect me to just live knowing you'll never love me? I'm determined. Call it denial if you want, but I call it hope," said Kawai, tearing up.

"You can't convince me to feel that way."

"Watch me," said Kawai, trying to pull off his crotch-plate.

"I know it's hard to take. But I'm not going to allow this situation to grow out of proportion."

"Are we thinking about the same thing?" asked Kawai, poking his crotch-plate with a dazed grin.

"I've got to end this now. Kawai, look at me. I will…I will never love you. I can't afford to."

"You mean you are incapable of love? How can such an incredible prize be unobtainable? You need to give romance a chance. I understand you have a hollow soul, but I'm never going to surrender to hopelessness. I want to fill that gaping hole with my unconditional love for you!" Kawai leaned in and kissed his cheek with gentle passion.

"It's not that I'm incapable of it. I choose to stay away from it. Love is a hero's biggest obstacle. It distracts them from their true goal."

"So that's what you see me as…a distraction?" asked Kawai, dropping to the floor.

"Don't get upset with me. You're telling me to try to love you, but what about Atatasuki? You never tried to love him. You never gave him even the slightest chance. Look, I'm not blaming you. I'm just making a point. Love creates favoritism and promotes hypocrisy. I want no part in it. Period."

"And why should I bother with him? He is a flawed failure. He's a mistake. He's like a miscarriage and you're the child prodigy! I love you and I always will. I will never give in to the despair." Kawai clenched her fists. "I am going to show you just how lovable I can be," she said as she licked her brother's cheeks.

"You're not listening to me. I am too rational to succumb to love."

"Then love me for my sake! It's the right thing to do, isn't it?" asked Kawai, her eyes watering up.

"If I did, I'd only be pretending. A loveless machine like me is not good enough for you. You need someone…who can fully appreciate your affection," said Exp 8 with a saddened tone.

"How can you say that? I'm the one who's not worthy," said Kawai, bowing repeatedly.

"It's not about worthiness! Look, there are tons of reasons. If I loved you, then I would be making Atatasuki suffer. Love always creates hatred and jealousy. My life is complex enough without love."

"Atatasuki wants us to be together. He's an idiot. He cares more about my happiness than his own. I do care deeply about your happiness. Really I do. But if you were in love with a girl besides me, I'd kill her," said Kawai, making a strangling motion with her tail.

"I don't want to love anyone. Love creates inequality. Love means favoring one over another. Love is an injustice!"

"Well then, be unjust. Be unequal. You are better than the laws of nature! Who decides what's just and unjust anyway? Morality is not innate. And if God made the concept of justice, then all the more reason to go against it. You are more than God. You are separate from God's creations! You're the one I love. You're as real as my swirling passion," said Kawai as she nestled his face.

"That passion is just going to keep going in a circle."

"I'm sorry, but I cannot stay quiet any longer! How can you be so cold-hearted?" asked Ada with a wounded voice.

"I'm trying to be moral. If being moral is immoral, then existence is hypocrisy!"

"Fine, be that way. Don't expect me to break you out," said Kawai, turning around and crossing her arms.

"You ask for me to accept your love when you deny Atatasuki's. Why don't you explain that?"

"I'd rather be a hypocrite than be without love," said Kawai as her eyes watered up.

"You made her cry again!" yelled Atatasuki from the cage all the way down the left corridor.

Kawai sharply turned to Atatasuki's direction. "Shut up! Why won't you stop loving me? You are creating your own pain, you idiot!"

"Pain is better than nothing! I will always love you! My purpose in life is to make you happy!" hollered Atatasuki.

"Well, you've failed…miserably. That's all you are, a big pathetic failure!" yelled Kawai, her stiff arms against her side.

"At least a failure has a heart, dysfunctional though it may be. Perfection is without emotion!" yelled Atatasuki.

Kawai flew out of the room angrily.

"I've made her cry again, waauhahahah," wailed Atatasuki.

"Look at what love has done to your sanity, brother! I want no part in such a thing!" hollered Exp 8.

"I'd rather be insane than heartless. Love is what keeps me going," said Atatasuki, determination breaking through his tears.

"Freedom is all I need to move me forward," said Exp 8, his eyes peering as far down the hallway as possible.

Meanwhile: Devlin was surveying the meeting room where the Viper Squad had their mission briefing. He meticulously grazed his hand on the surface of the table, checking it for any stray specks of dust. "This has to go perfectly," he said, combing back his hair. "You can come in now!"

The door opened up and all five new Exps sat down.

"Does anyone know why we are here?" asked Devlin, handing everyone a plate.

Matteria grabbed a pancake from the center.

Reflector watched with wide eyes as the syrup dripped on his girlfriend's face.

"Pancakes!" cheered D.S., quickly scarfing them down.

"Damn it! Kawai put a lot of...love in those pancakes!" yelled Devlin angrily, grabbing D.S. by his cheeks.

"Don't worry, Master Devlin. I don't eat," said Reflector, patting his reflective frame.

"Yeah and I just wanted to arouse you," said Matteria, sucking on the pancake.

"And I have recently taken a vow of photosynthesis! My Jain family is so proud of me!" exclaimed Violet, looking up at her creator for some sign of approval.

"The pancakes were more of a communion sort of thing. Well that and I wanted to test out my new microwave oven. Oh well. So, does anyone know why we are all here?" asked Devlin, walking around his new recruits.

"There are so many answers to your question," said Violet, sitting lotus-style on the floor.

"Ooh, ooh, pick me," said D.S., stretching out and waving his hand enthusiastically.

"Yes, Violet, do you have the answer?" asked Devlin, leaning toward her.

"We are here because the Gods want us to play our role in bringing the world into a new age of spiritual development. We are also here because our destinies have already been writ. Not only that, but our karmas are all connected to one another's. There's also—"

"No," said Devlin.

"Then it must be because we all love the Lord! We have come together to pray," said Violet, beaming up at him.

"We are here because seven of my Exps have betrayed me."

"What? Nobody betrays my little brother," said D.S., standing up from his chair.

"Sit down, please. But I like your enthusiasm. The traitors are Exp 8, Ada, Failed Experiment, Worthless Trash, Bob, Karson, and Nina. Ugh, do you have a question?" asked Devlin, turning to Reflector.

"Actually, I wanted to make a correction. Ada was not made by you. Neither were—"

"Do not interrupt me again!" Devlin breathed in deeply and then continued. "In order to stop any and all future back stabbings, I decided to have a

247

bonding circle with you all. We are not here to pray! Is that clear? So, who wants to share first?" asked Devlin, staring at the outgoing devotee with a fake smile.

"How did you know?" asked Violet amazed.

"Lucky guess," said Devlin, massaging his forehead.

Violet stood up, revealing her decorative garb. She was wearing a flowing white robe which draped over her feet. In the center of the robe was an intricate design that encompassed a spectrum of religious symbols into a single image.

"Hari-Om, I'm Violet Gold," she said with a loving smile.

"Hello Violet," said everyone in unison.

"I love every religion! I have monotheistic, polytheistic, henotheistic, deterministic, apocalyptic, animistic, satanic, deistic, theistic, atheistic, agnostic, and many other belief systems! I want to become a member of every religion because every religion holds universal truths! I also love reading Holy Scriptures in their original form. I one day hope to join with God and live out the rest of my lifetimes bringing salvation to all! I believe following my father's wishes will give me the necessary discipline to practice my free-spirited belief system."

"By that she means everyone's belief system," said Devlin, holding his forehead.

"I could never believe what everyone believes. There are infinite variations of worldviews, even within fundamentalist sects. There are as many belief systems as there are idiolects. I merely follow the prescribed practices and beliefs of an ever-expanding body of religions. Even though every religion is distinct, no path is mutually exclusive. There are hundreds of names for God and thousands of paths to enlightenment. All the religions follow core principles, so working on one- whether through belief, scriptural study, or action- brings you further along your path in another religion. They are all different, valid paths to true enlightenment. I am graced by all your divine presences," she said before sitting back down.

"Thank you for sharing, Violet. That was a wonderful introduction," said Devlin, starting up a circle of applause.

"You are most graciously welcome," said Violet with a bow.

"So, who would like to share next?" asked Devlin, putting a hand on D.S.'s back.

The huge muscle-bound man was now wearing a large, blue book bag. He was gripping a giant pair of scissors. "Sharing is for babies. Heheh."

"Well then, go ahead," said Devlin with a sweet smile.

"Wait, me?"

"Yes, you may speak."

"Um…okay. What do I say?" asked D.S., whispering to Matteria.

"Just introduce yourself, sheesh," said Devlin.

"Oh, okay. I got this. I am Destructus Supplious, but you can call me D.S. The other name is kind of long. I uh…" he said before stopping.

"Jesus be with you, brother D.S.," said Violet with closed eyes and a sweet smile.

"Um, yeah. So I enjoy drawing and cutting and pasting and kitties and taping and stapling and erasing and most of all killing! It's so much fun to cut people! Snip snip!" exclaimed D.S., almost smacking Devlin with his scissors as he swung them around.

"Thank you for your…um…words. Who's next?" asked Devlin.

The very shiny Exp stood up from his chair, reflecting light right in his master's eyes. "My name is Reflector."

"Hi Refels," said Matteria, blowing him a kiss.

"I like pretending to be a mirror so that people stare at me. It makes me feel special. This is my girlfriend," he said happily, gesturing to Matteria.

Devlin stood in between them and cleared his throat. "I guess I should share with everyone next. Hello, everyone, I am your creator, Devlin," he said, dramatically throwing his arms out.

"Hello Master Devlin!" they all exclaimed.

"I am a scientist seeking vengeance on this horrible world. I'm deeply in love with Kaity. Poetry is my passion and I just finished writing a song for my beloved. So, why don't you share," said Devlin, pointing to a disease-ridden corpse.

The only noise that came from the body was the squiggly maggots crawling inside it.

The diva saw a chance to debut and then stood up. "Hi everyone, I'm Matteria!"

"Hi Matteria."

"I like being beautiful," said Matteria with a girly twirl.

The sound of D.S. scribbling bore through the awkward silence.

"Go on," said Devlin.

Matteria looked at his current boyfriend and then back at Devlin. "Devi, why don't you desire me anymore? I want you so bad! Come on, play with me," said the pop star with a pouty tone.

"You know why. Now, hurry up. I have a date with Kaity," said Devlin, fixing his tie.

"Okay. As you all probably know, I am a successful fashion model. What you probably don't know is that I like getting caught in scandals because it brings me more attention. I believe that everyone should wear makeup so that they can all express themselves and become a beautiful work of art," said Matteria before reluctantly sitting down.

"I'm glad we had this talk. I'm sure we've rekindled the fires of our bonds. Farewell, my allies. I'm going to go check on the prisoners and try my luck with Kaity," said Devlin, freshening his breath.

"You said there would be candy!" yelled D.S., blocking his path.

"Go talk to Matteria. Goodbye, my dearly beloved and trusted Exps. Oh and just so we're clear, if any of you betray me…the rest of your existence will be remarkably unpleasant," said Devlin through gritted teeth.

"Good luck," said Violet, giving her creator a warm hug.

"Wait, you believe in luck? I thought you believed in karma," said Devlin with a raised eyebrow.

"I believe in both. And I wish you bountiful amounts of them."

"Waiiiiiit," said the disease-ridden corpse as it stood up.

Devlin squealed and then backed away from it.

The gruesome being had the overall shape of a human, but it was hideously distorted. Pulsating tumors created bulges throughout its body. Every inch of the monstrosity was rotting away. Its festering wounds oozed out pus and blood. A green murky fluid seeped out from the ill warrior's scabs, pooling back into its open gashes.

Matted, greasy white hair drew attention to its facial features. The leper's mouth was torn open and strewn diagonally. One eye bulged out, its color lost beneath a mist of cataracts and blood. The other had been partially swallowed up by the swollen flesh around it.

The right arm was larger than a motorcycle, its fingers all molding into a bludgeoning fist. The left arm was shrunken down to the size of a child's arm. The hulking monstrosity had powerful, tight muscles hidden just beneath the coating of disease.

"I aahm Amthraahksh! Ill whaahn too bea sheak saul thaaht mail paahtea kam pea shromkaahr!" The voice was pained, wet and guttural.

"Thank you all for sharing. Sayonara," said Devlin before leaving the room.

Devlin dragged a wedding cake into the prison chamber. He hid it behind the wall and then approached his dream girl.

"Hi Devi-kun, how did your little meeting go?" asked Kaity, leaning her head.

"Hi, Kaity. It went just fine. Hey, Kaity, I thought about you and made a cake," said Devlin as he rolled in her gift.

"Aww, thanks Devi-kun. Nina and I will eat it right away." Kaity sliced it with her plasma claws and then shoved the slice toward her crush's face.

"Think again, Devlin. I haven't maintained this body by poisoning it," said Nina, massaging her belly.

"I didn't get the cake for you. I made it for Kaity using my new microwave oven, with a little bit of Matteria's help, of course."

"You still have a crush on her. Oh, Devlin, one day you'll realize you need big breasts for your manly desires," said Nina, pushing out her chest.

"I wrote a poem about you," said Devlin suddenly turning to his beloved.

"You write poems! Let me see it," said Kaity, perking up with excitement.

"Uh, it's kind of written on the cake. In hindsight, it won't exactly be easy to read," said Devlin, shuffling his feet.

Kaity bounced up and gave the sweet boy a kiss on the cheek.

Devlin flared up in embarrassment, took a deep breath and then spoke. "But not to worry, I have it completely memorized. Kaity, you are the sunshine of my world. You are the music in my soul. You are my breath of fresh air. My inner sun revolves around your smile. I know that I can't express my love for you with words alone. Even so, you invoke sounds of beauty from within me. I feel as if I've known you forever, even though you're twelve. I think about you all the time. I hope that one day you'll be mine." He stroked her hair with a shaky hand.

Kaity gently pushed away from him. "Thanks, Devlin. That was really, really nice. But...you don't know anything about me. I'm not the kind of person someone wants to know anyway," she said, looking off to the side.

"But I want to get to know you. I really want to get to know you. That's why I wanted you to join me. I want to spend time with you. I love you, Kaity! I want to hold you in my arms and snuggle your breasts and have children with you!" exclaimed Devlin, before lighting up like a forest fire.

Kaity's eyes widened as she took another step back. "Wow. Um, Devlin, you're a really nice guy. And I...uh...appreciate your admiration. I don't want to hurt you. But I don't share the same feelings," she said, trying to look him in the eye.

"I don't know why I said that," said Devlin, covering his face.

"It's okay. You're not the first guy I've turned down. But you are the nicest," said Kaity with a warm smile.

"I wrote you a song. *In her eyes I see death. In her eyes I see pain. In her eyes I see sadness. So many emotions in her eyes. In her heart I see joy. In her heart I see pain. In her heart I see guilt. So many things make up her heart. In her hair I see the moon. In her hair I see blood. In her hair I see light. So many colors in her hair. She's as quick as a viper. She is a merciless sniper. Why can't her recticle be aimed at my heart? Why can't she shoot me with a bullet of love? From her smile I feel joy. From her frown, remorse. When she laughs, I light up. Why* can't she love me too? I know it doesn't rhyme, but I just came up with it," said Devlin, on the verge of crying.

"Please don't take this personally. I don't want to break your he—"

"My heart won't break. My heart has already been shattered to pieces innumerable times. My family, my girlfriend, my children! They all have betrayed me," said Devlin before bursting into tears.

"I'm so sorry, Devi-kun. *EVERYONE, LOVE, KAITY,*" she said softly.

All of the Freedom Forcers jumped for Kaity as they were overcome with a burning passion for her presence.

Nina ran to the cat-girl's side, thus escaping her prison.

Bob, Atatasuki, and Kawai also broke free of their trance as they were taken over by another one.

Exp 8 used all of his strength to break free and then ripped the back off of Karson's prison. "See sis, love doesn't work on me. I was just waiting for an opening," he said, helping Karson to his feet.

Devlin was already smitten with the adorable assassin and thus was unaffected by her ability. "I guess it was only a matter of time before I was betrayed again." He gripped his head and gazed downward. "I am reliving my despair! Everything was perfect and then it all fell to ruin!" He slammed his hands against the metal wall as tears raced down his face.

"*LOVE, CANCEL.*"

The Freedom Forcers broke out of the hex. They then split up and blocked the exits.

Atatasuki face palmed. "I knew I forgot something." He walked up to Exp 8. His fist then slammed into his brother's face.

Exp 8 was knocked off his feet.

"That was for making our little sister cry! Now...where was I supposed to stand guard?" asked Atatasuki, wandering around.

Exp 8 jumped back to his feet. "You good now? Got it out of your system?" he asked, cracking his jaw.

"Got what out of my system?" asked Atatasuki.

"Forget it. Ada, we need your help too," said Exp 8.

Ada dropped out and transformed before rushing to the fourth and final hallway entrance.

"You think you've won? You have absolutely no artifacts and you're outnumbered! I have five more Exps upstairs, so don't think you can escape this time. Why don't you all just go back to your prisons and do what I say?" yelled Devlin, desperately trying to intimidate the rebels.

"We don't know when the hell to give up," said Exp 8, cracking his fingers.

"Actually, going back to our cells doesn't sound so bad," said Nina, her head turning.

Atatasuki turned to her and nodded.

"Riufen, let's go! Kaity…I hope you have fun," said Devlin, trying to smile.

"I'm so sorry, Devi-kun."

Riufen zoomed into the room and picked up Devlin-sama. He then rushed out of sight before anyone could react.

"He won't get far. Kaity, aren't you're the only one who has an artifact on our team? Do you know if Devlin confiscated them?" asked Exp 8.

"What made you decide to betray Devlin?" asked Nina.

"You," said Kaity, latching onto her crush's arm.

"Wow, that's a good reason. I am extremely desirable and delicious and mmmmm…." Nina started fondling herself. "I miss that mirror cage already. Why must life be so cruel? Mwaaoh."

"I knew it," said a nearby dark voice. Tempo approached Kaity with a fiery glare, cracking his knuckles. "So all those years you spent with us meant nothing after all. Kanasta took you under his wing. Does some stupid crush really make all we've accomplished worthless? When you joined Kanasta you vowed never to leave the group. You aren't a part of our team anymore. I guess it falls upon me to kill you," he said coldly as his fist ignited.

"Hey, she never said she was leaving you guys!" hollered Atatasuki.

"No, he's right. I'm sticking with your group. I can't stay cooped up in this lab," said Kaity, standing tall.

Pharma emerged from a smoke cloud down the hallway. "We were unable to finish our battle. I refuse to die until you accept the truth." He flicked a cigarette at his rival.

"Are you kidding me? You've already died twice! Grooooah, why me?" asked Karson, his pistol hand to his forehead.

BoneSaw zoomed up to Atatasuki and revved up his saws.

Ego skated up to Nina. "I hear you have got quite the ego. But it is no match for mine. My self-love surpasses all obstacles," he said, kicking up his skateboard and catching it.

NoOne rose out from under Bob. He etched a smile on his blank face. "I don't stand a chance against you. You defeated Riufen! Prepare to win! Kehahahahaha!"

"I want a rematch," said Kanasta, dropping down from the ceiling and landing in front of the primary target.

"You want what? That's my line! I lost to you!" exclaimed Exp 8, pointing at the assassin boss with a trembling finger.

"I won't play around this time," said Kanasta with a smile.

"You...were playing around?" Exp 8 fell to the floor and curled up in the fetal position.

Kawai embraced her brother and helped him back to his feet. "Stand up and fight. You don't need to worry about him hurting you. I'm always here to help you, brother. We are going to kill him as a family!" she exclaimed, hopping onto his shoulder.

"Sis, about what I said earlier. I'm sorry for hurting you. I do love you. I love you dearly as my sister."

"It's a start," said Kawai, holding her chest with warm longing.

"Now let's go kick some ass!" exclaimed Exp 8, digging his knuckles into his palm.

Sefiwah dropped down from the ceiling, landing on Ada's back. "You deceived me when I pitied you. There is no forgiveness left in me. Die," she said, pulling out a dagger.

Chapter 24: Masters or Slaves

Tempo ran up and slammed his knee into the traitor's chest.

In the midst of the attack, Kaity stabbed her claws into his leg.

The plasma tore through the sinew and bone, but the seasoned killer didn't flinch.

Tempo punched the child's face, grabbed her arm, and then gripped her neck.

Kaity thrust her free hand at his chest.

Tempo snagged her arm between his, stopping the attack. With a single tug, he disjointed her arm. He then kicked the little girl off with his uninjured leg.

Kaity skidded across the ground, trying to regain her footing.

"*CLIMATE FEET, DUALITY!*"

Tempo's right leg became volcano hot, his left became tundra cold.

"*TEMPO, LOVE, KAITY!*"

Tempo rushed forth, unaffected by her attack. He kicked her disjointed arm, freezing it.

Kaity jumped into the air before dropkicking her opponent.

Tempo grabbed the leg before it could make contact and flung her aside.

"Why didn't my artifact work? Tempo, do you already love me? That's kind of sweet. Kind of creepy too," said Kaity as she regained her balance.

Tempo rushed forward and knocked the cat-girl off her feet with a slide. "You idiot, I hate you! My hatred is too strong to be distilled by your little artifact. You have ruined the Viper Squad! If you're going to leave, then, as your comrade, it is my duty to kill you. I have waited too long for this moment!" he yelled, kicking at the traitor furiously with his burning foot.

Kaity swiped her claw at his leg and then leaped to her feet.

Tempo flung his burning fist forth, stopping an inch from her face, before slamming his leg into her chest.

Kaity was sent rolling down the hallway as the heat melted through a portion of her suit, leaving her belly exposed to attack.

"*FROST KICK.*" Tempo quickly thrust his leg, sending a cold wave that froze the surface of the floor as it spread out.

Kaity's claws grew in size as she put them in front of her. They protected her from the cold wave, but the walls behind her became coated in ice.

"Good block. *SCORCHING KICK,*" said Tempo, flinging a heat wave forth.

Kaity jumped up and dodged the attack with precise timing.

Tempo flipped into a handstand and then kicked furiously at the spoiled child.

Kaity went down on all fours and ran around, dodging the barrage of temperature blasts.

Tempo jumped back to his feet. "**FIRE FIST**! **ICE FIST**! Let's see you dodge this!" He thrust both of his fists forward.

A massive heat wave emitted from his fists, followed by a cold wave.

Kaity back-flipped over Tempo and disengaged her sniper. While still in the air, she aimed at his forehead and fired.

His fists' aura froze the bullet before it could hit him.

Kaity landed, kicked off the ground and then lunged her claws at the enemy.

Tempo grabbed her arm before she could hit him and kneed her in the stomach.

Kaity's arm solidified in his icy grip. The cold traveled up to her shoulders.

Without another thought, Kaity shattered her arm to pieces. She then jumped back, dodging an upward kick.

"All things considered, you are a great assassin. But in the end, there can only be one master assassin. **ICY SANCTUARY**!" Tempo placed both hands on the floor, instantly freezing it along with the girl's feet.

Kaity stabbed at the ice but it kept reforming.

Tempo whistled a happy tune as he strolled up to his victim. "The little kitty can't run now," he said, grabbing her hair and pulling her up to him. He placed his other hand on her exposed belly.

A cold wave enveloped Kaity's body, leaving only her mouth and eyes unfrozen.

"Do you now see the consequences of disobeying Kanasta? The only way to leave the squad is in a body bag," said Tempo, whispering in her ear.

"You're the one disobeying Kanasta."

"You get adopted into our family, stay for awhile, and then just decide to leave! I have to kill you!" yelled Tempo, grabbing her throat.

"If you kill me, the Boss will never forgive you. Besides, I thought we were a family. You wouldn't kill your own sister, would you?" asked Kaity, worry outlining her emerald eyes.

"As long as it's fun," said Tempo, smacking her across the face.

"It is fun assassinating, isn't it? Hee-hee," said Kaity with a grin.

"It sure is. But you do have a point. I don't want to upset the Boss. But it's more important that I keep him on the proper path. So I guess he'll just have to grieve till he gets over you," said Tempo, his finger burning a hole into her chest.

"Hey Tempo, you should know that Kanasta sent me on a secret mission. I am still a part of the Viper Squad. Don't worry, I'll find a way to free all of you," said Kaity with a smile.

"Why didn't you say that earlier?" asked Tempo, his finger boring in deeper.

"Kanasta wanted to keep it just between the two of us."

Tempo pulled out his fiery finger. "Asshole! I've been by his side far longer than you have."

"So then, we're good."

"I hate to put the livelihood of the Viper Squad in the hands of a child, but shit, what else can I do. If Devlin catches me freeing you, he might just trigger that bomb he put inside me."

Kaity's eyes widened. She then shook herself to her senses. "Devlin wants me alive, so you should be worried about the damage you did not didn't do to me. Don't you see, Devlin's obsession with me is the reason Kanasta picked me for the job."

"Get out of here. If I see you again…I'll cremate you. Do you understand me?" asked Tempo, reluctantly unthawing her.

"You don't need to worry about me. I can handle myself. I was raised well," said Kaity, her arms behind her back.

"I hope we meet again soon," said Tempo, walking off with a grimace.

Pharma and Karson began their battle in a nearby hallway.

"I'm too toxic to die from a fatal overdose."

"If you go comatose again, I'll burn you to ashes."

"And when I win, I'll turn your body into a smoking pipe! This is our final fight! I won't hold back! It's time to break our tie," said Pharma before he upchucked a cigar and smoked it.

"What tie are you referring to? I beat you both times."

"Are you truly that foolish? Beh-kough-kough-beheh."

"You're the loon here!"

"The battle was drugs versus guns. Drugs killed me twice. If anything, you need to win two more times just to have a tie with me," said Pharma, blowing a smoky zero at the gunman.

"Let's just get this over with." Karson fired his Gatling gun at the enemy soldier.

"I still have the Slow-motion Artifact and you have nothing," said Pharma as the bullets crawled toward him. He lit up his thumb as the bullets pierced through his powdery skin.

Alcohol dripped out of the addict's wounds and onto the floor.

"I'm going to wipe that stain of superiority off your face once and for all!" exclaimed Karson as his hands transformed into rocket launchers.

"*Nicotine Smoke Bomb.*" Pharma coughed up cigarettes and tossed them to the ground. They created a smoke screen, masking his location. The drug lord ran behind his rival in the confusion.

Karson fired his Uzi feet, propelling him backwards toward the enemy. "Your military skill is abominable." He turned around and fired his chain-gun randomly as he skated across the floor.

"You're aim is off. *Cigarette Butt.*"

Various cigarettes singed Karson from within the smoke. They were more of an annoyance than a threat.

"Come out and fight me, you coward!" yelled Karson.

Pharma inhaled all of the smoke like a vacuum cleaner, exhaling out with a wide grin. "Last time we fought, I realized something. It was like an epiphany…whoa. I realized that I needed a weapon to kill you. So without further ado, meet my cigarette sword," he said before starting to choke. His choking became more and more intense.

"Again?" asked Karson.

"Kehough!" Pharma spit out a wad of tar. "Phew. This time my coughing is the ringing of your funeral bell."

"Was that supposed to be poetic? Why do I bother? It's only a matter of time before you kill yourself again," said Karson, turning around.

"Meet Nicky, the very first nicotine sword."

Nicky was shaped like a bastard sword and colored like a cigarette. The tip of the sword was glowing red and had smoke spewing from it.

"Nicky is the only sword on the globe that you can smoke," said Pharma as he puffed smoke circles at his adversary.

"Fascinating. Can we get on with this?"

Pharma jabbed Nicky at his rival furiously.

Karson stood still, untouched by the loon's amateur sword skills. "Pssh. Where did you learn how to use a sword?" he asked, covering his mouth in an attempt to hold in the laughter.

"Devlin created Nicky after I was resuscitated. I have been practicing ever since, thinking only of cutting you down. Sometimes I get a little distracted in the middle of training from my potent withdrawal symptoms and have to take a short smoking break. But now I have finally mastered the art of the sword," said Pharma, waving his weapon around.

"You're holding it upside down. Psahahahaha. What a moron."

Pharma looked down and quickly flipped the blade around, dropping it in the process. "You're a gun! You have no right to criticize my skill! You probably don't even know what a sword looks like," he said, poking Karson's face with the tip of the blade. He then shoved Nicky straight through the gunman's chest.

"Are you done yet?"

"I refuse to lose to you," said Pharma, puffing smoke in his rival's face.

"Swords are obsolete. Guns ended the samurai and they shall end you." Karson aimed his Uzi feet at a thirty-degree angle. He fired relentlessly, ripping through the bloke's knees.

Pharma collapsed, bleeding out coffee and alcohol.

"Even your blood is a drug. You're your own worst enemy. Ugh. Why couldn't I have gotten a cool rival?"

"You should know that it's also flammable!" yelled Pharma, leaping at Karson. His alcoholic blood spewed all over his rival. His shoulders opened up, revealing a lighter that ignited the puddle of blood.

Karson combusted as the flames overtook him. He jumped to a dry area on the floor, landing flat on it. He then rolled around, trying to put out the flames, careful not to hit his button in the process.

Pharma emerged, coated in flames. He inhaled deeply through all his pores, consuming the fire with his skin. He then slowly exhaled.

Fumes poured out of his body as he approached with a menacing smirk.

Pharma stopped, abruptly overtaken by fear. He then started coughing uncontrollably. After pounded his chest violently, the drug lord spit out a black wad on Karson's foot. "I've won now." He took out an empty bottle and put it on his bleeding knees to collect the flowing alcohol. The addict triumphantly raised the bottle to his mouth. His blood spilled all over him as he chugged it down. He gargled the alcohol before having it slide down his visible esophagus. "You can't even move. This calls for a victory smoke," he said, using his thumb to ignite Nicky. He burst into flames and collapsed to the floor.

Before long, Pharma's screams were silenced.

Karson leaped to his feet, just after ridding himself of the flames. "I won?" he asked, looking at the smoldering corpse curiously.

BoneSaw and Atatasuki's bout began in the adjacent metal hallway.

"I beat Ego. Taking care of you will be as easy as baking a pumpkin pie. It's only a matter of time before it's done," said Atatasuki, cracking his fingers.

BoneSaw cut the ground to read: "You have no artifacts, so neither shall I. This should be fun." The robot disengaged the Multiply Artifact and revved up its saws. It rushed at the target and launched off the ground.

Saws disconnected from the robot's sides, all shooting toward the cyborg's neck.

Atatasuki shielded his neck with his palms, but the force of the saws caused him to lose balance.

BoneSaw rode up the wall and then dive-bombed at its prey.

Atatasuki grabbed the killer box, trying to keep the giant saw as far away as possible from his neck. He dodged a jab and then flung the little robot into the wall.

BoneSaw landed and powered down.

"Did I break him? Whoohoo! I already won! You really didn't stand a chance after all. Don't feel bad, I am the greatest microwave of all time. But I've never finished a fight this fast! This calls for a ceremonial victory snack. I deserve to eat the Muffin of Victory," said Atatasuki as he brought his tail to his mouth.

Two saws came out from BoneSaw's metal body and dug into the ground. The saws propelled the assassin forward with incredible speed.

Atatasuki was just about to take a bite when the new Muffin of Victory was cut to shreds.

"She was innocent! You worthless treading piece of garbage…I'm going to destroy you! *SUPER MICROWAVE, FIST!*" Atatasuki's hands became scorching hot as the rage for his dearly departed pastry ignited his innate ability.

BoneSaw dug underground and disappeared from sight.

"I hate you! I am going to cook you alive you damn demon box!" Overtaken by his rage, Atatasuki thrust his fist into the ground.

The metal melted as it caved in.

BoneSaw popped out from the ceiling. It cut the target's chest as its saws stretched forward.

Atatasuki grabbed the saw, melting it as it cut his hand. He then slammed the murderer to the ground.

As soon as it recovered, the robot dug into the floor once more.

"Come out, you damn trashcan!"

BoneSaw stayed underground, waiting for the proper moment.

"If you aren't going to come out, then I'll just microwave everything to hell. I never thought I'd have to use this, but oooh I'm going to! *OVEN MITTS!*"

Iron-plated mitts enveloped in fire were burning on the plate inside his chest.

Atatasuki put on the flaming mitts triumphantly, striking them together. "*INFERNO GAUNTLETS!*" He slammed his burning fists against the ground.

The area around him burst with flames, even scorching the ceiling.
BoneSaw fell from its hiding place above the target.

The passionate prototype pulled back both fists and then punched his
opponent with explosive fury.

BoneSaw was flung into the ceiling, smashing straight through it before
melting into dust.

Atatasuki jumped up into the hole he made, arriving right in front of
Devlin and his new recruits.

"This is a delightful surprise! I needed someone to warm up this
cupcake," said Devlin, gesturing to the glamorized muffin with a sly grin.

Ego and Nina's confrontation was at the entrance to the northeast hallway.

"Your ego is just misrepresented insecurity. You feel worthless because
you don't have a girlfriend," said Nina with a half-smile.

Ego's artifact reacted to his belittlement, shrinking his skin as a result.
The skin ripped open, forming a gash across his chest.

"Did I hit a soft spot?" asked Nina, dragging her finger down the new
wound.

"I read everyone's file. And according to yours: your self-love is just a
program. My ego is natural. It is not forced by artificial means," said Ego,
launching a quick attack to strengthen his defenses. The skin enlarged as his
esteem was redeemed and thus the wound started to heal.

Nina pulled off her gloves compulsively and then took a deep breath.
"You're wrong. I love myself because I've worked on becoming a beloved
individual. It's not pre-programmed and it isn't vanity," she said, her finger
muscles tightening.

"If you're so great, then why do you have such a massive ego? Truly great
people have no egos," said Ego as his scar healed further.

Nina tore off her shoes at this insult and then smiled. "If that's true, then
you are nowhere near as great as you tell yourself," she said, circling around him.

Ego's shoulder split open, the wound almost cutting completely through.
He held in the pain and looked up at the enemy egotist.

"So you admit that I have greatness after all?" His shoulder slowly
reassembled.

Nina only ripped off one of her socks at this remark. "Your ego is so
weak, you are injured when you're insulted," she said, tapping his nose.

Ego coughed up blood, looking at it in disbelief.

"Poor little whiny boy. Never seen your own blood before, have you?
How pathetic," said Nina, dipping her finger in it and wiping it on his cheek.

261

Ego fell to the floor as his foot was sliced open. "You show off your body to everyone, only to fool yourself into thinking they are attracted to you. And when they aren't, you break down. Your self-confidence is laughable," he said, limping along the floor.

Nina not only stripped off her other sock, she also ripped her shirt open. "You're jealous because I have such a drop-dead gorgeous body. You're just an average unattractive little gear-head," she said, massaging her breasts through her bra.

The tattoo that said "It's Huge" on Ego's back suddenly formed a large scar.

"Oh, what's that tattoo for? Are you trying to compensate for something?" asked Nina, looking down at the ugly boy with a catty frown.

The scar fully healed in an instant.

"You couldn't be more wrong. I don't know what you're so happy about. The only reason you have great breasts is because they were designed by some horny scientist," said Ego, now back on his feet.

Nina ripped off her skirt, leaving her only in underwear.

"Whoa," said Ego with wide eyes.

Nina was too busy fondling herself to even notice the compliment.

Ego screamed out in pain as the reality of being ignored bore a massive hole into his back. "The only reason you molest yourself is because no one else wants to touch you."

Nina now ripped off her remaining clothes, leaving her naked. She crossed her legs and covered her breasts, trying to keep her sexy bits hidden as best she could.

"I told you my ego would prevail. It's huge!" said Ego as his self-esteem was healed by destroying hers.

Nina stuck out her tantalizing tongue. "Yes, I admit defeat," she said, grabbing a trigger from her hair. All of her clothes exploded around her opponent,

Ego fell to the ground as a smoldering mess. He raised his head, opened his mouth and then collapsed.

Nina pulled back her arm and then shoved it through his chest. She ripped out his capsule and examined it. "I won't use your worthless artifact. You can keep it." She slowly crushed his capsule under her foot. "Phew. Glad that's over. How could he ever think he is better than me? His ego is self-serving. Mine empowers me! My compulsive stripping was all a juicy part of my seductive strategy. And that strategy was—I feel cold." Her arms shivered over her bare breasts. She was then spontaneously wrapped in new clothing. The sexy survivalist took off her shirt and compulsively fondled herself.

NoOne's battle with Bob initiated at the hallway to the left.

"I didn't just beat Riufen. I also defeated Kanasta," said Bob.

"You're the one who conquered the mighty Kanasta! This ended before it began. I won't let it get me down. I will do my best before I fail miserably," said NoOne, standing tall with his shoulders up.

"Oh, show some backbone! Even if your name implies that you have no value, you must have faith in yourself," said Bob, patting the pitiful wretch with a spectral hand.

"You're right. I have to believe in myself! NoOne, you can do it. You can do it. You can…lose miserably. Ugh, I guess I just can't lie to myself," he said, sinking into the ground.

"This is pathetic! Attack me!" yelled Bob, pulling his opponent back up.

"Destroy him, my shadow sheep……or just get killed," said NoOne depressed as his shadow sheep were slaughtered by lasers. The shadow master punched a hole in his other hand.

"*SHADOW CANNON.*" NoOne fired shadow balls at the ground through the holes in his hand.

"*Eyeball Laser.*"

The shadow balls morphed into hands. The shadow hands then rose up and restrained the incoming laser.

The laser stopped inches away from their intended target. The hands then broke the laser apart and tossed the pieces at the eyeball.

Bob was assaulted by the shards, not bothering to pass through any of them.

NoOne fired shadow balls that floated around the unstoppable foe.

The shadow balls took the form of little eyeballs and fired tiny black lasers.

The mini-lasers passed through Bob and hit the shadow replicas behind him.

Bob floated up and rammed NoOne while still impaled by the laser shards.

The shards went deep into the shadow man's gooey skin.

NoOne molded his body around the unstoppable force, covering him. The shadow master then passed through his impregnable enemy.

Bob turned around as his foe fell to the floor. He aimed down and then fired forth a laser, piercing through his victim's body. He then summoned up the Atma Blade.

"Isn't that legendary blade forged by the souls of the dead?" asked NoOne, manually widening his eyes.

"It is the manifestation of my own essence. I can shape it in any way I want. This form is just the most pleasing to me," said Bob, admiring his spectral sword.

"Wow…I am so doomed," said NoOne, chuckling at his own despair.

Bob thrust his blade into the ground. "*Jiva Summon!*"

Material Jiva were created, looking around curiously with their spotlight eyes. The Jiva were wispy green beasts, poised on all fours. Their bodies were bare but had no skeletal structure. Wraith-like teeth outlined their mouth like a shark's. They walked toward their prey, engaging their spectral talons. The Jiva extracted its soul particles like a vacuum cleaner collects dust.

"*SHADOW STAIRS,*" said NoOne, walking on his own feet to get out of range of the attack.

Bob floated up to NoOne as he shot a laser upward.

NoOne split in two. He reassembled and then threw a shadow spear.

"*Soul Shield.*"

One of the Jiva selflessly ran into the laser and died. Its soul returned to the Atma Blade, yelping as it was reabsorbed.

"*SHADOW PILLAR,*" said NoOne.

The shadow balls under Bob created a pillar that elevated quickly, sending him on a path to the shadow master.

"*SHADOW MORPH.*" NoOne's body became a wall. He rammed Bob through the entire shadow pillar, splitting it in half. He then landed near the downed immortal, smiling victoriously. "Here it comes, your final attack," he said, his head drooping as his disappointment returned.

"*Soul Acquisition!*"

The Atma Blade swirled and gathered soul energy in its core.

Bob thrust it into his foe, exploding him into tens of thousands of particles.

"Do not underestimate the power of the Atma Blade," said Bob dramatically.

NoOne regenerated. "I didn't!"

The shadow man's pieces then sank into the ground. The shadow then moved down the hallway and out of sight.

"That was entertaining, I suppose," said Bob with a curious look.

Kanasta's struggle against Exp 8 and Kawai started in the center room where Exp 8 had been held captive.

"What makes you think you can win this time?" asked Kanasta.

Exp 8 approached him with powerful steps. "I won't play—"

"He has me on his side this time. Isn't that right, Brother?" asked Kawai, sitting on his shoulder.

"Yeah, that's what I meant. Kawai will keep me energized and I'll keep her safe," said Exp 8, clenching his fist.

"Until all the Freedom Forcers are out of commission, I am bound by my contract. It seems we are both fighting for our freedom now." Kanasta tossed a steel card at the primary target.

Kawai floated in front of her brother. The card hit her golden shoulder guard and then slid off. "Don't worry, Brother. I'll be your shield," she said, snuggling against his powerful arm.

Kanasta jumped past the primary target, turned around, and tossed a full hand of cards.

The cyber siblings both shot a laser net forward.

The cards cut through the nets and then hit the prototype. One of the cards sliced up her arm, leaving a bloody trail.

"Here, taste my blood," said Kawai, shoving her arm in her beloved's face.

"What the hell is wrong with you? This is no time to be screwing around!" he said, knocking her arm aside. He fired a lighting quick orb at Kanasta, who did a back-flip to dodge it.

"Soooo, when can we screw around?" asked Kawai, her tail stroking his crotch-plate.

"You can shoot out black orbs too, right?"

"Yeah, yeah. I can also perform air sex. I know, I'm revolutionary. Heeheehmph."

"I'm going to need your help. Be ready at my command," said Exp 8, grabbing her hand.

"I'm always ready," said Kawai, running her tail up his back.

Kanasta slammed down his foot, bringing up a stack of dominoes from the ground. He spun around and then slammed his palms into the domino in front of him.

The seven-foot stack was sent on a crash course towards the primary target.

"I won't let him hurt you again," said Kawai, getting smashed by the dominoes all the way to the wall.

Kanasta appeared behind the secondary target and thrust his fist forward.

Exp 8 pushed his sister out of the way, having the massive fist slam into him instead.

The wall behind him burst open from the force of the powerful punch.

"I've got you right where I want you," said Exp 8 with a wide smile.

"You mean you saved my life just to trick him?" asked Kawai with teary eyes.

Kanasta ripped his fist out and kicked the primary target like a football.

As her big brother was launched toward her, Kawai opened up her arms and snuggled his face.

"This is no time to molest me!" yelled Exp 8, breaking free of her grip.

"It's never time," said Kawai, crossing her arms and turning around.

"We can talk about this later. I need some back up," said Exp 8, strafing with his jets to rapidly dodge the assassin's attacks.

"Do you want me to drain his energy? Devlin made it so I don't lose energy anymore. I actually gain energy now. But I need to be careful not to take in too much. I wonder what enhancements he gave you," said Kawai, floating up to him.

"Eheh, what a perfect enhancement for such a lecherous little thing," said Exp 8, holding his head.

"So, should I give it a shot?" Using her tail, Kawai pulled her brother out of the way of Kanasta's forward jab.

"Go for it, Sis! Drain him dry," said Exp 8, quickly ducking a lighting quick strike.

"With pleasure," said Kawai, stretching her fingers. She flung herself on the enemy's leg. She embraced it tightly, sapping away its energy.

"Get off me," said Kanasta calmly, slamming the secondary target against the ground.

Exp 8 rushed up and socked the assassin boss in the face. "Hold onto him as if he were me."

Kawai strangled the leg with a sudden explosion of passion.

"Well played," said Kanasta, falling as his leg lost all energy. He rose up his head to be greeted by a giant black orb, pulsating with energy.

"Time to use my newest enhancement," said Exp 8 as his wrist ring disconnected.

The ring extended itself forward, overlapping his hand. The orb then connected to his levitating wrist ring.

"It's become an attachment to my body. How freaking cool is that?" Exp 8 slammed the orb against the assassin boss repeatedly. He then jumped backwards. "I can even shoot it off."

The orb shot out like a bullet into the trained killer. It exploded violently, filling the air with black murky smoke.

Kawai rushed in to the smoke cloud.

Exp 8 punched rapidly, blowing the smoke away and revealing Kanasta to be unconscious and severely wounded.

"Got every last bit he had. Now may I cuddle your face?" asked Kawai with her hands nestled to her chin.

"Yes, now is the time," said Exp 8, patting her head.

"Yay!" cheered Kawai, snuggling his face affectionately. "Did I do okay?" she asked, bouncing up and down.

"We make a great team! Now let's all escape from this hellhole."

"Can you carry me, Brother?" asked Kawai, bobbing side to side.

"Would you stop being so lazy? You can float!"

"Fine, I'll carry you then," said Kawai, smiling warmly as she lifted him up with her tail.

Sefiwah and Ada's battle started on the opposite side of the hallway where Kaity confronted Tempo.

Sefiwah jabbed her dagger at the enemy, who quickly flung her over her shoulder to deflect it.

Sefiwah rolled back to her feet. "You used my misery as an opening to knock me out. I will not forgive you. Your death shall bring you release from your own deceitful mind," she said, flinging various knives.

Two knives sliced into Ada's ankle, making her topple over.

"I felt bad after I hit you too. I don't want to hurt anyone ever again," said Ada, air-hugging the pale pacifist while on her knees.

"Don't worry. You won't," said Sefiwah, her eye twitching with anger.

"Truce?" asked Ada, standing up and outstretching her arm.

"This time you don't have any illusionary tricks. No artifact, no chance," said Sefiwah, checking the sharpness of a full set of knives.

"You're really upset, aren't you?" asked Ada, looking down.

Sefiwah dashed to her prey as swift as a cheetah. She slid down and kicked the unguarded legs. She stabbed a handful of knives into the knees. The nimble assassin then jabbed her fingertips through her target's chest. With her hand still in the chest, she stuck out her pointer finger with the other hand. "Snake style is very effective for killing. Snakes themselves are quick to the strike and then slowly strangle their prey. But I don't need to drag this out. I bet I can kill you with just this one finger," she said, stroking her victim's chin.

"I don't really like to bet. I never win," said Ada, twiddling her thumbs.

"But your life's on the line. How can we not make a bet when the stakes are so high, so…tempting?" asked Sefiwah, sliding her finger down her target's light blue lips. Her finger jabbed as fast as a bullet in rapid succession, poking holes throughout her opponent's body.

Ada kicked herself out of the kind killer's grip. "I don't want to hurt you," she said sadly, her wounds slowly healing.

"Neither do I. But I can't avoid it. I am sorry. You must die," said Sefiwah, bending down. She jumped behind the enemy and wrapped her arms around her neck. "Please die quickly," she said with tears flowing out onto her victim. "Why must this world force us to kill for survival? The very meaning of life is hypocritical. Why must we have to deprive others of life in order to live ourselves? I am doomed to have a life of murder to protect what is most dear to me. I don't want to ki—why aren't you dead yet?" she asked, turning to her stubborn victim.

"I didn't want to interrupt, but um…Exps don't need to breathe. I thought we went over this already."

"At least fight back. This doesn't even feel like a battle," said Sefiwah, wiping away a tear as it sprouted up.

"If I hurt you, then it would create a spiraling chain of vengeance. Kaity will hate me and if she kills me, then someone will hate her. But if you kill me, then Devlin will kill you! I don't want to be any part of something so horrible."

"You know Kaity?" asked Sefiwah.

"Yes. She's a really lovable person deep down," said Ada, folding her hands.

"I'm sorry to ruin your wonderful relationship," said Sefiwah softly. She placed a knife in the dangerous woman's hand and then thrust her own chest through it. "I can't allow Kaity to love anyone," she said, pushing the blade in deeper.

"No, Kaity and I are just friends. You've got the wrong idea!" said Ada, trying to pull the blade out.

"Oh…you should have told me sooner. It was only a matter of time, I guess. I suppose it is best if I die by your hand. It's about time for me to move on anyway. Please, protect Kaity from love. I'll see you in Heaven," said Sefiwah with a wide, caring smile.

Chapter 25: Crazy Kitty

Kaity rushed into the room where Sefiwah was, eager to catch her before she left. "Hi Ada, is Sefi…" she said before stopping in mid-hop. Her pupils shrank as they met her lover's lifeless eyes.

Ada was still holding the knife, lodged deep within Sefiwah's chest. "Give me a minute to explain. Hmm, well, to put it simply…she killed herself," she said, lowering her head.

Kaity took a deep breath. She pulled out her sniper rifle with a trembling hand.

"Sefiwah hates killing. She did this to stop herself from killing. She wanted you to blame me for her death because she thought I was your lover…or something," said Ada, making the body bleed more as she tried to yank the knife out.

"Stop talking." Kaity loaded up the rifle, while hoisting it with her leg. The recticle of the rifle shook as it inched toward the enemy's head. Kaity fired frantically, her aim impaired by her emotions.

"She really is a nice person!" exclaimed Ada, setting the body on the ground.

"Sefiwah kills mercilessly, without ever shedding a tear. Stop lying and die!" yelled Kaity as she fired once more.

The bullet shot through the Exp's chest, just barely missing her capsule.

"She is a good person," said Ada, walking toward the lost child.

"I'm the only one who understands her. And she…was the only one who understood me," said Kaity, blinded by tears. She tossed her rifle aside and pulled out a pistol. The prodigy assassin shot at the murderer's legs repeatedly, loading in clip after clip with her only hand.

Ada plummeted to the floor, still beaming up at the girl as more bullets pierced into her legs. "I'm so sorry this happened."

"I am Kanasta's strongest assassin, and you're the weakest Exp. I am going to enjoy bathing in your artificial blood," said Kaity, twitching frenetically.

Previously: In the room above them, Atatsuki met face-to-face with Devlin.

"Hellooooo, Failed Experiment. I have a cupcake that needs to be heated. Why are you so quiet?" asked Devlin.

"You know how much I hate those damn posers," said Atatsuki, turning away.

"You really are like a muffin…bland and fragile," said Devlin, walking closer.

"If you continue to mock the greatness of muffins, then I will show you their power!" yelled Atatasuki, clenching his fist.

"What greatness? Hahahaha."

Atatasuki's chest opened up and shot a muffin at the blasphemer.

Destructus Supplious dropped down from the ceiling, grabbed the muffin, and tossed it behind him.

Atatasuki flung his body forward, doing everything in his power to catch the muffin.

D.S. jumped above him and thrust his scissors down.

Atatasuki grabbed the edges of the scissors, stopping them from piercing his flesh.

D.S. opened the scissors, breaking the bad guy's grip. He then sliced the evildoer in half with a single cut.

Atatasuki screamed in undiluted agony as his upper half writhed compulsively on the ground.

"Don't worry. I missed your vitals," said Destructus Supplious, turning away with a proud grin.

"How exactly did you miss his vitals?" asked Devlin, covering his mouth.

"Yay, cutting time!" exclaimed Destructus Supplious as he continuously sliced up his spoils.

"That's enough. You can stop now. We don't need to kill him. I said stop!"

D.S. dropped his scissors and turned to his boss. "The bad guy has been defeated," he said with a thumbs-up.

All that was left of Atatasuki was a bloody mesh of metal and flesh.

"You didn't have to kill him!"

"Don't worry, he'll live," said Destructus Supplious, cleaning the blood off his scissors by wiping it on the wall.

Meanwhile: the Freedom Forcers met up on the floor below.

"There you are," said Karson, joining with Exp 8 and Kawai.

"How the hell did you beat Pharma?" asked Exp 8, smacking the gunman's shoulder.

"He set himself on fire this time. Uuugh. Wait a tick, how did you beat Kanasta!"

"I had Kawai's help and Devlin's badass upgrades!" exclaimed Exp 8, holding his sister up.

Nina rushed down the hallway and stopped, gazing into her reflection on the floor. "I want a mirror so bad," she said, trying to get the right angle.

Exp 8 waved at his distracted ally.

"Oh, it seems you won," said Nina, combing her hair with her fingertips.

"I think all of us won," said Exp 8, throwing his fist in the air.

"Well then, where's Bob?" asked Karson, looking around.

"Bob probably went ahead. Look, we need to find out where Kaity and Ada are. It's time to escape Devlin's lab a third time," said Exp 8, clenching his fist.

"You are just so cool," said Kawai with shimmering eyes.

"I'm glad Kaity betrayed Devlin. I knew an innocent girl like her couldn't be evil," said Exp 8.

"What about me?" asked Kawai with puffed out cheeks.

"I said innocent, didn't I?" asked Exp 8, rubbing her head.

"Yeah because murdering people for money is just sooo sweet," said Kawai with a strained smile.

"She was just raised wrong."

A bloody mass flew by them into the wall.

Kaity ran by them with Ada's blood dripping from her claws.

"Perfectly innocent," said Kawai, clasping her hands to her cheek.

"Ada!" Exp 8 ran as fast as he could to her aid. He looked in the distance, catching a glimpse of Kaity's plasma claws piercing into his comrade's chest.

Previously: after defeating NoOne, Bob was confronted by an old adversary.

"It is an honor to meet you again," said Riufen, dropping in from above.

"It's a good thing I didn't eradicate your soul. I haven't had a decent fight in a while," said Bob as a laser shot from his eye.

Riufen's body split in two, dodging the laser. "I couldn't be happier," said the samurai as he reassembled.

His rib cage shot out, ripping his stomach open and impaling his opponent.

Riufen rushed down the hallway, dragging his rival against the wall.

Bob fired a bulky laser, sending his opponent skidding backwards and releasing himself in the process. He then rammed the swordsman from above, plastering him to the ground.

Riufen's veins burst out of his arms and tangled around his rival.

Bob spun around, tugging on the veins and dragging the samurai closer.

The veins detached, sending the round Exp spinning into the wall.

Riufen ripped off his hands, exposing his bones.

The bones fired forward, pummeling the fellow swordsman gratuitously.

Bob's eye moved in a flash, cutting the bones to pieces.

Veins wrapped around the swordsman's newly grown bones, knitting them together.

The stalwart samurai ripped out his spine and flung it.

Bob swerved out of the way. The Atma Blade swirled with energy as he rushed forth. He thrust his weapon into the swordsman after darting out of the way of his fist.

Riufen spontaneously exploded into thousands of pieces.

"Goodbye Riufen. You were an honorable opponent," said Bob, bowing to the warrior's remains.

Riufen's bloody bits came together and reformed his body. "You are a great warrior. Though I don't know if I could call you honorable."

"B-b-but I destroyed you!"

"I have learned much. Thank you for taking time to spar with me." Riufen bowed. He then jumped into a hole in the ceiling and vanished.

"Was he mocking me? No, he is incapable of being insincere."

Bob flew down the hallway, meeting up with the Freedom Forcers.

Ada's blood-soaked body soared past him. "Aww. What did I miss this time?" asked Bob in hot pursuit.

Kaity appeared soon afterwards, a murderous intent gleaming in her eyes.

"Betrayal, from my own team? Go Kaity go!" cheered Bob, throwing his spectral arms in the air.

The rest of the Freedom Forcers followed the aerial blood trail to Ada.

"What the hell is wrong with you?!" asked Exp 8, grabbing the crazed girl's arm.

"Let go of me! She killed Sefiwah!" Kaity squeezed out of the iron grip and continued to pursue her enemy. She was then rammed into the wall by a pink blunt object.

"Don't touch my brother," said Kawai with an intense stare, pummeling the assassin with her tail.

Kaity leaped up and impaled her attacker with blood-drenched claws. "Get out of my way!" She kicked the nuisance off her plasma claws.

Bob floated out from the ground behind them. "Well, well, well, things are finally getting interesting," he said, eating spectral popcorn.

"Bob, stop her!" yelled Karson.

"As you command," said Bob, shooting a laser at the cat-girl's leg.

Kaity tumbled on the ground and then transitioned back into a sprint.

"Enough of this," said Nina, rushing ahead. She grabbed Kaity by the shoulders and turned her around. "If you don't stop, I will never let you look at my body again! And if you kill her, I will kill you," she said, pulling the crazed assassin right up to her.

Kaity reluctantly lowered her claws as her eyes teared up.

"Thank you!" exclaimed Ada, leaping up and embracing her savior.

"Oh my, even your blood is beautiful," said Nina, looking at the red digits now splattered on her hands.

Kaity backed away from the murderer, all the while hissing.

"Our team's very first betrayal…we've really come a long way, haven't we?" asked Bob, getting all watery.

Karson walked up to Bob. "Thank you. Thank you for bringing me to the medical bay. After fighting that monster assassin boss, I didn't think I'd survive."

"What are comrades for?" asked Bob with a sweet smile.

"Good job saving Karson," said Exp 8.

"That isn't all he did. After you were defeated, Bob nearly led us to victory. He's been a great leader," said Karson.

"A great temporary leader. I did defeat Tempo. But alas, Kanasta was too powerful for me to overcome," said Bob, turning away as his pupil turned red.

"Don't worry. Kawai and I brought him down together. Thank you Bob, for taking over in my absence," said Exp 8.

"It was an honor to follow in your footsteps," said Bob with a bow.

Kaity whipped out a gun as Ada approached her.

"We have to stick together. Devlin is going to do his best to divide us! We have to be alert at all times," said Exp 8, standing in the gun's shooting path.

A large, bloody mass of tape, paperclips, glue, thumbtacks, and staples landed in the middle of the team with a plop.

"I'm alive," said the bloody mass once recognized as Atatasuki.

"Told ya so," said Destructus Supplious from above. He then jumped down, landing in the circle of Freedom Forcers.

"Who the hell are you people?" asked Exp 8.

"Are you Devlin's new recruit?" asked Kawai, poking the bloody mass.

"You don't recognize your own brother?" asked Atatasuki.

"I'm Destructus Supplious! Devlin sent me here to—"

Exp 8 fired an orb at Destructus Supplious.

D.S. whipped out an eraser and eliminated the orb with upward strokes.

"Give him back to us!" yelled Exp 8 as he rushed at the foreign Exp.

"Stop yelling all the time! I came to return him. Stupid adults," said D.S., holding up what remained of Atatasuki.

"So, we don't have to fight you?" asked Exp 8, scratching his head.

"We'll play later. You guys gotta fight my friends first. Okay, so if I give you this guy, I want something too. Give me the mostest important person on your team."

"You can't have Bob!" yelled Exp 8.

"Not Bob. I want…Ada!"

"What! She's the least—"

"The last person we would want to give up," said Bob, approaching D.S.

"Why don't we just attack you now?" asked Exp 8, revealing his turrets.

"That's no fair! I came here to trade. You're a big meanie," said D.S., crossing his arms.

Ada turned to her brash leader with a look of disapproval. "How could you even suggest that? I'll go with you," she said, struggling to stand up.

"Good riddance," said Kaity with a dark glare.

"Please, sensei, don't go!" exclaimed Nina, her arm stretching out to Ada.

"I'll be okay, you need Atatasuki," said Ada.

"We can use him as a heater in case it gets cold, but otherwise he's kind of useless," said Kawai with a shrug.

"Is it a deal?" asked D.S., handing them Atatasuki.

"One blood-drenched body in exchange for another…seems as fair as trading apples for tomatoes. I say go for it," said Bob.

"It's a deal!" said Ada, leaving the Freedom Forcers' side.

"Pinkie promise?" asked D.S.

"Sure," said Ada, shaking his pinkie.

D.S. lifted his mom onto his shoulders. "See ya later." He leaped through the ceiling.

"What the heck is he doing here?" asked Kawai.

"Alright, everyone, let's get the hell out of this place. The exit should be right around the corner," said Exp 8, rushing with his teammates down the hall.

"Shouldn't we get our comrade some medical attention?" asked Karson, carrying the injured Exp.

"The only doctor here is owned by Devlin. I can go looking for him if you want. Ada needs post-haste medical attention," said Nina, scratching her knuckles.

"And so does Atatasuki. Sis, you should go with them too. Bob and I will work on an escape plan. Kaity, you should stay with us and—"

"Why does she get to stay with you? It's not fair," said Kawai, puffing out her cheeks.

"They might need you to give them an energy boost. Don't worry. I can take care of myself. We'll meet up right where we busted in to fight the assassins. Everyone, stay safe. We are all going to make it out of this alive," said Exp 8 with a clenched fist.

The Freedom Forcers saluted and then split up.

Chapter 26: The Mission

Kawai's group rushed through the narrow metal hallways.

Nina stopped abruptly, bringing the team to a sudden halt.

"What's wrong?" asked Karson, quickly scoping the area.

"I am really hot," said Nina, gazing at the reflective metallic walls.

"And he's really dying," said Kawai, dragging the big-breasted bimbo with her tail.

"I didn't know you cared. Gaaagh! Thanks sis. Mmmrph!"

"Don't get any weird ideas. Brother trusted me with this mission. I'm not going to fail him."

"Look at that ass! Have you ever seen a more refined butt?" asked Nina with wide eyes.

"I'm not going to pull you anymore! Let's get going," said Kawai, tapping the narcissist with her tail.

Devlin descended down from a platform that came out from the ceiling. "Whoa, whoa, whoa. What's the big hurry?"

Nina leaped onto the circular platform and picked the enemy leader up by his throat. "Where is Ada? If she doesn't get help, she could die," she said, staring into his eyes.

Devlin grabbed onto his ex-girlfriend and fried her with his electric glove. Nina fell to the ground, landing on her feet at the last instant.

"Ada is a program. She can't bleed out. As long as her capsule remains intact, she will be fine. Though I can't say the same for Atatsuki. Why don't you hand him over?" asked Devlin with an outstretched hand.

"We would never abandon our comrade!" yelled Karson.

"I'm offering to give him medical attention. There's only one doctor here and he works for me. You guys really need to stop treating me like some villain." Devlin hopped off his platform and approached them. "I made you. Show me some respect."

"Well, with all due respect, we don't need your help. My brother entrusted me with the task of healing Atatsuki. We'll find the doctor on our own," said Kawai, floating right past him.

"He's down the hall to your right in the medical bay. I don't think Exps can die from blood loss. But if you don't want to find out, I suggest you hurry," said Devlin before hopping back on his platform.

"Even as an enemy, Commander Devlin behaves so maturely. He is a true gentleman," said Karson as the Freedom Forcers raced down the hallway.

The team turned right and Nina rushed into the clinic.

Shelves of medical books spanned all the way around the room. There was an entire row of hospital beds and various medical supplies on fold-out metal tables. The lights flickered, illuminating a figure behind a white curtain. He was sitting in a swivel chair by an empty hospital bed.

Nina walked up to the curtain. "We have someone who's injured. If you don't heal him, then we will have to force you. Do you understand?"

"I'm sorry, but…it's terminal. You have twelve days left," said the doctor, his voice cracking.

"Did you hear me?" asked Nina as the she beckoned the rest of her group to enter.

"I know I can't understand how you feel, but I offer you my deepest condolences. Please, tell your children I am deeply sorry for their loss," said the doctor, on the verge of tears.

"We have a dying patient here!" yelled Karson.

"I'm with a patient right now. There are chairs on your right. I will be with you shortly," said the doctor with a distinguished, yet childish voice.

"If I have to come in there, this will be very unpleasant," said Kawai, her tail on the curtain.

"Come on, you bloke, he's dying! Are you really just going to let a patient die because of your inactivity?" asked Karson.

"First come, first served. Who am I to say which patient should be given priority?" He turned back to the medical bed. "I'm sorry for the interruption. I hope you enjoy your final days. Damn it, did that sound candid? My bedside manners still need improvement. Go ahead, bring him in," said the doctor, fixing his collar through the curtain.

The Freedom Forcers went through the medical curtain. They looked at the medical bed, noticing that the patient they were waiting on was a bunny plushy with bandages on it.

"Why did you keep us waiting?" asked Kawai, her tail around his scrawny neck.

The doctor slipped out of her grip. "I was practicing my discourse." His eyes met the patient's ravaged body. "Oh my Asclepius, is he dead?" asked the doctor in horror.

The doctor stood three feet eight inches and was presumably eleven years old. He had untidy white hair, some strands drooping past his shoulders. A light green mask protected his mouth from the harmful bacteria floating in the air.

The boy was in a white lab coat that was five sizes too big. His arms were buried beneath his bulky sleeves. On the front pocket of the coat was a red plus sign with two albino snakes entwined around it. A white-and-red medical bag was situated below the right arm held up by an elastic shoulder strap. He stood upright with his head up high. His white eyes were shining with a sense of endearment.

Karson knocked the plushy off the bed. "Are you deaf or just a bloody idiot?"

"I must have been in character. I apologize. When I get started, it's hard for me to stop. I'm not schizophrenic; I'm just a great actor," said the doctor, as Karson set the patient on the medical bed.

"I just hope your medical skills are as good as your characterization. Heheh-kough-argh," said Atatasuki, blood spurting from his mouth.

"You see all the books around here? I have access to all their information. But I don't trouble my patients with medical jargon. What seems to be the problem?" asked Anthrax with firm dignity and an air of kindness.

"He's dying, you nitwit!" yelled Karson.

"Hmm…severe lacerations from a serrated object, massive blood loss, staples impaled through the flesh—this looks pretty serious. How do you feel?" asked the doctor, slowly moving the patient's head left to right.

"Hmm, pretty good actually. My sister seemed to really care that I was dying. I'm in the hands of someone who hopefully knows what he's doing. Oh and all of my friends are alive and well," said Atatasuki with a blood-drenched grin.

"I'm a doctor, not your therapist. Do you have any headaches, loss of hearing, fever…anything bothering you?" asked Anthrax, connecting an IV bag of blood to the patient's arm. He slipped his left arm out from the long sleeve. It was covered by four layers of disposable gloves. He pulled off the tape, picked out the thumbtacks, removed the paper clips, dislodged the staples, burned away the glue, and then padded the bleeding areas.

"Incredible pain…and I'm a bit woozy, but other than that I feel as healthy as a sunflower," said Atatasuki as the doctor started cauterizing his wounds.

"Once your wounds are cauterized, I just need to bandage you up. Just rest for about an hour and you should be fully healed." He patted his patient on the head. "Here's your lollipop," said the doctor, pulling it out of his vest.

"This is incredible. How much do I owe you? My armor is made of bronze so I should be able to pay you," said Atatasuki as the doctor started to wrap his wounds.

"I don't charge my patients. Devlin takes care of all my living expenses, so I have no need for money. Besides, I became a doctor so I could help others. I will not benefit from their misfortune. Do be more careful around sharp objects in the future."

"I will. Thank you so much." Atatasuki stood up and stretched his arms out.

"Alright, you're dismissed." The doctor picked up the plush bunny and put it back on the bed. "What seems to be the problem?"

"The doc is a total loon. Are we done here?" asked Karson.

"Yep! Mission accomplished!" Kawai snatched the lollipop with her tail before popping it in her mouth.

"Alright, now let's meet up with the others and go save Ada," said Nina.

Previously: Exp 8's group decided to work on their escape plan.

"There's no way Devlin is going to just let us bust out like last time," said Exp 8.

"Are you sure? It didn't seem like his force field could stop anyone of us," said Bob.

"I don't know how long I've been out, but there's no reason to think Devlin didn't make any enhancements to it. What do you think, Kaity? You've been around Devlin, do you know anything?" asked Exp 8, turning to her.

"We've talked a little, but he never said anything about special exits. Either way, we're in the underground portion of his lab. We need to go up," said Kaity, her eyes sore from tears.

"I could easily get out of here, but I can't say the same for the rest. Come to think of it, Devlin's force fields rise out from the ground. It's safe to assume that the highest point of the lab would have the weakest defenses. But no doubt he has his strongest Exp waiting there for us," said Bob with a ponderous look.

"Don't worry. I can take whatever Devlin dishes out. Kaity, do you know where the staircase is?" asked Exp 8.

"There are only elevators as far as I know. Devlin's a total control freak, hee-hee," said Kaity, her voice cracking.

"She's right. There should be an elevator right down this corridor," said Bob, leading the way.

The Freedom Forcers rushed down the hallway.

Bob pressed the button for the elevator and waited patiently. "It was a good idea to bring Kaity along. You never know when a hostage will come in handy," he said, picking her up with spectral tentacles.

"That's not what she's here for. Set her down!" yelled Exp 8.

"For all we know, a powerful Exp could come ambush us as soon as these doors open. It's always good to plan ahead," said Bob, summoning the Atma Blade.

"It's fine. Good thinking, Bob," said Kaity, giving him a half-hearted smile.

The elevator doors opened, revealing three people in full-body black spandex. There was a large man, a small boy, and a young woman.

"I don't know who you are, but I've got a hostage. You wouldn't want to upset Master Devlin, would you?" asked Bob, his pupil glowing red and aiming at Kaity.

"Devlin, why does that sound familiar?" asked the young woman.

"Didn't you read the mission briefing? You see that guy there. We need to catch him, understood?" asked the young boy, pointing to the platinum-armored Exp.

"I know these guys. They work for Senator John. Don't worry, they're just a bunch of cowards," said Exp 8, powering up an energy orb.

"We are servants of the Lord. You cannot stop us, demon!" yelled the large man, hoisting up a rocket-launcher.

"Bob, let go of me. Holding me as a hostage won't help at all," said Kaity, gripping her sidearm.

"I understand," said Bob, quickly turning to the enemy and firing a laser beam.

The large man fired a rocket in the same instant.

The laser shot straight through the rocket before demolishing the man's gun.

"I'm scared, Gamma," screamed the young woman, hiding behind the boy.

"So am I, but we can do this," said Gamma, throwing a smoke bomb to the ground.

Kaity quickly leaped out of the way as rockets and machine gun fire came zooming out of the smoke cloud.

Exp 8 shot his orb into the smoke before being blasted by a missile.

Bob alternated between phasing through rockets and firing lasers.

The young woman rushed out of the smoke cloud. She ducked under the lasers and zoomed up to their assigned target. She dodged his midair punch and then slammed her palms into him before he could retaliate. The nimble woman then leaped up, grabbed onto his shoulders, and jettisoned herself behind him.

Kaity rushed into the smoke cloud.

The sound of a man screaming in agony soon followed.

Exp 8 slammed his head backwards into the young woman. When they hit the ground, he quickly rolled on top of her.

"Are you going to kill me?" she asked with glistening eyes.

"Ummm…do you want me to?" he asked with a scrunched forehead.

She slid out of his grip and then shot him with a revolver.

Exp 8 knocked the gun aside and grabbed her arm.

"You're so strong," she said, trying to break out of his grip.

"Please don't kill me!" yelled Gamma from within the smoke.

Kaity emerged from the cloud, keeping a steady aim on the boy.

Bob pulled out the blood-drenched men with ten spectral hands. "So, how should we kill them?"

"We aren't killing anyone. Tell your boss that I am not his property. I am an individual, not a tool," said Exp 8, looking into the young woman's eyes.

"We'll tell him whatever you want. Please don't kill us," said Gamma, hiding under his hands.

"If you value your soul, don't get in our way again," said Bob, holding the Atma Blade up to the man.

"We came unprepared. The demons are far stronger than we predicted. We must leave promptly." The large man walked up to Gamma and the young woman before picking them up.

"Wait, how did you guys get in here?" asked Exp 8.

"We dropped in from the roof," said Gamma, his face covered in sweat.

"Oh, Kaity, Koshi says hi by the way," said the young woman before the large man ran off with them.

"Do you know her?" asked Bob.

"She sure seems to know me," said Kaity, putting away her pistols.

"That's not much of an answer," said Bob.

"Lay off her a bit. It's likely that being an assassin makes her a target for government special agents," said Exp 8.

"Yeah, let's just leave it at that," said Kaity with a nervous smile.

The rest of the Freedom Forcers came rushing down the hallway.

"Brother! We did it! He's completely cured!" exclaimed Kawai, stretching out her arms.

"I knew you guys could do it," said Exp 8, walking toward the group before toppling over.

Kawai caught him with her tail just before he hit the ground. "What happened? Are you okay?" she asked, helping him back to his feet.

"When that girl hit me, I think she did something. I feel so tired," said Exp 8, wobbling in place.

"Don't worry, I'll make you feel better. *Energy Needle*"

Energy burst out from the tip of her tail into him, giving him a dramatic boost of energy.

Exp 8's eyes shot open and energy started gushing from his hands.

"Sorry, was that too much? I can take some back," said Kawai.

"No no, it's fine. I'll just use it up on our next opponent. Phew," said Exp 8, overly energized.

"Let's all get in the elevator. We've figured out that the only way out of this lab is through the roof. Be prepared; this route leaves us open to an ambush," said Bob, holding the elevator for his allies.

"Let's all get the hell out of here!" exclaimed Exp 8, rushing into the elevator.

The Freedom Forcers followed him into the elevator.

"Wait, there's something we have to do first." Exp 8 opened his arms out and turned to his the reliable assassin.

"I don't want a hug," said Kaity, turning away.

Nina put her arm around the cat-girl's shoulder. "Sorry, but you don't have a choice. This is how Freedom Forcers welcome you to the team. It's not official until we've hugged. I bet you've been dying to embrace me," she said, turning to their leader with a smile.

"Is Kaity really going to be a permanent member?" asked Kawai, rolling her eyes.

"Kaity fought alongside us valiantly when we were ambushed. She has shown that, even in hard times, she can keep a clear head. It will be our honor to have her on our team," said Exp 8, putting his arm around his sister.

"But she's a human. They always have some sort of ulterior motive. And are you just going to ignore that she almost killed Ada. That kitten's gotta find another home," said Kawai, crossing her arms.

Exp 8 pulled his sister in. "She lost someone very dear to her. She wasn't thinking straight. She's okay now; you can trust me."

"Oh, I always trust you. But can we honestly trust her?" asked Kawai, raising her voice.

"That is a very good question," said Bob, staring into assassin's cat-like eyes.

"You don't have to be an Exp to be a Freedom Forcer. We are all united by our ideals. If she fights for the freedom of our people, then she is one of us. Now, let's make it official," said Exp 8.

Kawai turned to the new girl with a smile. "If I catch you flirting with him, I'll tear out your tail," she whispered, before wrapping her tail around the girl's slender waist.

"It's time to officially welcome Bob, Nina, Kaity and Karson to the team! Group hug!" cheered Atatasuki, pulling in the gunman.

"Nothing like camaraderie among soldiers!" cheered Karson.

"I don't really see the point of all this, but I won't disrupt our team's unity," said Bob before joining in.

Exp 8 put his arm around Kaity and Kawai. "You're one of us now."

"Thanks for welcoming me," said Kaity with flustered cheeks.

The Freedom Forcers embraced.

Exp 8's excess energy flowed out to the entire group.

"Freedom Forcers, let's go find Ada and beat down any obstacle in our path!"

Exp 8 thrust his arm up in the air, followed by a cheer from his group. "I'm ready for anything!" He was jumping up and down, pumped up for battle.

"Alright we only need to go up ten floors and then we're out," said Bob, pressing the elevator button.

"I won't leave Ada behind," said Nina.

"We can come back for her later," said Bob with a dismissive wave of the hand.

"Nina's right, we are all leaving here together. But for all we know, Devlin is waiting with Ada on the top floor. If she isn't there, then we'll keep looking till we find her," said Exp 8.

The elevator suddenly stopped.

"We're only on floor five. Why did it stop?" asked Kaity, whipping out her guns.

"Devlin's probably got something else planned for us. I really hope it's not D.S.," said Atatasuki, hiding behind Karson.

The doors opened, revealing three hallways. The walls lit up with arrows pointing the way.

"You don't scare us, Devlin! Come on, everyone, let's go!" cheered Exp 8.

Following his lead, the Freedom Forcers rushed down the hallway. They arrived in front of a large door with "Here" painted on it with neon green paint.

"Don't you guys care that you're doing exactly what Devlin wants?" asked Kaity.

"We can only lose to him if we show fear! Let's charge in!" Exp 8 smashed an orb into the door.

The door broke off its hinges and shot forth.

"Does he know what subtlety is?" asked Kaity, readying her pistol.

"Charge!"

"I guess not, ugh," said Kaity.

Chapter 27: Matteria's Trap

The Freedom Forcers charged into the next room. It was a wide, nearly empty, cube with steel-plated walls and a low, pointed ceiling. In the center was Matteria, sitting on a sky-blue sphere while applying makeup.

"Hello, I'm Matteria. You probably recognize me. I'm on the front cover of *Fashionista*'s latest issue. I'm also a well-known pop-star, prominent actor, porn star, and legendary model. Not to mention, I am the most beautiful Exp." The jack of all trades stood up and approached the rebel's leader. "Now, if you all go back into the prison chamber, then I won't have to kill anyone. Sound good?"

Nina strutted in front of Exp 8. "I'm the sexiest Exp and you're just a poser," she said, running her fingers up her legs all the way to her lips.

"I don't recall seeing you as a nominee for the top ten sexi—"

"I don't need to enter some contest. My sexiness speaks for itself," said Nina, pushing up her breasts.

"Why do you pose to get attention? Isn't that a sign of insecurity?" asked Matteria with a slight grin.

"I'll rip you to shreds," said Nina, lunging at the powdered princess.

The cyborg brothers grabbed Nina's arms, holding her back from eviscerating the potential enemy.

"Beauty is in the eye of the beholder. I have proven my extravagance to millions of people. You're just a self-proclaimed goddess. You need to earn your beauty," said Matteria, while applying glossy lipstick.

"If we admit you're a beautiful girl, then will you let us pass?" asked Atatasuki.

"I don't really see what's stopping us from just going for the door," said Karson, standing by the exit.

"Beautiful girl, handsome man, feminine wiles, masculine strength, manpower, women's intuition…all these phrases impose discriminatory standards based on one's biological sex. Why must beauty only be socially acceptable for females? Why must we be fated to walk a path based on our biology? I have shown this world that boys can be just as beautiful as girls. I will destroy any gender boundary in my path!" exclaimed Matteria, combing his long pink hair.

"That's a man?" yelled Karson.

"If we admit you're beautiful for a guy, then can we leave?" asked Atatasuki.

"I had no idea boys could be so cute," said Kaity with wide eyes.

Nina slipped out of her allies' grip. "If boys are so beautiful, then why do you go to such lengths to look like a powdered girl?"

"Nina, you may be a knockout on the outside, but you have no inner beauty. You have no love to share with this world," said Matteria, throwing out his arms.

"So then you do agree that I have an incredibly sexy, scrumptious, and tantalizing body, right?" asked Nina, flicking her nipple through her shirt.

Matteria took a step forward. "Absolutely! Don't you think I'm pretty? Hee-hee-hoo-hoo."

"No…I don't. You try to conceal your face with makeup. You're poisoning your skin. You need to stop trying to look like a girl and just be natural," said Nina with a smile.

"By embellishing myself with makeup, I am transforming my face and body into a magnificent work of art," said Matteria, putting on an extra layer of blue lipstick.

"True art comes from nature. Mountains, hills, and breasts are all protrusions of beauty! You weren't endowed with a feminine body. You may have a slender figure for a man, but you're still as flat as a board," said Nina, patting his chest.

"I am as flat as a canvas and proud of it. The whole body is a canvas to draw on. You could never understand creativity because you have none," said Matteria, his eyes starting to water.

"Are you trying to get boys to fall in love with you because you could never have self-confidence with your unattractive male body?" asked Nina, sizing him up.

"You will never understand how beautiful boys can be."

"That's because they aren't beautiful! I, on the other hand…mmm…just look at me!"

Kawai grabbed onto Exp 8's arm. "That's not true at all! Brother is the most beautiful thing in existence!"

"Thanks, sis. Alright, everyone, let's keep moving," said Exp 8, beckoning his teammates.

"Master Devlin's will is my mission. None of you will escape this place," said Matteria, putting away his comb.

"And how are you going to stop us?" asked Karson.

"With the Matter Change artifact Master Devlin gave me upon creation. Matter cannot be created or destroyed, but it does undergo changes. With the white moonstone in my possession, I can bring about a state of condensation, vaporization, liquefaction and sublimation of any substance. Watch as the hideous ground beneath you dissipates. PHYSICAL CHANGE, LIQUEFACTION," said Matteria majestically.

The ground liquefied, instantly falling down and revealing a nearly bottomless pit beneath it.

Kawai grabbed onto Exp 8 while floating above the pit.

Kaity grabbed Nina, leaped off the watery floor, and stabbed her claws into the wall.

Bob's wings spread open as he swooped down, rescuing Karson from falling.

Atatasuki dragged his arm against the wall, screaming as he descended toward uncertain doom. His fingers quickly melted into the wall, creating a dip for him to grip onto.

Matteria was standing on a levitating, clear, bowling ball-sized sphere of ice. The sphere was halfway filled with water.

"You all managed to survive, color me very impressed," said Matteria, waving his long iridescent hair around.

"Why don't you come down here and fight me?" asked Nina, grabbing onto the wall with her fingertips.

"I'm fine right here," said Matteria, licking the frosting off a rainbow-sprinkled cupcake.

"How can you eat such a vile thing?" asked Atatasuki in disgust.

"Cupcakes are muffins that have been embellished to perfection. There is nothing vile about them," said Matteria before biting into the pastry.

"Cupcakes are posers!" yelled Atatasuki, slipping a bit.

"Why is everyone arguing?" asked Exp 8, powering up an orb.

Matteria floated down to the muffin lover as he licked the frosting off the tips of his fingers. "Cupcakes are muffins with added flair! They are muffins with an edge, with color and flavor. Cupcakes are a work of art, while muffins are just a blank canvas. Look at their beauty, Atatasuki. Look at how the frosting coats their mundane tops. Look at the rainbow sprinkles!"

"They're muffins that can't be content with their own existence. Their self-love comes only from embellishment. Nina is right…this time. You must learn to love who you are. Your beloved dessert is just a fallen muffin that has been sprinkled with vanity and iced with layer upon layer of denial. I will melt that fallen angel from your colored fingertips and release its soul from its wretched existence. *SUPER MICROWAVE, BODY!*"

Atatasuki's body became super heated, melting away his grip on the wall. With nothing to hold him up, the steaming prototype plummeted down into the somewhat bottomless pit.

"I can't believe that actually worked. Devlin was right, this is fun," said Matteria, tossing the cupcake aside.

"Kawai! You have to save him!" yelled Exp 8, shaking her.

"First of all, I don't really care if he dies, and secondly, I'm having enough trouble carrying you," said Kawai with a strained smile.

"I won't watch as he plummets to his doom," said Exp 8, struggling in her grip.

"Well then, close your eyes and kiss me," said Kawai, leaning forward.

Matteria waved his hair in a slow and majestic way. "That's one down. By the way, the prison offer still stands," he said, spinning on the floating orb with his tip toes.

"I will kill you before he goes *splat*." Bob's pupil glowed red as a laser shot forth. The laser became coated in a thin layer of ice as it zoomed forth.

"PHYSICAL CHANGE, SUBLIMATION."

The ice-coated laser beam transformed into a gaseous state. The newly formed wind flowed through Matteria's hair as he combed it gently with his hand.

By solidifying the water molecules in the air, the pop sensation formed a bridge of ice beneath him. He hopped off the ball and onto the bridge. The beautiful boy then picked up the icy orb. "PHYSICAL CHANGE, SOLIDIFICATION."

His blue lips softly kissed the dense ball, creating tiny ice blades inside it. After spinning in place, he tossed the ice bomb.

Kawai's tail slammed into the ball.

Tiny ice blades burst out like shrapnel, slicing her all over.

Exp 8's head slipped through Kawai's arms as she pulled back in pain. He fell into the seemingly bottomless pit, disappearing from sight.

"PHYSICAL STATE, PLASMA." Matteria snuggled the globe against his chest, culturing plasma inside it. He pulled his arm back before heaving the plasma ball.

The sphere passed through Bob and ricocheted off the wall behind him. It bounced at a forty-five degree angle and zoomed into Kawai's jets, setting them aflame.

"Sorry about that. Guess I shouldn't have gone into my Phase Form!" hollered Bob.

Kawai skyrocketed downwards into the almost bottomless pit, vanishing from sight.

Bob flew underneath Matteria as Karson launched his head forth.

"PHYSICAL CHANGE, LIQUEFACTION."

The missile exploded just before making contact.

The explosion liquefied, wetting the idol's glittery hair.

Matteria zoomed toward Karson on his newly created condensed ice ball. "Cast away your mechanized body and become one with the beauty of nature. 𝓟𝓗𝓨𝓢𝓘𝓒𝓐𝓛 𝓦𝓐𝓝𝓘𝓝𝓖, 𝓜𝓞𝓤𝓢𝓔𝓡𝓐𝓣𝓘𝓞𝓝!" he exclaimed, placing his hand on the gunman's chest.

"Farewell," said Karson, shooting off his shotgun at point-blank range.

The bullets became water as they touched the enemy's body.

Karson became liquid and dripped off of Bob to the near endless pit.

"All that's left is you two beautiful ladies and the pretty eyeball," said Matteria.

"Call me pretty again and you will be very sorry," said Bob, circling around the colorful nuisance.

"I meant that as a compliment. You have magnificent wings and a captivating pupil. Don't you see, we are all beautiful in our own ways," said Matteria with a sweet smile.

"You think I'm ladylike?" asked Kaity, her tail bobbing back and forth.

"What he meant to say is one mildly attractive flat-chested girl and one drop-dead gorgeous woman," said Nina, struggling to pose without releasing her grip.

"I like being flat. It makes me so much more aerodynamic. So, Matteria, if you think I'm beautiful, does that mean you'll join us?" asked Kaity.

"I am deeply devoted to Master Devlin. But don't worry, he wants you alive anyway."

"𝕰𝖞𝖊𝖇𝖆𝖑𝖑 𝕷𝖆𝖘𝖊𝖗," said Bob, seizing the moment to strike.

A laser shot out like a bullet, tearing straight through the deadly diva.

Devlin watched the scene from a monitor in the surveillance room while getting a massage. "Her breasts aren't flat, they're petite…soft and petite. They're wonderful! They're splendid!"

"I will…absolutely. I'm spending time with Devlin at the moment. I can't….Yesterday? Don't pull that on me….I was on a pilgrimage."

"Who are you talking to this time?" asked Devlin.

"Dionysus. He's getting jealous of the time I'm spending with you."

"Are you paying any attention to what's going on?" asked Devlin, snapping his fingers.

"Yes, and with great devotion. I was wondering…what happened to the Exps that fell? Did they die? Should I prepare a ceremony for them? Do I contact Hades or Set, perhaps Satan? No, maybe the Great Spirit would be best. What do you think?" asked Violet, rubbing her hands together.

"It doesn't matter. Matteria won't beat all of them." Devlin stood up from his chair. "Go to the eighth floor and eliminate them."

"I will. Please, pray to God for their safe passage into the next world," said Violet.

"Hmph, what God?"

"All of them, from every pantheon!"

"I'll pray to God that you shut up," said Devlin folding his hands to pray.

"You're off to a wonderful start." Violet kissed him on the cheek and then ran off.

Meanwhile: in the room with matte bender, only three Freedom Forcers remained.

Matteria held his side in pain. "Ahee-hee-hoo-hoo! You got me good. It's too bad you can't hurt me," he said, solidifying the blood and thus healing.

Nina leaped off the wall, kicking the ice ball out from under the powdered boy's feet. She grabbed onto Bob and propelled herself to the wall behind him.

Matteria frantically solidified the water molecules around him, but he was falling too fast to grab onto the ice platforms he created. "PHYSICAL CHANGE, CONDENSATION!"

The air going down the close-to-bottomless pit became water, stopping his descent toward death.

Nina and Kaity hopped down to the downed opponent.

"My makeup! No! It's running!" yelled Matteria as his blush, eye shadow and lipstick smeared all over his face.

Kaity put her hand on the bloodthirsty eyeball. "Don't kill him. We can make him an ally."

"Do what you want," said Bob, turning away.

Kaity leaped down and pulled Matteria out of the water and onto a nearby ice platform.

"Don't look at me. I'm naked," said Matteria, hiding his face under his hands.

Exp 8 surfaced, holding Atatasuki in his arms.

Kawai floated out from the water, offering her big brother a lift.

Exp 8 grabbed on while keeping a firm grip on his brother.

Kawai dropped them off on an ice platform and then nestled against her beloved brother.

"Where's Karson?" asked Atatasuki, looking at everyone.

"Pull it together, Matteria. You just need to wash up," said Kaity, cleaning up his face.

"So, I look okay?" asked Matteria, turning away.

"You look fine. We need you to bring back Karson. You can change him back, can't you?" asked Kaity, trying to look him in the eyes.

"Yeah, but I can't betray Devlin," said Matteria with watery eyes.

"Didn't Devlin abandon you for me? Don't you care that he's using you?" asked Nina.

"None of that matters! I love him. I don't want to lose him," said Matteria, wiping away his tears.

"We aren't going to kill Devlin. We're just going to break out of here, that's all. We could really use your help," said Exp 8, helping the potential ally to his feet.

"And if you'd rather die, we'd be more than happy to oblige you," said Bob, bringing out the Atma Blade.

"𝕻𝖍𝖞𝖘𝖎𝖈𝖆𝖑 𝕮𝖍𝖆𝖓𝖌𝖊, 𝕾𝖔𝖑𝖎𝖉𝖎𝖋𝖎𝖈𝖆𝖙𝖎𝖔𝖓!" exclaimed Matteria, pointing at a murky gray area below.

The water solidified into Karson.

The gunman quickly swam to the ice platform. "I never want to feel like that again. I was conscious, but unable to move. Is that how water feels?" he asked, draining the water out of his body.

"So, Matteria, will you help us escape?" asked Exp 8.

"I'll keep it simple. Either aid us, or you'll become the first model with a shattered spine," said Bob with a grin.

"Alright! I'll help you guys escape." Matteria created a staircase of ice all the way to the exit door. "Let's get moving," he said with a nervous smile.

The Freedom Forcers ran up the staircase, through the door, down the hallway, and into the next elevator.

"Be prepared, Violet Gold is probably going to be your next opponent," said Matteria, looking down.

"Does she have any weakness we should know about?" asked Exp 8.

"She is extremely religious. Her ability to change the beliefs of others is unnatural. The best way to beat her is to make her think you share the same views. We should join her in prayer and then strike swiftly."

"So you're really a guy? How do we know you aren't lying?" asked Karson, staring at the trickster suspiciously.

"Does it really matter?" asked Exp 8.

"Do you want me to strip and prove it?" asked Matteria, pulling down his skirt.

The elevator stopped on the eighth floor.

"Stay focused everyone! For all we know Violet could be waiting right outside this elevator," said Bob.

"If she's lying about his gender, then how can we trust anything he says?" Karson pressed his pistol to the girl's head in the midst of the young diva stripping.

"Gender is socially formed. I'm a boy in both gender and sex," said Matteria, slipping out of his panties.

"Devlin sure makes some strange creations," said Karson as the girly boy redressed himself.

The elevator doors opened, revealing another long hallway.

"Ugh. Why is this place so huge?" asked Exp 8.

"I think I found the room," said Atatasuki, pointing to an iron clad-door with "surrender" written with blood-red paint.

"You don't scare us, Devlin! Alright everyone, let's go with Matteria's plan. Be careful and we'll all make it out alive!" exclaimed Exp 8, slowly opening the door.

Chapter 28: Violet Gold's Mission

All the Freedom Forcers walked into the next room.

It looked nearly identical to the room where they had faced Matteria, but the ceiling was flat rather than pointed.

The Freedom Forcers sat lotus-style in a circle. They all folded their hands and prayed silently.

Violet Gold dropped down from a hole in the ceiling. "𝘽𝙀𝙇𝙄𝙀𝙁 𝘾𝙃𝘼𝙉𝙂𝙀𝙍, 𝙎𝙐𝙄𝘾𝙄...are you praying?" She took a deep breath and then sat down with the others, joining the circle of gratitude.

"Oh Lord, please save us from this religious zealot, amen," said Atatasuki as his blood pooled beneath the devotee.

"𝘾𝘼𝙏𝙎𝙄𝘾𝘼𝙇 𝘾𝘼𝙍𝘿𝙄𝘼𝘾 𝙎𝙊𝙇𝙄𝘿𝙄𝙁𝙄𝘾𝘼𝙏𝙄𝙊𝙉," said Matteria, stiffening the blood, thus anchoring her to the floor.

Violet continued to pray.

All the Freedom Forcers attacked her at once: Bob shot a laser; Karson fired off his head; Kaity shot her chest with a sniper rifle; Nina tossed her shirt and exploded it; and Exp 8 fired a souped-up orb. All the attacks hit her simultaneously, killing her in an instant. Kawai then rushed in and smacked the bloody remains with her tail.

"Guys. We went way too far," said Exp 8 with wide eyes.

"Wait, where's her artifact? It's supposed to be a lazurite stone. Maybe we didn't kill her after all," said Ada as she shook Violet's capsule.

D.S. dropped down from the ceiling and swiftly recovered her corpse. "Murderers! She was my friend!" he yelled in miserable rage. He then jumped back up into the hole in the ceiling.

"You cannot trust them. They only prayed so they catch you off guard and murder you," said Devlin from a speaker in the room.

"At least they prayed," whimpered Violet.

"Fine! We'll all rehearse 'Jesus Loves the Little Children' with you later," said Devlin, regretting every word.

"I'll stay aware and engaged."

"Soon the only real god will be me!" yelled Devlin.

"There are just so many gods," said Violet from above.

"We will all die if I don't get Exp 8. I can only save everyone when he is at maximum power. Now go back in there and kill them all!" exclaimed Devlin.

Violet jumped down through the hole into the room.

"How did she come back from the dead?" asked Karson.

"I don't know. Everyone keep your distance. But if she makes a move, go for a counter-attack," said Exp 8, dispersing the Freedom Forcers.

"That Violet you slaughtered was an illusion from an artifact. God, please grant me the power to eliminate these heretics," she said, pulling out a golden cross the size of a steering wheel.

The four sides of the cross fell off, revealing knives.

Violet took out a bottle of holy water and devotedly dripped the blessed water on the knives.

The knives all pointed to the Atatasuki as if by instinct.

Kawai floated in front of her prototype. "Don't worry, little brother. I won't let him die," she said, her tail poised.

Violet ducked under the tail and knocked the girl aside with an elbow jab. She then launched herself at Atatasuki and stabbed all the knives into him simultaneously.

The knives dispersed on the prototype's body, cutting trails into his flesh. They then drilled inside his palms and feet.

Atatasuki screamed out in agony as the blades bore deeper. He fell to the floor while the blades cut him open from within.

"We are not going to die here!" yelled Karson, revving up his Gatling gun arms.

Kawai rushed at the enemy, furiously attacking with her tail.

Violet grabbed her tail and pulled her in. She took the Sound Artifact out from her heart chakra and pressed it into the girl's chest. "Give in to the bliss of spirituality!" She gripped the child's head as energy seeped out from her fingertips. "*BELIEF CHANGER, DEVOTEE.*"

"Let her go!" yelled Exp 8, slamming an orb into the opponent.

Violet was sent flying backwards as the orb raged forth.

Bob fired a laser into the orb, exploding it and tearing through the zealot. Karson mowed her down with his Gatling gun.

Kawai floated into the bullet path, getting shot up in Violet's place.

"Move aside, you bloody idiot!" yelled Karson, redirecting his fire.

"This rebelllon is pointless. Devlin is our father. We must honor his wishes. *Sound Shot Snake,*" said Kawai with hollow eyes and empty words.

A condensed sound wave came out from her mouth and maneuvered through the Freedom Forcers like a phantom. It then went back, giving the Exps a second helping of sound-induced agony.

Violet stood up, draped head to toe in wounds. She closed her eyes and threw out her arms. Her body healed almost instantly as the Freedom Forcers screamed out in pain.

Kaity whipped out her pistol and aimed at Kawai, but it liquefied it before she could shoot.

"She's our teammate. Don't kill her!" yelled Matteria.

"Snap out of it, Sis, we're going to break free!" yelled Exp 8, walking toward her as he was tormented by the sound wave.

"You snap out of it! There's no reason we can't just live with Devlin! You're a rebel without a cause. Your insubordination is going to get us all killed!" yelled Kawai, enhancing the power of the sound wave.

"It is times like these I'm quite happy I have no ears," said Bob, knocking Kawai aside with a spectral tentacle to the face. He then zoomed up to Violet as he summoned up the Atma Blade.

"My erotic ears are bleeding!" screamed Nina.

"I'll provide supporting fire!" yelled Karson, forming his arms into a bazooka.

Bob thrust his blade into Violet and then entered his Phase Form as a rocket approached from behind.

The missile exploded on contact, knocking Violet off her feet and cutting into her with shards of shrapnel.

"Did you like the extra bang I put into that missile?" asked Karson.

Exp 8's jets activated, sending him flying into the opponent. He grabbed onto her and slammed her into the wall while remaining airborne. "Turn her back to normal!"

"The fate of the world is on my shoulders now. You must submit!" exclaimed Violet, putting out both her palms to subliminally fill his mind with restraint.

Nina ran up the wall and stabbed the battle nun's thigh with a concealed dagger.

"I am deeply sorry. Your death is for the greater good," said Violet in tears.

The knives inside Atatasuki burst out from his body. They then stabbed into Bob, Nina, and Exp 8.

"*ECSTASY!*" exclaimed Violet.

Religious spiritual power flowed from the tips of the blades, filling her enemies with spiritual bliss.

Exp 8 dropped Violet. Nina let go of the dagger and fell down.

Violet tore the dagger out from her thigh and fell to her knees.

Nina flailed about, gripping her temples. "What is this voice inside me?! Make it stop! The ego is the self! This is just another illusion!"

Bob looked up in an introspective state of mind.

Matteria started dancing as he was overcome with the incredible presence within.

Exp 8 pulled the blade out from his back and struggled to stand up.

Violet closed her eyes and began rapidly healing once more.

Exp 8 looked at his allies and realized the bleakness of the situation. "*DIVINE REVELATION!*"

All the bliss-filled Exps now turned to Exp 8, except for Matteria who continued to dance dramatically.

"Devlin is our only salvation," said the entranced Exps.

"I can't let Devlin win! Karson, shoot me!" yelled Exp 8, his talons boring into the ground.

"One rocket to jog your noggin coming right up!" yelled Karson, shooting a missile at his brave commander.

The rocket hit the back of his head and exploded violently.

Violet ran up to the military man as he loaded up another rocket.

"Your fancy persuasive techniques won't work on me! I'm made of metal!" said Karson before firing a missile at her.

Violet redirected the rocket away from her with a gentle push.

"Everything has a soul," she said, placing her finger on the living weapon's third eye.

Karson's eyes shot open with forced revelation. "I am a tool of God!" he exclaimed, quickly changing targets.

"I won't let you turn them against me! I've fought for these allies!" yelled Exp 8, rushing toward her.

"And soon you will all be united by the spirit within!"

"Kawai gave me a little gift before I came here!" yelled Exp 8.

A constant stream of energy erupted from his hand.

Violet was slammed against the wall as the energy sliced her skin like microscopic blades.

"I won't let you kill her!" yelled D.S. from above. He dropped down from the ceiling and closed his massive scissors down on the terrorist leader's arm.

The scissors tore through both the metal and flesh, severing his arm completely off.

Energy continued to shoot out from the bleeding stub. It sliced through D.S.'s flesh, soon reaching to the bones of his arm.

Destructus Supplious kicked Exp 8, escaping the continuous energy stream.

Bob repeatedly stabbed Exp 8 as Nina stripped and tossed her clothes on him.

Violet closed her eyes to heal before plasma claws shot out from her chest.

"Where were you?" asked Violet, turning to the young girl.

"Let her go!" yelled D.S., thrusting his scissors at the kitty-girl.

Devlin appeared in his path and grabbed the scissors with a gloved hand. "Do not hurt Kaity!"

Electricity flowed out from the glove and into the scissors before bursting into Destructus Supplious.

D.S. flailed about before finally releasing his weapon.

Devlin tickled Kaity, pulled Violet away, and then vanished from sight.

After getting back to his feet, D.S. leaped through a hole in the ceiling. "I thought you said if Exp 8 dies we lose the game," he said from above.

"If Kaity dies, I'll murder Ada right in front of you," said Devlin, his words muffled by D.S.'s screaming.

"Kaity, you stopped her. You saved us," said Exp 8, kicking Nina before she could blow up her clothes.

"I also got this," said Kaity, tossing Violet's artifact up with her foot. She caught the violet-blue lazurite in her hand and smiled. "*BELIEF CHANGER, RELIGIOUS DISILLUSIONMENT!*"

The Freedom Forcers slowly transitioned out of their spiritual trance.

"Did you piss me off or something?" asked Bob as he un-summoned his beloved Atma Blade.

"Why is my underwear on your arm?!" yelled Nina, yanking her bra off Exp 8.

"What happened to you?" asked Kawai as she rushed to her dear brother's side.

"I lost an arm, but we won. I've been through worse. Let's all keep going," said Exp 8, slipping on a puddle of blood and falling down.

"Do you want some more energy?" asked Kawai, touching his face affectionately.

"I'll manage," said Exp 8 with a smile.

"Um, guys…I don't know how to…well, you see, he's…he's dead," said Karson, his hand on Atatasuki's chest.

"Calm down Karson. I'm sure it's just a little hard for you to check his pulse. Come on, Bro, get up," said Exp 8, slowly rising to his feet.

"Yeah, he's a tough one. You can't get rid of him that easily, teehee." Kawai poked her annoying brother with her tail.

"Come on Bro, say something. We're so close to escaping. Get up," said Exp 8, shaking the body.

"I told you he's—" said Karson.

"Shut up! He's going to be just fine. Get up Bro. We're going to get out of here, okay? All of us are escaping together. Nobody is going to die."

"His capsule…it isn't making any noise. He just needs a jumpstart," said Kawai with watery eyes. She rubbed her hands together before slamming them into her little brother's chest.

Atatasuki's body convulsed upward, but his eyes did not open.

"Where is Violet? I'll murder her!" yelled Exp 8, his eyes darkening.

"We have to keep going! D.S. is injured and Devlin is busy. This is our best chance to escape. If you don't want him to have died in vain, let's get moving!" exclaimed Bob, pulling the brash leader up to him with spectral tentacles.

"I am not leaving him!" yelled Exp 8, struggling to break free.

"We don't have time for this. Karson, cremate the body," said Bob.

Karson's arms turned into flamethrowers.

"He isn't dead. He's just in a coma. He's really defective, that's all," said Kawai on the brink of tears.

A spectral tentacle grabbed onto Kawai and pulled her away.

Karson stood above his comrade's body and released jets of flame.

"Karson, don't do it! I'm warning you! Stop! Please stop! You're hurting him," wailed Exp 8 as the flames consumed his brother.

Karson kept burning his comrade until all that remained was a pile of ashes. "One dead soldier is no reason to surrender the war. Let's move along," he said, turning away.

"I will kill you, Devlin! You hear me, murderer? You're going to pay!" yelled Exp 8.

Devlin's voice emanated from the room. "I…I didn't want him to die. I warned you that there would be casualties. I warned you! Don't think I'm going to stop here. Surrender now unless you want everyone you care about to die."

"I give up. I'll do what you want. Just bring him back," said Exp 8 in tears.

Kawai rubbed the tears off his face. "We can't stop now. We have to keep going. He died so that we could be free," she said, petting her brother's head.

"He risked his life so I could be free. I'm the only one Devlin wants. I'm the reason he died," wailed Exp 8.

"I'm glad you're finally facing reality. Don't you see? Nobody had to die. You can end this right now," said Devlin.

"If Devlin gets a hold of you, everyone will suffer. We cannot afford to give up now! Stand up and be our leader!" yelled Bob.

"I'm not a leader. I just wanted to be free. I never should have dragged all of you into this. But you're right. I can't give up now. I'm going to stop Devlin on my own," said Exp 8 before falling over.

Kawai caught him just before he collapsed. "We're all fighting together. And we are all willing to give up our lives," she said, grabbing his hand.

"I'm not going to lose you too," said Exp 8, hugging his little sister tightly with his only arm.

"Ada is waiting for us. Devlin still has her captive, or did you forget?" asked Nina, opening the exit door.

"If I fight, then he'll kill Ada," said Exp 8.

"Fine then, two can play that game. If you don't fight Devlin, then I'll kill…Kawai," said Bob, suddenly grabbing her with a spectral tentacle.

"Let her go!" yelled Exp 8, charging at Bob.

"Devlin has to be stopped. I'll do what I must," said Bob as his hostage struggled to break free.

"Stop fighting!" yelled Kaity.

"Alright…I'll fight Devlin. Let her go. I can't live with myself if I let him get away with this. And I don't know what he plans to use me for. You're right, Bob. Let's…let's keep moving," said Exp 8, dragging his feet.

"Good," said Bob, releasing his little hostage and patting her on the head.

"Don't you ever threaten my brother again," said Kawai, staring furiously at Bob.

"I was merely encouraging him. Alright, Freedom Forcers, let's go take down Devlin!" cheered Bob.

The Freedom Forcers charged through the door and rushed down the hallway to the elevator.

"Do I even bother pushing floor ten? We all know it's not going to work. Uugh," said Bob.

"Who's our next opponent?" asked Karson, turning to their pretty informant.

Matteria grabbed onto the living tank's shoulders. "It's Reflector. Please, don't hurt him. He's a really nice guy."

"I'll be sure to kill him quickly then," said Bob as the door to the ninth floor opened.

"What's his weakness?" asked Exp 8 as they ran down the hall.

"He's unbreakable. But he isn't very powerful. Just watch out for his lasers and you should be fine. We can probably just knock him aside and move past him," said Matteria, grabbing the leader's arm.

"I thought we would all be fine. I never thought death was a possibility. I wasn't careful enough. I won't make that mistake again," said Exp 8, clenching his fist.

Chapter 29: Reflector's Image

"We shouldn't all go in at once. Let's send a group to scout the area," said Bob, floating at the entrance to the door.

"I'll do it. I've been yearning for a little alone time," said Nina, grabbing the doorknob.

"You're not going in alone. Matteria, Kaity, you should go with her. I need a moment to cool down," said Exp 8, sitting down against the wall.

"Karson, guard our backs. I'm going to see what's on the floor above us," said Bob before flying through the ceiling.

"You can rest easy." Karson's feet unfolded and bolted into the ground. His body folded in on itself, transforming into a turret.

"I'm so sorry," said Exp 8, holding his sister tightly.

"I don't blame you. I tried my best to protect him just like you did. I just can't believe he's really gone. He seemed…like he'd always be here to bother me. Nothing will ever be the same now," said Kawai, sitting in her brother's lap.

"We'll be careful. If it takes more than three minutes, come in and provide support," said Kaity, making sure her gun magazines were full.

"Understood. Stay safe," said Exp 8, embracing the young assassin.

Kaity knocked his arm away and then smiled. "We will be."

Kaity, Nina, and Matteria then rushed into the unknown room.

The ceiling and floor were covered by a twenty-five-foot mirror. The four walls of the rooms were made of glass, each one reflecting off the other.

Everywhere Nina looked her reflection was looking back at her. Overcome with bliss, she skipped around the room.

The bliss shot through her soul, impregnating her mind with a beloved song.

♫ "I feel sexy.
Oh so sexy.
I feel sexy and foxy and hot!
And I pity
everyone because they're not.
I am exotic.
Oh so exotic.
It's erotic how exotic I am.
And so sexy
that I can hardly believe…I can.
See those sexy girls in every mirror here.
Of course those hot girls are me.

Such a sexy face,
Such a sexy ass,
Such a sexy touch,
Such a sexy me!
I feel smoking,
And stunning.
Feel like groping and stroking with joy.
For I'm beloved
by every hot-blooded boy!" ♫

"Is she trying to give away our position?" asked Kaity, quickly scoping out the area.

"I'll shut her up," said Matteria, turning toward Nina.
♫ "Have you met the luscious Nina?
The most ego-filled girl on the clock.
You'll know her the second you see her.
She's the one who shows off her breasts made of rocks.
She thinks she is loved.
She thinks she is sane.
La la la.
She has no true love.
Her heart is too plain.
She's always in heat
Or needs to get laid.
La la la.
If you ask me,
She needs to be spayed.
Keep away from her.
Ignore her glow.
This is just the Nina that shows." ♫

"Don't be so mean!" exclaimed Kaity before joining in.
♫ "She's honest and pure.
Polite and refined.
So sweet and mature—"♫

Matteria cut Kaity off.
♫ "You're out of your mind!" ♫

Nina twirled around in delight before continuing.
♫ "I feel sexy.
Oh so sexy.
That natural is what must be.

A whole city should be created to honor me." ♫

Kaity sang in the background.

♫ "La la la la la la la la la la." ♫

Nina combed her hair sensuously with her fingers and then continued.

♫ "I feel tipsy.

I feel wispy.

I feel fizzy and funny and fine.

And so sexy

that everything should just be mine!" ♫

Matteria mocked her as she sang.

♫ "Blah blah blah blah blah blah blah blah blah blah." ♫

Nina ignored him and kept singing.

♫ "See that sexy girl in every mirror here." ♫

Kaity looked around precariously.

♫ "Which mirror where?" ♫

Nina patted her head and sang some more.

♫ "Of course that attractive girl's me." ♫

Kaity chimed in.

♫ "Of course it's you." ♫

Nina buts in front of her and caressed her own body.

♫ "Such a sexy ass,

Such a sexy set,

Such a sexy bod,

Such a sexy me!" ♫

Kaity hopped to Nina's side.

♫ "Such a sexy me." ♫

Matteria hopped in front of both of them.

♫ "Such a sexy me." ♫

Nina shoved Matteria aside.

♫ "Such a sexy me! ♫

Nina danced around the mirror, all the while Kaity echoed her and followed her stroll.

♫ "I feel elegant." ♫

♫ "And relevant." ♫

Nina continued, pulling off her shirt.

♫ "Feel like jumping and stripping with glee." ♫

Nina turned to Kaity and grabbed her cheeks.

♫ "And I'm beloved

by an assassin kitty." ♫

Nina hugged Kaity tightly as she ended her song.

"I don't want to hear any singing right now!" yelled Exp 8, storming into the room.

"You ruined our cuddle time!" yelled Kawai.

"Sorry, we kind of got swept up in the moment," said Matteria, looking down with a light blush.

"Only Nina can make *West Side Story* sound even more amazing," said Kaity with shimmering eyes.

"Did I miss anything?" asked Bob, entering the room from above.

"I'm here!" yelled Karson, rushing into the spacious room of mirrors.

"What do we have here?" asked Nina, peering at a lone mirror from the side. "You were hiding very well. But you can't escape me." She hugged the mirror and rubbed against it.

"Thank you for this contact. Your breasts are lovely by the way. Don't tell Matteria I said that," said Reflector, shattering his mirror disguise.

Nina looked at his reflective body with amazement. "You're a living mirror?" she asked before pouncing on him.

"Yes, I am, the one and only. I'm a distinguished member of a museum in France. I'm a living, breathing spectacle," said Reflector as the bodacious bade grinded against him.

Nina got up and turned away. "It just had to be a blabber-mouth. You're to respond only when I ask you a question. Understood?" she asked before turning back and patting his head.

"You did ask me a question and I'm a 'he' not an 'it!' Now, sad to say, I have to destroy your delicious body. It is my duty as Devlin's Exp to obey his orders. He has ordered me to stop anyone from getting through that door by any means necessary. I'm going to just go on a limb and assume that killing is permitted. Or you could just surrender and join my exclusive harem," said Reflector, standing in a dignified manner.

"Um, is that...the enemy?" asked Kawai, trying to see past Nina.

"You guys go on ahead. I want to be alone for this fight," said Nina, her hands ready to tear open her shirt.

"We're all staying together!" exclaimed Exp 8.

"I'm not leaving your side!" said Kaity with a salute.

"I'm not leaving either," said Matteria, grabbing the assassin's hand.

"You two better not interrupt my battle," said Nina, combing back her hair.

"The three of them can handle this. Devlin won't expect us so soon," said Bob, heading for the door.

"What if they can't handle it? I'm not going to just let them die," said Exp 8, standing in front of Bob.

"I know everything about Reflector. He is my boyfriend, after all. Don't worry, I'll make sure we're all okay," said Matteria, blowing a kiss and waving.

Exp 8 gripped Kaity's shoulder. "Devlin won't let you get hurt. Use that to protect Nina. We're going on ahead. Meet up with us as soon as you can."

"Understood," said Kaity.

Exp 8's group rushed past Reflector and went through the door.

"Wait! I'm not supposed to let anyone leave! I've already failed you, Master Devlin!" yelled Reflector, pounding his hands on the floor.

Nina spun in the air and slammed her foot down on his head. She then fell to the ground, holding her foot while gasping in pain.

"Direct attacks have no effect on me. You might as well give up now. It's pointless to fight me. Though you can all feel free to join my harem," said Reflector, opening his arms.

Nina jumped back to her feet. "I am the sexy, irresistible, enchanting, elegant, extravagant, beautiful, slender, succulent, alluring, seductive Nina. No man can own me!" she exclaimed, posing differently with each word.

"Indeed you are! I already know your name from your song. Nina, Nina, Nina…ah. But I have yet to introduce myself. I am Reflector. It is a pleasure to meet someone with such an amazing body. I consider it a bonus that you aren't a cross-dressing boy. No offense, my beloved!" hollered Reflector.

"The whole concept of cross-dressing is absurd. Where in our genetic structure does it say that boys shouldn't wear skirts and panties?" asked Matteria, throwing his head up.

"It doesn't. But keep in mind that skirts were made for girls to wear. Their shape and fabric don't serve any purpose for the male body. My body, on the other hand—" Nina's hands rode up her thighs.

"What's the male body? I don't remember there being a single template."

Nina was too busy looking at her reflection grope itself to care what he said. "My breasts look so shiny in your reflection," she said, pulling down her bra.

Reflector looked at the reflection and then beamed up at her. "Indeed they do! Behold, world, a woman is groping herself in my reflection. If I died, I would die slightly more fulfilled! But alas…you are the one who must die. *LASER BEAM*."

A thin beam shot forth from his chest and bounced off the mirrored walls. It headed straight for Nina, who quickly jumped out of the way. It ricocheted, shooting every which way across the arena.

"My laser will cover the whole arena in no time! There is no mistake…I mean escape, damn."

"Let's see how strong this laser is," said Nina, muttering to herself. She took off her gloves tauntingly and tossed them into the laser.

As soon as the gloves hit the laser, they disintegrated into dust.

Nina looked down at her shirt, realizing it was damp. "I don't know what you did, but my shirt is wet!" she exclaimed with a hop of excitement.

"Whatever happens to your reflection will in turn happen to you. If I cry on your reflection's shirt, then your own shirt gets wet. I love being me now that there's a hot babe on my skin. None are as fair as you, Nina," said Reflector as he poked the reflection of her beautiful breasts.

Nina kicked him in the face, smashing her foot yet again.

"You really need to stop hurting yourself," said Reflector, trying to adjust himself so he could see her breasts.

"I knew a living mirror was too good to be true. If I took you in, then you could touch my tantalizing body whenever you wanted. Only I'm allowed to touch! You've already indirectly defiled my erotic aura. I can't allow you to live," said Nina with a gallant pose.

Tears poured down Reflector's face, drenching Nina's clothes. "I thought we were the perfect match. A mirror and a narcissist…I thought we were meant to be together. But a narcissist is too selfish to have love in their heart. Am I doomed only to be allowed to watch! Actually…I think I can deal with that," he said, gawking at her bra.

"I still love you! You can do whatever you want to my reflection!" yelled Matteria from the other side of the room.

"Why does the trap have to be the understanding one? Am I doomed to become gay in my desperation?" asked Reflector, holding his chest dramatically.

"Gay is just a mindset? It's not a disease. You'll still always like girls," said Matteria.

"You're right. I'm sorry for being so emotional. I should be used to having my hopes and dreams dashed to pieces at this point in life. Things never really turn out how I envision them. Ah, you really are the only one that truly understands me," said Reflector, beaming at his partner.

"Wait…you like Matteria more than me! He has a cute butt granted, but mine has volume!" exclaimed Nina, sticking her butt out.

"He has a beauty that you could not fathom. He has inner beauty!" exclaimed Reflector, shining brightly from within.

Matteria ran to Reflector and embraced him tightly. "You are so sweet!"

"And you are sooooo squishy," said Reflector, grabbing his partner's butt.

"And I am so hot," said Nina, running her hands up her legs.

"There's really no difference as long as you don't poke under my skirt," said Matteria, rubbing noses with his shiny new boyfriend.

"Ah, what words of wisdom," said Reflector, nestling Matteria's crotch.

"It is not the same! He has no boobs!" exclaimed Nina.

"Can't you see I'm trying to be in denial here?" asked Reflector, turning to the femme fatale with a furious glare.

"So, are we still supposed to fight him?" asked Kaity as she instinctively chased after the laser.

"Nina, I have given up on trying to love you. Matteria is the most beautiful girl in the world! He has something no other girl has!" exclaimed Reflector, standing valiantly.

"Ohohoho. You mean a dick?" asked Nina.

"He has affection for me!" exclaimed Reflector before sobbing uncontrollably.

"He's a hypocrite in a dress! He talks about how beautiful men can be, yet he always dresses up like a teeny bopper girl! Your boyfriend wants to be a girl so bad because he can't come to grips with his homosexuality! He's insecure, while I fully accept each and every part of myself," said Nina, kissing her fingers one after the next.

"How dare you! Matteria started dressing up in more girly clothes after we started dating. And he doesn't really love me. His affection is unrefined pity. He looks at me to make me feel better. He is a selfless goddess that loves all equally!" exclaimed Reflector, rubbing his face against Matteria's chest.

"You mean he's a man-whore," said Nina, twisting her neck.

"Why is it man whore? Why can't "whore" be gender inclusive?" asked Matteria.

"See? Even he's not denying it," said Nina with a wide smirk.

"Love is something you cannot understand. Matteria, let me end this battle," said Reflector, grabbing his pretty partner's butt before walking past him.

Matteria skipped back to Kaity who was still chasing down the laser.

"I should inform that these lasers aren't a product of my artifact. They are as natural to me as stomach acid is to you," said Reflector.

"I don't eat. And I don't have stomach acid. My body is perfection both in and out," said Nina, sticking out her tongue.

"Perfection is absurd. Adequacy is all I shoot for. You are flawed, and it just so happens that I have knowledge of your little flaw," said Reflector, raising his arms in the air.

"Don't you dare," said Nina, her eyes shrinking in fear.

"I have the Darkness Artifact. Devlin gave me the Tiger's Eye! Behold its power. *LIGHT DESTRUCTION!*"

At the flick of a switch, the entire area was enshrouded in darkness. Even the lasers could scarcely be seen.

Nina was unable to see her hand mere inches from her face. She trembled as the terror crawled up her body. Her mind projected an image of her past in order to protect her from the approaching darkness.

The darkness dissolved as Nina's mind covered it in a projection of a flashback.

Chapter 30: The Benefits of Love

I was cloaked beneath the burgundy covers of my Master's queen-sized bed. Not a strand of my short hair dangled before my eyes. When I looked down, I could see my breasts were wrapped tightly and properly concealed. My mouth was covered by a dark purple cloth just barely visible in my peripheral vision.

I rolled around to face him. My whole body relaxed as I stared into his golden eyes.

He is more than my creator, more than my master. Devlin is my soul mate.

"You are so beautiful," he said, his hand caressing my cheek with gentle fingertips.

"I don't try to be," I said, turning away with a light blush.

"You don't need to try." He kissed my neck affectionately, climbing toward my lips.

I pulled away and then turned around to face him. "Devlin, something has been bothering me. It's been…bothering me for some time now." My voice was firm but unable to overcome apprehension. "I love you and…."

Every time I try to tell him, I lose command of my voice. I need to steady my mind.

"What's wrong?" asked Devlin, pulling me in closer.

I kissed his cheek and then leaned into his chest. "If I was…made to love you…then does that—my feelings aren't real?" I asked, tightly gripping my fingers.

"You need to stop worrying so much. Love is a chemical reaction. It is misinterpreted instinct. It's our body telling us we've found a means to continue our legacy. I engineered you in every way. Nature had no part in it. Therefore, the love you feel for me is part of your biology. It's no more unreal than the way I feel about you." Devlin put his arms around me and hugged me tightly.

So warm, but is this feeling real? Or is it just a pre-programmed response.

"Isn't love something formed through experience?" I asked, grabbing his hand.

"It is both strengthened and weakened through our experiences. The way we are nurtured cultivates our biology. With enough influence, we can even surpass our biology. Love can even turn into hate given the proper circumstances."

Hate? I don't hate him. How could I? Does he think I hate him? I have to explain it. I need him to understand what I'm feeling!

"When I don't get to see you all day, I get these terrible thoughts. I get so angry. I understand you have to work constantly, but I just feel so alone sometimes. I've meditated on those feelings for the past six weeks. I never want to hate you," I said, tightly gripping Devlin.

"We all get upset. You shouldn't try to contain that. Your emotions are an important part of you. They will bring you both happiness and pain."

"Emotions are an obstacle."

"Only if you look at them as such. My emotions are what inspired me to make you. Without feelings of loneliness, you wouldn't be here to brighten up my day," said Devlin as he combed my hair with his gentle fingers.

"Many wars have been waged because of fear. I don't want to be afraid, and I don't want to feel alone."

"Humans attack what they do not understand. They are unable to recognize true talent and true beauty. The only way they will overcome their insolence is if they become immersed in the oddity. Discrimination can only be overcome through experience. But I think we've talked enough. As much as I'd love to snuggle some more, I have to get some rest. Have a good night." Devlin kissed me on the forehead.

Ah, sometimes I forget the feeling of his fatherly affection. Oh no. Is my love for him as a father just a program too? No, I can't let him leave yet.

I grabbed his arm and looked up at him. "I don't want to be lonely, and I don't want to stop loving you."

"Then just relax. You're taking this too seriously. I'll always love you, so there's no need for concern. Now, why don't you get some rest?"

"I don't need to sleep…maybe you could hold me for just a bit longer? There are moments when I don't love you. Sometimes I feel completely apathetic to your suffering. I don't know why this is happening to me. Devlin, please don't leave me now."

I'm so scared. Please hold me.

"We've spent the whole day together. We had a really great time. I have a deadline coming up soon. I'm sorry, but I really am tired. We can snuggle first thing in the morning," said Devlin, walking to the door.

I jumped out of the bed and gripped onto his lab coat. "Why can't we ever sleep together? Please, Master…stay with me."

"I'm sorry, but I can't tonight. I am about to fall over." Devlin put out the scented candles with his fingertips.

"Then why not collapse in my arms. Today is special. Can't we share the bed just this once?" I asked, caressing his chest with passion.

"I know it's our six-month anniversary. I want to be with you, you know that. It's just that I sleep alone. It's how I operate. Don't take it personally. Try to get some rest for once. It might do you some good," said Devlin, kissing me on the forehead.

He makes me feel like a child. That kiss isn't the kiss I want. It isn't the kiss I need.

"I'm not going to waste valuable time. I'm going to spend the night training." I stood up tall and began my routine stretching exercises.

"Alright, do what you want. I'll be here first thing in the morning, I promise," he said before leaving me all alone.

As soon as the door closed, the lights went out.

"Devlin, turn on the lights! I need to train!" I walked toward the door, but then I stopped.

Maybe I should try to get some sleep.

I waved my hand in front of my face but could see nothing.

It's so dark. Ah, I can feel my stress fading.

I collapsed onto the bed and stretched my limbs. "If I'm going to get some rest, I'm going to need to work my body to exhaustion first."

Some exercise should help me think more clearly too.

I leaped off the bed and spun around before landing on the floor. After leaping backwards, I gripped onto the ceiling with my toes. I then pulled myself up while stretching out my arms. Once I released my grip, I landed on the bed without a sound.

"All this time I thought the key to connecting to the soul was concentration. What if it it's really relaxation? This is so fascinating." I closed my eyes and listened to the surrounding silence.

An unfamiliar presence!

I sat up abruptly.

"Who's there? Don't think the darkness can mask you. I can sense your presence. If you are an intruder, I will kill you."

"You two really are cute together," said the voice of a man from the darkness.

"I don't need a weapon to snap your neck," I said, leaping out of the bed. I grabbed the intruder's arm.

"You remind me of Ada. You are both so oblivious to your stunning beauty," said the voice.

"Identify yourself!"

"I'm sorry but I can't allow Devlin to fall in love. He has work to do. It's nothing personal," said the voice against my ear.

I tensed up my muscles as electricity shot into my body. *Once he's done, I'll just jab my fingers through his throat.*

"Don't be alarmed. It's just something to help you relax." He grabbed my head with his other hand.

How could I have left myself open?

The shock was unrelenting. I collapsed before I could retaliate.

I woke up above the covers, my body still sore from the electricity. I jumped out of the bed, looking around warily.

Was that a dream?

I checked my body for wounds. I looked down at my chest, seeing it all tied up.

Why would I hide something so voluptuous?

I tore off the wraps trapping my body. Now that they were free, I pushed up my bare breasts.

They are so full, so smooth, so incredibly smooth. They call to my fingers and my fingers naturally gravitate to them.

I caressed my nipples, breathing deeper as pleasure spread throughout my breasts.

"I never realized how sexy I am!" I exclaimed, spontaneously grouping myself for the first time.

The lights flickered in the room, creating an instant moment of darkness.

A chill ran down my sexy spine.

I better go ask Devlin to fix the lights.

I moved toward the door but stopped abruptly.

It's so silky.

I slowly dragged my fingers through my hair.

I should let my glorious hair flow freely.

I took off my headband and hair tie before tossing them aside.

As my hair was released I shook it left to right. My bangs dropped down over my face.

I licked the hair and then brushed it aside.

"I am smoking hot!"

What was I doing again? Oh yeah, got to go see Devlin.

I rushed to the living room.

Devlin was sprawled on the couch with his legs in opposite directions. He sat up from the couch, fixing up his messy hair. "Whoa, you look great with your hair down. But why did you take off your hair tie? I thought your hair hindered your concentration?"

"I got scared when the lights turned off. I couldn't see my body," I said, my hands trembling.

"You sure are acting strange. Though I think I'd lose my will to live if I couldn't see you," said Devlin sweetly before blowing me a kiss.

Strange, he doesn't look as attractive as I remembered. No matter, I need his help.

I grabbed his hands and stealthily pushed up my breasts as I feigned shyness. "Can you fix the darkness?"

"You are my shining angel, Nina. As the light of my life, I designed your body with a special feature. You're like a living flash bomb! Merely strip naked and you'll light the place up. I told you before, but you're just too shy to do it," said Devlin, tapping my nose.

He treats me like a child!

"Ugh, that sounds pointlessly complicated," I said, moving my silky hair aside.

"Oh, I completely forgot! Yesterday I wanted to give you something to celebrate our anniversary. Give me a moment," said Devlin, getting off the couch. He went to the corner of the room and pulled up the floorboards, revealing a stash of artifacts.

Don't worry, my darlings, soon you'll always be in my sight.

I pushed up my breasts and blew them sweet kisses.

"Alright, here we are! I give you the Gravity Artifact! Careful it's heavy," said Devlin, wobbling up to me with a rounded pearl white stone of barite.

I took it from his arms and absorbed it. "How will it help me?"

"Well, it will make your meditation easier. Plus you should be able to use it to enhance all your—are you listening?"

"My breasts feel so amazing!" I exclaimed, groping my breasts uncontrollably as a flood of passion took over.

"They sure are! But I thought you didn't want them to get in the way."

Why would I ever hide something so wonderful?

"So, do you want to snuggle some more?" he asked, kissing me on the cheek like I was his property.

I pulled away and grabbed a shirt off the floor. I slipped into it and turned around.

"You are not allowed to touch me. This body is a masterpiece. A single touch could shatter its perfection. Stay away."

"What the hell happened to you? Lie down. I need to check your system for bugs," said Devlin, reaching for my hand despite my warning.

I kicked his crotch and then backed away.

"Ow. Damn it Nina! What the hell has gotten into you?" asked Devlin, holding his crotch in pain.

Karson entered the room. "Commander, are you alright?"

"Yeah, I'm fine," said Devlin, taking a deep breath. "Nina, I would like to show you the newest enhancements I've made to Karson!"

The man made of guns posed proudly, showing off his bazooka arms.

What is he showing off? His entire body is so artificial and so unrefined.

311

"Hmm, what's this?" asked Devlin, looking at Karson's back.

"What's what?" asked Karson, turning around.

"There's a red button on your back…is this some kind of practical joke? Did you see any of the other Exps this morning?" asked Devlin.

"We were at the shooting range last night. If there was a red button, surely you would have noticed. Don't pull my leg," said Karson.

What happened to him needing his sleep? Devlin is such a liar.

"This is very strange. Hey, Nina, any ideas how this button got on Karson's back?" asked Devlin, careful not to touch me.

"Who cares?" I turned away from him.

"What's going on with her?" whispered Karson to his creator.

"It seems she is having a glitch, or she's PMSing. Hmm…do female Exps have periods? And, if so, what purpose would they serve?" asked Devlin, tapping his bottom lip.

"I should be the only thing that matters to you," I said, turning to face Devlin.

"I love all my Exps. You are all my children. But even among them, you are very special to me. I love you with all my heart."

Devlin's hand reached out to me only to be knocked aside.

I wonder, does he really care about me? Only one way to find out.

"If you love me, then I need you to get rid of these hideous distractions. Destroy the other Exps and prove your love!"

"I don't know what the hell is wrong with you, but I'm going to find out," said Devlin, reaching behind my head.

I grabbed his hand, spun his arm around, and put a dagger to his throat. "You touch me and I'll kill you."

There, that should get the point across.

Devlin's eyes watered up. "What happened to you?"

"I had a revelation. My sexiness is my soul!" I exclaimed, posing sexily for the very first time.

Nina's mind returned to the present, where she was enshrouded by darkness.

"I guess I wasn't paying attention before. But my miraculous mind knew exactly what memory I needed to revisit."

"What are you talking about? Did someone lock away your memories?" asked Reflector.

"No, I just blotted out Devlin's words and forgot about the artifact."

"What artifact?"

"Even after I betrayed him and joined the Freedom Forcers, Devlin left me with one artifact. Despite how obsessed he has become with revenge, he still cares about me. He still loves me. I won't let you cover my elegant body!" Nina took off her clothes with great determination. *"Softening Pull, Gravitation!"* Her body felt light as she rose off the ground. The less she weighed the more light she emitted. The light consumed the darkness, guided by the erotic warrior's willpower.

Reflector came into view, frozen in disbelief.

Nina used her gravity control to toss her shoe at her opponent.

The shoe exploded as it hit the glass man, but he was unfazed.

Nina was suddenly blown back as if the explosion had hit her. She slammed against the floor, reverting back into her normal form.

"You have defeated my darkness and my lasers all at once. Good for you. But you seem to have forgotten that your reflection serves as your body," said Reflector as he poked at the woman's breast in her reflection.

Nina covered her chest, only allowing the molester to poke her arm.

"Let me touch them! They are taunting me like giant delicious marbles!"

"I thought you only liked boys now!"

"I told you before, I'm not gay. Matteria is the only male I like. I'm not in denial and neither is he. If dressing up makes him happy and me happy, well then what's the problem?"

"The problem is that he's spreading his glamour gospel across the globe. The body is a temple, not a canvas! It is a natural gift. It is not a plaything," said Nina.

"It's his body. He can do with it whatever he wants! I don't need you, Nina. Matteria is all I'll ever need."

"Then leave me alone!"

"I can't resist your amazing body. Normally a guy like me would have no chance with a woman of your caliber. But we are enemies, so there's no problem with me forcibly touching your excellent body!" Reflector punched the reflection of Nina's arms furiously, trying to get them out of the way of her breasts.

"Your self-esteem is derived from the self-love of others, you are pathetic," said Nina as her arms withstood the blows.

"Don't hurt Nina and don't poke her boobs either!" exclaimed Kaity, aiming her sniper at him.

"Think about what you're doing. If you shoot me, she's the one who's going to feel it. Such is the power of the Mirror Artifact!" cheered Reflector as he tickled the reflection's arms.

"I developed immunity to tickling long ago. My body is perfection!" yelled Nina, rolling on her belly.

"Ah, your back is so tender," said Reflector, running his hands down her spine.

"I warned you!" Kaity aimed and pulled down the trigger.

The plasma bullet shot through his head, leaving a searing hole in its wake.

Nina was unharmed because his face had no part of her reflection on it.

"How could you?" asked Matteria, covering his mouth in shock.

"I love her! And, in case you forgot, he's the enemy!" yelled Kaity, about to fire again.

Matteria embraced the adorable girl tightly, crying tears of sympathy. "Oh, you poor thing, cursed to love the unlovable. Nina will only crush your youthful love. She should at least have the decency to wear a "do not touch" sign on her chest. At least then she would not encourage so many lustful hearts."

"Yeah, but she's still fun," said Kaity with a smile.

"You are too good for her," said Matteria, trying to knock the sniper out of the assassin's hand.

"I don't need a girlfriend! Matteria's twice the woman you'll ever be and more man than you'll ever get! I'm going to crush the heart that has crushed so many others!" yelled Reflector.

The mirror wall behind him shattered to pieces, revealing a wall made from hundreds of individual mirrors.

All the mirrors burst, revealing even more mirrors behind them.

"Go kick her finely tuned ass," cheered Matteria.

"You think she's hot too?" asked Reflector.

"It is the curse of every creature with eyes," said Matteria, covering his face in shame.

Nina's eyes widened as she gazed at the myriad of mirrors. "You are incredibly powerful. Now there are thousands of me! And now there are thousands of me groping myself!" she exclaimed as she fondled her breasts.

The small mirrors on the wall behind Reflector combined and formed into a dragon of glass.

The glass dragon opened its reflective mouth and emitted an array of lasers.

Nina jumped out of the way, dodging each laser with ease.

Kaity raced out of the line of fire.

Matteria made himself air and was thus unaffected by the lasers.

"I must do something I never thought I could do! I must break a mirror!" Nina tossed all her clothes in the mythical reptiles' mouth. "*Erotic Explosion!*"

Her clothes exploded the monster from inside, bursting the glass dragon to pieces.

Smoke shot out in the shape of Nina posing sexily.

"Wow, that was invigorating!" exclaimed Kaity, jumping on her partner's back.

Nina shook the girl off. "Now to deal with him!" she yelled, rushing at the mirror man. She ran through his array of lasers, deflecting them with the shards of glass in her hands.

The lasers bounced off his shiny body and simultaneously shot into her.

"You can't hurt me!" yelled Reflector as she closed in.

Nina leaped over him and then thrust both her palms into his back.

A small crack formed inside Reflector. "What did you do?" he asked, lunging at his attacker with a laser sword as the crack expanded.

"I bypassed your exterior. Don't think my sexiness is merely skin deep," said Nina as she rapidly dodged his sword.

Kaity aimed her gun and fired a bullet into the cracked area.

Reflector fell apart, shattering like glass.

Kaity hopped up to Matteria. "High five…oh yeah, he was your boyfriend. Sorry," she said, lowering her hand.

Matteria rushed to Reflector's side and picked up his head. "Are you okay?"

"I'll live," said the shattered head of Reflector.

"You fought well," said Matteria as he set down his boyfriend's head.

"I am a luscious lone wolf," said Nina, squeezing her breasts in delight.

"We should get going, Reflector reassembles pretty quickly," said Matteria, heading through the door.

"No, we should collect his artifacts first," said Nina, directing Kaity to search through the shards.

"Not so fast." Devlin suddenly dropped in. "Someone is here to see you."

Ada was behind him, captive in a clear spherical prison.

"Hi everyone!" exclaimed Ada, waving joyously.

"Nina, join me or I will personally send her to purgatory," said Devlin through clenched teeth.

Nina punched Kaity, showing her allegiance to the inventor's side.

Devlin rushed up to her and grabbed her by the throat. "Do that again and I will melt your breasts off," he said, slamming the detestable woman to the ground.

"I'm on your side," said Kaity, massaging her injured cheek.

"Not anymore. You're a Freedom Forcer and I'm an Omnipotent Overseer," said Nina with a hair flip.

"Then I guess we're a team again!" cheered Ada as her prison dissolved.

"Do you want me to capture Kaity?" asked Nina, ready to pull open her shirt.

"The reason I joined the Freedom Forcers is because I love you. I'll follow you anywhere," said Kaity, walking up to Nina and grabbing her hand.

"That is so beautiful," said Matteria with watery eyes.

"I didn't know you felt this strongly! I completely understand. I'm irresistible," said Nina, patting her little fan on the head.

Devlin released Nina and put his arm around Kaity's shoulder. "Both of you are joining me, how splendid! This is why I wanted Ada in the first place. Ada may be the weakest member of your group, but she is the starting point of this triangle of love," he said with a grin.

"Master Devlin, I'm sorry. I only joined them because I didn't want to die. I didn't betray you. I just gave them some advice, that's all," said Matteria with a bow.

"I know you wouldn't betray me. It was very kind of you to protect Kaity. But you don't need to worry anymore. She is now on my side."

"Can you help Reflector?" asked Matteria.

"Reflector can fix himself. I'm sorry, Kaity, but I'm going to have to ask you to wait on getting healed. My doctor is working on something vital. But worry not; he should have no problem helping you grow back your arm. Oooh, when I see Tempo again, he's going to beg for his death! Is there any way in particular you would like me to punish him?" asked Devlin with an endearing smile.

"I'm the one who cut it off. There's no need to punish anyone."

"Very well then, no harm shall come to him." Devlin patted his cute crush on the head. He then spun around. "As for you: if you oppose me again, I will kill Ada on the spot. Do I make myself clear?" he asked, grabbing the detestable woman by the chin.

"I understand. But please, don't fondle me," said Nina, shaking as she turned away from his gaze.

"I've been over you! I made Matteria after you broke my heart. But Kaity has opened up my heart again. Ah, love is so wondrous! There is no form of obedience stronger than love. After all, it is the Freedom Forcers' bonds that have allowed me to drive a wedge between them."

"You left me with an artifact. Now why would you do a thing like that if you didn't have feelings for me?" asked Nina, licking her lips.

"You're surprisingly perceptive. I left you with the Gravity Artifact because it was a precious gift to the other Nina. I hoped that, with this gift so close to your capsule, you would remember your old self," said Devlin, touching her cheek.

"You gave Reflector the Darkness Artifact for that specific reason, didn't you?" asked Nina with slanted eyes.

"Yes, I was hoping that your obedient, softer side would come out."

"Don't bother. She's gone," said Nina with a smirk.

"Don't you have any lingering feelings for me?" asked Devlin with a blush.

"I cut out those unnecessary thoughts long ago. I live for myself now," said Nina, pushing out her chest.

"Don't forget about Ada," said Devlin.

"The only reason I stick by Ada is because she has knowledge and experience that can increase my erotic aura of sexiness," said Nina, gripping her sensei's breasts.

"Is that really the only reason?" asked Ada, as her eyes watered up.

"Hey, um, Devi-kun, there's something I uh want to ask you," said Kaity, shifting her hips side to side.

"A-a-ask away. Kaity, I must say you look especially beautiful today," said Devlin, kissing her hand.

"You put bombs in my family. Remove them," said Kaity, pressing her pistol against his forehead.

The gun liquidated in the assassin's hand.

"Thank you, Matteria. I am sorry, Kaity, but I need to capture Exp 8. Your family is quite skilled."

"I won't ask again," said Kaity, her hand on her other sidearm.

"You got me. There are no bombs in them. If I didn't put them in my creations, why would I put them inside the assassins? I was bluffing. But in my defense, it did make them so much more cooperative," said Devlin with a smile.

"I'm keeping my eye on you," said Kaity with dagger-like eyes.

"That's wonderful news! Would you like to stay in my room? My bed is more than sufficient for the two of us," said Devlin, grabbing her hand.

"I can't stay here. I made a promise to Sefiwah that if she…I need to move on. But I can't leave my family trapped here," said Kaity, wiping her eyes.

Devlin crouched down to Kaity's level. "Once Exp 8 is under my control, they will be freed. You have my word," he said, shaking her hand.

"Then let's hurry up and bag him," said Kaity, stretching her fingers.

"I'll get right to it," said Devlin, patting her head.

"Is there any way to bring their friend back?" asked Matteria, turning to his master.

"Exp 8 needs to realize that I am not messing around. Reflector, get up!" hollered Devlin.

"I'm sorry, Master Devlin, sir. I tried my best to win, sir," said Reflector, now fully assembled.

"You did not injure Kaity, and all of your opponents have joined me. I don't see how this constitutes a loss. However, you have yet to defeat a Freedom Forcer. My deal still stands. If you beat the next opponent, then I'll buy you a harem. As for the now ex-Freedom Forcers, follow me," said Devlin, beckoning his newly created allies.

They all jumped onto a platform that rose up into the ceiling.

The top opened up, leading them to Devlin's operation room. Computers were monitoring the Freedom Forcers' every move from multiple angles.

"Wow, this is just like our security room," said Kaity with a wide smile.

"This is where Devlin spies on me in the shower," said Nina, lifting up a black cloth to reveal a hidden monitor.

"I have been far too busy recently. Now, let's separate the team even further. The Freedom Forcers will be killed, one by one," said Devlin darkly.

"Do you have to kill them?" asked Kaity, tugging on his shirt.

"Truthfully, I don't want any of them to die," said Devlin, his eyes narrowing.

"With all due respect, Master, didn't you order Violet to kill Atatasuki?" asked Matteria.

"Yes, I did. But I warned Exp 8 that there would be consequences. Still…it's a shame that Atatasuki died. I placed a muffin next to his ashes. I wanted to pay him my respects. It's the best I could do with the time I had. Who knows, maybe I'll be able to bring him back to life once I have captured Exp 8. One can only hope."

"You're so thoughtful," said Matteria as he embraced his master.

"I brought them into this world, so they are my responsibility. You can stop hugging me now," said Devlin, patting his child on the head.

"Sorry Master," said Matteria, backing away with flushed cheeks.

"Kaity, watch this! I will split up the Freedom Forcers with the press of a button. Then my forces can ki…defeat them one by one. Exp 8 underestimates me. He will run headfirst into any trap I set up just to prove that I have no power over him. It really makes things quite easy," said Devlin, throwing his legs over the table.

"He shouldn't think so low of you! You gave him life!" exclaimed Matteria.

"The hero always has an ego. Even the wily Odysseus had a moment of hubris. I just hope Exp 8 doesn't give up too soon."

Devlin pushed a button. The room the Freedom Forcers were in rotated, revealing four doors.

Chapter 31: Deceit

Previously: the Freedom Forcers ran past Reflector and out the door, leaving Nina, Matteria, and Kaity behind.

"Damn it, we don't have Matteria to tell us who we are up against. Everyone keep your distance. We need to find out what the enemy is capable of before we attack. Sis, stay close to me," said Exp 8 as they ran down yet another hallway.

"I will," said Kawai, floating above his shoulder.

The Freedom Forcers ran past a four-way intersection with a door in each direction.

"Bob, guard my back. As long as they don't know about the Button, I can defeat them," said Karson.

"So, which way do we go? Devlin didn't put up any signs for us to follow this time," said Kawai, her shoulders dropping.

"Let's go straight ahead. As long as we stick together, we won't lose," said Exp 8 with a firm fist. He then punched the door open.

The Freedom Forcers entered their next battlefield.

The room had no ceiling, allowing sunlight to enter from above. The gooey black walls rose up to unreachable heights. Black paint dripped from the walls onto the metallic floor below.

Exp 8 looked up at the sun with wonderment. "Ah, just feeling the sun's rays is invigorating. This is what we are fighting for! Soon we will all be free!" He cheered, grabbing his sister's hand.

"Wait, if there's no ceiling…we're free!" exclaimed Kawai, hugging her brother's face.

"You're right! Karson, hop on my back! " exclaimed Exp 8.

"This is too easy. I don't trust it." Karson aimed his pistol-hand at the opening and fired.

The bullet ricocheted, proving there was a barrier preventing their escape.

"So then…we aren't free yet. I just want to get out of this place," said Exp 8, lowering his head.

"It appears we would have to break through twenty feet of plexiglass in order to do so. Or I could just pass through it, hrm-hmm," said Bob.

"If only we all could," said Karson.

"So what the hell do we do? There isn't a door anywhere in this room!" yelled Exp 8.

"Devlin probably put this room here to taunt us. I guess we should head back. Um, Brother, there seems to be a problem," said Kawai, tapping his shoulder.

The door they came in vanished and the wall behind them was now black like the other three walls.

"How the hell are we going to get out of here?" asked Exp 8, slamming his only hand against the wall.

"This is a cheap move even for former Commander Devlin. I'll try to shoot us out," said Karson, turning his arms into a rocket launcher.

Kawai sat on her brother's shoulder.

"This is a miracle! We are locked in here together. I don't care if we ever get out, heeheehmph."

Exp 8 slammed the black wall continuously but couldn't put a dent in it.

"My rockets aren't doing a thing to the ceiling or the walls!" yelled Karson.

"I'm trapped forever! And now I'm not. And now I am...now I'm not! I love being me!" exclaimed Bob as he alternated between passing through the walls and the ceiling.

"A wall blocking your path...boxed in...not allowed to move on...doomed to fail no matter how hard you try. Now you know how it feels to be me," said NoOne, sulking into the room.

"Wait, where did you come from?" asked Exp 8, turning around before taking a step back.

"Probably from a puddle of failure. Ugh, I haven't won a single fight. Let's face it...I never will," said NoOne, sliding toward them.

"Come on, man, it's not that bad," said Karson, still trying to blow up the wall.

"You guys have lost to people who are weaker than me. Those human assassins won many fights against you. I'm an Exp, but that hasn't helped me one bit. Failure must be engraved in my DNA," said NoOne, lowering his head.

"The reason you keep on losing is because you have no self-confidence! Atatasuki had his faults, but he won many battles because he had determination. You have to accept your flaws so that you can blossom into a muffin. That sounds like something he'd say," said Exp 8, tearing up.

"Maybe you're right! Maybe I'm the only thing holding myself back. I mean shadow-bending is a really powerful ability!" exclaimed NoOne, raising his head up with his hands.

"Yeah and you did okay in our last battle. You still lost miserably, but the odds were against you," said Bob with a warm smile.

"You guys are too kind. I'm not going to let you down! I'm going to murder all of you...while suffering less than fatal injuries!" cheered NoOne.

"That's the spirit! But come on, you can still do better," said Exp 8, smacking the shadow man's back.

"I'm going to murder all of you without a scratch!" yelled NoOne, his talons gliding across the air.

"There we go. So, do you feel your confidence rising?" asked Exp 8.

"It's as if I'm blossoming from within. So self-deceit was the key to victory all along. If I thought: 'I'll defeat you no matter what,' then my deceit would become determination! I understand everything now! You guys are the best! Thanks to your help, I know I can kill you," said NoOne, sharpening his arm.

"I've come too far to lose to you," said Exp 8, getting into a fighting stance.

"You're right. I'm a loser," said NoOne, instantly drooping into a puddle.

Kawai smacked the puddle with her tail. "Don't give up so easily! You need to hold onto your deceit. Atatasuki overheated all the time, which nearly killed him on multiple occasions. He used that flaw to super heat his whole body, making it a powerful weapon. You must believe you can win or you'll never know what you're capable of," she said, getting a little teary-eyed.

"I thought you were heartless, but if you were heartless then you would have no self-love. I was a heartless wretch a mere minute ago! But now, your words have given me the benefit of deceit. Deceit is the key to being brave. Stupidly charging into battle, thinking you're invincible, that is what I must do if I want to win!" cheered NoOne.

"Um, none of us have hearts," said Kawai.

"That was really nice of you to help him out," said Exp 8, patting his sister's head.

"We did it together," said Kawai, shifting her hips.

"Come here and give me a hug," said Exp 8, snuggling her affectionately. Kawai giggled in his embrace, licking his face periodically.

"This is very sweet and all, but shouldn't we be killing him?" asked Bob.

"Wait a moment! I'm missing a key ingredient! I need some useless person to blindly protect," said NoOne, hitting his palm in revelation.

"Who are you calling useless?" asked Kawai with a snarl before continuing to snuggle her beloved brother.

"They don't have to be useless, it just helps. The more helpless they are, the stronger the will to protect them becomes!" cheered NoOne.

"Isn't NoOne our enemy? He's a swell guy and all, but he was sent here to kill us. Shouldn't we retaliate?" asked Karson, aiming both arms at the enemy soldier.

Exp 8 lowered the guns. "Let's all calm down. I'm tired of doing what Devlin wants. I'm not going to just mindlessly fight on. NoOne could become a great ally! And I think I can convince him to join us."

"You're talking like a true leader. I am impressed," said Bob, taken aback.

"Bob, I need you to join NoOne's team. Go cheer him on. Don't even deflect our attacks. Just…stand there. That way he will have to protect you," said Exp 8.

"That's genius! I won't let you hurt my little brother!" exclaimed NoOne, trying to get into character.

"I guess I'll play along. I hope this won't be boring," said Bob, rolling to the shadow man's side.

"So, NoOne, are you ready to fight now?" asked Exp 8, jumping in place to get pumped up.

"The Shadow Master is more than ready!" exclaimed NoOne, flinging his arms in the air.

"I'll fight you alone. Kawai, keep your distance. This could get dangerous," said Exp 8.

"Wait, I think I might have a better idea…maybe! You could act like the villain, that way I get the huge benefit of being the hero. Come to think of it, would it be alright if Kawai could cheer for me instead of Bob? Women always have more influence than men when it comes to this kind of stuff," said NoOne.

"That's a great idea! Bob, you and Karson can watch from the sidelines. Sis, will you please help him out?" asked Exp 8.

"I'll do anything for you," said Kawai, licking his cheek before turning toward NoOne.

Exp 8 grabbed the girl by the head and held her up. "Hero! Is this what you came for?"

NoOne ran up to Exp 8 and shot his fist forward.

Exp 8 caught the projectile fist. "You are too weak to protect her. You should have joined me when I gave you the chance," he said, using his best Devlin impersonation.

"I'll never join you! I will show you just how powerful love is!" exclaimed NoOne as he slammed his other fist in Exp 8's face.

The villain's head recoiled back. He chuckled in delight. "That's it, succumb to your hate," he said, gritting his teeth beneath his mouthpiece.

"*SHADOW MANIPULATION, SELF-BETRAYAL*," said NoOne.

Exp 8's shadow shot up and wrapped around him. It constricted his arms and legs like a python.

Kawai escaped his grip and rushed to NoOne's side.

Exp 8 laughed maniacally, not even trying to break free. "That might have worked before, but I have grown too strong. You should have killed me when you had the chance," he said, trying to add some back-story to the scene.

"I'm not like you. I refuse to kill!" exclaimed NoOne.

"You are right. You are not like me. You are weak!" Exp 8 burst out of his own shadow without the slightest effort. He hit NoOne with the back of his hand, sending the shadow master crashing into the wall. While NoOne recovered, he stepped toward the damsel in distress.

NoOne fired shadow balls from a hole in his hand, positioning them around the villain's feet.

"What's wrong? Is fear impairing your aim?" asked Exp 8, his eyes intensifying.

"What makes you think I missed?" asked NoOne, crossing his arms.

The shadow balls shot up from the ground, morphing into hands. The hands wrapped around the villain's legs, holding him in place.

"You might as well have missed. Your attempts are pathetic." Exp 8 walked out of the shadows' grip.

"Help me, my love, or are we supposed to be platonic?" asked Kawai, reaching out to NoOne as Exp 8 came closer.

"Leave my childhood friend alone!" yelled NoOne.

Exp 8 grabbed the girl by the neck. "Such a delicate flower…I can see why you love her. You know…I find such joy in plucking petals off pretty flowers."

"You bastard, let her go!" yelled NoOne.

Exp 8's hand let go of her neck and gripped her arm. "If I broke her, what would you do? She is the only one left who cares about you. Once you have lost everything…would you finally try to kill me? You should end this now! Hurry up before I crush your little flower," he said as he slowly pulled.

Blood shot out from her arm as the flesh stretched beyond its threshold.

"Okay. You can stop now," said Kawai, the pain bringing tears to her eyes.

Karson looked at the scene with worry. "Shouldn't I…umm…uh…stop him?"

Bob turned to him with an intense eye. "Don't spoil my fun!"

Exp 8 ripped her arm completely off and flung it aside.

The blood dripped down Kawai's body and onto her brother's hand.

Exp 8 licked the blood off his fingertips, smiling maniacally. "Oh, the nectar of a flower is truly delicious," he said as he gently touched Kawai's numbed-out face.

"Why did you do it!" yelled NoOne.

"I was bored. It's that simple."

NoOne lunged himself forward and flung around his serrated arm.

Exp 8 dodged each attempt with the slightest of movements and then knocked the hero off his feet.

"How could you just murder them all? They were our friends, our family!" NoOne jumped to his feet and then charged toward his nemesis.

"I grew tired of them." Exp 8 slammed his fist into the hero's face.

NoOne fell to the ground with a slam.

"You cannot beat me without hatred."

"Don't listen to him! Get up and win! Remember what you promised? You swore you'd always protect me no matter what! Get up, please. I can't bear to see you die like everyone else!" yelled Kawai, struggling in Exp 8's grip.

"I will never forget that wondrous day. A field of innocent flowers stood before me…and then nothing…but an empty field. How does that emptiness feel? You two were the only ones left. Do not think you were fated to live. I allowed the two of you to grow. I wanted you to lead me to the other fields so that I could wipe them clean," said Exp 8, grabbing his face with psychotic angst.

"How could you do something so horrible? We are not flowers. We are mobile beings!" yelled NoOne, struggling to raise his head up.

"Isn't it funny? It is all going to end at the very place it started," said Exp 8, cracking his wrist.

"Kawai, you remember what happened that day? That was the day I promised to protect you, no matter what!" NoOne's legs shook as he rose to his feet. He stood up straight, powered by determination. "No matter what happens, know that I love you!" yelled the hero as he charged forth.

"And I love you," said Kawai, her arm stretching out toward NoOne.

"Love…what a joke. Look how weak love has made you. Love cannot save you from me…nothing can!" exclaimed Exp 8, his voice overcome with rage.

"Love is what makes me powerful. You may have the stone of ultimate power, but you don't have love! It is something you will never understand!" yelled NoOne.

Energy burst out of him, blanketing him in a shadowy aura of power.

"The world shall end how it started, as a field with no life. It is time for me to end your feeble rebellion." Exp 8 tossed the girl aside.

NoOne fired shadow balls in the ground as the villain created a huge black orb.

"Come on, brother, let's finish what was started!" yelled Exp 8 as he charged toward the hero.

The shadow hand rose up, smashing through the plexiglass.

"How did you get so powerful?" exclaimed Exp 8, stepping back in fear.

"I fight to protect the ones I love. My family, my friends—you murdered them. Now Kawai is the only one left. I won't let you take her away from me!"

The hand slammed into the villain, smashing him into the ground.

"You won't win this!" yelled Exp 8, rising from his imprint.

"He got up!" exclaimed Kawai.

"We can clearly see that," said Bob.

NoOne punched his own back furiously, causing it to shoot forward and pummel his nemesis.

After charging forward, Exp 8 slammed his orb into the hero's chest.

The shadow master exploded into bits.

"How could I still have lost!" exclaimed NoOne, dropping his heroic accent.

"It must be genetic." Exp 8 turned to face his sister who was bleeding out from her missing arm. "Oh my god, are you okay? I didn't mean to hurt you!" he cried, blowing on her wound.

"I had no idea you had a dark side to you! When you pulled off my arm…I was in heaven. Look, twins," said Kawai, bumping her stub against his.

"This is insane. What the hell came over me? Was I being manipulated? Was Devlin controlling me!"

"Hush, hush, my darling. There's no need to freak out. It goes right back in, see?" Kawai put her broken arm to her stub and screwed it back in place.

"I don't know what came over me," said Exp 8, looking down in horror.

"I think I got a little wet when you tasted my blood," said Kawai with saliva dripping from her mouth.

"So the bad guy wins…good twist," said Karson with a nod.

"That was very entertaining!" exclaimed Bob, clapping with several sets of spectral hands.

"I can't believe I hurt her," said Exp 8, falling to his knees.

"I still lost," said NoOne, falling apart into a puddle.

"Yep, you sure did," said Kawai with a grin.

"Whatever, you guys won. I admit defeat. The glass is always half empty and cracked. What goes down stays down. The moon can only block the sun's light. Ugh, nothing changes," said NoOne as he slid under the door.

"Hey, Bob, check to see if NoOne broke through all the plexiglass. Hope that little charade paid off in the end," said Exp 8, pointing up.

Karson fired a bullet at the ceiling that bounced off. "Nope, still there. Look comrades, a door!"

"More like four doors. Ugh, why won't Devlin just tell us where to go?" asked Kawai with shrug.

"Maybe we should split up," said Bob.

"What if it's a trap?" asked Karson.

"We've handled our fair share of traps," said Exp 8 confidently.

"I don't want to split up," said Kawai in tears, latching onto his arm.

Bob loomed above the meek girl. "If we don't charge headfirst into this, then that means we fear Devlin. Isn't that what you always say?" he asked, turning to Exp 8 with a smile.

"It's our best bet. Besides, how many more Exps could Devlin possibly have?" asked Exp 8.

"I like the evil you more. He's smarter and he says my blood is tasty," said Kawai, smiling in bliss.

"Look, we'll probably just have a one-on-one battle. If I come across Violet, I'm going to avenge my brother!" said Exp 8, clenching his trembling fist.

"He's not worth the trouble," said Kawai, calming his hand.

"Nina and the others will be fine. Let's just defeat whatever's in our way!" exclaimed Bob.

"We'll meet up soon. I promise."

"When we do meet up…can I get a kiss?" asked Kawai, wagging her tail.

Exp 8 embraced her and gave her forehead a kiss. "Everyone, play it safe. We're almost out of this."

The Freedom Forcers each entered a separate arena. As soon as they arrived in the next room, the walls behind them rotated, leaving no entrance or exit.

"Wow, how cool! You've got loads of guns. Are they real or do they just shoot water?" asked Destructus Supplious, poking Karson's arms curiously.

"They're real enough to bust a cap in your ass," said Karson, flexing his arms.

"You said a bad word! I'm gonna tell Mommy right after you go bye-bye."

Bob was sent back to the hallway they came from. He went down the hall and into the room where Reflector had been. "A mirror puzzle?" he asked with a wide eye.

"More like a puzzle boss," said Reflector, camouflaged by hundreds of mirrors.

"Even better," said Bob with a smirk.

Kawai entered a small room with a familiar Exp waiting in the center. "You! You're the one who killed him!" she yelled furiously, lunging at Violet.

"What the hell are you?" asked Exp 8, looking at the most disease ridden thing he had ever seen.

"Amthraahksh," it said in a gurgled tone.

"Destroy them! No wait, knock them out!" yelled Devlin from above.

Chapter 32: New vs Old

The room Karson entered was identical to the room they had just exited from. It looked identical to the room that Exp 8 and Kawai were currently trapped in.

Destructus Supplious took an unsharpened pencil the length of a spear out from his book bag.

"Are you actually going to fight me with school supplies? Are you a lunatic? This is just absurd," said Karson, struggling to hold in his laughter.

D.S. took off the correction tape that covered his mouth. "I am Destructus Supplious!"

Five rows of jagged teeth encircled the inner walls of his mouth. The teeth rotated inside, quickly gaining speed.

D.S. plunged the pencil into his mouth, swiftly sharpening it.

Karson ran at the enemy with guns ablaze.

D.S. used quick but slight movements to dodge most of the bullets while sharpening his weapon. He leaped behind the gun guy and jabbed his head forward.

The pencil's eraser hit the shiny red button directly.

Karson combusted into flames, sending shrapnel flying every which way.

D.S. shielded his face with his arms before jumping back to his feet. He then took the pencil out of his mouth.

It was now razor-sharp, gleaming at its tip.

"Yay, explode again! Wait…why is your boom button so easy to hit?" Destructus Supplious reached into his book bag and pulled out an electronic pad.

Karson magically came back to life.

"Some prick broke into the lab and did this to me! I almost had the bastard too. You wouldn't happen to be him by any chance, would you?"

"Wh-wh-wha…how are you alive? Do it again! Look, I drew a cat," said D.S., showing off his creation.

"You want to know my secret! I can never die! I am immortal!" exclaimed Karson with a Herculean pose.

"But you go explodey a lot," said D.S. with his finger in his mouth.

"I come back after I'm killed, so I'm basically immortal. You should just give up. Kids belong in the schoolyard, not the battlefield."

"I hate school! They're all a bunch of meanie jerks!"

"You can't kill me, which means you can't win."

"Is that a challenge? I'm always up for a challenge!" D.S. ran at the bad guy like a knight, holding his pencil in front of him like a lance.

Karson deflected the pencil with his Gatling gun, hitting the enemy soldier off-balance. He then slammed his gun against his opponent's back, knocking him to the floor.

D.S. rolled out of the way of oncoming fire. He got back to his feet and then thrust his pencil blade at the bad guy's back.

The tip of the pencil barely missed the Button, poking the gunman's back instead. The graphite broke off, apparently not sharp enough to cut through metal.

Karson turned around, swiping his Gatling gun at the enemy in the process.

D.S. blocked the hit with his giant pencil. He ducked a forward jab, having the hulking piece of metal swoop over his head. Before Karson could throw a counterblow, he swung the pencil against the gun guy's head.

The attack knocked the gunman off his feet, but he quickly regained balance.

The pencil split in two.

D.S. tossed the pencil halves aside and took off his book bag. He rummaged through it and pulled out a giant stapler gun. "Let's play bang-bang," he said, loading staples into his gun.

"You're challenging me to a duel? Do you have a death wish?"

D.S. fired a staple that zoomed right over the bad guy's head.

"Very well then. Hmph, I accept. Just so we're clear, I'm not the same soldier I once was. Devlin has given me enhancements, and you appear to be worthy of them."

Karson's arms shifted through various types of guns until he was armed with dual portable Gatling guns.

Karson revved up, aiming in two directions at once. "Behold the refined form of the weapon that made World War I into a legend!"

The Gatling guns sent forth a barrage of bullets.

At the same time, D.S. fired staples that broke through the bullet storm and hit the bad guy.

The giant staples' momentum continued, impaling Karson to the wall.

D.S. was covered in bullet wounds from the assault. "Watch in amazement as my boo-boos go bye-bye!" He shot staples into his wounded areas.

The wounds closed up but did not stop bleeding.

"Does that really work?" asked Karson as he struggled to break free.

"Yep. Staples can hurt and heal! Staples are awesome! Now it's time for you to go bye-bye forever!" D.S. took out a huge roll of correction tape. He dragged the tape along the floor before tearing it off.

The top of the floor had been erased from existence, leaving a narrow opening to the room below.

"What kind of ridiculous power is that?" asked Karson, pulling back in disbelief.

"I have the sticky, um…make-believe and storage artifacts! Now it's time to correct you," said D.S., readying a strip of tape.

"I really don't want to do this. But I've run out of options!" Karson pushed his back up against the wall, triggering his self-destruct button. Missiles shot out as his body exploded.

D.S. emptied out his book bag's contents and pulled out a shotgun sized glue stick from the mound. He rubbed the glue stick on the top of his arms, giving them a glittery coating.

Two missiles from Karson's explosion zoomed to D.S.

The supply master ran up the wall and jumped off. He soared by the two missiles, catching them on his sticky arms. "SIMPLE FUSION," said D.S. posing with his new missile arms.

"Damn it, my missiles missed completely!" yelled Karson as soon as he re-materialized.

Karson's Gatling guns disengaged from his shoulders, falling to the floor. Flame throwers folded out, becoming the gunman's new arms.

"You won't be able to hit me now!" Karson sprayed the floor with flames, creating a burning circle of protection.

"I am Daddy's strongest Exp!" D.S. pulled his arms back and leaped up. The missiles stuck to his arms propelled him forward in midair. He tore through the fire and slammed into the gun guy's chest.

Karson used his defensive might to hold his ground, but the combined force was too much. He skyrocketed backward, still being rammed by the enemy soldier.

As soon as the bad guy was plastered against the wall, D.S. pummeled him with his strong fists.

"Hand to hand really isn't my style!" Karson fired a shotgun blast, stopping the assault. He then fell down from the wall, landing flat on the floor.

"DEFUSION," said D.S., taking off the missiles with a three-foot stapler remover.

Karson's head disconnected from his neck and shot straight up. The three missiles—two missiles and the gunman's head—collided into each other.

The monumental explosion flung Karson and D.S. in opposite directions, propelling them toward opposing walls.

D.S. regained his balance in midair. He ran down the wall into a full sprint toward the gun guy. He then stopped abruptly, realizing his left or right arm had melted off in the explosion. The retired gangster walked to the top half of his pencil and picked it up. He used its broken tip to draw himself a new arm.

Karson's new head popped out, an amazed look etched in his face. "You can't just draw your body parts back! That's cheating!"

"I got the create artifact too. Didn't I tell you already?" asked D.S., sucking on his thumb.

"No! You conveniently forgot!"

"It's not my fault. I can't remember them all. Mommy taught me a song to help me remember them. Here, I'll sing it for you. ♫This is your artifact song. Remember it, it's not too long. If things are getting sticky, so should you. If they shoot at you, erase. If you're gonna lose, then influence. To store your stuff, compact it. And if you get hurt, create! This is your artifact song. Remember it, it's not too long. Keep in mind that if you die. Mommy will forever cry!♫. Yep, now you know it too!" exclaimed D.S., doing the interpretive dance moves that went along with it.

"That's five artifacts! I don't even have one! Hand a couple over to me! Let's make this fair!"

"These artifacts are just for me! And used with my school supplies, I am undefeatable!"

Karson's feet fired rapidly, catching the Supply Master off guard.

A murderous glint appeared in D.S.'s eyes as he quickly spun around his pencil half.

The wood could not deflect a single bullet though, no matter how fast it was spun.

D.S. tossed the pencil half to the ground and then sprinted up to the gun guy. Bullets made holes in his body as he blindly ran forward into the torrent of metal.

"You don't learn, do you?" asked Karson.

"Not true. I love learning! But teaching people a lesson is what I'm really good at." D.S. ducked down, grabbing Karson's leg as more bullets shot into him. He lifted the bad guy off the ground, spinning him around furiously. He then let go, sending the evil doer really far away.

Karson kicked off the wall, propelling himself above the enemy soldier. "Well you're about to get a harsh lesson about the tragedy of war." His chest opened up.

A cannon inched out from the opening. It stretched out further and further, reaching out nearly a dozen feet. When fully engaged, the cannon's barrel pressed against the enemy's forehead.

The Supply Master stared in awe as the whole cannon glowed and collected energy at its top. A wave of energy shot forth, expanding as it branched out. It eliminated nearly every fiber of D.S.

"This is the future of warfare!"

The cannon receded into the gunman's chest.

A large portion of the floor had been obliterated.

Karson flung himself over the gap, landing face down on the ground. He saw D.S.'s thumb, the only remnant of his opponent. "Wow, I really destroyed him! He's the strongest of Devlin's new Exps and I annihilated him!" He leaped to his feet. "I love being invincible!"

As Karson began his fight against D.S., Bob looked around for his new opponent.

"It's times like this that being invisible really pays off," said Reflector.

"Oh, where could you be? Hmm, maybe here? No. I give up. You are just too elusive. Oooh," said Bob sarcastically, scanning the room cautiously. He shot a laser at one of the mirrors that bounced off.

"Guess again," said Reflector mysteriously.

"No, you guess again. Hrm-hmm."

The laser reflected off of fifteen mirrors and then hit Reflector right between the eyes.

The mirror man dropped off the wall, landing face first on the ground.

"Even though you're a mirror, it would appear you don't understand the concept of reflection. Shall I explain it to you?"

"Don't mock me! And keep in mind I have lasers of my own!" yelled Reflector, jumping to his feet.

A laser shot directly through the round Exp.

"Argghehehehahahaha! Pitiful imbecile, I can just phase through your attacks. No power you possess can even touch me, let alone kill me. But please don't surrender. I want to enjoy tormenting your soul in the very limited time I have," said Bob with a malicious grin.

"Honestly, I don't want to fight you. You could just pretend to lose, or I could. It really makes no difference to me," said Reflector, his legs trembling.

"Don't be absurd, I want to see you suffer for a bit longer," said Bob with a wide grin.

"I just need to be alone right now. I'm still healing from the last fight. And I was thinking of how to propose to Matteria."

"You want to marry him now. Well, I won't stop you. I just want to consume your soul. You can both be wedded inside the Atma Blade," said Bob, summoning up his weapon.

"That's damnation, not marriage!" yelled Reflector, backing away in fear.

"You are wasting my time," said Bob, floating up to him.

"Wait, aren't you on our side? You are just a spy on their team, right? There is no need for us to fight," said Reflector, walking toward his ally.

A laser slammed into Reflector's head, knocking him to the floor.

"Oh, about that, I decided to actually join the Freedom Forcers."

"What! I heard that you were Devlin's most trusted Exp!"

"I still am, as long as I kill you. Devlin is a fool to trust me. I betray whoever I want whenever I want. Right now, the Freedom Forcers have a lot less teammates than the Omnipotent Overseers. That means I get to consume more souls if I'm on their side," said Bob, his eye growing with delight.

"I am going to tell Master Devlin of your evil plot if you don't stop right now," said Reflector, his legs quaking.

Bob zoomed up to the mirror man. "No you won't." He pressed the Atma Blade against the mortal's face.

"What is that?" asked Reflector, enshrouded in fear.

"This is the Atma Blade. It is a spectral blade that can slice souls. Do you want to see how it works?" asked Bob, slowly pulling it back.

"Do not think so lightly of me! You don't have any artifacts! MIRROR OF FEAR!"

The mirrors floated off the wall. They surrounded Bob in a cube.

"Now you're stuck!" yelled Reflector.

Bob passed through them and moved up to the nuisance. "Now you're boring me," he said with a dark glare.

"You just went through my attack as if it was nothing. How did you do that?"

"Eyeball Ram."

"PLEXI PROTECTION!"

The components that made up Reflector's body altered and became far more durable.

Bob slammed into Reflector and bounced off as his force was tripled and thrown right back at him.

"MIRROR WALL PLEXI PRISON."

The mirrors from the room moved forward, making a wall of plexiglass.

Bob ricocheted off the mirrors continuously, increasing in force each time.

"Devlin said that, if I win this fight, he's going to get me my own harem. Just thinking about them looking at me while they are with each other is enough to give me a power boost. Matteria is going to be the star of my new harem! It is time for me to end this so my pursuit of happiness can finally begin! *LAIR OF LASERS, FLAWLESS FORMATION*."

All of the mirrors shot forth lasers at the eyeball as he bounced off the walls.

Bob passed through the lasers as he went through the wall of mirrors. He vanished into another room, moving through each wall until he was at the last wall of Devlin's underground lab. He then bounced forward, going through each oncoming wall with precise timing. In this way, he swiftly arrived back at Reflector's room. The Befriender of Betrayal then went through all the lasers until he was behind the mirror man. He spun in place for a while and then shot forward like a bullet, smashing into Reflector from behind. "I thought it was flawless!" he exclaimed, slowly losing momentum.

Reflector was shot forward, slamming hard into the plexiglass wall.

"I refuse to consume a soul as weak as yours," said Bob, turning away.

Reflector fell to the ground, shattering upon impact.

When Bob was locked in with Reflector, Kawai confronted Violet. She zoomed toward the murderer, hatred burning in her eyes. The vengeful little sister spun around like a wheel, smacking the enemy with her tail repeatedly.

"I'm sorry...I had no choice," said Violet, trying to shield herself with her arms.

"Ooooh, you most certainly had a choice! *Sound Shot!*" yelled Kawai.

Violet was hit by the sound burst but did not lose her footing.

"I'm going to make your death a fond memory!" Kawai aimed her fingertips at the brother killer. "*Sound Bullet Barrage!*" Condensed sound beams shot out from her fingertips and burst all over the murderer's body.

Violet's skin and outfit healed as it was destroyed. "You must be careful what you say. Words have great power." She pushed through the bullet storm and approached Kawai. "*RESTRAINT!*" she yelled, stopping the shooting spree.

"I'm not going to let you kill me too!" yelled Kawai, struggling to clap her hands together. Her quivering mouth relaxed into a smile. "You know what, it's better this way. I want to feel your bones crack."

"You don't understand what's at stake! If there were any other way, I would have gladly taken it," said Violet in tears.

"You knew him. We lived together, all of us. And yet you still murdered him!" yelled Kawai, clapping repeatedly.

A souped-up sound wave shot out vertically, knocking the devoted warrior off her feet.

"The world is going to come to an end if Devlin doesn't—"

A powerful sound wave smashed into the devotee's stomach.

Violet fell to the ground, gasping for air.

"How does killing my brother save the world?" yelled Kawai, smacking her brother's killer across the face with her tail.

"Exp 8 needs to get stronger. Devlin has done all he can. Exp 8 is the only hope we have left," said Violet, struggling to restrain Kawai.

"You didn't have to kill Atatasuki. He wasn't a bad guy. He was my brother," said Kawai, wiping away her tears.

"Devlin explained everything to me. Atatasuki's death was the push Exp 8 needed to break free of his restraints. It was the only way to unlock his true potential," said Violet, leaping out of the way of an incoming sound wave.

"That's absurd! My brother doesn't need a push! He's already super strong. If you just gave him a little time, I know he would uncover his latent strength," said Kawai in tears.

"We don't have time. The calamity is approaching swiftly. Devlin told me all about it!"

"What if he's lying? If this calamity doesn't come, then my brother died for nothing!"

"But if it does come, then his death has saved us all," said Violet with shimmering tears.

Kawai spun in the air, knocking Violet in the chin. She then latched onto her chest. "*Energy Drain!*"

The devoted Exp collapsed, her eyes moving around helplessly. "Go ahead and kill me. I understand how you feel. I can rest easy knowing the planet is safe," said Violet, closing her eyes.

"I'm not going to kill you! You are going to repent for what you've done. Your blood will be your payment. I'm going to beat you into absolution!" yelled Kawai, smashing her tail against the killer's back.

While Kawai confronted her older brother's murderer, her younger brother had a confrontation with a hulking monstrosity in the left adjacent room.

"Does it hurt to breathe? Are you incomplete?" asked Exp 8, taking a step closer.

"Thair ish shomthing whorsh thaim boolth gluhmsh ahmt truksh: teasheash!" exclaimed Amthraahksh.

"Okay, so I take it you have the Disease Artifact, right?" asked Exp 8 confused.

"Joo aahr kooraikt. *Teasheash Mealksh*," said Amthraahksh, stretching his arm out to touch the perfected invention.

Exp 8 ran around Amthraahksh, dodging his dripping fingers. "I'm glad you're using an artifact. I won't kill you. So if you could just give up, it will save us both a lot of trouble."

Amthraahksh flung his arm at the armored warrior, who barely ducked in time.

Exp 8 sped behind his opponent. He pulled back his fist and then stopped. "I'm kind of afraid of what I'll catch if I hit you. So prepare to lose to my ultimate attack!"

Amthraahksh turned around, staring at Exp 8 with his good eye. He swayed his arm back and forth.

Exp 8 ran away to the other side of the room as fast as he could. "Now prepare to lose to my ultimate attack," he said, glad to have some distance between them.

His arm shot out a single golf ball-sized orb. His wrist disengaged and floated above his fingertips. The floating circlet created a small gravity field, entrapping the orb.

Exp 8's shoulders opened up, revealing turrets. The turrets aimed at the orb and pumped it full of energy. The orb expanded immensely as each bullet entered it, becoming twice the size of Amthraahksh.

The Disease-Ridden Freak limped up to his opponent. "*Teasheash Aahmmeashuh.*"

"What the hell did you just say?"

Amthraahksh's hand shot off and splattered onto Exp 8's chest, pulsating as it spread sickness throughout his body.

Exp 8 raised the orb of colossal proportions and prepared to slam it down. His determination suddenly morphed into uncertainty. "Who the hell are you?"

"Amthraahksh! *Teasheash Airuhfaimtaiteas*," he said, grabbing his own arm in anguish.

The festering hand pulsated as the other arm inflated grotesquely.

"What is wrong with your arm?" asked Exp 8, trying to shake the sickness off his body.

Amthraahksh backhanded his enemy with his massive right arm.

Exp 8 fell to the ground and then quickly stood up. His palm fired an orb that his turrets quickly enlarged. "Let's do this!" He ran at Amthraahksh with the orb at his side. He then thrust it at the abomination's head, triggering an explosion.

Amthraahksh fell down, headless and defeated.

The force of the explosion sent Exp 8 off his feet. He toppled to the floor, falling right in front of the diseased man's corpse.

The decapitated body stood up from the floor. Its neck grew and then receded, revealing a new head beneath it.

Amthraahksh turned his head all the way around, making it face the wrong way.

"What the hell are you?" asked Exp 8 as he hopped back up.

"*Teasheash Shpralt!*" Amthraahksh grabbed Exp 8, his flesh melting onto his victim.

Exp 8 shot forth a laser net, but it was instantly absorbed by Amthraahksh's body. He tried to punch the monstrosity off of him, but his arm was stuck in the gooey skin.

"Joo aahr shteal choo wheak. Maaht raitee too pea Taifaim's hoasht jait," said Amthraahksh, releasing the Ultimate Exp.

"What the hell did you do to me?" asked Exp 8, looking down at a festering pile of flesh that once resembled an arm.

"Mai paahtea uhbshoarpt eat."

"I don't know what you're saying, but whatever it is, you are wrong."

Exp 8's arm fired off inside Amthraahksh's body, bloating his opponent.

"Shaf mea!" yelled Amthraahksh as he inflated from the inside.

"I don't know where the hell I am! I don't know who the hell you are! I don't know why I only have one arm! I don't know why the hell you are trying to kill me. But I do know something: you have lost!"

Just as he said the final word, the orb inside of Amthraahksh's stomach exploded.

The disease-ridden freak's body parts splattered all over the walls, coloring them with red, murky blood.

Exp 8 dodged the fleshy chunks with his eyes closed, not letting even a cell touch his armor.

"I'm sure he'll live. Okay, where's the exit?" Exp 8 looked the room up and down. "Whatever, I'll just destroy every wall in my path and find a way out of…wherever the hell I am."

Once the final Omnipotent Overseer was defeated, the rooms spun around. A door appeared, revealing an exit from each area.

The Freedom Forcers met up in the room where they had fought NoOne.

"Rejoice, comrades! I beat him! I beat Destructus Supplious!" yelled Karson.

"It looks like we all won our battles. I love being on the winning team," said Bob, putting a spectral hand on each of his partners.

"What happened to you?" asked Karson, turning to his smallest comrade.

"I found her. She's alive…but barely," said Kawai, with Violet's blood dripping down her body.

Exp 8 was the last to arrive. He turned to the blood-drenched chibi of himself and stopped in place. His eyes widened as he was seized by a sudden jolt of passion. "She's beautiful," he said, gripping his chest.

The room started shaking. It then moved up like an elevator. Suddenly it shot up at immense speeds. It then slowed down as it reached the top floor.

A door was slowly revealed.

"What could Devlin possibly have remaining?" asked Bob, his pupil sparking with intrigue.

"I just hope there's not another undead freak on the other side," said Exp 8, stretching his arm out.

The Freedom Forcers walked through the door to see an old enemy, Riufen.

Exp 8 looked at the bony samurai and lowered his head. "Oh great…here we go again."

Chapter 33: Escape

Meanwhile: Devlin was relaxing in the bed he once shared with Nina. He was getting a shirtless massage.

"You can stop groping my butt now. Huugh."

"I'm sorry, Master, it just looked so tight," said Matteria, now rubbing Devlin's shoulders.

"I am very tense. Things are working in my favor, but I can't help but worry."

"Master, you got Kaity back on your side. Cheer up a bit," said Matteria, rubbing up against his creator.

"Kaity only joined me because of Nina. To be honest, I don't know if she'll ever love me. What do you think?"

"I think you're incredibly beautiful. I'm sure she'll fall for you eventually."

"I've never fallen in love like this before. I most certainly had passion for Nina, but with Kaity it's like an obsession. I didn't even think this kind of love was real. It seized me in an instant and it won't let go. I don't want this feeling to ever leave me, but I must keep my priorities straight. I can't succumb to love when I have such an important task to fulfill," said Devlin with slanted eyes.

"I can't imagine why Kaity would go for Nina instead of you," said Matteria before nibbling on his master's ear.

"I made Nina too attractive and now I'm paying for it. It's too bad their relationship will never take off. I wonder just how sunny Kaity would be if they did get together. Hey, stop licking my ear and get my neck," said Devlin, slapping Matteria's hand.

"Nina is just a self-centered narcissist."

"Nina is a seasoned warrior. She doesn't allow physical contact because it will disrupt her aura. Her body is her weapon and she takes remarkable care of it," said Devlin, turning to face his loyal creation.

"I didn't know that. But don't you prefer the old Nina?"

"I most certainly do. She was so kind. She was so loving. But I can't bring her back. The personality virus inside Nina is too complex for even me to decode. Tampering with her personality chip could end up wiping her memory out altogether. I just have to accept that those happy days are behind me. Uugh."

"You still have me. And I'll always love you," said Matteria, hugging his master affectionately.

"I am well aware of this. I thought it was over…when Nina left me. I thought I was done with love once Nina turned sour…but Kaity found some way to open me up. And no matter how hard I try, I can't shut the doors. I'm not sure what to do. I can't let her light destroy my darkness completely. But…a little bit of light isn't a problem," said Devlin with a half-smile.

"So, Master, is there anything else I can do for you?" asked Matteria, kissing Devlin's neck.

"I don't want to get your hopes up. I am enamored with Kaity. Don't expect me to fall for you any time soon," said Devlin, grabbing the boy's chin.

"I was made for your enjoyment. I just want to make you happy. I don't need you to love me. I just want to touch you," said Matteria, rubbing his creator's bare chest.

Devlin sat up and embraced Matteria tightly. "I'm sorry. I was desperate after Nina. I was so lonely. It wasn't right to create you to be my slave. It isn't fair. I can't undo that mistake. I was pathetic back then. You don't need to do anything for me. You are free, Matteria," he said, caressing his creation's hair.

"I'm not upset with you. I like being this way. I have a strong libido, but I can handle it. I know I would have fallen in love with you regardless. You made me to be your sex doll and I don't mind it one bit," said Matteria, moving up and down.

"You are my creation, not my sex doll! I'm not going to use you for my pleasure. It isn't right," said Devlin, slowly breaking the hug.

"But I want you to. I want to be with you," said Matteria before he was silenced by his master's lips.

Matteria's tongue bounced around inside Devlin's mouth, licking every corner.

Devlin parted the kiss and pressed his hand to the boy's powdered cheek. "Soon I will be with Kaity. Before then, I want to make you feel good. It's about time I reciprocate your kindness," he said, leaning into Matteria and licking his neck.

"Master, this feels incredible."

"Don't call me Master. Just call me Devlin."

He gently pushed Matteria down on the bed and started rubbing his chest.

"You don't…have to do this," said Matteria with heavy breaths.

"I want to thank you for all you've done for me," said Devlin, pulling off his creation's shirt and pinching his nipples.

Matteria shook with pleasure, pushing his back up from the bed.

Devlin's arms slid behind Matteria's back and pulled him into his embrace.

"What do you want?" asked Devlin, whispering in his creation's ear.

"I want you to take me," said Matteria, turning away with a deep red blush.

Devlin turned Matteria to his side. "Then I shall." He pulled down the colorful skirt. With a quick whip of his hand, Devlin removed the striped rainbow panties. "Do you mind if I pull up the covers?" he asked with a light blush.

Matteria turned to face Devlin. "You're so adorable when you blush. Go right ahead," he said before giving his master a quick peck on the lips. He then turned around, wiggling his butt with delight.

Devlin pulled the covers up before grabbing Matteria's thighs and thrusting into him.

Matteria's voice cracked as he was overcome with a mix of both pain and pleasure.

"Are you alright...I've never done this before. Forgive my inexperience. Are you crying?" asked Devlin, gently touching just below the boy's eyes.

"I'm just so happy," said Matteria, moving his hips back and forth.

"It is a blessing to be able to bestow happiness with such a simple gesture," said Devlin, pounding Matteria as his hands crawled up his beloved creation's side.

"I love you!" exclaimed Matteria.

"Damn it! I slipped out," said Devlin, quickly readjusting.

"It's okay, Master. It happens to everyone. Woooh-whoah."

"I can't afford to slip up! Not when I'm this close to success!" exclaimed Devlin, thrusting in and pounding harder and harder.

"Just relax! Don't take things so seriously!" squealed Matteria in overwhelming pleasure.

Devlin stopped abruptly.

"Sorry, I forgot how sensitive I made your body. Your anal tract is especially receptive. And it's molded perfectly to my size," said Devlin, slowly pushing in.

"My pleasure is your pleasure. We are one," said Matteria, slowly moving his hips.

"I regret never having sex with Nina. I thought we would have an eternity to explore one another. Even though I made you for my sexual enjoyment...I never once made love to you. I felt guilty...no, I was a coward. I was afraid of becoming like my father. With Kaity, sex isn't even a part of the fantasy. I just need to hold her. I need her to love me." Devlin's breathing rapidly intensified.

"Don't think about the past. Just think about this moment. You're inside me. We're together. You'll never have to regret this moment," said Matteria with a smile.

"Never," said Devlin, hugging Matteria lovingly. He then slowly pulled out.

"Is something wrong?" asked Matteria, turning to face him.

"I made you bleed," said Devlin, lowering his head.

"It's okay. I'm okay. You made me tough. I can endure all sorts of things. You also made me bi," said Matteria, licking in between his fingers.

"I was so childish. Maybe we should stop," said Devlin, grabbing Matteria's hand.

"Nope. Not until you cum. I've got pride in my skills," said Matteria, grabbing his master's manhood from under the covers.

"Do what you wish. Hmm…I wonder what Violet would be like. That beautiful skin…so soft," said Devlin, licking his lips.

"Do you want to find out? I can call her over for a threesome," said Matteria, licking the center of Devlin's chest.

"I was merely fantasizing. I don't know why I even thought of that. What is wrong with me?"

"You're just horny. You know it's not a sin to enjoy yourself. Hee-hee."

"I'm not concerned with sins. Ah…you really are good at this," said Devlin, moaning like a little boy.

"I didn't know you could sound so cute, Devi," said Matteria, licking his fingers before rubbing Devlin's nipples with them.

"I thought my inner child was killed long ago. But ah…I think you found him," said Devlin, squirming in delight.

"You must have been so cute when you were young," said Matteria with glistening eyes.

"I was naive. I uh…used to have…a little crush on Kawai when I was young. I…wanted to marry her. I've grown a lot since then. Ahhh," said Devlin, struggling to keep his composure.

"I still think you two look cute together. So…ready to cum?" asked Matteria, licking his palms.

"Might as well. I need to relieve some stress anyway," said Devlin with a slight smile.

Matteria rubbed his palms on Devlin's chest vigorously while he did some fancy footwork under the covers.

Devlin squirmed around, opening his mouth in overwhelming pleasure. His eyes finally lost their coldness and warmed up. He pulled his legs up and started rubbing against the pretty boy's chest.

His breath bounced off his alveolar ridge and followed a fixed rhythm.

"Kheeh-huuh.Keeh-huuh."

"Master Devlin, you're acting like a kitty," said Matteria, now rubbing behind his ears.

Devlin didn't respond. He was consumed by the pleasure.

Reflector opened the door. "Master Devlin, the Freedom Forcers have nearly escaped. They are fighting Riufen as we speak. Should I mobilize everyone?" he asked with a salute.

Devlin continued to rub against Matteria, lost in another world.

"He'll be right with you," said Matteria.

"Oh, sorry for interrupting," said Reflector, bowing before shutting the door.

"Master Devlin, I'm going to send you to Heaven," said Matteria, before slipping under the covers.

Devlin convulsed in pleasure as he reached his climax.

Matteria popped up, kissing Devlin's lips repeatedly. "You're so tasty."

Devlin rubbed noses with the warm figure as he exhaled with heavy breaths.

Devlin's eyes then became cold once more.

"Enough." Devlin pulled Matteria off of him. He sat up, took a deep breath and then turned to his creation, gazing into his eyes. "You are not to speak of this to anyone," he said with cut and dry seriousness.

"So then, it's our little secret?" asked Matteria with shimmering eyes.

"Yes. Now, I need to get back to work." Devlin got up and grabbed his lab coat from the bedside. He slipped into it and went out the door.

Previously: the Freedom Forcers came face-to-face with the immortal samurai.

Riufen smiled and bowed to them. "I am all that is left of Devlin's Exps. I am all that stands in the way of your freedom. I know it is dishonorable to fight four opponents at once, but I must obey Devlin-sama. Please forgive me."

"Yes, yes, we forgive you," said Bob.

"Thank you. Now, draw your swords!" exclaimed Riufen.

Bob focused his spectral energy, forming the Atma Blade.

"Will this do?" asked Exp 8, shaping his orb into a sword before grabbing it.

Kawai wrapped her pink energy orbs in laser nets to create two swords.

Karson attached a knife to the tip of his Gatling guns.

"Good, now let our battle begin!" exclaimed Riufen.

Bob watched as his allies rushed forward.

Riufen jumped up, took out his spine, and shoved it through all three of their hands.

His spine lodged itself in the ground, rendering them all immobile.

"Bob, come on and fight me," said Riufen.

Karson quickly disengaged the gun impaled to the floor. He ran up to the swordsman and swiped his other Gatling gun at him furiously.

Riufen moved slightly, dodging each attack.

The samurai's rib cage burst through his chest, shooting through Karson's back. He tore out his rib cage and shoved it into the ground, pinning the gunman down.

A smile of joy spread across Kawai's face.

"Oh my! Our hands are touching each other!"

"Not just that…they're impaled together! Hey, I've been wondering…why do you look so much like me?" asked Exp 8.

"You think I'm as beautiful as you?" she asked, beaming at him.

"So…um…who are you?" asked Exp 8.

"You don't remember me?" asked Kawai, breaking into a fit of tears.

Bob frantically lashed the Atma Blade at the samurai.

Riufen quickly dodged each blow with ease.

"You don't remember me!" Fueled by her desperation, Kawai ripped her hand out from the spine. She floated up to the enemy and thrust her energy swords into his chest.

The blades exploded, blowing the samurai to bits.

Riufen instantly reassembled behind the compact warrior and slammed her against the floor. He tossed her away effortlessly and then sped toward Bob.

Kawai ripped the spinal cord out of the ground as she zoomed by her brother.

"Thanks!" hollered Exp 8, no longer pinned down.

Riufen slammed his fist forward at his rival.

Bob rammed into the fist but was sent flying back from the force. He bounced off the wall before crashing into Riufen.

The warrior tried to keep his ground but was shot backward into the air.

Exp 8 thrust his energy blade toward Riufen as the samurai went airborne.

Riufen caught the blade and stabbed it into the ground to stop his momentum. He kicked Exp 8 as he jumped off the blade toward Kawai.

Exp 8 was sent flying toward Bob, who luckily caught him with the Atma Blade.

Kawai fired a laser net, but the samurai quickly slid under it.

Riufen jumped up behind her and grabbed her by the neck. The ultimate swordsman then slammed her down, catching the laser net with her body. He spun around to see Bob rushing toward him.

Exp 8 was still impaled to Bob's blade and was holding a giant orb in front of him.

"*Explosive Sword!*" yelled Bob as he charged forward.

Riufen ran up the orb so softly that it did not burst. He kicked off of it, causing it to explode as he leaped through the air.

When Bob and Exp 8 were sent flying from the blast, Karson broke free of the swordsman's ribs.

"I know you said to fight honorably, but I'm not used to having a sword." Karson aimed his Gatling guns at Riufen and fired rapidly.

The Immortal Samurai ripped out his own intestines and spun them around in midair, deflecting most of the bullets.

As Karson regurgitated a clip to reload, Riufen hurled his intestines forward like a whip.

The samurai's entrails wrapped around the Gatling guns and ripped them off Karson's shoulders. The intestines then tightened their grip, crushing the guns.

Bob shoved his blade into Riufen's back. "I think you forgot about someone."

The samurai ripped out a new spine and stabbed it through his own stomach. It burst out his back, piercing Bob with its sharp, bony point. Riufen jerked it over and over, slamming his rival against his back while widening the hole.

Bob finally passed through him and then thrust the sword forth.

Riufen ducked and then flung his leg up, sending his rival crashing to the ceiling.

Holding a tiny orb in his hand, Exp 8 ambushed Riufen from behind.

The honorable warrior positioned himself so that the orb would go right through the hole in his back. He grabbed the arm once it popped out of his stomach. He then slammed his head back, smashing into the rebel leader's forehead.

Exp 8 plummeted to the ground in a daze.

Bob fell out from his indentation on the ceiling.

Fast as a falcon, Riufen grabbed Exp 8's arm and thrust it into Bob.

The orb exploded, sending Bob flying right back up to the same ceiling.

Karson ran up to the swordsman, firing his Uzi-feet in a frenzy.

Riufen tossed Exp 8 at Karson, causing the gunman to collapse under the weight.

Bob bounced off the ceiling and shot back down toward his opponent.

Riufen sped out of the way and then shot his fist forward like a cannon ball. His hand slammed into Bob, fighting against his downward momentum.

Bob was sent flying forward, slamming into Karson and Exp 8.

Kawai suddenly floated behind Riufen and hugged him.

Riufen thrust his spinal cord through his chest, piercing through the little warrior's knee guard. In a split second, he spun around, grabbed the spine from behind his back and tossed it down to the floor.

The spine became embedded in the ground, pinning Kawai down.

Riufen was hit upside the head by Exp 8's metallic body as it soared through the air.

"How do you like my projectile? Hrm-hmm." Bob rushed up to the samurai and thrust his sword.

Exp 8 turned around in midair with his jets, making a second trip up to Riufen.

The samurai smiled before slamming his head into the Exp's aerial body.

Exp 8 crashed into Bob.

Karson then came down from above and drop-kicked the swordsman's face.

Riufen's smile could be seen from beneath the foot. He grabbed Karson's leg, spun around and then flung his opponent aside.

Bob revolved in place rapidly before slamming into Riufen.

The samurai punched the rotating eyeball, initiating a power struggle.

Riufen's skin was torn off his hands as he slowed down his rival.

Bob's rotation was halted and he then shot off into the distance.

Exp 8 jumped to his feet only to be grabbed by Riufen and slammed to the floor.

"Die already!" Karson rushed at the swordsman. His head disconnected from his neck and shot forward like a missile.

Riufen grabbed the head with both hands. He kept his ground but was pushed back by the missile's momentum. His hand moved in a flash, flipping the missile. Propelled by the missile's speed, he ran up to Karson. He then let go of the head, letting it slam into its master's body.

The missile exploded, consuming Karson in its wake.

Then, like a phoenix, the gunman emerged from his own ashes.

Bob shot toward the samurai from behind.

Riufen dodged and punched his rival down. He hit Bob as soon as the eyeball rebounded, dribbling his rival like a basketball.

Karson's chest opened up, revealing his particle-cannon.

While dribbling Bob, Riufen ran toward the cannon as it collected energy. He slammed the eyeball into the cannon, making it backfire and creating a giant hole through Karson.

Bob was completely obliterated, not even ashes remained of him.

Riufen turned around as he was pummeled from behind.

Exp 8 was throwing powerful air punches, his talons boring into the ground to keep him in place.

Riufen charged toward his opponent as he was violently pummeled by the wind.

Kawai rolled up to the enemy and shoved his spine through his foot and into the floor.

Without forethought, the brave samurai thrust his foot forward, slicing it open to break free of his spine. His foot quickly healed as he charged toward Exp 8.

Kawai latched onto the enemy's leg as he ran forward. "*Energy Embrace Drain.*"

Riufen's leg became limp once it was drained of all its energy. "You have served me well, but it is time we part ways." He grabbed his leg and ripped it off. He then hopped up toward his primary target.

Exp 8 slammed a beach ball of an orb into the bony samurai.

The skilful swordsman caught the orb in his grip. He used all of his might to rip it out of Exp 8's floating wrist. He then slammed the orb into its creator.

Exp 8's body absorbed the massive explosion, leaving him unaffected.

Exp 8 grabbed Riufen's face. "Bye," he said, transferring the damage to the samurai.

As multiple tiny explosions ravaged Riufen from within, Bob rematerialized behind him. Once fully physical, he thrust his blade into the injured samurai.

Riufen grabbed his rival from behind and hurled him over his head.

The Befriender of Betrayal slammed into Exp 8, leaving the eyeball barely conscious.

Riufen fell to his knee, smoldering and exhausted.

Karson ran up to him and smashed his Gatling guns against the swordsman's head.

Riufen collapsed to the ground. He pushed off with his arms, standing back up on his only foot.

Bob rushed toward him in a daze.

Riufen hopped onto his rival and then kicked off, sending the eyeball skyrocketing into Karson.

Exp 8 rose from the ground and limped up to the bony samurai.

"I never got your name," said Exp 8, his hand on his knee.

"I thought we were already acquainted. No matter. I am Riufen, and this is the most exhilarating moment of my life! What am I saying? It is dishonorable to fight so many opponents," said Riufen, striking the side of his head.

Bob bounced off Karson, shooting back to his enemy. He zoomed by, sipping the samurai's soul with his spectral blade.

"It seems I can't beat all of you after all. I look forward to fighting you one-on-one when you get a sword, Exp 8," said Riufen with a warm smile.

"That's my name? Why can't I get a cool name?"

Kawai got up once more and hugged the enemy. "*Energy Embrace Complete Drain!*"

Riufen grabbed onto her. His whole arm went limp. The immortal samurai then collapsed, finally defeated.

Kawai grabbed her brother's cheeks, and shook his head. "How can you not remember this cute face?"

"I don't even remember this handsome face," said Exp 8, rubbing his quicksilver cheeks.

"Where is my wonderful brother?" she asked, hugging his crotch area.

"Who cares? I have you!" exclaimed Exp 8, hugging his chibi tightly.

"My love!" she exclaimed with shimmering eyes.

"Wait, I'm your lover? Is that true?" asked Exp 8, turning to his teammates.

Kawai stared threateningly at her allies, coaxing them to play along.

"Yes, of course. You've been together for years," said Karson, looking at the dry blood on the tip of her tail.

"You two are always in each other's arms," said Bob with a smile.

"I'm sorry, I don't remember you, my love," said Exp 8, gripping the gorgeous girl in a rush of passion.

Kawai embraced her brother with all her might. She was so overcome with happiness she lost control and drained him of all his power. "Damn it, now that I don't need to have fun while he's unconscious...he is."

"You can mope about your petty problems later. We need to leave," said Bob, already using his laser to cut through the wall.

Karson kicked the heated metal and it broke off, revealing the light of the outside world. "I do hope the others will find their own way out of here."

"Kaity, Nina, and Ada will meet up with us later. Let's get moving," said Bob.

"Kaity...that sounds familiar," said Exp 8, slowly standing back up.

"Wait, you remember her?!" asked Kawai, her eyes widening.

Karson peered over the edge. "Guys, come take a look. Oh by Britain, what have I done to deserve this?"

The Freedom Forcers looked down to see they were a fear-inducing two hundred seventy feet above the ground. They also saw that the extremely visible force field encompassed the entire lab. The only exception was a long, enclosed pathway beyond the front door.

"I thought that the top was the only way out," said Kawai, turning to Bob upset.

"Your brother is the one who said that. I just thought it made sense," said Bob, turning away as his pupil went red.

"Stop arguing. How will we get all the way down there?" asked Karson, pointing to the only exit.

"With no fear!" Exp 8 grabbed his cuddly chibi and leaped onto the side of the building.

Bob jumped next, rolling as soon as he hit the side of the lab.

"I don't think it's safe to go down a sixty degree angle! Damn it! Alright, I'm coming," yelled Karson, breaking into a sprint.

Chapter 34: Destructus Supplious

The Freedom Forcers ran down the side of Devlin's lab.

Giant scissors burst out from the metal below and impaled through Karson's chest.

Destructus Supplious emerged, hoisting the gun guy up as he slid down.

"I killed you! You were annihilated. All that remained of you was—"

"A finger," said D.S. with a wide grin. He then flung his scissors down the slope and the gun guy along with them.

"Who the hell are you?" asked Exp 8, looking at the large man while running down the wall.

Kawai grabbed his face. "Are you sure you don't remember him? You did remember the little cat girl! Are you at least going to tell me why you don't remember me?" she asked, breaking down into tears.

"I'm sorry, my beloved...I don't know why...but I don't remember you. I'm sure everything will come rushing back to me sooner or later," said Exp 8, snuggling her as he ran further down the side of the lab.

"You're going to get cooties, you idiot!" yelled D.S. as he slammed his fist into the main bad guy.

The two love birds lost their balance and skidded down the wall.

"You cannot win against the unrelenting power of school supplies!" D.S. quickly took out a sticky note and wrote the word "paralyzed" on it. He jumped up and slapped the note on the living marble.

The note passed through Bob.

The Befriender of Betrayal then repeatedly slammed into the man-child.

"As if I could lose to a marble," said D.S. as he held his ground.

"I'm an eyeball you simpleton!"

"Ew, gross," said D.S. as he poked Bob with his other hand. "That is so disgusting." He continuously poked the eyeball.

Bob slammed into D.S. with great force, nearly slowing his movement to a halt. He then lost the power struggle and was sent flying into the distance.

"You're a strong one," said Bob, zooming toward his new toy.

D.S. kicked off the building, launching into the air. He then slapped the sticky note on the eyeball's pupil.

Bob lost all mobility and plummeted down the slope all the way to the grass below.

"Your best player got beat so easily. You guys suck," said D.S., sticking out his tongue. He used his feet as a rudder, steering toward Exp 8.

Kawai fired laser nets as the enemy loomed closer.

D.S. erased each net before they could open. He zoomed up to main bad guy, quickly sliding to hit his legs.

With super fast reflexes, Exp 8 jumped onto the big guy and dug his talons into him. "Looks like we caught a ride," he said, riding the muscle man down the slope.

The supply master pushed off the ground and then tore Exp 8 off. He grabbed Kawai and then pummeled her brother's face with her body.

"Yes, harder! This is incredible!" gasped Kawai.

Exp 8 shoved his elbow talon into his attacker's neck and then kicked off of him.

D.S. fell off the side of the slope and out of sight.

"There's nothing like getting bloody in a fight, am I right?" asked Exp 8, patting his chibi's head.

"It's now or never." Kawai leaned up to him with rosy cheeks and lowered his mouthpiece. She pressed her lips against his.

D.S. leaped off the grass and back to his feet. He rushed up to Karson and yanked out his scissors.

Oil gushed out from Karson's body and spilled onto the grass.

The gunman fell to the ground, careful not to land on his button. "Don't move," said Karson, aiming his Gatling gun arms at the enemy soldier.

"My big brother once said a corpse is like a flash card. When you turn it over…the contents just might surprise you." D.S. flipped the gun guy over with childlike innocence. "I wanna press it," he said, staring at the Button with wide eyes.

"Push it now or I'll get really upset!" yelled Karson, using reverse psychology to toy with his opponent's childish mind.

"I'm not falling for that!" yelled D.S., whipping out a shotgun-sized glue gun from his book bag and firing it at the bad guy.

The glue spread over Karson's upper-half, connecting his arms together. The glue then spread to his legs, fusing them as well.

Karson struggled to break free but all in vain. He launched his head at D.S., but the supply master quickly fired the glue gun at the missile.

The glue hit the missile dead on and splattered on the floor, pinning it to the ground.

Exp 8 dropped down from above, finally breaking free of a passionate kiss.

Kawai's body convulsed with pleasure, a trail of saliva dangling from her lips.

"My adorable little snuggle muffin, allow me to take care of this nuisance," said Exp 8, his mouthpiece snapping into place.

"She's a girl, weirdo!" yelled D.S., cringing in disgust.

"As long as she looks this good, who can complain?" asked Exp 8, giving her a harsh slap on the bottom.

"Why does Devlin even want you alive? My host...ultimate power...don't kill him...I love Kaity. Destroy the world...blah blah blah! I'm tired of it! He's not here so I don't have to listen to his stupid orders. I'm going to make you go bye-bye! ERASER MODE."

D.S.'s skin turned pink and rubbery until his whole body became one huge living eraser.

"Things are really starting to get interesting," said Exp 8, instantly forming a massive orb. He fired the person-sized orb at D.S. as he tickled his chibi affectionately.

"ERASE," said D.S., moving up and down rapidly.

Within seconds, the orb was erased from existence.

"No power you got can harm me. I can make you go poof with a flick of my finger." D.S.'s head turned to the gun guy. His eyes were shimmering with curiosity. "So...will you go explodey again if I press it?"

"No! It umm...gives you a kiss," said Karson, surprised by his own statement.

"Ewie, I don't want to be kissed. What a stupid button," said D.S., turning around.

Karson pulled himself off the ground and broke his limbs free of the glue. "Stupid. Stupid doesn't begin to describe it! That button is a plague! I am tired of exploding!" He reconnected his head and started powering up his particle cannon.

"I love explosions!" yelled D.S., leaping over the blast and landing behind the gun guy. He then brought his finger down to push the Button.

Just then, a massive orb slammed into his back.

D.S. rubbed his back against the orb furiously, completely erasing it. "Nananananana. You can't hit me!" He plastered Karson down with another blast from the glue-gun.

"Gun-guy, leave this to me," said Exp 8, leaning down and patting Karson on the shoulder. He then turned to the large child and whispered in his ear. "You know, supposedly when the floating balls explode...candy shoots out."

"No way...I love candy!"

"So do I." Exp 8 turned around as he lowered his mouthpiece. He licked Kawai's leg and slowly brought his tongue all the way up to her mouth. He gently parted the kiss, and closed his mouthpiece.

D.S. turned his head and retched.

"Now it's only a rumor, but I think if you hit this orb really hard...you will be covered head to toe in candy!" exclaimed Exp 8 as he created a wrecking ball of an orb.

"Candy!" yelled D.S. as the orb slammed into him.

It burst open, but his rubbery body was unharmed. Also, no candy came out.

D.S. eyes gleamed with childlike fury. "Liar, liar, truth on fire...if you lie, your life will expire!" He jumped forward at the big fat liar and threw a punch.

Exp 8 slid under the punch as he powered up another orb.

D.S. fell over and skid on the ground, erasing an entire trail of grass. He quickly regained his balance and opened up his book bag. "I'm going to staple you to H-E-double hockey sticks," he said, pulling out his staple-gun.

A gentle breeze swooped by the fighters.

"Oh, you mean hell!" exclaimed Exp 8.

"Ooooh, you said a bad word. I'm going to tell Devlin and you're going to be in big trouble."

"Hell is a noun. It is a place with big fires. It is not, by any stretch of the imagination, a curse word. So, who the hell cares if I say hell?" asked Exp 8, bouncing in place to get pumped up.

"I can't hear you!" yelled D.S., covering his ears.

"What the hell is wrong with you? You act like a child, but you look like a hulking maniac."

"Are you calling me crazy? The last person who did that was just bloody confetti after I was done with him. No one calls Destructus Supplious crazy!" he yelled, reaching into his book bag and pulling out a double barrel staple gun. He aimed the gun sideways.

Six staples shot out like a shotgun blast into Exp 8.

"I know how to make things stop moving. You just pop staples in them till they're stuck, making pretty red on the wall, tehehugh."

The staples momentum slammed Exp 8 into a tree. The staples dug deep, embedding him in the bark.

"It's time to erase the biggerest mistake from existence, you!" D.S. jumped forward with a pair of extra sharp scissors, ready for the kill move.

Kawai jumped in the way and flung her tail at the massive scissors.

"*SUPER ULTIMATE OMEGA SUPREME EXPLOSION OF DESTRUCTION!*" yelled Devlin from nearby as his thumb pushed down on a bomb trigger.

D.S. exploded into eraser flakes.

Devlin walked through the rubbery remains of one of the strongest Exps and snatched the artifacts as they fell.

"Nice job! But how did you kill him?" asked Exp 8.

"You actually escaped…I can't believe I failed again," said Devlin on the brink of tears.

Bob yanked the scissors out of Exp 8. "Assemble, Freedom Forcers, let's kill him now. This seems like a good opportunity."

Devlin wiped his eyes and stood up tall. "Don't get cocky. This victory is hollow. I have almost completed Exp 11's battle training. And I still have more than enough obedient Exps at my disposal," he said, receding back into his lab.

Amthraahksh and Reflector exited from the front door, completely rejuvenated.

"I remember you," said Exp 8, his finger trembling while pointing at Amthraahksh.

"How can you remember this thing's face but not mine!" whined Kawai, pulling at her own cheeks.

"I'm sorry, my beloved syrupy pancake. The truth is…I woke up looking at that hideous face," said Exp 8, his hand against his forehead.

"Don't worry, Mommy's going to make it all better," said Kawai, snuggling him.

"Mommy? I thought you were my lover? Are you both? How did you give birth to me?" Exp 8 pulled her to his chest. "No, don't think about it. It must have been painful," he said, patting her head.

Kawai struggled out of the embrace. She looked up at him and then turned away. "Oh, I can't lie to that beautiful face. The truth is: I'm not your lover. I'm just your sister who has given her heart to you. You never loved me, so I took advantage of your sudden amnesia. I'm sorry, Brother, I shouldn't let my love hurt you," she said, hugging him while crying.

"Don't sweat it, Sis. You can't help who you love," he said, tickling her neck.

"This is very, very touching…incredibly so. But can someone please help me?" asked Karson, struggling to escape.

Bob ripped the gunman out from the glue puddle.

"*PLEXIGLASS DRAGON!*" yelled Reflector from behind. A dragon constructed of mirrors emerged out of his stomach and soared toward the devourer of souls.

Bob passed through the beast. He then rushed up to Amthraahksh and shoved the Atma Blade through him.

His blade pulsated, draining the monster of his soul.

Bob turned Amthraahksh around, now facing the glass dragon.

The hideous creature was now facing Reflector and the dragon.

The glass beast lost trajectory and crashed against the extremely visible force field.

Bob fired multiple lasers to protect his allies from the hailstorm of glass. He then turned to the fragile man.

"I surrender!" Reflector shattered into hundreds of fragments.

Bob tossed Amthraahksh aside, drained.

"My portable living mirror is gone forever!" wailed Nina, holding the glassy remains in her hand.

"Haven't seen you in a while. Good to have you back, soldier," said Karson with a salute.

"Remember me? Huhuhu," said Nina with slanted eyes.

"No, who the hell are you?" asked Exp 8.

Nina was knocked off her feet but quickly rolled back up. "First, you aren't affected by my sexy poses, and now you can't even remember my fantastic face! I'm glad I betrayed your team."

"You betrayed us? When did this happen?" asked Karson.

"Indeed she has!" exclaimed Devlin, who had supposedly left the area. "She's not the only one. Kaity and Matteria have joined me as well. You idiots traded Ada for Atatasuki and she was the beginning point for this little domino effect. You made one bad decision and now your whole team has been utterly demolished," he said, while beckoning the rest of his allies to come out.

Kaity and Matteria exited the lab and walked toward Devlin. Kaity had a brand new synthetic arm courtesy of Anthrax.

"Kaity! Why do I remember you? And who's this other girl?" asked Exp 8.

"I'm not a girl," said Matteria, crossing his arms.

"Where do I remember you from?" asked Exp 8, approaching the cat-girl.

"We were teammates," said Kaity softy, unwilling to make eye contact with him.

Ada walked out of the lab and skipped up to the Freedom Forcers. "Hi Exp 8. I'm glad to see you're okay. I'm sorry, but I'm not your ally anymore. You made the trade with D.S. That means I'm on Devlin's team now. But don't worry, I'll always be your friend!"

"That's alright. Devlin seems like a nice guy. He saved my life," said Exp 8, cracking his shoulder.

"That's my boy," she said, ruffling up Devlin's hair.

      Devlin backed away, fixed his hair and took out a knife. "Go my Exps! Kill them all…except for Exp 8. End their pathetic resistance!"

      "What have you done, you insolent child?" asked an unknown voice from behind.

Part 4
The Other Inventor

Chapter 35: Roots of Hatred

Devlin's eyes flared up upon recognition of the voice. His mouth opened, but rage clogged up his throat.

The man who inspired so much hatred in Devlin was a mere dozen feet away from him.

Devlin's head quaked as it turned to the voice's source. His eyes nearly burst upon seeing the man.

The man had short black hair that didn't cover any of his facial features. Rectangular glasses framed his captivating golden eyes. His genuine half-smile was harboring a lollipop. A necklace with a double helix was fastened reverently around his neck. His slender build, air of sophistication, and well-groomed goatee all came together to make him a very charming man. Long, flashy, black disco pants with glitter stars rode down to his white light-up sneakers. He was carrying a cooler in one hand and scolding Devlin with the other, which was harboring a wedding ring.

"Have you learned nothing from your father's mistakes? I told you how my life was ruined after I created Exps. Attachments lead down a path of ruin. Arrogance must be in our genes, heh." He spoke in a charming, relaxed tone outlined with scientific skepticism.

Devlin's fingers dug into his palms.

The man turned to Kaity with a glowing smile. "I am glad to see you have found such a youthful lover." He adjusted his glasses after catching something in his peripheral vision. "Oh, Ada, I didn't see you there. How are you doing, my love?" He opened his arms and moved into an embrace.

"I'm absolutely one hundred percent wonderful! Helping out the Freedom Forcers has been so much fun! I've even been in some battles. But I was very careful. I never lost sight of our wedding ring," said Ada, holding out her ring finger.

"It has been far too long since I've seen your beautiful face. Where's our other son? Hopefully he hasn't become a vengeful imbecile like Devlin. Hehehaha."

"Why are you here, Deceivant?" asked Devlin with a dark glare.

"I was hoping that, if all your plans blew up in your face, you would finally give up. However, it seems that you have another one of my tricky traits: stubbornness," said Deceivant with a shrug.

The front door to the lab shot open and Kanasta came rushing out. He was still wounded from before but not as badly as Exp 8 had originally thought.

"Dad?" he asked, looking at Deceivant with wide eyes.

"It's me, son. How have things been? Have you been getting along with your little brother?" asked Deceivant, putting an arm around his child.

"Yes, I've been looking after him since I got here. He has changed so much," said Kanasta, slightly lowering his head.

Kaity hopped up to Deceivant, her eyes shimmering. "You're the Boss' father. You look so young. Nice to meet you," she said, shaking his hand.

"You flatter me." Deceivant bent down, standing on the balls of his feet. "You know, you were just as cute the last time I saw you." He looked her up and down all the while smiling. "You look like you haven't aged a day," he said, patting her head.

"I don't remember ever introducing you," said Kanasta, stepping in between them.

"You never did."

"Then how do you know her?"

"How I know her is beside the point. The impact of our meeting is what has resonance," said Deceivant, tapping her adorable nose.

"Exactly how long have you known her?"

"So, son, what do you do for a living? Surely it can't be as unproductive as trying to wreak pointless havoc upon the world," said Deceivant, glaring at Devlin with heavy disappointment.

"I'm an assassin. Don't act surprised," said Kanasta under his breath.

The lollipop dropped from Deceivant's mouth. He caught it a mere inch before it fell in the dirt. "I guess you're better off than Devlin. Good job," he said, popping the candy stick back in his mouth.

"I'm so proud of how strong you've gotten," said Ada, leaping into an embrace with her big boy.

"She's your mom. I didn't know that. I could have killed her," said Kaity with wide eyes.

"Then I guess you made the right decision," said Kanasta, patting his apprentice's head.

Karson approached Deceivant. "Sir, it is an honor to meet you," he said, with a prolonged salute.

"Exp 2, it's a delight to finally meet you face-to-face. Sorry about putting that troublesome button on your back. I was hoping Devlin would push it and explode. It's a shame the blast didn't kill him when he did," said Deceivant, combing his hair back.

"You did this to me!" yelled Karson, aiming his Gatling guns at the man's face.

"Yes, but it was nothing personal. Don't worry. It comes right off." Deceivant wedged two thin screwdrivers into the sides of Exp 2's button and gave it a three-hundred-sixty degree turn.

The Button fell off into its creator's hand. Deceivant placed it on one of the Gatling guns.

Karson fell to his knees. Oil leaked from his eyelids. "Is this real? I am finally free of this curse!" he exclaimed, illuminating the deathly button by bringing it up to the sunlight. "You shall never torment another soul!" he yelled before flinging the Button into the distance. He turned to his savior, oil still flowing from his eyes. "Th-th-thank you."

"He's the one who put it on you in the first place. You do not owe him any thanks," said Devlin, gripping his fickle creation by the arm and lifting him up.

"You're right! I should kill you right now." Karson loaded his gun and pressed it to Deceivant's head. "But I'm too happy!" he exclaimed, jumping into an embrace.

Destructus Supplious burst out of his own eraser shavings, alive and well. "Daddy, you're back!" he exclaimed, running right past Devlin and into a hug with Deceivant.

"I thought I had killed you," said Devlin.

"I was just playing around. Can I have my artifacts back now?" asked D.S.

"You nearly killed Exp 8. You've shown that you aren't responsible enough for them," said Devlin, turning away.

"Come on, at least give me the Erase Artifact," said D.S. with googly eyes.

"Alright, but that's it," said Devlin, flinging a pink chunk of plume agate.

"Yay!" D.S. absorbed the artifact. "Hey, can I have my storage one too?"

"Don't forget who gave it to you," said Devlin, placing the gold nugget in the greedy child's hand.

"Yay I'm rich again!" cheered D.S. He then turned to Devlin. He rocked back and forth, put his finger in his mouth and rubbed his toes against the dirt. "Hey, um, little brother, can I have—"

"No! You can't, so don't bother asking," said Devlin through gritted teeth.

"Daaadyyy. Little brother's being stingy," said D.S., his finger in his mouth.

"Pay him no heed. So Exp 04, how are you doing? Have you been following Devlin like I ordered?" asked Deceivant, gripping his creation by the shoulders.

"Mhmh!" exclaimed D.S. with a nod.

"His name is Destructus Supplious. It's the name he gave himself after I gave him permission to have a name. Something you would never give him," said Devlin, pulling D.S. away.

"Only name the Exp that you are going to marry. You don't want to get attached to the other ones. They are not your family. They are just tools."

"You're wrong! They are my family! They are a product of me. I am their father. Even though I hate you with all that's left of my heart. I even treat your Exps like family. It is not their fault they had a prick for a creator," said Devlin with a cold stare.

"Ah, my adorable little prototype! I missed you, Kawai-chan," said Deceivant, his voice rising in pitch and growing with passion as he rushed up to her.

"Don't call her Exp 06! Her name is Worthless Trash!" yelled Devlin, grabbing his father's arm.

"I'm glad you didn't follow my idiot son," said Deceivant, patting his cutest creation's head.

"How dare you! He's not an idiot! He made my wonderful brother," said Kawai, her eyes sparkling and a trail of drool starting to form on her bottom lip.

"No, no, no. I made Exp 05, remember?" asked Deceivant, pinching her cheek.

"I said my "wonderful" brother," said Kawai, crossing her arms.

"Failed Experiment isn't here anymore, he died in combat," said Devlin, his voice dropping and his hands clasped.

"How can you get upset with me for calling him Exp 05 when you call him Failed Experiment? Giving him such a condescending name will damage his ego. Well, that is, if you believe in that sort of thing."

"Failed Experiment is a name that fits him perfectly. He is proud of that name…was proud," said Devlin, lowering his head.

"*Kawai-chan, kami ga kirei ni narimasu,*" said Deceivant in a sultry voice.

Kawai backed away. "*Urusai! Watashi wa chikan to hanashimasen!*"

"Aww, I love it when you speak nihongo. So Kawai-chan, do you want a…lollipop?" asked Deceivant, pulling one out of his vest.

"It's been forever since I've had sweets," said Kawai with shimmering eyes. "Devlin doesn't let us eat…anything…ever."

"That's because it is unnecessary. Exps are self-sufficient. Food is not a luxury."

"Little girls like sweets. How can you deny her what she wants? You are not her father. She is perfectly capable of making her own decisions." Deceivant popped the lollipop in her itty bitty mouth.

"Wow…it tastes like Brother's sweet lips," said Kawai, writhing in bliss.

"So you like it? Strawberry's my favorite flavor too. So, who is this wonderful brother you were talking about? Do I know him?" asked Deceivant, tapping his fingers together.

"She was talking about me," said Exp 8, walking in between his sister and the man.

Deceivant's golden eyes lit up with spontaneous wonderment. He took out some blueprints from his vest and compared it with Exp 8, looking back and forth between the two. "It's really you. I can't believe it! Devlin succeeded! He finished the ultimate weapon! He made Exp 08!" he exclaimed, leaping around.

"Exp 8!" retorted Devlin.

"You have your father's genius, after all. No, I shouldn't underplay this. Son…you have surpassed me!" exclaimed Deceivant, his hands riding up the arms of perfection itself.

"I like this guy," said Exp 8.

"Don't start praising me now! I haven't forgotten how you treated me, you bastard," said Devlin, grabbing his supposed father by the collar of his lab coat.

"Maybe you could show me how you did it. This is remarkable! You can tell me anything. Deceivant is a name you can trust, after all," said Devlin's father with a wink.

"You were the one who put the self-destruct button on my creation! You made Karson suffer for no reason!" yelled Devlin, flinging the detestable man forward.

Deceivant grabbed a tree branch just before falling. "But I did it for your own good, so it's okay," he said with a dismissive wave of his hand.

"How is killing me going to help me?" asked Devlin, his rage now reflected through his golden eyes.

"I was trying to get you to stop making Exps." Deceivant walked toward the aggressive boy but stopped before placing his hand on him. "I was trying to free you from your misguided path. Besides, even if you did die, at least I could save your soul before it was entirely corrupted by vengeance. If souls do indeed exist, that is, heheh."

"I'm fed up with your self-righteous nonsense." Devlin turned to the Omnipotent Overseers. "Kill them all!"

"I am sticking with Papa. He has candy," said D.S., walking right past Devlin and grabbing Deceivant's hand.

"Brother, my contract ends here. I will not allow you to do something you'd regret," said Kanasta, standing in front of his father.

Ada turned to Devlin. "Don't get upset. I just can't let you kill your father. You're going through a rebellious phase, but this is just too extreme. I'm going back to Exp 8," she said, condensing into a blue ball and floating into his chest. "Oh, by the way, now that the chicken is finally out of the coop, can I call you son?" She resonated with an inner light.

Devlin's teeth were grinding in his mouth as his eyes poured anger into the treacherous woman.

Ada patiently awaited his answer, not losing even an inkling of luminescence.

"I'm joining back with the Freedom Forcers too," said Nina, leaving Devlin's side yet again.

"I'm sticking with the Boss," said Kaity, rushing to Kanasta.

"I will not leave my master's side," said Matteria, his fingers entwining with Devlin's.

Devlin let go of Matteria's hand and pointed at Deceivant with quaking rage. "You're the one who made Matteria a guy, aren't you?" he asked furiously.

"Take a deep breath, Master. I've always been a guy, heehee," said Matteria.

"Sorry Devlin, I just couldn't allow you to fall in love with her. She used to be so cyuuuute," said Deceivant, his body wiggling like a caterpillar.

"I wouldn't fall in love with her; she's like sixteen! I'm not like you!" yelled Devlin.

"You made Exp 4 specifically for sex. I know hormones have something to do with that, but you must take responsibility for this!"

"I can't believe you would even dare say the word re—"

"And I can't believe my own son is capable of such a distasteful act. You are a pox to the Kagaku name," said Deceivant, his body stiff as a mountain.

"My heart was broken. I felt so alone! You can't judge me! I did have a moment of weakness. I did give into my desires. But when I was given the chance, I never took advantage of Matteria. I steadied my lust. I did not give in. I am not like you. I am not a pedophile!"

"So…I really was a girl! Is everything I know a lie?" asked Matteria, tugging at Devlin's shirt as his eyes welled up with tears.

Deceivant took a deep breath and fixed his glasses.

"You say pedophile like it's a bad thing."

"It is a very bad thing!"

"What about Kaity? Don't you love her? From the looks of it, she's around twelve years old? You do have your father's taste in girls," said Deceivant with a wide grin.

"You could never understand my feelings for Kaity. You can't love," said Devlin, his bottom lip flung beneath his top row of teeth.

"I'll admit, I can't fully understand it. But the same can be said for anything. That doesn't mean I haven't felt it. If I was incapable of love, then how have I married and raised children with this beautiful ray of sunshine right here?" Deceivant bent down to Ada and gave her a series of small kisses.

Kawai's eyes flared up. Her tail grabbed Deceivant's head and pulled his ear to her lips. "Don't touch Brother's chest."

"You are just darling," said Deceivant, poking her squishy belly and making her blush.

Just as Kawai's tail rose up with the intent to strike, her brother patted her head.

"There is no need to get upset. Deceivant was just displaying his affection. If anything, I am honored to feel his love through Ada," said Exp 8, his other hand holding his chest with reverence.

"Why don't you want to feel my love? Is it because I'm your sister?"

Exp 8's eyes were filled up with ego. His chest pushed out. His posture stiffened. "I do want to feel your love and I want you to feel mine," he said, pulling her up into a deep kiss.

"Aaah. It's great seeing kids get along," said Deceivant with a wispy smile.

Devlin grabbed the loathsome man's arm. "Don't change the subject! You asked how you could have possibly gotten married to Ada if you have no love. The answer is simple: marriage is a financial decision."

"True, but that is beside the point. Ada and I had a scientific union. No contract necessary. We merely opened the gateway for our electrons to be given and received by one another."

"You cheated! You designed Exp 03 to love everything. That is the only reason she loves a self-centered prick like you!"

"Please don't be upset with him. My hubby just has a different form of love, that's all. It's neither exclusive nor unconditional. It's something beyond our understanding," said Ada, turning red with passion.

"It's called pedophilia!" exclaimed Devlin, his hands abrasively turning to the child molester.

"Don't speak to me in that morally superior tone. Morality came from religion and was formatted into a law system. That system engenders a pseudo-biological sense of right and wrong."

"You take advantage of children."

Deceivant's nostrils rose and his eyebrows slanted. "Now you have gone too far." He took a deep breath and stepped up to Devlin. His fist tightened.

Ada plopped out of Exp 8's chest, rolled in between them, and materialized. "You two are father and son. You shouldn't fight so much. You both love each other, so move past your aggression. I bet you just need to hug it out. Turn that fiery emotion into one of love," she said, placing a relaxed hand on their chests.

"You think I forgot that you were spying for him? I never should have trusted you." Devlin pulled Ada's arm away and spat in her face. "You are not my mother. I have no parents," he said, his cold demeanor diluted by his quivering sadness.

"I was just making sure you were safe. We both were. That's why he told me to spy on you. We were looking out for you," said Ada, reaching out to her son.

Deceivant turned his beloved to him. He wiped the globule of spit off her face. "Don't bother with him. He'll believe what he wants to believe," he said, pulling Ada closer.

Matteria shook Deceivant's coat till it flapped like a frightened pigeon. A frown of worry was painted below his smeared eyes. "I don't remember ever being female. I was never a girl, right?" he asked, hope barely residing in his eyes.

"You were teetering between being a cute girl and an adorable woman. Of course, those stages are arbitrarily set up based on the recognition of patterns in certain age groups, but that's beside the point. I owe you an apology. I never wanted to change you into a boy. Doing so was against all my instincts, all rational thought. It was necessary but…so horrible! You were so cute before! A bit mature but still so…girly," said Deceivant, his hand curving on the boy's chest in remembrance of what once was.

"I am still cute, aren't I?" asked Matteria, his tears smudging his eyeliner.

"Hey, don't cry. I'm sure something here will cheer you up." Deceivant opened up his vest, revealing it to have a concealed stash of goodies. He had twelve deep pockets lining each side of his vest, each holding something different.

There were pockets overflowing with lollipops, candies, chocolates, balloons, kazoos, party poppers, crayons, origami sheets, panties, chalk, dolls, and stuffed animals.

"So then, what do you want?" asked Deceivant, squeezing the boy's nose.

"That Teddy bear is so cute!" exclaimed Matteria, his hand gravitating toward it.

"You mean your Teddy bear," said Deceivant, grabbing the plushy and firmly placing it in the boy's hands.

"Thank you," said Matteria, snuggling the pink bear affectionately.

"If you squeeze, it dances," said Deceivant.

"Really!"

"Daddy, what did you bring in the cooler?" asked D.S.

"It has popsicles, vegan ice-cream treats, water bottles, juice packs, snacks, and sodas."

"Can I have a swirly lollipop?" asked D.S.

"You most certainly can. Ah, you're just like me, a kid at heart." Deceivant handed him the lollipop but didn't let go.

D.S. pulled it out with ease.

"Just not in body. He-heh," said Deceivant his eyes widening.

D.S. thanked him with a sweets-filled smile.

Devlin approached from behind. He whipped out his knife and put it to Deceivant's throat. "You're the one who put that virus in Nina, weren't you?" he asked, drawing a little blood.

Ada leaped into action, but Deceivant stopped her with a calming hand and a relaxed smile. He then turned to Devlin. "I had my reasons. Nothing I do is to torment you. Like any good father, I do what's best for your development."

"How does crushing my heart help me grow?" asked Devlin, his tears trailing down his cheeks.

"I didn't crush your heart. Don't use abstractions in speech. It makes you sound simple-minded."

"I could slit your neck right now," said Devlin, grabbing the loathsome man by his hair.

"Now you're getting your point across. To put it simply, I made Nina egotistical so that the love between you two would end. Love is an obstacle, though it looks like you might need a few obstacles. Where did I go wrong? Huuugh."

Devlin pulled away, still gripping the blood-tipped knife. "Nina and I were in love…and you…you took that away from us. That isn't all you've done. All my suffering is a result of your influence."

"Now you're just being ridiculous. You can't live without taking any responsibility for yourself. My mistake, you can…but you really shouldn't."

"Kill every last one of them! But leave my father intact! I want him to die while staring at the corpses of his creations!" yelled Devlin, pointing the bladed weapon at his father.

"Violence prevails when reason fails," said Deceivant with a shrug.

"Kaity, I can't allow you to halt Devlin's ascension," said Violet Gold, suddenly appearing behind her.

"What ascension?" asked Kaity, her hand on her sidearm.

"How can you still be standing, I thought I killed you," said Kawai, gazing at Violet with flaring eyes.

"Don't worry, I excel at killing. She won't bother us again," said Kaity.

NoOne raced across the ground as a black puddle. He reassembled in front of Kawai.

"Let me handle NoOne. There's no way I can lose to him," said Kawai with determined eyes.

"I lost even as a hero," said NoOne, his head falling off his body. He picked it up and looked back at Kawai. "Uuuuugh."

"Reflector, stop playing dead," said Devlin with cold intensity.

The Exp's shards came together, reassembling Reflector in a mere moment.

"I was waiting for your command," said Reflector with terror in his voice.

"Take this artifact and win your battle!" yelled Devlin, tossing a shiny silver-gray, almost metallic chunk of cubic galena to his creation.

"I'll do my best," said Reflector, trembling as he absorbed the artifact.

"Leave the mirror to me," said Kanasta, walking up to his opponent with a widening grin.

"I am far more than a mirror!" exclaimed Reflector, beating his chest.

"Bob, let us fight one-on-one. This time, don't hold back," said Riufen, unsheathing his spine from his back.

"You've gotten a bit cocky. We can't have that now, can we?"

Matteria moved beyond Nina's comfort zone. Their noses were four centimeters from one another. "It is time for me to prove how beautiful men can be!"

"Just shut up already," said Nina, rolling her head.

D.S. approached Amthraahksh.

"Bring it on, zombie," said D.S., taking out his scissors.

"Shaahmpea?" asked Amthraahksh.

"This is great and all, but who the hell am I supposed to fight?" asked Exp 8, pounding his fists together.

Devlin walked up to Exp 8, smiling maniacally. "It's finally time for me to dirty my hands. Hurting you is going to feel almost as good as finally mincing my father. I am going to imprint my name into your flesh. I will destroy this oppressive world and anyone who dares defy me. And then...Kaity and I will get married and live happily ever after. Hehehehahaha!"

"C'mon, psycho-boy, let's get this party started!" exclaimed Exp 8, leaning back into a fighting stance.

"You will regret ever standing in my way," said Devlin, gripping the knife tightly.

"Is there no man brave enough to battle me? Very well. I'll just watch then," said Karson, sitting cross-legged and crossing his arms.

Ada sat down next to Karson. "Would you like to play Solitaire?" she asked, creating a holographic deck of playing cards.

"Solitaire is for loners. But I'm always up for a good game of War."

Chapter 36: Fights for Freedom

Violet Gold confronted Kaity and took out a cross the size of a steering wheel. She intensely gazed into the girl's eyes. "Devlin has divine work to complete. You must be at Devlin's side when he ascends! I will force you if I must!"

"Go ahead and try," said Kaity, her plasma claws jutting out.

The knives from the cross detached and shot out at Devlin's beloved.

Kaity deflected the flying knives with sideways swipes of her plasma claws.

"If I must break your will, then it shall break. *BELIEF CHANGER, DEPRESSIVE!*" The center of Violet's chest lit up with golden light.

The vigor drained out of the assassin's eyes.

Kaity sat down and grabbed a stray blade nestled between a patch of grass. She pressed the knife against her arm until she got a drop of blood. She then dragged the blade down the length of her arm.

Violet approached from behind. "You shall be transformed through sacrifice. Blood is power! Let it cleanse you of ego!" she exclaimed, placing her hands atop the girl's head.

"*VIOLET, LOVE, ATHEISM,*" said Kaity, using two fingers to grip the knife. She spun around and stabbed the knife into Violet's leg, allowing her artifact power to seep in.

Kaity grabbed another nearby knife and continued to slice open her arm.

Violet looked at her ritualistic cloth and pulled her head away. "Worshipers are fools who replace uncertainty with faith! I shall cleanse myself of this religious abomination!" she yelled, tearing at her clothes with her hands and teeth.

A bottle of holy water fell out from Violet's garb and rolled in front of the young assassin.

Kaity's backpack disengaged her sniper rifle.

The assassin prodigy opened up the chamber, took out the energy canister and poured out the liquid plasma onto the ground. She then poured the holy water into the canister, filling it all the way to the brim. The canister slid closed before she shoved it back into the gun.

"There is only one outcome for this fight! You must—" said Violet before the bullet shot through her chest.

"Give up! You don't want more holy water on your bare body. You have very nice breasts by the way, hee-hee," said Kaity with wide eyes.

Knives shot out from Violet's cross and sped past the girl.

369

Violet rushed up to the young assassin and then jumped up to a nearby tree. She kicked off the tree and pushed the gun up with her foot, making the bullet graze her shoulder as it fired. She landed on top of her attacker in the worshiper's position and karate-chopped the girl's hand as it reached for a sidearm.

Before Kaity could retaliate, the bladed cross was pressing against her neck.

"I am already part atheist. Atheism simply means one does not believe that God is a theistic being."

"And what does that mean?" asked Kaity, slowly moving her other hand beneath her leg.

"It means God is not a physical entity regulating the world from a separate realm. For some, it is the belief in an impersonal god, one which is not always watching. Another version of atheism is that God is not one thing, rather it is everything. Theologians call this pantheism. Then, there are the deists who believe God created the universe before moving on to more important things. Depending on the tradition they follow, there are Buddhists, Jains, and Naturalists that are atheist. Even those who claim to be irreligious are often swept up by secular ideologies such as nationalism, socialism and capitalism. It insults all my beliefs that people believe atheists are non-believers. They have sufficient faith to trust that their personal beliefs will not anger the Gods."

"That's really interesting, could you elaborate?" asked Kaity, stretching her fingers to grip the throwing knife on the side of her leg.

"I can and I shall! You see, some people do not give their gods enough credit. Thinking their god would send someone to damnation simply because they are lacking in belief is demeaning. Should agnostics be sentenced to eternal damnation because they choose to keep their minds open with a healthy amount of doubt? I have faith that God is not selfish enough to do something so horrid. It is the choices people make that send them to damnation, not the other way around."

"So then you were just acting, right?"

"I know I was deceptive, but I was trying to show you just how ridiculous your atheistic stereotypes are. I hope you understand now. God is everything, so all water is holy! Holy water is simply water that has had its prana aroused by an authenticated member of a religious institution. Don't you see? Every droplet came from God. And that includes every tiny drop making up your body," said Violet, closing her eyes with a smile.

Kaity flung the knife into Violet's eye. She then kicked her off and fired her sidearm, unloading a full clip into her target's bare chest.

Violet jettisoned behind a rock as Kaity reached for her sniper.

Kaity slid to grab her gun and instantly pulled the trigger. The bullet pierced through the rock. Blood dripped from the stone's side, signaling a direct hit.

The young assassin sprinted up to the rock, her hand on her extra sidearm. She vaulted over it and was now behind her opponent.

Violet turned around, the sniper barrel pressed against her forehead. "I am not afraid," she said, taking in a deep breath and closing her eyes.

Kaity fired all around Violet, piercing the rock instead of her opponent.

"Why won't you kill me?" asked Violet, reaching a hand out to the merciful killer.

"Give up now or I'll fill you full of holes!" yelled Kaity, dropping a canister as her eyes watered up.

Violet kicked Kaity's legs and grabbed her arm. She pulled the assassin up to her and then pressed her to the grass. She grabbed Kaity's hand and pushed the plasma claws toward the young girl's neck. "I shall not kill you no matter what you do. I am destined to join the Gods at some point, and I am faithful enough to believe they will not punish me for my impatience," she said, her eyes glowing with resoluteness.

Kaity jabbed her other hand at Violet, but the devotee grabbed her cross from the floor and struck Kaity's arm.

"I shall suffer for the Lord as penance for my self-sacrifice. My blood shall stain this cross, just as my beloved Jesus Christ's own blood once did to his own cross! I cannot free humanity of their sin; my blood is not precious enough. However, as my blood pours down this cross, you shall be purged of all of your sins. In this sin of impatience, I shall try at least to save one soul from damnation. I have faith that the Gods will understand my action," said Violet with tears like a river. She then stabbed her bladed cross into the center of her chest.

The blood spurted onto her cross, reddening it with absolution.

"I can see Heaven now…it radiates purity. Kaity, I hope you meet me there. Please…save Devlin's soul. Take my artifact. It will aid you. But in the end, only you can offer him salvation," said Violet, beaming as she faded from this world to the next. She then collapsed on top of Kaity, a smile of content on her lifeless face.

Kaity set Violet's body on the grass. "Devlin is beyond saving. And so am I. Keep your artifact. I don't need your belief to stop Devlin. All I need is my love to protect my family," she said, closing her opponent's eyelids.

As Violet tried to convert Kaity, Kawai fought the Shadow Master.

"So, are you ready to beg for mercy?" asked Kawai, smashing her tail against a rock.

"My love, you are alive. I thought you were killed. Oh no, I'm being controlled. I'm being forced to fight you," said NoOne, clenching his face melodramatically.

"We aren't going to play house! I only pretended to love you because Brother asked for it. Now it's just me and you. I'm going to crush you and you're going to beg for your life, understood?" asked Kawai, her tail smashing against a nearby tree.

"Okay fine, I'll be serious," said NoOne, his head drooping.

"Wait a moment! Won't you make a shadow of Exp 8 just for me?" asked Kawai, holding her hands to her chest.

"I can create shadows of whatever I want. However, helping you would be pointless…like my life…like everything."

"Maybe a little persuasion is all I need to make the point poignant," said Kawai, cracking her tail like a whip.

"You're a prototype of Exp 8. Unlike me, you're significant to Devlin's plot. You'll just end up as Exp 8's lover in the end anyway. And even if you don't, you are still going to beat me. Helping you would be imbecilic."

"I don't care about that! Make me a shadow of him now or I will make you make it!"

"I shall show you how powerful I truly am and then I shall miserably fail! *SHADOW SHEEP!*" NoOne's shadow branched off and created various sheep shadows over the floor. The shadows stretched until they resembled three-dimensional sheep.

Kawai shot a laser net at one of the sheep.

Just before the net hit, the shadow-sheep flattened out. All the sheep then opened up their mouths. Shadow balls poured out as they bleated and moved forward at a leisurely pace.

Kawai levitated above the balls. "You can't hit a floating target, can you?" she asked, sticking out her tongue and wiggling her fingers.

"I don't need to."

The shadow balls bunched together below her. They distorted to create a shadow of NoOne.

"As long as the sun projects light, I will be able to manipulate its absence." NoOne's shadow coiled around Kawai's shadow.

"Why can't I move!" yelled Kawai, her head bobbing back and forth.

"Now, by the law of cause and effect, you will come to me. I may not be able to break the laws of the universe, but I can bend them. It's something, I guess." NoOne's shadow pulled on her shadow, expanding it. "The bigger the shadow, the closer to the ground it is. By enlarging your shadow I bring you down to my level. And as long as I have hold of your shadow, you are powerless against me," he said with rising confidence that mirrored his posture.

Kawai's shadow expanded until she finally touched the floor. The shadow-sheep then ran into each other, combining into a fifteen-foot shadow-ball.

Insect-like legs jutted out from the front of NoOne's body. He then climbed up the shadow like a beetle. Once he was atop the shadow ball, he shoved his hands inside. He then pulled his hands out.

Two cylinders now protruded from the shadow-ball.

NoOne molded the two cylinders, sharpening them. He then grabbed the two cones, made spirals and punched two big holes into the front of the ball. He dragged his blade arm to make a long smile for his creation. Once the final touches were made, he molded a tail from the back portion of the ball. "Behold, my masterpiece. My shadow-sheep have combined to create a shadow-ram! It's too bad I'm still going to lose. Uugh, oh well." He slid down his shadow spawn, landing as a black puddle in the grass.

The giant ram looked down, depressed by its inevitable defeat.

NoOne's head rose up from the puddle. "Don't get all pessimistic, at least try or we won't even stand a chance," he said, patting the horned sheep effortlessly.

"Alright, you finished your little art show! Now let me go!" yelled Kawai, grunting motionlessly.

"Your resistance is so futile that you can't even budge your fingers," said NoOne as shadow hands caressed his prey's arms.

"Damn it, I'm the one who's supposed to immobilize people! You're supposed to be on the ground and I'm supposed to be making you writhe!"

"Don't worry. You're just going to get right back up after this attack and defeat me," said NoOne, sinking into the ground.

The ram kicked up dirt before charging at Kawai. It slammed into her, dragging NoOne's shadow along with her own.

"You can't escape now," said the shadow before ramming Kawai against the ground.

Kawai struggled to move as she was dragged along the prickly grass. "I refuse to die!"

"I veto that refusal," it said as it increased its speed.

"*Energy Drain*," yelled Kawai, her hands lighting up.

"You fool, shadows have unlimited energy!"

"You're wrong. You're an Exp. You made them with energy. That means they have a lot of power, but it's not endless!"

The ram slowed down. "What's the point then?" It stopped completely and rolled onto its back.

"Why am I not surprised?" asked NoOne as he glided up to the powerful prototype.

"You said I can't lose because I'm related to Exp 8. That does make sense. He's just so great. However, I also can't lose because my love shall make me victorious no matter the obstacle!" Kawai grabbed onto NoOne's shadow. "My devotion to him is my own blind determination!"

"How did you break free of my grasp?" asked the shadow beneath her.

"My shadow won't give up until it's been wrapped around his. No barrier on Earth can stand against the determination of my love! *Complete Drain!*"

Her arms lit up as she sucked out the shadow's energy.

NoOne's shadow collapsed and he fell soon after.

"Wow, I should feel tired right now. But I don't. I'm totally energized!" cheered Kawai, her tail bobbing back and forth.

"I can stand…but I don't really see the point in continuing this," said NoOne before collapsing into a puddle.

As Kawai fought for her brother, Kanasta took a stand for his family.

"You are an obstacle in my path. This will be the first time I killed someone for my own selfish reasons. Please forgive my unfairness," said Kanasta, cracking his knuckles.

"I assume you believe you had a reason before?" asked Reflector.

"I killed for suitcases worth of cash. I didn't judge, only executed. They were all just sacks of money, whether they were men, women, or children. I killed the targets with no exceptions. But this isn't business…it's self-defense. I am doing this for the sake of my family. It is not fair, but you must die," said Kanasta, whipping out a revolver and shooting a bullet at the innocent's forehead.

The bullet bounced off, not even leaving a dent.

Reflector charged into the hired gun, knocking him to the ground. He then tore the suitcase out from the man's grip.

"What's going on? I should have dodged that," said Kanasta, leaping to his feet and quickly finding cover behind a protruding boulder.

"You were hit because you are reluctant about this battle," said Reflector, firing a laser that shot right through the rock and grazed the assassin's shoulder.

"Give me back my suitcase!" yelled Kanasta, vaulting over the rock and charging into the thief. He smashed through, realizing it was a decoy as it shattered around him.

A laser went through a nearby tree and shot a hole into Kanasta's chest.

The assassin boss quickly reflected the laser with a shard in his hand, slicing the tree in half.

The tree collapsed on Reflector, pinning him beneath.

Kanasta continued his desperate pursuit. "Give me my suitcase! My world is in there!" he yelled, struggling to yank it out from the Exp's solid grip.

"It is my duty to kill you and I intend to. Even so, I am not insensitive to your problem. If I'm going to kill you, I at least want your head in the game. Fighting is one of my very few passions. Kanasta, I am hereby hiring you to kill me. If you succeed, then you may take this suitcase as payment," said Reflector, smacking the heavy case into the killer's knees.

"I accept your job offer," said Kanasta, looking into his client's eyes with a grin.

"That was quick. I thought you would have found it a tad strange," said Reflector as he crawled out from under the tree.

"I have been hired by those who are too spineless to do themselves in before. This is nothing new. It is merely an assignment now. Thank you, Reflector," said Kanasta with a warm smile.

"I am paying you. You owe me no thanks, ohohoho," said Reflector, standing up and backing away with trembling legs.

"Go ahead."

"You're letting me have the first move? That's very generous of you. But I thought you were going to take this seriously," said Reflector.

"Don't misunderstand. Allowing you the first move will give me a chance to counter-attack."

"Well then, what should I create? I've never used this artifact before, but I'm sure I'll get the hang of it." Reflector's body glowed.

The light shot out in front of him and formed into a dragon. The dragon then collapsed.

"What! It wasn't even three-dimensional! This artifact is useless!" yelled Reflector.

Kanasta sprinted up to the target and punched it with a clenched fist.

Reflector's plexiglass skin gleamed on impact.

Kanasta's hand shot back. He lost his balance and fell to the grass.

"You may be an experienced killer, but you're used to killing humans," said Reflector, shooting lasers out from his fingertips.

Kanasta jumped back to his feet, dodging the lasers. He took out a revolver from his vest as he rolled into the bushes.

The gun was colored like a checkerboard with small black-and-red squares around its surface. It had a sleek handle modified to fit the groove of the assassin's hand. The exit point for the gun was the size of a tadpole egg.

Kanasta jumped out from the bushes and fired at the center of the target's chest.

A checkered bullet skyrocketed into Reflector. The bullet ricocheted and shot through Kanasta's arm.

"My skin is the most durable plexiglass in existence. Not even your special bullets can penetrate it." Reflector created a mirror above, below, and in front of the assassin with mere motions of his arms.

"I have never failed a mission. I cannot fail now," said Kanasta, jumping out of the way of a laser as thin as a spider web.

The laser hit the mirror behind him and bounced off. After reflecting off yet another mirror, it careened into Kanasta's leg. It repeated the cycle, powering up with each revolution.

Kanasta pulled his leg away and the laser triangle followed. He leaped through the center as the laser converged on him. "I had hoped I would never have to use this, but circumstances have proven it necessary." He reached into a pocket on his utility belt and pulled out a fist-sized playing die.

"Are you toying with me?"

Kanasta rushed up to the target, hopped over it, and knocked the suitcase to the grass as he kicked off. "One move and it's over."

"Good thing I don't need to move to kill you," said Reflector, firing a laser at the killer's neck.

The master assassin used a jagged shard of glass in his hand to reflect the beam.

The laser moved Reflector back ever so slightly as it made contact.

"𝔇𝔢𝔞𝔱𝔥 𝔇𝔦𝔢," said Kanasta with apathetic eyes.

The die folded out and expanded.

"If I cannot kill you, then I shall at least make sure you can never escape," said Kanasta, jumping over four beams with a back-flip. He landed on his feet atop the target's rounded head.

"It's over now!"

Kanasta's feet gripped the target's head before flinging it to the ground.

Twenty beams converged at Reflector's chest before shooting forward. The souped-up beam nicked Kanasta's shoulder before piercing through a tree and shooting into the sky.

Kanasta snapped his fingers.

The die folded over the target, covering it completely. The dice was now an eight-by-eight-foot prison.

Reflector slammed the sides from within, but they would not budge.

"Normally this device dooms my targets to starvation. However, since you are an Exp, you will just stay trapped inside these impenetrable walls."

Kanasta pushed one of the dots, turning the whole thing invisible. "Once I am strong enough, I will return to complete the job." He grabbed his suitcase from the floor. He then walked away with his world hoisted over his shoulder.

"Let me out! I helped you! Let me out of here, you bastard!"

"I probably would have given up if you hadn't hired me. I have only lost to one target and that was Bob. However I still got paid in the end and the job's time limit expired, so the result was the same," said Kanasta with a wide grin.

"Wait, hear me out! You can't trust Bob! He betrayed Devlin to join the Freedom Forcers! I know more and I'll only tell you if you let me out of here. Please. Please..." Reflector's voice got more and more desperate as he continued to plead.

"I'm on the Freedom Forcers' side, or did you forget that?"

"Why won't you let me out, uhuhuhuhuh?"

"I'm sorry, but I couldn't risk failing your assignment. I will return when I am able to destroy you," said Kanasta with a salute.

"It really is true! No good deed goes unpunished! I hate you! I curse you and all your children!" yelled Reflector as he pounded against the walls.

"Try to entertain yourself. It may take a while before I can return."

Chapter 37: Old Enemies

While the Assassin Boss prepared to fight an immortal target, Riufen readied his blade for an unwinnable battle.

Bob summoned up his blade and circled around the samurai.

"Finally, we are able to fight without distractions. Unleash all your power!" hollered Riufen, charging toward Bob. He went into the fencer's stance and jabbed his spine at his rival twenty-four times.

His dishonorable opponent summoned a Jiva at each slash, deflecting it with their flesh.

"Cease protecting yourself with these weak shields! I want to fight you alone, blade-to-blade, Bob!" Riufen thrust his sword forward with greater intensity. It tore through the Jiva with ease.

Bob quickly countered the spine with his solidified Atma Blade.

The two blades simultaneously hit each other, clashing on impact.

Riufen lost the power struggle and fell to his knees. "Finally, you show me your might!" he exclaimed with a growing smile.

"You do not deserve the honor of fighting me. You are like a toddler playing with a stick. What makes you think you're a warrior?"

"I have trained every moment of my life."

"You have no real experience. You don't understand the fear of death. You are a mockery to all warriors. You can only keep up this act until reality pounds you into the ground," said Bob before ramming into the novice.

Bones jutted out from Riufen's legs and bore into the dirt. They broke off before he was flung into the air.

Riufen smashed into a tree, frightening a bird perched on a branch above. His fingers bore into the bark, holding him in place. "It is time for my training to bear its fruit for all to see. I will show you just how worthy I am!" He jumped off the tree, rolled on the grass and flung his spine at the dishonorable warrior.

The blade passed through the round Exp.

Riufen then raced behind Bob and grabbed his spinal cord. The Immortal Samurai stabbed his spine into Bob's pupil as soon as the eyeball turned around.

The wound leaked out a white fluid akin to egg white.

Bob passed through the ground and then popped up behind the samurai, who was now fully healed. "You really want a taste of my power?" His eye concentrated energy. For an instant, he became material and fired the laser.

The laser zoomed by, slicing the swordsman's arm clean off.

Before Riufen could react, Bob rammed into him. He knocked the samurai up before slamming down on him from above with a massive spectral fist. "It sickened me to act so useless when we last fought. I was told to let you win.

378

Even so, you failed like a miserable wretch. You lost to a defective prototype. You were defeated by a child. If you want to prove you are worthy, you mustn't lose when fighting multiple opponents. You must grow stronger!" He fired four lasers at once.

The lasers sliced off Riufen's arms and legs. His torso fell to the grass before Bob pulled it up to him with an unseen force.

"Does this mean you still aren't fighting me for real?" asked Riufen, gritting his teeth with rage.

"It matters not. I have already won. You have no sword. All you can do is bite me, hrm-hmm."

Riufen's veins pulled his severed limbs back to his body. The skin joined together, connecting his appendages. The samurai dug his hands into his chest and tore it open. He snapped his rib cage in two and gouged his gut open, letting his intestines drop to the grass. "How can I prove myself worthy? Is it a lack of inner strength or outer?" he asked, pulling out his organs as tears flowed out from his eyes.

"You have a deficiency of both. You lack the inner strength to have a purpose and the outer strength to carry one out," said Bob as his eye glowed red.

Riufen was flung off his feet and suspended in the air.

A beam shot forth from Bob's pupil, tearing through Riufen. The laser intensified, obliterating the swordsman's ribs.

Bob swayed his pupil left to right, cutting the weakling in two.

The two halves fell to the floor, pouring out blood. Riufen's veins burst out from both halves. They ensnared Bob in their grip and redirected his laser.

The laser sliced through the tree in front of Bob, toppling it on top of him. Riufen's veins then went through, signaling his adversary's escape.

The Befriender of Betrayal zoomed through the novice's upper half and materialized behind him.

Riufen's veins shot out, reconnecting his body once more. He rolled as he landed, dodging an incoming laser.

Bob continued firing his deadly beams as he fled from his opponent.

The Immortal Samurai dodged each beam with ease as he rushed in.

"You cannot defeat the Atma Blade and you can't defeat me." Bob shot forth and shoved his sword through the honor-bound simpleton.

The blade drained Riufen's soul essence once it breached his skin.

Bob tossed the feeble samurai aside with a contented grin.

"Don't think you've won yet!" yelled Riufen, pushing off his spine to help him rise to his feet.

"I am impressed you can still stand. Good job," said Bob, patting the potential warrior's head with an outstretched arm.

Riufen rushed up, tightened the muscles in his arms, and then punched his rival with full force.

Bob barely kept his ground as he continued to grin.

Riufen toppled over as his opponent went into Phase Form. He slammed his foot down and spun around. Each attack slid through as the samurai released a flurry of punches.

Bob rammed into the determined warrior over and over with precise timing.

The crater beneath Riufen enlarged as the attacks became increasingly brutal.

Ten spectral fists came out and barraged the samurai.

"If you do not know your limitations, you will end up dying a worthless death!" yelled Bob.

Riufen spat out a clot of blood that covered Bob's pupil. "Limitations are an obstacle I will overcome!" he yelled as he slammed his fist into his greatest obstacle.

The Befriender of Betrayal jumped into his Phase Form, but he was too late. He skyrocketed into the sky, vanishing from sight.

"Honor is not a matter of winning! It is the way you fight that counts! His arrogance was his downfall," said Riufen before collapsing backwards.

A flaming mortar rained down from above.

"You must never underestimate your opponent!" yelled Bob as he crashed down on the arrogant warrior.

The Immortal Samurai's body burst into flames as it exploded. The pieces then molded back together as he reformed behind Bob.

The Befriender of Betrayal shoved his sword into Riufen and drained him until he fell unconscious. "Ah, he's always just so much fun. I know one day he'll be a great warrior," he said with a contented smile.

When the swordfight started, the battle of the sexes commenced.

Matteria walked away from Nina and took out his matter sphere. "I don't know why men can't be dedicated to making themselves pretty. I guess I am the only man who can show the world true beauty," he said, patting his cheek.

"You used to be a woman. That's the only reason you're so attractive. You have no reason to protest about how sexy men can be. Your beliefs are a lie and your emotions are artificial," said Nina, slowly approaching.

"You're wrong! I did not just change my beliefs overnight. Deceivant must have altered my body before I was awakened. I have always been living as a man," said Matteria, flexing his muscles.

"Well apparently my egotism is just a program. It's something that should have naturally come about, but no…it's all programmed into me. The point I'm making is: my true self was a caring person. Which means, contrary to Reflector's misguided claim, I'm irresistible in both body and spirit. How can a gender-bender ever compare to that?" asked Nina, throwing her gloves at him before exploding them.

Matteria turned his body into fire, consuming the explosion. "Gender is socially constructed! It's an illusion that I must dispel! I'm not a gender-bender. I am a matter-bender." He tossed the water sphere.

The liquid ball slammed into her head. It latched on and encompassed her face.

"A gorgeous woman is no miracle. There a millions of women far more attractive than you. I am one of the select few. I am a member of the chosen clan. The chances of a beautiful man are one in a million. Drown in my tears. The world won't take any notice," said Matteria, powdering his cheeks.

Nina thrashed around, trying to shake off the water-ball. After her various attempts failed, she ran up to the embezzled boy and hugged him.

Matteria dropped his powder-puff and turned away.

Nina seductively ripped off her shirt and let it fall to the floor without breaking the embrace.

"Oh, I can't resist that beautiful face anymore! I must have a taste for myself," said Matteria, biting his lip. "We shall kiss in a sphere of our own sorrow." He shoved his head into the water-ball and locked lips with the gorgeous girl.

Nina slowly reached into her bra and pulled out a shuriken. She inched it to the boy's neck. She grabbed onto his head with her other hand, intensifying the kiss. The clever survivalist bit onto his tongue, holding it in place. She then dragged the shuriken across his throat while teasing her nipples.

Matteria held his neck as his blood gushed out into the water-ball.

Nina stepped away, the water-ball still covering her head.

Matteria plummeted to the grass as his blood spurted out from the gaping wound. His face fell into her open shirt. His pupils shrunk in fear as he realized there were explosive-tags throughout the inside.

The shirt exploded, taking Matteria along with it in a fiery blaze.

The sphere around Nina's head lost its hold on her neck. The water trickled down, moistening her clothing.

All that remained of Matteria were indistinct puddles of blood.

"*Seductive Ninjutsu, Irresistible Explosives*," said Nina blowing a kiss while pushing her moistened breasts up. "Did you forget that Exps don't need to breathe? I can't drown. And by the way, that kiss was purely tactical," she said, running her tongue up and down the blood-tipped edges of the shuriken.

Nina looked down at the red puddles. "Oooh, I can see my busty reflection in your blood." She twirled the shuriken around her fingers. "Old Nina was a ninja, and ninjas must remain unseen. It must have been so difficult for her. How could she have possibly hidden this boisterous body? How could she not be noticed by everyone who passed by? How could she tie up this beautiful hair? Oh, but it doesn't matter. She is never coming back. If I have to choose between a sexy interior and a sexy exterior, well then there's really no decision to be made. I cannot grope my personality, and I can't drag my fingers through my compassion. It is only natural for me to be an egotist. I am the reason that touch is one of the five senses," she said, giving her finger a kiss.

The puddles of blood moved toward Nina. They all came together, forming a silhouette of Matteria.

"I can't believe I have feelings for you," said the liquid Matteria.

"I distracted you with my irresistible body, and then sliced your throat open like a super seductive kunoichi," said Nina, slowly moving the shuriken across her body and cutting into her bra.

"That was the most amazing kiss I ever had. Even while my throat was being sliced open, the passion was undiluted! Nina, you don't just have an amazing body, you know how to use it too. So…did you like my blueberry-flavored lipstick?"

"I cannot love anything that tries to mask its true self. You must learn to love your natural body instead of poisoning it with beauty products. Our naked self is nature incarnate. It is intrinsically arousing. Any attempt to dress up the body, to beautify it, shows not only insecurity with one's natural endowments but also denial of one's natural form."

"But I use and promote all-natural products. They are environmentally friendly. And they are not tested on animals. I'm not hurting anyone."

"You're poisoning your cheeks, your eyelashes, your lips. You must cherish and adore your true body. Only then can you blossom into a fragrant flower of natural seduction." Nina dragged her hands up her legs, over her belly, and onto her breasts. She then carelessly tossed the shuriken aside.

Matteria stared at Nina in awe, drooling blood. The shuriken swiftly penetrated his liquid heart. "Love," he said as he changed into pink vapor. He then dispersed, carried away by the wind.

"My sexiness triumphs yet again," said Nina, the cuts in her bra stitching themselves shut.

As the battle of female and male started, the fight of freedom versus slavery commenced.

Devlin rushed forth with a steel dagger.

Exp 8 swiped the inventor off his feet and knocked the dagger out by striking the psycho's hand. He then grabbed it and stabbed it into his opponent's shoulder.

"You need to be a little faster," said Exp 8, turning around.

Devlin leaped back to his feet and whipped out a revolver from his coat pocket. "I remember when I first shot you with this gun."

"Really? What happened?"

"You tried to catch the bullet, like an imbecile."

"That does sound like me. But why don't I remember?"

"Maybe the pain will jog your memory," said Devlin as he cocked the gun.

"You are trying to help me. I knew you weren't evil. Alright, let's do this thing." Exp 8 closed his eyes. "Go ahead, I'm ready."

Devlin pressed the gun to Exp 8's head and fired. The bullet bounced off, not even leaving a dent.

"How the hell do you expect me to remember something so weak?" asked Exp 8, scratching his head.

Devlin tossed the gun aside. "Maybe you'll remember the sheer force of my fist!" He jumped and punched his creation in the face with great might. His whole body shook from the blow. "Ow," he said with a whimper before falling to the floor.

"If you think your punch is strong, then you're the one with the memory problem, heh."

"Enough of this!" Devlin pulled out a metal rod from his vest. It extended out, becoming a black steel sword. "I shall bestow you with a new memory. I will give you a mark to remember me by," he said, licking the blade maniacally. He pulled back his tongue and dropped the sword. Blood dripped out from his mouth to the grass.

"Looks like you're the one who's going to remember it. Pssshahhahahahah."

"Dat's not suppusr teh happen," said Devlin, covering his mouth.

"What's wrong, can't arti-kuh-late? Hehehehehahaha."

"I will haff your power! I may not beh able to stob you, but I won't lose!" exclaimed Devlin, backing up while holding his mouth in pain.

"Then bring it," said Exp 8, boosting up to his opponent.

The young scientist pulled out his Taser and thrust it into Exp 8's chest. His greatest creation's body convulsed from the incredible shock.

Exp 8 dug his talons into the dirt and pulled back his fist. He punched Devlin repeatedly, shocking him with each collision. He then gathered all the electricity into his head before slamming it into the madman's face.

Devlin screamed out as his body was fried. He fell to the ground as a smoldering mess.

Exp 8 checked the body's pulse and let out a sigh. "Good, he's still alive. It's too bad that shock didn't jog my memory. Oh well, at least it will help him remember not to mess with me," he said, cracking his neck. "Ooh, my muscles are so tight. Better loosen them up a bit. Ah, this should work perfectly," he said, gripping the scientist's collar.

Exp 8 hoisted the madman up. He then tossed him into a tree.

A branch pierced through the neck of Devlin's lab coat, leaving him suspended in the air.

"Looks like I found me a punching bag," said Exp 8, stretching out his only arm.

While Exp 8 showed Devlin his increased durability, D.S. began his battle with Amthraahksh.

"This will be my first time fighting a real live undead zombie! Eww…you are the most grossest thing I have ever seen!" yelled D.S. as he poked the sick guy's face.

"**Teasheash Tooumuh**." Amthraahksh's body bubbled. He screamed out in agony as tumors sprouted from inside his body, making large pulsating bulges.

"Eww, you're so gross. Cool," said D.S., poking the tumors.

"Theash teasheash eash whuht maiksh mea shtraahmguh. Ai whuhsh a wheakreamk peathoar, puht mau ai aaahm a hoorkeamk maahmshtraahshuhdea!" wailed Amthraahksh, pounding his chest.

"Aha! Here it is!" said D.S., pulling out a tire-sized role of correction tape.

"Ai whoamt rait joo peashtrau mai teasheash!" bleated Amthraahksh spasmodically. He slammed D.S. down with his cancerous elbow.

D.S. crashed to the ground but still kept his grip on the correction tape. Amthraahksh raised his elbow and slammed it down again.

The Supply Master put the correction tape in front of him like a shield.

Amthraahksh's elbow crashed down, becoming stuck to the correction tape.

D.S. jumped up, wrapping it completely around his opponent's elbow.

"**CRRECT**."

Amthraahksh's elbow was erased from existence. His severed arm fell to the floor, painting the grass with its murky blood.

D.S. whipped out a pistol-sized staple-gun and fired at the real live zombie from various angles.

Amthraahksh grabbed the man-child's stomach with his enlarged hand and slammed him to the ground ad nauseam.

D.S. finally lost his grip on the correction tape, allowing it to tumble out of reach.

Amthraahksh's hand deformed and expanded, pinning D.S.'s whole body to the ground.

"Ai whear keaf joo thuh keaft olf hillmess! Rait mai sheakmeash shprait too aifreatheamk! *Traamshpralmt!*"

All Amthraahksh's tumors moved to his little arm, making bloated welts in it. They then transferred from his toxic arm to his patient's body. "Toomuhsh aahr sheamprea shairsh thaaht haahf too much shaiksh .Tha aahr a maikroashkaahpeak oarchea eamshait aur paahtea. Mau fear thair raahth!

Toomuh Aimraahrch!"

D.S. screamed as the tumor cells rapidly migrated and connected to his blood vessels, feeding off of them like a baby. "*ERASER MODE*"

D.S.'s skin softened before becoming pink and rubbery.

"Eafeaim eaf joo kaahm earaish aifreatheamk aahm thuh autsait, joo kaahmmaaht uhreamuhraite thuh tooumuhsh wheatheam," said Amthraahksh, pointing to the man-child's chest.

"Stop babbling nonsense!" yelled D.S. as his skin started to tear open. He thrust his scissors into Amthraahksh as a last desperate attempt at survival.

The Disease-Ridden Freak's flesh spread to the scissors. His bubbling body then pulled them, making them into a gruesome attachment. "Ai gaish tha chuhst raik joo. Mau joo whear moa mea aahsh a teasheash-reataim freak!

Uhrteamalt Teasheash Meaksh!"

Chapter 38: A Taste of Freedom

Amthraahksh's and D.S.'s battle raged on.

The Disease Ridden Freak's hands shook gruesomely, transferring a plague of diseases into the weak man.

D.S. whined like as a child as his body was overthrown by the new dynasty of diseases. The expanding tumors felt trivial when compared to the pain he was in now.

"Too muhch teasheash!" screamed Amthraahksh, falling to the floor.

Destructus Supplious was ripped apart from the inside while throwing up and foaming at the mouth.

"Moa mooooar!" yelled Amthraahksh, tearing at his own body.

His deformed body shook hideously. The putrid skin washed off his body, revealing sleek soft skin beneath. The freak's massive arm shrank. His head flipped around and his eyeballs migrated back in place. Amthraahksh's yellow corrosive teeth expelled the plaque, readjusted themselves and now shined with whiteness.

The tumors inside him decayed, gradually revealing his true figure. Once his spine readjusted itself, he was barely four feet tall. His bloodshot eyes relaxed, revealing calm, white pupils. Amthraahksh was now the picture of perfect health.

"I can't take all this sickness anymore!" he said, holding his messy white hair. He yanked his medical bag out from a pile of muck. The young boy pulled out a lab coat and got dressed. Once he fixed his collar, he sat down next to D.S. "Don't fret sir, your disease isn't fatal," he said, putting a comforting hand on the patient's shoulder.

D.S.'s skin started to rip open as the tumors within him ran out of space. "Anthrax Elephantide will heal you in a jiffy."

D.S. was drowning in his own stomach acid as it filled up his throat.

Anthrax took out a shot from his pocket. "DISEASE EXPEL!" In an instant, he injected Destructus Supplious at every angle imaginable.

The disease was discarded like an exoskeleton.

D.S. emerged from his own festering flesh, completely cured of the onslaught of sickness. "Thanks for saving me doctor. Now it's time for me to play Operation!" He pulled his scissors out from the muck and aimed them at his attacker.

"I almost forgot. Here's your lollipop," said Anthrax as he popped it in the patient's mouth.

"It's tasty!" exclaimed D.S., dropping his scissors and sitting down.

"Now, onto the next patient," he said, picking up his medical bag. He turned around and his eyes widened. "Stop hitting him!"

"What, do you want a turn?" asked Exp 8, his fist now red with Devlin's blood.

Anthrax pulled Devlin off the tree and set him on the grass. He put his palms to his creator's chest. "ℝ𝔼𝕀𝕂𝕀." Energy came out from the tips of Anthrax's fingers and healed both electrical burns and bruises.

Devlin stood up, his skin no longer smoldering. "The pain, it's gone."

"That's a fancy skill you've got," said Exp 8, crouching down.

"I'm not done yet." Anthrax opened Devlin's mouth after putting on a latex glove. "You need to be careful of pointy objects," he said, taking out a needle and thread.

"Idn't dat pointuh?"

"Fret not; this will only hurt for an hour." He grabbed Devlin's tongue, pierced the needle through it and stitched it back together. The stitches fell out mere seconds afterwards.

"I thought you said it would hurt for an hour!" exclaimed Devlin, wiggling his tongue around.

"I exaggerate to lighten the pain," said Anthrax, popping a lollipop in Devlin's mouth. The young doctor then treaded up to Exp 8 with his head parallel to the ground. He dropped his medical bag once he was face-to-face with his patient.

"Um, what do want this time? You took away my punching bag, so now I'm bored," said Exp 8, sparring with the wind.

Anthrax jumped up and wrapped his arms around Exp 8's shoulders. His embrace tightened as he pet his victim's head. "You poor thing. It's all my fault. I destroyed the greatest treasure in the world, your mind. I'm so sorry, kitty," he said, rubbing his victim's chin.

"I may have amnesia, but I know I'm not a kitty," said Exp 8, grabbing the child's arm.

"He's delusional! What have I done! I am a plague on the planet. I hurt everyone around me!" yelled Anthrax, wiping away his tears.

Exp 8 backhanded the kid, knocking him to the grass. "Stop whining! You're a doctor, right? Can you help me remember who I am?" he asked, helping the doctor back to his feet.

"I'm sorry, Master Devlin, I am a doctor first and your creation second. Besides, this…is my responsibility."

"Giving him amnesia didn't really work in our favor anyway. Go ahead and bring him back," said Devlin, changing into a new lab coat.

"Thanks for being so understanding." Anthrax turned to Exp 8. "Don't worry, sir, Dr. Anthrax will fix your broken mind!"

"Wait, you're Amthraahksh?" asked Exp 8, his fist tightening.

"Oh, you didn't know. That big bubbling brute is actually me. I don't have dual identity disorder or anything. The thing is: when I am in my disease form I feel this uncontrollable need to spread my sickness to everyone."

"Is that so?" asked Exp 8, lifting up his attacker by his collar.

"It's not malicious really, it's so I can enlighten them from the deceit of perfect health. I was just trying to give you diseases to make you stronger, but sometimes I take it too far."

"You're damn right you do!" yelled Exp 8.

Anthrax slipped out of his doctor's coat and fell to the ground naked. "Let me explain! Whenever I am in my healthy form I feel the undying need to spread good health to everyone, almost like a virus. It's a bit ironic, heheh."

"Yeah, real funny. Hey, how about you give me a new arm while you're at it. You were the one who made me lose it, weren't you?" asked Exp 8 with a clenched fist.

"No, I wasn't. But I'll be more than happy to help." Anthrax pulled Exp 8's arm out of his medical bag. "I was going to study it, but I'll, uh, reconsider. Lie down."

"Alright, but you better not try anything," said Exp 8, lying flat on the grass.

"I wouldn't ponder it!" Anthrax pressed the arm to the stub. He then channeled healing energy through the arm.

Fibers sewed the arm back in place.

Exp 8 stretched his arm out. "Not bad kid."

"Enough talking! Time to purge you of your real ailment.

MEMORY JOG." Anthrax took out a ball-peen hammer from inside his coat on the ground. He smacked it against Exp 8's head with a bam!

"Who the hell are you?" exclaimed Exp 8, massaging the tiny spot on his forehead where he was hit.

"I'm sorry for hitting you, but head concussions are often both the cause and cure to amnesia," said Anthrax, slipping back into his coat.

Exp 8 looked at him precariously. "And…who the hell are you?"

"It seems it didn't work. I'm Dr. Anthrax and you are my patient," he said as he searched in his medical bag.

"Amthraahksh!" Exp 8 punched Anthrax in the face. "I won't let you touch me this time!"

The bruise on the boy's face instantly disappeared as he was sent flying off his feet.

He landed with a thud, healed the patch of grass, and turned to Exp 8 with shimmering eyes. "You do remember me! I may have given you amnesia, but now you're cured!" exclaimed Anthrax as he embraced his patient.

"So I've been unconscious all this time…and it's entirely your fault?" asked Exp 8, twisting his wrists.

"Correct," said Anthrax before he was punched again.

"Ow, violence is bad!" yelled Anthrax, shielding his face.

Kawai wrapped her tail around Exp 8's arm. "He's the one who saved Atatasuki. He saved your life too. This little doctor has saved a lot of our lives. Oooh, your arm is so buff, teeheehee."

"Wow! Then he would make a great ally," said Exp 8, picking the boy up by his collar.

"Yes…and it would be my p-p-p-pleasure to join you. I am loyal to Devlin, but not to worry. I've, uh, thought things through. It turns out that the best way to help Devlin is to help you guys. So, will you let me join you? I know I hurt you, but I'm not your enemy. I want to spread good health to the world! I'm really a nice guy, okay?" asked Anthrax, putting his arms over his head for protection.

"What, you're joining them too! Is there anyone who is still on my side?" asked Devlin, approaching them with his hand covering his face.

"What about D.S.?" asked Kawai.

"I follow candy," said D.S., sucking on a lollipop.

"That reminds me. Here you go," said Anthrax, pulling a lollipop out from the bag and pushing it toward Exp 8.

"I don't want your candied apology. What I want is your loyalty."

"I'll take it," said Kawai, snatching it from Anthrax's hand. After a bit of a struggle, she popped it in her tiny mouth, sucked off the candy, and handed the stick back to the doctor. "So, Brother, did that excite you?" asked Kawai, leaning into him.

"That's for patients only," said Anthrax, jumping at Kawai.

"Hello, I'm a traumatized member of the family. Don't I deserve some compensation?" asked Kawai, showing off the butterscotch candy with her tongue.

"Let her have it. Just know I'm keeping my eye on you," said Exp 8, bending down to the dangerous doctor.

"Hey Kanasta, you look like you could use some medical attention," said Anthrax.

Kanasta stripped out of his suit and dropped to the ground. "Very well, tend to my injuries."

Kaity jumped out from a nearby bush as Devlin tried to sneak away. "You should stop this right now. You don't need to get vengeance. You're stronger than that."

"Look, Kaity, I may not know your past, but you don't know mine either. It's not a problem. We can learn all about each other on a nice vacation in Hawaii. Right now I need you to show me your power and kill the Freedom Forcers!" yelled Devlin, his hands trembling.

"Calm down! You know I'm on their side!" exclaimed Kaity, grabbing his shoulders.

Devlin pulled away from Kaity. "I have no one! No one to love me, no one to care about me." Tears dripped out from the spaces between his fingers.

Ada dropped her cards and then rushed up to Devlin. "I'll always love you," she said, holding him to her chest.

"Fleeing the warzone already? Ah, another day, another battle, another victory," said Karson, leaning his head back.

Devlin knocked Ada to the ground and stared down at her with hatred. "You were helping Deceivant all along."

Deceivant put away his digital notepad. "And what more could a man ask from his loving wife?" he asked, pulling Ada up to him and kissing her neck.

"Oh my. Should we do it right here?" asked Ada, her whole body turning a bashful shade of pink.

"Ada, there are children here," said Deceivant with wide eyes before rubbing noses with her.

"Oh, you're right. Mmm, I love you so much," said Ada, giving him a peck on the lips.

"The only love I ever had was destroyed by my father! I don't care anymore if all the Freedom Forcers die. I must make priorities and it is my priority to win!" yelled Devlin, dropping bullets as he loaded up his revolver.

"Devlin, look at how your hatred has changed you. You made Violet kill Atatasuki. You're going down the wrong path!" Exp 8 knocked the gun out of his creator's hand.

"I don't care about him anymore. He was made by that bastard Deceivant. All his Exps can burn in hell forever! Enjoy this victory while you can!" yelled Devlin before running off.

Exp 8's jets started to heat up.

"Wait, Brother!" Kawai sped up to him. She looked him up and down. She floated between his legs and patted his crotch-plate.

Exp 8 grabbed her hand. "Why are you touching me there?"

Kawai beamed up at him, her eyes shimmering like the stars. "It's really you, isn't it?" she asked, before snuggling his chest.

"Yes, I'm back now. It's over, sis. We've won. We are finally free!" cheered Exp 8, seizing her in a sudden embrace.

"Actually, Devlin has another Exp. So, we should probably get moving," said Deceivant, putting away his phone and lifting up his cooler.

"And why should we trust you?" asked Kawai, grabbing Deceivant's arm with her tail.

Exp 8 grabbed Deceivant's other arm. "Yeah, who the hell are you anyway? Don't even think of lying to me!"

"Don't yell at Daddy!" yelled D.S., trying to pull Exp 8 off.

"Don't shout at my brother! And don't touch him!" yelled Kawai, smacking D.S.'s arm with her tail.

"Now now, kiddies, calm down," said Deceivant, patting Kawai's head.

"Hands off," said Kawai, wrapping her tail around Deceivant's arm.

"Kawai, sweetie, you should really listen to your father," said Ada, combing her daughter's hair.

"Wait, this man is your father? Just who is he?" asked Exp 8.

Deceivant adjusted his glasses for dramatic flair. "I am Deceivant Kagaku. I thought you knew already?"

"He's Devlin's father. And he also created me and our brother," said Kawai, lowering her head.

"Don't move Sis, Kanasta is approaching," said Exp 8, holding her to his chest.

"Relax, he's with us now. He's kind of my brother, by the way. But you're my favorite brother! Always will be!" exclaimed Kawai, snuggling Exp 8's chest.

"So you and Kanasta are related? How can that be? And that guy made you?" asked Exp 8, pointing at Deceivant.

"He made me too!" cheered D.S.

"Not buying it. Devlin said that he killed his father. Are you some kind of imposter?" asked Exp 8.

"My husband isn't lying. Devlin was making things up to intimidate you. He would never kill his father," said Ada, gripping Deceivant's arm.

"Your husband? Wait, you're his wife? Why didn't you ever mention this before? What else are you hiding from me?" asked Exp 8.

"I didn't want to upset Devlin. I made a promise I wouldn't mention…whoops. I guess I messed up," said Ada, turning light pink.

"You're Devlin's mom! Oh, now it's all starting to make sense. The more I learn about you, the less I trust you," said Exp 8 in a harsh tone, walking up to her.

"Ada's of no threat to anyone. As for Deceivant, I don't trust him either. That said, I have no objections to putting some distance between us and the lab," said Karson, standing up.

"It does seem like the best course of action," said Bob with a smile.

"Everyone, look how wet my clothes are," said Nina, pushing up her breasts.

"They are really wet," said Kaity, popping up behind her.

"So, what's the plan? How are we going to save Devlin?" asked Kanasta.

"What are you talking about? We aren't going to save Devlin. We are going to run away. How many miles do we have to run before we are out of his reach?" asked Exp 8, staring at Ada.

"Papa, is everyone else alright?" asked Kaity, tugging on Kanasta's arm.

"I don't know. Right now we need to come up with a plan," said Kanasta.

"We need to get away right now. We can figure out what to do next after we find refuge," said Bob, burning a hole through the exit door of the dome.

"Alright, everyone, follow me!" Exp 8 led the Freedom Forcers through the confined passageway while gazing at the greenery just beyond.

"So, what do you want to do after we're all free?" asked Kawai, covering her flustered cheeks as she floated by her brother's side.

"We've done it! Look...beyond that door is freedom," said Exp 8, his legs quaking.

"That isn't quite true. This entire area is under surveillance. Until we get out of the frungle, we are still in his domain," explained Bob.

"We will make it out! We will be free!" yelled Exp 8, bursting the door open with a souped-up orb.

"Ah, the air smells so fresh," said Kawai, sitting on her brother's shoulder.

"We need to wash off. I haven't been able to bathe all day," said Nina, covering her armpits.

"Hey Bob, once we get out of the frungle, we'll be free right?" asked Exp 8.

Anthrax trailed behind the leader. "Devlin won't allow you to escape. The only way to be free is to stop him," he said before tripping.

Deceivant picked up Anthrax and hoisted him on his shoulders. "Are you okay?"

"Just a bruise. Annnd it's gone now. Thanks. You're a lot nicer than Devlin said."

"Well, that's not exactly setting the bar...anywhere."

"Did you hear me? I need a bath," said Nina, running alongside her stubborn leader.

"It would be nice to have a refresher after all that fighting," said Deceivant, stretching his arm.

"You didn't even do anything. But he's right. I think a nice relaxing swim is just what we need," said Kawai, twirling in the air.

"Relaxation is the key to a clear mind," said Anthrax.

"Alright, I get it. We'll take a break. A short break. But then we need to get moving," said Exp 8, patting his sister's head.

"Don't think of it as a break! Think of it as enjoying your freedom," said Ada, grabbing his hand.

"You're right! Where is the lake we went to last time?" asked Exp 8, his eyes shimmering.

"Why go to a lake when you can have a bath in an authentic onsen?" asked Deceivant, pushing through a thicket of leaves.

Kawai floated up to him and her eyes lit up. "It's a hot spring!"

"The natural spring water should help us think more clearly," said Anthrax, hopping off Deceivant's shoulders before stripping down.

"I'm going in first," said Nina, pushing him out of the way.

"What? We don't have time for this," said Exp 8.

"He's right; we have to all go in at once," said Deceivant, smiling at his cutest creation.

"You'd like that, wouldn't you?" asked Kawai with suspicious eyes.

"Oh absolutely!" exclaimed Deceivant, hugging her abruptly.

Kawai yanked him off with her tail and waved it in front of him.

"Let's hurry it up then," said Exp 8, beckoning the rest of his team.

"I will not strip in front of you," said Nina with a turn of the head.

"You strip all the time. What the hell's your problem with it now?" asked Exp 8 as he slowly entered the hot spring.

"My body is a weapon. If I just show it off carelessly, then my enemies may become impervious to it," said Nina, crossing her legs.

"We are your allies. There's no need to worry. That is, unless you are planning on betraying us," said Karson, folding his uniform before leaping in.

"Every time my sexiness is exposed, my aura is slightly weakened. If I am seen too much, I will be unable to fight," said Nina her eyes to the ground.

"Then go in after us," said Kawai, stripping out of her clothes before making a cannonball into the hot spring.

"Wait for me!" exclaimed Deceivant, jumping in after her.

"I'm going to make the biggest cannonball!" exclaimed D.S., backing up. He ran at full speed before leaping forth. He rolled into a ball and made a huge splash.

"Come on, Papa, slip out of the suit," said Kaity, tugging on Kanasta's clothes.

"An assassin must always be prepared. We must both stay equipped," said Kanasta, picking up his protégé before leaping into the bath.

The splash he made reached the trees.

"Looks like I made the biggest," said Kanasta, landing behind D.S. with a wide grin.

The splash reached Matteria, who was standing at the edge of the hot spring.

Exp 8 pulled his sister behind him and turned to Matteria. "I knew Devlin would ambush us," he said, getting an orb ready.

"I'm not here to hurt anyone. I came to talk…to Deceivant," said Matteria, his voice quivering.

"Well then, come on in," said Deceivant tapping the water.

"It's just not the same," said Kaity, pulling at her suit with a frown.

"Ah, the water feels so wonderful," said Ada, floating on its surface.

"Matteria, the best way to help Devlin is to fight against him. You really should reconsider," said Anthrax.

The matter-changer walked out from the trees wearing a pink one-piece swimsuit.

"Where is your manly pride?" asked Karson with extended arms.

"Right here," said Matteria, pushing out his butt.

"It isn't natural," said Karson, turning away.

Nina walked out of the foliage, covering her chest.

"I found a lake nearby. Don't leave me behind," she said, before walking off.

"Just be careful!" hollered Exp 8.

"So, sweetie, why are you so upset with Deceivant?" asked Ada, petting Kawai's head.

"He made me to be a love doll. I am an individual. I don't exist for someone else's pleasure," said Kawai with puffed up cheeks.

"You make it sound so negative," said Deceivant, his hand to his chest.

"Father, I believe you owe someone an explanation," said Kanasta, pointing to Matteria.

"I don't owe Exp 4 anything. However, I would be more than happy to answer any questions he has," said Deceivant, sinking deeper into the spring water.

"I don't ever remember being a girl. Is what you claimed really true?" asked Matteria.

"I have no reason to lie to you. But I had a very good reason for what I did."

"So then, why don't I remember? You changed me before I was awakened, right?"

"By the time I arrived, you and Devlin had moved onto gropies. You weren't exactly in love, but he most certainly enjoyed your company. Like any caring father, I intervened and forced that relationship to end. Hmm…that sounded rather odd. Anyway, the reason you don't remember is because I made a little mistake. After changing you from a female Exp into a male Exp, I realized your brain needed to be rewired as well. I wiped away your previous memories to end the connection. It was a bit drastic, but hey it worked. Everything worked out rather well," said Deceivant, watching Kawai's tail wag back and forth.

Exp 8 turned to the inventor. "Why did you start making Exps? And why am I so important to Devlin?"

"How could you not be important?" asked Kawai, popping out from under him.

"I made Exps for many reasons. I wanted to fill a gap in my life, but I also had a duty to fulfill. We don't have the time to get into it and it doesn't matter anyway. The problem is that Devlin made Exps to be his companions, not his tools," explained Deceivant, before sitting in his wife's lap.

"How is that the problem! The whole reason we are fighting against him is so we won't be his tools. What are you even talking about?" asked Exp 8, throwing up his fists.

"Just because Exps don't age doesn't mean they don't die. Having attachments to them is a crutch. Isn't that right?" asked Deceivant, pinching Kawai's squishy cheeks.

"Get your hands off of me! Brother, are my cheeks okay?" asked Kawai, placing his hands against them.

"You're fine, don't worry." Exp 8 looked back at the inventor. "You were saying—"

"We've both created ten Exps, but we've done so with different intentions. Devlin makes Exps to be his partners. Exp 1, or NoOne, was made to be a catalyst for Devlin's depression. He wanted to move beyond it and made a melancholic Exp to tip his emotional scales. This backfired, of course, and brought him deeper into his misery. Exp 2, or what you call Karson, was made after Devlin let his hatred control him. This Exp was designed in order to kill anyone who opposed Devlin, and he was also made to be his loyal friend. I bet his betrayal must have really affected Devlin."

"I am a warrior at heart. And a warrior without a cause is a murderer! This rebellion is far more important than my prior responsibilities to ex-Commander Devlin," said Karson, standing up in the water.

"Shall I continue?" asked Deceivant.

"Please do," said Exp 8.

"Exp 3, also known as Nina, was his attempt at finding love amidst his hatred. She was made to save him from being consumed by his feelings of contempt. After she was modified by me—with exceptional results, I might add—he made Matteria. At this point, Devlin was through with love and wanted a sex partner. However, he got too attached and never really used Matteria for his original intentions."

"It's more than that! Devlin feels that creating me for sex was wrong. He said he didn't want to take advantage of me. He didn't want to be like you," said Matteria.

"I'm trying to explain things here. Please, no more interruptions. Exp 5, also known as Reflector, was made to boost his ego. Exp 6, who was named Anthrax for strictly ironic purposes, was made to be his lab assistant."

"About that, after I helped him create Violet, he kind of fired me. Devlin likes to work alone. He also wanted me to follow my dreams of being an international doctor," said Anthrax.

"Exp 7, or Violet, was made as a desperate attempt to become spiritually enlightened. When he gave up on this, he turned her into a loyal devotee. I assume that's when he got working on you. You were supposed to be the eighth. But he got sidetracked and made Exp 9 as a way to cope with his loss. Devlin delved into drugs with this new Exp aptly named Pharma, but eventually gave up when he didn't get addicted. This Exp wasn't even made for combat, as you have all seen."

"Yes, he truly is a pitiful excuse for a soldier," said Karson.

"Devlin then decided to try and find purpose through action. He made Exp 10 to help him guide his anger. You all know him as the Immortal Samurai, Riufen. Exp 10 has actually trained Devlin, fascinating isn't it? To sum it all up: Devlin has repeatedly tried to make Exps as tools to cope with his emotions and has become attached to them nearly every single time," said Deceivant, before slowly leaning back into his wife's embrace.

"How do you know all this?" asked Exp 8, shock outlining his words.

"These are observations made by my wifey. You did such a good job! Yes you did. Yes you did," said Deceivant, rubbing her sides.

"Well, I didn't tell you that Exp 8 was completed. I was worried you were going to sabotage him. Devlin was so happy. I couldn't ruin that. I'm so sorry," said Ada, holding her husband's cheek.

"Worry not, my beloved. Everything turned out splendidly," said Deceivant, wrapping his arm around her shoulders.

"I tried to be there for Devlin, but he still resents me," said Ada, looking down.

"What did you do to upset him? And how come nobody told me you were his mother? You all lived with him, didn't you?" asked Exp 8.

Kawai floated out from between Exp 8's legs. "I'm sorry, Brother, but Devlin made us promise never to speak of it. We do respect his feelings despite what he's done," she said with watery eyes.

Kaity turned to Kanasta. "I can't believe Devi-kun is your brother. You've told me so many stories about you and your brother. Why didn't you tell me it was Devlin?"

"Devlin despises me. I've tried to find out why, but he keeps it hidden inside. Besides, Devlin hired me to do a job. That made him my client until the mission was completed," said Kanasta, punching the air.

"Do any of you understand why Devlin hates you?" asked Exp 8, massaging his temples.

Ada shook her head.

"I have plenty of theories but no real proof. Either way, it doesn't matter why he hates us. We need to find a way to stop him," said Deceivant with a firm finger.

"Hey, Brother, do you think my breasts are good?" asked Kawai, pushing her chest out in his face.

"Kawai, I'm trying to have a serious conversation here," said Exp 8, gently pushing her aside.

"So am I," whined Kawai.

"I think they are pretty and petite," said Deceivant, lining up two fingers over her breasts and tapping the air. "Ah, they haven't grown a centimeter!"

"I didn't ask you," said Kawai, covering her chest and giving him an angry stare.

"Honey, come on, behave yourself," said Ada, combing his hair.

"I didn't mean to upset her," said Deceivant before his wifey kissed him on the lips.

"So, what do you think?" asked Kawai, now pressing her boobies against her brother's chest.

"Kawai, this is serious!" yelled Exp 8, yanking her off.

"So are my feelings," said Kawai, bursting into tears.

"Whoa, sis, don't cry," said Exp 8, moving up to her.

"Uuuuh, you can be so insensitive sometimes," said Ada, patting her lovesick child.

Exp 8 grabbed Kawai's hand and looked up at her. "Sis, you know I care about you. It's just that we are trying to figure things out right now. I'm sorry I hurt your feelings. I didn't mean to. I'm really overwhelmed right now. I would never try to hurt you," he said, holding her to his chest.

"I don't know when I'll be taken away from you. I want to be with you as much as I can," said Kawai, her tail joining in the embrace.

"Don't talk like that. You aren't going anywhere. We are getting out of this together. We'll find a nice little cave far away from this place. It will be right next to a lush green forest. We can spend the rest of eternity together. All of us can," said Exp 8, turning to his allies.

"I was actually thinking of joining the military. The British Armed Forces, of course. Too bad there aren't any wars going on. No matter, I'm sure it won't be too long till us soldiers will be called upon," said Karson.

"I'm already an established doctor. The only burdens on my shoulders are the ones I brought upon myself," said Anthrax, looking up at Matteria with a smile.

Exp 8 zoomed up to the young doctor. "Wait, you've been outside the lab. You've seen the world?"

"Indeed I have. Matteria has too. We are both bona fide members of society," said Anthrax, his head held up high.

"I'm a schoolteacher," chimed in Ada.

"What's the rest of the world like?" asked Exp 8.

"It's beautiful!" exclaimed Matteria, waving his arms up and down.

"It's no more beautiful than the marvel that is our body!" exclaimed Anthrax, standing tall in the water.

"I want to see the world…all of it! I want to walk every inch of this mystical planet," said Exp 8, dripping the warm water on his forehead.

"You're really dead set on this, aren't you?" asked Bob, gliding up to him.

"It is my deepest desire. Devlin needs to realize that it isn't right to put someone in a cage. A bird needs to fly, a fish needs to swim, and a cow needs to graze. We all deserve the choice of leaving our cages…even if it puts our lives into harm's way. The only confine that should exist is the atmosphere," said Exp 8, gazing out at the sky.

"I don't care where I am as long as I'm with you," said Kawai, grabbing his arm lovingly.

"Aww, that is just the sweetest thing," said Matteria, holding his hands to his cheek.

"Eeeeeee!" Deceivant held his chest and took a deep breath. "Wow…that was adorable," he said, trying to re-center himself.

Karson fired his pistol into the air. "Am I the only man here? Exp 8 missed out on a chance to grope a girl. Deceivant and Matteria squeal like little girls. And Bob...well, he's an eyeball. Uuugh, I guess Anthrax is still a man, but he's only a boy."

Anthrax swam up to Karson and looked him right in the eye. "Matteria is very sensitive about his masculinity. Don't insult my boyfriend again," he said with grave seriousness.

"Your boyfriend! I take it back, I am alone," said Karson, his head dropping.

"What about me?" asked Kanasta, towering behind the gunman.

"Bloody hell, I forgot you were there!" yelled Karson, leaping up.

"Why don't you think I'm manly?" asked Matteria, pushing out his chest.

"Because you're not! I doubt you've ever flexed a muscle other than your arse," said Karson with a pointed arm.

"I happen to be a very popular Speedo model," said Matteria, flexing his slender arms.

"You're practically a girl!"

"You have no right to judge him. You're a machine. You don't even have a nervous system. You also don't have a penis," said Anthrax, tapping his fingers together.

"Oooh, you said a bad word! I'm gonna tell Daddy!" D.S. turned to Deceivant and tugged on his arm. "Daddy, Daddy, he said a bad word."

"Son, penis is a socially acceptable scientific term. He said nothing improper."

"Mom, Daddy is talking weird. Oh, and he said a really bad word," said D.S., pointing at Deceivant while biting his thumb.

"Oh, come here. Mommy is going to teach you something new," said Ada, setting D.S. on her lap.

"Yay, learning!" cheered D.S.

"By the way, Doctor, I am very well endowed!" exclaimed Karson.

A tank cannon rose out from the bath, stretching out at least five feet.

Matteria's eyes glistened. "What an amazing dick. Fire when ready," he said, opening his mouth as wide as he could.

"Um...you'd die," said Karson bluntly.

"Au contraire, I'd die if I didn't get a taste." Matteria's hand inched closer to the rock-hard cannon.

"Keep it in your pants!" yelled Anthrax, slapping Matteria's hand.

"I was just proving that I'm not like Reflector," said Karson, pulling his cannon back in.

"Reflector may not have a tongue, a nose, or a dick, but he's still a man," retorted Matteria.

"You're awfully defensive, aren't you?" asked Karson, leaning against the side of the onsen.

"Well, you did just insult his boyfriend," said Bob while telepathically splashing D.S.

"His what! You mean you and Reflector were—Matteria!" yelled Anthrax, his eyes flaring up.

"Oh uh, heheh, well, it's…uh…there's a reason for it. It's a good reason, heh."

"I'm listening," said Anthrax, forcing a smile.

"Funny story, you see, we uh…we were both in France. He needed me. You weren't there. It was only a temporary thing. It didn't mean anything. I—"

"We need to talk," said Anthrax, beckoning his fickle boyfriend with his pointer finger.

"I need physical contact. I was made that way. I can't control how I feel. It isn't my fault," said Matteria as his jealous partner pulled him out of the bath.

"They bicker like they're married," said Karson, turning away with a frown.

"Why don't we bicker like that?" asked Kawai, snuggling up to her big brother.

"You have overflowing love for me. And I try to see things introspectively. There's no need to bicker," said Exp 8, rubbing her head sweetly.

"Sooo…wanna feel me up?" asked Kawai, pushing up her little breasts.

"No, I don't. Uuuh. I don't want to be a propagator of false hope," said Exp 8, straightening his back.

"Oh…okay. Um…they're really soft though. Deceivant, t-tell him," said Kawai, trying to hold back her tears.

"Think of a cold, rounded sheet of metal. Got it? Good. Now imagine this. The inside of this metal is filled with a viscous fluid. And at the tip of the metal sheet is a pink, perky node. Then it's overlaid with synthetic skin that smoothes out the whole structure. That is what her breasts are like. But it has been a while. Maybe a little gropey will offer new data," said Deceivant, his fingers moving closer to her.

Exp 8 stepped in his path and then turned to Kawai. His hands pressed against her soft chest. He moved them around while smiling at her.

Kawai started breathing heavily. "So…haaah…what do you think?" she asked, rubbing up against his hands.

"They are soft and bubbly, just like you," said Exp 8, tapping her nose affectionately.

Kawai pulled away and hid her blush in her tail.

"Alright, so what's the plan?" asked Exp 8, turning to his allies.

"The plan is to get relaxed so we can think clearly. Did I get it right?" asked Ada, turning to her hubby.

"You sure did," said Deceivant, pinching his wifey's cheeks.

Anthrax came back in the bath, his head held up high. "Ada's right. You need to relax. As long as you're covering up, you can't fully enjoy the bath," he said, stretching his legs out.

"I can't just get naked," said Exp 8, tightening his shoulders and covering his crotch.

"Why not? You're the one who told me that my body was a beautiful thing. That was very sweet of you. But, your body is a beautiful thing too," said Ada, putting her hand on his shoulder.

"It is a marvel of science!" cheered Deceivant.

"I'm not getting naked. We could get attacked. We need to be ready at a moment's notice," said Exp 8 with grave seriousness.

Kawai started clawing at his fortified crotch-plate. "I wanna see it. I've seen Karson's now. D.S. has been running around the bath naked. Anthrax just gave everyone an eyeful. Bob...well he doesn't have one—"

"I can have whatever I want," said Bob, lifting up D.S. with his spectral tentacles.

"Stop, that tickles," said D.S., struggling to break free.

"The point is...I wanna see it. Show it to me," said Kawai, now yanking at his crotch-plate.

"I am not taking it off. I don't even know how," said Exp 8, turning away.

"I want to see your whole body. I need to see it. Deceivant, you can do it, can't you?" asked Kawai, zooming up to him and bouncing in place.

"How could I refuse a request from that adorable little face?" asked Deceivant, pinching both cheeks.

"Please, I'll pay you back. I'll let you lick me wherever you want. Just please get it off," said Kawai, grinding against the side of the hot spring.

"I won't let you down," said Deceivant, clasping his hands around hers. He rushed out of the bath and grabbed a screwdriver and a crowbar from his vest.

"If you take one step closer, you will get hurt," said Exp 8, his fists poised for battle.

Kawai popped out from behind her beloved brother. "This is for the good of our relationship. *Energy Drain!*"

Exp 8 fell backwards, now floating on the water's surface.

Deceivant spun the screwdriver around as he walked back into the bath.

"Mom, Bob keeps cheating at Marco Polo," said D.S., looking up with a frown.

"That's just how he lives, sweetie. Thank you Bob, for playing with my son," said Ada with a warm smile.

"It's better than doing nothing, uugh."

"Tag, you're it!" exclaimed Kaity, tapping D.S. before running out of the bath.

"When did you join in?" asked D.S., getting out of the bath to chase her.

"Just now. Can't catch me," said Kaity, running on all fours around the hot spring.

D.S. tapped Kanasta on the shoulder. "You're it!" He then rushed out into the bushes.

Kanasta stood up from the bath and cracked each finger individually. "I'm always up for a challenge. Get ready," he said, leaping out of the hot spring and landing.

"Don't let him run off too far," said Deceivant, looking up as he pulled out a screw.

"I won't." Kanasta moved into the runner's pose. He then zoomed off into the bushes.

"Ah, it's so nice to see them getting along," said Ada, leaning against Deceivant.

"Social interaction is very important, especially during early childhood," said Anthrax, stretching his arms out.

D.S. rushed out of the bushes, screaming like a child.

Kanasta zoomed up to him and slammed both fists into his back.

D.S. tumbled to the ground, falling into the hot spring.

"Now, you're it," said Kanasta with a wide grin.

"Uh-uh, since I'm younger you have to tag me three times," said D.S., climbing out of the bath.

"Changing the rules, are we? It doesn't matter...the end result will be the same," said Kanasta, moving back into the runner's pose.

"Kanasta, sweetie, why can't you ever let your brother win?" asked Ada.

"Treat every game like a life or death scenario. Failure is death," said Kanasta, getting ready to lunge.

"Time out. We should make things more interesting." D.S. grabbed his scissors from a light green patch of grass. "You can use weapons to tag too," he said with a toothy grin.

"Heh, you are only making things more difficult for yourself," said Kanasta, his hand on his gun. He zoomed up to his competitor and shot him three times in the chest at point-blank range. "Now…you are it," he said, emptying the clip and loading it back up.

"I'm over here," said Kaity, leaping right over D.S.

"Owiiie! Mom, Kanasta shot me," whined D.S., showing her the bullet wound.

"Play nice with your little brother," said Ada with a stern finger.

"He brought this on himself," said Kanasta before vanishing in the bushes.

D.S. pulled the bullets out, glued his wounds shut, and then raced after Kaity.

"Kawai, I have fulfilled your request," said Deceivant with a heartfelt bow.

"You have! Eeeh!"

"Now I believe you were going to compensate me," said Deceivant, poking her belly.

"Oh yeah…I did say that, didn't I? Oh, alright. Let's just get this over with," said Kawai, closing her eyes.

Deceivant put his face to her squishy belly and started blowing against it.

"I only said you could lick," said Kawai, squirming about.

Deceivant started licking her belly button.

"That tickles," giggled Kawai.

Deceivant then rose up and gave his adorable little girl a sweet kiss on the forehead. "Have fun, but not too much fun," he said, flicking her nose.

"I know," said Kawai, rushing up to Exp 8. She opened his legs up like a Christmas present.

"It's majestic," said Kawai, her eyes sparkling as she gazed at his member.

"Calm down! Don't do anything weird. I can't move! This isn't right!" yelled Exp 8, struggling to struggle.

"Boop," said Kawai, poking his member. She then fell back, floating on the surface of the water. She was glowing with joy.

Matteria now came back in the bath. He slowly entered and sank until half his face was covered.

"What's wrong?" asked Ada, sliding up to him.

"I was created to crave sex…but it's hard to get Anthrax to even cuddle. I do love him…but it's just so hard," said Matteria, sobbing into his arms.

"Don't dwell on it. Think of something happy. Remember how you and Devlin recently made love," said Ada, caressing his shoulders.

"I'm not supposed to talk about that," said Matteria, pulling Ada close to him.

"What...Devlin too? Is there no one man enough to overcome this temptation?" yelled Karson.

"Why do you hate me?" asked Matteria, his makeup running.

"I don't hate you. It's just, ugh, I hate that I'm...turned on by you. You're a man and...it's not right," said Karson, turning away.

"Don't listen to him. Just think about Devlin. You made him so happy. You even got him to get all cuddly," said Ada, tickling Matteria's sides.

Kawai rose up from below, belly up. "Good job Matteria. It's hard to get him like that. He's so uptight. Even as a little one, he was so serious. But when you get him like that, he becomes a cuddly wuddly kitty witty. Tee-hee."

"Wait...you and Devlin...what did he make you do?" asked Exp 8, now fuming with rage.

"He didn't make me do anything. He had the cutest wittle crush on me. I'd tickle him sometimes. Oh and when I got lonely, we would snuggle a bit. It was sweet," said Kawai with a smile.

"You aren't ever supposed to talk about that," said Devlin's voice from behind them.

The Freedom Forcers turned around to see him standing outside the hot spring.

"Relax, Devlin. Who cares if you act like a cuddly wuddly kitty witty? I'm always cuddly," said Kawai, turning to her big brother and kissing him over and over.

"This is the end of the road," said Devlin, staring at his father with cold loathing.

"Devlin, this is the end for you! You've run out of Exps." Exp 8 pulled himself out of the bath. He stood up, took a deep breath, and then clenched his fist. "We are going to be free."

"I haven't run out. I still have one more Exp left. He is all that I need to put an end to your insipid rebellion," said Devlin with a twisted smile.

An exasperated scream was heard from the bushes in the back.

Exp 8's eyes popped open once he turned around and saw a figure emerge from the shrubs.

Chapter 39: Betrayal

The Atma Blade was impaled through Nina's bare body. Her eyes were hollow and her mouth agape. Her once vibrant purple hair was grayed out.

Bob tossed her lifeless shell before the Freedom Forcers. His smile stretched as he feasted on the shock of his allies.

Kaity rushed to Nina's aid, tears pouring out of her eyes.

Bob's entire eye glowed before a powerful beam shot forth. The laser shot encompassed Nina. It obliterated every fiber of her cherished body before Kaity could reach her.

Kaity's eyes shrank. She froze in place.

"You're lucky Devlin wants you alive," said Bob as he floated toward her.

"We have to run!" yelled Exp 8, grabbing onto the assassin girl.

"There's no use running," said Deceivant, slipping on his lab coat and pulling Ada toward him.

Kawai, still naked, zoomed into Exp 8 and embraced him. "I don't want to die. Promise you'll protect me," she said with trembling hands.

"No one else is going to die. So…don't worry," said Exp 8 softly as tears welled up in his eyes. "I'm going to stop Bob!" He struggled to run toward as he made an orb in his hand. Before he could reach the traitor, he collapsed face-first into the grass.

"What's wrong?" asked Kawai, lifting him up with her tail.

Devlin held his forehead, a twisted smile etched on his face. "You drained him so you could sneak a peek at his dick and now he's suffering for it. Ehehahaha!"

Exp 8 strained to get to his feet and then stood up tall. He closed his eyes, pulling out energy from within.

"He shouldn't even be able to stand. How interesting," said Devlin with wide eyes.

"Can I continue?" asked Bob.

"Wait for him to make the first move," whispered Devlin. He then walked away.

Exp 8 jetted up to Bob and slammed a shaky orb into him.

"I don't know why I must keep such a weakling alive," said Bob as he simply passed through the orb. He zoomed behind the rebel leader and materialized.

The Atma Blade pierced through Exp 8's metal armor, shooting through Kawai as well.

"There's no need to worry. I won't let go of you. As long as he's not allowed to kill me, you'll be safe," said Exp 8, caressing her head.

"Don't you ever tire of happy endings? I find them to be quite the bore," said Bob, his sword pulsing.

Kawai screamed in agony as she writhed around. She held in the pain and looked up at her brother. "I'll be okay, right?" she asked, clenching his hand as tight as possible. Her eyes slowly closed.

Kawai's bare limp body shot off the astral sword and careened into Exp 8's orb.

The orb exploded, sending Exp 8 smashing into a nearby tree.

He looked around frantically, tears welling up in his eyes.

"She wanted to die in your arms, but she ended up dying by your hand. That's close enough, isn't it? Sooo, are you ready to surrender now?" asked Bob, floating down to his prey.

"Kawai, where is she? Tell me where she is!" yelled Exp 8.

"I thought you didn't like her? Or was that just an annoying charade? Were you just hiding your love? I guess it makes no difference. Though I am curious about something else…how does it feel to be the instrument of her destruction?" asked Bob, his wide eye pulsing with cruelty.

Exp 8 embraced the spot where his sister once was as tears leaked out from his helmet.

"Love is a barrier one must overcome for true equality. Didn't you once say something along those lines? Hmm, turns out, Master Devlin agrees with you," said Bob with a sweet smile.

Exp 8 leaped up and thrust his fists at the traitor with all the power he could bring out.

He could not even make contact; his struggle was as futile as fighting a tornado.

"You said you were willing to die to free the Exps. But you knew you never had to worry about dying. You were well aware Devlin wanted you alive. How can you act so valiant when nothing is at stake? You carelessly risked their lives knowing you alone were safe. I will show you the error of your ways by killing each and every one of your expendable Freedom Forcers. Eheh-heh-heh."

Exp 8 threw desperate punches, hoping by a miracle one would connect.

"You are pathetic. You need strength if you want to have freedom. Do not hold on to such absurd goals unless you have the power to carry them out," said Bob, his words lined with sweet sarcasm.

"Die, you goddamned eyeball!" yelled Karson from behind.

Bob turned around to see Karson without both his uniform and his head.

Exp 8 used this moment of distraction to run away as fast as he could.

The missile slammed down on the round Exp. The explosion consumed the surrounding trees, setting them aflame.

Bob emerged from the flames with a wide smile. A spectral hand branched out from his side. In its wispy grip was the gunman's deathly button.

Karson's new head was disengaged, staring at the Button with all-encompassing fear.

Bob floated up to the cowardly soldier, pushing away any flame in his path.

Karson shot furiously with his Gatling gun arms.

The Befriender of Betrayal passed through the ground and appeared behind the trigger-happy fool. His spectral hand pressed the Button into Karson's back. He then turned the Button three-hundred-sixty degrees, locking it into place.

"This is all a joke, right? It's just a ploy to get Exp 8 to unleash his potential. You've got some sort of secret ability. You're going to revive us afterwards, right?" asked Karson, quivering in the treacherous eyeball's shadow.

Bob's spectral hand pushed the Button and then ripped it off.

Shrapnel burst out from within and shot out in all directions as Karson made one final war cry.

Bob passed right through the metal storm as he scanned the area for his next prey.

D.S., dressed in his school uniform, shoved his scissors through the liar and slammed him continuously against the charred grass.

Bob quickly adjusted to the situation and passed through the ground.

The Supply Master turned around to see the bad guy. "What are you doing to my friends?! And how did you escape Mr. Snippy?"

"How could you betray Devlin? He accepted you even though you were his father's Exp. Normally I would be proud of your betrayal, but you did it for candy. You are worthless," said Bob.

D.S. spun around and lashed his scissors at the bad guy.

The scissors passed through Bob as he smiled.

"You are merely a pawn going against the king's wishes. And I am the knight who will smite you," said Bob as he concentrated energy in his pupil.

Exp 8 jumped down from a nearby burning tree, landing in front of Bob. "Our lives have value! We are not just playing pieces that you can discard!" he yelled, holding a wrecking ball of an orb in his hand.

"You're one to talk," said Bob with contempt.

"Die!" Exp 8 slammed the orb down with all his might.

The explosion lifted the Ultimate Exp off his feet.

Exp 8 spun around before slamming into a burning tree trunk. He turned to the oak tree with trembling hands. "I think I got him. And even if I didn't, I'll make sure he pays for what he's done. I can't stop the fire. But I'll kill him. I swear I'll kill him. You all shall not die in vain." He stood up, panting.

The smoke cleared, and Bob was gone.

Exp 8 wanted to think it was over, but he knew otherwise. "We trusted you. How could you betray us?" His tears outlined his eyes, but his anger kept them from being released.

"Eheh-heh-heh-heh! I was never on your side. I was a spy the whole time. I am Bob, the Befriender of Betrayal. I befriended your little group for the sole sake of betraying them. It is moments like this that truly make me happy!" he exclaimed, spinning in place.

"How can you smile after killing your comrades? Nina may have been self-centered, but she was a reliable warrior. She was a great comrade. And she fought wholeheartedly for our freedom! And how the hell did you even kill Karson?" asked Exp 8, holding the sides of his head.

Bob circled around the foolish rebel. "I have powers beyond your greatest comprehension. You may see them as friends, but to me they were just pawns. One must sacrifice their pawns to protect the king. You mustn't lament when a pawn is discarded. It is all for the greater good. Yes, I did enjoy it a bit; what's wrong with enjoying what you do?"

"How can you take murder so lightly?" asked Exp 8, spitting out a wad of blood through his mouthpiece.

"I will do whatever is necessary to complete my purpose. It is something you could never understand. You will never succeed in life if you let trivial things get in the way. I have done far more atrocious things in the past, and I will continue to do so in the future. I am sorry to tell you, but you aren't really that important." Bob lifted Exp 8 up with the power of his mind. "This is my story, not yours."

The remaining Freedom Forcers ran to Exp 8's side.

"Exp 8 is the Ultimate Exp, not you. You are just Devlin's toy," said Deceivant.

"How dare you! Devlin treats me as his equal."

"He is just using you to get more power. Once he is done draining you of all your worth, you will be discarded like the pawn you are," said Deceivant through gritted teeth.

"If you think your insolent lies will cause a change of heart, then you are pathetically mistaken," said Bob, his pupil shrinking.

"Bob, please stop this. We don't want to hurt you," said Ada, trying to smile through the rush of tears.

"This is rich. No, I take it back…it is a joke in poor taste. You're the weakest Exp. Do you actually think you can harm me? Threats are empty without the power and the will needed to back them up." He slammed Exp 8 to the ground without even looking in his direction.

"Bob, you are sick…you are ill in the mind. Please, allow me to cure you," said Anthrax, fully clothed and slowly approaching.

"So now determination is a sickness? Your knowledge of disease only goes as far as Devlin's. You all only know exactly what Devlin wants you to know. Ehahahahaha!"

"Shut up! How could you murder Nina?" asked Kaity, her hands trembling as she loaded up her sniper rifle.

"What's wrong? Did you want me to leave her body intact so you could finally be with her? Don't act so upset…she was just something you wanted to play with. You never loved her…how could you?" asked Bob.

Kaity fired her sniper rifle, wiping away her tears between rounds.

Bob didn't even pass through her pitiful attacks.

Every single bullet missed.

"Do you see what emotions do? They impair your ability to carry out your purpose," explained Bob, closing in as the bullets zoomed by.

"Don't waste your bullets," said Kanasta, moving in front of his apprentice.

Kaity dropped her gun and gripped Kanasta. "You'll always be here for me, right Papa?"

"Yes, I will," said Kanasta, hugging his child with one arm.

Bob fired laser after laser at the assassin boss. "This is so pathetic. You couldn't even stop me when I was toying with you. Your words are just an empty promise."

Exp 8 ran up to the traitor only to get slammed back down to the dirt.

Bob's pupil revolved around, facing Exp 8. "Didn't you promise Kawai you'd keep her safe? Do not make promises unless you have the power to back them up."

Exp 8 rose to his knees before getting floored once again.

"Determination without power is a joke that quickly becomes monotonous. Do not bore me. Betrayal is supposed to be fun," said Bob, dragging Exp 8 up a burning tree.

Kanasta approached Bob, his feet firmly rooted in the ground. "I promised her I would make sure she would never have to cry again!" He grabbed onto the most powerful Exp.

His grip slipped as Bob went into Phase Form.

Bob watched as Exp 8 used a tree to hoist himself up. "You know what…I've changed my mind. I want you to promise all your teammates they'll be okay. Promise you'll protect them. Go on, do it," he said, poking the rebel leader's cheek.

Exp 8 turned to his fellow Freedom Forcers, standing as firm as his resolve. "Kaity, I promise I won't let him hurt you. Ada, I refuse to let Bob touch you. Deceivant, I will protect you. D.S., thank you for joining me…you're going to be just fine. Anthrax, you may have given me amnesia, but you're still part of my family. Kanasta, don't worry; you won't die from someone like him. I will make sure you are all protected."

"Such deceit, such…determination…now I truly see how closely linked they are," said Bob as he rushed up to Kanasta. He pierced the Atma Blade through him without even looking.

The Assassin Boss fell to his knees.

"Isn't it funny how your enemy is now perfectly accepted into your fake family? He tore you limb-from-limb and he kills for money. Yet in your desperation, you vow to save him? Why would you want to save this greedy murderer? He stands for everything you are against. He is your greatest foe," said Bob.

"You're my greatest foe, and I will kill you," said Exp 8 with a thumbs-down.

"What of Destructus Supplious? He was your enemy a while ago, but now you vow to protect him. Why must you be so self-centered? I was your teammate; aren't you going to promise me protection?" asked Bob with a googly eye.

"I will kill you," said Exp 8, gritting his teeth.

"I hope you live up to that. Empty threats annoy me," said Bob dismissively.

"I never break my promises," said Exp 8, slowly approaching.

"So then, you have others break them for you? That way you don't have to take any blame once they're broken. You truly are a selfish mastermind. Anyway, this conversation has distracted me. The Assassin Boss dies now," said Bob, his sword coursing with power.

"Stop! Don't kill him, he's my brother," said Devlin, entering through the smoke.

"Are you really going to let family bonds become an obstacle to your ambitions?" asked Bob, glaring at his shameful master.

"I want to kill him." Devlin's hands trembled. He turned to Bob. "You've killed enough Freedom Forcers today. I want to test out Exp 11. Just chill, okay?"

"Yes, Master, as you wish," said Bob with a devoted bow.

They both vanished in the smoke.

Chapter 40: Blame

Exp 8 fell to his knees, tears pouring out of his helmet. "I promised she would be safe."

"This is no way for the Ultimate Exp to act. You have to get a grip on your emotions," said Deceivant, sobbing uncontrollably.

Ada cradled Exp 8 to her chest. "It's good to cry. You have to release your pent up emotions or they'll eat away at you. Don't worry; I'm still here. I've been in you since the day you were made. I've always been with you and I always will be." She kissed him on the forehead.

"Can we really lose after all we've done?" asked Exp 8, grabbing her arm.

"Of course not. We'll all be okay. Devlin's a good kid. I know he'll come to his senses," said Ada with a tearful smile.

"I'm not in the mood for your blind motherly nonsense! He sent Bob to slaughter us." Exp 8 turned to Deceivant. "What changed Devlin?"

"We haven't the slightest clue," said Deceivant, continuously wiping away his tears.

"When his eyes met mine, I could feel his burning vengeance. He is blaming me for something, but I don't know what," said Kanasta, combing Kaity's hair.

"It was you, wasn't it? Devlin never wanted to kill us until you showed up!" said Exp 8, looking at Deceivant with eyes of spite.

"I have nothing to do with this. I'm just as sad as you are," said Deceivant, holding his chest.

"Don't act like you care. You think we are all just tools! Well, I have news for you: I am alive. We are all alive and our lives matter," said Exp 8, his tears dripping on the grass.

"Exp 02 said the same thing. He always spited me," said Deceivant softly.

Exp 8 stood up and walked toward Deceivant. "What did you do to him? Did you just throw him away once you were done using him?"

Deceivant turned his head away.

"We don't matter to you at all. You're just here to protect your sorry ass from your son!" Exp 8 grabbed the man's collar and lifted him off the ground.

"You don't understand at all. Put me down!" yelled Deceivant, struggling in his grip.

"You humans are all the same. You all use past hardships as an excuse for your misguided actions! If you hadn't ruined Devlin's life, then Nina, Karson, Kawai, and Atatasuki would all be alive right now. They would be right here by my side, supporting me."

"Let's not talk about what could have been."

"As far as I'm concerned you killed them!" Exp 8 slammed Deceivant to the floor.

Ada, threw herself on top of her husband. "Don't hurt him!"

"Why should I trust you? You were spying on us for Deceivant. You were making sure everything was going according to plan. I don't trust any of you! Destructus Supplious just joined us because you gave him candy. He'll probably do whatever you say. Kanasta is your son. As far as I know, he was in on this the whole time. Kaity only joined our team because she loved Nina!"

"Shut up! You aren't the only one who's lost someone," said Kaity, sitting up from Kanasta's lap.

"Stop making Kaity cry! I promised she would never have to cry again," said Kanasta, standing up from the ground and pushing out his chest.

"Bob is right. Why should I vow to protect any of you? All of my real allies are dead! You're all here for your own selfish needs! You don't care about our freedom!"

Deceivant stood up and approached Exp 8. "What about you? Aren't you having conflict for the sake of conflict? If you really wanted to escape, then you could have just run away! When the assassins gave you that invitation, you could have just ignored it!" he yelled, his spit spraying on the Exp's helmet.

"Where were you when Atatasuki was killed? You were probably watching in a surveillance room. You are a heartless coward," said Exp 8 through gritted teeth.

"How is that my fault? You were right next to him and yet you still couldn't protect him. If you hadn't gone to the lab to fight the assassins, then none of your precious friends would have died," said Deceivant with a cold stare.

Exp 8 punched the man's face, sending him skidding across the ground and into a tree. "If we didn't go back to fight the assassins, they would have just hunted us down later."

Deceivant rose to his feet, struggling to stand. "You thought that they weren't a threat! You went in to show Devlin you didn't fear him. All that pain and violence was for your own ego. Your family died because of your selfishness."

Exp 8 zoomed up to Deceivant with his jets as he pulled back his fist. He was impaled by D.S.'s scissors before his fist could connect.

"Stop hurting Daddy," said D.S., plunging the scissors in deeper.

Exp 8 slammed his head into the Supply Master, dislodging the scissors from his stomach. "You're probably just going to kill me later anyway. Is that what your plan is, Deceivant? Are you going to kill your own son and then destroy all the Exps? Do you want us eradicated?" he asked, holding his chest in pain.

"Father has done nothing wrong! You didn't really expect Karson's explosion to kill Devlin, did you?" asked Kanasta, turning to Deceivant with a look of suspicion.

"There's absolutely no way he would. Devlin is his son," said Ada, helping her husband to his feet.

"As far as I'm concerned, Hope and Kanasta are my only children…and Hope is dead," said Deceivant softly.

"You were trying to kill my brother!" Kanasta grabbed his father by the throat.

"I once believed in you. I thought you could change. But you are just a mindless killer like Devlin," said Deceivant, gripping Kanasta's arms.

"Devlin is suffering! Can't you see his pain? How could you? You never bothered to try to understand him." Kanasta intensified his grip as Ada tried to pull his hands off.

"Why did he turn on us?" asked Deceivant, struggling to breathe.

"Killing Devlin won't reveal the truth," said Kanasta, before tossing his father aside.

"He murdered my little sister! If we don't kill him, he'll destroy all of us!" exclaimed Exp 8.

"We need to help him!" yelled Kanasta.

"The so-called Ultimate Exp is right. The only way to stop Devlin is to kill him. This is far more than just a family matter," said Deceivant, wiping the dirt off his vest.

Ada turned to her beloved in tears. "Devlin is our child! We raised him together. How can you want to kill him?"

"We've run out of options. Killing him is the only way to stop him," said Deceivant, putting his hand on his wife's cheek.

"Killing should never be a solution! I've tried every day to convince Devlin to stop this. You're only making things worse," said Ada in tears.

"Why is everyone blaming me? I didn't create this situation, but I'm going to end it," said Deceivant, turning to D.S.

Exp 8 intercepted Deceivant's path. "Easy for you to say, I don't see you on the frontlines. Indirect killing is always easier, isn't it? Generals don't get nightmares about the people they've killed, the soldiers do. It's so much easier to kill someone if you send someone else to do it."

"He's right, isn't he? In the end, we are just tools for you to carry out your plan." Kanasta gripped Deceivant's shoulders "What do you gain from Devlin's death?"

"Don't accuse me of ulterior motives. You would kill your own mother if you got paid for it," said Deceivant with burning eyes.

"I don't murder for my own selfish reasons. There is no goal I wish to reach. I kill whoever I get paid to kill, family or otherwise," said Kanasta with quiet intensity.

Ada embraced Kanasta, tears rushing down her face. "Please don't say such horrible things."

Kanasta pried her off. "It's not horrible…it's fair," he said, looking into her eyes.

"Why are all my children completely insane?" yelled Deceivant, throwing his arms up.

Kanasta grabbed Deceivant's arm. "You weren't there for Devlin. While Ada was raising him, you were spending hours at your daycare. He may not be a cute little girl, but he's still your son. Take care of your own kids before you go off to please the children of others."

Ada stepped closer to her husband, her hands shaking. "Is it my fault? Am I the reason you wouldn't take care of the kids? Is my body not desirable?"

"Hey, where did this come from? Ada, I love you with all my heart. I just need a little variety in my life," said Deceivant, calming her hands.

"How can you love me with all your heart if you're not content with me?" asked Ada, about to cry.

"Good point; I shouldn't use abstractions. Look, I'm a complicated man. It takes a lot of a little to please me. Ada, you may not have a petite body or an adorable face, but I love you regardless. I love your unconditional kindness and your childlike innocence. I love your cute little smile. You're just a little girl in a woman's body. It's the little girl in you that I love, you know that," said Deceivant as he embraced her.

Exp 8's head turned to his ex-comrades. "You're a damn pedophile! You're both heartless assassins. You're just a spy for the pedophile. Anthrax, you could be Devlin's spy for all I know. That disease you gave me may have been a ploy to gain my trust. And D.S., you're just a stupid kid who follows Daddy's orders. I don't need any of you. I am going to stop Devlin with my own power!" he yelled, storming off.

"Go ahead, get yourself killed," said Kanasta, pulling Kaity close to him.

"I should have been by myself from the start. Teammates are just emotional baggage. I don't need anyone!" exclaimed Exp 8.

Kanasta bent down to Kaity and patted her head. "We are the only ones who can save Devlin. We need to come up with a strategy. How do you think we can reach him?"

"If we separate, then we are even less likely to be able to defeat Devlin," said Kaity softly.

"They aren't going to be of any help. Let's leave," said Kanasta, hoisting her onto his shoulders.

"Ada, you're staying with me, right? I am your loving husband. You wouldn't ever abandon me," said Deceivant, wrapping his arm around her.

Anthrax stood up abruptly. "Everyone stop! When cells combine they make tissue. Tissue combines to form functional organs. But only when the organs combine can the body operate effectively."

"What are you talking about, nerd?" asked D.S.

Ada broke out of Deceivant's grip and stood up. "Listen to Anthrax! Yes, Bob is powerful, but he's not unbeatable. And I wasn't spying on Devlin. I was watching over him, okay. I was just…watching over my son, like any mother would," she said in tears.

Anthrax turned to Kanasta. "You can't save Devlin on your own," he said before the assassin boss gently pushed him aside.

"If you want to beat Bob and save Devlin, then you'll need help!" yelled Ada, running after Kanasta.

Anthrax grabbed Deceivant's hand. "How can you just decide that killing Devlin is the only way? We are doing exactly what Devlin wants. We can't let him separate us!"

Exp 8 moved in front of the assassin boss, standing as firm as his resolve. "I…can't do this alone. Kanasta, if we want to save Devlin, then we are going to need to do it together." He outstretched his arm.

"He's my little brother. This is my responsibility," said Kanasta, walking past him.

"Please, don't go. I wasn't thinking. I need your help. You're the strongest fighter we have."

Kanasta turned to Exp 8. "Bob defeated me. I've lost to him twice. I can't win against him, not as I am now." He continued his leave.

Exp 8 looked out at his allies. He closed his eyes and put his hands to his chest.

Tears gushed from the seams of his helmet.

Exp 8 turned to Ada. "Even though you were spying for Deceivant…I trust you. You saved my life when I fought Nina. You've helped me through a lot," he said, trying to hold in his tears. He then turned to Deceivant. "I don't trust you nearly as far as I could throw you. However…if Ada believes in you, then I can at least give you the benefit of the doubt."

Ada walked to Exp 8's side. "We are the Freedom Forcers! We must force Devlin to free the other Exps. That's why you originally made this team, right?"

Exp 8 turned to face all his allies. "That's absolutely correct. We are fighting for our freedom! That is what we've always been fighting for. We can't let all their deaths be in vain. We owe it to them to see this to the end!" he exclaimed, throwing his arm up.

Ada grabbed Kanasta's hand. "If we separate, then we lose our only chance at saving him."

"I guess you really are the Ultimate Exp." Deceivant went down on his knees and bowed respectfully. "I want to save Devlin too. I'll help in any way I can."

Exp 8 turned to Kanasta as he cleaned the tears off his helmet. "I know you were just trying to save your brother. Anyone who cares about their brother so powerfully can't be all bad," he said, putting his hand on the assassin boss' shoulder.

"I'm sorry for dismembering you," said Kanasta with a smile.

"It's okay; you never killed anyone. Now that bitch Violet, oh…she is going to pay," said Exp 8, anger gathering in his fist.

"She's not a bitch!" blurted out Kaity.

"She killed my brother!"

"She was following orders." Kaity turned her gaze away from Exp 8.

"Her nonsensical loyalty to Devlin is the problem. And following orders doesn't excuse her actions!"

"She didn't want to kill him. She took her own life when I fought her. She believes that I can save Devlin. She was just trying to help the person she loved," said Kaity with a sniffle.

"I think Sefiwah was killing people so she could keep you safe," said Ada, touching Kaity's chest.

"I think she was just lying to get you to put down your guard. But…now that I know you…I don't think you killed her. She must have made that choice herself," said Kaity, wiping her eyes.

Kanasta stepped up to Exp 8 and lowered his head. "I've lost nearly all my family to your Freedom Forcers already. Promise me you won't kill my brother."

"I apologize for their actions. We were fighting for our lives. I can't promise I won't kill Devlin. I will try to avoid that option. But if the situation calls for it, then I will do what I must," said Exp 8 with a firm fist.

"He has such leadership, such strength. I've never seen an Exp act like this. Sure, they're stubborn, outspoken, and opinionated, but he's purely resolute," said Deceivant, his eyes gleaming beneath his glasses.

Tempo came rushing up to the Freedom Forcers, making them stand up in preparation. "Boss, where are the rest of the Viper Squad?" he asked with exasperated breaths.

"The Viper Squad is finished. We are now Freedom Forcers!" exclaimed Kanasta.

"You're still trying to save your brother? I don't get you. What's the point? What's the payoff?" asked Tempo, his fingers twitching with greed.

Tears poured out of Kanasta's face uncontrollably. "There is no pay. We are helping them for free."

"Never thought I'd hear you say that. Well, what the hell am I supposed to do now? It wasn't easy escaping that lab. I'm not going back there on my own."

"Do what you want. You no longer have any obligations to me," said Kanasta, putting his hands on Tempo's shoulders.

"I'm a fighter. I'm a killer. I ain't got a choice at this point. If you're with them…then so am I," said Tempo, pulling out his double-edged thermometer.

"Everyone, come closer," said Exp 8.

"Aren't I already initiated?" asked Kaity.

"Yeah, but it doesn't hurt to reinstate it," said Exp 8, his mouthpiece widening with his smile.

"Oh, it's time for the hug!" cheered Ada as she pulled Deceivant and Kanasta in.

Kaity joined in, reaching as far around Kanasta as she could.

"I don't do hugs," said Tempo before spitting in the grass.

"Hugs are safe if you disinfect right afterwards," said Anthrax, joining in.

"Hugs are for girls," said D.S., sticking out his tongue.

"Are you calling me a girl?" asked Kanasta, his arms wrapped around Exp 8 and Deceivant's shoulders.

"No. I just…alright, I'll do it," said D.S. with puffed out cheeks. He squeezed in between Ada and Deceivant.

"Let's just get this over with," said Tempo, practically strangling Anthrax and Exp 8 with his embrace.

"I hereby declare all of you honorary Freedom Forcers. Together we will preserve freedom for all out brethren," said Exp 8 before ending the hug.

"Now that the pleasantries are out of the way, we should plan our next course of action," said Deceivant, watching Kaity's tail.

"Hey, could you, um, reattach my crotch-plate?" asked Exp 8, looking away.

"Lie down. It should reconnect, no problem."

Exp 8 dropped to the grass. "Okay everyone, we need to figure out a plan of action. First things first: we need to find a way to stop Bob," he said, his hand tightening into a fist.

"We can't even touch him! He's a cheater!" exclaimed D.S.

"I have access to every piece of data about Bob. As long as Deceivant gives me the authorization to access the files, I'm sure we'll figure something out." Ada turned to Deceivant. Her lower lip curled up and her eyes became watery.

"You are so cute. At this point you don't need my authorization. We are in a crisis. Just open up the file," said Deceivant, rubbing her head.

"Alright then, let's see…aha! You need to time your attacks. Bob can only hit us when he isn't in his Phase Form. But watch out for his soul minions. They can attack you from another realm. The good news is the little guys aren't very fast. Keep track of your energy levels and you should be just fine."

"Hit him when he attacks. Sounds simple enough," said Kanasta, cracking his knuckles.

"Alright, your crotch-plate is reattached," said Deceivant, putting away his screwdriver.

"Thanks. Uh, I'm still feeling drained. I have to get stronger," said Exp 8, slamming his fist against his palm.

"I couldn't agree more," said Devlin, appearing before them. "I was hoping that you would have given in at this point. But I guess I overestimated your intelligence," he said with a smirk.

Exp 8 rushed at Devlin as he powered up an orb in his fist. "You murdered my comrades! You killed my sister!"

Devlin teleported away a mere inch before the orb could connect. He arrived behind Deceivant and spawned a knife in his grip.

"You have to stop this!" exclaimed Ada, running up to her son.

Devlin smacked her down with the back of his hand. He then wiped off the perceived filth on his pant leg. "I already warned Exp 8. I told him if he continued on this rebellious path, there would be casualties. I was deathly serious. I will not allow any of my creations to defy me without repercussions," he said, tightenlng his fingers.

Deceivant went to his beloved's side and caressed her cheek.

"Devlin, you need to stop before your vengeance consumes you," said Kaity.

"Heheh-ahahahaha! My vengeance has consumed me long ago. I beckoned it to devour all feelings of restraint. Do not try to save me now! The only way to stop me is to kill me. And as long as I have Exps to protect me, you won't even be able to approach." Devlin snapped his fingers.

"Did you know the whole time Bob was going to betray us? Was he your spy all along?" asked Exp 8.

"No. He left me in the dark about it. But after he beat Kanasta, he revealed his plan. I was impressed. Now I know you all miss Bob, but I brought someone new to fight you. Exp 11, show them your power," said Devlin, flinging his arms in the air dramatically.

"Have you decided to no longer name your Exps?" asked Deceivant with a shrug.

"Actually, he has three names," said Devlin with a curved grin.

Chapter 41: Opti and Pesi

Exp 11 approached from the thick bushels behind Devlin. He stood in a patch of sunlight that found an opening in the foliage.

He was slightly shorter than Exp 8 and looked to be about thirty years old. The man had long, playful white hair with blue tips at the end of each and every strand. Covering half his face was a snow-white drama mask. The mask had a thick blue-and-white rainbow above the heart-shaped eyehole. A snow-white iris with a friendly light-blue pupil was seen from the cutout. At the center of the mask was half of a blue diamond. A permanent black half-smile stretched from one edge of the plaster to the other. The Exp had a seamless white garb that folded out in the shape of angel wings. The tip of each white, powdery feather was sky blue. His skin was a spooky, ghostly pale.

He waved cheerfully at his adversaries. "Hello, Freedom Forcers! I am an overly pure truthful idealist. I am Opti. I must say, I am so super-excited to meet each and every one of you. Now, just so we're clear, it is my mission to kill you all. Well, not all of you. Thankfully I am not allowed to kill Kaity nor Exp 8. However, the rest of you aren't quite so lucky. But there's no need to worry at all! I will make your deaths fun, quick, and painless. Pop, like a balloon. I mean, there will be some agony, but nobody will suffer all that much. If that still isn't good enough for you, fret not, there's another way to resolve this! If you can convince Exp 8 to surrender and swear his unending and undying loyalty to Devlin, then nobody has to die at all. This is a once-in-a-lifetime chance. Just think it over…whup, time's up. So what is your decision?" asked Opti with an unchanging cheerful tone. He looked out at all of them with hope in his shimmering eyes.

Exp 8 walked out of the crowd and pointed to Exp 11. "We are going to take you down."

"That's easy for you to say; you're one of the ones I'm not supposed to kill," said Opti, his head resting on his knee.

"We are all going to take you down," said the Freedom Forcers in unison.

"So that's how it's gonna be. That's really too bad. I'm sure we would all have been great friends, the bestest. I am sorry, everyone, but many of you will die. But, like I said earlier, I'll try to do it with as little agony as possible," said Opti, waving his dainty hand dismissively.

Exp 11's garb was slowly corrupted by all-consuming blackness. His skin dyed from within, reemerging as pitch dark black. His long white hair withered and shot up like needle-thick spikes. The tips of his hair turned killer blood red. His feathers lost all their light, becoming black as coal. The tips of the wings were now a flaming, fiery red. Black irises with piercing murderous red pupils replaced his once gentle spheres. The mask became black with a red fiery outline atop its club-shaped eyehole. The stem of the club was a symbolic tear that served as an evil symbol of the horrid misery soon to come. At the center of the chaotic half mask was half of a spade, painted red like the blood of his victims. The black smile on the mask morphed and contorted into a jagged white frown.

"I shall kill all of you to death!" yelled Exp 11, flailing around his serrated fingernails.

"Great, another whack-job, uugh," said Exp 8, flicking his wrists.

"What happened to you, Opti?" asked Anthrax, his glasses gleaming with his intrigue.

"I am here to kill every last one of you, every single one! You're all going to die! Khehahahahah!"

"Yeah, we get it. So who the hell are you?" asked Exp 8.

"You mean you don't know?" asked the deranged Exp, his head twisting to his side.

"No, we don't. Hurry up and tell us," said Deceivant.

"I am the terminator of everything. The destroyer! The apocalypse! The entity of hatred and chaos! The annihilator! The purger! And the end! I am a pure evil sadistic idealist! I am Pesi!" he yelled, wailing his arms around in a frenzy as his black wings spread open.

"What kind of name is Pepsi?" asked D.S.

"Not Pepsi, damn it! It's Pesi! Pesi as in pessimistic!" yelled the Exp with a raspy, furious tone as he landed before them.

"So then, you're a mystical Pepsi?" asked Destructus Supplious, sucking his thumb.

"It means he prepares for the worst. He's a cynic. Or in layman's terms, he's hopeless," explained Deceivant, patting D.S. on the head.

"He's just like NoOne. Try to be more original next time, Devlin," said Exp 8, punching Exp 11 with a swift fist.

Pesi leaped back to his feet, wiping a line of blood off his face. "I am not pessimistic. I control pessimism," he said with a mystifying wave of his fingers.

"Okay, so your ability is to hate things?" asked D.S. as he sharpened his scissors.

"Yes, I hate everything! Nothing can dare stand in my way! No Exp is more powerful than me!" yelled Pesi, pounding his chest.

"You should be called Ignorant, not Pesi," said Exp 8, knocking down his opponent with a well-timed kick.

Pesi rebounded back up the instant he hit the ground. "Your insults are as empty as your fists," he said, pushing his chest out in pride.

"Where did the assassins run off to?" asked Exp 8, looking around confused.

"They are assassins, what did you expect?" asked Deceivant, slowly backing away from the rest of the group.

"Where did the kitty girl go?" asked D.S.

"Sweetie, she's an assassin too," said Ada.

"Whoa, I had no idea. She's really good," said D.S. with a nod.

"Stop ignoring me!" Pesi looked around to make sure everyone was listening. "You all think I'm bluffing. You better hope I'm bluffing. But I'm not! I really will kill all of you," he said, clenching his fist.

"Just shut up already. If you want to kill us, then bring it!" yelled Exp 8, powering up an energy orb.

"Watch this!" Pesi reached into his shirt and pulled out a cat plushy. He bit its head off with his teeth and then spit it out in disgust.

The sound of a switch being flipped emitted from Pesi's head. He then fully transformed back into Opti.

"What happened to Fuzzle?!" asked Opti in despair, looking at the decapitated plushy.

"Ada, if you compliment him, he might not fight us at all," said Exp 8, surveying the area for the ex-Viper Squad members.

"I'll try my best. Opti, your hair is so beautiful!" exclaimed Ada, caressing it lovingly.

"You really think so? I think your hair is awe-ful, as in full of awe," he said, petting her head with gentle fingertips.

"Nina's hair was so pretty," said Kaity from a nearby tree.

Opti looked up to see Kaity crying. "What's bothering you?" he asked, hopping up to her tree branch.

Devlin knocked him off the tree and approached his beloved with a handkerchief. "Please don't cry, Kaity." He brought the handkerchief to her watery eyes.

Kaity smacked his hand aside. "You're the one who sent Bob to kill Nina!" she exclaimed before shooting him.

Devlin held the hole in his chest before falling out of the tree.

Anthrax was by his side the second he landed. "Don't worry, you're going to be okay," he said, already pulling out the bullet.

Devlin sat up. "Kaity, I'm sorry. I can't blame you for being upset with me. I lost sight of what matters most to me. I've endangered your happiness. I know I don't deserve your forgiveness, but I want to make it up to you."

"You've finally come to! Oh, thank goodness!" exclaimed Ada, running toward her son with open arms.

Devlin turned to her with piercing eyes. He rushed up and grabbed her by the throat. "I am going to kill you, my father, and my brother! I came here to give

Kaity a gift. The rest of you can burn in hell for all I care." He tossed Ada to the ground.

"I don't want a present. I can't forgive you," said Kaity, turning away from him.

"I don't expect you to. I just want to make it so you don't cry anymore. It hurts me to see you cry," said Devlin, his hands to his chest.

"Spoken like a true pedophile. I am proud of you, son," said Deceivant, wiping away tears.

"Bring it out!" yelled Devlin to the bushes.

Riufen rolled out an eight-foot cake from between the trees.

The words "Happy Re-Birthday" were iced on its vanilla cream surface.

"I don't want anything from you," said Kaity with a sniffle.

The cake burst open, icing flying everywhere. Nina emerged, naked and coated in frosting.

Kaity's jaw dropped before she fell off the tree.

Devlin caught her in his arms and gently set her down.

Kaity gazed at the living miracle with shimmering eyes.

Nina dragged her fingers across her chest and then licked the icing off them. "The goddess of sexiness has been reborn!" she exclaimed, flinging her head back.

"Tears just don't do your eyes justice," said Devlin, wiping the young girl's cheeks.

Kaity leaped on Devlin and embraced him. "You did it! You brought her back!" she exclaimed as she rubbed her cheeks against his face.

"Kaity, I appreciate this…sooo much! However…I do not deserve it. I was the reason for your tears. You don't owe me anything," said Devlin as he reluctantly pried her hands off. He put his hand on her shoulder, crouched to her level and held her hands between his. "If you ever embrace me, I want it to be for something I've done for you. This was just to apologize for my mistake."

Kaity turned away with a light blush. "How is she alive?" she asked, stepping toward Nina.

"Bob never killed her." Devlin then turned to Opti, who was giving Ada a massage. "Opti, I need you to finish this. Kill them…please," he said with cupped hands.

"Only because you said *please*. I'll use my Temperature Artifact," said Opti with a twirl.

"Hey, asshole, I have the Temperature Artifact," said Tempo, popping out of the ground. He leaped to his feet as his hand heated up.

Opti shoved his hand through Tempo's chest and ripped out his capsule. He smashed the capsule in his fist. He then thrust the greasy crimson chunk of mercury into his chest and absorbed it. "Now I have the Temperature Artifact. *SUPER HEAT*!" he yelled, placing his hands to the ground.

"Did he just…kill Tempo?" asked Kanasta, overcome with stillness.

The grass beneath them burst into flames. The dirt became mud as the ground melted.

The Freedom Forcers fell into the newly formed muddy pool.

Tempo's corpse sunk to the bottom, slightly reddening the muddy lake.

"Don't let your guard down!" yelled Exp 8.

The Freedom Forcers made a break for the shore.

(Switch) Pesi looked down at them and laughed, his wings flapping to keep him airborne. "You are making this too easy! Wait a minute, one…two…three…four…five…six…seven. Hmm, where's that temperature guy?" he asked as he counted his fingers.

"You killed him and took his artifact. Now hurry, they're escaping." Devlin leaned back in a chair while he watched Kaity lick the frosting off her present.

"I have a dastardly plan. *TEMPERATURE FALL*!" yelled Pesi, outstretching his hand.

The mud-pool froze, leaving all of the Freedom Forcers poking out of it.

(Switch) "Who attacked you guys?" asked Opti, his hands over his mouth.

"Pesi did!" exclaimed Deceivant, his head protruding from the brown sheet of ice.

(Switch) Pesi landed on the ground and slowly approached D.S. who was halfway free. "You look to be the strongest of all of them."

D.S. was in his eraser form and was moving back and forth, trying to get rid of the ice around him. "You're right about that!" He jumped out from the ice and up to Pesi. He pulled out his scissors and thrust them forward.

Exp 11 shoved his thumb into D.S. "*DESTROY*!"

D.S. exploded into bits. His blood splattered all over Pesi.

(Switch) "Who did this?" asked Opti, looking at the blood with horror.

"I'm going to kill you!" exclaimed Exp 8, his feet and head outcropping from the ice.

"No. No! He can't be dead," cried Ada.

(Switch) "I have killed D.S. with only my thumb! Kehahahahaha!"

"So did I," said Devlin, showing off his bomb trigger.

"So, who wants to die next?" asked Pesi, miming a throat slitting.

"Don't forget you have the Influence Artifact. Be careful what you say. In the hands of a simpleton, it is more powerful and dangerous," said Devlin, his head arching back over the chair.

"I don't worry. I am Pesi!" he exclaimed, sticking out his tongue and patting his cheeks.

"Don't you know that evil is a disease?" asked Anthrax, his hands fruitlessly flailing about.

"Well then, I must be deathly ill," said Pesi with a smile, exposing his jagged teeth. He then burst out into crazed cackling. His laughter transformed into fear as he coughed up a wad of blood.

"And now you are. Looks like we won," said Anthrax, giving his team a thumbs-up.

"I'm not deathly ill, you are!" yelled Pesi, his fingers tearing into his chest. His coughing instantly stopped.

Anthrax held his chest as he gasped. A drop of blood dripped down his lip.

(Switch) "Are you okay? Who did this?" exclaimed Opti as he ripped the white-haired boy out of the ice.

Anthrax's head fell down. His eyes were glazed over and his mouth was foaming.

"Who killed my friend?" asked Opti, holding the boy's limp body tight to his chest.

"Stop it already!" yelled Exp 8, trying to burst out of the ice.

(Switch) "This has been postponed long enough," said Pesi, taking out a handful of bomb triggers.

"So much attention! Ada was right, I need to spread joy! Careful now, just the icing. Aaah!" gasped Nina as Kaity licked the icing off her cheeks. "Wait…is that what I think it is?" she asked with hollow eyes. She pushed the cat-girl off and instantly got redressed.

"These are all of the Freedom Forcers' detonation triggers. Now, who should I kill first? Ada or Nina?" asked Pesi, his thumb moving back and forth between the two detonators.

"Neither!" yelled Nina, rushing toward him.

"Another step and I push both! That goes for any of you!" yelled Pesi.

Nina stopped in place, looking at Ada with worry.

"How the hell did you get those?" asked Devlin, jumping out of his chair.

"I stole them from you. I can't kill Exp 8, huh? You shouldn't underestimate me. Prepare to be proven wrong!" exclaimed Pesi, as he pushed down the button.

Exp 8 closed his eyes, bracing for the worst. When he opened them, he was still alive.

"I really can't kill him! Whatever, I still have Ada's and Nina's buttons," exclaimed Pesi, smashing Exp 8's detonator in his grip.

Pesi suddenly screamed and fell down to his knees.

Devlin loomed over him. He grabbed Pesi's spiky hair. He pulled him up till he was staring into his creator's only visible eye. "I am going to kill Ada! And if you kill Nina, then Kaity will cry. I don't want her to cry ever again," he said through his teeth. He then smashed the defiant Exp's head into the ground and smothered it in the dirt. The young scientist reached into his coat pocket and found nothing. He checked inside his vest.

Pesi jumped to his feet and flew above his creator. "Is this what you were looking for?" He held out a trigger with his own name on it. "You thought you could blow me up, but you were wrong." He zoomed down and snatched two detonators from the ground. "Now, as I was saying, whose death comes first, Ada's or Nina's?" he asked, twirling them in his hand.

"You can't push either of them," said Exp 8, his neck now poking out.

"Oh, I can't!" he said, bringing his thumb down.

His thumb somehow missed. It was as if the bright red button had a repulsive magnetic field.

Pesi tried again and again, but each time his thumb was averted. He then switched to Opti who looked at the triggers with curious eyes.

"We're sorry, but we have to kill you in order to kill Pesi." Deceivant beckoned Opti with his protruding pointer finger just above the icy surface. "Would you be a dear and not struggle?"

"Wait, who's Pesi?" asked Opti, tapping his bottom lip.

"Ada, would you do the honors?" asked Deceivant.

Ada projected a hologram of Pesi destroying D.S. She then turned away with tearful eyes.

"I'm a killer?" asked Opti, his eyes widening in disbelief.

"You did murder Tempo, so yes. Yes you are," said Deceivant with an unchanged smile.

"When did Tempo die?" asked Kaity with watery eyes.

"Don't cry. He died fighting," said Kanasta, appearing behind Kaity.

"I'll never forget him," said Kaity as she wiped her eyes.

"There there, it will be alright," said Deceivant.

"I'm sorry, Master Devlin, but I can't do this. I refuse to ever kill again!" yelled Opti, stamping his foot down.

"You think I'd get used to it by now," said Kaity, wiping away a stray tear.

"Wait! I know how to fix this! Everybody Pesi and I killed is miraculously alive!" said Opti joyfully.

Anthrax rose from the ground, holding his chest with a smile. D.S.'s eraser flakes came together and reformed him. Tempo's limp body did not rise up.

"Two out of three; that's not bad," said Deceivant with a shrug.

"Tempo, you were a true assassin," said Kanasta with a firm salute.

"I'm joining you guys," said Opti, liquefying the ice lake. He then jumped in.

"What's going on?" asked Devlin, falling to his knees.

"It's over, that's what," said Exp 8, climbing out of the lake.

"Your betrayal has no impact on my plans. Opti, why don't you be a sport and hand your artifacts back to D.S.?" asked Devlin with a smirk.

"Yeah, they belong to me! Hand them over!" exclaimed D.S.

"I didn't know. Devlin said they were mine. I didn't mean to upset you," said Opti, pulling out the artifacts.

He tossed both artifacts to D.S.

"*TELEPORT, INFLUENCE ARTIFACT*," said Devlin with an open hand. The burgundy, glossy garnet gemstone was instantly relocated to his open palm.

D.S. grabbed the Fusion Artifact. "That's mine!" he yelled, running toward Devlin.

"Farewell. My last Exp will meet up with you all in just a bit," said Devlin, vanishing before the eyes of the Freedom Forcers.

"Um…how did he do that?" asked Exp 8, tapping Deceivant's shoulder.

"With the Teleport Artifact. You didn't notice the traveler's stone in Devlin's hand? I thought the Ultimate Exp would be a bit more aware. Heh."

"That's how that bastard keeps appearing everywhere!" yelled Exp 8, pounding his fists against the surface of the lake.

"I thought it was obvious," said Deceivant with a shrug.

Opti swam out of the pool and stood up. (Switch) "Hah, I'm back. All of you suddenly explode!" yelled Pesi evilly.

"Devlin took away your Influence Artifact, but I don't think it would be that easy either way," said Ada, caressing his hand.

"That bastard thinks he can tame destruction itself! I will show him just how powerful I am. You can join me for now, but once he's dead you're all next. And by that I mean you're all next on the chopping block. Khuhuhuhu."

"So then, you're joining us?" asked Exp 8, offering his hand.

"No, but you can join me. You can get rid of Devlin's minions, but he's mine," said Pesi, stretching out his wings.

"Have it your way," said Exp 8.

"My team shall be called the Calamity Cadavers!" exclaimed Pesi, moving his tongue up and down.

"What about the Freedom Forcers?" asked Exp 8 with a nod.

"I guess that's okay, but I don't like the word freedom." (Switch) "Who did I kill now?" asked Opti, falling to his knees in tears.

"You didn't kill anyone. Pesi just joined our team," said Exp 8 with a thumbs-up.

"That's wonderful, I knew he couldn't be all bad," said Opti, wiping away his tears.

"I knew it too," said Ada, holding D.S. to her chest.

"So, Deceivant, you've made a lot of Exps, correct?" asked Exp 8.

"You're looking at quite a few of my creations. I've done my fair share of inventing. It's really rather simple if you understand bioengineering, mechanics, and physics, though you do need surface knowledge of chemistry in order to grasp the nuances of a capsule's capabilities."

"Then, you're the smartest person in our group."

"Beyond a reasonable doubt," said Deceivant, pushing up his glasses.

"So, do we go to Devlin or should we let him come to us?"

"If we are to catch Devlin, we will need to ambush him. I suggest we go back to the lab."

"You don't think he would really kill us, right?" asked Kanasta.

"Don't be ridiculous," said Ada, patting Kanasta on the back.

"I wouldn't put it past Devlin. To him we are just obstacles. We need to capture him and try to convince him that his hatred is misplaced. If all else fails, we'll have to kill him," said Deceivant.

"We aren't going to kill our son," said Ada, petting D.S.'s head.

"If he hurt you, I wouldn't know what to do," said Deceivant, putting his arm around her.

"He's our little boy, he would never hurt us," said Ada, her hands to her chest.

"We just need to cure Devlin of his mental sickness and then everything else will fall into place," said Anthrax, catching up to them.

"Can we still cut him a little bit?" asked D.S., tapping his fingers together.

"He's really on the ropes now. We need to be extra cautious from here on out," said Exp 8, turning around to address his team.

"Yep, yep, extra cautious," said Kaity, licking away the last bit of frosting off Nina's cheek.

"Extra cautious won't save us from Bob," said Nina, wiping away the saliva off her cheek with trembling fingers.

"We should have no problem dealing with Bob," said Deceivant, cleaning his glasses.

"Uh, how is that the case?" asked Exp 8.

"That reminds me. D.S., could you hand over the Fusion Artifact?" asked Deceivant.

"But it's mine," said D.S. with a pouty face.

"Devlin haphazardly gave it to you. It belongs to me. Now hand it over," said Deceivant with a smile.

"Mommy! Daddy's being greedy," pouted D.S.

"You know your father only does what's best for us. Come on, sweetie, be a dear and give it to him," said Ada.

"Alright. But you're going to give it back later, right?" asked D.S., pulling a branchy copper stone out from his chest.

"It won't be up to me. But I'm sure we can find some useful artifacts once we've killed Devlin," said Deceivant, patting D.S.'s head.

"How can you say that?" asked Ada aghast.

"Relax Mother, I'm sure we can convince Devlin to stop this madness," said Kanasta, uncertainty outlining his stoic voice.

"If this body can't sway him, then nothing can," said Nina, biting into her bottom lip as she grasped her breasts.

"We're all going to die!" sobbed Opti.

"You're supposed to be the optimistic one!" yelled Anthrax.

"I'm just being realistic. When Devlin gets angry, he stays angry," said Opti, shivering in his own embrace.

"Guys, we need to figure this out! I can't beat Bob as I am now. We can't even hit him. How are we going to take him down?" asked Exp 8.

"I'm not worried about Bob. I'm worried about Exp 12," said Opti with fear-stricken eyes.

"Who's Exp 12? Ada, do you have any data concerning the matter?" asked Deceivant.

"Exp 12 is Devlin's latest Exp, according to what he said. I have no other data, sorry," said Ada, grabbing Deceivant's arm.

"Wait a minute. We have nine members on our side. How many allies does Devlin have?" asked Exp 8.

"There's Matteria, Bob, and Exp 12. I'm not missing anyone, am I?" asked Anthrax.

"What about NoOne? I don't think you can kill that guy," said Exp 8.

"Yeah, he's still alive and so is Riufen," said Opti.

"That's right. He delivered the cake, right?" asked Exp 8.

"Correct," said Nina, pinching her nipples.

"So then Devlin has a team of six and we have nine. Those are odds I can deal with," said Exp 8 with a punch.

"I'm sure we can convince Matteria to join us," said Anthrax, combing his hair.

There was a rustling in the bushes. The Freedom Forcers looked around attentively.

Matteria walked out of the bushes, wearing only his underwear.

"The most beautiful man in the world has arrived," said Matteria, blowing them a kiss.

"You're a guy!" exclaimed Opti, his hands to the sides of his head.

"Yes. We've been over this. But...I was a girl at first. Deceivant changed me into a boy," said Matteria, lowering his head.

"And I regret it every day. You had such cute wittle boobies," said Deceivant.

Anthrax rushed to Matteria's side. "I don't care and you shouldn't either. You're anatomy isn't as important as your mind. I'm sorry about being distant. Maybe we just don't work together," he said, cupping his boyfriend's hands in his own.

"Devlin sent you here to kill us. So, we'll just have to kill you first," said Nina, ready to pull off her shirt.

Matteria crouched down to Anthrax. "It is hard and I know I can be promiscuous. But there's no one I love more than you," he said, kissing him on the lips.

"So is he our ally now...or not?" asked Nina, twirling her shirt on her finger.

Anthrax broke apart from the kiss and hugged Matteria. "If you care about Devlin, you have to help us stop him." He sprayed disinfectant on his tongue after turning away from his lover's gaze.

"I saw what he ordered Bob to do. I never saw that side of him. I tried to comfort him, but he doesn't trust me anymore. He's lost trust in everyone," said Matteria, looking down.

"We won't let you get the jump on us," said Nina, keeping her distance.

"There's nothing I can do for Devlin at his side. I'm joining up with you guys. If we all work together, I know we can help him through this," said Matteria, grabbing Exp 8's hand.

Nina grabbed Matteria by the wrist. "We need to talk. Now," she said, dragging him into the bushes.

"Hey! Get your hand off my—"

"Don't worry, Thraxy, we're just going to talk. That's all," said Matteria with a nervous smile.

"If I see the slightest injury on him, every organ in your beloved body will turn against you!"

"I'll be fine!" hollered Matteria.

Once they were out of sight, Nina slammed Matteria to the ground.

"Should I get undressed or are you going to do it for me?" asked Matteria, his hands on his colorful panties.

"Don't play around with me. I don't know whose side you're really on, but I don't really give a damn right now."

"So then I guess you weren't swept up in a wave of passion. Uuuh, oh well."

"Did you think I was confiding in you? The only reason I showed off my true nature is because I really wanted to kill you. The thing that pisses me off is that…I can't kill you! I slit your throat, blew you up, and yet you're still alive!"

"As long as Devlin needs me, I can't die," said Matteria with a wave of his hair.

"I need you to swear to me that you won't mention my ninjutsu to anyone, ever. If you let my secret identity slip, I'll kill Anthrax. And, yes, I can kill him."

"You need to calm down. There is no reason to threaten me. Ninjas are secretive; I completely understand. Don't worry, Nina, your secret is safe with me."

"Swear on his life!"

"I promise you I won't speak of it to anyone. In return, I'll tell you a secret. Devlin made me to be his sex slave, pretty naughty right?" asked Matteria with a smirk.

"Why would I care?"

"That sort of information could ruin my life as a celebrity if it got out. But, I trust you with it," said Matteria, putting his hand on her shoulder.

"I already knew that. Now, let's get back to the team. And just so you know, I'll be watching your every move," said Nina with wide eyes.

"You know, only really close friends share deep secrets with each other," said Matteria, putting his arm around her.

"Don't bother harboring affection for me. It won't go anywhere," said Nina, shrugging off his arm. "Follow me and don't try anything."

They joined up with the team.

"So, is he really on our side?" asked Exp 8.

"Seems like it," said Nina with a shrug.

"Hey Matteria, come here. You're the last one," said Anthrax.

Matteria rushed over. "The last one for what?"

Exp 8 walked up to Matteria and gave him a hug. "Welcome to the Freedom Forcers."

Matteria gave him a kiss on the cheek. "Thanks for being so sweet about it. Just keep in mind; I'm doing this for Devlin."

"I understand. He means a lot to you. Devlin must have a side I have yet to see. Glad to have you on the team," said Exp 8, shaking his newest ally's hand.

"So now we have ten teammates and Devlin only has five," said Kanasta before vanishing.

"What the hell just happened!" asked Exp 8, jumping back in response.

"Devlin probably teleported Kanasta up to him," said Deceivant, stretching out his arms.

"Is he going to be okay?" asked Exp 8, taking careful steps.

"Devlin would never hurt his brother. He probably just wanted to ask Kanasta about Kaity," said Ada with a wrinkled forehead.

"Or he wants to recruit him. That could be a problem," said Exp 8, holding his forehead.

"Kanasta can handle anything," said Kaity, standing firm.

"Regardless, we need to head back to the lab," said Deceivant, patting the adorable assassin's head.

"Yeah, it's time to finish this," said Exp 8, picking up the pace.

Part 5
Return to the Lab

Chapter 42: Demonica

Previously: after vanishing before the Freedom Forcers, Devlin reappeared in an extravagant bedroom.

Windows stretched across the left side of the room, giving Devlin a perfect view of the frungle from between the parted lavender curtains. The sleek wooden floor complemented the scarlet walls. A picture of him as a child gripping his mother's hand stood upright on the bedside table.

Devlin collapsed on the queen-sized bed, throwing his arms out with a smile on his face. "That was so incredible! I've only dreamed of Kaity's loving embrace. It felt...so warm," he said, blood rushing to his cheeks. He sat up abruptly and grabbed a TV remote.

As the one-hundred-twenty-inch monitor descended, Devlin wiped some dirt off his shirt. "Since Bob can't be completely trusted, I'm going to need some extra muscle. Time to initialize the backup plan," he said, combing back his hair. "Etah, God of Sel, I summon you!"

The TV turned on and showed only static. "Who dares speak my name?" asked the deep, echoing voice of Etah.

"It's Devlin, remember? You gave me a proposition."

"I give many propositions. Specify or be silent!"

"I send you enough souls and you make me into a god. Does that ring any bells?" asked Devlin with a nervous smile.

"Enough souls to take over Lum?" asked Etah, his inflection rising.

"That was the plan. Things have gotten a bit more complicated. I need a little assistance to fulfill my end of the bargain."

"You want my assistance. Why should I help you?"

"It's in our best interests."

"I suppose it is."

"I give you souls and all you have to give me is some assistance. What's the problem?"

"Nothing to lose and everything to gain. Hmm. Very well...what do you want from me? Don't expect me to come down there myself."

"Oh, of course not. I need someone to take care of Bob in case he gets overconfident. So, do you have anyone in mind? Anyone who excels at killing? Someone who can end an immortal?" asked Devlin with a glint in his eye.

"I do. She's been eager to meet you for a while. Her constant pestering is quite irritating. You may borrow her. Demonica!"

Devlin's eyes widened upon hearing the name.

"I'm already here. So...you're finally going to let me meet Devlin?" she asked, her voice outlined with arousal.

"How powerful is she? I've heard of her, but I've never met her. I don't want a low-level demon working for me," said Devlin, channel-surfing through static.

"She is the best I have."

The TV turned off. Blood leaked from the walls, slowly filling the room and forming an upside down pentagram that stretched from one corner of the room to the other. The blood then shot up, forming into Etah's demon.

The liquid solidified into skin as she took form. Her long, black-and-red mane parted, revealing six dark horns erecting from her crown. They gradually sharpened into scythes. She had black sickle pupils, neon-purple irises, and a black sclera with blood-red lines radiating throughout.

The demon's lips were a misty purple, giving them a venomous, tempting glow. Her scarlet fingernails shot out like daggers. Her sleek, pale, purple skin showed off the couture of her full, busty build. She had powerful wide hips, a solid, thick waist, and a womanly cavern of fiery demonic delights.

Her garment was the last thing to materialize. Her feet transformed into dagger stilettos. The iron dominatrix outfit that bled into existence made her staggering six-foot-six height all the more imposing. The jagged mistress-mask intensified her gaze. Her shoulders, elbows, and knees were now armored with jagged blades. The thick spikes over her nipples were sharp enough to pierce through flesh and her mountainous bosom was held up with thin strings. Iron lingerie was situated just below her red needle pubes, which accentuated rather than covered her gateway to Sel.

"Can you stop the Freedom Forcers' resistance, Exp 12?" asked Devlin, captivated by her eyes.

Exp 12 tapped her belly button, making a spiked and studded piercing appear and leaving an enticing drip of blood. Her smile stretched maliciously across her face. "Don't call me Exp 12. You are to call me Htaed, human," she said, her breathy voice trailing off at the end of her sentences, giving every utterance an air of bewitchment. "Oh wait…it's you. Demonica will be just fine," she exhaled, showing off her sharp teeth and serpent tongue.

"I need to call you Exp 12 in order to deceive the Freedom Forcers," said Devlin, moving to the edge of the bed.

"Then call me Demonica…when we're alone," she said softly, touching his face with her long, sharpened fingernails.

"How do you know me?" asked Devlin with a raised eyebrow.

"We were destined to be together," breathed Demonica as she stroked his jet black hair.

"So, uh…I'll just tell you where the Freedom Forcers are and then you go kill them, okay?"

"It's been a lifetime since I've been on Earth. It would be nice to relax for a bit," said Demonica as she lowered herself onto the bed.

"But once you've finished relaxing, you'll kill them?" asked Devlin, cautiously scooting away from her.

"You should relax with me." Demonica grabbed Devlin and pulled him on top of her. "Your muscles are so tense," she said, massaging his shoulders.

"Demonica, would you please honor my personal space? Do you mind not caressing me?" asked Devlin, getting up from the bed.

Demonica pulled him back down onto the bed. "Yes, I mind it. How am I supposed to have fun with you if I can't touch?" she asked as she dragged her finger across his enticing lips.

He wiped his lips clean, hoping he wasn't poisoned. "So...uh, how can I make you comfy?" asked Devlin, backing up until he slipped off the bed.

"You are so shy. That's a trait I loathe in men. However...because it's you, I'm turned on." Demonica slid off the bed, landing on top of the bashful boy.

"So what can I do for you?" asked Devlin, tensing up.

"Draw me a bath," said Demonica, sitting up on his lap.

"Okay, I'll get it ready right away," said Devlin, squeezing out from beneath her.

Demonica leaped back to her feet. "Make it a blood bath. It's good for my complexion." She dragged her hands down her sides while biting her lip. She then dug her fingernails into his arm, just deep enough to get some blood.

"Right away," said Devlin, almost falling over.

Demonica collapsed into blood. She rematerialized beneath the handsome boy, catching him in her arms. "You need to relax." She shoved her finger in his mouth. "How do you taste?"

"It tastes bloody," said Devlin, his legs trembling.

"Delicious!" exclaimed Demonica as she savored the remnants of his blood.

"So uh...you want a blood bath, right?" asked Devlin, backing away from her.

"Your blood is the sweetest I've ever tasted. It's so nostalgic." Demonica appeared right in front of him. "I want the bath made with your blood."

"I don't think I have that much blood," said Devlin, gripping his arm nervously.

"You'll just have to dig deep," whispered Demonica as she jabbed her nails into her own chest.

The fear left Devlin's eyes and a smile returned to his face.

"I have a better idea. *TELEPORT, KANASTA*," said Devlin with an outstretched hand.

Kanasta appeared before them, leaping back upon arrival.

"You must be Devlin's brother," said Demonica as she massaged the man's firm chest.

"Who are you?" asked Kanasta, gripping her by the wrist.

"I'm Devlin's mistress, Demonica."

"It looks like he's all grown up now," said Kanasta with watery eyes.

"I didn't bring you here so we could chat. So...what's Kaity's favorite flower?" asked Devlin.

"That would be hibiscus," said Kanasta with a nod.

"Good. You are no longer needed. Demonica, I offer you my brother as a sacrifice," said Devlin, bowing down.

"That's not much of a sacrifice. You hate him," said Demonica, pulling Devlin up by his chin.

"How did you know that? How long have you been spying on me?" asked Devlin, knocking her off.

"I can see the hatred in your eyes," said Demonica, licking the boy's eyelids.

Devlin pulled away. "Stop doing weird things."

"You are so adorable," said Demonica, petting his head.

"Kanasta, remember how we bathed together when we were little?" asked Devlin, leading them into the bathroom.

"I would never forget," said Kanasta with a smile.

Devlin turned to Demonica with a smirk. "I can't give you my blood. But I offer you the next best thing." He pushed his brother into the indoor Jacuzzi and slammed his hand against a button on the wall.

Wires shot out from beneath the assassin, wrapping around him.

"You aren't going to kill me. You're not capable of such an act," said Kanasta, sitting up in the bath.

"I am going to extract every last drop of your deceitful blood," said Devlin with a hollow tone.

The wires moved in a flash, tearing at the assassin viciously.

"Devlin, I don't know what I did to you...but I am sorry," said Kanasta contritely, not flinching as the wires tore him apart.

"A simple apology could never atone for the pain you have forced upon me. I'll meet you in hell to continue your torture," said Devlin as the wires became more vicious.

Devlin stared at Kanasta until there was no longer a recognizable piece of his brother left. Small chunks of meat were floating in the blood water, raising the water level to the brim.

Demonica rubbed up against Devlin in arousal.

"Your bath is ready," said Devlin, blood on his cheeks.

Demonica breathed heavy as she clawed at his lab coat. Her clothes disintegrated as she rammed into him.

Devlin toppled backwards into the bath, landing with Demonica on top.

"Push that button again! Auuwh!" exclaimed Demonica, fiddling with her nipples.

"He's really gone," said Devlin with a tearful smile.

"We'll be ripped to shreds together," said Demonica as she bit into his earlobe.

Devlin pulled away and grabbed his ear. "What the hell is wrong with you? That really hurt."

"Ooh, the blood's nice and warm. I love it when it's fresh," said Demonica as her fingers glided across her body.

"Glad I could make you happy. Now, I really should be getting back to work," said Devlin as he tried to exit the bath.

Demonica's teeth bore into his leg, causing Devlin to topple onto the edge of the tub. "I always knew we were destined to be together. You are darker than I ever imagined. Let's have some fun," she said as she pulled him back in.

Devlin looked away from her with flustered cheeks. "I've always wanted to meet a demon. It's really cool to meet you," he said, bowing his head as he struggled to break free of her grasp.

"Why must you hide your amazing body?" asked Demonica as she tore open his lab coat.

Devlin lowered his head. "My body isn't amazing."

"Oh yes it is. It's the one and only hunk of flesh I want all to myself. Its unique charm gets me riled up all over. Ahhhh! Blood baths are too delicious," she said, seductively licking her fingers one by one.

"Yeah, tasty. Heheh."

Demonica shoved her fingers inside his open mouth. "How does your brother taste? How does it feel to taste him?" she asked, moving up and down in excitement.

"Is this…turning you on?" asked Devlin, backing up until his back was pressed against the edge of the bath.

"Obviously. Doesn't it turn you on?" asked Demonica, dragging her claws down his coat.

"He was my brother," said Devlin, his eyes tearing up.

"I saw the way you tore him to shreds. I saw the blood lust in your eye. Killing does turn you on. Though it's cute how you act so innocent," said Demonica as her fingers made laps around his exposed nipples.

"Perhaps vengeance does get me a bit excited. But pointless killing is just sick," said Devlin, pushing away from her.

Demonica burst into laughter and hissed into his ear. "Vengeance is pointless killing."

"I gave you your bath. When are you going to help me?" asked Devlin, grabbing her by the shoulders.

"Why are you so worried? You just need to relax," she said as she shoved her hand down his pants.

"I need to go," said Devlin, quickly getting out of the bath.

"Etah, Devlin's being mean," cried out Demonica, her hands rubbing the corners of her eyes.

"Goooo, take off my pants," said Devlin, quickly stripping out of them. He jumped right back into the bath in his underwear.

"I guess it's an improvement. Now come on, just relax on my chest. Let your brother's blood wash away all your worries," said Demonica as she cradled her love to her voluptuous bosom.

"Mom used to snuggle with me in the bath," said Devlin as his shoulders relaxed.

"You are just too cute. You're thinking about your mommy while you're resting on my breasts. You don't have a perverted bone in your body. Well, maybe one," said Demonica as she grabbed his boner.

"Hey, I was just starting to relax!" exclaimed Devlin, knocking her hand off.

Demonica put her hand up to his heart. "Your heart's racing. Is that the beat of love?" she asked, turning to him with hope in her eyes.

"No, that's definitely fear," said Devlin, turning away from her.

"Good. You should fear me," said Demonica, gripping his neck.

"Sometimes I wonder if vengeance is worth it. I know justice is important, but...it's still painful," said Devlin, examining Kanasta's eye in his fingers.

Demonica's grip tightened and she pulled him out of the water.

"Vengeance is always worth the pain. It's only fair that they suffer! You can't let them just get away with what they've done," said Demonica through clenched teeth.

Devlin ripped her hand off his neck and stood in the bath. "You're absolutely correct. It's just that the thought of killing my family is...frightening. I can't believe I murdered my own brother. Ahahaha-hugh-hugh-hugh."

"Fretting over fratricide, that's just so adorable," said Demonica as she snuggled the worrisome child to her chest.

Devlin wiped his tears away. "Killing is a big deal to me. Revenge isn't a road of flowers, but it's a road I must travel," he said with a righteous fist.

"That's right. Vengeance is paved with blood and anguish. I know what you're going through. Just give in to the hatred. Let it become you. Savor their pain. Then all those sweet memories will strengthen your resolve," said Demonica, petting him lovingly.

"I know it must be done. But that doesn't mean I have to enjoy it," said Devlin, grabbing a towel.

"I try to enjoy everything I do. Bliss is a mindset, not a destination," said Demonica, grabbing his hand.

"You do have a point," said Devlin, dropping the towel and turning to her.

"Don't think of this blood as the remains of your brother. Think of it as the taste of sweet revenge," said Demonica, letting a handful pour down her bare breasts.

"I should detach myself from the act, not bask in it," said Devlin, looking at his bloody hands contemplatively.

"Don't be like that. It's not about how the blood tastes. All that matters is who it's from. Flesh is all the sweeter when it's rendered from your favorite cow," said Demonica, rubbing her breasts.

"No. It's not about Kanasta. This blood isn't his. This is the fruit of my vengeance. This is the glory of revenge!" Devlin stretched his arms and legs out, letting the blood blanket his body. "I am surrounded by righteous judgment. This is a communion of righteousness!" He bit into a chunk of his brother's flesh. He then cupped his hands and sipped the blood.

Demonica gasped before pressing against Devlin.

"It's not my brother…it is justice," said Devlin as he swallowed the flesh.

Demonica pushed him under the surface. Her tongue ravaged the corners of his mouth as she sucked up his breath.

Devlin writhed around as her claws dug into his shoulders. He escaped her grip and ran out the bath. He sped into his bedroom, falling over after bumping into Demonica.

"Why are you avoiding me?" she asked, lifting him up by his leg.

"I am already devoted to someone else."

"What is it, a woman, a man, a tentacle?" asked Demonica, shaking him around.

"Tentacle?" asked Devlin with a raised eyebrow.

"I can use tentacles!" she exclaimed, releasing her grip. She slit her stomach open with her fingernail.

Tentacles raged forth, wrapping around the young scientist.

"It's a girl, okay," squealed Devlin, covering his crotch.

The tentacles kissed the boy goodbye before receding back into her belly.

"A girl? As in a little girl? How old?"

"She's…in middle school, I think. I should have asked Kanasta," said Devlin, slowly getting back on his feet.

"So then you're a pedophile. This makes things difficult. I can grow a cock, but I can't make myself younger. Auuh," said Demonica, rolling her head back.

"I…uh…didn't need to know that," said Devlin, as his hand secretly rummaged through his underwear drawer.

"Actually, I was reborn only about fifteen years ago. Does that excite you?" asked Demonica, her tongue stretching out to lick her cheeks.

"Really, how fascinating," said Devlin, slipping on a dry pair of underwear.

"Since I'm actually quite young, will you love me?" asked Demonica, her hand to her heart.

"I'm not a pedophile! I just like one little girl," said Devlin, quickly putting on an undershirt.

"Your father said the same thing. That's how they all start out. So how old is she, eight?"

"She's twelve, but, like I said, I don't know if she's going to middle school or not. She would look so cute in uniform. Eee!"

"Your father's first little lover was in grade school."

"How do you know so much about my father?" asked Devlin, grabbing her hand.

Demonica's hand overlapped his. "I've been waiting for you since before you were born," she said with a heavy breath.

"I'm not going to buy all this nonsense. I've researched succubi, you can't trick me," said Devlin, slipping into his lab coat.

"So, who is the little bitch?" asked Demonica, grinding her teeth.

"Kaity is a catlike assassin, not a dog. You're lucky your insults are nonsensical," said Devlin, pulling a gun out from his lab coat.

"It's Kaity." Demonica took in a deep breath. "It just had to be her. Why is everyone so interested in her?" she asked through clenched teeth.

"What are you talking about?"

Demonica pressed up against Devlin. "When I return, I'll be drenched in her blood. If you behave yourself, I'll give you a taste," she said, biting her lip.

Devlin shot the demon right in the forehead with his Colt pistol. He then rammed into her, knocking her onto the bed. He put the gun to her neck as his hands trembled. "You touch her and I will mutilate you!"

Demonica's head recoiled. The wound vanished. A twisted smirk spread across her face.

Demonica pulled him up with her legs into a forced embrace. "I love a man who's a little violent. All I needed to do to get on your bad side is hurt Kaity. You make this way too easy," she said, rubbing his boyish cheeks.

"If you hurt her, I will never love you," said Devlin, gripping her by the throat.

"I'm sure I can find other ways to make you cry," said Demonica, her breath becoming heavy. She then flung him to the ground. "Get down on your knees!"

Devlin obeyed the command as if under a hex.

"You will marry me!"

"Um, don't you mean, will you marry me?" asked Devlin with quivering legs.

"Why ask, when you can tell? Say goodbye to your little squeeze. Sehuhuhuhu."

Devlin grabbed her shoulders and slammed her down on the bed. "Go back to hell! I don't need your help. I'll stop the Freedom Forcers without you!"

Chains shot through the bed and fastened the delectable boy to the ceiling.

"Let me go!" yelled Devlin, slamming his knuckles against the ceiling.

Demonica flew up to Devlin, grappling onto him with her sharp nails. "Let's do it upside down like a bat. Once you're tired, I'll go kill your little girlfriend."

Devlin broke free of the chains and repeatedly punched the demon as he fell back to the bed.

Demonica bounced off the bed, catching Devlin in midair. "You can relax. I'm not really going to kill Kaity. I was assigned to follow your orders. I was just messing around. You are just so much fun to play with. Now, command me! I'll do anything you want," she said, grabbing his hand and pressing it to her chest.

"Anything?" asked Devlin, licking his lips.

"Whatever you command…Master," said Demonica, breathing heavily in his ear.

"I order you to…kill the Freedom Forcers! Like I said when you first arrived!" exclaimed Devlin, grabbing her by the chin.

"Are you serious? I thought maybe I could try being on the bottom for a change," said Demonica, getting off the bed and fixing her hair.

"You're on the bottom now. Kill all the Freedom Forcers. Break their spirit."

"Fine, but first I want a kiss," said Demonica, perking up her lips.

"I'm saving my first kiss for Kaity," said Devlin, turning away in embarrassment.

"Even your lips haven't been de-virginized? You are just too innocent. I want to ravage you right now," said Demonica, grabbing his crotch.

"I'll give you a hug," said Devlin with a smile.

"Deal!" Demonica embraced him tightly. "And once your plan succeeds, you'll go on a date with me. I choose where," she said, bouncing up and down.

Devlin slipped out of her arms and then pulled a file off his dresser. "Fine, but you are not allowed to kill Kaity or Exp 8 or Nina or Deceivant or Ada. Is that clear?" he asked, showing her their pictures.

"Why so many? Have you grown soft?"

"You can't kill Nina because Kaity will cry. You can't kill Kaity because I love her. You can't kill Exp 8 because I need him for power. And you can't kill Deceivant or Ada because I am going to kill them," said Devlin, touching her face with his cold fingers.

"Your dark side is so hot. I'll be back in a little while; watch me in your surveillance room," said Demonica with a wink.

"You know about that too?"

"I know so much about you. I'm your dark stalker." Demonica then leaped out the window.

Devlin ran to the window and saw a bloody puddle where Demonica landed.

"I'm not falling for it!"

The blood then reassembled into Demonica.

"Not even a tear!" she hollered back with a wounded voice.

"Get moving already. I'm going to go prepare for our date," said Devlin, before shutting the window.

Demonic held her heart longingly before taking flight.

Chapter 43: Bloodlust

Previously: after Matteria joined the Freedom Forcers and Kanasta vanished, the group began their journey back to Devlin's lab.

"So, what's the big plan to stop Devlin once we get there?" asked Matteria.

"We are going to try and ambush him. If we capture him, we plan to convince him to stop this foolishness," said Deceivant.

"Devlin is as stubborn as you are. It won't work."

"So, what's your plan?" asked Exp 8.

"Well, what does Devlin care more about than anything?"

"That would be vengeance, ugh," said Deceivant.

"Engh, wrong. He cares about Kaity above all else."

"Hmm, you might have a point. I've always tried to separate him from love to keep his initiative going. Perhaps settling down will pacify him a bit," said Deceivant, stroking his chin hairs.

"Exactly, all we need is for Kaity to make Devlin's dreams come true," said Matteria with his hands clasped to his cheeks.

"I'm not going to prostitute myself out," said Kaity with puffed out cheeks.

"Devlin's love for you is as real as my abs. What he wants more than anything is for you to accept his love. Once he is in this state of bliss, he will realize how empty vengeance is. Kaity, you are our only hope at stopping this," said Matteria, grabbing her hand.

"If this doesn't work out, then I'll knock some sense into him," said Exp 8, rolling his wrists.

Kaity put her arms behind her head. "I don't see why it wouldn't. I've done this gig before. You just make them feel special. I just won't dive in for the kill this time, hee-hee."

"Aren't we asking too much of her?" asked Ada with a frown.

"I am an assassin; acting is no problem. Plus, Devlin's got a sweet side to him. This should go off without a hitch, right, Boss?" Kaity turned around, but he wasn't there. Her head dropped and she sighed. "I hope he's okay."

"We're going to defeat Devlin with the power of love? How incredibly boring?" said Pesi.

"It's not like we're holding hands and our friendship makes us immortal. Heheh. That would be so cool," said D.S., drawing on his electronic pad.

"It's rather practical, actually. We're dissolving Devlin's negative delusions. Finding him a love partner will give him a brighter aspect of the world," said Anthrax, turning to Matteria with a warm smile.

"Everyone! I have a perfect plan to destroy Devlin!" exclaimed Pesi, rubbing his palms together.

"Huuh. Destruction solves nothing," said Matteria.

"We should run right into his lab and then smash his face in!" hollered Pesi, looking at his team for signs of appreciation.

"How like a man to jump to violence," said Matteria, lowering his shoulders.

"Don't be so sexist. There are plenty of peaceful men. Men may have come from women, but that doesn't mean men are inferior. Both are slightly different anatomically, but they have equal potential," said Anthrax with a stern finger.

"Your wisdom is infinite," said Matteria, grabbing his lover's hand.

"I'm only as smart as Devlin programmed me to be," said Anthrax with a light blush.

"That isn't entirely true. You were programmed for the capacity of acquiring and applying new information," said Deceivant.

"Stop talking about us like we're software! We are living, feeling beings!" yelled Exp 8.

"But of course, most Exps were engineered with the basic senses," said Deceivant.

"We weren't made so that you creators could use us. We have feelings and thoughts; all of us do. I don't know what comes after death, but Exps can't be excluded from it. We have a soul, don't we?"

"If you believe in that sort of thing, then I guess so. If souls do exist, then all things living and non-living will have them. Some argue that nothing can function without a consciousness. I'm still skeptical about this assumption."

"So then...the souls of our comrades...will they be watching us?" asked Exp 8 with a gentle tone.

"I hardly see how that matters. I don't know what happens after death other than decay. There are enough phenomena in this world, so I don't really concern myself with the afterlife. Conjecture can be dangerous. Religious fanaticism spawns from strict presuppositions, after all," said Deceivant.

"Obsession can come from anything. There is this burning instinct inside me, yearning for freedom. I have to be careful or I could end up like Devlin," said Exp 8, holding his chest.

"Don't worry about what happens. As long as you make the right choices, you will remain in control regardless," said Deceivant, patting him on the shoulder.

"Who says what's right or wrong?"

"My bad. As long as you evaluate your course of action, then you won't stray from the desired path."

"Exactly! It's my choice," said Exp 8 with fierce eyes.

"I never said you couldn't make choices. I just think you should be aware that Devlin's programming is the foundation for the choices you make."

"Then I'll deprogram myself and every Exp."

"You can't eliminate your biology. What an absurd notion."

Kaity hopped up in front of them. "So, why don't we all just rush into Devlin's lab and surrender? After that, I'll try to convince him to stop this. How does that sound?"

"We can't surrender; even if it's just an act. We have to relentlessly fight while you convince Devlin. If his beliefs are unshaken, we must be ready to overtake him. But there's no need to worry. We've got your back," said Exp 8 with a thumbs-up.

"I really do think I can stop him. You guys don't need to fight anymore. I don't want to lose anyone else," said Kaity with watery eyes.

"If this works...then all the fighting was pointless. They didn't need to die. Kawai and Atatasuki could be by my side right now. If you could have convinced Devlin...I'm not blaming you. I'm just having some regrets, that's all," said Exp 8, tears dripping down his mask.

"Violence prevails when diplomacy fails. It's been that way for so long. But as long as there is compromise, there will be peace. Kaity is our little compromise," said Ada sweetly, fiddling with the cat-girl's nose.

"Are you going to stand by and fight with us, Ada?" asked Exp 8.

"I really don't like to fight. That's why I like to stay cooped up in your chest," said Ada, touching the center of his concave chest.

"But if Kaity can't change him, we will all fight," said Exp 8, gripping Ada's hand.

"Whoa, calm down. I'm not an Exp. I'm human. There's no reason I should have to fight," said Deceivant.

"I'll fight if it comes down to it," said Kaity, checking if her pistols were fully loaded.

"Your metallic kitty tail is just too cute," said Deceivant, grabbing her tail and rubbing it against his face.

"We've wasted enough time, let's kick this into high gear," said Exp 8, activating his jets.

Ada went back into Exp 8's chest.

Matteria picked up Anthrax and rode a self-made wave.

"Kanasta hasn't come back yet. Is he going to be okay?" asked Kaity as she ran on all fours.

"He is probably taking Devlin hostage as we speak," said Deceivant, failing to follow.

"You're slowing us down," said Exp 8 as he calmed his jets.

"I'm sorry I can't fly," said Deceivant, bent over with his hands on his knees.

"As long as you're sorry, we'll forgive you," said Opti, lifting the elderly man onto his shoulders.

"Hey, Deceivant, do you know why one side of Devlin's lab is a canyon and the other is a frungle?" asked Exp 8.

"That was my choice. I found an oasis in the canyon and decided that I wanted my base right between the two. I was hoping the government wouldn't track me in a canyon in New Mexico. Senator John sure is persistent though. You should be grateful Devlin didn't sell you off. You should be grateful," said Deceivant, holding onto his glasses.

"I broke out. Devlin didn't let me go. What did you owe the government anyway?"

"A lot of bail money, but Hope got me out of most of it," said Deceivant with a tender smile.

"That's not all," said Ada.

"Right you are. You see, apparently I am not responsible enough to own the weapons I create. The government wanted to confiscate them. Senator John is particularly patriotic. According to him, only America should have that kind of firepower. I was thinking of selling them to the Japanese if things got tough. I was born there and they actually value peace. They've been through the horrors of nuclear warfare. They don't act like the world police."

"So am I a nuclear weapon?" asked Exp 8 softly.

"You are a weapon of energy. Devlin wants full control of your power. But first he wants to unlock your latent abilities. That's what I think at least."

"But what do you owe Senator John?"

"To be honest, I don't really owe him anything. I struck a deal a while back. I promised him Exp 8 if he would leave me be. Well, looks like he came to collect, heheh."

"So I'm just money under the table then?"

"You make it sound so crude. Haha."

"Um, honey, where were you while I watched over Devlin?" asked Ada.

"I was tending to my daycares. I struck a deal and got some inexpensive ones set up in Tokyo."

"Why didn't you just spend time with Devlin?" asked Exp 8.

"My time is best spent with little girls," said Deceivant, his hand to his chest.

"He's our son. You shouldn't talk like that," said Ada, her voice cracking.

"So you just abandoned Devlin at the lab?" asked Exp 8.

"It wasn't his fault. Devlin left us. We raised Devlin with love and compassion," said Ada, beaming at her husband.

"Everyone, we've arrived," said Exp 8, looking up at the lab through the thick foliage.

"It's been too long since I've been here," said Deceivant, overcome with warmth.

Ada popped out of Exp 8's chest and rematerialized. She leaned against Deceivant and kissed his cheek.

"Don't move. Let's scope out the area," said Nina.

"Look everyone!" Opti pointed up high at the side of the lab.

Demonica now had blood wings that were pierced into the wall, holding her in place. She looked down at her prey and licked her lips.

"That must be Exp 12. It looks like a girl," said Opti squinting.

"Well, whatever it is, I think it sees us!" exclaimed Exp 8.

Demonica swooped down.

"She saw us from way up there? Do you think she has super eyes?" asked D.S., hopping in place.

Demonica hit the ground, becoming a puddle of blood.

"Are you serious? She died? That was…quite convenient," said Deceivant with a grin.

"Devlin said he'd give the new Exp all the artifacts. We should hurry and collect them before reinforcements show up," said Opti with double thumbs-up.

The Freedom Forcers rushed up to the puddle of blood but no artifacts were there.

"I guess he didn't give her any artifacts. I'm sorry you had to die for Devlin. Don't worry…you will be the last," said Exp 8, lowering his head to the ground with a bow.

The blood shot up, making a red silhouette. Demonica's skin formed, showing her grand physique.

"Did Devlin get lonely again?" asked Nina, rolling her eyes.

"Isn't he always? Sehuhuhu," said Demonica as she stood up.

"Why did he make you?" asked Nina with a scowl.

"To kill all of you," she said, blowing a kiss.

"I know you. You're not an Exp! Isn't your name…Tsul?" asked Deceivant with a snap of the fingers.

"No, I am Htaed. Tsul is my sister. You're the one who turned her down because she wasn't young enough," she said with a condescending look.

"You know her? How do you know Devlin's newest Exp?" asked Exp 8, turning to the suspicious scientist.

"She's not an Exp. She's a demon."

"Wait, so souls are ridiculous, but you believe in demons?"

"I don't believe in them, but…trust me, she's not an Exp."

"Are demons stronger than Exps?"

"I'm not just a demon. I am the most powerful demon of them all," said Demonica, running her hands down her body.

"She's just a poser. I'm still the sexiest," said Nina, rubbing her breasts.

"You're just a girl. I'm a full-grown woman," said Demonica, stroking her thighs. "*Blood Bondage*."

Chains of blood shot out from the ground and wrapped around Nina. They then receded, pinning her down.

"I don't care what you are, you're in the way!" yelled Exp 8, rushing to Demonica.

Chains shot out all around the Freedom Forcers. Exp 8, Matteria, Anthrax, and D.S. were all pulled to the ground and held in place.

Demonica strutted up to Nina, not noticing Kaity in the tree above her.

"Devlin told me not to kill you, but I don't really care. You're just another obstacle. It's best to get rid of you now." Her hand turned blood-red as it molded into a blade.

"I'm too drop-dead gorgeous to die!" exclaimed Nina, struggling in futility.

Kaity jumped at Demonica. She stabbed her plasma claws into her viciously.

The claws tore straight through the demon's body.

"Don't you dare hurt Nina!" exclaimed Kaity, her jabs weakened by her emotions.

"It's so cute how you try to stop me," said Demonica, blowing the girl a kiss. She then plunged her blade-like arm into Nina. Blood seeped off her arm and onto her victim, spreading over her whole body.

Nina gradually dissolved into a bloody puddle.

Demonica ripped Kaity off and tossed her aside. A cage of chains then enveloped the little girl. "Devlin wanted to kill Deceivant…but that's not my problem," she said, her head abruptly turning to him.

A single fingernail elongated, zooming past Opti before slicing into Deceivant.

Deceivant's body convulsed as her blood bore its way through him. He then liquidated into blood.

Demonica's fingernail retracted. She licked the remnants of blood off her fingertip with the tip of her tongue. "Next on my list is Devlin's mother," she said as her malicious eyes targeted Ada.

"He can't be dead," said Ada, her eyes hollow with horror.

Demonica grabbed Ada by the throat. Blood poured into her victim's open mouth.

Ada then exploded into blood.

Demonica ravenously licked the blood off her arm.

D.S. rammed her from behind, shoving his scissors through her back.

Demonica grabbed onto the scissors and pulled them in deeper, gasping orgasmically as she played with herself.

D.S. screamed in horror. He let go of his scissors and made a run for it.

The demon's tail wrapped around D.S.'s legs, causing him to trip. Her tail then shot up, lifting her prey above the ground.

D.S. shielded his eyes as she dangled him back and forth.

Demonica made her arm extra sharp before thrusting it into him.

D.S. gripped the blood blade, struggling to pull it out.

Chains of blood shot into him and ripped out his capsule.

"*DESERT KICK*!" yelled Opti, recovering from the shock of Exp 12's power.

A heat wave slammed into Demonica, melting the skin off her chest. Blood gushed out from her chest and solidified into skin.

"That felt amazing!" gasped Demonica. She crushed D.S.'s capsule in her grip, absorbed his artifacts, and tossed his limp body aside.

"*ICE SHOT*!" yelled Opti, forming a large icicle from a heart-shaped hand-sign.

Demonica strafed to the side and then thrust her hand into the ground.

Her finger's burst out from below, piercing into Opti's body. The razor sharp nails then quickly receded.

Opti fell to his knees, shivering in pain.

"Next, I'll go for the cute little boy," said Demonica, releasing her next plaything from her chains.

Anthrax got up as his whole body trembled in fear. "D...duh...don't worry, sir. Dr. Anthrax will ff...fff...fix you up in a jiffy." He tried to move forward but fear paralyzed him.

"Those concerned about others are doomed to a premature death," said Demonica, flying up to him.

Matteria jumped in the way, throwing his arms out to shield his lover.

Demonica's blade arm sliced into Matteria's chest, cracking the surface of his capsule. The blade's momentum continued, piercing all the way through. It then shot out his back and bore through Anthrax's chest.

Demonica tore her arm out.

Anthrax fell to the floor, grabbing the hole in his chest.

"I'm bored of this. Huugh." A blood scythe was conjured up into Demonica's grip. She sliced off Anthrax's head with one sweep. She snatched the two artifacts from the shattered capsules. Demonica then stepped on Anthrax's head with her razor-sharp heel, twisting her foot as she gasped with pleasure.

"Stop killing my friends!" Opti soared through the air and up to the nasty lady.

"I follow my master's orders; you should've done the same."

Demonica's stomach burst open, revealing a swirling red vortex. Tentacles came out and latched onto the bird-man, ripping him out of the air.

Opti grabbed onto the ground with all his might. He lost his grip and was reeled toward the vortex.

The jagged teeth around the edges of her stomach chomped on his flesh. Her tentacles shoved his whole body inside the vortex. Her stomach shut close.

Demonica rubbed her belly while biting her lip. "Mmm, that's everyone! I am definitely going on that date," she said with a little hop of excitement.

The chain cage around Kaity crumbled.

Kaity fell out and touched the bloody puddle that once resembled Nina.

"You are coming with me," said Demonica, strutting up to Devlin's little squeeze.

Kaity reached for Nina as Demonica ripped her from the ground and took to the skies with black wings.

Exp 8 was trapped beneath the blood-red shackles the entire time. He could only watch as his final comrade was taken from him.

Chapter 44: Devlin's Weakness

Demonica flew through the air with Kaity in her grip, nearly forty feet above ground.

Kaity's backpack disengaged her sniper rifle.

In a flash, she slipped out, grabbed the falling gun, cocked it, and fired.

The energy bullet shot up into Demonica's jaw, and out her head.

Kaity propelled herself toward the lab.

Demonica crashed to the ground with a gaping hole in her mouth.

Kaity stabbed her claws into the side of the lab as she slid down. She fell to the grass, catching Devlin in the corner of her eye. She steadied her hands and aimed her sights.

Devlin was suddenly right in front of her. He ripped the gun out of her hands and teleported it out of sight. He rushed his hands up her legs as she reached for her sidearm. Their hands touched and her guns were whisked away.

"You can't disarm me! I'm a living weapon!" yelled Kaity, stabbing her plasma claws into his side.

Devlin cringed in pain and exhaled sharply. "Kaity, I told Demonica not to kill Nina," he said, looking at the demon's fallen body with a dark glare.

"Aww, I still couldn't trick you." Demonica stood back up. The hole in her head healed as she strutted up to Devlin. "I didn't kill Nina, I just changed her form," she said, holding a ball of blood between her fingernails.

Kaity's eyes shimmered as she reached out to the blood ball.

"What about Ada and Deceivant? They were mine to kill!" yelled Devlin, tearing the plasma claws out from his side.

"I was just tricking Exp 8 so he would lose all remaining hope. Ada and Deceivant have been changed as well. I'll go lock them up for you," said Demonica, turning away.

"What happened to the others?" asked Devlin, teleporting in front of her.

Demonica's smile slowly widened. She handed Devlin all the artifacts of the dead Exps.

"The rest of them are dead, right?" asked Devlin as he absorbed them.

"They will never bother you again," said Demonica, giving him a kiss.

"That's…wonderful," said Devlin, lowering his head.

"I followed your orders and tricked Exp 8. There's no reason to be so pouty," said Demonica, massaging his shoulders.

Devlin pulled away from her. "I feel responsible for them. Matteria in particular was very special to me," he said, wiping his eyes.

"Instead of lamenting over your Exps' demise, you should be anticipating your parents' murder. I want front-row seating for your patricidal exhibition," said Demonica before flying off through the open window above.

Devlin teleported up to Kaity while holding his side in pain. He summoned a medical wrap and covered his wound.

"Kaity, I'm sorry about all of this. But don't worry…things are coming to a close," said Devlin, clenching the teleport artifact tightly.

"You can't undo this! They're dead. I can't believe you wanted this," said Kaity in tears.

"This is all necessary. Please, Kaity, you have to trust me," said Devlin, offering her his hand.

"What exactly is your plan?" asked Kaity, slowly getting up.

"To sacrifice enough souls so that I can bribe my way to godhood. I want real power and I will get it."

"I thought you were after vengeance, not power. You're talking like a maniac," said Kaity, backing away from him.

"My vengeance shall pave the path to my acquisition of power."

"You don't have to do this," said Kaity, sitting up.

"I deserve vengeance! To forgive them after what they did to me would be an injustice."

Kaity grabbed his hand. "You can work through this. It's never too late."

"If I gave up now, then all their deaths are in vain." Devlin placed his hand atop Kaity's. "I owe it to the fallen Freedom Forcers to complete my plan."

"They die in vain only if your plan works. If you quit now…then they died to save you."

Devlin and Kaity vanished, reappearing in his bedroom.

"I don't need saving," said Devlin, letting go of her hand.

"Leave your plan unfinished, like you did with Atatasuki," said Kaity with a forced smile.

"He was Deceivant's Exp; all I did was give him a silver coating."

"Think this through," said Kaity, grabbing his arm.

"The end is in sight. Exp 8 will not let me live after I murdered all his comrades. He will come for me," said Devlin, holding his side to calm a surge of pain.

"You're wrong."

"Am I now?"

"Even after Kawai and Atatasuki were killed, Exp 8 didn't seek vengeance. The plan was for me to come here and convince you to stop."

"There is no stopping. You can stop pretending to care about me. I don't need pity," said Devlin, turning away from her.

"I really do want to help you," said Kaity, hugging his arm.

Devlin sat down on the bed. "I'm sorry for doubting you. I'm just so afraid."

"What are you afraid of?"

"I'm afraid I've lost myself. By remaining cold and detached in the pursuit of justice, I thought I could preserve my identity. But I've changed. I've become hollowed out. It won't matter once I'm a god though, nothing will." Devlin stripped out of his lab coat.

"Devlin…where is Kanasta?" asked Kaity, looking at the trail of blood leading to the bathroom.

Devlin dropped his head.

"Where is he?" asked Kaity, her voice trembling.

Devlin looked her in the eye. "He's…dead."

"You killed him?" asked Kaity, her bottom lip trembling.

Devlin nodded and then turned away.

"You killed my Papa," said Kaity softly, almost like a question.

"You don't know what he did to me. It was payback," said Devlin, wiping away a stray tear off his cheek.

"He raised me when my parents died. He loved me."

"He would've killed me. I had to do it!"

"He can't be dead. He's too strong to die," said Kaity with still eyes.

"It's so much harder to kill with your own hands," said Devlin, looking at his palms reflexively.

Kaity pressed her plasma claws to Devlin's neck. She glared at him with cold hatred. "You don't deserve to live."

"Regardless, I must complete my plan," said Devlin, his eye firm with resolve.

"If I killed you right now, then it would all be over," said Kaity, her claws now drawing blood.

"Do what you must," said Devlin, moving his hair aside and looking at her with both eyes.

"How could you kill Kanasta?" asked Kaity, her tears now rushing freely.

"Don't cry, Kaity. It hurts me to see you like this," said Devlin, putting his hand on her shoulder.

"How could you do it?" asked Kaity, pushing him away.

"My grudges are between me and my family. I wasn't trying to drag anyone else into this."

"The second you called Kanasta, you brought my entire family into your mess," said Kaity with flaring eyes.

"There's no room for regret on the road to revenge. I did what I had to."

"You didn't have to do it. He cared about you. He took care of me," said Kaity, now wiping her tears.

"I care about him too. He's my brother. But I had to put my feelings aside. You understand, don't you?" asked Devlin, touching her hand.

"What, you think you're working for some higher power! You think you can just kill someone in the name of justice?"

"That's exactly what Kanasta believed in! We have to quench the flames of vengeance, else we'll be consumed. I killed him with his own damned philosophy."

"He was your brother! He is my father!"

"I killed him despite my blood ties! Is that not altruism?"

"You should only kill to survive!"

"This is my survival! You think I don't love him? You think I'm not burning inside right now. I'm regretting it. I'm wishing I could take it back; but at the same time, I know what I did was purposeful."

"How can you love him and still hate him enough to kill him?"

"I hate what he's done to me. But I can't forget about all the times he was there for me as my big brother. It's like there were two completely different Kanasta's. I don't expect you to understand."

"I...I do understand. Kanasta...he killed someone very dear to me. Even after all this time...I still have some resentment. I know I shouldn't, but I just can't help it."

"Hatred created a demon inside of me. Vengeance is the only way to cleanse me of my demons."

"He helped calm my inner demons."

"No, he unleashed them further. He took your weakness and made it his strength. You learned how to control it," said Devlin, putting his arm around her.

"And now I'm all alone with those demons."

Devlin pet her head. "You're not alone, Kaity."

"I don't know why, but I trust you," said Kaity, leaning into him.

Devlin's eyes watered up as he embraced her.

"Power and revenge can't be the only thing motivating you. I know your plan isn't so shortsighted."

"Once I become a god I am going to make the world a better place. Equality shall be enforced worldwide," said Devlin, his embrace tightening.

"How can you be sure you'll have that kind of power? What if it consumes you?" asked Kaity, peering up at him.

"I can't do it alone, Kaity. I used to think that love would be an obstacle, but it's absolutely necessary. I need your help to change the world," said Devlin, touching her cheek.

"How can I help?" asked Kaity tenderly.

"Well, I'd be asking a lot of you. Too much, actually. Heheh," said Devlin, turning red and twiddling his thumbs.

"Devlin, I want to help you in any way I can," said Kaity, exiting the embrace and gripping his hand.

Devlin went down on bended knee. He looked up at his beloved with overwhelming passion. "Will you join me in unholy matrimony?"

Kaity almost fell off the bed, but Devlin caught her hand and pulled her back up.

"Will you marry me and join me on the podium of the gods?" asked Devlin, pulling her up to his chest.

"Are you really asking me this?" asked Kaity, turning away with a deep blush.

"Will you marry me?" asked Devlin, hope twinkling in his eyes.

"I'm only twelve years old. I…uh…" Kaity pulled her hand out of his grip.

"My love for you transcends time," said Devlin, beaming at her.

"Is that even allowed?" asked Kaity, her hands to her chest.

"In Hell it is," said Devlin with a grin.

"The marriage is in Hell?" asked Kaity, sliding off the bed.

"The only way to stop anguish is from its core. Will you join me?" asked Devlin with an outstretched arm.

"Wait, you mean you want to marry me…like right now?" asked Kaity, stopping in her tracks.

Demonica suddenly entered in through the doorway. "Are you guys serious?" she asked, putting her hands on the little girl's shoulders.

"Yes, Demonica, I am very serious."

"Then why don't you just take her here and now?" asked Demonica, grabbing Kaity's arms.

"Let go of her. Kaity will either agree or she won't. This is her choice, not mine," said Devlin, jumping off the bed.

Demonica pinched Kaity's nipples. "If you talk like that, you'll die a virgin." She ran her hand up Kaity's crotch. "If you want something, then take it," she said, pushing the child into her beloved's arms.

Devlin caught her in a gentle embrace. "I will be content with whatever choice Kaity makes. Kaity, what is your answer?" he asked, bouncing in place.

"I thought you would want to take things slow. I never expected you to be one to jump into sex. You know, I wouldn't mind a threesome," said Demonica, sandwiching Kaity between her and Devlin with a sudden embrace.

"The question was about marriage," said Devlin, holding Kaity closer to his chest.

Demonica fell backwards to the floor.

"I don't have time to take things slow! I will only be able to control my godly powers if you are by my side. If you marry me, then my ascension is absolute," said Devlin, releasing Kaity from his embrace.

Kaity looked down, her cheeks ablaze with embarrassment. "Um, well...if it's the only way...then I accept," she said, fidgeting with her fingers.

"Yeeeeeeeeeees!" Devlin jumped up and threw his fist in the air. He rushed up to Kaity and lifted her into his arms. He spun around with her and pulled her into a loving embrace.

Kaity kissed him on the forehead and smiled awkwardly.

Demonica rose from the ground, her eyes aflame. "No! No! No! This is all wrong! You're supposed to love me! I'm the one you're going to be with. Everything was going to work out perfectly. We were supposed to be side-by-side," she said, breaking down into furious tears.

"Who decided this?" asked Devlin with a blissful smile.

"She may have your heart, but the rest of your body is mine," snapped Demonica as she dragged her fingers across his chest.

"Kaity, it's time to go to Sel...together," said Devlin, gently grabbing her hand. "Ow!" He grabbed Demonica's wrist. "Stop hurting me."

"I was just getting your attention. You don't have time to waste gazing into each other's eyes. Let's just have your marriage here!" hissed Demonica before flying through the wall.

"Um...should I go get dressed?" asked Kaity, looking down.

"You can do whatever you want, Kaity. I'm going to go check on my parents," said Devlin, turning to the door.

"Where are they?"

"In the prison cell. Locked up. Tight."

"Is Nina there too?" asked Kaity, her eyes lighting up.

"Indeed she is. Would you like to join me?" asked Devlin, offering his hand.

"Absolutely," said Kaity, rushing on ahead.

Devlin grabbed Kaity's hand and the next instant they were both in the prison chamber.

It was as if they had traveled to the medieval times. The walls were made out of old gray bricks. The floor was gritty and dusty. The cages had rusted bars.

"Where are we?" asked Kaity.

"At the lowest level of the lab. It was once an underground torture chamber. It's amazing the things one can find when they dig deep enough," said Devlin, brushing the dust off an iron maiden.

"There she is!" exclaimed Kaity, rushing off.

Nina was asleep in her cell. A few rats were nibbling at her toes.

Kaity licked her lips, causing the rats to disperse.

Devlin took an iron rod from the side of the prison and banged it against the bars.

Nina sprung up. She gasped, looked around, saw Devlin, and smiled. "I knew it. You just couldn't destroy this delicious body. You still yearn for it, don't you? You'll always yearn for it," she said, seductively wiping the dust off her chest.

"The only reason you're alive is because Kaity loves you. The feelings I once had for you are long gone," said Devlin, brushing the dust off his shirt.

"Kaity, can you break me out?" asked Nina with worrisome eyes.

"You will be freed after our wedding ceremony," said Devlin, grabbing Kaity's hand.

"Wedding ceremony…with her? She's a little girl. Besides, she likes me much, much more," said Nina, rubbing her nipples.

"Do you want a kiss?" asked Kaity, her tail perking up.

"I'm just feeling a bit jilted, that's all," said Nina, placing her head on her knuckles.

"After we're married, Nina will be all yours," said Devlin, putting his arm around his fiancé.

"Really?" asked Kaity with shimmering eyes.

"Absolutely!" exclaimed Devlin, tickling her affectionately.

"Don't I get a say in this?" asked Nina, her hands on the bars.

"That's entirely up to Kaity," said Devlin, flicking Nina's nose.

"Devlin, I knew you wouldn't kill us!" hollered Ada from a nearby cell.

Devlin stepped toward her prison, the gentleness in his eyes all but vanquished.

Ada was pinned down with her belly to the ground, getting a good stretch. Her arms and legs were all chained together like one big, happy family.

Ada raised her head and smiled upon seeing Devlin. "The other Freedom Forcers must be A-okay as well. Demonica must have just transformed all of them, right? You were trying to scare Exp 8, weren't you? You're so smart. Hmmhmmhymm."

Devlin crouched down to her while Nina and Kaity continued to chat. He looked into her hope-filled eyes and grinned. "They are all dead now. The only reason you are still alive is because I am going to kill you after the wedding ceremony."

Ada's eyes watered up. "You're getting married! Oh, my little boy's all grown up!"

Deceivant's feet were chained together along with his hands. He hobbled up to Devlin like a caterpillar. "You mean with little Kaity, right? You may not have a lot in common with me, but at least you have my taste in girls," he said with a grin.

"Oh, I am going to enjoy slowly killing the both of you so very, very much. Kanasta's death was far too quick," said Devlin, with a click of the tongue.

Ada's pupils shrank. Her smile dropped.

"Kanasta would never harm you! After you left, he went searching for you! This is all one huge misunderstanding," said Deceivant, rattling his bars.

"You didn't really kill Kanasta. He's your brother. Where is the sweet little boy I raised?" asked Ada, breaking down into tears.

"The sweet little boy you raised was murdered by society. I am a vengeful young man now," said Devlin, proudly combing back his hair.

"Damn it, Devlin, please…don't hurt Ada. I've already lost enough." Deceivant sat on his knees and pressed his head down to the damp floor. "I'll take double the punishment, just please let her live."

"Honey, don't say that." Ada stretched out her chains, trying to reach her husband.

Devlin leaned down and looked into the desperate man's eyes. "I want you to watch as I rip her body to shreds. I want you to realize her death is all your fault. Aheheh-hahahaha!"

Tears poured uncontrollably from Deceivant's golden eyes, forming into a small puddle.

"Devlin, I'm so sorry! Please, don't do it! I'll do whatever you want."

"It's such a rare sight to see you in such a pitiful state. Once I'm done torturing Ada, I'll see what you look like when you've reached the depths of despair!"

"I was trying to protect you! I didn't want you to end up like me! Just let me explain!"

"Shut up! I have wasted enough time with you. You are ruining my good mood," said Devlin, slowly transitioning back into a blissful state.

"Devlin…congratulations!" exclaimed Ada through her tears.

"Yes, congratulations indeed," said Devlin as he skipped to Kaity.

Devlin's phone vibrated in his pocket. He curiously pulled it out of his vest.

"The marriage ceremony is about to start. We even scorched the ground so it feels like Sel. Meet us behind the lab at the theatre. Don't keep me waiting," said Demonica from the other line, before hanging up.

"Wait, how did you...get my phone number?"

"Come on, just a little touch," said Kaity, reaching her arms into Nina's cage.

"That's it...just a little bit further," said Nina, slowly scooting back.

Devlin teleported inside Nina's prison cell. He grabbed her arms and pressed her against the bars.

Kaity rubbed her face against her crush's breasts, sighing with bliss.

Devlin then pulled Nina away and flung her back. He appeared in front of Kaity and grabbed her hand.

"They're waiting on us," said Devlin, smiling down at her.

"Okay, bye Nina! I'll see you after the ceremony!" cheered Kaity, waving playfully.

Nina looked in between her breasts to see a slightly damp key to her prison. "Bye, Kaity. I'll see you again soon," she said with a smile.

Devlin picked up Kaity in his arms and rushed through various exit doors. He ran up the stairs, holding her firmly in his grip. He then sped down a long hallway. When he finally arrived at the last door, he stopped. He set Kaity down to her feet and then slowly gripped the doorknob. "This is the door to my happiness."

His eyes widened as they watered up.

Devlin kicked the door, causing it to shoot open.

Chapter 45: Black Wedding

Devlin bowed and offered his hand to Kaity. To his delight, she firmly grasped it. They then began their descent down the stairs to the scorched stage.

There must have been around two-thousand demons in the metal pews. Damned souls from all corners of Sel had gathered for the ceremony, happy to finally get a break from their eternal damnation. They filled up six long rows and twelve columns. The demons looked like mutilated humans. A permanent flame erupted from their body which was held together by spiked vines. Their flesh was charred and their skin bubbled from an inner heat. Many of them were hunched over, their every breath filled with pain. Some of them had spokes stabbing into their legs. Others had appendages that were melted together. They were a diverse bunch.

The fiery pits around them shot out flames of joy as Kaity and Devlin walked hand-in-hand onto the stage.

Standing behind the black podium was Demonica, shrouded in a black cloak.

"I shall be the minister for this glorious day!" she exclaimed, hiding her jealous face beneath her hood.

"Demonica, I have the vows I wrote right here," said Devlin, taking out what looked like a college dissertation.

"Devlin, I think they've suffered enough. The last thing they want is an eight-hour lovey-dovey wedding. Besides, time is of the essence. Don't worry your brilliant mind; these demons will love the vows I wrote," said Demonica with a shady grin.

"Weddings aren't supposed to be entertaining. They are supposed to be long and grueling. They are a sort of a prelude of what's to come. A preparation of sorts."

"Don't be so pessimistic. Weddings are fun!"

"Yes, this wedding will be different. It will foster a fond memory in our minds that will be gradually embellished as time goes on. Every year this moment will be better and better!"

"And if it goes on too long, then we'll just get your sappy sermon stuck in our heads. My wedding was supposed to be short and to the point. Besides, when you are on a stage, your priority is to please the audience not yourself. They came here for some entertainment, and that is exactly what I am going to give them. These are the vows I wrote for our marriage. I'll just say her mortal name instead of mine," said Demonica, gritting her teeth.

"Thank you for setting this up for me," said Devlin with a slight bow.

"It's the least I could do for you. After all, you helped me escape from the boredom of Sel."

The bride and groom turned to each other.

Devlin looked down into her eyes with overwhelming admiration.

Kaity peeked up at him with an embarrassed smile.

Demonica crumbled her vows in her fist. She then frantically tried to straighten them out. "You know, Devlin, marriage is temporary. Once you've been immortalized as a god, you won't age alongside Kaity. Eventually you'll need a new wife," she said, rubbing his chest.

The demons hooted and hollered.

"I'll deal with that when it comes up. Demonica, you may begin," said Devlin with a gentlemanly bow.

Demonica smiled and opened her black book of vows. "All of us gods started out as wretched, feeble people. We were only able to cause misery on a personal level. However, as our trivial sins piled up, we were consumed by them. The ashes of sin burnt away our bodies and rebirthed our minds. We transformed into deities of malevolence! Devlin is to be a new god in Sel. He shall sacrifice innumerous souls to our Lord. Once his sins have reached a global scale, he shall be reborn as a god." She clasped her hands together and began a prayer. "Sel, welcome the future god, and my one true love…Devlin."

The stadium screeched with cheers from various demons. A group near the front of eight female demons let out a particularly loud roar of excitement.

"Now for the other one. Kaity's life was tragically rewritten at a tender age. She then joined the infamous Viper Squad assassins. Since then, she has given our Lord quite a few souls. Welcome Devlin's queen, the lucky little plaything, Kaity!" exclaimed Demonica, her fingers tensing up.

"How dare you!" yelled Devlin, his fingers tightening into a fist.

"Don't interrupt the minister. Now, let me continue. We must all eventually unite one day. Do not be dismayed, because without unity we would not know division. Without love, hate would cease to exist. Without happiness, sadness could not spread boundlessly. Without pleasure, pain would be meaningless. Without creation, there would be nothing to fuel destruction. Without Lum, Sellum would be unbalanced. And without balance, we would all go to ruin. We are not just uniting in this ceremony. We are separating as well. By joining a group, you are dividing yourself from everyone outside that group. By uniting with Kaity, Devlin has cut off his ties with all other perfectly legitimate candidates! The only tears that should be shed now are tears of joy. For without them, tears of anguish would have no potency. Unholy matrimony is a divine separation from the material world and should be entered with a wholesome understanding of its sacrilegiousness. Whether divine or secular, marriage is a

462

union. This inner perception of oneness brings forth external unity through thoughts and actions. By shaping the interior and exterior selves, chaos will flow effortlessly. On this glorious day, for Kaity, your separate minds and goals shall be unified into one consciousness. Will you Kaity and you Devlin take from this world life, each for your sake and for the other, to the best of your abilities?"

"I will," said Devlin, his hand on his chest.

"Am I vowing to kill now?" asked Kaity with raised eyebrows.

"You've already killed a lot…just say I will," said Demonica, under her breath.

"I will," said Kaity, shuffling in place.

"Know that misery cannot emerge from the external world, for it is your mind that projects its misery outward. Love is timeless and thus unaffected by decay and death. Realize that nonconsensual love between a man and a little twelve-year-old girl will be everlasting, as long as it is sinful and one-sided. She's just a little girl, Devlin. Don't you want a woman?" asked Demonica, pushing up her breasts.

"Continue," said Devlin, rolling his eyes.

"Be wary of your thoughts; allow no dissonance to penetrate them. Be stubborn in your love toward the one whom you have decided upon…which should have been me," said Demonica with a frown. "Ahem! Let love guide you and allow the darkness you spread to grow boundlessly. The light you feel inside shall be projected as darkness to the world that has forsaken you!" yelled Demonica, triggering a roar of approval from the audience.

"Hey, this is supposed to be a happy moment," said Devlin with watery eyes.

"Always remember that no life should be lived for merely its own sake. In times of tribulations, as a wholesome entity, come together through will, emotion, and reason to surpass the hardships. Your love must be catastrophic, yet progressive in its regression. In other words, the more partners…the better," whispered Demonica in the groom's ear.

"No, it means that if you try to live only your goals you will be consumed by selfishness and lead a dense life," said Devlin reflexively.

"Oooh, I like that even better. Anyway, back to the vows. Realize that marriage is like a slave: forever bound and permanently employed. It is nurtured by the lashings which you yourselves bestow upon it. Therefore, embed love and servitude in each other. Have faith in your marriage but pure devotion to the awesome power of Sel. Devlin, will you take this twelve-year-old little girl to be your wife, after Lord Sel's law, to live as one in the unholy state of matrimony? Will you love her, treasure her, keep her, and guide her at all times…" Demonica clenched her finger and exhaled sharply "…and forsaking all others keep onto her?"

"I will," said Devlin, looking at his bride with overflowing warmth.

"And will you give her a couple of lashes every so often?"

Devlin gave Demonica a condescending look.

"Demonica, I mean Kaity, will you take this hunk of a man to be your husband, after Lord Sel's law, to live as one in the unholy state of matrimony? Will you love him, worship him, please him, and follow him at all times and forsaking all others keep only unto him?"

"No," said Kaity, taking a step back.

The demons in the pews gasped harmonically.

"What?" asked Devlin, his lips already puckered.

"I'm not going to worship him! And well…I still love Nina and I want to spend time with her," said Kaity softly.

"I wouldn't agree to it either. Well, will you love him, please him, and follow him at all times; and every so often have fun with others?" asked Demonica with a smirk.

"I will," said Kaity with a grin.

"Devlin, what token have you of your vows?"

"My soul," said Devlin, opening up his vest.

"It has to be something material and expensive, like a ring," said Demonica, caressing his finger.

"Oh, of course," said Devlin with a little blush. He took out a glimmering ring with a lavender stone and handed it to the dark minister.

"Devlin, let this glorious circle be your eternal symbol of underage love," said Demonica.

"It's not a circle. It's a ring," said Devlin.

"It's poetic. Here, read this, echoes annoy me," said Demonica, handing him a paper.

"With this ring I wed thee—It shall be a token of our immortal love—a never-ending, imperishable symbol of our devotion. I give it place now upon your hand," said Devlin, offering the ring.

"That wasn't what it said, but I guess it's good enough. Here, hurry up and read it," said Demonica, snatching the book from Devlin's hand and giving it to Kaity.

"As a token of your feelings for me—I give it place now upon my hand," said Kaity as she slipped the ring on her finger.

"Now she's supposed to give you a ring. However she doesn't have it and it's the same blessed vows anyway," said Demonica with a wave of her hand.

"If we don't do that, then it's sexist," said Devlin.

"I think of it as symbolic. The man is the giver and the woman the receiver. He gives her the sperm, which in turn makes her pregnant. The pressure of the ring's weight symbolizes the burden of carrying a child. The man gives a beautiful gift that is, in truth, a burden to the woman. I think it's very poetic this way, hmmhmm," said Demonica, running her hand down Devlin's arm.

"What?" asked Devlin, smacking her arm aside.

"Now for the prayer. Oh thou Lord, torturer and waster of all mankind and propagator of hatred and fear. We, the residents of Sel, know that thou art always damning us. It is through our damnation that we become your kindred. All genders, colors, class, and species are irrelevant to thee. We are all thy children at the moment of our damnation. And we must all come together to keep our world afloat. At this moment each of us has gathered here to initiate new members into our infernal family. May you damn this man and this little girl, in thy name, so that they, too, can spread despair and hatred to all corners of the Earth. May their journey of torment be illuminated through their bond and may it bring forth many new souls into our home. May their space inside your realm propagate the spread of calamity, discord, and balance. True marriage is ownership, and though one of them may own the other, both are the property of you, our Lord. This union is more than a bonding of souls; it is a testament to thy laws. May their new bonds enable them to murder faithfully and dutifully. They must follow the covenant made between themselves and, in turn, live out the vows they have made to you, our Lord. These words now declare that they will remain in a perfect balance of love and discord. From this day and all days beyond, may you trust and cooperate with one another to spread despair throughout Sel. Do you Devlin, take Kaity to be your wife until the sun ceases to burn and the universe is consumed?" asked Demonica, pulling Devlin close to her.

"Even then I do!" said Devlin, gripping his bride's hand.

"And do you Kaity, take Devlin to be your husband till the flow of time ceases to move?" asked Demonica, crying from jealousy.

"I do," said Kaity with a firm nod.

Demonica put her hand between both Devlin and Kaity. Dark energy coursed through her as a circuit, connecting to both of them. She then released her grip and the energy vanished.

"I pronounce you eternally linked in unholy matrimony. You may fuck the bride!" exclaimed Demonica, throwing her arms up.

"What!" exclaimed Devlin and Kaity simultaneously.

"Sorry, that last part was for my wedding. You may kiss," said Demonica, weeping uncontrollably.

Devlin wrapped his arms around Kaity, trembling from anticipation. Kaity put her arms around him reluctantly.

Their lips locked.

Devlin became overwhelmed with passion. His arms squeezed Kaity's back. His body quaked with bliss, pressing into her as the kiss continued.

The demons whistled and shouted vulgarities, but Devlin was too entranced to even be aware of their intrusion. He felt Kaity's body against his. He felt isolated from the world and one with his beloved.

Once Devlin parted the kiss, he toppled over to the ground. "I will never forget this moment. This is my true first kiss!" he exclaimed, holding his chest.

"Before Sel's witness, the Seven Deadly Sisters and the Queen of the Sins—along with the presence of Sel's residents—I hereby join these two souls. We shall all bask in this grand union in this spirit of revelry and discord. Let us all share this declaration: may balance forever reign throughout the cosmos. Nema!"

Flaming confetti shot into the air, littering the stage. The tormented souls cheered as the unholy bonding was completed.

"I call dibs on his virginity," said Demonica, her finger pointed up.

Devlin was smiling wispily. "My life is complete now. I can go to Heaven," he said, looking up at the sky.

"This was a Seltanic marriage. If you die, you'll go straight to Sel." Demonica's fingernail shot into Devlin's collar. She then pulled him to her and kissed his cheek.

"That was the first time I've kissed a guy," said Kaity, blushing bright red.

"And probably the last time," said Demonica, tapping the girl's lips.

Devlin jumped up to Kaity and embraced her once more. "My dream has come true, and it's all thanks to you!" he exclaimed, tears flowing freely.

"I...um...I'm glad to help," said Kaity with a bright red blush.

"I have my parents trapped...Exp 8 is all by himself...I'm married to Kaity! All that's left now is to overthrow Etah," said Devlin to himself.

"I hear you loud and clear," said Demonica with a wink.

Devlin grabbed Demonica's arm and pulled her aside.

"You're not going to tell him, are you?" asked Devlin, his grip tightening.

"Are you kidding? I've grown tired of his rule. Sel needs a new god and you're the perfect candidate," said Demonica, flicking his nose.

"So, is there a wedding cake?" asked Devlin, searching the area.

"No, that's it. I wanted our marriage to be fast so you could get back to your work. I know, I'm so considerate," said Demonica, touching his cheek.

"Oh, so it's over then?" asked Devlin, brushing the searing confetti off his pant leg.

"Indeed it is. And that means all of you need to leave!" yelled Demonica, turning to the tormented souls.

The residents of Sel all vanished into a puff of black smoke.

"So does this mean I'm legally wed to Kaity?" exclaimed Devlin, jumping up and down.

"Who cares about legality? Your souls are eternally linked, isn't that enough?" asked Demonica with a groan.

"It's more than I could ever ask! Auuu," said Devlin his hands cupped to his chest. He then turned to Demonica. "Keep an eye on Deceivant. He's always got a backup plan."

"Understood, my Lord," gasped Demonica, as she rushed back into the lab.

"It's time for us to fulfill my destiny!" exclaimed Devlin as he grabbed his wife's hand.

"Whatever you say, umm, darling," said Kaity with a nervous smile.

"How I've longed for this day," said Devlin, wiping away his tears in bliss. He skipped into the lab, holding Kaity's hand tightly. "Once Exp 8 submits, then all things will fall into their proper place." His smile then vanished and his eyes watered up. "I can't believe they're all dead."

"Don't worry about it. We're together now," said Kaity as she hugged his arm.

"Yes we are; all is right now," said Devlin, putting an arm around his beloved.

Chapter 46: Alone

Previously: Exp 8 was helpless but to watch as Kaity, his final comrade, vanished from sight.

Exp 8 looked around at the puddles of blood and stretched his arm out. He dipped his fingers in Ada's puddle, and pressed it to his forehead. "Ada, please comfort me. Say something…anything. A laugh, a giggle…I just need to know you're okay." He rolled his hand around in the puddle. "You were always so confident Devlin cared about us. You even started to convince me it was true. I thought maybe he was just a lost child looking for a purpose. But you were wrong. It was all just a ploy. He never cared for any of us. He murdered his children heartlessly!"

His blood-drenched hand quaked. "How can you just blindly trust him? How can you always smile no matter what happens? Are you just in a constant state of denial? But when I look at your smile…I don't see a façade. I see true happiness, true purity. I need you Ada! Talk to me!" yelled Exp 8, dragging his fingers on the grass.

His hand became still. "You would tell me not to give up, that there is still a way for Devlin to redeem himself. I don't want him to be redeemed! I want him to be broken and desperate! I want him to die with all his sins tearing into his karmic self. I want him to suffer for what he's done!" yelled Exp 8, slamming his fist against the ground furiously. "I will kill him…but only when he begs for it! I'll rip off that sinister smile of his. I'll gouge out those holier-than-thou eyes! And I'll make Bob and Demonica suffer for all the pain they've caused my comrades. It will be so wonderful! It will be so righteous. Ahehahaha." He pulled at the blood chains surrounding his body. "I'll show Devlin the full wrath of the Ultimate Exp! I may be alone, but I can still kill him!"

Exp 8 froze in place. The constant stream of tears stopped abruptly. "I'm not alone. Demonica took Kaity away. That means Kaity is still alive. I have to break into Devlin's lab and free her so we can stop that madman together," he said, slipping his other arm out from under the chains. He tried to pull the rest of his body free but couldn't budge an inch. "Devlin would never kill Kaity. He loves her. I'm sure she will be fine," he said, before a wind of doubt swept over him. "What if it's just a ruse? That's it! It's all a lie! He can't love. Anyone who could…do what he's done…is incapable of love. He wants to sacrifice Kaity. I have to save her before she gets killed. I still have someone to protect. I'm not done yet!" he yelled, trying to squirm out from under the wires.

The commander of the black-suit soldiers approached from behind. The young man crouched in front of Exp 8, his face covered with a helmet. "So…this is the Ultimate Exp. I'm not impressed," he said, flicking Exp 8's skull.

"You came here to bring me back to your boss! Well go ahead and try! I'm not going without a fight!" yelled Exp 8, struggling to swing his fist at the special agent.

"We were waiting, you know. Gamma and the others acted without orders to capture you earlier. Me and the Boss…we were waiting."

"Waiting for what? Waiting till I was defenseless to capture me?" asked Exp 8, yanking on the blood chains.

"No. I would have had captured you long ago if that were the case. We were waiting for Devlin to lose it. We were waiting for your comrades to die. My boss doesn't like Exps. He thinks the world is better off without them."

"The world is better off without speciesist people like him!"

"It was very kind of you to lead a rebellion and kill off most of your kind. Couldn't have done it better myself," he said, stretching his arms back.

"If I wasn't stuck here, I'd break your neck!"

"You aren't stuck. Give me a break. You're a super weapon, dumbass! No chains can hold you down. You tore a wall out to escape Devlin's lab before. You just aren't trying hard enough now. You've lost your spark."

"These chains won't budge! I am stuck, dumbass!"

"You can stay trapped here like a failure, or you can break out and get that freedom you so covet."

"Don't taunt me!"

"You've been playing tug-of-war with Devlin the whole time. When he pulls, you pull. When he let's go, you let go. The time for pulling against his wishes is over. Now, why don't you tighten that fist and start smashing?" asked the commander, standing up.

Exp 8 raised his arms and slammed his fists down on the chains. He punched them over and over but didn't even dent them.

"Hurry it up! My boss doesn't want a piece of shit weapon. We want you to tap into that pool of strength you allegedly have," said the commander, twirling a pistol on his finger.

Exp 8 continued to punch the chains. He then put his hands together.

The jewels on his hands glowed as the energy inside them swirled around. A tiny black orb formed between his palms.

"This is the manifestation of my will to be free!" Exp 8 pressed the orb against the chains.

The commander hopped back to avoid the explosion.

Exp 8 rose from the ground, damaged and smoldering. "I will not let you capture me," he said, firing tiny orbs like bullets.

The commander dodged left and then leaped toward Exp 8. "I was sent here to capture you…but you might be able to stop Devlin. And that will be one more problem I don't have to deal with. Considering how pissed off you are right now, you might just kill the rest of his Exps. I'll come pick you up after the battle. Don't you die now," said the commander, slugging the living weapon's shoulder.

"I'm going to kill Devlin. And when you come back to fetch me, I'm going to kill you," said Exp 8, grabbing the commander's arm.

"Looking forward to it. Oh, and next time, I'll be prepared," he said, shrugging Exp 8 off. "Can't believe I put off a dinner date for this." He then walked off into the frungle.

"Alright, who wants to die? Come at me!" yelled Exp 8, running toward Devlin's lab. He then tripped and fell flat on the ground.

All his bravado vanished and he started crying again. "How am I going to beat Riufen? I can't even touch Bob! I can't win. I'm not strong enough on my own. My family is dead and…I can't even avenge them. What am I saying! I'm talking about vengeance. Devlin's changed me. He's already won. What can I do to stop him?" he asked, rubbing his tears off on the grass.

He then slammed his fist to the ground. "No! I don't have an excuse anymore! I'm not chained down! I'm free! There's no reason I shouldn't fight Devlin! If I die, then I will die free. I will die fighting! But…I've got no intention to die. I've got to put Devlin in his place." The Ultimate Exp rose back to his feet.

Exp 8 heard a rustling in the bushes. He turned around and looked right into the eyes of NoOne.

"That was quite the rebound. I'm sorry to trouble you. Devlin has ordered me to kill you. Things have changed it seems. I won't be holding back, not like it will make any difference. Uugh."

Exp 8 lifted NoOne up by his throat and slammed him against a nearby tree. "How can you still serve him? He murdered all or your brethren. Doesn't that matter to you at all?" He tossed his enemy aside.

NoOne regained his balance and sharpened his arms into blades. "My chances of survival are even slimmer if I join you. I don't want to die."

"There are more important things at stake here! Do you really think your life matters that much? Don't worry about Devlin. If you stand in my way, I'll kill you myself," said Exp 8 as he approached the enemy.

"Shut up! I'm at a dead-end no matter where I turn! You can't understand the fear I feel! Devlin never once threatened your life! You're not a hero! You put others in danger, never yourself. You don't know what it means to survive. If I kill you, then I get to live…It's my only option," said NoOne, his bottom half trembling.

"There's no need for you to worry, I will defeat Devlin. I promise," said Exp 8 as he embraced his fellow Exp.

The shadow master pushed him off. "Your promise is empty. You are as helpless before Devlin as I am before you. It is impossible for either of us to succeed at this point." NoOne thrust his bladed arm into Exp 8's chest.

"I have to win! I must stop Devlin no matter what," said Exp 8, ripping out NoOne's arm. He gripped it tightly, tore it off, and threw it to the ground.

"Stop talking like that. This is terrifying enough as it is. That determination, it is the ring to my funeral bell," said NoOne, his whole body shaking.

"You never joined me because you're a coward. You never had the courage to stand up to Devlin. Either find that courage or die here and now!" Exp 8 fired orbs rapidly into the air.

The balls of energy joined together into a single wrecking ball-sized orb.

NoOne punched his back furiously, causing his chest to shoot forward like a machine gun.

Exp 8 took the hits as he pulled back his fist. He jumped up and socked the orb, serving it like a volley ball.

The orb exploded, flinging Exp 8 backwards into a tree. The tree split in half.

Exp 8 got back to his feet and put his hand on the dying tree. He closed his eyes.

NoOne reappeared next to him, not wounded in the least. He then thrust his serrated arm forth.

Exp 8 stopped NoOne's arm between his palms. He then kicked the shadow man's lower portion and flung him over.

The two Exps fell to the floor at the same time.

Exp 8 rolled right back to his feet, but NoOne was still down. He kicked at the shadow man furiously, tearing at him with his talons.

The shadow master's body rapidly shot up, pummeling the broken hero.

Exp 8 was knocked off his feet and launched in the air.

NoOne's body then pulled Exp 8 back down. He shoved his arm into his adversary's chest. His arm popped out the back and slowly spread over the broken hero's body.

Exp 8's tail slammed into NoOne's arm, breaking it off. The Ultimate Exp's jet boosters then started up. They melted the shadowy goop and sent him above his opponent.

Exp 8 shot down with maximum thrust.

The Shadow Master's body sped forward, shaped like a wall.

Exp 8 was rammed into NoOne's body and then fell down toward the ground. "That really hurt, you bastard."

NoOne's goopy body crawled up to his downed adversary and pummeled him ruthlessly.

Exp 8 struggled to get to his knees as the shadow man barraged him.

"Do not pretend you can't stand up. You are far stronger than this." NoOne's body shot into the hero like a shotgun.

Exp 8 was knocked flat on his back. "I guess I don't have the drive to do this anymore," he said, not even bothering to get up.

"Do not dare act defeated. The second I turn my back, you're going to get right back up. Then you're going to defeat me with some new and flashy attack."

Exp 8 struggled up to his feet and stood up gallantly. "I give up, NoOne. Take me to Devlin. You win," he said, putting his hands out to be cuffed.

NoOne gave him a blank stare. "You're serious?" he asked, pulling his head back in suspicion.

"I can't beat you. I've lost the will to keep on fighting," said Exp 8, lowering his head in surrender.

"I won? That's impossible. The chances of me winning do not exist. How could I...me...NoOne have won?" he asked, grabbing his forehead.

"I had to find some way to lose to you. With a zero percent chance of failure, I had no choice but to cheat. Surrender has never been an option for me, which made it the perfect decision," said Exp 8, stretching his arms over his head.

"If you cheated, then I didn't really win," said NoOne, starting to sink into the ground.

"Does it really matter how you won? The end result is the same, isn't it?" asked Exp 8, closing his eyes.

NoOne created shadow cuffs and fastened them around the defeated hero's wrists. "I really did it. I won. The ends justify the means!" he exclaimed, throwing his arm in the air.

Exp 8 looked up at him. "Didn't you say the chances of you winning were the same as me defeating Devlin?"

"Something along those lines, but what does that matter? My victory doesn't change your predicament. Devlin is still unbeatable."

"And so was I. Thanks to you, I know how to win an unwinnable battle."

"By having Devlin pointlessly surrender?"

"Nope. The only way to beat Devlin is to cheat," said Exp 8 with a thumbs-up.

"How do we do that?"

"I already have. Getting you, one of his most faithful subordinates on my side, would definitely count as cheating," said Exp 8, breaking out of the handcuffs.

"Do you think we stand a fighting chance?"

"Not at all, but neither did you. I promise, I will protect you," said Exp 8, putting his hand on his comrade's shoulder.

"You've made your point. Alright, I'll fight with you. Oh, I just hope this kind of works out," said NoOne, his shoulders drooping.

"If I have someone to protect, then I can deceive myself into believing that I can protect them. The deceit then transmutes into determination and then it evolves into a self-fulfilling prophecy."

"You're right! Deceit is determination, and determination is power," said NoOne with a confident fist.

"That's the spirit! Now come on, let's barge right through the front door."

"That would be completely idiotic. Are you trying to get us killed?" whispered NoOne.

"A brash strategy like this will only strengthen my resolve!"

"I think I'm beginning to grasp it. You never show fear to psych out your opponent," said NoOne, his eyes widening.

"And to psych myself up. Now let's go," said Exp 8 as he kicked the door to the lab open.

The door shot forward, skidding down the hall. The door slid by, revealing Bob before them. He exited his Phase Form as soon as the door went through him. A sinister smile stretched across his eye.

"We're going to die!" yelled NoOne, leaping into Exp 8's arms.

Bob floated up to them, his smile unchanging. "I see you're as pessimistic as ever. However…your justified pessimism will not give me an ounce of pity. Tell me, what is your purpose?" He raised the Atma Blade.

"My purpose is to be loved, that is all," said NoOne.

"To want love is an act of selfishness. To give unconditional love is selfless. You covet love, but give out none. Why should I spare your self-serving existence?" asked Bob, floating around him.

"You can't kill him, Bob. I promised to protect him," said Exp 8, powering up an orb in his fist.

"Oh yes, because that's really worked out for your other friends recently, hasn't it?" asked Bob with a chortle.

"What is he talking about?" asked NoOne.

"Don't listen to a single treacherous word he says! We're going to get through this together!" yelled Exp 8.

"Ugh. It was your idea to kick the front door open, wasn't it?" asked Bob with a condescending look.

"I refuse to give you or Devlin the satisfaction of my fear," said Exp 8, cracking each individual finger.

"You never learn, do you? Ehehahaha! Once again, you've let your egotism doom your allies."

"Not this time. This time, it is my egotism which will save them," said Exp 8, holding his chest.

"So, what's your purpose? Is it to make false promises? Or are you actually corrupted by your own idealism?"

"Neither. My purpose is to free my family from enslavement."

"Only concerned about your own species, are you? You're no better than the humans. But the other Exps were never really enslaved. The only ones forbidden to leave this lab were Kawai, Karson, and Atatasuki. They were killed exactly for this reason. Devlin and I both thought a rational being such as yourself would realize that, once they had died, you had nothing to fight for. After my attack, you were the only Exp without freedom. There really was no reason to get the others involved in your selfish quest."

"Shut up! Devlin is just going to keep making more slaves if I don't stop him now!" yelled Exp 8, shooting an orb in a split second.

Bob swerved out of the way and picked up Exp 8 without even touching him. "Do you really believe this, or are you just lying to comfort yourself? Once Devlin has you under his control, no more Exps would have to die. He cares about all of you. Why don't you realize that?"

"He sent Demonica to murder all of them!"

"I don't know why he didn't ask me to do it. But it doesn't matter. Your purpose is too weak to pull you through this. My prime goal is to better the universe for everyone and everything under a new visionary god. All will unify under the rule of one being. That's thinking big. You're only concerned with yourself."

"That is not equality, it is imprisonment!"

"There is always a price for peace. I swore absolute loyalty to my creator," said Bob, his pupil intensifying as it turned red. "All I ask from you as payment is acceptance. If you will not accept, I will make you submit."

Exp 8 was slammed to the ground. He was forced to grovel as Bob looked down on him. "You ask for denial, not acceptance. True freedom breaks the shackles of morality. There shouldn't be any kings or rules! When you are truly free, then nothing holds you down," he said, rising to his feet.

"Freedom and peace are the antitheses of each other. To have peace you must have control. Only an idealist can imagine the two as one. Hrmhmmhmm."

"I will search for the right path. Slavery creates feelings of contempt. Eventually the contempt will start a rebellion. That rebellion will disturb the peace until a new ruler takes control. And then the process repeats itself all over again.

As long as there are rulers, peace will be transient," said Exp 8, flinging his fists at the traitor.

"If you are born into slavery, then you will be complacent with it. You will never understand the shackles freedom imbeds into you: the mental shackles that have bore into your mind, forcing you to be fixated on freedom. When one is free, they have no morals and no responsibilities. They will create chaos. Freedom is too dangerous."

A laser beam crashed into the rebel leader's chest.

Exp 8 held back the laser with both hands. "Freedom is the way of the universe! Order is imposed by those who seek power! Those too weak to uphold their own freedom gave it away when they requested a social contract. My people never agreed to this!"

The laser zoomed by, the force of it knocking Exp 8 off his feet.

"Those caught up in this torrent will be imprisoned in an idealistic state of mind. The only thing your brand of freedom will bring is ascension to the heavens. Ugh, why am I wasting my time trying to reason with you? Brainless brutes can only speak with their fists." Bob sank into the ground and then popped up in front of NoOne. "I will ask you once more…what is your purpose?"

"To feel loved, just once more. I want to be more than just an artificial product…just to feel that I matter to someone," said NoOne, his head drooping.

"You will never matter with such a pointless purpose," said Bob with a cold glare. He then plunged the Atma Blade through NoOne. "Come to think of it, didn't you promise to protect him? Eheh, oh well."

Exp 8 leaped into a rising uppercut, but his fist passed right through Bob. He turned around in midair, his face a mere three inches from the murderer's pupil.

"I will never be able to defeat you, Bob," said Exp 8. He then jetted down and grabbed NoOne.

Bob just stood there with a blank stare.

Exp 8 ran to the door with NoOne on his back.

NoOne's head drooped over his savior's shoulder. "I thought you said you must believe you can win?"

"I deceived myself into believing the truth of our futility in order to assure our victory. Make sense?" asked Exp 8, scratching his own head.

Bob zoomed up to them, readying his blade. "I won't fall for your pathetic tricks."

"It wasn't pathetic if you fell for it, right?" asked Exp 8 as he powered up an orb behind his back.

"Hmm, I guess you're right, it was oddly ingenious," said Bob with a smile.

"Thanks," said Exp 8 as he powered up another orb.

"Did I...just compliment you?" asked Bob, trying to shake away his disgust.

"Complementing your opponent justifies your struggle with them. Insulting your opponent is what makes you seem weak," said Exp 8, combining the two orbs behind his back and then condensing them into the size of a marble.

"I never thought of it that way," said Bob with reflexive contemplation.

Exp 8 jetted forward and slammed the tiny orb into his enemy.

The orb grew to an immense size as it shot Bob outside the lab and into the distance.

"Told you we'd win," said Exp 8, giving NoOne a high five.

The door to a nearby room shot open, revealing Riufen before them.

Bob popped out of the ceiling, using his spectral hands to pull out some twigs that had gotten lodged in his body.

Exp 8 stared into the eyes of his enemies. His deceit faded away and with it, his determination. He collapsed to his knees, tears pouring out from the holes in his helmet.

Chapter 47: Double Agent

"Riufen, are you ready?" asked Bob with a cruel smile.

"I will fight Exp 8. Do not interrupt," said Riufen, pulling out his spine.

"Let's fight them both at once; NoOne alone is no challenge," said Bob, stretching out his spectral arms.

"Understood." Riufen turned to NoOne. "I hope you will show me your true might."

"You've already lost. I have your shadow. I'm going to win with my own power!"

Riufen looked down to see NoOne's shadow constricting his own. "Well played, but your shadow is far too weak," he said, cracking his neck.

The master samurai's shadow flipped NoOne's shadow over its back.

"My shadow cannot be destroyed, no matter what!" exclaimed NoOne, taking a step back.

"Then I will simply slice your body until you can no longer cast a shadow," said Riufen, spinning his spine on his finger.

"I don't want to die!" NoOne turned around and ran away.

Riufen hurled his spine forward. It shot through his adversary's back and out his front.

The samurai rushed up and grabbed his spine. He thrust it upward, ripping NoOne's upper half in two. He then rapidly slashed left to right, cutting his opponent to pieces until he vanished altogether.

"I promised he'd be safe!" yelled Exp 8. He thrashed his huge orb at Bob, who dodged it with ease.

"I knew that would end quickly. Riufen, come over here and assist me. However, be careful, we don't want to kill him," said Bob, ramming into his opponent.

"Can't you handle him alone?" asked Riufen, sitting down and cleaning his spine.

"Devlin wants us to use whatever force is necessary. He wants you to assist me. You don't want to go against his wishes, do you?" asked Bob as he popped out of the ground before going back in.

"If I must dishonor myself, then I will not dishonor my blade," said Riufen, sharpening his knuckles.

Exp 8 turned around and slammed the orb into the approaching samurai.

Riufen spun out of the way and slapped Exp 8's arm down.

The orb slammed into the floor and exploded.

Exp 8 shot upward into the ceiling.

Bob soared up and thrust the Atma Blade through him.

Exp 8's arms flailed around as his soul was ravaged by the blade. In the midst of the attack, he grabbed Bob and slammed his head into him relentlessly.

Bob fell in a dazed state, allowing Exp 8 to slip off his blade.

Exp 8 kicked off the wall and landed on Bob. He created a huge orb in his hand and slammed it against him.

The orb sent Bob flying downwards into Riufen.

The samurai pulled his fist back and then shot it forward. It slammed into Bob, sending him right back at Exp 8.

Bob shot into Exp 8's head, causing his opponent to spin in midair.

Riufen jumped up and grabbed onto Exp 8's face. He then dive-bombed and slammed him into the ground.

"How dare you use me as a cue-ball!" yelled Bob, turning to his arrogant ally with a dark glare.

Exp 8 raised his head before Riufen stepped down on it.

The Immortal Samurai grabbed Exp 8 and tossed him up. He pulled his fist back and thrust it forward.

Exp 8 was propelled like a pinball, bouncing back after smashing into the wall. He was about to fall down when Bob suddenly rammed into him, leaving an imprint upon contact.

Exp 8 closed his eyes as he plummeted.

Riufen turned to his ally and lowered his head. "I meant no offense. I merely saw an opportunity for a counterattack."

"Don't do it again. Hmm, it looks like he's already done. I hope I haven't killed him, hmhm."

"He's not done yet. Devlin-sama wanted him for a reason. He was trying to make him more powerful. If he was this weak…Devlin-sama would have told us to vanquish him long ago," said Riufen, holding his sword out.

Exp 8 stood up with an orb clenched in each fist. "I won't lose as long as I have a shred of hope left." He slammed one of the orbs against the ground. He was propelled toward the samurai by the blast and primed the other orb for impact.

Riufen shot his fist forward into the orb.

The orb exploded, sending Exp 8 toward the ceiling.

Bob slammed him down before Exp 8 could reach the ceiling.

As soon as Exp 8 hit the ground, Riufen slammed his head against the floor furiously. "Give up! I am sick of dishonoring myself. Surrender your power to Devlin-sama now."

"I will never surrender," said Exp 8. He then retched a mound of blood all over himself.

Riufen grabbed Exp 8's neck and slammed him against the wall. He then jumped out of the way as Bob's laser shot forth.

The laser pressed Exp 8 against the wall and burned into his armor. The wall collapsed and broke apart.

Exp 8 fell down an elevator shaft. He activated his jets when he was a mere moment away from a brutal collision. He soared down the hallway and into the prison chamber, crashing through the iron bars of a cell.

"Ada, damage report." Exp 8 gripped his head and sobbed. "I miss you."

Footsteps closed in on his location.

Riufen was right in front of him, just outside the cell. "Your suffering is pointless. It is only harming my honor," he said, gripping the rebel's arms.

Exp 8 prepared to shoot a laser net.

The samurai knocked Exp 8's hand aside, causing the net to miss.

Riufen's ribs pierced through Exp 8's arms and legs, pinning him to the wall.

"Let's go. He is no longer a threat to anyone," said Riufen, turning away from the broken warrior.

"I have to stop Devlin. I can't lose," said Exp 8, his head bobbing back and forth.

"Fine, I'll just torture him until he's unconscious," said Bob, entering the room by passing through the ceiling.

"There is no need. I will fetch Devlin-sama promptly," said Riufen with a bow.

"Hmm, that's funny. I don't remember asking your permission," said Bob, creating spectral drills.

"He is defenseless. It would be dishonorable to—"

"Do not forget that I defeated you! You have no right to give me orders," said Bob as his eye focused a laser.

"You are right. Disobeying you would be dishonorable," said Riufen as he sheathed his blade.

"You are so easy to manipulate." Bob fired a laser into his helpless victim.

Within seconds, the laser burned through the rebel's armor.

Exp 8 gasped through clenched teeth as the laser seared into his flesh.

"This is so pathetic. Under all that armor he's soft and tender. He hides his true self beneath these chunks of metal. How can he pretend to be chivalrous when he conceals his identity?" asked Bob, redirecting his laser to melt various segments of the armor.

"Knights follow a complex code of honor. Perhaps he does as well?"

"Really and what code is that? They preach about honor and justice while killing in the name of their king. They are cowards incapable of taking responsibility for their actions. Sure, they are useful as tools, but they lack the initiative it takes to be a leader."

"Soldiers have an initiative of their own."

"It's called a follower's mentality. You take away their individuality and take control of all aspects of their identity. You treat them all equally, and in return, they serve under you." Bob fired another laser, melting Exp 8's armor further. "I wonder what's behind this mask. Shall we have a look?" he asked with a glint of curiosity.

"That's enough," said Riufen, putting a hand on his ally.

"What, are you going to try to defend his honor? He has no honor. You would only dishonor yourself by defying me."

Riufen put his fingers to the *giri* kanji on his headband. "No...this is wrong. My honor has always been my guide. And right now it is telling me this is cruel and unfair. If I allow you to shame him, then I don't deserve honor." Riufen ripped out his spine and plunged it into Bob.

The spine passed through.

"You made the wrong choice," said Bob with a shaky grin. He thrust the Atma Blade into the foolish warrior. "Do you feel your soul slipping away?" he asked, pushing it in deeper.

"I cannot die."

"True, but that doesn't mean your soul can't be harvested."

Riufen fell to his knees, but Bob was unrelenting.

"Riufen, don't give up," said Exp 8 weakly.

"You are all so pathetic!" yelled Bob, tearing the Atma Blade out.

Riufen gasped and then closed his eyes.

Bob lifted the samurai's body up like a marionette. "Without the soul holding things together, the body just falls apart." He fired a psychic blast into Riufen, bursting his body into pieces.

"It's over; I've lost," said Exp 8 as the bones impaled in his hands dissipated into vapors.

"What do you mean? All you have to do is defeat me and then you're free. I'm all that stands in your path now," said Bob, pulling Exp 8 up with a spectral hand.

"You win Bob, take me to Devlin," said Exp 8, his whole body limp with hopelessness.

"You can't just give up now. When the two of us teamed up on you, your determination was so strong. Why are you copping out on me?" whined Bob.

"You defeated Riufen with one attack," said Exp 8 with wide eyes.

"But of course. He is nothing compared to me."

"And I was nothing compared to him," said Exp 8, lowering his shoulders.

"I don't know why Devlin thinks you're the Ultimate Exp. It is exceedingly apparent I am the superior one," said Bob, his pupil raised with pride.

"Where did Devlin want you to take me?" asked Exp 8, falling backwards.

"To the prison," said Bob with a welcoming gesture.

"Well, here we are. Lock me up and leave me be," said Exp 8, closing his eyes.

Deceivant stood up inside his prison cell. He was holding his head in pain. "That's one way of breaking me out."

"I…I thought you were dead," said Exp 8 with shimmering eyes.

Deceivant hunched under the broken bars. "So did I, heh."

"Run now. You can't beat him," said Exp 8, grabbing the inventor's arm.

"Good job stalling him," said Deceivant with a warm smile.

"I wasn't stalling him. I was just trying to survive."

"I was talking to Bob," said Deceivant, walking past Exp 8.

"You've been on Devlin's side the whole time?" asked Exp 8, holding his head, his eyes hollowed out.

"I already told you I want what's best for Devlin," said Deceivant, using a pen laser to melt through his remaining chains.

Exp 8 lifted up Deceivant and pressed him against the wall. "You lied to me. You lied to all of us!"

"I never lied. I just didn't tell you the truth," said Deceivant with a sly smile.

"You've been acting weak the whole time, haven't you?" asked Exp 8, slamming him against the wall.

"Nope. I really am useless in combat."

"So, Master, are things going smoothly? I did a good job fooling him, right?" asked Bob, shaking up and down.

Exp 8 created an orb in his hand and pressed it to Deceivant's chest. "Surrender or he dies."

"I truly am sorry he killed your sister. She was so sweet. She was too young to die. To be honest, I wasn't sure if he was still on my side," said Deceivant, tears brewing in his eyes.

"I even fooled you. I never cease to impress myself." Bob placed his spectral hands on Exp 8's shoulders. "Now, why don't you calm down a bit?" he asked, giving the shoulders a massage.

"This is the only way to beat you," said Exp 8 with a dark glare.

"Look, I was only acting to be on Devlin's side. Deceivant is my true master. He's the one who really created me. Exp 10 at your service," said Bob with a bow.

"He regrets murdering your teammates, but he had to convince Devlin to trust him. Exp 10, I order you to apologize," said Deceivant.

"I really am truly sorry. Now can we put this stuff behind us and move on?" asked Bob, wiping the blood off of his Exp 8.

"You're really on my side?" asked Exp 8, dropping Deceivant. His arms stayed in place and his eyes became still.

"He had better be, or else we're done for. Hahaha," said Deceivant, holding his forehead.

Exp 8 pressed the orb up to Deceivant's chest. "I will only forgive you, if you help me stop Devlin."

"But of course," said Deceivant, holding his neck in pain.

"Sounds good to me," said Bob with a nod.

Exp 8's hand pulled in the energy, dissolving the orb.

"I'm glad we understand each other. Exp 10, I want a full report on the information obtained while you spied on Devlin," said Deceivant, turning to his creation.

"I didn't spy. I was on his side. I tend to get absorbed in the character I portray," said Bob modestly.

"Fine. Is there any information which could be of service to us?" asked Deceivant.

"Devlin has one more Exp in reserve that could even destroy me…in theory of course," said Bob, his hands opening to keep them calm.

"I promised everyone I would stop him," said Exp 8, lowering his head.

"Just add it to your list of empty promises. We are going to stop him," said Bob, pulling his arrogant ally up to him.

"There are only three of us. How many teammates does Devlin have?" asked Exp 8.

"There's him, Demonica, and Kaity," said Bob.

"Kaity joined Devlin?" asked Exp 8.

"They got married, so I assume that would be a yes," said Deceivant.

Exp 8's neck shot back. "What? When did they get married?"

"Not important. We need to concentrate on the problem at hand," said Bob.

"Is Ada alive?" asked Exp 8.

"Alive and well. You have impeccable accuracy, freeing me and my husband in one glorious crash," said Ada as she embraced Exp 8 from behind.

"Ada, I…I thought you were dead," said Exp 8, tearing up as he looked into her eyes.

"Then you must be pleasantly surprised. Demonica spared us. Oh, I knew that she couldn't be all bad. Hmmhmmhymm."

"Are the others alive?" asked Exp 8, his head rising alongside his hope.

"They are dead. Oh and by the way, Devlin's coming back to kill us after the wedding ceremony," said Deceivant.

"Which should be pretty soon," said Bob with a grin.

"So then we're the only ones left then," said Exp 8 solemnly.

"My children are gone," said Ada, breaking down into tears.

Deceivant pulled her up to him and pet her lovingly. "We're alive. And I won't let anything happen to you. Still, I…I can't believe they're really dead."

"No! We can't give into despair!" yelled Exp 8, on the verge of bursting into tears.

"You have no right to say that! Kawai didn't have to die!" yelled Deceivant.

"Lamenting won't bring them back. I think…I think we should give them a tribute and then…let's move on and figure out what to do next," said Exp 8.

"He's right. We need to work through this," said Ada, grabbing her husband's hand.

"Do what you want. I'll keep watch. Be back soon," said Bob before sinking into the floor.

Exp 8 looked up and took a deep breath. "First of all I would like to apologize on behalf of my team to the assassins and Exps that lost their lives when battling us. Even if it was in self-defense, killing them was still wrong. Their lives mattered and we owe them our condolences." He closed his eyes.

"Your allies were protecting themselves, they did nothing wrong," said Deceivant, wiping away his tears.

"If they had tried to avoid killing then…there would at least be one less life lost in this struggle. And that is something worth regretting."

"Wow. You're really something else. You really live by your morals."

"Atatasuki, Kawai, the two of you…are my family. You made me smile and laugh and get upset. I don't know how I've kept on fighting without the two of you, but…I will keep on doing so until I die. I hope the two of you know just how much I love you."

Tears rushed down Exp 8's armored cheeks.

"She was too young to die. My little girl shouldn't have left so early," said Deceivant, his voice cracking.

Ada put her hand on her husband's shoulder. "We will always remember you. We will always love you."

"Nina, Karson, the two of you were the greatest fighters I've had the honor of fighting alongside. You were always aware and always ready for battle. I hope that the two of you never stop fighting for what you believe in."

"Nina, I always looked up to you. The way you took care of your body was inspiring. I know I was your sensei, but you taught me so much," said Ada in tears.

"Anthrax, Matteria, D.S., Kanasta, Opti, Pesi, Riufen, and NoOne…you all were enemies at first. You were very powerful enemies. There were so many times I thought you were too strong to defeat. But with my allies by my side, we found a way to overcome you. And then somehow you all ended up joining in my struggle. I thought I could protect if I shouted loud enough, if I believed hard enough. But that isn't the way things work. I'm sorry you all died under my command. I…I'm so sorry."

"Kanasta, you were more than my son. You were my best friend. If it weren't for you, I would have given up hope long ago. Thank you," said Deceivant with a bow.

Ada sobbed uncontrollably, unable to wipe away the tears faster than they came up.

Deceivant held her in his arms and kissed her forehead.

"To all my fallen Freedom Forcers, I give my thanks. Know that your deaths were not wasted. Devlin is going to be stopped!" Exp 8 flung his fist in the air.

Ada wiped away her tears, grabbed Exp 8's hand and smiled at him. "You've grown so much," she said, hugging him tightly.

"Okay. We finished the tribute. What are we going to do now?" asked Deceivant, cleaning the tears off his glasses.

"I'm not sure. Should we fight him head on or lure him here?" asked Exp 8.

Bob popped out from below. "We need to get rid of Demonica first."

"Yes, but how are we supposed to do that?" asked Exp 8.

"I have an idea. Let's go get some reinforcements," said Deceivant, rubbing his palms together.

"What reinforcements?" asked Bob with a glint of curiosity.

"I still have two of my old Exp's hidden in the lab," explained Deceivant, leading them out of the prison.

They all froze in place as a white portal formed before them.

A woman emerged, covered in moss. A beaming smile, accompanied by gentle green-and-brown eyes, emanated from beneath her seaweed hair. On the corner of her head was a cherished white Madonna lily held in place by the marine algae and her devotion.

Her body was meek and humble. It bent naturally like a flower. Her chest was modestly protected by pink lotus lilies which had yet to bloom. Rather than a skirt, a light-pink, Canterbury bell flower grew from her hips and stretched to her fragile knees. Two wings made of dandelions sprouted from her back, bending humbly to a higher power.

Chapter 48: Reinforcements

"You are the ones who oppose Devlin, correct?" asked the woman as she walked toward the Freedom Forcers.

"Yes, that is us," said Bob with a grin.

She looked at Bob, her face tensing up with worry. "What are you doing here? I thought you were with Devlin. Is he really helping you?" she asked, touching Ada's hand.

"He is…at the moment," said Ada, leaning back a little.

"He's my Exp, you can trust him," said Deceivant, putting an arm around his beloved.

"And…who are you?" asked Bob, pointing at her with four hands.

"My deepest pardons, I mustn't be so hasty. Without proper hospitality even the planets would fall out of alignment."

"No they wouldn't," said Bob, rolling his eye.

She opened her arms and beamed at them. "Hello, I am called Efil, Goddess of Life. I have come to offer thou uh, you pardon." Her voice was like a gentle whisper. She spoke in a humble tone that lacked self-assurance.

"Pardon from what?" asked Exp 8.

"Well, from going to Sel. You are currently on a path that leads to damnation. Except for Ada," said Efil, looking up at her with a smile.

"What did I do wrong?" asked Exp 8, grabbing the angel's hand.

She pulled away from him. "You've been doing exactly what Devlin wants. You've gotten many Exps needlessly involved in your personal struggle. Not to mention your foul language and brutishness, hmph," said Efil, turning away from him.

"If we stop Devlin, then can we cancel our reservations in Sel?" asked Deceivant.

"Yes. All the Freedom Forcers will be pardoned. Which brings me back to the reason I was sent here: to lend you my powers. I hope they can be of service," said Efil, lowering her head.

"Do all of us get cool powers?" asked Exp 8.

"No, only one of you can receive this unsurpassable blessing," said Efil with a smile.

"I should take it. It's the only way I'll be able to fight against Devlin's forces," said Deceivant as he fixed his glasses.

"I don't want her pointless ability anyway," said Bob with a sneer.

"And I can crush Devlin with my own power," said Exp 8, grinding his knuckles into his palm.

"Just give him your useless power and leave. We don't need a messenger to slow us down," said Bob, turning away.

"Very well. I apologize for not assisting directly. It's forbidden for gods to tamper with the material world. Just because Sel has broken this rule doesn't mean Lum should. That is why the receiver is only allowed to use these powers on himself and against Demonica. Any other use is strictly prohibited. Uh, do you understand?" asked Efil, twiddling her thumbs.

"Yes, thank you for equalizing the playing field," said Deceivant with a warm smile.

"I wish I could help more, but any further intervention could start up a war. Things are already very tense. But, um, off the record, I…uh…I wish you all the luck of the Goddess," said Efil with a shaky bow.

"Don't worry about it. I wanted to settle this battle myself anyway," said Exp 8, stretching out his arms.

"We are all going to help in our own little way," said Ada, giving Exp 8 a warm smile.

"No. I don't want anyone else to die," said Exp 8, standing tall.

"Alright, you can go first. But once you're dead, it will be my turn to fight Devlin's ultimate Exp," said Bob.

"What ultimate Exp? I thought Demonica was the last one," said Exp 8.

"Are you really surprised? Devlin always has several aces up his sleeves. So if you don't want to die, then let me fight it."

"I won't die. Now that you're no longer an enemy, I can do this," said Exp 8 with a confident fist.

"Fine, you two can go fight the Ultimate Exp, but we're going to take out Demonica." Deceivant turned to the goddess and cupped his hands. "Efil, I am ready to receive my power."

Efil embraced the man, wrapped her fingers around his and pressed her forehead against his.

Light permeated inside his body, making him gleam with a blinding aura. Efil then collapsed with exhaustion.

Deceivant caught her in his arms. "I feel my cells filling up with energy. They're evolving!"

Flowers spontaneously bloomed all over his body.

"Could you toss me in the portal?" asked Efil with a weak smile.

"Are you going to be okay?" asked Deceivant, moving the seaweed away from her eyes.

"Don't worry about me. Once you die, my powers will return," said Efil, her mossy skin now a dead brown.

"Then I won't keep you waiting," said Deceivant with a nervous smile. He tossed her into the portal of light. As soon as she was no longer visible, the portal dissipated.

"So, about those extra Exps, where did you put them?" asked Ada.

"You never met them, did you? I made them after the…uh…incident. I put them deep underground. Exp 10, if you would go fetch them, I'd really appreciate it," said Deceivant with a half-hearted smile.

"He already left," said Exp 8, looking around.

"So, do you think they have enough oomph to stop Demonica?" asked Ada.

"Knowing you, they probably attack with their undeveloped bodies. Heh," said Exp 8, throwing his arms back.

"That is not funny. Hope made me promise not to make another little girl. As much as it pains me, I will keep the oath as long as I draw breath," said Deceivant, intensely gripping his chest.

"They better not be as useless as you are," said Bob as he appeared, lifting up two metal spheres with his spectral hands.

"Well, I haven't had a chance to test them in combat yet," said Deceivant with a nervous grin.

The spheres shook the ground as Bob dropped them down right in front of Deceivant.

Exp 8 peered through the glass window of their incubators, but couldn't see through the murky green liquid. "Have they been trapped in these prisons their whole lives?" asked Exp 8, turning to their careless creator with a clenched fist.

"Naturally. I had no use for them until now. But relax, they'll taste freedom soon enough."

"Enter password, Daddy," said one incubator in the voice of a little girl.

Bob gave Deceivant a condescending look.

"Waka Laka!" exclaimed Deceivant, tossing his hands in the air.

The glass window shot up. Green gooey liquid poured on the ground, and the Exp with it.

A baseball-sized silver ball rolled out of the incubator.

"So, um, is that it? Or does it transform?" asked Exp 8.

"This is it," said Deceivant, gesturing toward the ball-shaped Exp.

"He looks weak," said Bob.

"It is not a he. Exp 08 has no sex."

"Wait, it has the same name as me?" asked Exp 8.

"Exp 08, not 8. All my Exps have a zero before their number, except for Bob. I didn't think I'd make it to the triple digits so it seemed unnecessary. You were supposed to be Devlin's last Exp, but it appears he had to make some up just to capture you."

"So my rebellion actually brought some Exps into existence?"

"Yes, but don't be so happy about it. You also brought them to their doom," said Bob, patting Exp 8 on the back.

"Now now, don't taunt him, Exp 10," said Deceivant.

"I'm going to take responsibility for their deaths by stopping Devlin once and for all."

"Ugh, would you quit with the morale speeches," said Bob with a roll of his pupil.

"So, what does Exp 08 do?" asked Exp 8.

"It can levitate," said Deceivant with a shrug.

"That's it!"

"Calm down, it's an Exp. Bob, hand over the Multiply Artifact," said Deceivant with an outstretched hand.

"When did you get that?" asked Exp 8.

"Once I finished my second fight with Riufen, I had a Jiva fetch it from BoneSaw's smoldering remains. Here you are, Master," said Bob, flicking the gray gypsum to the inventor.

Deceivant caught it and shoved it into Exp 08, who promptly absorbed it.

"So now he can multiply himself, right?" asked Exp 8.

"Don't expect an answer to such an obvious question. Exp 08 was designed specifically to tap into the potential of the Multiply Artifact. It is also very fond of geometry. The personality came of its own accord. I intended for Exp 08 to be without any emotions, desires, feelings, et cetera. I still don't know how that little glitch came to be."

Deceivant turned to the other incubation sphere. "Enter password, Teacher," said the other incubator in a girly voice.

"Mika!" cried Deceivant dramatically.

The glass rose up and another ball rolled out. This one was a frenetic mesh of colors and looked very sticky.

"And this is Exp 09. This one was made in order to aid my research on synthetic organs. With the Fusion Artifact in its possession, Exp 09 has the power to combine anything." Deceivant set the copper stone on the ground.

Exp 09 rolled down the slight incline over the artifact and absorbed it.

"Victory is now an option," said Deceivant, fixing his glasses.

"Why don't we give them names?" asked Exp 8.

"For all we know they could be dead by the end of the day. But, do what you want," said Deceivant with a careless sway of the hand.

Exp 8 sat down and picked up the little silver ball. "Hello, brother, since you like geometry so much…I'll call you Demo. Welcome to life," he said, touching the ball.

"Does Demo stand for Dimensional Energy Manipulating Orb?" asked Ada with shimmering eyes.

"It will stand for whatever the hell he wants. As for you…." Exp 8 turned to the sticky ball. "Let's see. You combine things…so how about Fusion? It's simple but to the point. Welcome to life, sister," he said, putting his hand just above his fellow Exp. "The two of you are now honorary Freedom Forcers. You're family. Together we will fight against Devlin to free our future brethren."

"How very kind of you to impose your ideals onto them," said Bob with a fake smile.

"So, when are they going to open up?" asked Ada, hovering over them in intrigue.

"They're not. They're just balls, like Exp 10," said Deceivant, gesturing to Bob.

"From making little girls to making balls, what a change," said Bob with a smirk.

"I lost my creative spark after Hope left. I miss her," wailed Deceivant.

"Oh, don't worry. You'll be joining her soon enough," said Demonica, appearing from the shadows.

"No…it's you," said Exp 8, his eyes shrinking in horror.

"I truly enjoyed watching your brethren burst into delicious blood," said Demonica, dragging her fingernails down her chest. She then turned her head to Bob. "I'll give you one last chance to rethink the situation. You know Devlin's going to win in the end. Why side with the mortals when you could stand with a future god?" she asked, looking deeply into his pupil.

"Whatever team I'm on will be the victor," said Bob blatantly.

"Devlin gave me the okay to kill all of you! I will make Devlin the king of this world. He will be all mine once you have all perished," said Demonica, flicking her tongue like a snake.

"Exp 8, slam an orb into the dormant Exps!" yelled Deceivant.

"What?"

"Just trust me!" yelled Deceivant, before rushing at Demonica.

Exp 8 created two tiny orbs and shot them into the new Exps.

The Exps absorbed the energy and then sprang to life.

Fusion rolled out of the room at supersonic speed.

"You can't run from me!" Demonica pushed off Devlin's father and spread her wings. She rushed out of the prison chamber in hot pursuit of Fusion.

"Let's get out of here. If Fusion takes control of the lab, we could all end up dead," said Deceivant, pushing them along.

Demonica's wings sharpened into swords. She sliced through the walls with ease.
A sentry gun popped out from the wall and aimed at her.
"Even your lab denies me," said Demonica with flowing tears.
Blood shot out from her eyes and consumed the turret. The walls then started to close in on her.
"That thing is trying to destroy my beloved's lab. I cannot allow that." Demonica cut through the walls and found the perpetrator.
Fusion's body was melded with the lab floor. It now had full control over the entire building.
"I will not disgrace my hands with your blood! *Blood Spawn*."

A swarm of blood bats shot out of Demonica's bosom and surrounded the new Exp. The bats combined with Fusion, lifting it up along with the building's foundation.
"I won't let you ruin my future home." Blood shot out of her arms and formed into a scythe.
"Die." Demonica slashed at the sticky ball before getting slammed into a wall by a ray of light.
Her scythe fell to the ground.
"Fusion may not be my daughter, but I still made it. If you don't leave Earth, I will destroy you with the fanciful power of Lum," said Deceivant, light energy collecting in his palm.
"Now there's an oxymoron: power of Lum. What are you going to do...drown me in flowers?" asked Demonica.
"Is that your weakness?" asked Deceivant.
"How dare you mock me!"
Demonica's fingertips melted away. Blood erupted out of them, solidifying into long spikes. They burst through the mortal's arms and impaled him to the wall.
"You're a mere nuisance." Demonica shoved her other set of bloody fingertips into Fusion.
The blood enveloped the ball and consumed Fusion, leaving no trace of its existence.
Demonica swapped the artifact from the floor and then strutted up to Deceivant, swaying her hips back and forth. "All my desires have been festering inside me, begging to be freed. I need a sexual outlet! You are his father, so you'll

do just fine. Take me now! Auuh." She moaned as she rubbed her breasts against Deceivant and played with his crotch.

"Get your hands—"

Ada punched Demonica with all her might. "Get your hands off my husband!"

Demonica didn't even flinch from the pathetic blow. "I shouldn't have spared your lives. You are all just obstacles to Devlin's descent." Her fingernails shot out as blood-like daggers.

The sharpened blood tore through Ada, pinning her right next to her husband.

"I refuse to let you harm my beloved!" yelled Deceivant, tears flowing from his furious eyes.

"You already failed. Open your eyes, fool."

"I won't let her die…she's all I have left."

"She's just property to you. I'll have fun destroying your tool. Then I will free you of your pathetic existence," said Demonica, her nails dragging across his chest.

"Didn't Devlin tell you to spare us?" asked Ada.

"It doesn't matter at this point. He's already married Kaity. He already ruined everything. Oh I bet he'll be devastated 'cause he didn't get to kill his mommy and daddy. I am going to lick his delicious tears as they pour down his soft cheeks," said Demonica, licking her fingers.

Deceivant's aura shot out of his body, forming wings of absolute light.

Demonica cringed in pain as the pureness of the wings radiated over her.

Her blood-stained fingers retracted as flowers enveloped her hands. "Damn it, I hate these things!" The demon queen brushed off the flowers in disgust.

"Ada, run away!" yelled Deceivant, frantically pushing her forward.

"No one escapes me!" hissed Demonica before shoving her hand into the ground.

Her fingers erupted from the floor as bloody spikes. The spear-like fingers then curled inward, forming a prison of blood around Deceivant.

Demonica slammed her spiked heel against the ground.

A single thin spear shot out from beneath Deceivant. It then retracted with lightning-quick speed. The only trace of its presence was the hole through his chest. Dark energy coated the wound, blocking off the angelic energy from healing the injury.

Deceivant put his hand over the hole, trying to conceal the wound from Ada. The look in his eyes betrayed him; he knew he had no hope of survival. He looked up at his beloved, offering his hand to her. "Get as far away from here as you can," said Deceivant weakly, grabbing onto her hand.

"No…I won't. I'll die with you if I have to," said Ada with trembling arms.

"Please, Ada, you can still survive if you leave now," he said, holding her hand as he coughed up blood.

Demonica walked to the couple with a cruel smile across her face. "I probably should kill her, but this is just priceless," she said, creating a chair out of solidified blood.

"I love you so much," said Deceivant with one last warm smile.

His eyes closed. His hand became limp in her grip.

Ada gave him a gentle kiss. She then turned to face his killer. "I'm sorry, but our son's well-being is at stake! I will stop her and I will save Devlin."

"Sehuhuhuhuhu! You, defeat me? That is as impossible as Deceivant arising from the dead," said Demonica, standing up from her chair.

Chapter 49: The Last Resistance

A white cloud of light exited Deceivant's frail body and shot into Ada.

Light energy spontaneously erupted out of Ada, forming angelic wings which illuminated the room.

"You think a little light can destroy me? I am far beyond your comprehension," said Demonica, her stomach opening up.

Ada's angelic feathers detached and shot out. The feathers hit Demonica with full force but did no damage.

"You can't tickle me to death. Lum is useless and Sel is all-powerful," said Demonica as she lashed her nails viciously.

Ada dodged some of the slices and her powers healed the wounds that cropped up. "I don't care. My love for him is real."

"So is my power." Demonica pierced her nails through the woman's chest.

"Devlin is counting on me, whether he knows it or not! I won't let you turn my son into your puppet!"

"Hmm, I don't want to ruin my beloved's lab. Let's leave this place and finish this elsewhere," said Demonica, looking at the battle-worn room.

Her black wings shot open before she flew out the window. She tossed Ada off her nails and toward her doom.

At the moment of impact, all of Ada's wounds healed.

"Lum powers may be able to mend wounds, but I can cut faster than they can heal!" Demonica leaped through the window and dive-bombed.

"I must stop you to save Devlin," said Ada, standing up with pure determination.

"Save Devlin? From what…being consumed by vengeance? He is far beyond saving. Besides, I like the new Devlin. His undying hatred makes me so hot inside. Auugh," said Demonica, running her hands up her thighs.

"I will save my son." Ada became coated in an aura of light.

"I've had enough of your baseless optimism. I do hope Devlin forgives me for killing you. It's nothing personal, honestly. I just won't allow his hatred to hinder his journey," said Demonica, landing before the weak woman.

Light shot out as beams from Ada's body.

Demonica dodged through them as she soared up to Ada. Blood coated her hand as she thrust it through her victim. She pulled out her hand and then gripped onto her victim's face.

Blood poured out, crawling into Ada's eyes, ears, nose, and mouth.

"Don't worry. I'll take care of Devlin," said Demonica, combing Ada's hair with her fingertips.

The clouds above them parted. A strong echoing voice emanated from the void. "Gods are not allowed to trifle in the affairs of the living. However, I shalt not allow the forces of Sel to intervene without opposition from Lum!" boomed the deity's voice.

"Oh heaven! How can she be here! This isn't fair!" yelled Demonica, pulling the blood back into her body.

"I will make it rain purity!" yelled the heavens.

The clouds parted further and the entire sky lit up with energy. The energy focused into a radiant cloud of absolute light.

"PURIFYING RAY."

A mountainous ray of pureness crashed down from the cloud. The light engulfed Demonica. It spread over her body like a vicious flame.

The demon queen frantically created a black portal and flung herself inside.

"Now things are fair," said the godly voice.

"I've never felt something so pure," said Ada, her eyes glistening.

Devlin appeared a foot in front of Ada, a dagger twirling in his grip. "What pureness? Nothing is fully anything. When broken down to a molecular level, the illusion of pureness is shattered. In essence, everything is corrupt!"

Bob rose out from the ground, bowing to Devlin.

"Demonica is no more. Yet another problem has vanished. This is no longer a battleground for Heaven and Hell! This is a personal fight. Bob, show no mercy. Destroy Ada!" yelled Devlin, gripping his face with angst.

Bob looked back and forth between Ada and Devlin. His eye gathered energy as he prepared to fire. He then turned to Devlin and released his laser.

The nimble scientist dodged the laser with a side-step.

"I was with Deceivant the whole time. Now hurry up and unleash your ultimate Exp. I've grown tired of absorbing weak souls," said Bob, flexing his spectral arms.

"You would rather side with him than me! Ahahahaha! I never could fully trust you, but it no longer matters. With all the artifacts at my disposal, I can destroy you." Devlin snapped his fingers, making Kaity appear in his arms. "I don't know if I can handle killing my own mother; could you do the honors and kill her for me?" he asked, caressing his wife's cheek.

"Kaity, if you love him, tell him to stop this," said Ada in tears.

Kaity hopped out of his arms. "Master wants me to kill you, so I will," she said with a nod.

A heavenly shield surrounded Ada as she stood proudly and pushed out her chest. "I refuse to fight you."

"Whether you struggle or not, I will kill you," said Kaity as she aimed her sniper rifle. She pulled the trigger with a glazed look in her eyes.

The bullet shot into the shield of pure light before bouncing off. Dark energy grew from the point of impact and spread across the shield. The Lum shield then shattered, leaving Ada defenseless.

Kaity tossed her sniper rifle aside and ran toward her enemy.

Ada turned around to make a run for it.

Kaity thrust her claws in the enemy's chest, twisted them, and ripped them out.

Blood erupted out from Ada's body as she collapsed. She limped away, pulling herself along with one arm.

"Get off her! Traitor!" Nina rushed in and rammed into the bloodthirsty killer, knocking her to the ground. "Ada, are you okay?" she asked, helping her beloved sensei to her feet.

Kaity stabbed her claws into Nina's foot. "I can't fail Master." She pierced holes in Nina's leg, slowly moving up to her thighs.

"What is going on!" asked Devlin, his eyes wide with disbelief.

"Is something wrong, Master?" asked Kaity as she continuously stabbed her victim's stomach.

"You would never hurt Nina." Devlin stomped the ground furiously. "Etah, what did you do to Kaity!"

The ground split in two as it shook violently. Fire shot out from it and the godly voice of Etah boomed at Devlin. "I made her your doll. When she said 'I do,' she allowed herself to be eternally bound to your will. In a Seltanic marriage, there is always a master and always a slave. Hmmhmmhmmmhuhuh!"

"Bring her back!" yelled Devlin, flinging his arms out.

"Once you succeed, she will return to being herself. But only once you succeed. I will not allow your feelings to get in the way of your plan," said Etah, cruelty outlining every syllable.

"Kaity, please stop this!" yelled Devlin, gripping her shoulders.

The bewitched assassin's body froze. Blood dripped from her claws.

Devlin opened up his arms as his eyes watered up. "Come here, Kaity. I never wanted this to happen," he said, holding her to his chest.

"What's wrong, Master?" asked Kaity, her head tilting to him.

"I was so overcome with happiness that I forgot who you were. I'm so sorry." Devlin gripped her hand. "I promise I am going to kill Etah for this, even if I die in the process!"

Ada cradled her wounded friend to her chest. "I'm so happy you're alive. Nina, the final lesson on how to be sexy is: enjoy life. Don't bother fighting Devlin, just live on," she said, failing to hold back her tears.

"No! I need you! I still haven't learned enough. You're supposed to teach me!" yelled Nina, shaking her sensei.

Devlin appeared and fried Nina with his Taser. He ripped her off of Ada and flung her aside. He took a deep breath and then looked right into Ada's eyes. "Goodbye, mother," he said in a whisper. He slammed his foot down on Ada's head.

A crack was heard, but she was still alive.

Nina wailed as she crawled back to her teacher.

"Please stop this! I love you," said Ada in tears, grabbing onto her son's leg.

"That's it…beg!" Devlin slammed his foot down again and again.

"I love you!"

His mother's head cracked open.

Devlin continued to stomp. "Die! Die! Die!"

The hologram faded and the tiny blue ball appeared, split wide open.

"Ada!" Nina grabbed onto Devlin's leg, unable to see through her drenched eyes.

Devlin looked down at Nina and then back at Ada's crushed core. "I…I did it," he said, holding his face with tears and a twisted smile.

"Bring her back!" wailed Nina.

Demo rolled toward Devlin, preparing to attack.

"Kaity, you kill that spherical thing. I'll deal with the treacherous eyeball!" said Devlin, quaking in misery.

"Wait up, I'm curious to see Deceivant's new Exps in action. We'll fight when it's over," said Bob, creating himself a spectral chair.

"Very well…I could use a breather anyway," said Devlin, teleporting himself a bed. He flung himself onto the bed and sat up to watch Kaity's fight.

Kaity shot Demo with her rifle as it rolled closer to her master. The ball swerved out of the way, dodging the bullet.

A black point spawned behind Kaity, floating in the air.

A line shot out from both Demo and the point almost instantly.

Kaity leaped to the side, allowing the line to only graze her arm.

"**LINE SEGMENT**," said Demo in a robotic voice.

The segment then shifted until it faced Kaity.

"**RAY**."

An arrow branched from the segment and traveled onward. The arrow impaled the assassin, keeping a steady pattern of velocity.

Kaity severed the large arrow, causing it to become a segment as well.

"**INTERSECT**."

Another line appeared perpendicular to the first. It spawned and shot into the assassin's right side.

Kaity shoved her claws into the line and pushed herself off.

"⊡IMΞΠƧI⊡Π ⊡Ξ.M⊡TI⊡Π." Demo's body flattened into a circle before passing by the assassin.

Kaity leaped backwards but Demo pursued, grazing her arm as it sped by.

After locking onto Demo, Kaity pulled her sniper trigger.

Demo became a microscopic dot, causing the bullet to zoom by.

The assassin held her side in pain as she loaded up her gun. "I refuse to let Master down! *ELEMENTAL KITTIES!*"

A litter of cute little kitties were summoned, each with their own elemental properties.

The fire kitty ran around frantically, trying to get away from his flames. The water kitty leaped about, terrified of its own existence. The ice kitty fell down, covered in ice and unable to move. The electric kitty ran in circles as lightning struck behind it. The earth kitty was too busy rolling in its own mud to fight.

"⊡IMΞΠƧI⊡Π ⊡IƧT⊡RTI⊡Π.ΠΞT LΛⵘ⊡UT." Demo unfolded, making its surface area visible from a single perspective. All its sides were laid out next to each other like a grid.

"Minus." Demo charged toward the assassin with robotic conviction.

Kaity poured energy into her plasma claws as her enemy closed in.

Demo was sliced in half as it made contact, turning into two rectangles.

The shapes wrapped around Kaity, minimizing her mobility.

"Are you sure you don't need any assistance?" asked Devlin, cleaning the blood off his boot.

Kaity tore through Demo and rolled to the ground. "I've got it under control, Master." She turned around and pumped the enemy full of bullets.

Twenty dots appeared behind Kaity like a grid, spaced equidistant from one another.

Lines instinctively shot out of Demo to connect the dots.

Kaity leaped through the line frenzy, swinging up one to dodge another. She flung herself above the line mesh as more dots appeared behind her. "Go kitties, attack!" she yelled, pointing her arm at her enemy.

The kitties made no response to her command. They were too preoccupied with their own elements.

Kaity grabbed onto an incoming line and flung herself on top. She turned on the sights of her sniper, creating a visible laser dot on her enemy.

The fire and lightning elemental kitties turned to the dot. They rushed into Demo, setting the Exp aflame and electrifying it all at once.

The combined elemental attacks were greater than the rectangles' defenses. Demo reverted into a ball and fell to the ground.

Kaity rushed up to her enemy and shoved her claws right through it.

A shattering sound was heard from within Demo, signaling its demise.

Kaity grabbed the artifact in her mouth and ran to Devlin on all fours. She dropped it in his hand and wagged her tail back and forth.

"Kaity, you've performed exceptionally!" Devlin took the artifact and patted her on the head. "Watch me get rid of Bob with a single attack!" he said, putting out his palm.

"That is hilarious. You won't even be able to touch me," said Bob, zooming toward Devlin. He fired a souped-up laser in midflight.

Devlin's hand turned pink and shook back and forth erasing the laser as it balled up.

"I don't need to Go to Sel. *TELEPORT, BOB*," said Devlin with a smirk.

Bob vanished, being instantly spirited away to another realm.

"Well, that was easy," said Devlin, stretching his arms back.

Nina fell to her knees. "How can we win if Bob lost?"

"You won't. Now don't get in my way," said Devlin, smacking her down.

Nina stood up. "No, it's not over yet. I am too luscious to lose," she said, lunging at Devlin.

"How did you escape?" Devlin kneed the stubborn woman under her chin and then backhanded her.

Nina fell to the ground with a red mark on her face. "I still have my artifacts. I guess you overlooked that."

"Can I kill her?" asked Kaity, grabbing Devlin's arm while bouncing up and down.

"No, I won't force you to kill someone you love," said Devlin, kicking Nina before she could get up.

"As long as my breasts bounce, my sexiness shall shield me," said Nina, rolling back onto her feet.

"Egotistic to the very end," said Devlin with a wide grin.

"I have no one left to fight for but myself. My selfishness is stronger than ever! And that selfishness will only heighten my erotic aura. Prepare to be destroyed by my dynamite body," said Nina, her hand ready to rip open her shirt.

Devlin teleported up to her and hooked her leg, knocking her off her feet.

In the same instant, Nina ripped open her shirt with one hand and pulled Devlin down with the other. She slipped out of her shirt and wrapped it around him. In a split second she was on top of Ada's killer, holding her bomb trigger.

"Why didn't you just leave? Did you come back for Ada?"

"I fight for myself and by myself. My feelings for Ada may have weakened my aura, but now that she's gone…my self-love is almost absolute."

"What feelings? Your jealousy for Ada hasn't turned into love, you're just misrepresenting it."

"Maybe I am, but I feel liberated now that she's gone."

"And what about me? Don't you still love me, even a little bit?" asked Devlin, reaching for the trigger.

Nina pinned his arm down with her foot. "The other Nina's feelings for you are still holding me back. With your death, my seduction will blossom into a pure substance. I will be unstoppable," she said, digging her foot into his head.

"Is that why you joined the Freedom Forcers, just to kill me?" asked Devlin, slamming his fist into her leg. He flung his other fist up, knocking the trigger out of her hand.

Nina kicked off of Devlin and grabbed the trigger. "Maybe," she said with a sly smile. She then dive-bombed into him.

Devlin rolled out of the way and grabbed her leg. He flung it up, making her flip in midair. The clever creator teleported in her path, grabbed her face, and slammed her to the ground. "I never should have shown you any mercy, traitor! I won't make that mistake again. You die now!"

"Oh, I wouldn't be so sure about that. I beat the Exp that still eludes you even now," said Nina before Devlin slammed his foot down on her stomach.

He sat on top of her and fried her with his Taser. "To think that I once yearned for your body…I was so desperate. I see you for what you are now. You are a hideous creature," whispered Devlin as he pulled her up by her hair.

Nina flipped him over her; now she was on top. "The only reason I ever loved you was because I was programmed to. Same goes for Matteria, same for Violet, Ada, and even Kaity at this point. You are incapable of being loved." She spat in his face.

Devlin's fists struck her face over and over. He slammed his head into her face and grabbed her by the nipples. After twisting them, he gripped her breasts tightly. "Pathetic." He slammed his elbow into Nina's chest, knocking her off.

"Let's make your body a mirror image of your soul. Soon you will be so hideous your own reflection will make you retch. Not even you will love yourself. I won't kill you here. You'll kill yourself later," said Devlin, stepping on her gut.

Nina rolled out from under his foot and jumped off the ground. She barraged Devlin's face with a dozen kicks and then landed on his stomach. She pulled her legs up and kicked his face furiously.

Devlin bit her foot and stabbed her leg, causing her to collapse on him. He put one arm behind her head while his other coiled around to her throat. "Do you remember how my embrace feels?" he asked, his hands trembling.

Nina slammed her head into Devlin's and then cringed in pain.

He slammed his head into her face repeatedly. Her nose was crushed, blood now leaking down her face.

Devlin rolled on top of her, pushing against her. "Kaity only loves you for your body; it blinds her from seeing the true you. I am merely making the distinction vividly apparent," he said, grabbing her by the hair.

He slammed her against the ground repeatedly, reddening the grass with her blood.

"Stop!" yelled Kaity, grabbing the top of her head.

Devlin's hand froze and he looked up at Kaity. He teleported up to her and held her in a gentle embrace. "I'm sorry, Kaity. I knew this would be the only way to get you back. I didn't want you to cry," he said, shaking with misery.

"Why would I cry, Master?" asked Kaity with an empty smile and watery eyes.

"I guess things aren't going to be that simple. Kaity...I will get you back to normal. Nina, you may live." Devlin thrust his arm into Nina's chest. He pulled out the Gravity Artifact and absorbed it.

"Just kill me," cried Nina.

"Nope," said Devlin, snapping his fingers.

Nina was teleported away to an unspecified location.

"Master, what is that?" asked Kaity, peering in the distance.

A barrage of explosions appeared all around them.

Devlin pulled Kaity into his arms and held out his hand.

A large orb shot into the grass, making the dust shoot up.

Devlin was suddenly knocked off his feet by an unseen force.

Exp 8 turned around in mid-flight and flung a massive orb into the smoke cloud.

Devlin appeared right behind Exp 8, setting his wife down. "Run along, Kaity. It is now time for the final battle. Tell me, Exp 8, are you ready to become a true weapon of mass destruction?" he asked with a beckoning hand.

"I'm here to break the shackles of slavery and strangle you with them!" yelled Exp 8, flying at him with a massive orb in each hand.

Chapter 50: Exp 8

"*GRAVITY FALL*," said Devlin as he walked toward his enemy.

Exp 8 crashed to the ground. He fired off the two orbs at Devlin, who vanished and then appeared behind him.

Devlin flipped his creation over with his foot.

Exp 8 pushed off the ground but wasn't even able to rise to his knees.

"All these trees will just get in the way." Devlin snapped his fingers, teleporting them both to the deserted side of the lab.

The ground was flat and stretched on for miles. Exp 8 could see a familiar hill in the distance and beyond it the lab that once imprisoned him.

"Look at me when I'm fighting you! Well, well, this one might seem familiar to you. *SHIELD*." Devlin raised his hands up.

A light blue force field was emitted, creating a twenty-by-twenty-five-foot dome around them.

"Now, I want you to stay here," said Devlin, grinding his foot into the stubborn rebel.

The Ultimate Exp smashed his fists into Devlin's knees. He rose while punching up his captor's body.

Devlin was knocked off of Exp 8 but quickly got back to his feet. "You're able to deter the effects of artifacts. You've finally reached my expectations. But don't think for a second that you've won."

The sand beneath Exp 8 collapsed into a puddle.

Devlin sped up to his creation and flung his leg up. The powerful kick sent Exp 8 crashing into the top of the dome.

Devlin took the opportunity to plant an energy sword upright in the ground.

Exp 8 shot down with immense force as soon as he hit the barrier. He was then propelled back into the protruding blade. He pushed off the ground and rose to his feet. He then lunged at his enemy with a souped-up orb.

Devlin twirled around the attack. He enlarged his arm before smashing it into his greatest creation.

Exp 8 was sent flying forward toward the barrier. He reflected off the wall only to be knocked right back into it.

Devlin spun out of the way as Exp 8 was repelled once more. He gripped the hilt of the energy sword and tore it out of from his creation's chest.

The final Freedom Forcer shot back toward Devlin as he hit the light blue wall.

"No matter where you go, you are trapped!" Devlin thrust the sword into the defiant invention's shoulder and pinned him to the ground.

Exp 8 grabbed the sword and pulled its energy into his body. He then knocked Devlin off with a sudden backhand.

"That was very good. Now, it's time to see how much you've really improved." Devlin teleported behind his creation and pulled back his fist.

Exp 8 engaged his elbow talons and spun around.

Devlin's fist slammed into Exp 8's chest just before the talons drew blood. The nimble scientist teleported behind him, coated his hands in ice, and slammed his fists into Exp 8's crown.

With a loud crash, Exp 8 was plastered to the ground. He spun his feet in a flurry, stabbing into Devlin's legs with his talons. After creating an orb, he immediately fired it.

Devlin kicked off the ground and landed behind Exp 8. "I didn't get to torture Ada or Deceivant, so I'm going to make you suffer in their place," he said as he thrust two Tasers into his creation.

Ice came out from Devlin's feet, creating a small trail.

Exp 8 turned around with a large orb ready to fire, but his enemy had vanished.

After dropping from above and landing on his invention, Devlin thrust another energy sword through his own foot and Exp 8's chest. "You will learn your place," he said with a scowl. The youthful scientist pushed off the icy ground, skating on Exp 8's body. He hopped as he approached the barrier. He then kicked off the force field, gaining momentum as he skated toward the other wall. "Enough fun," he said as they arrived at the next wall. He raised his foot and slammed his stubborn child against the barrier vigorously. "You were supposed to give up after Bob's attack. Why did you still fight? Your despair had already uncovered your latent powers. Your other allies didn't have to die."

"Every single living thing has a family that loves it dearly. A mother cow loves her calf just as much as Ada loved you. A young tiger loves its sister just as dearly as I love Kawai! I loved them all as comrades. I cared about each and every one of them. But there are far more important things than the lives of those you care about. By stopping you, I will save so many lives, so many families. And I owe it to my comrades to see this through to the end. I have to defeat you, Devlin. And I will." Exp 8 purposely slammed his head forward into the force field. His head instantaneously recoiled, slamming into his creator's face with incredible force.

Devlin held his head in pain as blood spurted out of it. "Don't act so noble. I created all of your morals. I wanted you to escape. That burning feeling inside you is just a program. The freedom you yearn for is a hoax. I planned on you gathering allies. I needed to bring you to the depths of despair to unlock your true power. You only seek freedom so that I can take it from you. You are only disobedient so that I can make you obey," he said, shooting a heat wave at the rebel.

Exp 8 absorbed the heat wave and fired it off as energy. "I don't care! It doesn't matter if it's artificial or not. My morals guide me. And they will guide me to freedom," he said as turrets popped out from his shoulders.

Wires burst out from the ground and sliced the turrets to pieces.

"You are going to be so fun to break. Don't worry, once I've made you obedient, no more Exps will have to die. I need to send souls to Sel and the only souls headed down that path are those of humans. I'm not going to destroy the planet. I'm just going to level a few cities, that's all. The Earth knows that humans must die if it is to thrive. Mankind has caused so much anguish! So much destruction!" yelled Devlin as he rapidly dodged projectile energy orbs.

A single orb hit the scientist, tearing right through him.

Five Devlins appeared all around the foolish rebel. "I have all the artifacts and you have none! You are all alone and stand no chance!"

The real Devlin impaled a new energy sword through Exp 8's concave chest and into the barrier.

Exp 8 shook violently as his insides were sliced up by the blade.

"This is payback for going against the plan! Demonica was supposed to be a last resort! And once I told you the truth about your morals, you were supposed to be crushed. I created the foundation for every thought you've ever had. After your sister's death, you were supposed to give in. But no, you had to be a stupid hero with no trust, no hope, and no purpose." Devlin twisted the blade. "You are a soulless machine that relies on its every action being righteous!" He yanked the blade out only to shove it back in.

"I've just been following my instincts and I will continue to do so!" yelled Exp 8 as the barrier repeatedly smashed against his back.

"I will become a god! I shall eliminate Etah and take his place. But that's not all. After I've harnessed my powers as the ruler of Sel, I will incarnate on Earth and impose justice on a global scale! This is your last chance. Will you obey your master?" Devlin pressed his creation against the barrier.

"My only master is Nature. I will bask in its glory and you can't stop me!"

Devlin gripped the rebel's shoulders. "Such valor, even now. And it's all going to be mine!" He pulled Exp 8 up to the blade's hilt and then slammed him against the barrier.

Ripples dispersed from the point of impact.

Devlin fell to his knees, holding his chest. Blood spurted out through his clenched teeth.

Exp 8 fell flat on his face and then slowly stood up. He looked down with contempt as his creator swayed back and forth. "I am the master of my own destiny! I didn't even have to kill you. You killed yourself with your own toxic rage. And it was my sister's artifact that ended you!"

"No, it…it isn't over yet," said Devlin, struggling to stand.

"I thank you for creating me and my people. You gave us life…but we don't owe it to you. I'll never be indebted to you, Devlin. Think about all the lives that were pointlessly wasted during your climb for conquest. Spend your last moments sorting out what you've done." Exp 8 turned away once the pool of blood reached his feet.

Devlin stood up.

Exp 8 turned around with wide eyes. "No way."

Devlin yanked a knife out of his lab coat and pressed it to the bottom of his stomach. He dragged the blade up, cutting into his own skin. "All the hatred I obtained from the world shall seep back into it. I shall set it aflame with chaos and destruction. And you are going to be my weapon! You escaped my lab, and you thought you had won! You thought you were free! You are such a fool! In the end, your struggle was meaningless! All of it was worthless! All your comrades are dead and you will still become my weapon. It was completely pointless to defy me from the beginning!" he yelled, plunging the blade in deeper.

Exp 8 turned to the pitiful creature, his eyes shaking with anger. "Why can't you admit that you're wrong? Why can't you just apologize for killing my family? Why the hell won't you get down on your knees and repent!"

A trail of tears flowed down to his mouthpiece.

"I don't regret anything! If I give up, then it's all in vain!" Devlin's eyes glowed blood red.

"What happened to you?" asked Exp 8, crouching down.

"I was nurtured with hatred. I was alone! I was abandoned by all I loved and forsaken by all that I believed!" Devlin grabbed the parted area of his skin and tore it off like a shirt.

His exposed flesh was black. Wires shot out from it, tearing away any leftover skin. Blades sliced open his hands from within. His teeth fell out, promptly replaced by knives. The scientist's eyes were the only things that remained unaltered. The wires flailed about as he released a shrill mechanical screech.

"Why hide your true self for so long? Devlin…we're family," said Exp 8, grabbing the Exp's jet-black talons.

Devlin went down on all fours, his talons piercing into the earth. His fox-like ears pointed back. As his back arched upward, his spinal cord shot out as serrated blades. Wires all over his body spread out, making him nearly three times his original size. "I hid myself in order to survive. But I don't want to survive in this world! I want to rule in the next! I am the true Ultimate Exp, and I will become the one true God!" His stomach burst open, wires erupting out.

The wires coiled around every inch of Exp 8.

"I'm going to use you to blow up everything in my path! So come on, bomb, let me harness your power," said Devlin as the wires tightened their grip.

"I'm a living thing, not a weapon!" yelled Exp 8, his voice muffled into a whisper by the wires. He flung his arms and legs around haphazardly as he tried to break free.

"You're both!" yelled Devlin, shooting more wires into his masterpiece.

Energy shot out from Exp 8's capsule and gathered in his fists. He created two energy orbs and then slammed his hands together.

Devlin jumped back, dodging the explosion.

Exp 8 rocketed out of the mesh of wires. Turrets popped out of his shoulders and fired furiously.

A single wire spun around in front of Devlin, deflecting every bullet. An array of wires then erupted from his shoulder.

Exp 8 strafed with his jet boosters, but the wires kept up their pursuit. They wrapped around his leg and pulled him in.

A sleek, black, bladed tail with a razor-sharp tip shot out from Devlin. It burst into Exp 8, penetrating his stomach. Wires then gushed out of the tail, wrapping around the rebel leader's back.

"Ada, I need help!" yelled Exp 8 as he fired an array of energy orbs.

"She's dead," said Devlin before teleporting away from the assault.

Devlin's tail swung back and forth, slamming Exp 8 into the hardened clay.

The ground quaked as the freedom seeker was smashed against it.

Exp 8 tore out the wires and jet boosted off the sharp tail. He crashed into the extremely visible force field, plastering against it. The next second, he was shot back toward Devlin. He created an orb in his fist and thrust it at his creator.

A mere centimeter before contact, wires shot up like a wall. Once Exp 8's fist hit the wall, the wires adjusted to the groove of the fist and wrapped around his wrist. They then retracted, ripping off the living weapon's hand effortlessly.

"Oh the irony, you used my hand to dispel the extremely visible force field and now I'm going to use yours to make it stronger," said Devlin, spinning the hand on the tip of his bladed finger. He then pressed the orb held by the dismembered hand against the barrier.

The orb was absorbed, giving the barrier a slightly darker tint.

The wrist of Exp 8's dismembered hand detached, levitating above his fingertips.

Exp 8 concentrated and made a tiny orb come out of his stub.

"I was hoping you'd do that," said Devlin, turning to his creation with a jagged grin.

In a split second, Devlin's wires sliced off Exp 8's turrets. They wrapped around the auto-guns, and slammed them into the orb.

The turrets exploded, releasing all the energy inside them. The energy fused with the orb, bloating it to the size of a stadium.

The wires slammed the orb into the force field, which absorbed the orb for energy. The hue of the field darkened further.

Exp 8 watched the spectacle with a blank stare.

"Don't give up now. Let's find out just how much you've improved. The first test is strength. Go on, hit me like old times," said Devlin, patting his cheek.

The jewel on Exp 8's right hand coursed with energy. The energy coated his fist as it smashed into Devlin's cheek.

Devlin skid back with a dent on his metallic face. "I see much improvement. Now, on to durability."

The wires tossed the hand at the wall. It shot backward at the second of impact. The dismembered hand then pierced through Exp 8's chest, leaving a hole in its wake. The hand's momentum continued, slamming into Devlin. This stopped the hand's movement and created a small crater in his metal chest.

Devlin's wires wrapped around Exp 8's legs and then reeled him in.

"I can think of an even better way to test your durability," said Devlin as he slowly walked to the force field. He grabbed Exp 8 by the back of his head while his wires yanked on his victim's arms and legs. "I always wondered if torture could break your spirit," he said, moving his creation toward the souped-up defense wall.

The wires brought Exp 8's right hand up and slowly inched it closer to the force field.

"The finger of opposition, always standing above the rest, shall be the first put to rest. The tallest and most vulgar of the family is always trying to get attention. The center of the crowd will be the first one out."

Exp 8's middle finger softly touched the force field. In the blink of an eye, it was gone. The only indication of its departure was the rebel's cringe of anguish.

"Don't want to give me the satisfaction of hearing your pain? Let's see how long you can keep this up. Can you guess what finger is next? Why it is the finger of conformity, the ring finger. Its constriction illuminates the essence of matrimony: lifelong suffering. Yet the pain is so slight it shan't ever be done away with. My marriage has already met its first conflict. No doubt there will be many more to come. You desire freedom, so let me divorce you from the finger of bondage," said Devlin.

A gush of blood shot out where Exp 8's ring finger once was.

"Now the finger of blame and indication shall next be sent to incineration. Always informing the location of something or other, acting as a neutral indicator. Yet when there is blame, it seldom points to the owner. And it is often used in various dirty jobs, like pulling the trigger of a gun. Must you blame me for all of your trifles? You know the blame is yours as well," said Devlin before the next finger vanished.

"Now, the outcast shall be cast away. The shortest and weakest of the fingers; it just barely lingers. Being the shortest, it is the most useless. It is always cowering behind the other fingers. You probably won't even notice its departure."

With his pinky severed, all of Exp 8's fingers were gone. All that remained was his thumb.

"Thumbs-up indeed! Finally the greatest of all the phalanges shall be freed. It is no longer even considered to be a finger. It has surpassed its brethren through evolution. And since it is opposable, it is used frequently and thus has become the strongest. It is able to give a crippling critique in an instant. In a coliseum, its direction is the difference of life and death."

Exp 8 screamed in agony as his thumb vanished.

Devlin flung the wretch to the ground and pinned him down with a flood of wires. "You've lost. But fret not, for we have won," he said with a light-hearted smile.

The wires tugged on Exp 8, dragging him toward his maker's stomach.

Exp 8 firmly placed his talons in the ground and powered up the orbs inside his levitating wrists.

"I've had my fun." Devlin teleported a trigger into his hand and pressed the button.

Exp 8 collapsed to the sand, unable to move a muscle. "If you could stop me just like that, why didn't you do it before?"

"I wanted to have the pleasure of breaking you with my own power. I could have stopped you in your tracks long ago, but you had work to do! You've grown through your battles and your despair. Become a part of me! Become a part of the future God!"

Exp 8 vainly tried to hold onto the ground with his feet. The Penultimate Exp was unable to save himself and was shoved inside Devlin.

His creator's wires soon enveloped Exp 8 completely.

"You shall be melded within me, becoming my innards. I shall gain your immeasurable power! Everything you've done is for this moment. Everyone who died did not do so in vain. You've surpassed your limits! The dichotomy of your desire to be free and my mantra of servitude, along with the despair of losing your allies, broke your inhibitors. And now, because of it, I will surpass all barriers!" yelled Devlin, flinging his arms around dramatically.

"I won't let you!"

"It isn't your choice. Thanks to Anthrax's artifact, your defenses are being eaten away at a microscopic level!"

"I don't care! I will not give in! I refuse to become your tool!" yelled Exp 8 from within.

The consciousness of Exp 8 wrestled within Devlin's psyche. The rebel's mental self was trapped in a black void.

Devlin's consciousness approached Exp 8's, manifesting as his human façade.

"What the hell is going on?" asked Exp 8's mental representation, trying to tear the darkness off of him.

"You are in the process of melding with me. This is the realm of my mind. I don't just want to assimilate your body…your knowledge, your emotions, your power, your bravery, your soul! Everything! I want it all."

"You don't have the right. They all belong to me!"

"All that is left is for me to crush your mind. The darkness around you is doubt. I stored it all so that it would not interfere with my ascension. Now it will drain away your drive until you submit!" yelled Devlin, clenching his fist.

"If our willpowers clash, mine shall be victorious!" yelled Exp 8, tearing out of the darkness.

"You think your will is stronger than mine. I have never lost faith that I would succeed, not even once. While you have a burst of doubt every time one of your teammates dies. I have the stronger will! Now it's time for your final test: intelligence."

The doubt dispersed beneath Devlin's feet, revealing shimmering white resolve below.

Devlin's arm detached and fell to the ground. It separated into multiple wires that stampeded forward at Exp 8. The wires dug into the invention's skin and slowly expanded within his flesh.

Exp 8 grabbed his chest in overwhelming anguish as he ran toward his final opponent.

"Are you prepared for that seed of pain to bloom into a flower of suffering?"

The wires sent electricity through their currents, brutally shocking the rebel leader.

Exp 8 fell to his knees, his whole body trembling from the powerful voltage.

The other side of the wires lengthened and attached to Devlin's stomach. The wires then retracted, bringing Exp 8 to his creator.

"All that energy! It is mine now!" The True Ultimate Exp bit into Exp 8's chest as soon as his bladed teeth cropped out.

Exp 8 punched Devlin off of him and fired an orb.

Devlin's wires shot out and sucked up the orb's energy until it was gone.

Exp 8 wrapped his arm around the wires and planted his feet in the resolve. His arm shook as he yanked the wires out.

The wires disconnected from Devlin, causing Exp 8 to tumble backwards. The ends of the wires revealed knives. They then swung at the intruder, slicing him up.

Shadows shaped like his fallen comrades came out from the resolve. They grabbed onto Exp 8, holding him against the ground.

"These husks don't resemble them in the least! They have no will and no purpose!"

"I have all the artifacts at my disposal, all you have is a thick head. Your willpower shall be crushed. TEMPERATURE RISE." The sharp edges instantly became searing hot as they continued to assault the pathetic rebel.

"This is nothing! I won't be stopped so easily!" yelled Exp 8.

"Fine then; I'll crush you both physically and emotionally! Feel Kawai's power! Know that your sister is dead! She tried to stop you, but you never listened! You led her to her grave!"

Devlin barraged his creation with a continuous stream of sound blasts.

"You won't win!" yelled Exp 8 as he tried to resist the pain.

"Oh, I won't! Hahahahooh, you're really full of it," said Devlin, holding his head.

A burst of energy emitted from Exp 8's capsule, rendering the wires inert. He stood up with power coursing through his body.

Devlin fired out more bladed wires, but they couldn't pierce through Exp 8's energy aura.

Exp 8 walked to Devlin as he slowly raised his fist.

"Where are you drawing your power from?" asked Devlin with trembling legs.

"I have to win and I will," said Exp 8, his talons channeling the resolve beneath him.

Devlin backed up and lost his footing.

Exp 8 flung his fist into his captor with immense force. Energy erupted out of his fist as a violent torrent.

Devlin's metallic skin crumbled under the force of the blow. The next instant he vanished. He crashed into the edge of the mindscape into a wall of black doubt.

The doubt enveloped his body as he fell down to the ground.

Exp 8 jet-boosted toward Devlin, his aura repelling any and all doubt.

Devlin crashed down in front of Exp 8's feet. Wires burst out of his body, slicing away the doubt. He got up drowsily in his Exp form, trembling with rage. "I have come too far to fail now! I refuse to have lived in vain!" Wires shot out from his every pore, lunging themselves at the enemy without mercy.

As soon as each wire came in contact with Exp 8, they fell to the floor in defeat.

"The wires are me! Why are they giving up?" yelled Devlin, grasping his face in anguish. His tail shot forward, slicing into the rebel.

Exp 8 yanked on the tail, pulling Devlin in. He slammed his captor to the ground with one hand and crashed an orb into him with the other.

Devlin was plastered to the ground. The crater grew larger and larger as he screamed out in fury. He teleported behind Exp 8. He held his chest while wheezing in pain.

Devlin's resolve molded around the defiant invention's legs, holding him in place.

"I have all the artifacts! Stop resisting the inevitable! *GROWING SELF RESPECT, SELF!*" His metallic body enlarged to mountainous proportions. He towered over his creation like a skyscraper to a bush.

Exp 8's eyes stared him down as energy continued to swirl around his body.

Devlin's hand moved like a whip, catching the rebel in its grip.

"You've sealed your own fate!" yelled Exp 8 as his head swung around in futility.

"This is my mind! How can you think you've won? *TEMPERATURE FALL!*" yelled Devlin, freezing Exp 8 spontaneously. He pressed his thumb against the defiant weapon's head. "*BELIEF CHANGER, DEVOTEE!*"

Thoughts of submission poured out of Devlin's thumb and bore into Exp 8's mind.

"Your body will soon be completely absorbed. While we've been fighting in here, we've been assimilating out there. It's only a matter of time now! Once your body is mine, your mind will soon follow. After your mind submits to me, all your power will be my own."

"You'll have to take my flaws too!" Exp 8's body shook rapidly, building up heat. His whole body emitted a powerful heat wave, melting all the ice around him.

Exp 8's arm pushed out of Devlin's grip. It then shot a marble-sized orb. It was so small that it was completely unnoticed by the scientist.

"Just stay frozen! *TEMPERATURE FALL!*"

No ice formed on Exp 8; his body was too scorching hot to be frozen.

"Devlin...thanks. I couldn't have done it without you," said Exp 8, his mouthpiece stretching as he smirked.

Exp 8's turrets popped out from his shoulders. They concentrated all their firepower on the orb, bloating it with energy until it was as large as Devlin's head. The Freedom Forcers' wrist expanded and overlapped the orb, making it an attachment to his body. He pulled back his fist and gathered swirling energy in his arm. The orb shot forward like a geyser, slamming into his captor's face.

Devlin was sent flying into the ceiling of doubt. The black energy tore away at his body as he crashed back to the ground.

Exp 8 boosted up to his final enemy as tiny orbs were spawned within his palm. The tiny orbs joined together, becoming a single swirling sphere of energy. His entire aura enveloped the orb as he lunged it forth.

The orb went through Devlin's chest and exploded. Energy shot out and spread throughout the scientist's mountain-like body.

Devlin's entire body lit up before disintegrating into nothingness.

Exp 8 awoke in the physical world completely shrouded by darkness. He was still inside of Devlin and encompassed in wires. The sentient weapon couldn't figure out where his legs and arms were. He no longer knew which body parts belonged to him.

Exp 8's melding with his creator had reached the final stage.

Devlin put his hand to his belly with a contented grin. "You have been trapped yet again. Your body has become a prison in and of itself. It was my energy that kick-started your capsule. Now I'm getting that energy back. You're returning to the source. Rejoice! You are merging with the new god of this world!" he yelled, tears pouring out from his blood-red eyes.

"I refuse to let you succeed," said Exp 8 softly from within. His concave chest opened up outside of Devlin, revealing a timer inside it. "*SELF-DESTRUCT, ACTIVATE*! If I'm going to die, I'm taking you with me!" he yelled, projecting his thoughts out loud.

"Is that your final desperate attempt at defying me? Why would I build a manual self-destruct for a creation that was made to be a part of me?" asked Devlin with a grin.

"It's my body and my life. With enough energy I can destroy myself from within! Better think of something, Devlin, you've got about a minute to scheme your way out of this. Thanks for the reverse stopwatch feature, by the way."

Devlin looked down at the digital 6 and 0 on his chest. His eyes shrank. He slammed his body against the ground, desperately trying to stop the countdown.

"There is nothing you can do now but wait. Use these last few seconds to regret all you've sacrificed!" yelled Exp 8 as the numbers counted down.

"How could I have lost?" asked Devlin, frozen in disbelief.

"You just had to be right," said Exp 8.

Devlin's eyes widened as he saw Kaity in the corner of his eye. "I have to save Kaity! I have to save her before it's too late," he said, covering the descending numbers with his hand. He rushed toward her on all fours and charged through the force field at full speed. His body was mangled, but he managed to break through to the other side. Now in tatters, he looked up to see the love of his life. She was alive and well.

"I will die by your side, Master," said Kaity with a childish salute.

Devlin looked at the empty devotion outlining the girl's eyes. "I will save you, Kaity. Don't worry. I will never allow my vengeance to consume you," he said, grabbing her hand. He stood up and embraced her as his body fell to pieces. "*TELEPORT*," he said before his love vanished in his arms.

"I guess Nina will be the only Exp left now. How can you not see the folly of your actions?" asked Exp 8.

"I somehow miscalculated. But there's nothing I can do now. Why do I feel happy? I feel warm," said Devlin, holding his chest as sheets of metal shed from his body.

"The bond you formed with Kaity has rusted away the chains of your vengeance. That bond has cleansed your soul," said Exp 8.

"That's ridiculous. The bond…it merely helped me find myself again," said Devlin before closing his eyes.

"Time's up," said Exp 8.

A long *beep* pierced Exp 8's mind with finality.

The final Freedom Forcer's body emitted a white ray of light that consumed him as it expanded. He did not know how far it would spread, but it didn't matter. The struggle had ended.

Exp 8 was consumed in oblivion. The blast spread across the frungle and desert, expanding exponentially.

There was a dot in the center of the blast. Someone appeared inside the explosion. The figure was shrouded in a black cloak. It glided through the explosion as if it was a mild wind. The figure approached the mass of artifacts left by Devlin's corpse. "There you are, my brethren. Join with me," it said with a glint in its eye.

Exp 8 was destroyed, but with his death he proved that all chains can be broken. His shackles had driven him to attain the ultimate freedom: death. He refused to accept being born into slavery. When faced with eternal imprisonment, Exp 8 chose everlasting freedom.

To be continued in book 2, ***Resurrection of the Exps: The Hero of Sel***

About the Author

Alexander McCarty is an animal born on Earth who actively seeks freedom for his fellow animals. He enjoys watching anime, playing video games, reading books by other independent authors, being an activist, writing anime-style stories, and living a vegan life. Having graduated from college with a focus on Asian and Religious Studies, he now spends his time as a writer and as an abolitionist vegan advocate. He listens to any and all comments, suggestions, reflections and criticism.

Please contact me with a link to where you placed a review for any of my books and I will answer any single question as one of my characters for **FREE**. If you do a review (and point out where) in addition to submitting fan art, I will write a **FREE** short 2–4 page story (with my characters) in a scenario of your choosing. =(:3)*

Bloggers who wish to review *Exp 8: Rebellion of the Exps* may request "Review Copies" at the links below.
authoralexandermccarty@gmail.com
alexanderjmccarty@facebook.com

<u>The Fight for Freedom Continues with You</u>

Slavery has not ended for our fellow animals who share this planet. It is time to get informed about the planetary suffering of non-human animals. Once informed, we can end our involvement in the exploitation and enslavement of our fellow living beings by transitioning to a VEGAN lifestyle. Living a vegan life is the moral way to treat our fellow animals with the respect they deserve. When you make a conscious choice to not purchase or eat meat and animal products and/or spread vegan awareness through activism, you make a difference in the lives of those who are enslaved and executed for the crime of not being born human. Every time we make a purchase, we make a vote to either support or oppose slavery. If we all do our part, we can end systemic slavery worldwide!

Below are some links to places where we can get informed and get involved.
http://www.adaptt.org/
http://www.abolitionistapproach.com/
veganeducationgroup.com

www.ingramcontent.com/pod-product-compliance
Lightning Source LLC
Chambersburg PA
CBHW051934020726
47501CB00001B/114